Alfred Tennyson

The Complete Poetical Works of Alfred Tennyson

Alfred Tennyson

The Complete Poetical Works of Alfred Tennyson

ISBN/EAN: 9783337400385

Printed in Europe, USA, Canada, Australia, Japan

Cover: Foto ©Andreas Hilbeck / pixelio.de

More available books at **www.hansebooks.com**

THE

COMPLETE POETICAL WORKS

OF

ALFRED TENNYSON.

AUTHOR'S HOUSEHOLD EDITION.

BOSTON:
JAMES R. OSGOOD AND COMPANY,
LATE TICKNOR & FIELDS, AND FIELDS, OSGOOD, & CO.
1872.

CONTENTS.

	PAGE
TO THE QUEEN	1
CLARIBEL	1
LILIAN	1
ISABEL	2
MARIANA	2
TO ——	4
MADELINE	4
SONG. — THE OWL	5
SECOND SONG. — TO THE SAME	5
RECOLLECTIONS OF THE ARABIAN NIGHTS	5
ODE TO MEMORY	7
SONG	9
ADELINE	9
A CHARACTER	10
THE POET	10
THE POET'S MIND	11
THE SEA-FAIRIES	11
THE DESERTED HOUSE	12
THE DYING SWAN	13
A DIRGE	13
LOVE AND DEATH	14
THE BALLAD OF ORIANA	14
CIRCUMSTANCE	15
THE MERMAN	15
THE MERMAID	16
SONNET TO J. M. K.	16
THE LADY OF SHALOTT	17
MARIANA IN THE SOUTH	19
ELEÄNORE	20
THE MILLER'S DAUGHTER	22
FATIMA	24
ŒNONE	25
THE SISTERS	28
TO ——	29
THE PALACE OF ART	29
LADY CLARA VERE DE VERE	33
THE MAY QUEEN	34
NEW YEAR'S EVE	36
CONCLUSION	37
THE LOTOS-EATERS	38
CHORIC SONG	39
A DREAM OF FAIR WOMEN	41
MARGARET	46
THE BLACKBIRD	47

CONTENTS.

The Death of the Old Year	47
To J. S.	48
"You ask me, why, tho' ill at ease"	49
"Of old sat Freedom on the heights"	49
"Love thou thy land, with love far-brought"	50
The Goose	51
English Idyls and other Poems :—	
The Epic	52
Morte d'Arthur	52
The Gardener's Daughter; or, The Pictures	58
Dora	62
Audley Court	64
Walking to the Mail	66
Edwin Morris; or, The Lake	68
St. Simeon Stylites	70
The Talking Oak	73
Love and Duty	77
The Golden Year	78
Ulysses	79
Locksley Hall	81
Godiva	87
The Two Voices	88
The Day-Dream :—	
Prologue	94
The Sleeping Palace	95
The Sleeping Beauty	95
The Arrival	96
The Revival	96
The Departure	96
Moral	97
L'Envoi	97
Epilogue	98
Amphion	98
St. Agnes' Eve	99
Sir Galahad	100
Edward Gray	101
Will Waterproof's Lyrical Monologue	102
To ——, after reading a Life and Letters	105
To E. L., on his Travels in Greece	105
Lady Clare	106
The Lord of Burleigh	107
Sir Launcelot and Queen Guinevere	108
A Farewell	109
The Beggar Maid	109
The Vision of Sin	109
"Come not when I am dead"	112
The Eagle	113
"Move eastward, happy earth, and leave"	113
"Break, break, break"	113
The Poet's Song	113
"My life is full of weary days"	114
The Captain; a Legend of the Navy	114
Three Sonnets to a Coquette	114
Song	115
Song	115
On a Mourner	115
Northern Farmer. New Style	116
The Golden Supper	117

CONTENTS.

The Victim	123
Wages	123
The Higher Pantheism	124
"Flower in the crannied wall"	124
Lucretius	124
Idylls of the King:—	
Dedication	128
The Coming of Arthur	129
Geraint and Enid	135
Merlin and Vivien	162
Lancelot and Elaine	175
The Holy Grail	199
Pelleas and Ettarre	211
Guinevere	220
The Passing of Arthur	231
The Princess: a Medley	238
In Memoriam	288
Maud, and other Poems:—	
Maud	323
The Brook; an Idyl	343
The Letters	348
Ode on the Death of the Duke of Wellington	348
The Daisy	352
To the Rev. F. D. Maurice	353
Will	353
The Charge of the Light Brigade	354
Enoch Arden, and other Poems:—	
Enoch Arden	355
Aylmer's Field	370
Sea Dreams	382
The Grandmother	387
Northern Farmer. Old Style	390
Tithonus	391
The Voyage	392
In the Valley of Cauteretz	393
The Flower	394
Requiescat	394
The Sailor-Boy	394
The Islet	394
Literary Squabbles	395
The Ringlet	395
A Welcome to Alexandra	396
Ode sung at the Opening of the International Exhibition	396
A Dedication	397
Experiments:—	
Boädicea	397
In Quantity	398
Specimen of a Translation of the Iliad in Blank Verse	399
Additional Poems:—	
Timbuctoo	400
Elegiacs	403
The "How" and the "Why"	403
Supposed Confessions of a second-rate Sensitive Mind not in Unity with itself	404
The Burial of Love	406
To ——	406
Song	406
Song	407
Song	407
Nothing will die	407

ALL THINGS WILL DIE	408
HERO TO LEANDER	408
THE MYSTIC	409
THE GRASSHOPPER	409
LOVE, PRIDE, AND FORGETFULNESS	410
CHORUS IN AN UNPUBLISHED DRAMA, WRITTEN VERY EARLY	410
LOST HOPE	410
THE TEARS OF HEAVEN	410
LOVE AND SORROW	411
TO A LADY SLEEPING	411
SONNET	411
SONNET	411
SONNET	411
SONNET	412
LOVE	412
THE KRAKEN	412
ENGLISH WAR-SONG	413
NATIONAL SONG	413
DUALISMS	413
WE ARE FREE	414
THE SEA FAIRIES	414
Οἱ ῥέοντες	415
SONNET	415
TO ——	415
BONAPARTE	416
SONNETS	416
THE HESPERIDES	416
ROSALIND	418
SONG	418
KATE	419
SONNET WRITTEN ON HEARING OF THE OUTBREAK OF THE POLISH INSURRECTION	419
SONNET ON THE RESULT OF THE LATE RUSSIAN INVASION OF POLAND	419
SONNET	419
O DARLING ROOM	420
TO CHRISTOPHER NORTH	420
NO MORE	420
ANACREONTICS	420
A FRAGMENT	421
SONNET	421
SONNET	421
THE SKIPPING-ROPE	421
THE NEW TIMON AND THE POETS	421
STANZAS	422
SONNET TO WILLIAM CHARLES MACREADY	422
BRITONS, GUARD YOUR OWN	422
THE THIRD OF FEBRUARY, 1852	423
HANDS ALL ROUND	424
THE WAR	425
ON A SPITEFUL LETTER	425
1865-1866	425
THE WINDOW, OR THE SONGS OF THE WRENS	426
THE LAST TOURNAMENT	429

POEMS.

(PUBLISHED 1830.)

TO THE QUEEN.

REVERED, beloved — O you that hold
  A nobler office upon earth
  Than arms, or power of brain, or birth
Could give the warrior kings of old,

Victoria, — since your Royal grace
  To one of less desert allows
  This laurel greener from the brows
Of him that utter'd nothing base;

And should your greatness, and the care
  That yokes with empire, yield you time
  To make demand of modern rhyme
If aught of ancient worth be there;

Then — while a sweeter music wakes,
  And thro' wild March the throstle calls,
  Where all about your palace-walls
The sun-lit almond-blossom shakes —

Take, Madam, this poor book of song;
  For tho' the faults were thick as dust
  In vacant chambers, I could trust
Your kindness. May you rule us long,

And leave us rulers of your blood
  As noble till the latest day!
  May children of our children say,
"She wrought her people lasting good;

"Her court was pure; her life serene;
  God gave her peace; her land reposed;
  A thousand claims to reverence closed
In her as Mother, Wife, and Queen;

"And statesmen at her council met
  Who knew the seasons when to take
  Occasion by the hand, and make
The bounds of freedom wider yet

"By shaping some august decree,
  Which kept her throne unshaken still
  Broad-based upon her people's will,
And compass'd by the inviolate sea."

MARCH, 1851.

CLARIBEL.

A MELODY.

I.

WHERE Claribel low-lieth
  The breezes pause and die,
    Letting the rose-leaves fall:
But the solemn oak-tree sigheth,
  Thick-leaved, ambrosial,
  With an ancient melody
  Of an inward agony,
Where Claribel low-lieth.

II.

At eve the beetle boometh
  Athwart the thicket lone:
At noon the wild bee hummeth
  About the moss'd headstone:
At midnight the moon cometh,
  And looketh down alone.
  Her song the lintwhite swelleth,
The clear-voiced mavis dwelleth,
  The callow throstle lispeth,
  The slumbrous wave outwelleth,
  The babbling runnel crispeth,
  The hollow grot replieth
Where Claribel low-lieth.

LILIAN.

I.

AIRY, fairy Lilian,
Flitting, fairy Lilian,
When I ask her if she love me,
Claps her tiny hands above me,
  Laughing all she can;
She'll not tell me if she love me,
  Cruel little Lilian.

II.

When my passion seeks
Pleasance in love-sighs,
She, looking thro' and thro' me
Thoroughly to undo me,
  Smiling, never speaks:

So innocent-arch, so cunning-simple,
 From beneath her gather'd wimple
  Glancing with black-beaded eyes,
 Till the lightning laughters dimple
  The baby-roses in her cheeks;
   Then away she flies.

III.

Prythee weep, May Lilian!
 Gayety without eclipse
  Wearieth me, May Lilian:
 Thro' my very heart it thrilleth
  When from crimson-threaded lips
   Silver-treble laughter trilleth:
    Prythee weep, May Lilian.

IV.

Praying all I can,
 If prayers will not hush thee,
  Airy Lilian,
 Like a rose-leaf I will crush thee,
  Fairy Lilian.

ISABEL.

I.

EYES not down-dropt nor over bright,
  but fed
 With the clear-pointed flame of chastity,
 Clear, without heat, undying, tended by
  Pure vestal thoughts in the translucent fane
Of her still spirit; locks not wide-dispread,
 Madonna-wise on either side her
  head;
  Sweet lips whereon perpetually did
   reign
 The summer calm of golden charity,
Were fixed shadows of thy fixed mood,
 Revered Isabel, the crown and head,
The stately flower of female fortitude,
 Of perfect wifehood and pure lowlihead.

II.

The intuitive decision of a bright
 And thorough-edged intellect to part
  Error from crime; a prudence to
   withhold;
  The laws of marriage character'd in
   gold
 Upon the blanched tablets of her heart;
 A love still burning upward, giving light
To read those laws; an accent very low
 In blandishment, but a most silver flow
  Of subtle-paced counsel in distress,
 Right to the heart and brain, tho' undescried,
  Winning its way with extreme gentleness
Thro' all the outworks of suspicious pride;
 A courage to endure and to obey;
 A hate of gossip parlance, and of sway,
 Crown'd Isabel, thro' all her placid life,
 The queen of marriage, a most perfect wife.

III.

The mellow'd reflex of a winter moon;
 A clear stream flowing with a muddy one,
  Till in its onward current it absorbs
   With swifter movement and in purer
    light
    The vexed eddies of its wayward
     brother:
   A leaning and upbearing parasite,
   Clothing the stem, which else had
    fallen quite,
   With cluster'd flower-bells and ambrosial orbs
   Of rich fruit-bunches leaning on each
    other —
    Shadow forth thee — the world hath
     not another
(Tho' all her fairest forms are types of
  thee,
And thou of God in thy great charity)
Of such a finish'd chasten'd purity.

MARIANA.

"Mariana in the moated grange."
Measure for Measure.

WITH blackest moss the flower-plots
 Were thickly crusted, one and all:
The rusted nails fell from the knots
 That held the pear to the gable-wall.
The broken sheds look'd sad and strange:
 Unlifted was the clinking latch;
 Weeded and worn the ancient thatch
Upon the lonely moated grange.
  She only said, "My life is dreary,
   He cometh not," she said;
  She said, "I am aweary, aweary,
   I would that I were dead!"

Her tears fell with the dews at even;
 Her tears fell ere the dews were dried;
She could not look on the sweet heaven,
 Either at morn or eventide.

MARIANA.

*"Her tears fell with the dews at even;
Her tears fell ere the dews were dried."*

After the flitting of the bats,
  When thickest dark did trance the sky,
She drew her casement-curtain by,
And glanced athwart the glooming flats.
    She only said, "The night is dreary,
      He cometh not," she said;
    She said, "I am aweary, aweary,
      I would that I were dead!"

Upon the middle of the night,
  Waking she heard the night-fowl crow:
The cock sung out an hour ere light:
  From the dark fen the oxen's low
Came to her: without hope of change,
  In sleep she seem'd to walk forlorn,
  Till cold winds woke the gray-eyed
      morn
About the lonely moated grange.
    She only said, "The day is dreary,
      He cometh not," she said;
    She said, "I am aweary, aweary,
      I would that I were dead!"

About a stone-cast from the wall
  A sluice with blacken'd waters slept,
And o'er it many, round and small,
  The cluster'd marish-mosses crept.
Hard by a poplar shook alway,
  All silver-green with gnarled bark:
  For leagues no other tree did mark
The level waste, the rounding gray.
    She only said, "My life is dreary,
      He cometh not," she said;
    She said, "I am aweary, aweary,
      I would that I were dead!"

And ever when the moon was low,
  And the shrill winds were up and away,
In the white curtain, to and fro,
  She saw the gusty shadow sway.
But when the moon was very low,
  And wild winds bound within their cell,
The shadow of the poplar fell
Upon her bed, across her brow.
    She only said, "The night is dreary,
      He cometh not," she said;
    She said, "I am aweary, aweary,
      I would that I were dead!"

All day within the dreamy house,
  The doors upon their hinges creak'd;
The blue fly sung in the pane; the mouse
  Behind the mouldering wainscot shriek'd,
Or from the crevice peer'd about.
  Old faces glimmer'd thro' the doors,
  Old footsteps trod the upper floors,
Old voices called her from without.
    She only said, "My life is dreary,
      He cometh not," she said;
    She said, "I am aweary, aweary,
      I would that I were dead!"

The sparrow's chirrup on the roof,
  The slow clock ticking, and the sound
Which to the wooing wind aloof
  The poplar made, did all confound
Her sense; but most she loathed the hour
  When the thick-moted sunbeam lay
  Athwart the chambers, and the day
Was sloping toward his western bower.
    Then, said she, "I am very dreary,
      He will not come," she said;
    She wept, "I am aweary, aweary,
      O God, that I were dead!"

TO ———.

I.

CLEAR-HEADED friend, whose joyful scorn,
  Edged with sharp laughter, cuts atwain
  The knots that tangle human creeds,
  The wounding cords that bind and strain
  The heart until it bleeds,
Ray-fringed eyelids of the morn
  Roof not a glance so keen as thine:
  If aught of prophecy be mine,
  Thou wilt not live in vain.

II.

Low-cowering shall the Sophist sit;
  Falsehood shall bare her plaited brow:
  Fair-fronted Truth shall droop not now
With shrilling shafts of subtle wit.
Nor martyr-flames, nor trenchant swords
  Can do away that ancient lie;
  A gentler death shall Falsehood die,
Shot thro' and thro' with cunning words.

III.

Weak Truth a-leaning on her crutch,
  Wan, wasted Truth in her utmost need,
  Thy kingly intellect shall feed,
    Until she be an athlete bold,
And weary with a finger's touch
  Those writhed limbs of lightning speed;
Like that strange angel which of old,
  Until the breaking of the light,
Wrestled with wandering Israel,
  Past Yabbok brook the livelong night,
And heaven's mazed signs stood still
  In the dim tract of Penuel.

MADELINE.

I.

THOU art not steep'd in golden languors,
  No tranced summer calm is thine,
    Ever varying Madeline.
Thro' light and shadow thou dost range,
  Sudden glances, sweet and strange,
Delicious spites and darling angers,
  And airy forms of flitting change.

II.

Smiling, frowning, evermore,
Thou art perfect in love-lore.
Revealings deep and clear are thine
Of wealthy smiles: but who may know
Whether smile or frown be fleeter?
Whether smile or frown be sweeter,
    Who may know?
Frowns perfect-sweet along the brow
Light-glooming over eyes divine,
Like little clouds sun-fringed, are thine,
    Ever varying Madeline.
Thy smile and frown are not aloof
    From one another,
  Each to each is dearest brother;
Hues of the silken sheeny woof
  Momently shot into each other.
    All the mystery is thine;
  Smiling, frowning, evermore,
  Thou art perfect in love-lore,
    Ever varying Madeline.

III.

A subtle, sudden flame,
  By veering passion fann'd,
    About thee breaks and dances ;
  When I would kiss thy hand,
The flush of anger'd shame
  O'erflows thy calmer glances,
And o'er black brows drops down
A sudden-curved frown :
But when I turn away,
  Thou, willing me to stay,
Wooest not, nor vainly wranglest ;
  But, looking fixedly the while,
All my bounding heart entanglest
  In a golden-netted smile ;
Then in madness and in bliss,
  If my lips should dare to kiss
Thy taper fingers amorously,
  Again thou blushest angerly ;
And o'er black brows drops down
A sudden-curved frown.

SONG. — THE OWL.

I.

When cats run home and light is come,
  And dew is cold upon the ground,
And the far-off stream is dumb,
  And the whirring sail goes round,
  And the whirring sail goes round ;
    Alone and warming his five wits,
    The white owl in the belfry sits.

II.

When merry milkmaids click the latch,
  And rarely smells the new-mown hay,
And the cock hath sung beneath the thatch
  Twice or thrice his roundelay,
  Twice or thrice his roundelay ;
    Alone and warming his five wits,
    The white owl in the belfry sits.

SECOND SONG.

TO THE SAME.

I.

Thy tuwhits are lull'd, I wot,
  Thy tuwhoos of yesternight,
Which upon the dark afloat,
  So took echo with delight,
  So took echo with delight,
    That her voice untuneful grown,
    Wears all day a fainter tone.

II.

I would mock thy chant anew ;
  But I cannot mimic it ;
Not a whit of thy tuwhoo,
  Thee to woo to thy tuwhit,
  Thee to woo to thy tuwhit,
    With a lengthen'd loud halloo,
    Tuwhoo, tuwhit, tuwhit, tuwhoo-o-o.

RECOLLECTIONS OF THE ARABIAN NIGHTS.

When the breeze of a joyful dawn blew free
  In the silken sail of infancy,
The tide of time flow'd back with me,
  The forward-flowing tide of time ;
And many a sheeny summer-morn,
Adown the Tigris I was borne,
By Bagdat's shrines of fretted gold,
High-walled gardens green and old ;
True Mussulman was I and sworn,
  For it was in the golden prime
    Of good Haroun Alraschid.

Anight my shallop, rustling thro'
The low and bloomed foliage, drove
The fragrant, glistening deeps, and clove
The citron-shadows in the blue :
By garden porches on the brim,
The costly doors flung open wide,
Gold glittering thro' lamplight dim,
And broider'd sofas on each side :
  In sooth it was a goodly time,
  For it was in the golden prime
    Of good Haroun Alraschid.

Often, where clear-stemm'd platans guard
The outlet, did I turn away
The boat-head down a broad canal
From the main river sluiced, where all
The sloping of the moon-lit sward
Was damask-work, and deep inlay
Of braided blooms unmown, which crept
Adown to where the water slept.
  A goodly place, a goodly time,
  For it was in the golden prime
    Of good Haroun Alraschid.

A motion from the river won
Ridged the smooth level, bearing on
My shallop thro' the star-strown calm,
Until another night in night
I enter'd, from the clearer light,

"Adown the Tigris I was borne,
By Bagdat's shrines of fretted gold."

Imbower'd vaults of pillar'd palm,
Imprisoning sweets, which, as they clomb
Heavenward, were stay'd beneath the dome
Of hollow boughs. — A goodly time,
For it was in the golden prime
  Of good Haroun Alraschid.

Still onward; and the clear canal
Is rounded to as clear a lake.
From the green rivage many a fall
Of diamond rillets musical,
Thro' little crystal arches low
Down from the central fountain's flow
Fall'n silver-chiming, seem'd to shake
The sparkling flints beneath the prow.
  A goodly place, a goodly time,
  For it was in the golden prime
  Of good Haroun Alraschid.

Above thro' many a bowery turn
A walk with vary-color'd shells
Wander'd engrain'd. On either side
All round about the fragrant marge

From fluted vase, and brazen urn
In order, eastern flowers large,
Some dropping low their crimson bells
Half-closed, and others studded wide
  With disks and tiars, fed the time
  With odor in the golden prime
  Of good Haroun Alraschid.

Far off, and where the lemon grove
In closest coverture upsprung,
The living airs of middle night
Died round the bulbul as he sung;
Not he: but something which possess'd
The darkness of the world, delight,
Life, anguish, death, immortal love,
Ceasing not, mingled, unrepress'd,
  Apart from place, withholding time,
  But flattering the golden prime
  Of good Haroun Alraschid.

Black the garden-bowers and grots
Slumber'd: the solemn palms were ranged
Above, unwoo'd of summer wind:
A sudden splendor from behind

Flush'd all the leaves with rich gold-green,
And, flowing rapidly between
Their interspaces, counterchanged
The level lake with diamond-plots
    Of dark and bright. A lovely time,
    For it was in the golden prime
        Of good Haroun Alraschid.

Dark-blue the deep sphere overhead,
Distinct with vivid stars inlaid,
Grew darker from that under-flame:
So, leaping lightly from the boat,
With silver anchor left afloat,
In marvel whence that glory came
Upon me, as in sleep I sank
In cool soft turf upon the bank,
    Entranced with that place and time,
    So worthy of the golden prime
        Of good Haroun Alraschid.

Thence thro' the garden I was drawn —
A realm of pleasance, many a mound,
And many a shadow-chequer'd lawn
Full of the city's stilly sound,
And deep myrrh-thickets blowing round
The stately cedar, tamarisks,
Thick rosaries of scented thorn,
Tall orient shrubs, and obelisks
    Graven with emblems of the time,
    In honor of the golden prime
        Of good Haroun Alraschid.

With dazed vision unawares
From the long alley's latticed shade
Emerged, I came upon the great
Pavilion of the Caliphat.
Right to the carven cedarn doors,
Flung inward over spangled floors,
Broad-baséd flights of marble stairs
Ran up with golden balustrade,
    After the fashion of the time,
    And humor of the golden prime
        Of good Haroun Alraschid.

The fourscore windows all alight
As with the quintessence of flame,
A million tapers flaring bright
From twisted silvers look'd to shame
The hollow-vaulted dark, and stream'd
Upon the mooned domes aloof
In inmost Bagdat, till there seem'd
Hundreds of crescents on the roof
    Of night new-risen, that marvellous time
    To celebrate the golden prime
        Of good Haroun Alraschid.

Then stole I up, and trancedly
Gazed on the Persian girl alone,
Serene with argent-lidded eyes
Amorous, and lashes like to rays
Of darkness, and a brow of pearl
Tressed with redolent ebony,
In many a dark delicious curl,
Flowing beneath her rose-hued zone;
    The sweetest lady of the time,
    Well worthy of the golden prime
        Of good Haroun Alraschid.

Six columns, three on either side,
Pure silver, underpropt a rich
Throne of the massive ore, from which
Down-droop'd, in many a floating fold,
Engarlanded and diaper'd
With inwrought flowers, a cloth of gold.
Thereon, his deep eye laughter-stirr'd
With merriment of kingly pride,
    Sole star of all that place and time,
    I saw him — in his golden prime,
        THE GOOD HAROUN ALRASCHID!

ODE TO MEMORY.

I.

    THOU who stealest fire,
    From the fountains of the past,
    To glorify the present; O, haste,
    Visit my low desire!
    Strengthen me, enlighten me!
    I faint in this obscurity,
    Thou dewy dawn of memory.

II.

    Come not as thou camest of late,
Flinging the gloom of yesternight
On the white day; but robed in soften'd light
    Of orient state.
Whilome thou camest with the morning mist,
    Even as a maid, whose stately brow
The dew-impearled winds of dawn have kiss'd,
    When she, as thou,
Stays on her floating locks the lovely freight
Of overflowing blooms, and earliest shoots
Of orient green, giving safe pledge of fruits,
Which in wintertide shall star
The black earth with brilliance rare.

III.

Whilome thou camest with the morning mist,
And with the evening cloud,
Showering thy gleaned wealth into my open breast
(Those peerless flowers which in the rudest wind
Never grow sere,
When rooted in the garden of the mind,
Because they are the earliest of the year).
Nor was the night thy shroud.
In sweet dreams softer than unbroken rest
Thou leddest by the hand thine infant Hope.
The eddying of her garments caught from thee
The light of thy great presence; and the cope
Of the half-attain'd futurity,
Tho' deep not fathomless,
Was cloven with the million stars which tremble
O'er the deep mind of dauntless infancy.
Small thought was there of life's distress:
For sure she deem'd no mist of earth could dull
Those spirit-thrilling eyes so keen and beautiful:
Sure she was nigher to heaven's spheres,
Listening the lordly music flowing from
The illimitable years.
O strengthen me, enlighten me!
I faint in this obscurity,
Thou dewy dawn of memory.

IV.

Come forth, I charge thee, arise,
Thou of the many tongues, the myriad eyes!
Thou comest not with shows of flaunting vines
Unto mine inner eye,
Divinest Memory!
Thou wert not nursed by the waterfall
Which ever sounds and shines
A pillar of white light upon the wall
Of purple cliffs, aloof descried:
Come from the woods that belt the gray hill-side,
The seven elms, the poplars four
That stand beside my father's door,
And chiefly from the brook that loves
To purl o'er matted cress and ribbed sand,
Or dimple in the dark of rushy coves,
Drawing into his narrow earthen urn,
In every elbow and turn,
The filter'd tribute of the rough woodland.
O, hither lead thy feet!
Pour round mine ears the livelong bleat
Of the thick-fleeced sheep from wattled folds,
Upon the ridged wolds,
When the first matin-song hath waken'd loud
Over the dark dewy earth forlorn,
What time the amber morn
Forth gushes from beneath a low-hung cloud.

V.

Large dowries doth the raptured eye
To the young spirit present
When first she is wed;
And like a bride of old
In triumph led,
With music and sweet showers
Of festal flowers,
Unto the dwelling she must sway.
Well hast thou done, great artist Memory,
In setting round thy first experiment
With royal frame-work of wrought gold;
Needs must thou dearly love thy first essay,
And foremost in thy various gallery
Place it, where sweetest sunlight falls
Upon the storied walls;
For the discovery
And newness of thine art so pleased thee,
That all which thou hast drawn of fairest
Or boldest since, but lightly weighs
With thee unto the love thou bearest
The first-born of thy genius. Artist-like,
Ever retiring thou dost gaze
On the prime labor of thine early days:
No matter what the sketch might be;
Whether the high field on the bushless Pike,
Or even a sand-built ridge
Of heaped hills that mound the sea,
Overblown with murmurs harsh,
Or even a lowly cottage whence we see
Stretch'd wide and wild the waste enormous marsh,
Where from the frequent bridge,
Like emblems of infinity,
The trenched waters run from sky to sky;
Or a garden bower'd close
With plaited alleys of the trailing rose,

Long alleys falling down to twilight grots,
Or opening upon level plots
Of crowned lilies, standing near
Purple-spiked lavender:
Whither in after life retired
From brawling storms,
From weary wind,
With youthful fancy reinspired,
We may hold converse with all forms
Of the many-sided mind,
And those whom passion hath not blinded,
Subtle-thoughted, myriad-minded.
My friend, with you to live alone,
Were how much better than to own
A crown, a sceptre, and a throne!
O strengthen me, enlighten me!
I faint in this obscurity,
Thou dewy dawn of memory.

SONG.

I.

A SPIRIT haunts the year's last hours
Dwelling amid these yellowing bowers:
    To himself he talks;
For at eventide, listening earnestly,
At his work you may hear him sob and sigh
    In the walks;
    Earthward he boweth the heavy stalks
Of the mouldering flowers:
    Heavily hangs the broad sunflower
    Over its grave i' the earth so chilly;
    Heavily hangs the hollyhock,
    Heavily hangs the tiger-lily.

II.

The air is damp, and hush'd, and close,
As a sick man's room when he taketh repose
    An hour before death;
My very heart faints and my whole soul grieves
At the moist rich smell of the rotting leaves,
    And the breath
    Of the fading edges of box beneath,
And the year's last rose.
    Heavily hangs the broad sunflower
    Over its grave i' the earth so chilly;
    Heavily hangs the hollyhock,
    Heavily hangs the tiger-lily.

ADELINE.

I.

MYSTERY of mysteries,
  Faintly smiling Adeline,
Scarce of earth nor all divine,
  Nor unhappy, nor at rest,
  But beyond expression fair
  With thy floating flaxen hair;
Thy rose-lips and full blue eyes
  Take the heart from out my breast.
Wherefore those dim looks of thine,
Shadowy, dreaming Adeline?

II.

Whence that aery bloom of thine,
  Like a lily which the sun
Looks thro' in his sad decline,
  And a rose-bush leans upon,
Thou that faintly smilest still,
  As a Naiad in a well,
  Looking at the set of day,
Or a phantom two hours old
Of a maiden past away,
Ere the placid lips be cold?
Wherefore those faint smiles of thine,
Spiritual Adeline?

III.

What hope or fear or joy is thine?
Who talketh with thee, Adeline?
  For sure thou art not all alone:
  Do beating hearts of salient springs
  Keep measure with thine own?
    Hast thou heard the butterflies
    What they say betwixt their wings?
    Or in stillest evenings
With what voice the violet wooes
To his heart the silver dews?
  Or when little airs arise,
  How the merry bluebell rings
    To the mosses underneath?
    Hast thou look'd upon the breath
Of the lilies at sunrise?
Wherefore that faint smile of thine,
Shadowy, dreaming Adeline?

IV.

Some honey-converse feeds thy mind,
  Some spirit of a crimson rose
In love with thee forgets to close
  His curtains, wasting odorous sighs
All night long on darkness blind.
What aileth thee? whom waitest thou
With thy soften'd, shadow'd brow,
  And those dew-lit eyes of thine,
  Thou faint smiler, Adeline?

V.

Lovest thou the doleful wind
　　When thou gazest at the skies?
Doth the low-tongued Orient
　　Wander from the side of the morn,
　　　　Dripping with Sabæan spice
On thy pillow, lowly bent
　　With melodious airs lovelorn,
Breathing Light against thy face,
While his locks a-drooping twined
　　Round thy neck in subtle ring
Make a carcanet of rays,
　　And ye talk together still,
In the language wherewith Spring
　　Letters cowslips on the hill?
Hence that look and smile of thine,
　　Spiritual Adeline.

A CHARACTER.

WITH a half-glance upon the sky
At night he said, "The wanderings
Of this most intricate Universe
Teach me the nothingness of things."
Yet could not all creation pierce
Beyond the bottom of his eye.

He spake of beauty: that the dull
Saw no divinity in grass,
Life in dead stones, or spirit in air;
Then looking as 't were in a glass,
He smooth'd his chin and sleek'd his hair,
And said the earth was beautiful.

He spake of virtue: not the gods
More purely, when they wish to charm
Pallas and Juno sitting by:
And with a sweeping of the arm,
And a lack-lustre dead-blue eye,
Devolved his rounded periods.

Most delicately hour by hour
He canvass'd human mysteries,
And trod on silk, as if the winds
Blew his own praises in his eyes,
And stood aloof from other minds
In impotence of fancied power.

With lips depress'd as he were meek,
Himself unto himself he sold:
Upon himself himself did feed:
Quiet, dispassionate, and cold,
And other than his form of creed,
With chisell'd features clear and sleek.

THE POET.

THE poet in a golden clime was born,
　　With golden stars above;
Dower'd with the hate of hate, the scorn
　　　　of scorn,
　　The love of love.

He saw thro' life and death, thro' good
　　　　and ill,
　　He saw thro' his own soul.
The marvel of the everlasting will,
　　An open scroll,

Before him lay: with echoing feet he
　　　　threaded
　　The secretest walks of fame:
The viewless arrows of his thoughts were
　　　　headed
　　And wing'd with flame,

Like Indian reeds blown from his silver
　　　　tongue,
　　And of so fierce a flight,
From Calpe unto Caucasus they sung,
　　Filling with light

And vagrant melodies the winds which
　　　　bore
　　Them earthward till they lit;
Then, like the arrow-seeds of the field
　　　　flower,
　　The fruitful wit

Cleaving, took root, and springing forth
　　　　anew
　　Where'er they fell, behold,
Like to the mother plant in semblance,
　　　　grew
　　A flower all gold,

And bravely furnish'd all abroad to fling
　　The winged shafts of truth,
To throng with stately blooms the breath-
　　　　ing spring
　　Of Hope and Youth.

So many minds did gird their orbs with
　　　　beams,
　　Tho' one did fling the fire.
Heaven flow'd upon the soul in many
　　　　dreams
　　Of high desire.

Thus truth was multiplied on truth, the
　　　　world
　　Like one great garden show'd,

And thro' the wreaths of floating dark upcurl'd,
    Rare sunrise flow'd.

And Freedom rear'd in that august sunrise
    Her beautiful bold brow,
When rites and forms before his burning eyes
    Melted like snow.

There was no blood upon her maiden robes
    Sunn'd by those orient skies;
But round about the circles of the globes
    Of her keen eyes

And in her raiment's hem was traced in flame
WISDOM, a name to shake
All evil dreams of power—a sacred name.
    And when she spake,

Her words did gather thunder as they ran,
    And as the lightning to the thunder
Which follows it, riving the spirit of man,
    Making earth wonder,

So was their meaning to her words. No sword
    Of wrath her right arm whirl'd,
But one poor poet's scroll, and with *his* word
    She shook the world.

THE POET'S MIND.

I.

Vex not thou the poet's mind
    With thy shallow wit:
Vex not thou the poet's mind;
    For thou canst not fathom it.
Clear and bright it should be ever,
Flowing like a crystal river;
Bright as light, and clear as wind.

II.

Dark-brow'd sophist, come not anear;
    All the place is holy ground;
Hollow smile and frozen sneer
    Come not here.
Holy water will I pour
Into every spicy flower
Of the laurel-shrubs that hedge it around.
The flowers would faint at your cruel cheer.

In your eye there is death,
    There is frost in your breath
    Which would blight the plants.
Where you stand you cannot hear
    From the groves within
    The wild-bird's din.
In the heart of the garden the merry bird chants,
It would fall to the ground if you came in.
    In the middle leaps a fountain
    Like sheet lightning,
    Ever brightening
    With a low melodious thunder;
All day and all night it is ever drawn
From the brain of the purple mountain
Which stands in the distance yonder:
It springs on a level of bowery lawn,
And the mountain draws it from Heaven above,
And it sings a song of undying love;
And yet, tho' its voice be so clear and full,
You never would hear it; your ears are so dull;
So keep where you are: you are foul with sin;
It would shrink to the earth if you came in.

THE SEA-FAIRIES.

Slow sail'd the weary mariners and saw,
    Betwixt the green brink and the running foam,
Sweet faces, rounded arms, and bosoms prest
To little harps of gold; and while they mused,
Whispering to each other half in fear,
Shrill music reach'd them on the middle sea.

Whither away, whither away, whither away? fly no more.
Whither away from the high green field, and the happy blossoming shore?
Day and night to the billow the fountain calls;
Down shower the gambolling waterfalls
From wandering over the lea:
Out of the live-green heart of the dells
They freshen the silvery-crimson shells,
And thick with white bells the clover-hill swells
High over the full-toned sea:
O hither, come hither and furl your sails,
Come hither to me and to me:

Hither, come hither and frolic and play ;
Here it is only the mew that wails ;
We will sing to you all the day :
Mariner, mariner, furl your sails,
For here are the blissful downs and dales,
And merrily, merrily carol the gales,
And the spangle dances in bight and bay,
And the rainbow forms and flies on the land
Over the islands free ;
And the rainbow lives in the curve of the sand ;
Hither, come hither and see ;
And the rainbow hangs on the poising wave,
And sweet is the color of cove and cave,
And sweet shall your welcome be :
O hither, come hither, and be our lords,
For merry brides are we :
We will kiss sweet kisses, and speak sweet words :
O listen, listen, your eyes shall glisten
With pleasure and love and jubilee :
O listen, listen, your eyes shall glisten
When the sharp clear twang of the golden chords
Runs up the ridged sea.
Who can light on as happy a shore
All the world o'er, all the world o'er ?
Whither away ? listen and stay : mariner, mariner, fly no more.

THE DESERTED HOUSE.

I.

LIFE and Thought have gone away
   Side by side,
     Leaving door and windows wide :
Careless tenants they !

II.

All within is dark as night :
In the windows is no light ;
And no murmur at the door,
So frequent on its hinge before.

"Life and Thought have gone away
Side by side."

III.

Close the door, the shutters close,
 Or thro' the windows we shall see
 The nakedness and vacancy
Of the dark deserted house.

IV.

Come away: no more of mirth
 Is here or merry-making sound.
The house was builded of the earth,
And shall fall again to ground.

V.

Come away: for Life and Thought
 Here no longer dwell;
 But in a city glorious —
A great and distant city — have bought
 A mansion incorruptible.
  Would they could have stayed with us!

THE DYING SWAN.

I.

THE plain was grassy, wild and bare,
 Wide, wild, and open to the air,
 Which had built up everywhere
An under-roof of doleful gray.
With an inner voice the river ran,
Adown it floated a dying swan,
 And loudly did lament.
It was the middle of the day.
Ever the weary wind went on,
 And took the reed-tops as it went.

II.

Some blue peaks in the distance rose,
And white against the cold-white sky,
 Shone out their crowning snows,
 One willow over the river wept,
And shook the wave as the wind did sigh;
Above in the wind was the swallow,
 Chasing itself at its own wild will,
 And far thro' the marish green and still
 The tangled water-courses slept,
Shot over with purple, and green, and yellow.

III.

The wild swan's death-hymn took the soul
Of that waste place with joy
Hidden in sorrow: at first to the ear
The warble was low, and full and clear;
And floating about the under-sky,

Prevailing in weakness, the coronach stole
Sometimes afar, and sometimes anear;
But anon her awful jubilant voice,
With a music strange and manifold,
Flow'd forth on a carol free and bold;
As when a mighty people rejoice
With shawms, and with cymbals, and harps of gold,
And the tumult of their acclaim is roll'd
Thro' the open gates of the city afar,
To the shepherd who watcheth the evening star.
And the creeping mosses and clambering weeds,
And the willow-branches hoar and dank,
And the wavy swell of the soughing reeds,
And the wave-worn horns of the echoing bank,
And the silvery marish-flowers that throng
The desolate creeks and pools among,
Were flooded over with eddying song.

A DIRGE.

I.

Now is done thy long day's work;
Fold thy palms across thy breast,
Fold thine arms, turn to thy rest.
 Let them rave.
Shadows of the silver birk
Sweep the green that folds thy grave.
 Let them rave.

II.

Thee nor carketh care nor slander;
Nothing but the small cold worm
Fretteth thine enshrouded form.
 Let them rave.
Light and shadow ever wander
O'er the green that folds thy grave.
 Let them rave.

III.

Thou wilt not turn upon thy bed;
Chanteth not the brooding bee
Sweeter tones than calumny?
 Let them rave.
Thou wilt never raise thine head
From the green that folds thy grave.
 Let them rave.

IV.

Crocodiles wept tears for thee;
The woodbine and eglatere
Drip sweeter dews than traitor's tear.
 Let them rave.

Rain makes music in the tree
O'er the green that folds thy grave.
    Let them rave.

V.

Round thee blow, self-pleached deep,
Bramble roses, faint and pale,
And long purples of the dale.
    Let them rave.
These in every shower creep
Thro' the green that folds thy grave.
    Let them rave.

VI.

The gold-eyed kingcups fine ;
The frail bluebell peereth over
Rare broidry of the purple clover.
    Let them rave.
Kings have no such couch as thine,
As the green that folds thy grave.
    Let them rave.

VII.

Wild words wander here and there :
God's great gift of speech abused
Makes thy memory confused :
    But let them rave.
The balm-cricket carols clear
In the green that folds thy grave.
    Let them rave.

LOVE AND DEATH.

WHAT time the mighty moon was gathering light
Love paced the thymy plots of Paradise,
And all about him roll'd his lustrous eyes ;
When, turning round a cassia, full in view
Death, walking all alone beneath a yew,
And talking to himself, first met his sight :
"You must begone," said Death, "these walks are mine."
Love wept and spread his sheeny vans for flight ;
Yet ere he parted said, "This hour is thine :
Thou art the shadow of life, and as the tree
Stands in the sun and shadows all beneath,
So in the light of great eternity
Life eminent creates the shade of death ;
The shadow passeth when the tree shall fall,
But I shall reign for ever over all."

THE BALLAD OF ORIANA.

MY heart is wasted with my woe,
    Oriana.
There is no rest for me below,
    Oriana.
When the long dun wolds are ribb'd with snow,
And loud the Norland whirlwinds blow,
    Oriana,
Alone I wander to and fro,
    Oriana.

Ere the light on dark was growing,
    Oriana,
At midnight the cock was crowing,
    Oriana :
Winds were blowing, waters flowing,
We heard the steeds to battle going,
    Oriana ;
Aloud the hollow bugle blowing,
    Oriana.

In the yew-wood black as night,
    Oriana,
Ere I rode into the fight,
    Oriana,
While blissful tears blinded my sight
By star-shine and by moonlight,
    Oriana,
I to thee my troth did plight,
    Oriana.

She stood upon the castle wall,
    Oriana :
She watch'd my crest among them all,
    Oriana :
She saw me fight, she heard me call,
When forth there stept a foeman tall,
    Oriana,
Atween me and the castle wall,
    Oriana.

The bitter arrow went aside,
    Oriana :
The false, false arrow went aside,
    Oriana :
The damned arrow glanced aside,
And pierced thy heart, my love, my bride,
    Oriana !
Thy heart, my life, my love, my bride,
    Oriana !

Oh ! narrow, narrow was the space,
    Oriana.
Loud, loud rung out the bugle's brays,
    Oriana.

Oh! deathful stabs were dealt apace,
The battle deepen'd in its place,
    Oriana;
But I was down upon my face,
    Oriana.

They should have stabb'd me where I lay,
    Oriana!
How could I rise and come away,
    Oriana?
How could I look upon the day?
They should have stabb'd me where I lay,
    Oriana —
They should have trod me into clay,
    Oriana.

O breaking heart that will not break,
    Oriana!
O pale, pale face so sweet and meek,
    Oriana!
Thou smilest, but thou dost not speak,
And then the tears run down my cheek,
    Oriana:
What wantest thou? whom dost thou seek,
    Oriana?

I cry aloud: none hear my cries,
    Oriana.
Thou comest atween me and the skies,
    Oriana.
I feel the tears of blood arise
Up from my heart unto my eyes,
    Oriana.
Within thy heart my arrow lies,
    Oriana.

O cursed hand! O cursed blow!
    Oriana!
O happy thou that liest low,
    Oriana!
All night the silence seems to flow
Beside me in my utter woe,
    Oriana.
A weary, weary way I go,
    Oriana.

When Norland winds pipe down the sea,
    Oriana,
I walk, I dare not think of thee,
    Oriana.
Thou liest beneath the greenwood tree,
I dare not die and come to thee,
    Oriana.
I hear the roaring of the sea,
    Oriana.

CIRCUMSTANCE.

Two children in two neighbor villages
Playing mad pranks along the heathy
    leas;
Two strangers meeting at a festival;
Two lovers whispering by an orchard wall;
Two lives bound fast in one with golden
    ease;
Two graves grass-green beside a gray
    church-tower,
Wash'd with still rains and daisy-
    blossomed;
Two children in one hamlet born and bred;
So runs the round of life from hour to
    hour.

THE MERMAN.

I.

Who would be
A merman bold,
Sitting alone,
Singing alone
Under the sea,
With a crown of gold,
On a throne?

II.

I would be a merman bold;
I would sit and sing the whole of the day;
I would fill the sea-halls with a voice of
    power;
But at night I would roam abroad and
    play
With the mermaids in and out of the
    rocks,
Dressing their hair with the white sea-
    flower;
And holding them back by their flowing
    locks
I would kiss them often under the sea,
And kiss them again till they kiss'd me
    Laughingly, laughingly;
And then we would wander away, away
To the pale-green sea-groves straight and
    high,
Chasing each other merrily.

III.

There would be neither moon nor star;
But the wave would make music above
    us afar —
Low thunder and light in the magic
    night —

Neither moon nor star.
We would call aloud in the dreamy dells,
Call to each other and whoop and cry
  All night, merrily, merrily;
They would pelt me with starry spangles
    and shells,
Laughing and clapping their hands between,
  All night, merrily, merrily:
But I would throw to them back in
    mine
Turkis and agate and almondine:
Then leaping out upon them unseen
I would kiss them often under the sea,
And kiss them again till they kiss'd me
    Laughingly, laughingly.
O, what a happy life were mine
Under the hollow-hung ocean green!
Soft are the moss-beds under the sea;
We would live merrily, merrily.

THE MERMAID.

I.

Who would be
A mermaid fair,
Singing alone,
Combing her hair
Under the sea,
In a golden curl
With a comb of pearl,
On a throne?

II.

I would be a mermaid fair;
I would sing to myself the whole of the
    day;
With a comb of pearl I would comb my
    hair;
And still as I comb'd I would sing and
    say,
"Who is it loves me? who loves not
    me?"
I would comb my hair till my ringlets
    would fall
  Low adown, low adown,
From under my starry sea-bud crown
  Low adown and around,
And I should look like a fountain of
    gold
    Springing alone
  With a shrill inner sound,
    Over the throne
  In the midst of the hall;

Till that great sea-snake under the sea
From his coiled sleeps in the central deeps
Would slowly trail himself sevenfold
Round the hall where I sate, and look in
    at the gate
With his large calm eyes for the love of me.
And all the mermen under the sea
Would feel their immortality
Die in their hearts for the love of me.

III.

But at night I would wander away, away,
  I would fling on each side my low-
    flowing locks,
And lightly vault from the throne and
    play
  With the mermen in and out of the
    rocks;
We would run to and fro, and hide and
    seek,
  On the broad sea-wolds in the crimson
    shells,
  Whose silvery spikes are nighest the sea.
But if any came near I would call, and
    shriek,
And adown the steep like a wave I would
    leap
  From the diamond-ledges that jut from
    the dells;
For I would not be kiss'd by all who would
    list,
Of the bold merry mermen under the sea;
They would sue me, and woo me, and
    flatter me,
In the purple twilights under the sea;
But the king of them all would carry me,
Woo me, and win me, and marry me,
In the branching jaspers under the sea;
Then all the dry pied things that be
In the hueless mosses under the sea
Would curl round my silver feet silently,
All looking up for the love of me.
And if I should carol aloud, from aloft
All things that are forked, and horned,
    and soft
Would lean out from the hollow sphere
    of the sea,
All looking down for the love of me.

SONNET TO J. M. K.

My hope and heart is with thee — thou
    wilt be
A latter Luther, and a soldier-priest
To scare church-harpies from the master's
    feast;

Our dusted velvets have much need of
    thee:
Thou art no sabbath-drawler of old saws,
Distill'd from some worm-canker'd
    homily;
But spurr'd at heart with fieriest energy
To embattail and to wall about thy cause
With iron-worded proof, hating to hark
The humming of the drowsy pulpit-drone
Half God's good sabbath, while the worn-
    out clerk
Brow-beats his desk below. Thou from
    a throne
Mounted in heaven wilt shoot into the dark
Arrows of lightnings. I will stand and
    mark.

POEMS.

(PUBLISHED 1832.)

[This division of this volume was published in the winter of 1832. Some of the poems have been considerably altered. Others have been added, which, with one exception, were written in 1833.]

THE LADY OF SHALOTT.

PART I.

On either side the river lie
Long fields of barley and of rye,
That clothe the wold and meet the sky;
And thro' the field the road runs by
    To many-tower'd Camelot;
And up and down the people go,
Gazing where the lilies blow
Round an island there below,
    The island of Shalott.

Willows whiten, aspens quiver,
Little breezes dusk and shiver
Thro' the wave that runs for ever
By the island in the river
    Flowing down to Camelot.
Four gray walls, and four gray towers,
Overlook a space of flowers,
And the silent isle imbowers
    The Lady of Shalott.

By the margin, willow-veil'd,
Slide the heavy barges trail'd
By slow horses; and unhail'd
The shallop flitteth silken-sail'd
    Skimming down to Camelot:
But who hath seen her wave her hand?
Or at the casement seen her stand?
Or is she known in all the land,
    The Lady of Shalott?

Only reapers, reaping early
In among the bearded barley,
Hear a song that echoes cheerly
From the river winding clearly,
    Down to tower'd Camelot:
And by the moon the reaper weary,
Piling sheaves in uplands airy,
Listening, whispers "'T is the fairy
    Lady of Shalott."

PART II.

There she weaves by night and day
A magic web with colors gay.
She has heard a whisper say,
A curse is on her if she stay
    To look down to Camelot.
She knows not what the curse may be,
And so she weaveth steadily,
And little other care hath she,
    The Lady of Shalott.

And moving thro' a mirror clear
That hangs before her all the year,
Shadows of the world appear.
There she sees the highway near
    Winding down to Camelot:
There the river eddy whirls,
And there the surly village-churls,
And the red cloaks of market-girls,
    Pass onward from Shalott.

Sometimes a troop of damsels glad,
An abbot on an ambling pad,
Sometimes a curly shepherd-lad,
Or long-hair'd page in crimson clad,
    Goes by to tower'd Camelot;
And sometimes thro' the mirror blue

The knights come riding two and two:
She hath no loyal knight and true,
      The Lady of Shalott.

But in her web she still delights
To weave the mirror's magic sights,
For often thro' the silent nights
A funeral, with plumes and lights,
      And music, went to Camelot:
Or when the moon was overhead,
Came two young lovers lately wed;
"I am half sick of shadows," said
      The Lady of Shalott.

PART III.

A BOW-SHOT from her bower-eaves,
He rode between the barley-sheaves,
The sun came dazzling thro' the leaves,
And flamed upon the brazen greaves
      Of bold Sir Lancelot.
A red-cross knight for ever kneel'd
To a lady in his shield,
That sparkled on the yellow field,
      Beside remote Shalott.

The gemmy bridle glitter'd free,
Like to some branch of stars we see
Hung in the golden Galaxy.
The bridle bells rang merrily
      As he rode down to Camelot:
And from his blazon'd baldric slung
A mighty silver bugle hung,
And as he rode his armor rung,
      Beside remote Shalott.

All in the blue unclouded weather
Thick-jewell'd shone the saddle-leather,
The helmet and the helmet-feather
Burned like one burning flame together,
      As he rode down to Camelot.
As often thro' the purple night,
Below the starry clusters bright,
Some bearded meteor, trailing light,
      Moves over still Shalott.

His broad clear brow in sunlight glow'd;
On burnish'd hooves his war-horse trode;
From underneath his helmet flow'd
His coal-black curls as on he rode,
      As he rode down to Camelot.
From the bank and from the river
He flash'd into the crystal mirror,
"Tirra lirra," by the river
      Sang Sir Lancelot.

She left the web, she left the loom,
She made three paces thro' the room,
She saw the water-lily bloom,
She saw the helmet and the plume,
      She look'd down to Camelot.
Out flew the web and floated wide;
The mirror crack'd from side to side;
"The curse is come upon me," cried
      The Lady of Shalott.

PART IV.

IN the stormy east-wind straining,
The pale yellow woods were waning,
The broad stream in his banks complaining,
Heavily the low sky raining
      Over tower'd Camelot;
Down she came and found a boat
Beneath a willow left afloat,
And round about the prow she wrote
      The Lady of Shalott.

And down the river's dim expanse—
Like some bold seër in a trance,
Seeing all his own mischance—
With a glassy countenance
      Did she look to Camelot.
And at the closing of the day
She loosed the chain, and down she lay;
The broad stream bore her far away,
      The Lady of Shalott.

Lying, robed in snowy white
That loosely flew to left and right—
The leaves upon her falling light—
Thro' the noises of the night
      She floated down to Camelot:
And as the boat-head wound along
The willowy hills and fields among,
They heard her singing her last song,
      The Lady of Shalott.

Heard a carol, mournful, holy,
Chanted loudly, chanted lowly,
Till her blood was frozen slowly,
And her eyes were darken'd wholly,
      Turn'd to tower'd Camelot;
For ere she reach'd upon the tide
The first house by the water-side,
Singing in her song she died,
      The Lady of Shalott.

Under tower and balcony,
By garden-wall and gallery,
A gleaming shape she floated by,
Dead-pale between the houses high,
      Silent into Camelot.
Out upon the wharfs they came,

"'The curse is come upon me,' cried
The Lady of Shalott."

Knight and burgher, lord and dame,
And round the prow they read her name,
  The Lady of Shalott.

Who is this? and what is here?
And in the lighted palace near
Died the sound of royal cheer;
And they cross'd themselves for fear,
 All the knights at Camelot:
But Lancelot mused a little space;
He said, "She has a lovely face;
God in his mercy lend her grace,
  The Lady of Shalott."

MARIANA IN THE SOUTH.

WITH one black shadow at its feet,
 The house thro' all the level shines,
Close-latticed to the brooding heat,
 And silent in its dusty vines:
A faint-blue ridge upon the right,
 An empty river-bed before,
And shallows on a distant shore,
 In glaring sand and inlets bright.
  But "Ave Mary," made she moan,
  And "Ave Mary," night and morn,
  And "Ah," she sang, "to be all alone,
   To live forgotten, and love forlorn."

She, as her carol sadder grew,
 From brow and bosom slowly down
Thro' rosy taper fingers drew
 Her streaming curls of deepest brown
To left and right, and made appear,
 Still-lighted in a secret shrine,
 Her melancholy eyes divine,
The home of woe without a tear.

And "Ave Mary," was her moan,
  "Madonna, sad is night and
    morn";
And "Ah," she sang, "to be all alone,
  To live forgotten, and love for-
    lorn."

Till all the crimson changed, and past
  Into deep orange o'er the sea,
Low on her knees herself she cast,
  Before Our Lady murmur'd she;
Complaining, "Mother, give me grace
  To help me of my weary load."
And on the liquid mirror glow'd
The clear perfection of her face.
  "Is this the form," she made her
    moan,
  "That won his praises night and
    morn?"
And "Ah," she said, "but I wake
    alone,
  I sleep forgotten, I wake forlorn."

Nor bird would sing, nor lamb would bleat,
  Nor any cloud would cross the vault,
But day increased from heat to heat,
  On stony drought and steaming salt;
Till now at noon she slept again,
  And seem'd knee-deep in mountain
    grass,
And heard her native breezes pass,
And runlets babbling down the glen.
  She breathed in sleep a lower moan,
    And murmuring, as at night and
      morn,
  She thought, "My spirit is here
    alone,
    Walks forgotten, and is forlorn."

Dreaming, she knew it was a dream:
  She felt he was and was not there.
She woke: the babble of the stream
  Fell, and, without, the steady glare
Shrank one sick willow sere and small.
  The river-bed was dusty-white;
And all the furnace of the light
Struck up against the blinding wall.
  She whisper'd, with a stifled moan
    More inward than at night or morn,
  "Sweet Mother, let me not here alone
    Live forgotten and die forlorn."

And, rising, from her bosom drew
  Old letters, breathing of her worth,
For "Love," they said, "must needs be
    true,
  To what is loveliest upon earth."
An image seem'd to pass the door,

To look at her with slight, and say,
  "But now thy beauty flows away,
So be alone for evermore."
  "O cruel heart," she changed her
    tone,
  "And cruel love, whose end is
    scorn,
Is this the end to be left alone,
  To live forgotten, and die forlorn!"

But sometimes in the falling day
  An image seem'd to pass the door,
To look into her eyes and say,
  "But thou shalt be alone no more."
And flaming downward over all
  From heat to heat the day decreased,
And slowly rounded to the east
The one black shadow from the wall.
  "The day to night," she made her
    moan,
  "The day to night, the night to
    morn,
  And day and night I am left alone
    To live forgotten, and love for-
      lorn."

At eve a dry cicala sung,
  There came a sound as of the sea;
Backward the lattice-blind she flung,
  And lean'd upon the balcony.
There all in spaces rosy-bright
  Large Hesper glitter'd on her tears,
And deepening thro' the silent spheres,
Heaven over Heaven rose the night.
  And weeping then she made her
    moan,
  "The night comes on that knows
    not morn,
  When I shall cease to be all alone,
    To live forgotten, and love for-
      lorn."

ELEÄNORE.

I.

Thy dark eyes open'd not,
  Nor first reveal'd themselves to English
    air,
  For there is nothing here,
Which, from the outward to the inward
    brought,
Moulded thy baby thought.
Far off from human neighborhood,
  Thou wert born, on a summer morn,
A mile beneath the cedar-wood.
Thy bounteous forehead was not fann'd

With breezes from our oaken glades,
But thou wert nursed in some delicious
  land
Of lavish lights, and floating shades:
And flattering thy childish thought
  The oriental fairy brought,
  At the moment of thy birth,
From old well-heads of haunted rills,
And the hearts of purple hills,
And shadow'd coves on a sunny shore,
  The choicest wealth of all the earth,
  Jewel or shell, or starry ore,
  To deck thy cradle, Eleänore.

II.

Or the yellow-banded bees,
Thro' half-open lattices
Coming in the scented breeze,
Fed thee, a child, lying alone,
  With whitest honey in fairy gardens cull'd —
A glorious child, dreaming alone,
In silk-soft folds, upon yielding down,
With the hum of swarming bees
  Into dreamful slumber lull'd.

III.

Who may minister to thee?
Summer herself should minister
  To thee, with fruitage golden-rinded
On golden salvers, or it may be,
Youngest Autumn, in a bower
Grape-thicken'd from the light, and
  blinded
  With many a deep-hued bell-like
  flower
Of fragrant trailers, when the air
  Sleepeth over all the heaven,
  And the crag that fronts the Even,
  All along the shadowy shore,
Crimsons over an inland mere,
  Eleänore!

IV.

How may full-sail'd verse express,
  How may measured words adore
  The full-flowing harmony
    Of thy swan-like stateliness,
      Eleänore?
  The luxuriant symmetry
Of thy floating gracefulness,
  Eleänore?
Every turn and glance of thine,
Every lineament divine,
  Eleänore,

And the steady sunset glow,
That stays upon thee? For in thee
  Is nothing sudden, nothing
  single;
Like two streams of incense free
  From one censer, in one
  shrine,
Thought and motion mingle,
Mingle ever. Motions flow
To one another, even as tho'
  They were modulated so
    To an unheard melody,
Which lives about thee, and a sweep
Of richest pauses, evermore
Drawn from each other mellow-deep;
  Who may express thee, Eleänore?

V.

I stand before thee, Eleänore;
  I see thy beauty gradually unfold,
Daily and hourly, more and more.
I muse, as in a trance, the while
  Slowly, as from a cloud of gold,
Comes out thy deep ambrosial smile.
I muse, as in a trance, whene'er
  The languors of thy love-deep eyes
Float on to me. I would I were
  So tranced, so rapt in ecstasies,
To stand apart, and to adore,
Gazing on thee for evermore,
Serene, imperial Eleänore!

VI.

Sometimes, with most intensity
Gazing, I seem to see
Thought folded over thought, smiling
  asleep,
Slowly awaken'd, grow so full and deep
In thy large eyes, that, overpower'd quite,
I cannot veil, or droop my sight,
But am as nothing in its light:
As tho' a star, in inmost heaven set,
  Ev'n while we gaze on it,
Should slowly round his orb, and slowly
  grow
To a full face, there like a sun remain
Fix'd — then as slowly fade again,
  And draw itself to what it was before;
  So full, so deep, so slow,
  Thought seems to come and go
In thy large eyes, imperial Eleänore.

VII.

As thunder-clouds that, hung on high,
  Roof'd the world with doubt and fear,
Floating thro' an evening atmosphere,
Grow golden all about the sky;

In thee all passion becomes passionless,
Touch'd by thy spirit's mellowness,
Losing his fire and active might
   In a silent meditation,
Falling into a still delight,
   And luxury of contemplation :
As waves that up a quiet cove
Rolling slide, and lying still
      Shadow forth the banks at will :
Or sometimes they swell and move,
   Pressing up against the land,
   With motions of the outer sea :
   And the self-same influence
   Controlleth all the soul and sense
   Of Passion gazing upon thee.
His bow-string slacken'd, languid Love,
   Leaning his cheek upon his hand,
   Droops both his wings, regarding thee,
   And so would languish evermore,
   Serene, imperial Eleänore.

VIII.

But when I see thee roam, with tresses
    unconfined,
While the amorous, odorous wind
   Breathes low between the sunset and
     the moon ;
   Or, in a shadowy saloon,
On silken cushions half reclined ;
   I watch thy grace ; and in its place
My heart a charmed slumber keeps,
   While I muse upon thy face ;
   And a languid fire creeps
Thro' my veins to all my frame,
Dissolvingly and slowly : soon
   From thy rose-red lips MY name
Floweth ; and then, as in a swoon,
   With dinning sound my ears are rife,
   My tremulous tongue faltereth,
   I lose my color, I lose my breath,
   I drink the cup of a costly death,
Brimm'd with delirious draughts of
    warmest life.
I die with my delight, before
   I hear what I would hear from
    thee ;
   Yet tell my name again to me,
I *would* be dying evermore,
So dying ever, Eleänore.

THE MILLER'S DAUGHTER.

I SEE the wealthy miller yet,
   His double chin, his portly size,
And who that knew him could forget
   The busy wrinkles round his eyes ?
The slow wise smile that, round about
   His dusty forehead drily curl'd,
Seem'd half-within and half-without,
   And full of dealings with the world ?

In yonder chair I see him sit,
   Three fingers round the old silver cup—
I see his gray eyes twinkle yet
   At his own jest — gray eyes lit up
With summer lightnings of a soul
   So full of summer warmth, so glad,
So healthy, sound, and clear and whole,
   His memory scarce can make me sad.

Yet fill my glass : give me one kiss :
   My own sweet Alice, we must die.
There 's somewhat in this world amiss
   Shall be unriddled by and by.
There 's somewhat flows to us in life,
   But more is taken quite away.
Pray, Alice, pray, my darling wife,
   That we may die the self-same day.

Have I not found a happy earth ?
   I least should breathe a thought of pain.
Would God renew me from my birth
   I'd almost live my life again.
So sweet it seems with thee to walk,
   And once again to woo thee mine —
It seems in after-dinner talk
   Across the walnuts and the wine —

To be the long and listless boy
   Late-left an orphan of the squire,
Where this old mansion mounted high
   Looks down upon the village spire :
For even here, where I and you
   Have lived and loved alone so long,
Each morn my sleep was broken thro'
   By some wild skylark's matin song.

And oft I heard the tender dove
   In firry woodlands making moan ;
But ere I saw your eyes, my love,
   I had no motion of my own.
For scarce my life with fancy play'd
   Before I dream'd that pleasant dream —
Still hither thither idly sway'd
   Like those long mosses in the stream.

Or from the bridge I lean'd to hear
   The milldam rushing down with noise,
And see the minnows everywhere
   In crystal eddies glance and poise,
The tall flag-flowers when they sprung
   Below the range of stepping-stones,
Or those three chestnuts near, that hung
   In masses thick with milky cones.

But, Alice, what an hour was that,
  When after roving in the woods
('T was April then), I came and sat
  Below the chestnuts, when their buds
Were glistening to the breezy blue ;
  And on the slope, an absent fool,
I cast me down, nor thought of you,
  But angled in the higher pool.

A love-song I had somewhere read,
  An echo from a measured strain,
Beat time to nothing in my head
  From some odd corner of the brain.
It haunted me, the morning long,
  With weary sameness in the rhymes,
The phantom of a silent song,
  That went and came a thousand times.

Then leapt a trout. In lazy mood
  I watch'd the little circles die ;
They past into the level flood,
  And there a vision caught my eye ;
The reflex of a beauteous form,
  A glowing arm, a gleaming neck,
As when a sunbeam wavers warm
  Within the dark and dimpled beck.

For you remember, you had set,
  That morning, on the casement-edge
A long green box of mignonette,
  And you were leaning from the ledge :
And when I raised my eyes, above
  They met with two so full and bright —
Such eyes ! I swear to you, my love,
  That these have never lost their light.

I loved, and love dispell'd the fear
  That I should die an early death :
For love possess'd the atmosphere,
  And fill'd the breast with purer breath.
My mother thought, What ails the boy ?
  For I was alter'd, and began
To move about the house with joy,
  And with the certain step of man.

I loved the brimming wave that swam
  Thro' quiet meadows round the mill,
The sleepy pool above the dam,
  The pool beneath it never still,
The meal-sacks on the whiten'd floor,
  The dark round of the dripping wheel,
The very air about the door
  Made misty with the floating meal.

And oft in ramblings on the wold,
  When April nights began to blow,
And April's crescent glimmer'd cold,
  I saw the village lights below ;

I knew your taper far away,
  And full at heart of trembling hope,
From off the wold I came, and lay
  Upon the freshly-flower'd slope.

The deep brook groan'd beneath the mill ;
  And "by that lamp," I thought, "she sits !"
The white chalk-quarry from the hill
  Gleam'd to the flying moon by fits.
" O that I were beside her now !
  O, will she answer if I call ?
O, would she give me vow for vow,
  Sweet Alice, if I told her all ?"

Sometimes I saw you sit and spin ;
  And, in the pauses of the wind,
Sometimes I heard you sing within ;
  Sometimes your shadow cross'd the blind.
At last you rose and moved the light,
  And the long shadow of the chair
Flitted across into the night,
  And all the casement darken'd there.

But when at last I dared to speak,
  The lanes, you know, were white with May,
Your ripe lips moved not, but your cheek
  Flush'd like the coming of the day ;
And so it was — half-sly, half-shy,
  You would, and would not, little one !
Although I pleaded tenderly,
  And you and I were all alone.

And slowly was my mother brought
  To yield consent to my desire :
She wish'd me happy, but she thought
  I might have look'd a little higher ;
And I was young — too young to wed :
  "Yet must I love her for your sake ;
Go fetch your Alice here," she said :
  Her eyelid quiver'd as she spake.

And down I went to fetch my bride :
  But, Alice, you were ill at ease ;
This dress and that by turns you tried,
  Too fearful that you should not please.
I loved you better for your fears,
  I knew you could not look but well ;
And dews, that would have fall'n in tears,
  I kiss'd away before they fell.

I watch'd the little flutterings,
  The doubt my mother would not see ;
She spoke at large of many things,
  And at the last she spoke of me ;

And turning look'd upon your face,
  As near this door you sat apart,
And rose, and, with a silent grace
  Approaching, press'd you heart to heart.

Ah, well — but sing the foolish song
  I gave you, Alice, on the day
When, arm in arm, we went along,
  A pensive pair, and you were gay
With bridal flowers — that I may seem,
  As in the nights of old, to lie
Beside the mill-wheel in the stream,
  While those full chestnuts whisper by.

It is the miller's daughter,
  And she is grown so dear, so dear,
That I would be the jewel
  That trembles at her ear :
For hid in ringlets day and night,
  I 'd touch her neck so warm and white.

And I would be the girdle
  About her dainty dainty waist,
And her heart would beat against me,
  In sorrow and in rest :
And I should know if it beat right,
  I 'd clasp it round so close and tight.

And I would be the necklace,
  And all day long to fall and rise
Upon her balmy bosom,
  With her laughter or her sighs,
And I would lie so light, so light,
  I scarce should be unclasp'd at night.

A trifle, sweet ! which true love spells —
  True love interprets — right alone.
His light upon the letter dwells,
  'For all the spirit is his own.
So, if I waste words now, in truth
  You must blame Love. His early rage
Had force to make me rhyme in youth,
  And makes me talk too much in age.

And now those vivid hours are gone,
  Like mine own life to me thou art,
Where Past and Present, wound in one,
  Do make a garland for the heart :
So sing that other song I made,
  Half-anger'd with my happy lot,
The day, when in the chestnut shade
  I found the blue Forget-me-not.

    Love that hath us in the net,
    Can he pass, and we forget ?
    Many suns arise and set.
    Many a chance the years beget.
    Love the gift is Love the debt.
      Even so.
    Love is hurt with jar and fret.
    Love is made a vague regret.
    Eyes with idle tears are wet.
    Idle habit links us yet.
    What is love ? for we forget:
      Ah, no ! no !

Look thro' mine eyes with thine. True wife,
  Round my true heart thine arms entwine ;
My other dearer life in life,
  Look thro' my very soul with thine !
Untouch'd with any shade of years,
  May those kind eyes forever dwell !
They have not shed a many tears,
  Dear eyes, since first I knew them well.

Yet tears they shed : they had their part
  Of sorrow : for when time was ripe,
The still affection of the heart
  Became an outward breathing type,
That into stillness past again,
  And left a want unknown before ;
Although the loss that brought us pain,
  That loss but made us love the more,

With farther lookings on. The kiss,
  The woven arms, seem but to be
Weak symbols of the settled bliss,
  The comfort, I have found in thee :
But that God bless thee, dear — who wrought
  Two spirits to one equal mind —
With blessings beyond hope or thought,
  With blessings which no words can find.

Arise, and let us wander forth,
  To yon old mill across the wolds ;
For look, the sunset, south and north,
  Winds all the vale in rosy folds,
And fires your narrow casement glass,
  Touching the sullen pool below :
On the chalk-hill the bearded grass
  Is dry and dewless. Let us go.

FATIMA.

O Love, Love, Love ! O withering might !
O sun, that from thy noonday height
Shudderest when I strain my sight,
Throbbing thro' all thy heat and light,

Lo, falling from my constant mind,
Lo, parch'd and wither'd, deaf and blind,
I whirl like leaves in roaring wind.

Last night I wasted hateful hours
Below the city's eastern towers:
I thirsted for the brooks, the showers:
I roll'd among the tender flowers:
I crush'd them on my breast, my mouth:
I look'd athwart the burning drouth
Of that long desert to the south.

Last night, when some one spoke his name,
From my swift blood that went and came
A thousand little shafts of flame
Were shiver'd in my narrow frame.
 O Love, O fire! once he drew
 With one long kiss my whole soul thro'
 My lips, as sunlight drinketh dew.

Before he mounts the hill, I know
He cometh quickly: from below
Sweet gales, as from deep gardens, blow
Before him, striking on my brow.
 In my dry brain my spirit soon,
 Down-deepening from swoon to swoon,
 Faints like a dazzled morning moon.

The wind sounds like a silver wire,
And from beyond the noon a fire
Is pour'd upon the hills, and nigher
The skies stoop down in their desire;
 And, isled in sudden seas of light,
 My heart, pierced thro' with fierce delight,
 Bursts into blossom in his sight.

My whole soul waiting silently,
All naked in a sultry sky,
Droops blinded with his shining eye:
I *will* possess him or will die.
 I will grow round him in his place,
 Grow, live, die looking on his face,
 Die, dying clasp'd in his embrace.

ŒNONE.

THERE lies a vale in Ida, lovelier
Than all the valleys of Ionian hills.
The swimming vapor slopes athwart the glen,
Puts forth an arm, and creeps from pine to pine,
And loiters, slowly drawn. On either hand
The lawns and meadow-ledges midway down
Hang rich in flowers, and far below them roars
The long brook falling thro' the clov'n ravine
In cataract after cataract to the sea.
Behind the valley topmost Gargarus
Stands up and takes the morning: but in front
The gorges, opening wide apart, reveal
Troas and Ilion's column'd citadel,
The crown of Troas.
 Hither came at noon
Mournful Œnone, wandering forlorn
Of Paris, once her playmate on the hills.
Her cheek had lost the rose, and round her neck
Floated her hair or seem'd to float in rest.
She, leaning on a fragment twined with vine,
Sang to the stillness, till the mountain-shade
Sloped downward to her seat from the upper cliff.

"O mother Ida, many-fountain'd Ida,
Dear mother Ida, harken ere I die.
For now the noonday quiet holds the hill:
The grasshopper is silent in the grass:
The lizard, with his shadow on the stone,
Rests like a shadow, and the cicala sleeps.
The purple flowers droop: the golden bee
Is lily-cradled: I alone awake.
My eyes are full of tears, my heart of love,
My heart is breaking, and my eyes are dim,
And I am all aweary of my life.

"O mother Ida, many-fountain'd Ida,
Dear mother Ida, harken ere I die.
Hear me, O Earth, hear me, O Hills, O Caves
That house the cold crown'd snake! O mountain brooks,
I am the daughter of a River-God,
Hear me, for I will speak, and build up all
My sorrow with my song, as yonder walls
Rose slowly to a music slowly breathed,
A cloud that gather'd shape: for it may be
That, while I speak of it, a little while
My heart may wander from its deeper woe.

"O mother Ida, many-fountain'd Ida,
Dear mother Ida, harken ere I die.
I waited underneath the dawning hills,
Aloft the mountain lawn was dewy-dark,
And dewy-dark aloft the mountain pine:

Beautiful Paris, evil-hearted Paris,
Leading a jet-black goat white-horn'd, white-hooved,
Came up from reedy Simois all alone.

"O mother Ida, harken ere I die.
Far-off the torrent call'd me from the cleft :
Far up the solitary morning smote
The streaks of virgin snow. With down-dropt eyes
I sat alone : white-breasted like a star
Fronting the dawn he moved ; a leopard skin
Droop'd from his shoulder, but his sunny hair
Cluster'd about his temples like a God's :
And his cheek brighten'd as the foam-bow brightens
When the wind blows the foam, and all my heart
Went forth to embrace him coming ere he came.

"Dear mother Ida, harken ere I die.
He smiled, and opening out his milk-white palm
Disclosed a fruit of pure Hesperian gold,
That smelt ambrosially, and while I look'd
And listen'd, the full-flowing river of speech
Came down upon my heart.
                    "'My own Œnone,
Beautiful-brow'd Œnone, my own soul,
Behold this fruit, whose gleaming rind ingrav'n
"For the most fair," would seem to award it thine,
As lovelier than whatever Oread haunt
The knolls of Ida, loveliest in all grace
Of movement, and the charm of married brows.'

"Dear mother Ida, harken ere I die.
He prest the blossom of his lips to mine,
And added 'This was cast upon the board,
When all the full-faced presence of the Gods
Ranged in the halls of Peleus ; whereupon
Rose feud, with question unto whom 't were due :
But light-foot Iris brought it yester-eve,
Delivering, that to me, by common voice,
Elected umpire, Herè comes to-day,
Pallas and Aphrodite, claiming each
This meed of fairest. Thou, within the cave

Behind yon whispering tuft of oldest pine,
Mayst well behold them unbeheld, unheard
Hear all, and see thy Paris judge of Gods.'

"Dear mother Ida, harken ere I die.
It was the deep midnoon : one silvery cloud
Had lost his way between the piney sides
Of this long glen. Then to the bower they came,
Naked they came to that smooth-swarded bower,
And at their feet the crocus brake like fire,
Violet, amaracus, and asphodel,
Lotos and lilies : and a wind arose,
And overhead the wandering ivy and vine,
This way and that, in many a wild festoon
Ran riot, garlanding the gnarled boughs
With bunch and berry and flower thro' and thro'.

"O mother Ida, harken ere I die.
On the tree-tops a crested peacock lit,
And o'er him flow'd a golden cloud, and lean'd
Upon him, slowly dropping fragrant dew.
Then first I heard the voice of her, to whom
Coming thro' Heaven, like a light that grows
Larger and clearer, with one mind the Gods
Rise up for reverence. She to Paris made
Proffer of royal power, ample rule
Unquestion'd, overflowing revenue
Wherewith to embellish state, 'from many a vale
And river-sunder'd champaign clothed with corn,
Or labor'd mines undrainable of ore.
Honor,' she said, 'and homage, tax and toll,
From many an inland town and haven large,
Mast-throng'd beneath her shadowing citadel
In glassy bays among her tallest towers.'

"O mother Ida, harken ere I die.
Still she spake on and still she spake of power,
'Which in all action is the end of all ;
Power fitted to the season ; wisdom-bred
And throned of wisdom — from all neighbor crowns
Alliance and allegiance, till thy hand

Fail from the sceptre-staff. Such boon from me,
From me, Heaven's Queen, Paris, to thee king-born,
A shepherd all thy life but yet king-born,
Should come most welcome, seeing men, in power,
Only, are likest gods, who have attain'd
Rest in a happy place and quiet seats
Above the thunder, with undying bliss
In knowledge of their own supremacy.'

"Dear mother Ida, harken ere I die.
She ceased, and Paris held the costly fruit
Out at arm's-length, so much the thought of power
Flatter'd his spirit ; but Pallas where she stood
Somewhat apart, her clear and bared limbs
O'erthwarted with the brazen-headed spear
Upon her pearly shoulder leaning cold,
The while, above, her full and earnest eye
Over her snow-cold breast and angry cheek
Kept watch, waiting decision, made reply.

"'Self-reverence, self-knowledge, self-control,
These three alone lead life to sovereign power.
Yet not for power, (power of herself
Would come uncall'd for) but to live by law,
Acting the law we live by without fear ;
And, because right is right, to follow right
Were wisdom in the scorn of consequence.'

"Dear mother Ida, harken ere I die.
Again she said : 'I woo thee not with gifts.
Sequel of guerdon could not alter me
To fairer. Judge thou me by what I am,
So shalt thou find me fairest.
Yet, indeed,
If gazing on divinity disrobed
Thy mortal eyes are frail to judge of fair,
Unbiass'd by self-profit, O, rest thee sure
That I shall love thee well and cleave to thee,
So that my vigor, wedded to thy blood,
Shall strike within thy pulses, like a God's,
To push thee forward thro' a life of shocks,
Dangers, and deeds, until endurance grow
Sinew'd with action, and the full-grown will,
Circled thro' all experiences, pure law,
Commeasure perfect freedom.'
"Here she ceased,
And Paris ponder'd, and I cried, 'O Paris,
Give it to Pallas !' but he heard me not,
Or hearing would not hear me, woe is me !

" O mother Ida, many-fountain'd Ida,
Dear mother Ida, harken ere I die.
Idalian Aphrodite beautiful,
Fresh as the foam, new-bathed in Paphian wells,
With rosy slender fingers backward drew
From her warm brows and bosom her deep hair
Ambrosial, golden round her lucid throat
And shoulder : from the violets her light foot
Shone rosy-white, and o'er her rounded form
Between the shadows of the vine-bunches
Floated the glowing sunlights, as she moved.

"Dear mother Ida, harken ere I die.
She with a subtle smile in her mild eyes,
The herald of her triumph, drawing nigh
Half-whisper'd in his ear, 'I promise thee
The fairest and most loving wife in Greece.'
She spoke and laugh'd : I shut my sight for fear :
But when I look'd, Paris had raised his arm,
And I beheld great Herè's angry eyes,
As she withdrew into the golden cloud,
And I was left alone within the bower ;
And from that time to this I am alone,
And I shall be alone until I die.

"Yet, mother Ida, harken ere I die.
Fairest — why fairest wife ? am I not fair ?
My love hath told me so a thousand times.
Methinks I must be fair, for yesterday,
When I past by, a wild and wanton pard,
Eyed like the evening star, with playful tail
Crouch'd fawning in the weed. Most loving is she ?
Ah me, my mountain shepherd, that my arms
Were wound about thee, and my hot lips prest
Close, close to thine in that quick-falling dew
Of fruitful kisses, thick as Autumn rains
Flash in the pools of whirling Simois.

"O mother, hear me yet before I die.
They came, they cut away my tallest pines,
My dark tall pines, that plumed the craggy ledge
High over the blue gorge, and all between
The snowy peak and snow-white cataract
Foster'd the callow eaglet—from beneath
Whose thick mysterious boughs in the dark morn
The panther's roar came muffled, while I sat
Low in the valley. Never, never more
Shall lone Œnone see the morning mist
Sweep thro' them; never see them overlaid
With narrow moon-lit slips of silver cloud,
Between the loud stream and the trembling stars.

"O mother, hear me yet before I die.
I wish that somewhere in the ruin'd folds,
Among the fragments tumbled from the glens,
Or the dry thickets, I could meet with her,
The Abominable, that uninvited came
Into the fair Peleïan banquet-hall,
And cast the golden fruit upon the board,
And bred this change; that I might speak my mind,
And tell her to her face how much I hate
Her presence, hated both of Gods and men.

"O mother, hear me yet before I die.
Hath he not sworn his love a thousand times,
In this green valley, under this green hill,
Ev'n on this hand, and sitting on this stone?
Seal'd it with kisses? water'd it with tears?
O happy tears, and how unlike to these!
O happy Heaven, how canst thou see my face?
O happy earth, how canst thou bear my weight?
O death, death, death, thou ever-floating cloud,
There are enough unhappy on this earth,
Pass by the happy souls, that love to live:
I pray thee, pass before my light of life,
And shadow all my soul, that I may die.
Thou weighest heavy on the heart within,
Weigh heavy on my eyelids: let me die.

"O mother, hear me yet before I die.
I will not die alone, for fiery thoughts
Do shape themselves within me, more and more,
Whereof I catch the issue, as I hear
Dead sounds at night come from the inmost hills,
Like footsteps upon wool. I dimly see
My far-off doubtful purpose, as a mother
Conjectures of the features of her child
Ere it is born: her child!—a shudder comes
Across me: never child be born of me,
Unblest, to vex me with his father's eyes!

"O mother, hear me yet before I die.
Hear me, O earth. I will not die alone,
Lest their shrill happy laughter come to me
Walking the cold and starless road of Death
Uncomforted, leaving my ancient love
With the Greek woman. I will rise and go
Down into Troy, and ere the stars come forth
Talk with the wild Cassandra, for she says
A fire dances before her, and a sound
Rings ever in her ears of armed men.
What this may be I know not, but I know
That, wheresoe'er I am by night and day,
All earth and air seem only burning fire."

THE SISTERS.

WE were two daughters of one race:
She was the fairest in the face:
   The wind is blowing in turret and tree.
They were together, and she fell;
Therefore revenge became me well.
   O the Earl was fair to see!

She died: she went to burning flame:
She mix'd her ancient blood with shame.
   The wind is howling in turret and tree.
Whole weeks and months, and early and late,
To win his love I lay in wait:
   O the Earl was fair to see!

I made a feast; I bade him come;
I won his love, I brought him home.
   The wind is roaring in turret and tree.
And after supper, on a bed,
Upon my lap he laid his head:
   O the Earl was fair to see!

I kiss'd his eyelids into rest:
His ruddy cheek upon my breast.
   The wind is raging in turret and tree.

I hated him with the hate of hell,
But I loved his beauty passing well.
O the Earl was fair to see!

I rose up in the silent night:
I made my dagger sharp and bright.
   The wind is raving in turret and tree.
As half-asleep his breath he drew,
Three times I stabb'd him thro' and thro'.
   O the Earl was fair to see!

I curl'd and comb'd his comely head,
He look'd so grand when he was dead.
   The wind is blowing in turret and tree.
I wrapt his body in the sheet,
And laid him at his mother's feet.
   O the Earl was fair to see!

TO ———

WITH THE FOLLOWING POEM.

I SEND you here a sort of allegory,
(For you will understand it) of a soul,
A sinful soul possess'd of many gifts,
A spacious garden full of flowering weeds,
A glorious Devil, large in heart and brain,
That did love Beauty only, (Beauty seen
In all varieties of mould and mind)
And Knowledge for its beauty; or if Good,
Good only for its beauty, seeing not
That Beauty, Good, and Knowledge, are three sisters
That doat upon each other, friends to man,
Living together under the same roof,
And never can be sunder'd without tears.
And he that shuts Love out, in turn shall be
Shut out from Love, and on her threshold lie
Howling in outer darkness. Not for this
Was common clay ta'en from the common earth,
Moulded by God, and temper'd with the tears
Of angels to the perfect shape of man.

THE PALACE OF ART.

I BUILT my soul a lordly pleasure-house,
   Wherein at ease for aye to dwell.
I said, "O Soul, make merry and carouse,
   Dear soul, for all is well."

A huge crag-platform, smooth as burnish'd brass
I chose. The ranged ramparts bright
From level meadow-bases of deep grass
   Suddenly scaled the light.

Thereon I built it firm. Of ledge or shelf
   The rock rose clear, or winding stair.
My soul would live alone unto herself
   In her high palace there.

And "while the world runs round and round," I said,
"Reign thou apart, a quiet king,
Still as, while Saturn whirls, his stedfast shade
   Sleeps on his luminous ring."

To which my soul made answer readily:
"Trust me, in bliss I shall abide
In this great mansion, that is built for me,
   So royal-rich and wide."

* * * *

* * * *

Four courts I made, East, West and South and North,
In each a squared lawn, wherefrom
The golden gorge of dragons spouted forth
   A flood of fountain-foam.

And round the cool green courts there ran a row
Of cloisters, branch'd like mighty woods,
Echoing all night to that sonorous flow
   Of spouted fountain-floods.

And round the roofs a gilded gallery
   That lent broad verge to distant lands,
Far as the wild swan wings, to where the sky
   Dipt down to sea and sands.

From those four jets four currents in one swell
   Across the mountain stream'd below
In misty folds, that floating as they fell
   Lit up a torrent-bow.

And high on every peak a statue seem'd
   To hang on tiptoe, tossing up
A cloud of incense of all odor steam'd
   From out a golden cup.

So that she thought, "And who shall
gaze upon
My palace with unblinded eyes,
While this great bow will waver in the sun,
And that sweet incense rise?"

For that sweet incense rose and never
fail'd,
And, while day sank or mounted
higher
The light aërial gallery, golden-rail'd,
Burnt like a fringe of fire.

Likewise the deep-set windows, stain'd
and traced,
Would seem slow-flaming crimson fires
From shadow'd grots of arches interlaced,
And tipt with frost-like spires.

* * * *

* * * *

Full of long-sounding corridors it was,
That over-vaulted grateful gloom,
Thro' which the livelong day my soul did
pass,
Well-pleased, from room to room.

Full of great rooms and small the palace
stood,
All various, each a perfect whole
From living Nature, fit for every mood
And change of my still soul.

For some were hung with arras green and
blue,
Showing a gaudy summer-morn,
Where with puff'd cheek the belted
hunter blew
His wreathed bugle-horn.

One seem'd all dark and red — a tract of
sand,
And some one pacing there alone,
Who paced for ever in a glimmering land,
Lit with a low large moon.

One show'd an iron coast and angry waves.
You seem'd to hear them climb and fall
And roar rock-thwarted under bellowing
caves,
Beneath the windy wall.

And one, a full-fed river winding slow
By herds upon an endless plain,
The ragged rims of thunder brooding low,
With shadow-streaks of rain.

And one, the reapers at their sultry
toil.
In front they bound the sheaves. Be-
hind
Were realms of upland, prodigal in oil,
And hoary to the wind.

And one, a foreground black with stones
and slags,
Beyond, a line of heights, and higher
All barr'd with long white cloud the
scornful crags,
And highest, snow and fire.

And one, an English home — gray twi-
light pour'd
On dewy pastures, dewy trees,
Softer than sleep — all things in order
stored,
A haunt of ancient Peace.

Nor these alone, but every landscape fair,
As fit for every mood of mind,
Or gay, or grave, or sweet, or stern, was
there
Not less than truth design'd.

* * * *

* * * *

Or the maid-mother by a crucifix,
In tracts of pasture sunny-warm,
Beneath branch-work of costly sardonyx
Sat smiling, babe in arm.

Or in a clear-wall'd city on the sea,
Near gilded organ-pipes, her hair
Wound with white roses, slept St. Cecily;
An angel look'd at her.

Or thronging all one porch of Paradise
A group of Houris bow'd to see
The dying Islamite, with hands and eyes
That said, We wait for thee.

Or mythic Uther's deeply-wounded son
In some fair space of sloping greens
Lay, dozing in the vale of Avalon,
And watch'd by weeping queens.

Or hollowing one hand against his ear,
To list a foot-fall, ere he saw
The wood-nymph, stay'd the Ausonian
king to hear
Of wisdom and of law.

THE PALACE OF ART.

Or over hills with peaky tops engrail'd,
  And many a tract of palm and rice,
The throne of Indian Cama slowly sail'd
  A summer fann'd with spice.

Or sweet Europa's mantle blew unclasp'd,
  From off her shoulder backward borne:
From one hand droop'd a crocus: one hand grasp'd
  The mild bull's golden horn.

Or else flushed Ganymede, his rosy thigh
  Half-buried in the Eagle's down,
Sole as a flying star shot thro' the sky
  Above the pillar'd town.

Nor these alone: but every legend fair
  Which the supreme Caucasian mind
Carved out of Nature for itself, was there,
  Not less than life, design'd.

*   *   *   *

*   *   *   *

Then in the towers I placed great bells that swung,
  Mov'd of themselves, with silver sound;
And with choice paintings of wise men I hung
  The royal dais round.

For there was Milton like a seraph strong,
  Beside him Shakespeare bland and mild;
And there the world-worn Dante grasp'd his song,
  And somewhat grimly smiled.

And there the Ionian father of the rest;
  A million wrinkles carved his skin;
A hundred winters snow'd upon his breast,
  From cheek and throat and chin.

Above, the fair hall-ceiling stately-set
  Many an arch high up did lift,
And angels rising and descending met
  With interchange of gift.

Below was all mosaic choicely plann'd
  With cycles of the human tale
Of this wide world, the times of every land
  So wrought, they will not fail.

The people here, a beast of burden slow,
  Toil'd onward, prick'd with goads and stings;

Here play'd, a tiger, rolling to and fro
  The heads and crowns of kings;

Here rose, an athlete, strong to break or bind
  All force in bonds that might endure,
And here once more like some sick man declined,
  And trusted any cure.

But over these she trod: and those great bells
  Began to chime. She took her throne:
She sat betwixt the shining Oriels,
  To sing her songs alone.

And thro' the topmost Oriels' colored flame
  Two godlike faces gazed below;
Plato the wise, and large-brow'd Verulam,
  The first of those who know.

And all those names, that in their motion were
  Full-welling fountain-heads of change,
Betwixt the slender shafts were blazon'd fair
  In diverse raiment strange:

Thro' which the lights, rose, amber, emerald, blue,
  Flush'd in her temples and her eyes,
And from her lips, as morn from Memnon, drew
  Rivers of melodies.

No nightingale delighteth to prolong
  Her low preamble all alone,
More than my soul to hear her echo'd song
  Throb thro' the ribbed stone;

Singing and murmuring in her feastful mirth,
  Joying to feel herself alive,
Lord over Nature, Lord of the visible earth,
  Lord of the senses five;

Communing with herself: "All these are mine,
  And let the world have peace or wars,
'T is one to me." She — when young night divine
  Crown'd dying day with stars,

Making sweet close of his delicious toils —
  Lit light in wreaths and anadems,
And pure quintessences of precious oils
  In hollow'd moons of gems,

THE PALACE OF ART.

To mimic heaven ; and clapt her hands
    and cried,
"I marvel if my still delight
In this great house so royal-rich, and wide,
    Be flatter'd to the height.

"O all things fair to sate my various eyes !
    O shapes and hues that please me well !
O silent faces of the Great and Wise,
    My Gods, with whom I dwell !

"O God-like isolation which art mine,
    I can but count thee perfect gain,
What time I watch the darkening droves
      of swine
    That range on yonder plain.

"In filthy sloughs they roll a prurient
      skin,
They graze and wallow, breed and sleep ;
And oft some brainless devil enters in,
    And drives them to the deep."

Then of the moral instinct would she prate
    And of the rising from the dead,
As hers by right of full-accomplish'd Fate ;
    And at the last she said :

"I take possession of man's mind and
      deed.
I care not what the sects may brawl.
I sit as God holding no form of creed,
    But contemplating all."

    *   *   *   *

    *   *   *   *

Full oft the riddle of the painful earth
    Flash'd thro' her as she sat alone,
Yet not the less held she her solemn mirth,
    And intellectual throne.

And so she throve and prosper'd : so three
      years
    She prosper'd : on the fourth she fell,
Like Herod, when the shout was in his
      ears,
    Struck thro' with pangs of hell.

Lest she should fail and perish utterly,
    God, before whom ever lie bare
The abysmal deeps of Personality,
    Plagued her with sore despair.

When she would think, where'er she
      turn'd her sight
The airy hand confusion wrought,
Wrote "Mene, mene," and divided quite
    The kingdom of her thought.

Deep dread and loathing of her solitude
    Fell on her, from which mood was born
Scorn of herself ; again, from out that mood
    Laughter at her self-scorn.

"What ! is not this my place of strength,"
    she said,
"My spacious mansion built for me,
Whereof the strong foundation-stones
    were laid
    Since my first memory ?"

But in dark corners of her palace stood
    Uncertain shapes ; and unawares
On white-eyed phantasms weeping tears
      of blood,
    And horrible nightmares,

And hollow shades enclosing hearts of
      flame,
And, with dim fretted foreheads all,
On corpses three-months-old at noon she
      came,
    That stood against the wall.

A spot of dull stagnation, without light
    Or power of movement, seem'd my soul,
'Mid onward-sloping motions infinite
    Making for one sure goal.

A still salt pool, lock'd in with bars of
      sand ;
    Left on the shore ; that hears all night
The plunging seas draw backward from
      the land
    Their moon-led waters white.

A star that with the choral starry dance
    Join'd not, but stood, and standing saw
The hollow orb of moving Circumstance
    Roll'd round by one fix'd law.

Back on herself her serpent pride had
      curl'd.
"No voice," she shriek'd in that lone
      hall,
"No voice breaks thro' the stillness of
    this world :
    One deep, deep silence all !"

She, mouldering with the dull earth's
      mouldering sod,
    Inwrapt tenfold in slothful shame,
Lay there exiled from eternal God,
    Lost to her place and name ;

And death and life she hated equally,
   And nothing saw, for her despair,
But dreadful time, dreadful eternity,
   No comfort anywhere;

Remaining utterly confused with fears,
   And ever worse with growing time,
And ever unrelieved by dismal tears,
   And all alone in crime:

Shut up as in a crumbling tomb, girt round
   With blackness as a solid wall,
Far off she seem'd to hear the dully sound
   Of human footsteps fall.

As in strange lands a traveller walking slow,
   In doubt and great perplexity,
A little before moon-rise hears the low
   Moan of an unknown sea;

And knows not if it be thunder or a sound
   Of rocks thrown down, or one deep cry
Of great wild beasts; then thinketh, "I have found
   A new land, but I die."

She howl'd aloud, "I am on fire within.
   There comes no murmur of reply.
What is it that will take away my sin,
   And save me lest I die?"

So when four years were wholly finished,
   She threw her royal robes away.
"Make me a cottage in the vale," she said,
   "Where I may mourn and pray.

"Yet pull not down my palace towers, that are
   So lightly, beautifully built:
Perchance I may return with others there
   When I have purged my guilt."

LADY CLARA VERE DE VERE.

Lady Clara Vere de Vere,
   Of me you shall not win renown:
You thought to break a country heart
   For pastime, ere you went to town.
At me you smiled, but unbeguiled
   I saw the snare, and I retired:
The daughter of a hundred Earls,
   You are not one to be desired.

Lady Clara Vere de Vere,
   I know you proud to bear your name,
Your pride is yet no mate for mine,
   Too proud to care from whence I came.
Nor would I break for your sweet sake
   A heart that doats on truer charms.

A simple maiden in her flower
   Is worth a hundred coats-of-arms.

Lady Clara Vere de Vere,
   Some meeker pupil you must find,
For were you queen of all that is,
   I could not stoop to such a mind.
You sought to prove how I could love,
   And my disdain is my reply.
The lion on your old stone gates
   Is not more cold to you than I.

Lady Clara Vere de Vere,
   You put strange memories in my head.
Not thrice your branching limes have blown
   Since I beheld young Laurence dead.
O, your sweet eyes, your low replies:
   A great enchantress you may be;
But there was that across his throat
   Which you had hardly cared to see.

Lady Clara Vere de Vere,
   When thus he met his mother's view,
She had the passions of her kind,
   She spake some certain truths of you.
Indeed I heard one bitter word
   That scarce is fit for you to hear;
Her manners had not that repose
   Which stamps the caste of Vere de Vere.

Lady Clara Vere de Vere,
   There stands a spectre in your hall:
The guilt of blood is at your door:
   You changed a wholesome heart to gall.
You held your course without remorse,
   To make him trust his modest worth,
And, last, you fix'd a vacant stare,
   And slew him with your noble birth.

Trust me, Clara Vere de Vere,
   From yon blue heavens above us bent
The gardener Adam and his wife
   Smile at the claims of long descent.
Howe'er it be, it seems to me,
   'T is only noble to be good.
Kind hearts are more than coronets,
   And simple faith than Norman blood.

I know you, Clara Vere de Vere,
   You pine among your halls and towers:
The languid light of your proud eyes
   Is wearied of the rolling hours.
In glowing health, with boundless wealth,
   But sickening of a vague disease,
You know so ill to deal with time,
   You needs must play such pranks as these.

"The daughter of a hundred Earls,
You are not one to be desired."

Clara, Clara Vere de Vere,
  If Time be heavy on your hands,
Are there no beggars at your gate,
  Nor any poor about your lands?
Oh! teach the orphan-boy to read,
  Or teach the orphan-girl to sew,
Pray Heaven for a human heart,
  And let the foolish yeoman go.

THE MAY QUEEN.

You must wake and call me early, call
  me early, mother dear;
To-morrow 'ill be the happiest time of
  all the glad New-year;
Of all the glad New-year, mother, the
  maddest merriest day;

For I 'm to be Queen o' the May, mother,
  I 'm to be Queen o' the May.

There 's many a black black eye, they say,
  but none so bright as mine;
There 's Margaret and Mary, there 's Kate
  and Caroline:
But none so fair as little Alice in all the
  land they say,
So I 'm to be Queen o' the May, mother,
  I 'm to be Queen o' the May.

I sleep so sound all night, mother, that
  I shall never wake,
If you do not call me loud when the day
  begins to break:
But I must gather knots of flowers, and
  buds and garlands gay,
For I 'm to be Queen o' the May, mother,
  I 'm to be Queen o' the May.

THE MAY QUEEN.

"You must wake and call me early, call me early, mother dear,
To-morrow 'll be the happiest time of all the glad New-year."

As I came up the valley whom think ye should I see,
But Robin leaning on the bridge beneath the hazel-tree?
He thought of that sharp look, mother, I gave him yesterday, —
But I 'm to be Queen o' the May, mother, I 'm to be Queen o' the May.

He thought I was a ghost, mother, for I was all in white,
And I ran by him without speaking, like a flash of light.
They call me cruel-hearted, but I care not wha they say,
For I 'm to be Queen o' the May, mother, I 'm to be Queen o' the May.

They say he 's dying all for love, but that can never be:
They say his heart is breaking, mother — what is that to me?
There 's many a bolder lad 'ill woo me any summer day,
And I 'm to be Queen o' the May, mother, I 'm to be Queen o' the May.

Little Effie shall go with me to-morrow to the green,
And you 'll be there, too, mother, to see me made the Queen;
For the shepherd lads on every side 'ill come from far away,
And I 'm to be Queen o' the May, mother, I 'm to be Queen o' the May.

The honeysuckle round the porch has
wov'n its wavy bowers,
And by the meadow-trenches blow the
faint sweet cuckoo-flowers;
And the wild marsh-marigold shines like
fire in swamps and hollows gray,
And I 'm to be Queen o' the May, mother,
I 'm to be Queen o' the May.

The night-winds come and go, mother,
upon the meadow-grass,
And the happy stars above them seem to
brighten as they pass;
There will not be a drop of rain the whole
of the livelong day,
And I 'm to be Queen o' the May, mother,
I 'm to be Queen o' the May.

All the valley, mother, 'ill be fresh and
green and still,
And the cowslip and the crowfoot are
over all the hill,
And the rivulet in the flowery dale 'ill
merrily glance and play,
For I 'm to be Queen o' the May, mother,
I 'm to be Queen o' the May.

So you must wake and call me early, call
me early, mother dear,
To-morrow 'ill be the happiest time of all
the glad New-year:
To-morrow 'ill be of all the year the
maddest merriest day,
For I 'm to be Queen o' the May, mother,
I 'm to be Queen o' the May.

NEW-YEAR'S EVE.

If you 're waking call me early, call me
early, mother dear,
For I would see the sun rise upon the
glad New-year.
It is the last New-year that I shall ever
see,
Then you may lay me low i' the mould
and think no more of me.

To-night I saw the sun set: he set and
left behind
The good old year, the dear old time,
and all my peace of mind;
And the New-year 's coming up, mother,
but I shall never see
The blossom on the blackthorn, the leaf
upon the tree.

Last May we made a crown of flowers:
we had a merry day;
Beneath the hawthorn on the green they
made me Queen of May;
And we danced about the may-pole and
in the hazel copse,
Till Charles's Wain came out above the
tall white chimney-tops.

There 's not a flower on all the hills:
the frost is on the pane:
I only wish to live till the snowdrops
come again:
I wish the snow would melt and the sun
come out on high:
I long to see a flower so before the day I die.

The building rook 'ill caw from the windy
tall elm-tree,
And the tufted plover pipe along the
fallow lea,
And the swallow 'ill come back again
with summer o'er the wave,
But I shall lie alone, mother, within the
mouldering grave.

Upon the chancel-casement, and upon
that grave of mine,
In the early early morning the summer
sun 'ill shine,
Before the red cock crows from the farm
upon the hill,
When you are warm-asleep, mother, and
all the world is still.

When the flowers come again, mother,
beneath the waning light
You 'll never see me more in the long
gray fields at night;
When from the dry dark wold the summer airs blow cool
On the oat-grass and the sword-grass,
and the bulrush in the pool.

You 'll bury me, my mother, just beneath
the hawthorn shade,
And you 'll come sometimes and see me
where I am lowly laid.
I shall not forget you, mother, I shall
hear you when you pass,
With your feet above my head in the
long and pleasant grass.

I have been wild and wayward, but you 'll
forgive me now;
You 'll kiss me, my own mother, and
forgive me ere I go;

Nay, nay, you must not weep, nor let
  your grief be wild,
You should not fret for me, mother, you
  have another child.

If I can I'll come again, mother, from
  out my resting-place;
Tho' you'll not see me, mother, I shall
  look upon your face;
Tho' I cannot speak a word, I shall
  harken what you say,
And be often, often with you when you
  think I'm far away.

Good-night, good-night, when I have
  said good-night for evermore,
And you see me carried out from the
  threshold of the door;
Don't let Effie come to see me till my
  grave be growing green:
She'll be a better child to you than
  ever I have been.

She'll find my garden-tools upon the
  granary floor:
Let her take 'em: they are hers: I shall
  never garden more:
But tell her, when I'm gone, to train
  the rose-bush that I set
About the parlor-window and the box
  of mignonette.

Good-night, sweet mother: call me be-
  fore the day is born.
All night I lie awake, but I fall asleep at
  morn;
But I would see the sun rise upon the
  glad New-year,
So, if you're waking, call me, call me
  early, mother dear.

CONCLUSION.

I THOUGHT to pass away before, and yet
  alive I am;
And in the fields all round I hear the
  bleating of the lamb.
How sadly, I remember, rose the morn-
  ing of the year!
To die before the snowdrop came, and
  now the violet's here.

O sweet is the new violet, that comes
  beneath the skies,
And sweeter is the young lamb's voice
  to me that cannot rise,

And sweet is all the land about, and all
  the flowers that blow,
And sweeter far is death than life to me
  that long to go.

It seem'd so hard at first, mother, to
  leave the blessed sun,
And now it seems as hard to stay, and
  yet His will be done!
But still I think it can't be long before
  I find release;
And that good man, the clergyman, has
  told me words of peace.

O blessings on his kindly voice and on
  his silver hair!
And blessings on his whole life long,
  until he meet me there!
O blessings on his kindly heart and on
  his silver head!
A thousand times I blest him, as he
  knelt beside my bed.

He taught me all the mercy, for he
  show'd me all the sin.
Now, tho' my lamp was lighted late,
  there's One will let me in:
Nor would I now be well, mother, again,
  if that could be,
For my desire is but to pass to Him that
  died for me.

I did not hear the dog howl, mother, or
  the death-watch beat,
There came a sweeter token when the
  night and morning meet:
But sit beside my bed, mother, and put
  your hand in mine,
And Effie on the other side, and I will
  tell the sign.

All in the wild March-morning I heard
  the angels call;
It was when the moon was setting, and
  the dark was over all;
The trees began to whisper, and the
  wind began to roll,
And in the wild March-morning I heard
  them call my soul.

For lying broad awake I thought of you
  and Effie dear;
I saw you sitting in the house, and I no
  longer here;
With all my strength I pray'd for both,
  and so I felt resign'd,
And up the valley came a swell of music
  on the wind.

I thought that it was fancy, and I listen'd
    in my bed,
And then did something speak to me —
    I know not what was said ;
For great delight and shuddering took
    hold of all my mind,
And up the valley came again the music
    on the wind.

But you were sleeping ; and I said, "It's
    not for them : it's mine."
And if it comes three times, I thought,
    I take it for a sign.
And once again it came, and close beside
    the window-bars,
Then seem'd to go right up to Heaven
    and die among the stars.

So now I think my time is near. I trust
    it is. I know
The blessed music went that way my
    soul will have to go.
And for myself, indeed, I care not if I go
    to-day.
But, Effie, you must comfort *her* when I
    am past away.

And say to Robin a kind word, and tell
    him not to fret ;
There's many a worthier than I, would
    make him happy yet.
If had lived — I cannot tell — I might
    have been his wife ;
But all these things have ceased to be,
    with my desire of life.

O look ! the sun begins to rise, the
    heavens are in a glow ;
He shines upon a hundred fields, and all
    of them I know.
And there I move no longer now, and
    there his light may shine —
Wild flowers in the valley for other hands
    than mine.

O sweet and strange it seems to me, that
    ere this day is done
The voice, that now is speaking, may be
    beyond the sun —
For ever and for ever with those just
    souls and true —
And what is life, that we should moan ?
    why make we such ado ?

For ever and for ever, all in a blessed
    home —
And there to wait a little while till you
    and Effie come —
To lie within the light of God, as I lie
    upon your breast —
And the wicked cease from troubling,
    and the weary are at rest.

THE LOTOS-EATERS.

"Courage !" he said, and pointed
    toward the land,
"This mounting wave will roll us shore-
    ward soon."
In the afternoon they came unto a land,
In which it seemed always afternoon.
All round the coast the languid air did
    swoon,
Breathing like one that hath a weary
    dream.
Full-faced above the valley stood the
    moon ;
And like a downward smoke, the slender
    stream
Along the cliff to fall and pause and fall
    did seem.

A land of streams ! some, like a downward
    smoke,
Slow-dropping veils of thinnest lawn, did
    go ;
And some thro' wavering lights and
    shadows broke,
Rolling a slumbrous sheet of foam below.
They saw the gleaming river seaward
    flow
From the inner land : far off, three
    mountain-tops,
Three silent pinnacles of aged snow,
Stood sunset-flush'd : and, dew'd with
    showery drops,
Up-clomb the shadowy pine above the
    woven copse.

The charmed sunset linger'd low adown
In the red West : thro' mountain clefts
    the dale
Was seen far inland, and the yellow down
Border'd with palm, and many a winding
    vale
And meadow, set with slender galingale ;
A land where all things always seem'd
    the same !
And round about the keel with faces pale,
Dark faces pale against that rosy flame,
The mild-eyed melancholy Lotos-eaters
    came.

"To lie within the light of God, as I lie upon your breast, —
And the wicked cease from troubling, and the weary are at rest."

Branches they bore of that enchanted
    stem,
Laden with flower and fruit, whereof they
    gave
To each, but whoso did receive of them,
And taste, to him the gushing of the wave
Far far away did seem to mourn and rave
On alien shores ; and if his fellow spake,
His voice was thin, as voices from the
    grave ;
And deep-asleep he seem'd, yet all awake,
And music in his ears his beating heart
    did make.

They sat them down upon the yellow sand,
Between the sun and moon upon the shore ;
And sweet it was to dream of Father-land,
Of child, and wife, and slave ; but ever-
    more
Most weary seem'd the sea, weary the oar,
Weary the wandering fields of barren foam.
Then some one said, "We will return
    no more " ;
And all at once they sang, "Our island
    home
Is far beyond the wave ; we will no longer
    roam."

CHORIC SONG.

I.

There is sweet music here that softer falls
Than petals from blown roses on the grass,
Or night-dews on still waters between
    walls
Of shadowy granite, in a gleaming pass ;
Music that gentlier on the spirit lies,
Than tir'd eyelids upon tir'd eyes ;
Music that brings sweet sleep down from
    the blissful skies.
Here are cool mosses deep,
And thro' the moss the ivies creep,
And in the stream the long-leaved flowers
    weep,
And from the craggy ledge the poppy
    hangs in sleep.

II.

Why are we weigh'd upon with heaviness,
And utterly consumed with sharp distress,
While all things else have rest from
    weariness ?
All things have rest : why should we
    toil alone,
We only toil, who are the first of things,

And make perpetual moan,
Still from one sorrow to another thrown:
Nor ever fold our wings,
And cease from wanderings,
Nor steep our brows in slumber's holy balm;
Nor harken what the inner spirit sings,
"There is no joy but calm!"
Why should we only toil, the roof and crown of things?

III.

Lo! in the middle of the wood,
The folded leaf is woo'd from out the bud
With winds upon the branch, and there
Grows green and broad, and takes no care,
Sun-steep'd at noon, and in the moon
Nightly dew-fed; and turning yellow
Falls, and floats adown the air.
Lo! sweeten'd with the summer light,
The full-juiced apple, waxing over-mellow,
Drops in a silent autumn night.
All its allotted length of days,
The flower ripens in its place,
Ripens and fades, and falls, and hath no toil,
Fast-rooted in the fruitful soil.

IV.

Hateful is the dark-blue sky,
Vaulted o'er the dark-blue sea.
Death is the end of life; ah, why
Should life all labor be?
Let us alone. Time driveth onward fast,
And in a little while our lips are dumb.
Let us alone. What is it that will last?
All things are taken from us, and become
Portions and parcels of the dreadful Past.
Let us alone. What pleasure can we have
To war with evil? Is there any peace
In ever climbing up the climbing wave?
All things have rest, and ripen toward the grave
In silence; ripen, fall and cease:
Give us long rest or death, dark death, or dreamful ease.

V.

How sweet it were, hearing the downward stream,
With half-shut eyes ever to seem
Falling asleep in a half-dream!
To dream and dream, like yonder amber light,
Which will not leave the myrrh-bush on the height;
To hear each other's whisper'd speech;
Eating the Lotos day by day,
To watch the crisping ripples on the beach,
And tender curving lines of creamy spray;
To lend our hearts and spirits wholly
To the influence of mild-minded melancholy;
To muse and brood and live again in memory,
With those old faces of our infancy
Heap'd over with a mound of grass,
Two handfuls of white dust, shut in an urn of brass!

VI.

Dear is the memory of our wedded lives,
And dear the last embraces of our wives
And their warm tears: but all hath suffer'd change;
For surely now our household hearths are cold:
Our sons inherit us: our looks are strange:
And we should come like ghosts to trouble joy.
Or else the island princes over-bold
Have eat our substance, and the minstrel sings
Before them of the ten years' war in Troy,
And our great deeds, as half-forgotten things.
Is there confusion in the little isle?
Let what is broken so remain.
The Gods are hard to reconcile:
'T is hard to settle order once again.
There *is* confusion worse than death,
Trouble on trouble, pain on pain,
Long labor unto aged breath,
Sore task to hearts worn out by many wars
And eyes grown dim with gazing on the pilot-stars.

VII.

But, propt on beds of amaranth and moly,
How sweet (while warm airs lull us, blowing lowly)
With half-dropt eyelids still,
Beneath a heaven dark and holy,
To watch the long bright river drawing slowly
His waters from the purple hill —
To hear the dewy echoes calling
From cave to cave thro' the thick-twined vine —

To watch the emerald-color'd water falling
Thro' many a wov'n acanthus-wreath
    divine !
Only to hear and see the far-off sparkling
    brine,
Only to hear were sweet, stretch'd out
    beneath the pine.

VIII.

The Lotos blooms below the barren peak :
The Lotos blows by every winding creek :
All day the wind breathes low with
    mellower tone :
Thro' every hollow cave and alley lone
Round and round the spicy downs the
    yellow Lotus-dust is blown.
We have had enough of action, and of
    motion we,
Roll'd to starboard, roll'd to larboard,
    when the surge was seething free,
Where the wallowing monster spouted his
    foam-fountains in the sea.
Let us swear an oath, and keep it with
    an equal mind,
In the hollow Lotos-land to live and lie
    reclined
On the hills like Gods together, careless
    of mankind.
For they lie beside their nectar, and the
    bolts are hurl'd
Far below them in the valleys, and the
    clouds are lightly curl'd
Round their golden houses, girdled with
    the gleaming world :
Where they smile in secret, looking over
    wasted lands,
Blight and famine, plague and earth-
    quake, roaring deeps and fiery
    sands,
Clanging fights, and flaming towns, and
    sinking ships, and praying hands.
But they smile, they find a music centred
    in a doleful song
Steaming up, a lamentation and an ancient
    tale of wrong,
Like a tale of little meaning tho' the
    words are strong ;
Chanted from an ill-used race of men that
    cleave the soil,
Sow the seed, and reap the harvest with
    enduring toil,
Storing yearly little dues of wheat, and
    wine and oil ;
Till they perish and they suffer — some,
    't is whisper'd — down in hell
Suffer endless anguish, others in Elysian
    valleys dwell,
Resting weary limbs at last on beds of
    asphodel.
Surely, surely, slumber is more sweet
    than toil, the shore
Than labor in the deep mid-ocean, wind
    and wave and oar ;
O rest ye, brother mariners, we will not
    wander more.

A DREAM OF FAIR WOMEN.

I READ, before my eyelids dropt their
    shade,
    "*The Legend of Good Women,*" long
      ago
Sung by the morning star of song, who
    made
    His music heard below ;

Dan Chaucer, the first warbler, whose
    sweet breath
Preluded those melodious bursts,
    that fill
The spacious times of great Elizabeth
    With sounds that echo still.

And, for a while, the knowledge of his art
    Held me above the subject, as strong
      gales
Hold swollen clouds from raining, tho'
    my heart,
    Brimful of those wild tales,

Charged both mine eyes with tears. In
    every land
    I saw, wherever light illumineth,
Beauty and anguish walking hand in hand
    The downward slope to death.

Those far-renowned brides of ancient song
    Peopled the hollow dark, like burn-
      ing stars,
And I heard sounds of insult, shame, and
    wrong,
    And trumpets blown for wars ;

And clattering flints batter'd with clang-
    ing hoofs :
    And I saw crowds in column'd sanc-
      tuaries ;
And forms that pass'd at windows and
    on roofs
    Of marble palaces ;

Corpses across the threshold ; heroes tall
    Dislodging pinnacle and parapet

"O rest ye, brother mariners, we will not wander more."

Upon the tortoise creeping to the wall;
    Lances in ambush set;

And high shrine-doors burst thro' with
    heated blasts
      That run before the fluttering tongues
      of fire;
White surf wind-scatter'd over sails and
    masts,
    And ever climbing higher;

Squadrons and squares of men in brazen
    plates,
    Scaffolds, still sheets of water, divers
      woes,

Ranges of glimmering vaults with iron
    grates,
    And hushed seraglios.

So shape chased shape as swift as, when
    to land
      Bluster the winds and tides the self-
      same way,
Crisp foam-flakes scud along the level
    sand,
    Torn from the fringe of spray.

I started once, or seem'd to start in pain,
    Resolved on noble things, and strove
      to speak,

As when a great thought strikes along
    the brain,
And flushes all the cheek.

And once my arm was lifted to hew down
    A cavalier from off his saddle-bow,
That bore a lady from a leaguer'd town ;
    And then, I know not how,

All those sharp fancies, by down-lapsing
    thought
Stream'd onward, lost their edges,
    and did creep
Roll'd on each other, rounded, smooth'd,
    and brought
Into the gulfs of sleep.

At last methought that I had wander'd far
    In an old wood : fresh-wash'd in
    coolest dew
The maiden splendors of the morning star
    Shook in the stedfast blue.

Enormous elmtree-boles did stoop and lean
    Upon the dusky brushwood under-
    neath
Their broad curved branches, fledged
    with clearest green,
New from its silken sheath.

The dim red morn had died, her journey
    done,
    And with dead lips smiled at the
    twilight plain,
Half-fall'n across the threshold of the sun,
    Never to rise again.

There was no motion in the dumb dead air,
    Not any song of bird or sound of rill ;
Gross darkness of the inner sepulchre
    Is not so deadly still

As that wide forest. Growths of jasmine
    turn'd
    Their humid arms festooning tree to
    tree,
And at the root thro' lush green grasses
    burn'd
The red anemone.

I knew the flowers, I knew the leaves, I
    knew
    The tearful glimmer of the languid
    dawn
On those long, rank, dark wood-walks
    drench'd in dew,
    Leading from lawn to lawn.

The smell of violets, hidden in the green,
    Pour'd back into my empty soul and
    frame
The times when I remember to have been
    Joyful and free from blame.

And from within me a clear under-tone
    Thrill'd thro' mine ears in that un-
    blissful clime,
"Pass freely thro' : the wood is all thine
    own,
Until the end of time."

At length I saw a lady within call,
    Stiller than chisell'd marble, stand-
    ing there ;
A daughter of the gods, divinely tall,
    And most divinely fair.

Her loveliness with shame and with sur-
    prise
    Froze my swift speech : she turning
    on my face
The star-like sorrows of immortal eyes,
    Spoke slowly in her place.

" I had great beauty : ask thou not my
    name :
No one can be more wise than destiny.
Many drew swords and died. Where'er
    I came
I brought calamity."

" No marvel, sovereign lady : in fair field
    Myself for such a face had boldly
    died,"
I answer'd free ; and turning I appeal'd
    To one that stood beside.

But she, with sick and scornful looks
    averse,
    To her full height her stately stature
    draws ;
" My youth," she said, "was blasted
    with a curse :
This woman was the cause.

" I was cut off from hope in that sad place,
    Which yet to name my spirit loathes
    and fears :
My father held his hand upon his face ;
    I, blinded with my tears,

"Still strove to speak : my voice was
    thick with sighs
    As in a dream. Dimly I could descry
The stern black-bearded kings with
    wolfish eyes,
    Waiting to see me die.

"The high masts flicker'd as they lay
    afloat ;
The crowds, the temples, waver'd, and
    the shore ;
The bright death quiver'd at the victim's
    throat ;
Touch'd ; and I knew no more."

Whereto the other with a downward brow:
"I would the white cold heavy-
    plunging foam,
Whirl'd by the wind, had roll'd me deep
    below,
Then when I left my home."

Her slow full words sank thro' the silence
    drear,
As thunder-drops fall on a sleeping
    sea :
Sudden I heard a voice that cried, "Come
    here,
That I may look on thee."

I turning saw, throned on a flowery rise,
    One sitting on a crimson scarf un-
    roll'd ;
A queen, with swarthy cheeks and bold
    black eyes,
    Brow-bound with burning gold.

She, flashing forth a haughty smile,
    began :
"I govern'd men by change, and so
    I sway'd
All moods. 'T is long since I have seen
    a man.
    Once, like the moon, I made

"The ever-shifting currents of the blood
    According to my humor ebb and flow.
I have no men to govern in this wood :
    That makes my only woe.

"Nay — yet it chafes me that I could
    not bend
    One will ; nor tame and tutor with
    mine eye
That dull cold-blooded Cæsar. Prythee,
    friend,
    Where is Mark Antony ?

"The man, my lover, with whom I rode
    sublime
    On Fortune's neck : we sat as God
    by God :
The Nilus would have risen before his time
    And flooded at our nod.

"We drank the Libyan Sun to sleep,
    and lit
    Lamps which outburn'd Canopus.
    O my life
In Egypt ! O the dalliance and the wit,
    The flattery and the strife,

"And the wild kiss, when fresh from
    war's alarms,
    My Hercules, my Roman Antony,
My mailed Bacchus leapt into my arms,
    Contented there to die !

"And there he died : and when I heard
    my name
    Sigh'd forth with life I would not
    brook my fear
Of the other : with a worm I balk'd his
    fame.
    What else was left ? look here !"

(With that she tore her robe apart, and
    half
    The polish'd argent of her breast to
    sight
Laid bare. Thereto she pointed with a
    laugh,
    Showing the aspick's bite.)

"I died a Queen. The Roman soldier
    found
    Me lying dead, my crown about my
    brows,
A name for ever ! — lying robed and
    crown'd,
    Worthy a Roman spouse."

Her warbling voice, a lyre of widest range
    Struck by all passion, did fall down
    and glance
From tone to tone, and glided thro' all
    change
    Of liveliest utterance.

When she made pause I knew not for
    delight ;
    Because with sudden motion from
    the ground
She raised her piercing orbs, and fill'd
    with light
    The interval of sound.

Still with their fires Love tipt his keenest
    darts ;
    As once they drew into two burning
    rings
All beams of Love, melting the mighty
    hearts
    Of captains and of kings.

Slowly my sense undazzled. Then I heard
   A noise of some one coming thro'
      the lawn,
And singing clearer than the crested
      bird,
   That claps his wings at dawn.

"The torrent brooks of hallow'd Israel
   From craggy hollows pouring, late
      and soon,
Sound all night long, in falling thro' the
      dell,
   Far-heard beneath the moon.

"The balmy moon of blessed Israel
   Floods all the deep-blue gloom with
      beams divine :
All night the splinter'd crags that wall
      the dell
   With spires of silver shine."

As one that museth where broad sunshine
      laves
   The lawn by some cathedral, thro'
      the door
Hearing the holy organ rolling waves
   Of sound on roof and floor

Within, and anthem sung, is charm'd
      and tied
   To where he stands, — so stood I,
      when that flow
Of music left the lips of her that died
   To save her father's vow ;

The daughter of the warrior Gileadite,
   A maiden pure ; as when she went
      along
From Mizpeh's tower'd gate with wel-
      come light,
   With timbrel and with song.

My words leapt forth : "Heaven heads
      the count of crimes
   With that wild oath." She render'd
      answer high :
"Not so, nor once alone ; a thousand
      times
   I would be born and die.

"Single I grew, like some green plant,
      whose root
   Creeps to the garden water-pipes
      beneath,
Feeding the flower ; but ere my flower to
      fruit
   Changed, I was ripe for death.

"My God, my land, my father — these
      did move
Me from my bliss of life, that Nature
      gave,
Lower'd softly with a threefold cord of love
   Down to a silent grave.

"And I went mourning, 'No fair Hebrew
      boy
   Shall smile away my maiden blame
      among
The Hebrew mothers'—emptied of all joy,
   Leaving the dance and song,

"Leaving the olive-gardens far below,
   Leaving the promise of my bridal-
      bower,
The valleys of grape-loaded vines that
      glow
   Beneath the battled tower.

"The light white cloud swam over us.
      Anon
   We heard the lion roaring from his
      den ;
We saw the large white stars rise one by
      one,
   Or, from the darken'd glen,

"Saw God divide the night with flying
      flame,
   And thunder on the everlasting hills.
I heard Him, for He spake, and grief
      became
   A solemn scorn of ills.

"When the next moon was roll'd into
      the sky,
   Strength came to me that equall'd
      my desire.
How beautiful a thing it was to die
   For God and for my sire !

"It comforts me in this one thought to
      dwell,
   That I subdued me to my father's
      will ;
Because the kiss he gave me, ere I fell,
   Sweetens the spirit still.

"Moreover it is written that my race
   Hew'd Ammon, hip and thigh, from
      Aroer
On Arnon unto Minneth." Here her face
   Glow'd, as I look'd at her.

She lock'd her lips: she left me where
    I stood:
  "Glory to God," she sang, and past
    afar,
Thridding the sombre boskage of the wood,
  Toward the morning-star.

Losing her carol I stood pensively,
  As one that from a casement leans
    his head,
When midnight bells cease ringing sud-
    denly,
  And the old year is dead.

"Alas! alas!" a low voice, full of care,
  Murmur'd beside me: "Turn and
    look on me:
I am that Rosamond, whom men call
    fair,
  If what I was I be.

"Would I had been some maiden coarse
    and poor!
  O me, that I should ever see the
    light!
Those dragon eyes of anger'd Eleanor
  Do hunt me, day and night."

She ceased in tears, fallen from hope and
    trust:
  To whom the Egyptian: "O, you
    tamely died!
You should have clung to Fulvia's waist,
    and thrust
  The dagger thro' her side."

With that sharp sound the white dawn's
    creeping beams,
  Stol'n to my brain, dissolved the
    mystery
Of folded sleep. The captain of my
    dreams
  Ruled in the eastern sky.

Morn broaden'd on the borders of the
    dark,
  Ere I saw her, who clasp'd in her
    last trance
Her murder'd father's head, or Joan of
    Arc,
  A light of ancient France;

Or her, who knew that Love can vanquish
    Death,
  Who kneeling, with one arm about
    her king,

Drew forth the poison with her balmy
    breath,
  Sweet as new buds in Spring.

No memory labors longer from the deep
    Gold-mines of thought to lift the
      hidden ore
That glimpses, moving up, than I from
    sleep
  To gather and tell o'er

Each little sound and sight. With what
    dull pain
  Compass'd, how eagerly I sought to
    strike
Into that wondrous track of dreams again!
  But no two dreams are like.

As when a soul laments, which hath been
    blest,
  Desiring what is mingled with past
    years,
In yearnings that can never be exprest
  By signs or groans or tears;

Because all words, tho' cull'd with choicest
    art,
  Failing to give the bitter of the sweet,
Wither beneath the palate, and the heart
  Faints, faded by its heat.

MARGARET.

I.

O SWEET pale Margaret,
  O rare pale Margaret,
What lit your eyes with tearful power,
Like moonlight on a falling shower?
Who lent you, love, your mortal dower
  Of pensive thought and aspect pale,
  Your melancholy sweet and frail
As perfume of the cuckoo-flower?
From the westward-winding flood,
From the evening-lighted wood,
  From all things outward you have
    won
A tearful grace, as tho' you stood
  Between the rainbow and the sun.
The very smile before you speak,
That dimples your transparent cheek,
Encircles all the heart, and feedeth
The senses with a still delight
  Of dainty sorrow without sound,
  Like the tender amber round,
  Which the moon about her spreadeth,
Moving thro' a fleecy night.

II.

You love, remaining peacefully,
  To hear the murmur of the strife,
  But enter not the toil of life.
Your spirit is the calmed sea,
  Laid by the tumult of the fight.
You are the evening star, alway
  Remaining betwixt dark and bright:
Lull'd echoes of laborious day
  Come to you, gleams of mellow light
  Float by you on the verge of night.

III.

What can it matter, Margaret,
  What songs below the waning stars
  The lion-heart, Plantagenet,
  Sang looking thro' his prison bars?
  Exquisite Margaret, who can tell
The last wild thought of Chatelet,
  Just ere the falling axe did part
  The burning brain from the true
    heart,
  Even in her sight he loved so well?

IV.

A fairy shield your Genius made
  And gave you on your natal day.
Your sorrow, only sorrow's shade,
  Keeps real sorrow far away.
You move not in such solitudes,
  You are not less divine,
But more human in your moods,
  Than your twin-sister, Adeline.
Your hair is darker, and your eyes
  Touch'd with a somewhat darker hue,
  And less aërially blue,
  But ever trembling thro' the dew
Of dainty-woful sympathies.

V.

O sweet pale Margaret,
  O rare pale Margaret,
Come down, come down, and hear me
    speak:
Tie up the ringlets on your cheek:
  The sun is just about to set,
The arching limes are tall and shady,
  And faint, rainy lights are seen,
    Moving in the leavy beech.
Rise from the feast of sorrow, lady,
  Where all day long you sit between
    Joy and woe, and whisper each.
Or only look across the lawn,
  Look out below your bower-eaves,
Look down, and let your blue eyes dawn
  Upon me thro' the jasmine-leaves.

THE BLACKBIRD.

O BLACKBIRD! sing me something well:
  While all the neighbors shoot thee
    round,
  I keep smooth plats of fruitful ground,
Where thou may'st warble, eat and dwell.

The espaliers and the standards all
  Are thine; the range of lawn and park:
  The unnetted black-hearts ripen dark,
All thine, against the garden wall.

Yet, tho' I spared thee all the spring,
  Thy sole delight is, sitting still,
  With that cold dagger of thy bill
To fret the summer jenneting.

A golden bill! the silver tongue,
  Cold February loved, is dry:
  Plenty corrupts the melody
That made thee famous once, when young:

And in the sultry garden-squares,
  Now thy flute-notes are changed to
    coarse,
  I hear thee not at all, or hoarse
As when a hawker hawks his wares.

Take warning! he that will not sing
  While yon sun prospers in the blue,
  Shall sing for want, ere leaves are new,
Caught in the frozen palms of Spring.

THE DEATH OF THE OLD YEAR.

FULL knee-deep lies the winter snow,
And the winter winds are wearily sighing:
Toll ye the church-bell sad and slow,
And tread softly and speak low,
  For the old year lies a-dying.
    Old year, you must not die;
    You came to us so readily,
    You lived with us so steadily,
    Old year, you shall not die.

He lieth still: he doth not move:
He will not see the dawn of day.
He hath no other life above.
He gave me a friend, and a true true-love,
  And the New-year will take 'em away.
    Old year, you must not go;
    So long as you have been with us,
    Such joy as you have seen with us,
    Old year, you shall not go.

He froth'd his bumpers to the brim;
A jollier year we shall not see.
But tho' his eyes are waxing dim,
And tho' his foes speak ill of him,
He was a friend to me.
    Old year, you shall not die;
    We did so laugh and cry with you,
    I've half a mind to die with you,
    Old year, if you must die.

He was full of joke and jest,
But all his merry quips are o'er.
To see him die, across the waste
His son and heir doth ride post-haste,
But he'll be dead before.
    Every one for his own.
    The night is starry and cold, my friend,
    And the New-year blithe and bold, my friend,
    Comes up to take his own.

How hard he breathes! over the snow
I heard just now the crowing cock.
The shadows flicker to and fro:
The cricket chirps: the light burns low:
'T is nearly twelve o'clock.
    Shake hands, before you die.
    Old year, we'll dearly rue for you:
    What is it we can do for you?
    Speak out before you die.

His face is growing sharp and thin.
Alack! our friend is gone.
Close up his eyes: tie up his chin:
Step from the corpse, and let him in
That standeth there alone,
    And waiteth at the door.
    There's a new foot on the floor, my friend,
    And a new face at the door, my friend,
    A new face at the door.

TO J. S.

THE wind, that beats the mountain, blows
    More softly round the open wold,
And gently comes the world to those
    That are cast in gentle mould.

And me this knowledge bolder made,
    Or else I had not dared to flow
In these words toward you, and invade
    Even with a verse your holy woe.

'T is strange that those we lean on most,
    Those in whose laps our limbs are nursed,
Fall into shadow, soonest lost:
    Those we love first are taken first.

God gives us love. Something to love
He lends us; but, when love is grown
To ripeness, that on which it throve
    Falls off, and love is left alone.

This is the curse of time. Alas!
    In grief I am not all unlearn'd;
Once thro' mine own doors Death did pass;
    One went, who never hath return'd.

He will not smile — not speak to me
    Once more. Two years his chair is seen
Empty before us. That was he
    Without whose life I had not been.

Your loss is rarer; for this star
    Rose with you thro' a little arc
Of heaven, nor having wander'd far
    Shot on the sudden into dark.

I knew your brother: his mute dust
    I honor and his living worth:
A man more pure and bold and just
    Was never born into the earth.

I have not look'd upon you nigh,
    Since that dear soul hath fall'n asleep.
Great Nature is more wise than I:
    I will not tell you not to weep.

And tho' mine own eyes fill with dew,
    Drawn from the spirit thro' the brain,
I will not even preach to you,
    "Weep, weeping dulls the inward pain."

Let Grief be her own mistress still.
    She loveth her own anguish deep
More than much pleasure. Let her will
    Be done — to weep or not to weep.

I will not say, "God's ordinance
    Of Death is blown in every wind";
For that is not a common chance
    That takes away a noble mind.

His memory long will live alone
    In all our hearts, as mournful light

That broods above the fallen sun,
   And dwells in heaven half the night.

Vain solace! Memory standing near
   Cast down her eyes, and in her throat
Her voice seem'd distant, and a tear
   Dropt on the letters as I wrote.

I wrote I know not what. In truth,
   How *should* I soothe you anyway,
Who miss the brother of your youth?
   Yet something I did wish to say:

For he too was a friend to me:
   Both are my friends, and my true breast
Bleedeth for both; yet it may be
   That only silence suiteth best.

Words weaker than your grief would make
   Grief more. 'T were better I should cease
Although myself could almost take
   The place of him that sleeps in peace.

Sleep sweetly, tender heart, in peace:
   Sleep, holy spirit, blessed soul,
While the stars burn, the moons increase,
   And the great ages onward roll.

Sleep till the end, true soul and sweet.
   Nothing comes to thee new or strange.
Sleep full of rest from head to feet;
   Lie still, dry dust, secure of change.

You ask me, why, tho' ill at ease,
   Within this region I subsist,
   Whose spirits falter in the mist,
And languish for the purple seas?

It is the land that freemen till,
   That sober-suited Freedom chose,
   The land, where girt with friends or foes
A man may speak the thing he will;

A land of settled government,
   A land of just and old renown,
   Where Freedom broadens slowly down
From precedent to precedent:

Where faction seldom gathers head,
   But by degrees to fulness wrought,
   The strength of some diffusive thought
Hath time and space to work and spread.

Should banded unions persecute
   Opinion, and induce a time
   When single thought is civil crime,
And individual freedom mute;

Tho' Power should make from land to land
   The name of Britain trebly great —
   Tho' every channel of the State
Should almost choke with golden sand —

Yet waft me from the harbor-mouth,
   Wild wind! I seek a warmer sky,
   And I will see before I die
The palms and temples of the South.

Of old sat Freedom on the heights,
   The thunders breaking at her feet:
Above her shook the starry lights:
   She heard the torrents meet.

There in her place she did rejoice,
   Self-gather'd in her prophet-mind,
But fragments of her mighty voice
   Came rolling on the wind.

Then stept she down thro' town and field
   To mingle with the human race,
And part by part to men reveal'd
   The fulness of her face —

Grave mother of majestic works,
   From her isle-altar gazing down,
Who, God-like, grasps the triple forks,
   And King-like, wears the crown:

Her open eyes desire the truth.
   The wisdom of a thousand years
Is in them. May perpetual youth
   Keep dry their light from tears;

That her fair form may stand and shine,
   Make bright our days and light on dreams,
Turning to scorn with lips divine
   The falsehood of extremes!

LOVE THOU THY LAND.

Love thou thy land, with love far-brought
From out the storied Past, and used
Within the Present, but transfused
Thro' future time by power of thought.

True love turn'd round on fixed poles,
Love, that endures not sordid ends,
For English natures, freemen, friends,
Thy brothers and immortal souls.

But pamper not a hasty time,
Nor feed with crude imaginings
The herd, wild hearts and feeble wings,
That every sophister can lime.

Deliver not the tasks of might
To weakness, neither hide the ray
From those, not blind, who wait for
 day,
Tho' sitting girt with doubtful light.

Make knowledge circle with the winds;
But let her herald, Reverence, fly
Before her to whatever sky
Bear seed of men and growth of minds.

Watch what main-currents draw the
 years:
Cut Prejudice against the grain:
But gentle words are always gain:
Regard the weakness of thy peers:

Nor toil for title, place, or touch
Of pension, neither count on praise:
It grows to guerdon after-days:
Nor deal in watch-words overmuch:

Not clinging to some ancient saw;
Not master'd by some modern term;
Not swift nor slow to change, but firm:
And in its season bring the law;

That from Discussion's lip may fall
With Life, that, working strongly,
 binds—
Set in all lights by many minds,
To close the interests of all.

For Nature also, cold and warm,
And moist and dry, devising long,
Thro' many agents making strong,
Matures the individual form.

Meet is it changes should control
Our being, lest we rust in ease.
We all are changed by still degrees,
All but the basis of the soul.

So let the change which comes be free
To ingroove itself with that, which flies,
And work, a joint of state, that plies
Its office, moved with sympathy.

A saying, hard to shape in act;
For all the past of Time reveals
A bridal dawn of thunder-peals,
Wherever Thought hath wedded Fact.

Ev'n now we hear with inward strife
A motion toiling in the gloom—
The Spirit of the years to come
Yearning to mix himself with Life.

A slow-develop'd strength awaits
Completion in a painful school;
Phantoms of other forms of rule,
New Majesties of mighty States—

The warders of the growing hour,
But vague in vapor, hard to mark;
And round them sea and air are dark
With great contrivances of Power.

Of many changes, aptly join'd,
Is bodied forth the second whole.
Regard gradation, lest the soul
Of Discord race the rising wind;

A wind to puff your idol-fires,
And heap their ashes on the head;
To shame the boast so often made,
That we are wiser than our sires.

O yet, if Nature's evil star
Drive men in manhood, as in youth,
To follow flying steps of Truth
Across the brazen bridge of war—

If New and Old, disastrous feud,
Must ever shock, like armed foes,
And this be true, till Time shall close,
That Principles are rain'd in blood;

Not yet the wise of heart would cease
To hold his hope thro' shame and guilt,
But with his hand against the hilt,
Would pace the troubled land, like Peace;

Not less, tho' dogs of Faction bay,
Would serve his kind in deed and word,
Certain, if knowledge bring the sword,
That knowledge takes the sword away—

Would love the gleams of good that broke
  From either side, nor veil his eyes:
And if some dreadful need should rise
Would strike, and firmly, and one stroke:

To-morrow yet would reap to-day,
  As we bear blossoms of the dead;
Earn well the thrifty months, nor wed
  Raw Haste, half-sister to Delay.

THE GOOSE.

I KNEW an old wife lean and poor,
  Her rags scarce held together;
There strode a stranger to the door,
  And it was windy weather.

He held a goose upon his arm,
  He utter'd rhyme and reason,
"Here, take the goose, and keep you warm,
  It is a stormy season."

She caught the white goose by the leg,
  A goose — 't was no great matter.
The goose let fall a golden egg
  With cackle and with clatter.

She dropt the goose, and caught the pelf,
  And ran to tell her neighbors;
And bless'd herself, and cursed herself,
  And rested from her labors.

And feeding high, and living soft,
  Grew plump and able-bodied;
Until the grave churchwarden doff'd,
  The parson smirk'd and nodded.

So sitting, served by man and maid,
  She felt her heart grow prouder:

But ah! the more the white goose laid
  It clack'd and cackled louder.

It clutter'd here, it chuckled there;
  It stirr'd the old wife's mettle:
She shifted in her elbow-chair,
  And hurl'd the pan and kettle.

"A quinsy choke, thy cursed note!"
  Then wax'd her anger stronger.
"Go, take the goose, and wring her throat,
  I will not bear it longer."

Then yelp'd the cur, and yawl'd the cat;
  Ran Gaffer, stumbled Gammer.
The goose flew this way and flew that,
  And fill'd the house with clamor.

As head and heels upon the floor
  They flounder'd all together,
There strode a stranger to the door,
  And it was windy weather:

He took the goose upon his arm,
  He utter'd words of scorning;
"So keep you cold, or keep you warm,
  It is a stormy morning."

The wild wind rang from park and plain,
  And round the attics rumbled,
Till all the tables danced again,
  And half the chimneys tumbled.

The glass blew in, the fire blew out,
  The blast was hard and harder.
Her cap blew off, her gown blew up,
  And a whirlwind clear'd the larder:

And while on all sides breaking loose
  Her household fled the danger,
Quoth she, "The Devil take the goose,
  And God forget the stranger!"

ENGLISH IDYLS AND OTHER POEMS.

(PUBLISHED 1842.)

THE EPIC.

At Francis Allen's on the Christmas-
    eve, —
The game of forfeits done — the girls all
    kiss'd
Beneath the sacred bush and past away —
The parson Holmes, the poet Everard
    Hall,
The host, and I sat round the wassail-
    bowl,
Then half-way ebb'd : and there we held
    a talk,
How all the old honor had from Christ-
    mas gone,
Or gone, or dwindled down to some odd
    games
In some odd nooks like this ; till I, tired out
With cutting eights that day upon the
    pond,
Where, three times slipping from the
    outer edge,
I bump'd the ice into three several stars,
Fell in a doze ; and half-awake I heard
The parson taking wide and wider sweeps,
Now harping on the church-commission-
    ers,
Now hawking at Geology and schism ;
Until I woke, and found him settled down
Upon the general decay of faith
Right thro' the world, "at home was
    little left,
And none abroad : there was no anchor,
    none,
To hold by." Francis, laughing, clapt
    his hand
On Everard's shoulder, with "I hold by
    him."
"And I," quoth Everard, "by the was-
    sail-bowl."
"Why yes," I said, "we knew your
    gift that way
At college : but another which you had,
I mean of verse (for so we held it then,)
What came of that?" "You know,"
    said Frank, "he burnt
His epic, his King Arthur, some twelve
    books "—
And then to me demanding why? "O,
    sir,

He thought that nothing new was said,
    or else
Something so said 't was nothing — that
    a truth
Looks freshest in the fashion of the day :
God knows : he has a mint of reasons : ask.
It pleased *me* well enough." "Nay, nay,"
    said Hall,
"Why take the style of those heroic times?
For nature brings not back the Mastodon,
Nor we those times ; and why should any
    man
Remodel models ? these twelve books of
    mine
Were faint Homeric echoes, nothing-
    worth,
Mere chaff and draff, much better burnt."
    "But I,"
Said Francis, "pick'd the eleventh from
    this hearth,
And have it : keep a thing, its use will
    come.
I hoard it as a sugar-plum for Holmes."
He laugh'd, and I, though sleepy, like a
    horse
That hears the corn-bin open, prick'd my
    ears ;
For I remember'd Everard's college fame
When we were Freshmen : then at my
    request
He brought it ; and the poet little urged,
But with some prelude of disparagement,
Read, mouthing out his hollow oes and aes,
Deep-chested music, and to this result.

MORTE D'ARTHUR.

So all day long the noise of battle roll'd
Among the mountains by the winter sea ;
Until King Arthur's table, man by man,
Had fall'n in Lyonness about their Lord,
King Arthur : then, because his wound
    was deep,
The bold Sir Bedivere uplifted him,
Sir Bedivere, the last of all his knights,
And bore him to a chapel nigh the field,
A broken chancel with a broken cross,
That stood on a dark strait of barren land.
On one side lay the Ocean, and on one

MORTE D'ARTHUR.

Lay a great water, and the moon was full.
   Then spake King Arthur to Sir Bedivere:
"The sequel of to-day unsolders all
The goodliest fellowship of famous knights
Whereof this world holds record. Such a sleep
They sleep — the men I loved. I think that we
Shall nevermore, at any future time,
Delight our souls with talk of knightly deeds,
Walking about the gardens and the halls
Of Camelot, as in the days that were.
I perish by this people which I made, —
Tho' Merlin sware that I should come again
To rule once more — but let what will be, be,
I am so deeply smitten thro' the helm
That without help I cannot last till morn.
Thou therefore take my brand Excalibur,
Which was my pride: for thou rememberest how
In those old days, one summer noon, an arm
Rose up from out the bosom of the lake,
Clothed in white samite, mystic, wonderful,
Holding the sword, — and how I row'd across
And took it, and have worn it, like a king:
And, wheresoever I am sung or told
In aftertime, this also shall be known:
But now delay not: take Excalibur,
And fling him far into the middle mere:
Watch what thou seëst, and lightly bring me word."
   To him replied the bold Sir Bedivere:
"It is not meet, Sir King, to leave thee thus,
Aidless, alone, and smitten thro' the helm.
A little thing may harm a wounded man.
Yet I thy hest will all perform at full,
Watch what I see, and lightly bring thee word."
   So saying, from the ruin'd shrine he stept
And in the moon athwart the place of tombs,
Where lay the mighty bones of ancient men,
Old knights, and over them the sea-wind sang
Shrill, chill, with flakes of foam. He, stepping down
By zig-zag paths, and juts of pointed rock,
Came on the shining levels of the lake.
   There drew he forth the brand Excalibur,
And o'er him, drawing it, the winter moon,
Brightening the skirts of a long cloud, ran forth
And sparkled keen with frost against the hilt:
For all the haft twinkled with diamond sparks,
Myriads of topaz-lights, and jacinth-work
Of subtlest jewellery. He gazed so long
That both his eyes were dazzled, as he stood,
This way and that dividing the swift mind,
In act to throw: but at the last it seem'd
Better to leave Excalibur conceal'd
There in the many-knotted waterflags,
That whistled stiff and dry about the marge.
So strode he back slow to the wounded King.
   Then spake King Arthur to Sir Bedivere:
"Hast thou perform'd my mission which I gave?
What is it thou hast seen? or what hast heard?"
   And answer made the bold Sir Bedivere:
"I heard the ripple washing in the reeds,
And the wild water lapping on the crag."
   To whom replied King Arthur, faint and pale:
"Thou hast betray'd thy nature and thy name,
Not rendering true answer, as beseem'd
Thy fëalty, nor like a noble knight:
For surer sign had follow'd, either hand,
Or voice, or else a motion of the mere.
This is a shameful thing for men to lie.
Yet now, I charge thee, quickly go again
As thou art lief and dear, and do the thing
I bade thee, watch, and lightly bring me word."
   Then went Sir Bedivere the second time
Across the ridge, and paced beside the mere,
Counting the dewy pebbles, fix'd in thought;
But when he saw the wonder of the hilt,
How curiously and strangely chased, he smote
His palms together, and he cried aloud,
"And if indeed I cast the brand away,
Surely a precious thing, one worthy note,

"An arm
Rose up from out the bosom of the lake
Clothed in white samite."

Should thus be lost for ever from the earth,
Which might have pleased the eyes of
    many men.
What good should follow this, if this were
    done?
What harm, undone? deep harm to dis-
    obey,
Seeing obedience is the bond of rule.
Were it well to obey then, if a king demand
An act unprofitable, against himself?

The King is sick, and knows not what
    he does.
What record, or what relic of my lord
Should be to aftertime, but empty breath
And rumors of a doubt? but were this
    kept,
Stored in some treasure-house of mighty
    kings,
Some one might show it at a joust of arms,
Saying, 'King Arthur's sword, Excalibur,

Wrought by the lonely maiden of the Lake.
Nine years she wrought it, sitting in the deeps
Upon the hidden bases of the hills.'
So might some old man speak in the aftertime
To all the people, winning reverence.
But now much honor and much fame were lost."
  So spake he, clouded with his own conceit,
And hid Excalibur the second time,
And so strode back slow to the wounded King.
  Then spoke King Arthur, breathing heavily :
" What is it thou hast seen ? or what hast heard ?"
And answer made the bold Sir Bedivere :
" I heard the water lapping on the crag,
And the long ripple washing in the reeds."
  To whom replied King Arthur, much in wrath :
" Ah, miserable and unkind, untrue,
Unknightly, traitor-hearted ! Woe is me !
Authority forgets a dying king,
Laid widow'd of the power in his eye
That bow'd the will. I see thee what thou art,
For thou, the latest-left of all my knights,
In whom should meet the offices of all,
Thou wouldst betray me for the precious hilt ;
Either from lust of gold, or like a girl
Valuing the giddy pleasure of the eyes.
Yet, for a man may fail in duty twice,
And the third time may prosper, get thee hence :
But, if thou spare to fling Excalibur,
I will arise and slay thee with my hands."
  Then quickly rose Sir Bedivere, and ran,
And, leaping down the ridges lightly, plunged
Among the bulrush-beds, and clutch'd the sword,
And strongly wheel'd and threw it. The great brand
Made lightnings in the splendor of the moon,
And flashing round and round, and whirl'd in an arch,
Shot like a streamer of the northern morn,
Seen where the moving isles of winter shock
By night, with noises of the northern sea.
So flash'd and fell the brand Excalibur :
But ere he dipt the surface, rose an arm
Clothed in white samite, mystic, wonderful,
And caught him by the hilt, and brandish'd him
Three times, and drew him under in the mere.
And lightly went the other to the King.
  Then spoke King Arthur, drawing thicker breath :
" Now see I by thine eyes that this is done.
Speak out : what is it thou hast heard, or seen ?"
  And answer made the bold Sir Bedivere :
" Sir King, I closed mine eyelids, lest the gems
Should blind my purpose, for I never saw,
Nor shall see, here or elsewhere, till I die,
Not tho' I live three lives of mortal men,
So great a miracle as yonder hilt.
Then with both hands I flung him, wheeling him ;
But when I look'd again, behold an arm,
Clothed in white samite, mystic, wonderful,
That caught him by the hilt, and brandish'd him
Three times, and drew him under in the mere."
  And answer made King Arthur, breathing hard :
" My end draws nigh ; 't is time that I were gone.
Make broad thy shoulders to receive my weight,
And bear me to the margin ; yet I fear
My wound hath taken cold, and I shall die."
  So saying, from the pavement he half rose,
Slowly, with pain, reclining on his arm,
And looking wistfully with wide blue eyes
As in a picture. Him Sir Bedivere
Remorsefully regarded thro' his tears,
And would have spoken, but he found not words,
Then took with care, and kneeling on one knee,
O'er both his shoulders drew the languid hands,
And rising bore him thro' the place of tombs.
But, as he walk'd, King Arthur panted hard,
Like one that feels a nightmare on his bed

When all the house is mute. So sigh'd
   the King,
Muttering and murmuring at his ear,
   "Quick, quick !
I fear it is too late, and I shall die."
But the other swiftly strode from ridge
   to ridge,
Clothed with his breath, and looking, as
   he walk'd,
Larger than human on the frozen hills.
He heard the deep behind him, and a
   cry
Before. His own thought drove him like
   a goad.
Dry clash'd his harness in the icy caves
And barren chasms, and all to left and
   right
The bare black cliff clang'd round him,
   as he based
His feet on juts of slippery crag that rang
Sharp-smitten with the dint of armed
   heels —
And on a sudden, lo ! the level lake,
And the long glories of the winter moon.
   Then saw they how there hove a dusky
      barge,
Dark as a funeral scarf from stem to stern,
Beneath them ; and descending they were
   ware
That all the decks were dense with stately
   forms
Black-stoled, black-hooded, like a dream
   — by these
Three Queens with crowns of gold — and
   from them rose
A cry that shiver'd to the tingling stars,
And, as it were one voice, an agony
Of lamentation, like a wind, that shrills
All night in a waste land, where no one
   comes,
Or hath come, since the making of the
   world.
   Then murmur'd Arthur, "Place me in
      the barge,"
And to the barge they came. There those
   three Queens
Put forth their hands, and took the King,
   and wept.
But she, that rose the tallest of them all
And fairest, laid his head upon her lap,
And loosed the shatter'd casque, and
   chafed his hands,
And call'd him by his name, complaining
   loud,
And dropping bitter tears against his brow
Striped with dark blood : for all his face
   was white

And colorless, a
   moon
Smote by the fresh
   east ;
And all his grea
   with drops
Of onset ; and t
   curls —
That made his for
High from the daïs
   with dust ;
Or, clotted into po
Mix'd with the
   fringed his
So like a shatter'd
Not like that Art
   rest,
From spur to plun
Shot thro' the
   charged
Before the eyes of
   Then loudly cr
      vere,
"Ah ! my Lord
   go ?
Where shall I hid
   eyes ?
For now I see t
   dead,
When every mor
   chance,
And every chance
   knight.
Such times have
   that led
The holy Elders
But now the who
   solved
Which was an ima
And I, the last, g
And the days dar
   years,
Among new men
   minds."
   And slowly ans
      barge :
"The old order cl
   to new,
And God fulfils h
Lest one good cus
   world.
Comfort thyself :
I have lived my
   have done
May He within hi
   thou,
If thou shouldst n

"All the decks were dense with stately forms,
Black-stoled, black-hooded, like a dream — by these
Three Queens with crowns of gold."

Pray for my soul. More things are wrought by prayer
Than this world dreams of. Wherefore, let thy voice
Rise like a fountain for me night and day.
For what are men better than sheep or goats
That nourish a blind life within the brain,
If, knowing God, they lift not hands of prayer
Both for themselves and those who call them friend?
For so the whole round earth is every way
Bound by gold chains about the feet of God.
But now farewell. I am going a long way

With these thou seëst — if indeed I go —
(For all my mind is clouded with a doubt)
To the island-valley of Avilion ;
Where falls not hail, or rain, or any snow,
Nor ever wind blows loudly ; but it lies
Deep - meadow'd, happy, fair with or-
   chard-lawns
And bowery hollows crown'd with sum-
   mer sea,
Where I will heal me of my grievous
   wound."
  So said he, and the barge with oar and
   sail
Moved from the brink, like some full-
   breasted swan
That, fluting a wild carol ere her death,
Ruffles her pure cold plume, and takes
   the flood
With swarthy webs. Long stood Sir
   Bedivere
Revolving many memories, till the hull
Look'd one black dot against the verge
   of dawn,
And on the mere the wailing died away.

  Here ended Hall, and our last light,
   that long
Had wink'd and threaten'd darkness,
   flared and fell :
At which the Parson, sent to sleep with
   sound,
And waked with silence, grunted
   " Good ! " but we
Sat rapt : it was the tone with which he
   read —
Perhaps some modern touches here and
   there
Redeem'd it from the charge of nothing-
   ness —
Or else we loved the man, and prized his
   work ;
I know not : but we sitting, as I said,
The cock crew loud ; as at that time of
   year
The lusty bird takes every hour for dawn :
Then Francis, muttering, like a man ill-
   used,
" There now — that's nothing ! " drew
   a little back,
And drove his heel into the smoulder'd
   log,
That sent a blast of sparkles up the flue :
And so to bed ; where yet in sleep I seem'd
To sail with Arthur under looming shores,
Point after point ; till on to dawn, when
   dreams

Begin to feel the truth and stir of day,
To me, methought, who waited with a
   crowd,
There came a bark that, blowing forward,
   bore
King Arthur, like a modern gentleman
Of stateliest port ; and all the people cried,
" Arthur is come again : he cannot die."
Then those that stood upon the hills be-
   hind
Repeated — "Come again, and thrice as
   fair " ;
And, further inland, voices echoed —
   " Come
With all good things, and war shall be
   no more."
At this a hundred bells began to peal,
That with the sound I woke, and heard
   indeed
The clear church-bells ring in the Christ-
   mas morn.

THE GARDENER'S DAUGHTER ; OR, THE PICTURES.

THIS morning is the morning of the day,
When I and Eustace from the city went
To see the Gardener's Daughter ; I and he,
Brothers in Art ; a friendship so complete
Portion'd in halves between us, that we
   grew
The fable of the city where we dwelt.
  My Eustace might have sat for Hercules;
So muscular he spread, so broad of breast.
He, by some law that holds in love, and
   draws
The greater to the lesser, long desired
A certain miracle of symmetry,
A miniature of loveliness, all grace
Summ'd up and closed in little ; — Juliet,
   she
So light of foot, so light of spirit, — O, she
To me myself, for some three careless
   moons,
The summer pilot of an empty heart
Unto the shores of nothing ! Know you
   not
Such touches are but embassies of love,
To tamper with the feelings, ere he found
Empire for life ? but Eustace painted
   her,
And said to me, she sitting with us then,
" When will *you* paint like this ? " and I
   replied,
(My words were half in earnest, half in
   jest,)

"'T is not your work, but Love's. Love,
   unperceived,
A more ideal Artist he than all,
Came, drew your pencil from you, made
   those eyes
Darker than darkest pansies, and that
   hair
More black than ashbuds in the front of
   March."
And Juliet answer'd laughing, "Go and
   see
The Gardener's daughter: trust me, after
   that,
You scarce can fail to match his master-
   piece."
And up we rose, and on the spur we
   went.
   Not wholly in the busy world, nor
     quite
Beyond it, blooms the garden that I love.
News from the humming city comes to it
In sound of funeral or of marriage bells;
And, sitting muffled in dark leaves, you
   hear
The windy clanging of the minster clock;
Although between it and the garden lies
A league of grass, wash'd by a slow broad
   stream,
That, stirr'd with languid pulses of the
   oar,
Waves all its lazy lilies, and creeps on,
Barge-laden, to three arches of a bridge
Crown'd with the minster-towers.
                   The fields between
Are dewy-fresh, browsed by deep-udder'd
   kine,
And all about the large lime feathers low,
The lime a summer home of murmurous
   wings.
   In that still place she, hoarded in her-
     self,
Grew, seldom seen: not less among us
   lived
Her fame from lip to lip. Who had not
   heard
Of Rose, the Gardener's daughter?
   Where was he,
So blunt in memory, so old at heart,
At such a distance from his youth in grief,
That, having seen, forgot? The common
   mouth,
So gross to express delight, in praise of
   her
Grew oratory. Such a lord is Love,
And Beauty such a mistress of the world.
   And if I said that Fancy, led by Love,
Would play with flying forms and images,

Yet this is also true, that, long before
I look'd upon her, when I heard her name
My heart was like a prophet to my heart,
And told me I should love. A crowd of
   hopes,
That sought to sow themselves like
   winged seeds,
Born out of everything I heard and saw,
Flutter'd about my senses and my soul;
And vague desires, like fitful blasts of
   balm
To one that travels quickly, made the air
Of Life delicious, and all kinds of
   thought,
That verged upon them, sweeter than the
   dream
Dream'd by a happy man, when the dark
   East,
Unseen, is brightening to his bridal
   morn.
   And sure this orbit of the memory folds
For ever in itself the day we went
To see her. All the land in flowery
   squares,
Beneath a broad and equal-blowing wind,
Smelt of the coming summer, as one
   large cloud
Drew downward: but all else of Heaven
   was pure
Up to the Sun, and May from verge to
   verge,
And May with me from head to heel.
   And now,
As tho' 't were yesterday, as tho' it were
The hour just flown, that morn with all
   its sound,
(For those old Mays had thrice the life
   of these,)
Rings in mine ears. The steer forgot to
   graze,
And, where the hedge-row cuts the path-
   way, stood,
Leaning his horns into the neighbor field,
And lowing to his fellows. From the
   woods
Came voices of the well-contented doves.
The lark could scarce get out his notes
   for joy,
But shook his song together as he near'd
His happy home, the ground. To left
   and right,
The cuckoo told his name to all the hills;
The mellow ouzel fluted in the elm;
The redcap whistled; and the nightingale
Sang loud, as tho' he were the bird of day.
   And Eustace turn'd, and smiling said
   to me,

"Hear how the bushes echo! by my life,
These birds have joyful thoughts. Think
  you they sing
Like poets, from the vanity of song?
Or have they any sense of why they sing?
And would they praise the heavens for
  what they have?"
And I made answer, "Were there noth-
  ing else
For which to praise the heavens but only
  love,
That only love were cause enough for
  praise."
  Lightly he laugh'd, as one that read
  my thought,
And on we went; but ere an hour had
  pass'd,
We reach'd a meadow slanting to the
  North;
Down which a well-worn pathway courted
  us
To one green wicket in a privet hedge;
This, yielding, gave into a grassy walk
Thro' crowded lilac-ambush trimly
  pruned;
And one warm gust, full-fed with per-
  fume, blew
Beyond us, as we enter'd in the cool.
The garden stretches southward. In the
  midst
A cedar spread his dark-green layers of
  shade.
The garden-glasses shone, and momently
The twinkling laurel scatter'd silver
  lights.
  "Eustace," I said, "this wonder keeps
  the house."
He nodded, but a moment afterwards
He cried, "Look! look!" Before he
  ceased I turn'd,
And, ere a star can wink, beheld her there.
For up the porch there grew an Eastern
  rose,
That, flowering high, the last night's gale
  had caught,
And blown across the walk. One arm
  aloft —
Gown'd in pure white, that fitted to the
  shape —
Holding the bush, to fix it back, she stood.
A single stream of all her soft brown hair
Pour'd on one side: the shadow of the
  flowers
Stole all the golden gloss, and, wavering
Lovingly lower, trembled on her waist —
Ah, happy shade — and still went waver-
  ing down,
But, ere it touch'd a foot, that might have
  danced
The greensward into greener circles, dipt,
And mix'd with shadows of the common
  ground!
But the full day dwelt on her brows, and
  sunn'd
Her violet eyes, and all her Hebe bloom,
And doubled his own warmth against her
  lips,
And on the bounteous wave of such a
  breast
As never pencil drew. Half light, half
  shade,
She stood, a sight to make an old man
  young.
  So rapt, we near'd the house; but she,
  a Rose
In roses, mingled with her fragrant toil,
Nor heard us come, nor from her ten-
  dance turn'd
Into the world without; till close at hand,
And almost ere I knew mine own intent,
This murmur broke the stillness of that
  air
Which brooded round about her:
                     "Ah, one rose,
One rose, but one, by those fair fingers
  cull'd,
Were worth a hundred kisses press'd on
  lips
Less exquisite than thine."
             She look'd: but all
Suffused with blushes — neither self-
  possess'd
Nor startled, but betwixt this mood and
  that,
Divided in a graceful quiet — paused,
And dropt the branch she held, and turn-
  ing, wound
Her looser hair in braid, and stirr'd her
  lips
For some sweet answer, tho' no answer
  came,
Nor yet refused the rose, but granted it,
And moved away, and left me, statue-
  like,
In act to render thanks.
             I, that whole day,
Saw her no more, altho' I linger'd there
Till every daisy slept, and Love's white
  star
Beam'd thro' the thicken'd cedar in the
  dusk.
  So home we went, and all the livelong
  way
With solemn gibe did Eustace banter me.

THE GARDENER'S DAUGHTER; OR, THE PICTURES.

"Now," said he, "will you climb the top of Art.
You cannot fail but work in hues to dim
The Titianic Flora. Will you match
My Juliet? you, not you, — the Master,
Love,
A more ideal Artist he than all."
So home I went, but could not sleep for joy,
Reading her perfect features in the gloom,
Kissing the rose she gave me o'er and o'er,
And shaping faithful record of the glance
That graced the giving — such a noise of life
Swarm'd in the golden present, such a voice
Call'd to me from the years to come, and such
A length of bright horizon rimm'd the dark.
And all that night I heard the watchman peal
The sliding season: all that night I heard
The heavy clocks knolling the drowsy hours.
The drowsy hours, dispensers of all good,
O'er the mute city stole with folded wings,
Distilling odors on me as they went
To greet their fairer sisters of the East.
Love at first sight, first-born, and heir to all,
Made this night thus. Henceforward squall nor storm
Could keep me from that Eden where she dwelt.
Light pretexts drew me: sometimes a Dutch love
For tulips; then for roses, moss or musk,
To grace my city-rooms; or fruits and cream
Served in the weeping elm; and more and more
A word could bring the color to my cheek;
A thought would fill my eyes with happy dew;
Love trebled life within me, and with each
The year increased.
   The daughters of the year,
One after one, thro' that still garden pass'd:
Each garlanded with her peculiar flower
Danced into light, and died into the shade;
And each in passing touch'd with some new grace
Or seem'd to touch her, so that day by day,
Like one that never can be wholly known,
Her beauty grew; till Autumn brought an hour
For Eustace, when I heard his deep "I will,"
Breathed, like the covenant of a God, to hold
From thence thro' all the worlds: but I rose up
Full of his bliss, and following her dark eyes
Felt earth as air beneath me, till I reach'd
The wicket-gate, and found her standing there.
   There sat we down upon a garden mound,
Two mutually enfolded; Love, the third,
Between us, in the circle of his arms
Enwound us both; and over many a range
Of waning lime the gray cathedral towers,
Across a hazy glimmer of the west,
Reveal'd their shining windows: from them clash'd
The bells; we listen'd; with the time we play'd;
We spoke of other things; we coursed about
The subject most at heart, more near and near,
Like doves about a dovecote, wheeling round
The central wish, until we settled there.
Then, in that time and place, I spoke to her,
Requiring, tho' I knew it was mine own,
Yet for the pleasure that I took to hear,
Requiring at her hand the greatest gift,
A woman's heart, the heart of her I loved;
And in that time and place she answer'd me,
And in the compass of three little words,
More musical than ever came in one,
The silver fragments of a broken voice,
Made me most happy, faltering, "I am thine."
   Shall I cease here? Is this enough to say
That my desire, like all strongest hopes,
By its own energy fulfill'd itself,
Merged in completion? Would you learn at full
How passion rose thro' circumstantial grades
Beyond all grades develop'd? and indeed
I had not stayed so long to tell you all,
But while I mused came Memory with sad eyes,

Holding the folded annals of my youth;
And while I mused, Love with knit brows
    went by,
And with a flying finger swept my lips,
And spake, "Be wise: not easily forgiven
Are those, who, setting wide the doors
    that bar
The secret bridal chambers of the heart,
Let in the day." Here, then, my words
    have end.
  Yet might I tell of meetings, of fare-
    wells —
Of that which came between, more sweet
    than each,
In whispers, like the whispers of the leaves
That tremble round a nightingale — in
    sighs
Which perfect Joy, perplex'd for utter-
    ance,
Stole from her sister Sorrow. Might I
    not tell
Of difference, reconcilement, pledges
    given,
And vows, where there was never need
    of vows,
And kisses, where the heart on one wild
    leap
Hung tranced from all pulsation, as above
The heavens between their fairy fleeces
    pale
Sow'd all their mystic gulfs with fleeting
    stars;
Or while the balmy glooming, crescent-
    lit,
Spread the light haze along the river-
    shores,
And in the hollows; or as once we met
Unheedful, tho' beneath a whispering rain
Night slid down one long stream of sigh-
    ing wind,
And in her bosom bore the baby, Sleep.
  But this whole hour your eyes have
    been intent
On that veil'd picture — veil'd, for what
    it holds
May not be dwelt on by the common day.
This prelude has prepared thee. Raise
    thy soul;
Make thine heart ready with thine eyes:
    the time
Is come to raise the veil.
                Behold her there,
As I beheld her ere she knew my heart,
My first, last love; the idol of my youth,
The darling of my manhood, and, alas!
Now the most blessed memory of mine
    age.

DORA.

WITH farmer Allan at the farm abode
William and Dora. William was his son,
And she his niece. He often look'd at
    them,
And often thought, "I'll make them man
    and wife."
Now Dora felt her uncle's will in all,
And yearn'd towards William; but the
    youth, because
He had been always with her in the house,
Thought not of Dora.
              Then there came a day
When Allan call'd his son, and said,
    "My son:
I married late, but I would wish to see
My grandchild on my knees before I die:
And I have set my heart upon a match.
Now therefore look to Dora: she is well
To look to: thrifty too beyond her age.
She is my brother's daughter: he and I
Had once hard words, and parted, and he
    died
In foreign lands; but for his sake I bred
His daughter Dora: take her for your
    wife;
For I have wish'd this marriage, night
    and day,
For many years." But William answer'd
    short:
"I cannot marry Dora; by my life,
I will not marry Dora." Then the old
    man
Was wroth, and doubled up his hands,
    and said:
"You will not, boy! you dare to answer
    thus!
But in my time a father's word was law,
And so it shall be now for me. Look to it;
Consider, William: take a month to
    think,
And let me have an answer to my wish;
Or, by the Lord that made me, you shall
    pack,
And never more darken my doors again."
But William answer'd madly; bit his
    lips,
And broke away. The more he look'd at
    her
The less he liked her; and his ways were
    harsh;
But Dora bore them meekly. Then before
The month was out he left his father's
    house,
And hired himself to work within the
    fields;

And half in love, half spite, he woo'd and wed
A laborer's daughter, Mary Morrison.
  Then, when the bells were ringing, Allan call'd
His niece and said : "My girl, I love you well ;
But if you speak with him that was my son,
Or change a word with her he calls his wife,
My home is none of yours. My will is law."
And Dora promised, being meek. She thought,
"It cannot be : my uncle's mind will change!"
  And days went on, and there was born a boy
To William ; then distresses came on him ;
And day by day he pass'd his father's gate,
Heart-broken, and his father help'd him not.
But Dora stored what little she could save,
And sent it them by stealth, nor did they know
Who sent it ; till at last a fever seized
On William, and in harvest time he died.
  Then Dora went to Mary. Mary sat
And look'd with tears upon her boy, and thought
Hard things of Dora. Dora came and said :
"I have obey'd my uncle until now,
And I have sinn'd, for it was all thro' me
This evil came on William at the first.
But, Mary, for the sake of him that's gone,
And for your sake, the woman that he chose,
And for this orphan, I am come to you :
You know there has not been for these five years
So full a harvest : let me take the boy,
And I will set him in my uncle's eye
Among the wheat ; that when his heart is glad
Of the full harvest, he may see the boy,
And bless him for the sake of him that's gone."
  And Dora took the child, and went her way
Across the wheat, and sat upon a mound
That was unsown, where many poppies grew.
Far off the farmer came into the field
And spied her not ; for none of all his men
Dare tell him Dora waited with the child ;
And Dora would have risen and gone to him,
But her heart fail'd her ; and the reapers reap'd,
And the sun fell, and all the land was dark.
  But when the morrow came, she rose and took
The child once more, and sat upon the mound ;
And made a little wreath of all the flowers
That grew about, and tied it round his hat
To make him pleasing in her uncle's eye.
Then when the farmer pass'd into the field
He spied her, and he left his men at work,
And came and said : "Where were you yesterday ?
Whose child is that ? What are you doing here ?"
So Dora cast her eyes upon the ground,
And answer'd softly, "This is William's child !"
"And did I not," said Allan, "did I not
Forbid you, Dora ?" Dora said again :
"Do with me as you will, but take the child
And bless him for the sake of him that's gone !"
And Allan said, "I see it is a trick
Got up betwixt you and the woman there.
I must be taught my duty, and by you !
You knew my word was law, and yet you dared
To slight it. Well — for I will take the boy ;
But go you hence, and never see me more."
  So saying, he took the boy, that cried aloud
And struggled hard. The wreath of flowers fell
At Dora's feet. She bow'd upon her hands,
And the boy's cry came to her from the field,
More and more distant. She bow'd down her head,
Remembering the day when first she came,
And all the things that had been. She bow'd down
And wept in secret ; and the reapers reap'd,
And the sun fell, and all the land was dark.
  Then Dora went to Mary's house, and stood
Upon the threshold. Mary saw the boy
Was not with Dora. She broke out in praise

To God, that help'd her in her widowhood.
And Dora said, "My uncle took the boy;
But, Mary, let me live and work with you:
He says that he will never see me more."
Then answer'd Mary, "This shall never be,
That thou shouldst take my trouble on thyself:
And, now I think, he shall not have the boy,
For he will teach him hardness, and to slight
His mother; therefore thou and I will go,
And I will have my boy, and bring him home;
And I will beg of him to take thee back:
But if he will not take thee back again,
Then thou and I will live within one house,
And work for William's child, until he grows
Of age to help us."
            So the women kiss'd
Each other, and set out, and reach'd the farm.
The door was off the latch: they peep'd, and saw
The boy set up betwixt his grandsire's knees,
Who thrust him in the hollows of his arm,
And clapt him on the hands and on the cheeks,
Like one that loved him: and the lad stretch'd out
And babbled for the golden seal, that hung
From Allan's watch, and sparkled by the fire.
Then they came in: but when the boy beheld
His mother, he cried out to come to her:
And Allan set him down, and Mary said:
"O Father! — if you let me call you so —
I never came a-begging for myself,
Or William, or this child; but now I come
For Dora: take her back; she loves you well.
O Sir, when William died, he died at peace
With all men; for I ask'd him, and he said,
He could not ever rue his marrying me —
I had been a patient wife: but, Sir, he said
That he was wrong to cross his father thus:
'God bless him!' he said, 'and may he never know
The troubles I have gone thro'!' Then he turn'd
His face and pass'd — unhappy that I am!
But now, Sir, let me have my boy, for you
Will make him hard, and he will learn to slight
His father's memory; and take Dora back,
And let all this be as it was before."
So Mary said, and Dora hid her face
By Mary. There was silence in the room;
And all at once the old man burst in sobs:—
"I have been to blame — to blame.
I have kill'd my son.
I have kill'd him — but I loved him —
my dear son.
May God forgive me! — I have been to blame.
Kiss me, my children."
            Then they clung about
The old man's neck, and kiss'd him many times.
And all the man was broken with remorse;
And all his love came back a hundred-fold;
And for three hours he sobb'd o'er William's child,
Thinking of William.
            So those four abode
Within one house together; and as years
Went forward, Mary took another mate;
But Dora lived unmarried till her death.

AUDLEY COURT.

"THE Bull, the Fleece are cramm'd, and not a room
For love or money. Let us picnic there
At Audley Court."
            I spoke, while Audley feast
Humm'd like a hive all round the narrow quay,
To Francis, with a basket on his arm,
To Francis just alighted from the boat,
And breathing of the sea. "With all my heart,"
Said Francis. Then we shoulder'd thro' the swarm,

AUDLEY COURT.

*"I have been to blame — to blame. I have kill'd my son,
I have kill'd him — but I loved him — my dear son."*

And rounded by the stillness of the beach
To where the bay runs up its latest horn.
  We left the dying ebb that faintly lipp'd
The flat red granite; so by many a sweep
Of meadow smooth from aftermath we reach'd
The griffin-guarded gates, and pass'd thro' all
The pillar'd dusk of sounding sycamores,
And cross'd the garden to the gardener's lodge,
With all its casements bedded, and its walls
And chimneys muffled in the leafy vine.
  There, on a slope of orchard, Francis laid
A damask napkin wrought with horse and hound,
Brought out a dusky loaf that smelt of home,
And, half-cut-down, a pasty costly-made,
Where quail and pigeon, lark and leveret lay,
Like fossils of the rock, with golden yolks
Imbedded and injellied; last, with these,
A flask of cider from his father's vats,
Prime, which I knew; and so we sat and eat
And talk'd old matters over; who was dead,
Who married, who was like to be, and how
The races went, and who would rent the hall:
Then touch'd upon the game, how scarce it was
This season; glancing thence, discuss'd the farm,
The fourfield system, and the price of grain;
And struck upon the corn-laws, where we split,
And came again together on the king
With heated faces; till he laugh'd aloud;

And, while the blackbird on the pippin
    hung
To hear him, clapt his hand in mine and
    sang —
"Oh! who would fight and march and
    countermarch,
Be shot for sixpence in a battle-field,
And shovell'd up into a bloody trench
Where no one knows? but let me live
    my life.
"Oh! who would cast and balance at
    a desk,
Perch'd like a crow upon a three-legg'd
    stool,
Till all his juice is dried, and all his joints
Are full of chalk? but let me live my life.
"Who 'd serve the state? for if I
    carved my name
Upon the cliffs that guard my native land,
I might as well have traced it in the sands;
The sea wastes all: but let me live my
    life.
"Oh! who would love? I woo'd a
    woman once,
But she was sharper than an eastern wind,
And all my heart turn'd from her, as a thorn
Turns from the sea; but let me live my life."
He sang his song, and I replied with
    mine:
I found it in a volume, all of songs,
Knock'd down to me, when old Sir Robert's pride,
His books — the more the pity, so I said —
Came to the hammer here in March —
    and this —
I set the words, and added names I knew.
"Sleep, Ellen Aubrey, sleep, and
    dream of me:
Sleep, Ellen, folded in thy sister's arm,
And sleeping, haply dream her arm is
    mine.
"Sleep, Ellen, folded in Emilia's arm;
Emilia, fairer than all else but thou,
For thou art fairer than all else that is.
"Sleep, breathing health and peace
    upon her breast:
Sleep, breathing love and trust against
    her lip:
I go to-night: I come to-morrow morn.
"I go, but I return: I would I were
The pilot of the darkness and the dream.
Sleep, Ellen Aubrey, love, and dream
    of me."
So sang we each to either, Francis Hale,
The farmer's son, who lived across the bay,
My friend; and I, that having wherewithal,

And in the fallow leisure of my life
A rolling stone of here and everywhere,
Did what I would; but ere the night we
    rose
And saunter'd home beneath a moon,
    that, just
In crescent, dimly rain'd about the leaf
Twilights of airy silver, till we reach'd
The limit of the hills; and as we sank
From rock to rock upon the glooming
    quay,
The town was hush'd beneath us: lower
    down
The bay was oily calm; the harbor-buoy
Sole star of phosphorescence in the calm,
With one green sparkle ever and anon
Dipt by itself, and we were glad at heart.

WALKING TO THE MAIL.

John. I 'm glad I walk'd. How fresh
    the meadows look
Above the river, and, but a month ago,
The whole hillside was redder than a fox.
Is yon plantation where this byway joins
The turnpike?
James. Yes.
John. And when does this come by?
James. The mail? At one o'clock.
John. What is it now?
James. A quarter to.
John. Whose house is that I see?
No, not the County Member's with the
    vane:
Up higher with the yewtree by it, and half
A score of gables.
James. That? Sir Edward Head's:
But he 's abroad: the place is to be sold.
John. O, his. He was not broken.
James. No, sir, he,
Vex'd with a morbid devil in his blood
That veil'd the world with jaundice, hid
    his face
From all men, and commercing with
    himself,
He lost the sense that handles daily life —
That keeps us all in order more or less —
And sick of home went overseas for change.
John. And whither?
James. Nay, who knows? he 's here
    and there.
But let him go; his devil goes with him,
As well as with his tenant, Jocky Dawes.
John. What 's that?
James. You saw the man — on Monday, was it? —

There by the humpback'd willow; half stands up
And bristles; half has fall'n and made a bridge;
And there he caught the younker tickling trout —
Caught in *flagrante* — what 's the Latin word ?—
Delicto: but his house, for so they say,
Was haunted with a jolly ghost, that shook
The curtains, whined in lobbies, tapt at doors,
And rummaged like a rat: no servant stay'd:
The farmer vext packs up his beds and chairs,
And all his household stuff; and with his boy
Betwixt his knees, his wife upon the tilt,
Sets out, and meets a friend who hails him, "What!
You 're flitting!" "Yes, we 're flitting," says the ghost,
(For they had pack'd the thing among the beds,)
"O well," says he, "you flitting with us too —
Jack, turn the horses' heads and home again."
  John. He left *his* wife behind; for so I heard.
  James. He left her, yes. I met my lady once:
A woman like a butt, and harsh as crabs.
  John. O yet but I remember, ten years back —
'T is now at least ten years — and then she was —
You could not light upon a sweeter thing:
A body slight and round, and like a pear
In growing, modest eyes, a hand, a foot
Lessening in perfect cadence, and a skin
As clean and white as privet when it flowers.
  James. Ay, ay, the blossom fades, and they that loved
At first like dove and dove were cat and dog.
She was the daughter of a cottager,
Out of her sphere. What betwixt shame and pride,
New things and old, himself and her, she sour'd
To what she is: a nature never kind!
Like men, like manners: like breeds like, they say.

Kind nature is the best: those manners next
That fit us like a nature second-hand;
Which are indeed the manners of the great.
  John. But I had heard it was this bill that past,
And fear of change at home, that drove him hence.
  James. That was the last drop in the cup of gall.
I once was near him, when his bailiff brought
A Chartist pike. You should have seen him wince
As from a venomous thing: he thought himself
A mark for all, and shudder'd, lest a cry
Should break his sleep by night, and his nice eyes
Should see the raw mechanic's bloody thumbs
Sweat on his blazon'd chairs; but, sir, you know
That these two parties still divide the world —
Of those that want, and those that have: and still
The same old sore breaks out from age to age
With much the same result. Now I myself,
A Tory to the quick, was as a boy
Destructive, when I had not what I would.
I was at school — a college in the South:
There lived a flayflint near; we stole his fruit,
His hens, his eggs; but there was law for *us;*
We paid in person. He had a sow, sir. She,
With meditative grunts of much content,
Lay great with pig, wallowing in sun and mud.
By night we dragg'd her to the college tower
From her warm bed, and up the corkscrew stair
With hand and rope we haled the groaning sow,
And on the leads we kept her till she pigg'd.
Large range of prospect had the mother sow,
And but for daily loss of one she loved,

As one by one we took them — but for
  this —
As never sow was higher in this world —
Might have been happy: but what lot is
  pure?
We took them all, till she was left alone
Upon her tower, the Niobe of swine,
And so return'd unfarrow'd to her sty.
John. They found you out?
  James.   Not they.
  John.   Well — after all —
What know we of the secret of a man?
His nerves were wrong. What ails us,
  who are sound,
That we should mimic this raw fool the
  world,
Which charts us all in its coarse blacks
  or whites,
As ruthless as a baby with a worm,
As cruel as a schoolboy ere he grows
To Pity — more from ignorance than will.
  But put your best foot forward, or I fear
That we shall miss the mail: and here
  it comes
With five at top: as quaint a four-in-hand
As you shall see — three pyebalds and a
  roan.

EDWIN MORRIS; OR, THE LAKE.

O ME, my pleasant rambles by the lake,
My sweet, wild, fresh three quarters of a
  year,
My one Oasis in the dust and drouth
Of city life! I was a sketcher then:
See here, my doing: curves of mountain,
  bridge,
Boat, island, ruins of a castle, built
When men knew how to build, upon a
  rock,
With turrets lichen-gilded like a rock:
And here, new-comers in an ancient hold,
New-comers from the Mersey, million-
  naires,
Here lived the Hills — a Tudor-chimneyed
  bulk
Of mellow brickwork on an isle of bowers.

O me, my pleasant rambles by the lake
With Edwin Morris and with Edward Bull
The curate; he was fatter than his cure.

  But Edwin Morris, he that knew the
    names,
Long learned names of agaric, moss and
  fern,
Who forged a thousand theories of the
  rocks,
Who taught me how to skate, to row, to
  swim,
Who read me rhymes elaborately good,
His own — I call'd him Crichton, for he
  seem'd
All-perfect, finish'd to the finger nail.

And once I ask'd him of his early life,
And his first passion; and he answer'd me;
And well his words became him: was he
  not
A full-cell'd honeycomb of eloquence
Stored from all flowers? Poet-like he
  spoke.

"My love for Nature is as old as I;
But thirty moons, one honeymoon to that,
And three rich sennights more, my love
  for her.
My love for Nature and my love for her,
Of different ages, like twin-sisters grew,
Twin-sisters differently beautiful.
To some full music rose and sank the sun,
And some full music seem'd to move and
  change
With all the varied changes of the dark,
And either twilight and the day between;
For daily hope fulfill'd, to rise again
Revolving toward fulfilment, made it
  sweet
To walk, to sit, to sleep, to wake, to
  breathe."

  Or this or something like to this he
    spoke.
Then said the fat-faced curate, Edward
  Bull,
"I take it, God made the woman for
  the man,
And for the good and increase of the world.
A pretty face is well, and this is well,
To have a dame indoors, that trims us up,
And keeps us tight; but these unreal
  ways
Seem but the theme of writers, and indeed
Worn threadbare. Man is made of solid
  stuff.
I say, God made the woman for the man,
And for the good and increase of the
  world."

  "Parson," said I, "you pitch the pipe
    too low:
But I have sudden touches, and can run
My faith beyond my practice into his:
Tho' if, in dancing after Letty Hill,

I do not hear the bells upon my cap,
I scarce have other music: yet say on.
What should one give to light on such a
  dream?"
I ask'd him half-sardonically.
                              "Give?
Give all thou art," he answer'd, and a light
Of laughter dimpled in his swarthy cheek;
"I would have hid her needle in my heart,
To save her little finger from a scratch
No deeper than the skin: my ears could
  hear
Her lightest breaths: her least remark
  was worth
The experience of the wise. I went and
  came;
Her voice fled always thro' the summer
  land;
I spoke her name alone. Thrice-happy
  days!
The flower of each, those moments when
  we met,
The crown of all, we met to part no more."

Were not his words delicious, I a beast
To take them as I did? but something
  jarr'd;
Whether he spoke too largely; that there
  seem'd
A touch of something false, some self-
  conceit,
Or over-smoothness: howsoe'er it was,
He scarcely hit my humor, and I said:

"Friend Edwin, do not think yourself
  alone
Of all men happy. Shall not Love to me,
As in the Latin song I learnt at school,
Sneeze out a full God-bless-you right and
  left?
But you can talk: yours is a kindly vein;
I have, I think, — Heaven knows — as
  much within;
Have, or should have, but for a thought
  or two,
That like a purple beech among the greens
Looks out of place: 't is from no want in
  her:
It is my shyness, or my self-distrust,
Or something of a wayward modern mind
Dissecting passion. Time will set me
  right."

  So spoke I knowing not the things
    that were.
  Then said the fat-faced curate, Edward
    Bull:

"God made the woman for the use of man,
And for the good and increase of the
  world."
And I and Edwin laugh'd; and now we
  paused
About the windings of the marge to hear
The soft wind blowing over meadowy
  holms
And alders, garden-isles; and now we left
The clerk behind us, I and he, and ran
By ripply shallows of the lisping lake,
Delighted with the freshness and the
  sound.

But, when the bracken rusted on their
  crags,
My suit had wither'd, nipt to death by him
That was a God, and is a lawyer's clerk,
The rentroll Cupid of our rainy isles.
'T is true, we met; one hour I had, no more:
She sent a note, the seal an *Elle vous suit*,
The close "Your Letty, only yours"; and
  this
Thrice underscored. The friendly mist
  of morn
Clung to the lake. I boated over, ran
My craft aground, and heard with beating
  heart
The Sweet-Gale rustle round the shelving
  keel;
And out I stept, and up I crept: she moved,
Like Proserpine in Enna, gathering
  flowers:
Then low and sweet I whistled thrice;
  and she,
She turn'd, we closed, we kiss'd, swore
  faith, I breathed
In some new planet: a silent cousin stole
Upon us and departed: "Leave," she cried,
"O leave me!" "Never, dearest, never:
  here
I brave the worst": and while we stood
  like fools
Embracing, all at once a score of pugs
And poodles yell'd within, and out they
  came
Trustees and Aunts and Uncles. "What,
  with him!
Go" (shrill'd the cotton-spinning chorus);
  "him!"
I choked. Again they shriek'd the bur-
  den — "Him!"
Again with hands of wild rejection "Go!—
Girl, get you in!" She went — and in
  one month
They wedded her to sixty thousand
  pounds,

To lands in Kent and messuages in York,
And slight Sir Robert with his watery smile
And educated whisker. But for me,
They set an ancient creditor to work:
It seems I broke a close with force and arms:
There came a mystic token from the king
To greet the sheriff, needless courtesy!
I read, and fled by night, and flying turn'd:
Her taper glimmer'd in the lake below:
I turn'd once more, close-buttoned to the storm;
So left the place, left Edwin, nor have seen
Him since, nor heard of her, nor cared to hear.

Nor cared to hear? perhaps: yet long ago
I have pardon'd little Letty; not indeed,
It may be, for her own dear sake but this,
She seems a part of those fresh days to me;
For in the dust and drouth of London life
She moves among my visions of the lake,
While the prime swallow dips his wing, or then
While the gold-lily blows, and overhead
The light cloud smoulders on the summer crag.

ST. SIMEON STYLITES.

ALTHO' I be the basest of mankind,
From scalp to sole one slough and crust of sin,
Unfit for earth, unfit for heaven, scarce meet
For troops of devils, mad with blasphemy,
I will not cease to grasp the hope I hold
Of saintdom, and to clamor, mourn and sob,
Battering the gates of heaven with storms of prayer,
Have mercy, Lord, and take away my sin.
Let this avail, just, dreadful, mighty God,
This not be all in vain, that thrice ten years,
Thrice multiplied by superhuman pangs,
In hungers and in thirsts, fevers and cold,
In coughs, aches, stitches, ulcerous throes and cramps,
A sign betwixt the meadow and the cloud,
Patient on this tall pillar I have borne
Rain, wind, frost, heat, hail, damp, and sleet, and snow;

And I had hoped that ere this period closed
Thou wouldst have caught me up into thy rest,
Denying not these weather-beaten limbs
The meed of saints, the white robe and the palm.
 O take the meaning, Lord: I do not breathe,
Not whisper, any murmur of complaint.
Pain heap'd ten-hundred-fold to this, were still
Less burden, by ten-hundred-fold, to bear,
Than were those lead-like tons of sin, that crush'd
My spirit flat before thee.
 O Lord, Lord,
Thou knowest I bore this better at the first,
For I was strong and hale of body then;
And tho' my teeth, which now are dropt away,
Would chatter with the cold, and all my beard
Was tagg'd with icy fringes in the moon,
I drown'd the whoopings of the owl with sound
Of pious hymns and psalms, and sometimes saw
An angel stand and watch me, as I sang.
Now am I feeble grown; my end draws nigh;
I hope my end draws nigh: half deaf I am,
So that I scarce can hear the people hum
About the column's base, and almost blind,
And scarce can recognize the fields I know;
And both my thighs are rotted with the dew;
Yet cease I not to clamor and to cry,
While my stiff spine can hold my weary head,
Till all my limbs drop piecemeal from the stone,
Have mercy, mercy: take away my sin.
 O Jesus, if thou wilt not save my soul,
Who may be saved? who is it may be saved?
Who may be made a saint, if I fail here?
Show me the man hath suffer'd more than I.
For did not all thy martyrs die one death?
For either they were stoned, or crucified,
Or burn'd in fire, or boil'd in oil, or sawn
In twain beneath the ribs; but I die here
To-day, and whole years long, a life of death.
Bear witness, if I could have found a way

(And heedfully I sifted all my thought)
More slowly-painful to subdue this home
Of sin, my flesh, which I despise and hate,
I had not stinted practice, O my God.
 For not alone this pillar-punishment,
Not this alone I bore: but while I lived
In the white convent down the valley
 there,
For many weeks about my loins I wore
The rope that haled the buckets from the
 well,
Twisted as tight as I could knot the
 noose ;
And spake not of it to a single soul,
Until the ulcer, eating thro' my skin,
Betray'd my secret penance, so that all
My brethren marvell'd greatly. More than
 this
I bore, whereof, O God, thou knowest all.
 Three winters, that my soul might grow
 to thee,
I lived up there on yonder mountain side.
My right leg chain'd into the crag, I lay
Pent in a roofless close of ragged stones ;
Inswathed sometimes in wandering mist,
 and twice
Black'd with thy branding thunder, and
 sometimes
Sucking the damps for drink, and eating
 not,
Except the spare chance-gift of those
 that came
To touch my body and be heal'd, and live :
And they say then that I work'd miracles,
Whereof my fame is loud amongst man-
 kind,
Cured lameness, palsies, cancers. Thou,
 O God,
Knowest alone whether this was or no.
Have mercy, mercy ; cover all my sin.
 Then, that I might be more alone with
 thee,
Three years I lived upon a pillar, high
Six cubits, and three years on one of
 twelve ;
And twice three years I crouch'd on one
 that rose
Twenty by measure ; last of all, I grew
Twice ten long weary weary years to this,
That numbers forty cubits from the soil.
 I think that I have borne as much as
 this —
Or else I dream — and for so long a time,
If I may measure time by yon slow light,
And this high dial, which my sorrow
 crowns —
So much — even so.

And yet I know not well,
For that the evil ones come here, and
 say,
"Fall down, O Simeon : thou hast suf-
 fer'd long
For ages and for ages !" then they prate
Of penances I cannot have gone thro',
Perplexing me with lies ; and oft I fall,
Maybe for months, in such blind lethar-
 gies,
That Heaven, and Earth, and Time are
 choked.
 But yet
Bethink thee, Lord, while thou and all
 the saints
Enjoy themselves in heaven, and men on
 earth
House in the shade of comfortable roofs,
Sit with their wives by fires, eat whole-
 some food,
And wear warm clothes, and even beasts
 have stalls,
I, 'tween the spring and downfall of the
 light,
Bow down one thousand and two hun-
 dred times,
To Christ, the Virgin Mother, and the
 Saints ;
Or in the night, after a little sleep,
I wake : the chill stars sparkle ; I am wet
With drenching dews, or stiff with crack-
 ling frost.
I wear an undress'd goatskin on my back ;
A grazing iron collar grinds my neck ;
And in my weak, lean arms I lift the
 cross,
And strive and wrestle with thee till I
 die :
O mercy, mercy ! wash away my sin.
 O Lord, thou knowest what a man I
 am ;
A sinful man, conceived and born in sin :
'T is their own doing ; this is none of
 mine ;
Lay it not to me. Am I to blame for
 this,
That here come those that worship me ?
 Ha ! ha !
They think that I am somewhat. What
 am I ?
The silly people take me for a saint,
And bring me offerings of fruit and
 flowers :
And I, in truth (thou wilt bear witness
 here)
Have all in all endured as much, and
 more

Than many just and holy men, whose names
Are register'd and calendar'd for saints.
Good people, you do ill to kneel to me.
What is it I can have done to merit this?
I am a sinner viler than you all.
It may be I have wrought some miracles,
And cured some halt and maim'd; but what of that?
It may be, no one, even among the saints,
May match his pains with mine; but what of that?
Yet do not rise; for you may look on me,
And in your looking you may kneel to God.
Speak! is there any of you halt or maim'd?
I think you know I have some power with Heaven
From my long penance: let him speak his wish.
  Yes, I can heal him. Power goes forth from me.
They say that they are heal'd. Ah, hark! they shout
"St. Simeon Stylites." Why, if so,
God reaps a harvest in me. O my soul,
God reaps a harvest in thee. If this be,
Can I work miracles and not be saved?
This is not told of any. They were saints.
It cannot be but that I shall be saved;
Yea, crown'd a saint. They shout, "Behold a saint!"
And lower voices saint me from above.
Courage, St. Simeon! This dull chrysalis
Cracks into shining wings, and hope ere death
Spreads more and more and more, that God hath now
Sponged and made blank of crimeful record all
My mortal archives.
          O my sons, my sons,
I, Simeon of the pillar, by surname
Stylites, among men; I, Simeon,
The watcher on the column till the end;
I, Simeon, whose brain the sunshine bakes;
I, whose bald brows in silent hours become
Unnaturally hoar with rime, do now
From my high nest of penance here proclaim
That Pontius and Iscariot by my side
Show'd like fair seraphs. On the coals I lay,
A vessel full of sin: all hell beneath
Made me boil over. Devils pluck'd my sleeve;
Abaddon and Asmodeus caught at me.
I smote them with the cross; they swarm'd again.
In bed like monstrous apes they crush'd my chest:
They flapp'd my light out as I read: I saw
Their faces grow between me and my book;
With colt-like whinny and with hoggish whine
They burst my prayer. Yet this way was left,
And by this way I 'scaped them. Mortify
Your flesh, like me, with scourges and with thorns;
Smite, shrink not, spare not. If it may be, fast
Whole Lents, and pray. I hardly, with slow steps,
With slow, faint steps, and much exceeding pain,
Have scrambled past those pits of fire, that still
Sing in mine ears. But yield not me the praise:
God only thro' his bounty hath thought fit,
Among the powers and princes of this world,
To make me an example to mankind,
Which few can reach to. Yet I do not say
But that a time may come — yea, even now,
Now, now, his footsteps smite the threshold stairs
Of life — I say, that time is at the doors
When you may worship me without reproach;
For I will leave my relics in your land,
And you may carve a shrine about my dust,
And burn a fragrant lamp before my bones,
When I am gather'd to the glorious saints.
  While I spake then, a sting of shrewdest pain
Ran shrivelling thro' me, and a cloudlike change,
In passing, with a grosser film made thick
These heavy, horny eyes. The end! the end!
Surely the end! What's here? a shape, a shade,
A flash of light. Is that the angel there
That holds a crown? Come, blessed brother, come.

I know thy glittering face. I waited long;
  My brows are ready. What! deny it now?
Nay, draw, draw, draw nigh. So I clutch
    it. Christ!
'T is gone : 't is here again ; the crown !
    the crown !
So now 't is fitted on and grows to me,
  And from it melt the dews of Paradise,
Sweet ! sweet ! spikenard, and balm, and
    frankincense.
Ah ! let me not be fool'd, sweet saints : I trust
That I am whole, and clean, and meet
    for Heaven.
  Speak, if there be a priest, a man of God,
Among you there, and let him presently
Approach, and lean a ladder on the shaft,
And climbing up into my airy home,
Deliver me the blessed sacrament ;
For by the warning of the Holy Ghost,
I prophesy that I shall die to-night,
A quarter before twelve.
                But thou, O Lord,
Aid all this foolish people ; let them take
Example, pattern : lead them to thy light.

THE TALKING OAK.

ONCE more the gate behind me falls ;
  Once more before my face
I see the moulder'd Abbey-walls,
  That stand within the chace.

Beyond the lodge the city lies,
  Beneath its drift of smoke ;
And ah ! with what delighted eyes
  I turn to yonder oak.

For when my passion first began,
  Ere that, which in me burn'd,
The love, that makes me thrice a man,
  Could hope itself return'd ;

To yonder oak within the field
  I spoke without restraint,
And with a larger faith appeal'd
  Than Papist unto Saint.

For oft I talk'd with him apart,
  And told him of my choice,
Until he plagiarized a heart,
  And answer'd with a voice.

Tho' what he whisper'd, under Heaven
  None else could understand ;

I found him garrulously given,
  A babbler in the land.

But since I heard him make reply
  Is many a weary hour ;
'T were well to question him, and try
  If yet he keeps the power.

Hail, hidden to the knees in fern,
  Broad Oak of Sumner-chace,
Whose topmost branches can discern
  The roofs of Sumner-place !

Say thou, whereon I carved her name,
  If ever maid or spouse,
As fair as my Olivia, came
  To rest beneath thy boughs. —

"O Walter, I have shelter'd here
  Whatever maiden grace
The good old Summers, year by year,
  Made ripe in Sumner-chace :

"Old Summers, when the monk was fat,
  And, issuing shorn and sleek,
Would twist his girdle tight, and pat
  The girls upon the cheek,

"Ere yet, in scorn of Peter's-pence,
  And number'd bead, and shrift,
Bluff Harry broke into the spence,
  And turn'd the cowls adrift :

"And I have seen some score of those
  Fresh faces, that would thrive
When his man-minded offset rose
  To chase the deer at five ;

"And all that from the town would stroll,
  Till that wild wind made work
In which the gloomy brewer's soul
  Went by me, like a stork :

"The slight she-slips of loyal blood,
  And others, passing praise,
Strait-laced, but all-too-full in bud
  For puritanic stays :

"And I have shadow'd many a group
  Of beauties, that were born
In teacup-times of hood and hoop,
  Or while the patch was worn ;

"And, leg and arm with love-knots gay,
  About me leap'd and laugh'd
The modest Cupid of the day,
  And shrill'd his tinsel shaft.

"I swear (and else may insects prick
 Each leaf into a gall)
This girl, for whom your heart is sick,
 Is three times worth them all;

"For those and theirs, by Nature's law,
 Have faded long ago;
But in these latter springs I saw
 Your own Olivia blow,

"From when she gamboll'd on the greens,
 A baby-germ, to when
The maiden blossoms of her teens
 Could number five from ten.

"I swear, by leaf, and wind, and rain,
 (And hear me with thine ears,)
That, tho' I circle in the grain
 Five hundred rings of years —

"Yet, since I first could cast a shade,
 Did never creature pass
So slightly, musically made,
 So light upon the grass:

"For as to fairies, that will flit
 To make the greensward fresh,
I hold them exquisitely knit,
 But far too spare of flesh."

O, hide thy knotted knees in fern,
 And overlook the chace;
And from thy topmost branch discern
 The roofs of Sumner-place.

But thou, whereon I carved her name,
 That oft hast heard my vows,
Declare when last Olivia came
 To sport beneath thy boughs.

"O yesterday, you know, the fair
 Was holden at the town;
Her father left his good arm-chair,
 And rode his hunter down.

"And with him Albert came on his.
 I look'd at him with joy:
As cowslip unto oxlip is,
 So seems she to the boy.

"An hour had past — and, sitting straight
 Within the low-wheel'd chaise,
Her mother trundled to the gate
 Behind the dappled grays.

"But, as for her, she stay'd at home
 And on the roof she went,
And down the way you used to come,
 She look'd with discontent.

"She left the novel half-uncut
 Upon the rosewood shelf;
She left the new piano shut:
 She could not please herself.

"Then ran she, gamesome as the colt,
 And livelier than a lark
She sent her voice thro' all the holt
 Before her, and the park.

"A light wind chased her on the wing,
 And in the chase grew wild,
As close as might be would he cling
 About the darling child:

"But light as any wind that blows
 So fleetly did she stir,
The flower, she touch'd on, dipt and rose,
 And turn'd to look at her.

"And here she came, and round me play'd,
 And sang to me the whole
Of those three stanzas that you made
 About my 'giant bole';

"And in a fit of frolic mirth
 She strove to span my waist:
Alas, I was so broad of girth,
 I could not be embraced.

"I wish'd myself the fair young beech
 That here beside me stands,
That round me, clasping each in each,
 She might have lock'd her hands.

"Yet seem'd the pressure thrice as sweet
 As woodbine's fragile hold,
Or when I feel about my feet
 The berried briony fold."

O muffle round thy knees with fern,
 And shadow Sumner-chace!
Long may thy topmost branch discern
 The roofs of Sumner-place!

But tell me, did she read the name
 I carved with many vows
When last with throbbing heart I came
 To rest beneath thy boughs?

"O yes, she wander'd round and round
 These knotted knees of mine,
And found, and kiss'd the name she found,
 And sweetly murmur'd thine.

THE TALKING OAK.

"A teardrop trembled from its source,
  And down my surface crept.
My sense of touch is something coarse,
  But I believe she wept.

"Then flush'd her cheek with rosy light,
  She glanced across the plain;
But not a creature was in sight:
  She kiss'd me once again.

"Her kisses were so close and kind,
  That, trust me on my word,
Hard wood I am, and wrinkled rind,
  But yet my sap was stirr'd:

"And even into my inmost ring
  A pleasure I discern'd,
Like those blind motions of the Spring,
  That show the year is turn'd.

"Thrice-happy he that may caress
  The ringlet's waving balm —
The cushions of whose touch may press
  The maiden's tender palm.

"I, rooted here among the groves,
  But languidly adjust
My vapid vegetable loves
  With anthers and with dust:

"For ah! my friend, the days were brief
  Whereof the poets talk,
When that, which breathes within the leaf,
  Could slip its bark and walk.

"But could I, as in times foregone,
  From spray, and branch, and stem,
Have suck'd and gather'd into one
  The life that spreads in them,

"She glanced across the plain;
But not a creature was in sight:
She kiss'd me once again."

"She had not found me so remiss;
　But lightly issuing thro',
I would have paid her kiss for kiss,
　With usury thereto."

O flourish high, with leafy towers,
　And overlook the lea,
Pursue thy loves among the bowers,
　But leave thou mine to me.

O flourish, hidden deep in fern,
　Old oak, I love thee well;
A thousand thanks for what I learn
　And what remains to tell.

" 'T is little more: the day was warm;
　At last, tired out with play,
She sank her head upon her arm
　And at my feet she lay.

" Her eyelids dropp'd their silken eaves.
　I breathed upon her eyes
Thro' all the summer of my leaves
　A welcome mix'd with sighs.

" I took the swarming sound of life —
　The music from the town —
The murmurs of the drum and fife
　And lull'd them in my own.

" Sometimes I let a sunbeam slip,
　To light her shaded eye;
A second flutter'd round her lip
　Like a golden butterfly;

" A third would glimmer on her neck
　To make the necklace shine;
Another slid, a sunny fleck,
　From head to ankle fine.

" Then close and dark my arms I spread,
　And shadow'd all her rest —
Dropt dews upon her golden head,
　An acorn in her breast.

" But in a pet she started up,
　And pluck'd it out, and drew
My little oakling from the cup,
　And flung him in the dew.

" And yet it was a graceful gift —
　I felt a pang within
As when I see the woodman lift
　His axe to slay my kin.

" I shook him down because he was
　The finest on the tree.
He lies beside thee on the grass.
　O kiss him once for me.

" O kiss him twice and thrice for me,
　That have no lips to kiss,
For never yet was oak on lea
　Shall grow so fair as this."

Step deeper yet in herb and fern,
　Look further thro' the chace,
Spread upward till thy boughs discern
　The front of Sumner-place.

This fruit of thine by Love is blest,
　That but a moment lay
Where fairer fruit of Love may rest
　Some happy future day.

I kiss it twice, I kiss it thrice,
　The warmth it thence shall win
To riper life may magnetize
　The baby-oak within.

But thou, while kingdoms overset,
　Or lapse from hand to hand,
Thy leaf shall never fail, nor yet
　Thine acorn in the land.

May never saw dismember thee,
　Nor wielded axe disjoint,
That art the fairest-spoken tree
　From here to Lizard-point.

O rock upon thy towery top
　All throats that gurgle sweet!
All starry culmination drop
　Balm-dews to bathe thy feet!

All grass of silky feather grow —
　And while he sinks or swells
The full south-breeze around thee blow
　The sound of minster bells.

The fat earth feed thy branchy root,
　That under deeply strikes!
The northern morning o'er thee shoot,
　High up, in silver spikes!

Nor ever lightning char thy grain,
　But, rolling as in sleep,
Low thunders bring the mellow rain,
　That makes thee broad and deep!

And hear me swear a solemn oath,
　That only by thy side
Will I to Olive plight my troth,
　And gain her for my bride.

And when my marriage morn may fall,
  She, Dryad-like, shall wear
Alternate leaf and acorn-ball
  In wreath about her hair.

And I will work in prose and rhyme,
  And praise thee more in both
Than bard has honor'd beech or lime,
  Or that Thessalian growth,

In which the swarthy ringdove sat,
  And mystic sentence spoke;
And more than England honors that,
  Thy famous brother-oak,

Wherein the younger Charles abode
  Till all the paths were dim,
And far below the Roundhead rode,
  And humm'd a surly hymn.

LOVE AND DUTY.

Of love that never found his earthly close,
What sequel? Streaming eyes and break-
    ing hearts?
Or all the same as if he had not been?
  Not so. Shall Error in the round of
    time
Still father Truth? O shall the braggart
    shout
For some blind glimpse of freedom work
    itself
Thro' madness, hated by the wise, to law
System and empire? Sin itself be found
The cloudy porch oft opening on the Sun?
And only he, this wonder, dead, become
Mere highway dust? or year by year alone
Sit brooding in the ruins of a life,
Nightmare of youth, the spectre of him-
    self?
  If this were thus, if this, indeed, were
    all,
Better the narrow brain, the stony heart,
The staring eye glazed o'er with sapless
    days,
The long mechanic pacings to and fro,
The set gray life, and apathetic end.
But am I not the nobler thro' thy love?
O three times less unworthy! likewise thou
Art more thro' Love, and greater than thy
    years.
The Sun will run his orbit, and the Moon
Her circle. Wait, and Love himself will
    bring
The drooping flower of knowledge changed
    to fruit

Of wisdom. Wait: my faith is large in
    Time,
And that which shapes it to some perfect
    end.
  Will some one say, Then why not ill for
    good?
Why took ye not your pastime? To that
    man
My work shall answer, since I knew the
    right
And did it; for a man is not as God,
But then most Godlike being most a man.
  — So let me think 't is well for thee and
    me —
Ill-fated that I am, what lot is mine
Whose foresight preaches peace, my heart
    so slow
To feel it! For how hard it seem'd to me,
When eyes, love-languid thro' half-tears,
    would dwell
One earnest, earnest moment upon mine,
Then not to dare to see! when thy low
    voice,
Faltering, would break its syllables, to
    keep
My own full-tuned, — hold passion in a
    leash,
And not leap forth and fall about thy neck,
And on thy bosom, (deep-desired relief!)
Rain out the heavy mist of tears, that
    weigh'd
Upon my brain, my senses and my soul!
  For Love himself took part against
    himself
To warn us off, and Duty loved of Love —
O this world's curse, — beloved but hated
    — came
Like Death betwixt thy dear embrace and
    mine,
And crying, "Who is this? behold thy
    bride,"
She push'd me from thee.
                If the sense is hard
To alien ears, I did not speak to these —
No, not to thee, but to thyself in me:
Hard is my doom and thine: thou know-
    est it all.
  Could Love part thus? was it not well
    to speak,
To have spoken once? It could not but
    be well.
The slow sweet hours that bring us all
    things good,
The slow sad hours that bring us all
    things ill,
And all good things from evil, brought
    the night

In which we sat together and alone,
And to the want, that hollow'd all the
 heart,
Gave utterance by the yearning of an eye,
That burn'd upon its object thro' such
 tears
As flow but once a life.
                The trance gave way
To those caresses, when a hundred times
In that last kiss, which never was the last,
Farewell, like endless welcome, lived and
 died.
Then follow'd counsel, comfort, and the
 words
That make a man feel strong in speaking
 truth ;
Till now the dark was worn, and overhead
The lights of sunset and of sunrise mix'd
In that brief night ; the summer night,
 that paused
Among her stars to hear us ; stars that
 hung
Love-charm'd to listen : all the wheels
 of Time
Spun round in station, but the end had
 come.
    O then like those, who clench their
 nerves to rush
Upon their dissolution, we two rose,
There — closing like an individual life —
In one blind cry of passion and of pain,
Like bitter accusation ev'n to death,
Caught up the whole of love and utter'd it,
And bade adieu for ever.
                      Live — yet live —
Shall sharpest pathos blight us, knowing
 all
Life needs for life is possible to will —
Live happy ; tend thy flowers ; be tended
 by
My blessing ! Should my Shadow cross
 thy thoughts
Too sadly for their peace, remand it thou
For calmer hours to Memory's darkest
 hold,
If not to be forgotten — not at once —
Not all forgotten. Should it cross thy
 dreams,
O might it come like one that looks content,
With quiet eyes unfaithful to the truth,
And point thee forward to a distant light,
Or seem to lift a burden from thy heart
And leave thee freër, till thou wake refresh'd,
Then when the first low matin-chirp hath
 grown

Full quire, and morning driv'n her plough
 of pearl
Far furrowing into light the mounded
 rack,
Beyond the fair green field and eastern sea.

THE GOLDEN YEAR.

WELL, you shall have that song which
 Leonard wrote :
It was last summer on a tour in Wales :
Old James was with me : we that day
 had been
Up Snowdon ; and I wish'd for Leonard
 there,
And found him in Llanberis : then we
 crost
Between the lakes, and clamber'd half
 way up
The counter side ; and that same song of
 his
He told me ; for I banter'd him, and swore
They said he lived shut up within himself,
A tongue-tied Poet in the feverous days,
That, setting the *how much* before the *how*,
Cry, like the daughters of the horseleech,
 "Give,
Cram us with all," but count not me the
 herd !
    To which "They call me what they
 will," he said :
"But I was born too late : the fair new
 forms,
That float about the threshold of an age,
Like truths of Science waiting to be
 caught —
Catch me who can, and make the catcher
 crown'd —
Are taken by the forelock. Let it be.
But if you care indeed to listen, hear
These measured words, my work of yestermorn.
    "We sleep and wake and sleep, but all
 things move ;
The Sun flies forward to his brother Sun ;
The dark Earth follows wheel'd in her
 ellipse ;
And human things returning on themselves
Move onward, leading up the golden year.
    "Ah, tho' the times, when some new
 thought can bud,
Are but as poets' seasons when they flower,
Yet seas, that daily gain upon the shore,
Have ebb and flow conditioning their
 march,

And slow and sure comes up the golden
  year.
"When wealth no more shall rest in
  mounded heaps,
But smit with freër light shall slowly melt
In many streams to fatten lower lands,
And light shall spread, and man be liker
  man
Thro' all the season of the golden year.
"Shall eagles not be eagles? wrens be
  wrens?
If all the world were falcons, what of that?
The wonder of the eagle were the less,
But he not less the eagle. Happy days
Roll onward, leading up the golden year.
"Fly, happy happy sails and bear the
  Press;
Fly happy with the mission of the Cross;
Knit land to land, and blowing havenward
With silks, and fruits, and spices, clear
  of toll,
Enrich the markets of the golden year.
"But we grow old. Ah! when shall
  all men's good
Be each man's rule, and universal Peace
Lie like a shaft of light across the land,
And like a lane of beams athwart the sea,
Thro' all the circle of the golden year?"
Thus far he flow'd, and ended; where-
  upon
"Ah, folly!" in mimic cadence an-
  swer'd James —
"Ah, folly! for it lies so far away,
Not in our time, nor in our children's time,
'T is like the second world to us that live;
'T were all as one to fix our hopes on
  Heaven
As on this vision of the golden year."
  With that he struck his staff against
  the rocks
And broke it, — James, — you know him,
  — old, but full
Of force and choler, and firm upon his feet,
And like an oaken stock in winter woods,
O'erflourish'd with the hoary clematis:
Then added, all in heat:
        "What stuff is this!
Old writers push'd the happy season
  back, —
The more fools they, — we forward:
  dreamers both:
You most, that in an age, when every hour
Must sweat her sixty minutes to the death,
Live on, God love us, as if the seedsman,
  rapt
Upon the teeming harvest, should not
  plunge

His hand into the bag: but well I know
That unto him who works, and feels he
  works,
This same grand year is ever at the doors."
  He spoke; and, high above, I heard
  them blast
The steep slate-quarry, and the great
  echo flap
And buffet round the hills from bluff to
  bluff.

ULYSSES.

It little profits that an idle king,
By this still hearth, among these barren
  crags,
Match'd with an aged wife, I mete and
  dole
Unequal laws unto a savage race,
That hoard, and sleep, and feed, and
  know not me.
I cannot rest from travel: I will drink
Life to the lees: all times I have enjoy'd
Greatly, have suffer'd greatly, both with
  those
That loved me, and alone; on shore, and
  when
Thro' scudding drifts the rainy Hyades
Vext the dim sea: I am become a name;
For always roaming with a hungry heart
Much have I seen and known; cities of men
And manners, climates, councils, govern-
  ments,
Myself not least, but honor'd of them all;
And drunk delight of battle with my peers,
Far on the ringing plains of windy Troy.
I am a part of all that I have met;
Yet all experience is an arch wherethro'
Gleams that untravell'd world, whose
  margin fades
For ever and for ever when I move.
How dull it is to pause, to make an end,
To rust unburnish'd, not to shine in use!
As tho' to breathe were life. Life piled
  on life
Were all too little, and of one to me
Little remains: but every hour is saved
From that eternal silence, something
  more,
A bringer of new things; and vile it were
For some three suns to store and hoard
  myself,
And this gray spirit yearning in desire
To follow knowledge like a sinking star,
Beyond the utmost bound of human
  thought.

This is my son, mine own Telemachus,
To whom I leave the sceptre and the isle —
Well-loved of me, discerning to fulfil
This labor, by slow prudence to make mild
A rugged people, and thro' soft degrees
Subdue them to the useful and the good.
Most blameless is he, centred in the sphere
Of common duties, decent not to fail
In offices of tenderness, and pay
Meet adoration to my household gods,
When I am gone. He works his work,
 I mine.
  There lies the port: the vessel puffs
 her sail :
There gloom the dark broad seas. My
 mariners,
Souls that have toil'd, and wrought, and
 thought with me —
That ever with a frolic welcome took
The thunder and the sunshine, and op-
 posed
Free hearts, free foreheads — you and I
 are old ;
Old age hath yet his honor and his toil ;
Death closes all : but something ere the
 end,
Some work of noble note, may yet be done,
Not unbecoming men that strove with
 Gods.
The lights begin to twinkle from the rocks :
The long day wanes : the slow moon
 climbs : the deep
Moans round with many voices. Come,
 my friends,
'T is not too late to seek a newer world.
Push off, and sitting well in order smite
The sounding furrows ; for my purpose
 holds

"There lies the port : the vessel puffs her sail :
There gloom the dark broad seas."

To sail beyond the sunset, and the baths
 Of all the western stars, until I die.
It may be that the gulfs will wash us
 down:
It may be we shall touch the Happy Isles,
And see the great Achilles, whom we
 knew.
Tho' much is taken, much abides: and
 tho'
We are not now that strength which in
 old days
Moved earth and heaven; that which we
 are, we are;
One equal temper of heroic hearts,
Made weak by time and fate, but strong
 in will
To strive, to seek, to find, and not to yield.

LOCKSLEY HALL.

COMRADES, leave me here a little, while
 as yet 't is early morn:
Leave me here, and when you want me,
 sound upon the bugle horn.

'T is the place, and all around it, as of old,
 the curlews call,
Dreary gleams about the moorland flying
 over Locksley Hall;

Locksley Hall, that in the distance over-
 looks the sandy tracts,
And the hollow ocean-ridges roaring into
 cataracts.

" 'T is the place, and all around it, as of old, the curlews call,
Dreary gleams about the moorland flying over Locksley Hall."

Many a night from yonder ivied casement,
   ere I went to rest,
Did I look on great Orion sloping slowly
   to the West.

Many a night I saw the Pleiads, rising
   thro' the mellow shade,
Glitter like a swarm of fire-flies tangled in
   a silver braid.

Here about the beach I wander'd, nour-
   ishing a youth sublime
With the fairy tales of science, and the
   long result of Time;

When the centuries behind me like a
   fruitful land reposed;
When I clung to all the present for the
   promise that it closed:

When I dipt into the future far as human
   eye could see;
Saw the Vision of the world, and all the
   wonder that would be. ——

In the Spring a fuller crimson comes upon
   the robin's breast;
In the Spring the wanton lapwing gets
   himself another crest;

In the Spring a livelier iris changes on
   the burnish'd dove;
In the Spring a young man's fancy lightly
   turns to thoughts of love.

Then her cheek was pale and thinner than
   should be for one so young,
And her eyes on all my motions with a
   mute observance hung.

And I said, "My cousin Amy, speak, and
   speak the truth to me,
Trust me, cousin, all the current of my
   being sets to thee."

On her pallid cheek and forehead came a
   color and a light,
As I have seen the rosy red flushing in the
   northern night.

And she turn'd — her bosom shaken with
   a sudden storm of sighs —
All the spirit deeply dawning in the dark
   of hazel eyes —

Saying, "I have hid my feelings, fearing
   they should do me wrong";
Saying, "Dost thou love me, cousin?"
   weeping, "I have loved thee long."

Love took up the glass of Time, and turn'd
   it in his glowing hands;
Every moment, lightly shaken, ran itself
   in golden sands.

Love took up the harp of Life, and smote
   on all the chords with might;
Smote the chord of Self, that, trembling,
   pass'd in music out of sight.

Many a morning on the moorland did we
   hear the copses ring,
And her whisper throng'd my pulses with
   the fulness of the Spring.

Many an evening by the waters did we
   watch the stately ships,
And our spirits rush'd together at the
   touching of the lips.

O my cousin, shallow-hearted! O my
   Amy, mine no more!
O the dreary, dreary moorland! O the
   barren, barren shore!

Falser than all fancy fathoms, falser than
   all songs have sung,
Puppet to a father's threat, and servile to
   a shrewish tongue!

Is it well to wish thee happy? — having
   known me — to decline
On a range of lower feelings and a nar-
   rower heart than mine!

Yet it shall be: thou shalt lower to his
   level day by day,
What is fine within thee growing coarse
   to sympathize with clay.

As the husband is, the wife is: thou art
   mated with a clown,
And the grossness of his nature will have
   weight to drag thee down.

He will hold thee, when his passion shall
   have spent its novel force,
Something better than his dog, a little
   dearer than his horse.

What is this? his eyes are heavy: think
   not they are glazed with wine.
Go to him: it is thy duty: kiss him:
   take his hand in thine.

It may be my lord is weary, that his brain
   is overwrought:
Soothe him with thy finer fancies, touch
   him with thy lighter thought.

"Many an evening by the waters did we watch the stately ships,
And our spirits rush'd together at the touching of the lips."

He will answer to the purpose, easy things
to understand —
Better thou wert dead before me, tho' I
slew thee with my hand!

Better thou and I were lying, hidden from
the heart's disgrace,
Roll'd in one another's arms, and silent
in a last embrace.

Cursed be the social wants that sin against
the strength of youth!
Cursed be the social lies that warp us from
the living truth!

Cursed be the sickly forms that err from
honest Nature's rule!
Cursed be the gold that gilds the straiten'd
forehead of the fool!

Well — 't is well that I should bluster! —
Hadst thou less unworthy proved —
Would to God — for I had loved thee
more than ever wife was loved.

Am I mad, that I should cherish that
which bears but bitter fruit?
I will pluck it from my bosom, tho' my
heart be at the root.

Never, tho' my mortal summers to such
length of years should come
As the many-winter'd crow that leads the
clanging rookery home.

Where is comfort? in division of the
records of the mind?
Can I part her from herself, and love her,
as I knew her, kind?

I remember one that perish'd : sweetly
did she speak and move :
Such a one do I remember, whom to look
at was to love.

Can I think of her as dead, and love her
for the love she bore ?
No — she never loved me truly : love is
love for evermore.

Comfort ? comfort scorn'd of devils ! this
is truth the poet sings,
That a sorrow's crown of sorrow is re-
membering happier things.

Drug thy memories, lest thou learn it,
lest thy heart be put to proof,
In the dead unhappy night, and when
the rain is on the roof.

Like a dog, he hunts in dreams, and thou
art staring at the wall,
Where the dying night-lamp flickers, and
the shadows rise and fall.

Then a hand shall pass before thee, point-
ing to his drunken sleep,
To thy widow'd marriage-pillows, to the
tears that thou wilt weep.

Thou shalt hear the "Never, never,"
whisper'd by the phantom years,
And a song from out the distance in the
ringing of thine ears ;

And an eye shall vex thee, looking an-
cient kindness on thy pain.
Turn thee, turn thee on thy pillow : get
thee to thy rest again.

Nay, but Nature brings thee solace ; for
a tender voice will cry.
'T is a purer life than thine ; a lip to
drain thy trouble dry.

Baby lips will laugh me down : my latest
rival brings thee rest.
Baby fingers, waxen touches, press me
from the mother's breast.

O, the child too clothes the father with
a dearness not his due.
Half is thine and half is his : it will be
worthy of the two.

O, I see thee old and formal, fitted to thy
petty part,
With a little hoard of maxims preaching
down a daughter's heart.

"They were dangerous guides the feelings
— she herself was not exempt —
Truly, she herself had suffer'd " — Perish
in thy self-contempt !

Overlive it — lower yet — be happy !
wherefore should I care ?
I myself must mix with action, lest I
wither by despair.

What is that which I should turn to,
lighting upon days like these ?
Every door is barr'd with gold, and opens
but to golden keys.

Every gate is throng'd with suitors, all
the markets overflow.
I have but an angry fancy : what is that
which I should do ?

I had been content to perish, falling on
the foeman's ground,
When the ranks are roll'd in vapor, and
the winds are laid with sound.

But the jingling of the guinea helps the
hurt that Honor feels,
And the nations do but murmur, snarl-
ing at each other's heels.

Can I but relive in sadness ? I will turn
that earlier page.
Hide me from my deep emotion, O thou
wondrous Mother-Age !

Make me feel the wild pulsation that I
felt before the strife,
When I heard my days before me, and
the tumult of my life ;

Yearning for the large excitement that
the coming years would yield,
Eager-hearted as a boy when first he leaves
his father's field,

And at night along the dusky highway
near and nearer drawn,
Sees in heaven the light of London flar-
ing like a dreary dawn ;

And his spirit leaps within him to be
gone before him then,
Underneath the light he looks at, in
among the throngs of men ;

Men, my brothers, men the workers, ever
reaping something new :
That which they have done but earnest
of the things that they shall do :

*"Baby lips will laugh me down: my latest rival brings thee rest.
Baby fingers, waxen touches, press me from the mother's breast."*

For I dipt into the future, far as human eye could see,
Saw the Vision of the world, and all the wonder that would be;

Saw the heavens fill with commerce, argosies of magic sails,
Pilots of the purple twilight, dropping down with costly bales;

Heard the heavens fill with shouting, and there rain'd a ghastly dew
From the nations' airy navies grappling in the central blue;

Far along the world-wide whisper of the south-wind rushing warm,
With the standards of the peoples plunging thro' the thunder-storm;

Till the war-drum throbb'd no longer, and the battle-flags were furl'd
In the Parliament of man, the Federation of the world.

There the common sense of most shall hold a fretful realm in awe,
And the kindly earth shall slumber, lapt in universal law.

So I triumph'd ere my passion sweeping thro' me left me dry,
Left me with the palsied heart, and left me with the jaundiced eye;

Eye, to which all order festers, all things here are out of joint:
Science moves, but slowly slowly, creeping on from point to point:

Slowly comes a hungry people, as a lion,
    creeping nigher,
Glares at one that nods and winks behind
    a slowly-dying fire.

Yet I doubt not thro' the ages one in-
    creasing purpose runs,
And the thoughts of men are widen'd
    with the process of the suns.

What is that to him that reaps not
    harvest of his youthful joys,
Tho' the deep heart of existence beat for
    ever like a boy's?

Knowledge comes, but wisdom lingers,
    and I linger on the shore,
And the individual withers, and the
    world is more and more.

Knowledge comes, but wisdom lingers,
    and he bears a laden breast,
Full of sad experience, moving toward
    the stillness of his rest.

Hark, my merry comrades call me, sound-
    ing on the bugle-horn,
They to whom my foolish passion were a
    target for their scorn:

Shall it not be scorn to me to harp on
    such a moulder'd string?
I am shamed thro' all my nature to have
    loved so slight a thing.

Weakness to be wroth with weakness! wo-
    man's pleasure, woman's pain —
Nature made them blinder motions
    bounded in a shallower brain:

Woman is the lesser man, and all thy
    passions, match'd with mine,
Are as moonlight unto sunlight, and as
    water unto wine —

Here at least, where nature sickens, noth-
    ing. Ah, for some retreat
Deep in yonder shining Orient, where my
    life began to beat;

Where in wild Mahratta-battle fell my
    father evil-starr'd; —
I was left a trampled orphan, and a self-
    ish uncle's ward.

Or to burst all links of habit — there to
    wander far away,
On from island unto island at the gate-
    ways of the day.

Larger constellations burning, mellow
    moons and happy skies,
Breadths of tropic shade and palms in
    cluster, knots of Paradise.

Never comes the trader, never floats an
    European flag,
Slides the bird o'er lustrous woodland,
    swings the trailer from the crag;

Droops the heavy-blossom'd bower,
    hangs the heavy-fruited tree —
Summer isles of Eden lying in dark-pur-
    ple spheres of sea.

There methinks would be enjoyment
    more than in this march of mind,
In the steamship, in the railway, in the
    thoughts that shake mankind.

There the passions cramp'd no longer shall
    have scope and breathing-space;
I will take some savage woman, she shall
    rear my dusky race.

Iron-jointed, supple-sinew'd, they shall
    dive, and they shall run,
Catch the wild goat by the hair, and
    hurl their lances in the sun;

Whistle back the parrot's call, and leap
    the rainbows of the brooks,
Not with blinded eyesight poring over
    miserable books —

Fool, again the dream, the fancy! but I
    know my words are wild,
But I count the gray barbarian lower than
    the Christian child.

I, to herd with narrow foreheads, vacant
    of our glorious gains,
Like a beast with lower pleasures, like a
    beast with lower pains!

Mated with a squalid savage — what to
    me were sun or clime?
I the heir of all the ages, in the foremost
    files of time —

I that rather held it better men should
    perish one by one,
Than that earth should stand at gaze
    like Joshua's moon in Ajalon!

Not in vain the distance beacons. For-
    ward, forward let us range.
Let the great world spin for ever down
    the ringing grooves of change.

Thro' the shadow of the globe we sweep
 into the younger day:
Better fifty years of Europe than a cycle
 of Cathay.

Mother-Age (for mine I knew not) help
 me as when life begun:
Rift the hills, and roll the waters, flash
 the lightnings, weigh the Sun—

O, I see the crescent promise of my spirit
 hath not set.
Ancient founts of inspiration well thro'
 all my fancy yet.

Howsoever these things be, a long fare-
 well to Locksley Hall!
Now for me the woods may wither, now
 for me the roof-tree fall.

Comes a vapor from the margin, black-
 ening over heath and holt,
Cramming all the blast before it, in its
 breast a thunderbolt.

Let it fall on Locksley Hall, with rain
 or hail, or fire or snow;
For the mighty wind arises, roaring sea-
 ward, and I go.

"Comes a vapor from the margin, blackening over heath and holt,
Cramming all the blast before it in its breast a thunderbolt."

GODIVA.

I waited for the train at Coventry;
I hung with grooms and porters on the
 bridge,
To watch the three tall spires; and there
 I shaped
The city's ancient legend into this:—
 Not only we, the latest seed of Time,
New men, that in the flying of a wheel
Cry down the past, not only we, that prate
Of rights and wrongs, have loved the
 people well,
And loathed to see them overtax'd; but
 she
Did more, and underwent, and overcame,
The woman of a thousand summers back,
Godiva, wife to that grim Earl, who ruled
In Coventry: for when he laid a tax

Upon his town, and all the mothers
 brought
Their children, clamoring, "If we pay,
 we starve!"
She sought her lord, and found him,
 where he strode
About the hall, among his dogs, alone,
His beard a foot before him, and his hair
A yard behind. She told him of their
 tears,
And pray'd him, "If they pay this tax,
 they starve."
Whereat he stared, replying, half-amazed,
"You would not let your little finger ache
For such as *these?*"—"But I would
 die," said she.
He laugh'd, and swore by Peter and by
 Paul:
Then fillip'd at the diamond in her ear;

"O ay, ay, ay, you talk!"—"Alas!"
  she said,
"But prove me what it is I would not do."
And from a heart as rough as Esau's hand,
He answer'd, "Ride you naked thro' the
  town,
And I repeal it"; and nodding, as in
  scorn,
He parted, with great strides among his
  dogs.
  So left alone, the passions of her mind,
As winds from all the compass shift and
  blow,
Made war upon each other for an hour,
Till pity won. She sent a herald forth,
And bade him cry, with sound of trum-
  pet, all
The hard condition; but that she would
  loose
The people: therefore, as they loved her
  well,
From then till noon no foot should pace
  the street,
No eye look down, she passing; but that
  all
Should keep within, door shut, and win-
  dow barr'd.
  Then fled she to her inmost bower,
  and there
Unclasp'd the wedded eagles of her belt,
The grim Earl's gift; but ever at a breath
She linger'd, looking like a summer moon
Half-dipt in cloud: anon she shook her
  head,
And shower'd the rippled ringlets to her
  knee;
Unclad herself in haste; adown the stair
Stole on; and, like a creeping sunbeam,
  slid
From pillar unto pillar, until she reach'd
The gateway; there she found her pal-
  frey trapt
In purple blazon'd with armorial gold.
  Then she rode forth, clothed on with
  chastity:
The deep air listen'd round her as she rode,
And all the low wind hardly breathed
  for fear.
The little wide-mouth'd heads upon the
  spout
Had cunning eyes to see: the barking cur
Made her cheek flame: her palfrey's
  footfall shot
Light horrors thro' her pulses: the blind
  walls
Were full of chinks and holes; and
  overhead

Fantastic gables, crowding, stared: but
  she
Not less thro' all bore up, till, last, she saw
The white-flower'd elder-thicket from the
  field
Gleam thro' the Gothic archways in the
  wall.
  Then she rode back, clothed on with
  chastity:
And one low churl, compact of thankless
  earth,
The fatal byword of all years to come,
Boring a little augur-hole in fear,
Peep'd—but his eyes, before they had
  their will,
Were shrivell'd into darkness in his head,
And dropt before him. So the Powers,
  who wait
On noble deeds, cancell'd a sense misused;
And she, that knew not, pass'd: and all
  at once,
With twelve great shocks of sound, the
  shameless noon
Was clash'd and hammer'd from a hun-
  dred towers,
One after one: but even then she gain'd
Her bower; whence reissuing, robed and
  crown'd,
To meet her lord, she took the tax away
And built herself an everlasting name.

THE TWO VOICES.

A STILL small voice spake unto me,
"Thou art so full of misery,
Were it not better not to be?"

Then to the still small voice I said;
"Let me not cast in endless shade
What is so wonderfully made."

To which the voice did urge reply;
"To-day I saw the dragon-fly
Come from the wells where he did lie.

"An inner impulse rent the veil
Of his old husk: from head to tail
Came out clear plates of sapphire mail.

"He dried his wings: like gauze they
  grew:
Thro' crofts and pastures wet with dew
A living flash of light he flew."

I said, "When first the world began,
Young Nature thro' five cycles ran,
And in the sixth she moulded man.

"Then fled she to her inmost bower, and there
Unclasp'd the wedded eagles of her belt."

"She gave him mind, the lordliest
Proportion, and, above the rest,
Dominion in the head and breast."

Thereto the silent voice replied ;
"Self-blinded are you by your pride :
Look up thro' night : the world is wide.

"This truth within thy mind rehearse,
That in a boundless universe
Is boundless better, boundless worse.

"Think you this mould of hopes and fears
Could find no statelier than his peers
In yonder hundred million spheres ?"

It spake, moreover, in my mind :
"Tho' thou wert scatter'd to the wind,
Yet is there plenty of the kind."

Then did my response clearer fall :
"No compound of this earthly ball
Is like another, all in all."

To which he answer'd scoffingly ;
"Good soul ! suppose I grant it thee,
Who'll weep for thy deficiency ?

"Or will one beam be less intense,
When thy peculiar difference
Is cancell'd in the world of sense ?"

I would have said, "Thou canst not know,"
But my full heart, that work'd below,
Rain'd thro' my sight its overflow.

Again the voice spake unto me :
"Thou art so steep'd in misery,
Surely 't were better not to be.

"Thine anguish will not let thee sleep,
Nor any train of reason keep:
Thou canst not think, but thou wilt
    weep."

I said, "The years with change advance:
If I make dark my countenance,
I shut my life from happier chance.

"Some turn this sickness yet might take,
Ev'n yet." But he: "What drug can
    make
A wither'd palsy cease to shake?"

I wept, "Tho' I should die, I know
That all about the thorn will blow
In tufts of rosy-tinted snow;

"And men, thro' novel spheres of thought
Still moving after truth long sought,
Will learn new things when I am not."

"Yet," said the secret voice, "some time,
Sooner or later, will gray prime
Make thy grass hoar with early rime.

"Not less swift souls that yearn for light,
Rapt after heaven's starry flight,
Would sweep the tracts of day and night.

"Not less the bee would range her cells,
The furzy prickle fire the dells,
The foxglove cluster dappled bells."

I said that "all the years invent;
Each month is various to present
The world with some development.

"Were this not well, to bide mine hour,
Tho' watching from a ruin'd tower
How grows the day of human power?"

"The highest-mounted mind," he said,
"Still sees the sacred morning spread
The silent summit overhead.

"Will thirty seasons render plain
Those lonely lights that still remain,
Just breaking over land and main?

"Or make that morn, from his cold crown
And crystal silence creeping down,
Flood with full daylight glebe and town?

"Forerun thy peers, thy time, and let
Thy feet, millenniums hence, be set
In midst of knowledge, dream'd not yet.

"Thou hast not gain'd a real height,
Nor art thou nearer to the light,
Because the scale is infinite.

"'T were better not to breathe or speak,
Than cry for strength, remaining weak,
And seem to find, but still to seek.

"Moreover, but to seem to find
Asks what thou lackest, thought resign'd,
A healthy frame, a quiet mind."

I said, "When I am gone away,
'He dared not tarry,' men will say,
Doing dishonor to my clay."

"This is more vile," he made reply,
"To breathe and loathe, to live and sigh,
Than once from dread of pain to die.

"Sick art thou — a divided will
Still heaping on the fear of ill
The fear of men, a coward still.

"Do men love thee? Art thou so bound
To men, that how thy name may sound
Will vex thee lying underground?

"The memory of the wither'd leaf
In endless time is scarce more brief
Than of the garner'd Autumn-sheaf.

"Go, vexed Spirit, sleep in trust;
The right ear, that is fill'd with dust,
Hears little of the false or just."

"Hard task, to pluck resolve," I cried,
"From emptiness and the waste wide
Of that abyss, or scornful pride!

"Nay — rather yet that I could raise
One hope that warm'd me in the days
While still I yearn'd for human praise.

"When, wide in soul and bold of tongue,
Among the tents I paused and sung,
The distant battle flash'd and rung.

"I sung the joyful Pæan clear,
And, sitting, burnish'd without fear
The brand, the buckler, and the spear —

"Waiting to strive a happy strife,
To war with falsehood to the knife,
And not to lose the good of life —

"Some hidden principle to move,
To put together, part and prove,
And mete the bounds of hate and love —

"As far as might be, to carve out
Free space for every human doubt,
That the whole mind might orb about —

"To search thro' all I felt or saw,
The springs of life, the depths of awe,
And reach the law within the law :

"At least, not rotting like a weed,
But, having sown some generous seed,
Fruitful of further thought and deed,

"To pass, when Life her light withdraws,
Not void of righteous self-applause,
Nor in a merely selfish cause —

"In some good cause, not in mine own,
To perish, wept for, honor'd, known,
And like a warrior overthrown ;

"Whose eyes are dim with glorious tears,
When, soil'd with noble dust, he hears
His country's war-song thrill his ears :

"Then dying of a mortal stroke,
What time the foeman's line is broke,
And all the war is roll'd in smoke."

"Yea !" said the voice, "thy dream was good,
While thou abodest in the bud.
It was the stirring of the blood.

"If Nature put not forth her power
About the opening of the flower,
Who is it that could live an hour ?

"Then comes the check, the change, the fall,
Pain rises up, old pleasures pall.
There is one remedy for all.

"Yet hadst thou, thro' enduring pain,
Link'd mouth to mouth with such a chain
Of knitted purport, all were vain.

"Thou hadst not between death and birth
Dissolved the riddle of the earth.
So were thy labor little-worth.

"That men with knowledge merely play'd,
I told thee — hardly nigher made,
Tho' scaling slow from grade to grade ;

"Much less this dreamer, deaf and blind,
Named man, may hope some truth to find,
That bears relation to the mind.

"For every worm beneath the moon
Draws different threads, and late and soon,
Spins, toiling out his own cocoon.

"Cry, faint not : either Truth is born
Beyond the polar gleam forlorn,
Or in the gateways of the morn.

"Cry, faint not, climb : the summits slope
Beyond the furthest flights of hope,
Wrapt in dense cloud from base to cope.

"Sometimes a little corner shines,
As over rainy mist inclines
A gleaming crag with belts of pines.

"I will go forward, sayest thou,
I shall not fail to find her now.
Look up, the fold is on her brow.

"If straight thy track, or oblique,
Thou know'st not. Shadows thou dost strike,
Embracing cloud, Ixion-like ;

"And owning but a little more
Than beasts, abidest lame and poor,
Calling thyself a little lower

"Than angels. Cease to wail and brawl !
Why inch by inch to darkness crawl ?
There is one remedy for all."

"O dull, one-sided voice," said I,
"Wilt thou make everything a lie,
To flatter me that I may die ?

"I know that age to age succeeds,
Blowing a noise of tongues and deeds,
A dust of systems and of creeds.

"I cannot hide that some have striven,
Achieving calm, to whom was given
The joy that mixes man with Heaven :

"Who, rowing hard against the stream,
Saw distant gates of Eden gleam,
And did not dream it was a dream ;

"But heard, by secret transport led,
Ev'n in the charnels of the dead,
The murmur of the fountain-head —

"Which did accomplish their desire,
Bore and forebore, and did not tire,
Like Stephen, an unquenched fire.

THE TWO VOICES.

"He heeded not reviling tones,
Nor sold his heart to idle moans,
Tho' cursed and scorn'd, and bruised with stones:

"But looking upward, full of grace,
He pray'd, and from a happy place
God's glory smote him on the face."

The sullen answer slid betwixt :—
"Not that the grounds of hope were fix'd,
The elements were kindlier mix'd."

I said, "I toil beneath the curse,
But, knowing not the universe,
I fear to slide from bad to worse.

"And that, in seeking to undo
One riddle, and to find the true,
I knit a hundred others new :

"Or that this anguish fleeting hence,
Unmanacled from bonds of sense,
Be fix'd and froz'n to permanence :

"For I go, weak from suffering here ;
Naked I go, and void of cheer :
What is it that I may not fear ?"

"Consider well," the voice replied,
"His face, that two hours since hath died ;
Wilt thou find passion, pain or pride ?

"Will he obey when one commands ?
Or answer should one press his hands ?
He answers not, nor understands.

"His palms are folded on his breast :
There is no other thing express'd
But long disquiet merged in rest.

"His lips are very mild and meek :
Tho' one should smite him on the cheek,
And on the mouth, he will not speak.

"His little daughter, whose sweet face
He kiss'd, taking his last embrace,
Becomes dishonor to her race —

"His sons grow up that bear his name,
Some grow to honor, some to shame, —
But he is chill to praise or blame.

"He will not hear the north-wind rave,
Nor, moaning, household shelter crave
From winter rains that beat his grave.

"High up the vapors fold and swim :
About him broods the twilight dim :
The place he knew forgetteth him."

"If all be dark, vague voice," I said,
"These things are wrapt in doubt and dread,
Nor canst thou show the dead are dead.

"The sap dries up : the plant declines.
A deeper tale my heart divines.
Know I not Death ? the outward signs ?

"I found him when my years were few ;
A shadow on the graves I knew,
And darkness in the village yew.

"From grave to grave the shadow crept :
In her still place the morning wept :
Touch'd by his feet the daisy slept.

"The simple senses crown'd his head :
'Omega ! thou art Lord,' they said,
'We find no motion in the dead.'

"Why, if man rot in dreamless ease,
Should that plain fact, as taught by these,
Not make him sure that he shall cease ?

"Who forged that other influence,
That heat of inward evidence,
By which he doubts against the sense ?

"He owns the fatal gift of eyes,
That read his spirit blindly wise,
Not simple as a thing that dies.

"Here sits he shaping wings to fly :
His heart forebodes a mystery :
He names the name Eternity.

"That type of Perfect in his mind
In Nature can he nowhere find.
He sows himself on every wind.

"He seems to hear a Heavenly Friend,
And thro' thick veils to apprehend
A labor working to an end.

"The end and the beginning vex
His reason : many things perplex,
With motions, checks, and counterchecks.

"He knows a baseness in his blood
At such strange war with something good,
He may not do the thing he would.

"Heaven opens inward, chasms yawn,
Vast images in glimmering dawn,
Half shown, are broken and withdrawn.

"Ah! sure within him and without,
Could his dark wisdom find it out,
There must be answer to his doubt.

"But thou canst answer not again.
With thine own weapon art thou slain,
Or thou wilt answer but in vain.

"The doubt would rest, I dare not solve.
In the same circle we revolve.
Assurance only breeds resolve."

As when a billow, blown against,
Falls back, the voice with which I fenced
A little ceased, but recommenced.

"Where wert thou when thy father play'd
In his free field, and pastime made,
A merry boy in sun and shade?

"A merry boy they called him then,
He sat upon the knees of men
In days that never come again.

"Before the little ducts began
To feed thy bones with lime, and ran
Their course, till thou wert also man:

"Who took a wife, who rear'd his race,
Whose wrinkles gather'd on his face,
Whose troubles number with his days:

"A life of nothings, nothing worth,
From that first nothing ere his birth
To that last nothing under earth!"

"These words," I said, "are like the rest,
No certain clearness, but at best
A vague suspicion of the breast:

"But if I grant, thou might'st defend
The thesis which thy words intend —
That to begin implies to end;

"Yet how should I for certain hold,
Because my memory is so cold,
That I first was in human mould?

"I cannot make this matter plain,
But I would shoot, howe'er in vain,
A random arrow from the brain.

"It may be that no life is found,
Which only to one engine bound
Falls off, but cycles always round.

"As old mythologies relate,
Some draught of Lethe might await
The slipping thro' from state to state.

"As here we find in trances, men
Forget the dream that happens then,
Until they fall in trance again.

"So might we, if our state were such
As one before, remember much,
For those two likes might meet and touch.

"But, if I lapsed from nobler place,
Some legend of a fallen race
Alone might hint of my disgrace;

"Some vague emotion of delight
In gazing up an Alpine height,
Some yearning toward the lamps of night.

"Or if thro' lower lives I came —
Tho' all experience past became
Consolidate in mind and frame —

"I might forget my weaker lot;
For is not our first year forgot?
The haunts of memory echo not.

"And men, whose reason long was blind,
From cells of madness unconfined,
Oft lose whole years of darker mind.

"Much more, if first I floated free,
As naked essence, must I be
Incompetent of memory:

"For memory dealing but with time,
And he with matter, should she climb
Beyond her own material prime?

"Moreover, something is or seems,
That touches me with mystic gleams,
Like glimpses of forgotten dreams —

"Of something felt, like something here;
Of something done, I know not where;
Such as no language may declare."

The still voice laugh'd. "I talk," said he,
"Not with thy dreams. Suffice it thee
Thy pain is a reality."

"But thou," said I, "hast miss'd thy mark,
Who sought'st to wreck my mortal ark,
By making all the horizon dark.

"Why not set forth, if I should do
This rashness, that which might ensue
With this old soul in organs new?

"Whatever crazy sorrow saith,
No life that breathes with human breath
Has ever truly long'd for death.

"'T is life, whereof our nerves are scant,
O life, not death, for which we pant;
More life, and fuller, that I want."

I ceased, and sat as one forlorn.
Then said the voice, in quiet scorn,
"Behold, it is the Sabbath morn."

And I arose, and I released
The casement, and the light increased
With freshness in the dawning east.

Like soften'd airs that blowing steal,
When meres begin to uncongeal,
The sweet church bells began to peal.

On to God's house the people prest:
Passing the place where each must rest,
Each enter'd like a welcome guest.

One walk'd between his wife and child,
With measured footfall firm and mild,
And now and then he gravely smiled.

The prudent partner of his blood
Lean'd on him, faithful, gentle, good,
Wearing the rose of womanhood.

And in their double love secure,
The little maiden walk'd demure,
Pacing with downward eyelids pure.

These three made unity so sweet,
My frozen heart began to beat,
Remembering its ancient heat.

I blest them, and they wander'd on:
I spoke, but answer came there none:
The dull and bitter voice was gone.

A second voice was at mine ear,
A little whisper silver-clear,
A murmur, "Be of better cheer."

As from some blissful neighborhood,
A notice faintly understood,
"I see the end, and know the good."

A little hint to solace woe,
A hint; a whisper breathing low,
"I may not speak of what I know."

Like an Æolian harp that wakes
No certain air, but overtakes
Far thought with music that it makes:

Such seem'd the whisper at my side
"What is it thou knowest, sweet voice?"
I cried.
"A hidden hope," the voice replied:

So heavenly-toned, that in that hour
From out my sullen heart a power
Broke, like the rainbow from the shower,

To feel, altho' no tongue can prove,
That every cloud, that spreads above
And veileth love, itself is love.

And forth into the fields I went,
And Nature's living motion lent
The pulse of hope to discontent.

I wonder'd at the bounteous hours,
The slow result of winter showers:
You scarce could see the grass for flowers.

I wonder'd, while I paced along:
The woods were fill'd so full with song,
There seem'd no room for sense of wrong.

So variously seem'd all things wrought,
I marvell'd how the mind was brought
To anchor by one gloomy thought;

And wherefore rather I made choice
To commune with that barren voice,
Than him that said, "Rejoice! rejoice!"

THE DAY-DREAM.

PROLOGUE.

O LADY FLORA, let me speak:
  A pleasant hour has past away
While, dreaming on your damask cheek,
  The dewy sister-eyelids lay.
As by the lattice you reclined,
  I went thro' many wayward moods
To see you dreaming — and, behind,
  A summer crisp with shining woods.
And I too dream'd, until at last
  Across my fancy, brooding warm,
The reflex of a legend past,
  And loosely settled into form.
And would you have the thought I had,
  And see the vision that I saw,

Then take the broidery-frame, and add
  A crimson to the quaint Macaw,
And I will tell it. Turn your face,
  Nor look with that too-earnest eye —
The rhymes are dazzled from their place,
  And order'd words asunder fly.

THE SLEEPING PALACE.

I.

The varying year with blade and sheaf
  Clothes and reclothes the happy plains;
Here rests the sap within the leaf,
  Here stays the blood along the veins.
Faint shadows, vapors lightly curl'd,
  Faint murmurs from the meadows come,
Like hints and echoes of the world
  To spirits folded in the womb.

II.

Soft lustre bathes the range of urns
  On every slanting terrace-lawn.
The fountain to his place returns
  Deep in the garden lake withdrawn.
Here droops the banner on the tower,
  On the hall-hearths the festal fires,
The peacock in his laurel bower,
  The parrot in his gilded wires.

III.

Roof-haunting martins warm their eggs :
  In these, in those the life is stay'd.
The mantles from the golden pegs
  Droop sleepily : no sound is made,
Not even of a gnat that sings.
  More like a picture seemeth all
Than those old portraits of old kings,
  That watch the sleepers from the wall.

IV.

Here sits the Butler with a flask
  Between his knees, half-drain'd ; and there
The wrinkled steward at his task,
  The maid-of-honor blooming fair ;
The page has caught her hand in his :
  Her lips are sever'd as to speak :
His own are pouted to a kiss :
  The blush is fix'd upon her cheek.

V.

Till all the hundred summers pass,
  The beams, that thro' the Oriel shine,
Make prisms in every carven glass,
  And beaker brimm'd with noble wine.

Each baron at the banquet sleeps,
  Grave faces gather'd in a ring.
His state the king reposing keeps.
  He must have been a jovial king.

VI.

All round a hedge upshoots, and shows
  At distance like a little wood ;
Thorns, ivies, woodbine, mistletoes,
  And grapes with bunches red as blood ;
All creeping plants, a wall of green
  Close-matted, burr and brake and brier,
And glimpsing over these, just seen,
  High up, the topmost palace-spire.

VII.

When will the hundred summers die,
  And thought and time be born again,
And newer knowledge, drawing nigh,
  Bring truth that sways the soul of men ?
Here all things in their place remain,
  As all were order'd, ages since.
Come, Care and Pleasure, Hope and Pain,
  And bring the fated fairy Prince.

THE SLEEPING BEAUTY.

I.

Year after year unto her feet,
  She lying on her couch alone,
Across the purpled coverlet,
  The maiden's jet-black hair has grown,
On either side her tranced form
  Forth streaming from a braid of pearl :
The slumbrous light is rich and warm,
  And moves not on the rounded curl.

II.

The silk star-broider'd coverlid
  Unto her limbs itself doth mould
Languidly ever ; and, amid
  Her full black ringlets downward roll'd,
Glows forth each softly-shadow'd arm
  With bracelets of the diamond bright :
Her constant beauty doth inform
  Stillness with love, and day with light.

III.

She sleeps : her breathings are not heard
  In palace chambers far apart.
The fragrant tresses are not stirr'd
  That lie upon her charmed heart.
She sleeps : on either hand upswells
  The gold-fringed pillow lightly prest :
She sleeps, nor dreams, but ever dwells
  A perfect form in perfect rest.

THE ARRIVAL.

I.

ALL precious things, discover'd late,
  To those that seek them issue forth ;
For love in sequel works with fate,
  And draws the veil from hidden worth.
He travels far from other skies —
  His mantle glitters on the rocks —
A fairy Prince, with joyful eyes,
  And lighter-footed than the fox.

II.

The bodies and the bones of those
  That strove in other days to pass,
Are wither'd in the thorny close,
  Or scatter'd blanching on the grass.
He gazes on the silent dead :
  "They perish'd in their daring deeds."
This proverb flashes thro' his head,
  "The many fail : the one succeeds."

III.

He comes, scarce knowing what he seeks :
  He breaks the hedge : he enters there :
The color flies into his cheeks :
  He trusts to light on something fair ;
For all his life the charm did talk
  About his path, and hover near
With words of promise in his walk,
  And whisper'd voices at his ear.

IV.

More close and close his footsteps wind :
  The Magic Music in his heart
Beats quick and quicker, till he find
  The quiet chamber far apart.
His spirit flutters like a lark,
  He stoops — to kiss her — on his knee.
"Love, if thy tresses be so dark,
  How dark those hidden eyes must be !"

THE REVIVAL.

I.

A TOUCH, a kiss ! the charm was snapt.
  There rose a noise of striking clocks,
And feet that ran, and doors that clapt,
  And barking dogs, and crowing cocks ;
A fuller light illumined all,
  A breeze thro' all the garden swept,
A sudden hubbub shook the hall,
  And sixty feet the fountain leapt.

II.

The hedge broke in, the banner blew,
  The butler drank, the steward scrawl'd,
The fire shot up, the martin flew,
  The parrot scream'd, the peacock squall'd,
The maid and page renew'd their strife,
  The palace bang'd, and buzz'd and clackt,
And all the long-pent stream of life
  Dash'd downward in a cataract.

III.

And last with these the king awoke,
  And in his chair himself uprear'd,
And yawn'd, and rubb'd his face, and spoke,
  "By holy rood, a royal beard !
How say you ? we have slept, my lords.
  My beard has grown into my lap."
The barons swore, with many words,
  'T was but an after-dinner's nap.

IV.

"Pardy," return'd the king, "but still
  My joints are somewhat stiff or so.
My lord, and shall we pass the bill
  I mention'd half an hour ago ?"
The chancellor, sedate and vain,
  In courteous words return'd reply :
But dallied with his golden chain,
  And, smiling, put the question by.

THE DEPARTURE.

I.

AND on her lover's arm she leant,
  And round her waist she felt it fold,
And far across the hills they went
  In that new world which is the old :
Across the hills, and far away
  Beyond their utmost purple rim,
And deep into the dying day
  The happy princess follow'd him.

II.

"I 'd sleep another hundred years,
  O love, for such another kiss" ;
"O wake for ever, love," she hears,
  "O love, 't was such as this and this."
And o'er them many a sliding star,
  And many a merry wind was borne,
And, stream'd thro' many a golden bar,
  The twilight melted into morn.

III.

"O eyes long laid in happy sleep !"
"O happy sleep, that lightly fled !"

*"How say you? we have slept, my lords.
My beard has grown into my lap."*

"O happy kiss, that woke thy sleep!"
"O love, thy kiss would wake the dead!"
And o'er them many a flowing range
Of vapor buoy'd the crescent-bark,
And, rapt thro' many a rosy change,
The twilight died into the dark.

IV.

"A hundred summers! can it be?
And whither goest thou, tell me where?"
"O seek my father's court with me,
For there are greater wonders there."
And o'er the hills, and far away
Beyond their utmost purple rim,
Beyond the night, across the day,
Thro' all the world she follow'd him.

MORAL.

I.

So, Lady Flora, take my lay,
And if you find no moral there,
Go, look in any glass and say,
What moral is in being fair.
O, to what uses shall we put
The wildweed-flower that simply blows?
And is there any moral shut
Within the bosom of the rose?

II.

But any man that walks the mead,
In bud or blade, or bloom, may find,
According as his humors lead,
A meaning suited to his mind.
And liberal applications lie
In Art like Nature, dearest friend;
So 't were to cramp its use, if I
Should hook it to some useful end.

L'ENVOI.

I.

You shake your head. A random string
Your finer female sense offends.

Well — were it not a pleasant thing
  To fall asleep with all one's friends ;
To pass with all our social ties
  To silence from the paths of men ;
And every hundred years to rise
  And learn the world, and sleep again ;
To sleep thro' terms of mighty wars,
  And wake on science grown to more,
On secrets of the brain, the stars,
  As wild as aught of fairy lore ;
And all that else the years will show,
  The Poet-forms of stronger hours,
The vast Republics that may grow,
  The Federations and the Powers ;
Titanic forces taking birth
  In divers seasons, divers climes ;
For we are Ancients of the earth,
  And in the morning of the times.

II.

So sleeping, so aroused from sleep
  Thro' sunny decads new and strange,
Or gay quinquenniads would we reap
  The flower and quintessence of change.

III.

Ah, yet would I — and would I might !
  So much your eyes my fancy take —
Be still the first to leap to light
  That I might kiss those eyes awake !
For, am I right, or am I wrong,
  To choose your own you did not care ;
You 'd have *my* moral from the song,
  And I will take my pleasure there :
And, am I right or am I wrong,
  My fancy, ranging thro' and thro',
To search a meaning for the song,
  Perforce will still revert to you ;
Nor finds a closer truth than this
  All-graceful head, so richly curl'd,
And evermore a costly kiss
  The prelude to some brighter world.

IV.

For since the time when Adam first
  Embraced his Eve in happy hour,
And every bird of Eden burst
  In carol, every bud to flower,
What eyes, like thine, have waken'd hopes ?
What lips, like thine, so sweetly join'd ?
Where on the double rosebud droops
  The fulness of the pensive mind ;
Which all too dearly self-involved,
  Yet sleeps a dreamless sleep to me ;
A sleep by kisses undissolved,
  That lets thee neither hear nor see :

But break it. In the name of wife,
  And in the rights that name may give,
Are clasp'd the moral of thy life,
  And that for which I care to live.

EPILOGUE.

So, Lady Flora, take my lay,
  And, if you find a meaning there,
O whisper to your glass, and say,
  "What wonder, if he thinks me fair ?"
What wonder I was all unwise,
  To shape the song for your delight
Like long-tail'd birds of Paradise,
  That float thro' Heaven, and cannot light ?
Or old-world trains, upheld at court
  By Cupid-boys of blooming hue —
But take it — earnest wed with sport,
  And either sacred unto you.

AMPHION.

My father left a park to me,
  But it is wild and barren,
A garden too with scarce a tree,
  And waster than a warren :
Yet say the neighbors when they call,
  It is not bad but good land,
And in it is the germ of all
  That grows within the woodland.

O had I lived when song was great
  In days of old Amphion,
And ta'en my fiddle to the gate,
  Nor cared for seed or scion !
And had I lived when song was great,
  And legs of trees were limber,
And ta'en my fiddle to the gate,
  And fiddled in the timber !

'T is said he had a tuneful tongue,
  Such happy intonation,
Wherever he sat down and sung
  He left a small plantation ;
Wherever in a lonely grove
  He set up his forlorn pipes,
The gouty oak began to move,
  And flounder into hornpipes.

The mountain stirr'd its bushy crown.
  And, as tradition teaches,
Young ashes pirouetted down
  Coquetting with young beeches ;

And briony-vine and ivy-wreath
　Ran forward to his rhyming,
And from the valleys underneath
　Came little copses climbing.

The linden broke her ranks and rent
　The woodbine wreaths that bind her,
And down the middle buzz! she went
　With all her bees behind her:
The poplars, in long order due,
　With cypress promenaded,
The shock-head willows two and two
　By rivers gallopaded.

Came wet-shot alder from the wave,
　Came yews, a dismal coterie;
Each pluck'd his one foot from the grave,
　Poussetting with a sloe-tree:
Old elms came breaking from the vine,
　The vine stream'd out to follow,
And, sweating rosin, plump'd the pine
　From many a cloudy hollow.

And was n't it a sight to see,
　When, ere his song was ended,
Like some great landslip, tree by tree,
　The country-side descended;
And shepherds from the mountain-eaves
　Look'd down, half-pleased, half-frighten'd,
As dash'd about the drunken leaves
　The random sunshine lighten'd!

O, nature first was fresh to men,
　And wanton without measure;
So youthful and so flexile then,
　You moved her at your pleasure.
Twang out, my fiddle! shake the twigs!
　And make her dance attendance;
Blow, flute, and stir the stiff-set sprigs,
　And scirrhous roots and tendons.

'T is vain! in such a brassy age
　I could not move a thistle;
The very sparrows in the hedge
　Scarce answer to my whistle;
Or at the most, when three-parts-sick
　With strumming and with scraping,
A jackass heehaws from the rick,
　The passive oxen gaping.

But what is that I hear? a sound
　Like sleepy counsel pleading;
O Lord! — 't is in my neighbor's ground,
　The modern Muses reading.
They read Botanic Treatises,
　And Works on Gardening thro' there,
And Methods of transplanting trees,
　- To look as if they grew there.

The wither'd Misses! how they prose
　O'er books of travell'd seamen,
And show you slips of all that grows
　From England to Van Diemen.
They read in arbors clipt and cut,
　And alleys, faded places,
By squares of tropic summer shut
　And warm'd in crystal cases.

But these, tho' fed with careful dirt,
　Are neither green nor sappy;
Half-conscious of the garden-squirt,
　The spindlings look unhappy.
Better to me the meanest weed
　That blows upon its mountain,
The vilest herb that runs to seed
　Beside its native fountain.

And I must work thro' months of toil,
　And years of cultivation,
Upon my proper patch of soil
　To grow my own plantation.
I'll take the showers as they fall,
　I will not vex my bosom:
Enough if at the end of all
　A little garden blossom.

ST. AGNES' EVE.

DEEP on the convent-roof the snows
　Are sparkling to the moon:
My breath to heaven like vapor goes:
　May my soul follow soon!
The shadows of the convent-towers
　Slant down the snowy sward,
Still creeping with the creeping hours
　That lead me to my Lord:
Make Thou my spirit pure and clear
　As are the frosty skies,
Or this first snowdrop of the year
　That in my bosom lies.

As these white robes are soil'd and dark,
　To yonder shining ground;
As this pale taper's earthly spark,
　To yonder argent round;
So shows my soul before the Lamb,
　My spirit before Thee;
So in mine earthly house I am,
　To that I hope to be.
Break up the heavens, O Lord! and far,
　Thro' all yon starlight keen,
Draw me, thy bride, a glittering star,
　In raiment white and clean.

*"My breath to heaven like vapor goes:
May my soul follow soon!"*

He lifts me to the golden doors;
   The flashes come and go;
All heaven bursts her starry floors,
   And strews her lights below,
And deepens on and up! the gates
   Roll back, and far within
For me the Heavenly Bridegroom waits,
   To make me pure of sin.
The sabbaths of Eternity,
   One sabbath deep and wide —
A light upon the shining sea —
   The Bridegroom with his bride!

SIR GALAHAD.

My good blade carves the casques of men,
   My tough lance thrusteth sure,
My strength is as the strength of ten,
   Because my heart is pure.
The shattering trumpet shrilleth high,
   The hard brands shiver on the steel,
The splinter'd spear-shafts crack and
     fly,
   The horse and rider reel:
They reel, they roll in clanging lists,
   And when the tide of combat stands,
Perfume and flowers fall in showers,
   That lightly rain from ladies' hands.

How sweet are looks that ladies bend
   On whom their favors fall!
For them I battle till the end,
   To save from shame and thrall:
But all my heart is drawn above,
   My knees are bow'd in crypt and shrine:

I never felt the kiss of love,
　Nor maiden's hand in mine.
More bounteous aspects on me beam,
　Me mightier transports move and thrill;
So keep I fair thro' faith and prayer
　A virgin heart in work and will.

When down the stormy crescent goes,
　A light before me swims,
Between dark stems the forest glows,
　I hear a noise of hymns :
Then by some secret shrine I ride ;
　I hear a voice, but none are there ;
The stalls are void, the doors are wide,
　The tapers burning fair.
Fair gleams the snowy altar-cloth,
　The silver vessels sparkle clean,
The shrill bell rings, the censer swings,
　And solemn chants resound between.

Sometimes on lonely mountain-meres
　I find a magic bark ;
I leap on board : no helmsman steers :
　I float till all is dark.
A gentle sound, an awful light !
　Three angels bear the holy Grail :
With folded feet, in stoles of white,
　On sleeping wings they sail.
Ah, blessed vision ! blood of God !
　My spirit beats her mortal bars,
As down dark tides the glory slides,
　And star-like mingles with the stars.

When on my goodly charger borne
　Thro' dreaming towns I go,
The cock crows ere the Christmas morn,
　The streets are dumb with snow.
The tempest crackles on the leads,
　And, ringing, springs from brand and mail ;
But o'er the dark a glory spreads,
　And gilds the driving hail.
I leave the plain, I climb the height ;
　No branchy thicket shelter yields ;
But blessed forms in whistling storms
　Fly o'er waste fens and windy fields.

A maiden knight — to me is given
　Such hope, I know not fear ;
I yearn to breathe the airs of heaven
　That often meet me here.
I muse on joy that will not cease,
　Pure spaces clothed in living beams,
Pure lilies of eternal peace,
　Whose odors haunt my dreams ;
And, stricken by an angel's hand,
　This mortal armor that I wear,

This weight and size, this heart and eyes,
　Are touch'd, are turn'd to finest air.

The clouds are broken in the sky,
　And thro' the mountain-walls
A rolling organ-harmony
　Swells up, and shakes and falls.
Then move the trees, the copses nod,
　Wings flutter, voices hover clear :
"O just and faithful knight of God !
　Ride on ! the prize is near."
So pass I hostel, hall, and grange ;
　By bridge and ford, by park and pale,
All-arm'd I ride, whate'er betide,
　Until I find the holy Grail.

EDWARD GRAY.

Sweet Emma Moreland of yonder town
　Met me walking on yonder way,
"And have you lost your heart ?" she said ;
"And are you married yet, Edward Gray ?"

Sweet Emma Moreland spoke to me :
　Bitterly weeping I turn'd away :
"Sweet Emma Moreland, love no more
　Can touch the heart of Edward Gray.

"Ellen Adair she loved me well,
　Against her father's and mother's will :
To-day I sat for an hour and wept,
　By Ellen's grave, on the windy hill.

"Shy she was, and I thought her cold ;
　Thought her proud, and fled over the sea ;
Fill'd I was with folly and spite,
　When Ellen Adair was dying for me.

"Cruel, cruel the words I said !
　Cruelly came they back to-day :
'You're too slight and fickle,' I said,
　'To trouble the heart of Edward Gray.'

"There I put my face in the grass —
　Whisper'd, 'Listen to my despair :
I repent me of all I did :
　Speak a little, Ellen Adair !'

"Then I took a pencil, and wrote
　On the mossy stone, as I lay,
'Here lies the body of Ellen Adair ;
　And here the heart of Edward Gray !'

*"All-arm'd I ride, whate'er betide,
Until I find the holy Grail."*

"Love may come, and love may go,
   And fly, like a bird, from tree to tree:
But I will love no more, no more,
   Till Ellen Adair come back to me.

"Bitterly wept I over the stone:
   Bitterly weeping I turn'd away:
There lies the body of Ellen Adair!
   And there the heart of Edward Gray!"

WILL WATERPROOF'S LYRICAL MONOLOGUE.

MADE AT THE COCK.

O PLUMP head-waiter at The Cock,
   To which I most resort,
How goes the time? 'T is five o'clock.
   Go fetch a pint of port:

But let it not be such as that
   You set before chance-comers,
But such whose father-grape grew fat
   On Lusitanian summers.

No vain libation to the Muse,
   But may she still be kind,
And whisper lovely words, and use
   Her influence on the mind,
To make me write my random rhymes,
   Ere they be half-forgotten;
Nor add and alter, many times,
   Till all be ripe and rotten.

I pledge her, and she comes and dips
   Her laurel in the wine,
And lays it thrice upon my lips,
   These favor'd lips of mine;
Until the charm have power to make
   New lifeblood warm the bosom,

And barren commonplaces break
  In full and kindly blossom.

I pledge her silent at the board ;
  Her gradual fingers steal
And touch upon the master-chord
  Of all I felt and feel.
Old wishes, ghosts of broken plans,
  And phantom hopes assemble ;
And that child's heart within the man's
  Begins to move and tremble.

Thro' many an hour of summer suns,
  By many pleasant ways,
Against its fountain upward runs
  The current of my days :
I kiss the lips I once have kiss'd ;
  The gas-light wavers dimmer ;
And softly, thro' a vinous mist,
  My college friendships glimmer.

I grow in worth, and wit, and sense,
  Unboding critic-pen,
Or that eternal want of pence,
  Which vexes public men,
Who hold their hands to all, and cry
  For that which all deny them —
Who sweep the crossings, wet or dry,
  And all the world go by them.

Ah yet, tho' all the world forsake,
  Tho' fortune clip my wings,
I will not cramp my heart, nor take
  Half-views of men and things.
Let Whig and Tory stir their blood ;
  There must be stormy weather ;
But for some true result of good
  All parties work together.

Let there be thistles, there are grapes ;
  If old things, there are new ;
Ten thousand broken lights and shapes,
  Yet glimpses of the true.
Let raffs be rife in prose and rhyme,
  We lack not rhymes and reasons,
As on this whirligig of Time
  We circle with the seasons.

This earth is rich in man and maid ;
  With fair horizons bound :
This whole wide earth of light and shade
  Comes out, a perfect round.
High over roaring Temple-bar,
  And, set in Heaven's third story,
I look at all things as they are,
  But thro' a kind of glory.

Head-waiter, honor'd by the guest
  Half-mused, or reeling ripe,
The pint, you brought me, was the best
  That ever came from pipe.
But tho' the port surpasses praise,
  My nerves have dealt with stiffer.
Is there some magic in the place ?
  Or do my peptics differ ?

For since I came to live and learn,
  No pint of white or red
Had ever half the power to turn
  This wheel within my head,
Which bears a season'd brain about,
  Unsubject to confusion,
Tho' soak'd and saturate, out and out,
  Thro' every convolution.

For I am of a numerous house,
  With many kinsmen gay,
Where long and largely we carouse
  As who shall say me nay :
Each month, a birthday coming on,
  We drink defying trouble,
Or sometimes two would meet in one,
  And then we drank it double ;

Whether the vintage, yet unkept,
  Had relish fiery-new,
Or, elbow-deep in sawdust, slept,
  As old as Waterloo ;
Or stow'd (when classic Canning died)
  In musty bins and chambers,
Had cast upon its crusty side
  The gloom of ten Decembers.

The Muse, the jolly Muse, it is !
  She answer'd to my call,
She changes with that mood or this,
  Is all-in-all to all :
She lit the spark within my throat,
  To make my blood run quicker,
Used all her fiery will, and smote
  Her life into the liquor.

And hence this halo lives about
  The waiter's hands, that reach
To each his perfect pint of stout,
  His proper chop to each.
He looks not like the common breed
  That with the napkin dally ;
I think he came like Ganymede,
  From some delightful valley.

The Cock was of a larger egg
  Than modern poultry drop,
Stept forward on a firmer leg,
  And cramm'd a plumper crop ;

Upon an ampler dunghill trod,
  Crow'd lustier late and early,
Sipt wine from silver, praising God,
  And raked in golden barley.

A private life was all his joy,
  Till in a court he saw
A something-pottle-bodied boy,
  That knuckled at the taw:
He stoop'd and clutch'd him, fair and good,
  Flew over roof and casement:
His brothers of the weather stood
  Stock-still for sheer amazement.

But he, by farmstead, thorpe and spire,
  And follow'd with acclaims,
A sign to many a staring shire,
  Came crowing over Thames.
Right down by smoky Paul's they bore,
  Till, where the street grows straiter,
One fix'd for ever at the door,
  And one became head-waiter.

———

But whither would my fancy go?
  How out of place she makes
The violet of a legend blow
  Among the chops and steaks!
'T is but a steward of the can,
  One shade more plump than common;
As just and mere a serving-man
  As any, born of woman.

I ranged too high: what draws me down
  Into the common day?
Is it the weight of that half-crown,
  Which I shall have to pay?
For, something duller than at first,
  Nor wholly comfortable,
I sit (my empty glass reversed),
  And thrumming on the table:

Half fearful that, with self at strife
  I take myself to task;
Lest of the fulness of my life
  I leave an empty flask:
For I had hope, by something rare,
  To prove myself a poet:
But, while I plan and plan, my hair
  Is gray before I know it.

So fares it since the years began,
  Till they be gather'd up;
The truth, that flies the flowing can,
  Will haunt the vacant cup:
And others' follies teach us not,
  Nor much their wisdom teaches;
And most, of sterling worth, is what
  Our own experience preaches.

Ah, let the rusty theme alone!
  We know not what we know.
But for my pleasant hour, 't is gone,
  'T is gone, and let it go.
'T is gone: a thousand such have slipt
  Away from my embraces,
And fall'n into the dusty crypt
  Of darken'd forms and faces.

Go, therefore, thou! thy betters went
  Long since, and came no more;
With peals of genial clamor sent
  From many a tavern-door,
With twisted quirks and happy hits,
  From misty men of letters;
The tavern-hours of mighty wits—
  Thine elders and thy betters.

Hours, when the Poet's words and looks
  Had yet their native glow;
Nor yet the fear of little books
  Had made him talk for show;
But, all his vast heart sherris-warm'd,
  He flash'd his random speeches;
Ere days, that deal in ana, swarm'd
  His literary leeches.

So mix for ever with the past,
  Like all good things on earth!
For should I prize thee, couldst thou last,
  At half thy real worth?
I hold it good, good things should pass:
  With time I will not quarrel:
It is but yonder empty glass
  That makes me maudlin-moral.

Head-waiter of the chop-house here,
  To which I most resort,
I too must part: I hold thee dear
  For this good pint of port.
For this, thou shalt from all things suck
  Marrow of mirth and laughter;
And, wheresoe'er thou move, good luck
  Shall fling her old shoe after.

But thou wilt never move from hence,
  The sphere thy fate allots:
Thy latter days increased with pence
  Go down among the pots:
Thou battenest by the greasy gleam
  In haunts of hungry sinners,
Old boxes, larded with the steam
  Of thirty thousand dinners.

We fret, *we* fume, would shift our skins,
  Would quarrel with our lot ;
Thy care is, under polish'd tins,
  To serve the hot-and-hot ;
To come and go, and come again,
  Returning like the pewit,
And watch'd by silent gentlemen,
  That trifle with the cruet.

Live long, ere from thy topmost head
  The thick-set hazel dies ;
Long, ere the hateful crow shall tread
  The corners of thine eyes :
Live long, nor feel in head or chest
  Our changeful equinoxes,
Till mellow Death, like some late guest,
  Shall call thee from the boxes.

But when he calls, and thou shalt cease
  To pace the gritted floor,
And, laying down an unctuous lease
  Of life, shalt earn no more ;
No carved cross-bones, the types of Death,
  Shall show thee past to Heaven :
But carved cross-pipes, and, underneath,
  A pint-pot, neatly graven.

TO ――――,

AFTER READING A LIFE AND LETTERS.

"Cursed be he that moves my bones."
        Shakespeare's Epitaph.

You might have won the Poet's name,
  If such be worth the winning now,
  And gain'd a laurel for your brow
Of sounder leaf than I can claim ;

But you have made the wiser choice,
  A life that moves to gracious ends
  Thro' troops of unrecording friends,
A deedful life, a silent voice :

And you have miss'd the irreverent doom
  Of those that wear the Poet's crown :
  Hereafter, neither knave nor clown
Shall hold their orgies at your tomb.

For now the Poet cannot die
  Nor leave his music as of old,
  But round him ere he scarce be cold
Begins the scandal and the cry :

"Proclaim the faults he would not show :
  Break lock and seal : betray the trust :
  Keep nothing sacred : 't is but just
The many-headed beast should know."

Ah shameless ! for he did but sing
  A song that pleased us from its worth ;
  No public life was his on earth,
No blazon'd statesman he, nor king.

He gave the people of his best :
  His worst he kept, his best he gave.
  My Shakespeare's curse on clown and knave
Who will not let his ashes rest !

Who make it seem more sweet to be
  The little life of bank and brier,
  The bird that pipes his lone desire
And dies unheard within his tree,

Than he that warbles long and loud
  And drops at Glory's temple-gates,
  For whom the carrion vulture waits
To tear his heart before the crowd !

TO E. L., ON HIS TRAVELS IN GREECE.

ILLYRIAN woodlands, echoing falls
  Of water, sheets of summer glass,
  The long divine Peneïan pass,
The vast Akrokeraunian walls,

Tomohrit, Athos, all things fair,
  With such a pencil, such a pen,
  You shadow forth to distant men,
I read and felt that I was there :

And trust me while I turn'd the page,
  And track'd you still on classic ground,
  I grew in gladness till I found
My spirits in the golden age.

For me the torrent ever pour'd
  And glisten'd — here and there alone
  The broad-limb'd Gods at random thrown
By fountain-urns ; — and Naiads oar'd

A glimmering shoulder under gloom
  Of cavern pillars ; on the swell
  The silver lily heaved and fell ;
And many a slope was rich in bloom

From him that on the mountain lea
  By dancing rivulets fed his flocks,
  To him who sat upon the rocks,
And fluted to the morning sea.

LADY CLARE.

It was the time when lilies blow,
    And clouds are highest up in air,
Lord Ronald brought a lily-white doe
    To give his cousin, Lady Clare.

I trow they did not part in scorn:
    Lovers long-betroth'd were they:
They two will wed the morrow morn:
    God's blessing on the day!

"He does not love me for my birth,
    Nor for my lands so broad and fair;
He loves me for my own true worth,
    And that is well," said Lady Clare.

In there came old Alice the nurse,
    Said, "Who was this that went from thee?"
"It was my cousin," said Lady Clare,
    "To-morrow he weds with me."

"O God be thank'd!" said Alice the nurse,
    "That all comes round so just and fair:
Lord Ronald is heir of all your lands,
    And you are not the Lady Clare."

"Are ye out of your mind, my nurse, my nurse?"
    Said Lady Clare, "that ye speak so wild?"

"Lord Ronald brought a lily-white doe
To give his cousin, Lady Clare."

"As God's above," said Alice the nurse,
  "I speak the truth : you are my child.

"The old Earl's daughter died at my
    breast ;
  I speak the truth, as I live by bread !
I buried her like my own sweet child,
  And put my child in her stead."

"Falsely, falsely have ye done,
  O mother," she said, "if this be true,
To keep the best man under the sun
  So many years from his due."

"Nay now, my child," said Alice the
    nurse,
  "But keep the secret for your life,
And all you have will be Lord Ronald's,
  When you are man and wife."

"If I'm a beggar born," she said,
  "I will speak out, for I dare not lie.
Pull off, pull off, the brooch of gold,
  And fling the diamond necklace by."

"Nay now, my child," said Alice the
    nurse,
  "But keep the secret all ye can."
She said, "Not so : but I will know
  If there be any faith in man."

"Nay now, what faith ?" said Alice the
    nurse,
  "The man will cleave unto his right."
"And he shall have it," the lady replied,
  "Tho' I should die to-night."

"Yet give one kiss to your mother dear !
  Alas, my child, I sinn'd for thee."
"O mother, mother, mother," she said,
  "So strange it seems to me.

"Yet here's a kiss for my mother dear,
  My mother dear, if this be so,
And lay your hand upon my head,
  And bless me, mother, ere I go."

She clad herself in a russet gown,
  She was no longer Lady Clare :
She went by dale, and she went by down,
  With a single rose in her hair.

The lily-white doe Lord Ronald had
    brought
  Leapt up from where she lay,
Dropt her head in the maiden's hand,
  And follow'd her all the way.

Down stept Lord Ronald from his tower :
  "O Lady Clare, you shame your worth !
Why come you drest like a village maid,
  That are the flower of the earth ?"

"If I come drest like a village maid,
  I am but as my fortunes are :
I am a beggar born," she said,
  "And not the Lady Clare."

"Play me no tricks," said Lord Ronald,
  "For I am yours in word and in deed.
Play me no tricks," said Lord Ronald,
  "Your riddle is hard to read."

O and proudly stood she up !
  Her heart within her did not fail :
She look'd into Lord Ronald's eyes,
  And told him all her nurse's tale.

He laugh'd a laugh of merry scorn :
  He turn'd and kiss'd her where she
    stood :
"If you are not the heiress born,
  And I," said he, "the next in blood—

"If you are not the heiress born,
  And I," said he, "the lawful heir,
We two will wed to-morrow morn,
  And you shall still be Lady Clare."

THE LORD OF BURLEIGH.

In her ear he whispers gayly,
  "If my heart by signs can tell,
Maiden, I have watch'd thee daily,
  And I think thou lov'st me well."
She replies, in accents fainter,
  "There is none I love like thee."
He is but a landscape-painter,
  And a village maiden she.
He to lips, that fondly falter,
  Presses his without reproof :
Leads her to the village altar,
  And they leave her father's roof.
"I can make no marriage present :
  Little can I give my wife.
Love will make our cottage pleasant,
  And I love thee more than life."
They by parks and lodges going
  See the lordly castles stand :
Summer woods, about them blowing,
  Made a murmur in the land.
From deep thought himself he rouses,
  Says to her that loves him well,
"Let us see these handsome houses
  Where the wealthy nobles dwell."

So she goes by him attended,
   Hears him lovingly converse,
Sees whatever fair and splendid
   Lay betwixt his home and hers ;
Parks with oak and chestnut shady,
   Parks and order'd gardens great,
Ancient homes of lord and lady,
   Built for pleasure and for state.
All he shows her makes him dearer :
   Evermore she seems to gaze
On that cottage growing nearer,
   Where they twain will spend their days.
O but she will love him truly !
   He shall have a cheerful home ;
She will order all things duly,
   When beneath his roof they come.
Thus her heart rejoices greatly,
   Till a gateway she discerns
With armorial bearings stately,
   And beneath the gate she turns ;
Sees a mansion more majestic
   Than all those she saw before :
Many a gallant gay domestic
   Bows before him at the door.
And they speak in gentle murmur,
   When they answer to his call,
While he treads with footstep firmer,
   Leading on from hall to hall.
And, while now she wonders blindly,
   Nor the meaning can divine,
Proudly turns he round and kindly,
   "All of this is mine and thine."
Here he lives in state and bounty,
   Lord of Burleigh, fair and free,
Not a lord in all the county
   Is so great a lord as he.
All at once the color flushes
   Her sweet face from brow to chin :
As it were with shame she blushes,
   And her spirit changed within.
Then her countenance all over
   Pale again as death did prove :
But he clasp'd her like a lover,
   And he cheer'd her soul with love.
So she strove against her weakness,
   Tho' at times her spirit sank :
Shaped her heart with woman's meekness
   To all duties of her rank :
And a gentle consort made he,
   And her gentle mind was such
That she grew a noble lady,
   And the people loved her much.
But a trouble weigh'd upon her,
   And perplex'd her, night and morn,
With the burden of an honor
   Unto which she was not born.

Faint she grew, and ever fainter,
   And she murmur'd, "O, that he
Were once more that landscape-painter,
   Which did win my heart from me !"
So she droop'd and droop'd before him,
   Fading slowly from his side :
Three fair children first she bore him,
   Then before her time she died.
Weeping, weeping late and early,
   Walking up and pacing down,
Deeply mourn'd the Lord of Burleigh,
   Burleigh-house by Stamford-town.
And he came to look upon her,
   And he look'd at her and said,
"Bring the dress and put it on her,
   That she wore when she was wed."
Then her people, softly treading,
   Bore to earth her body, drest
In the dress that she was wed in,
   That her spirit might have rest.

SIR LAUNCELOT AND QUEEN GUINEVERE.

A FRAGMENT.

LIKE souls that balance joy and pain,
With tears and smiles from heaven again
The maiden Spring upon the plain
   Came in a sun-lit fall of rain.
In crystal vapor everywhere
Blue isles of heaven laugh'd between,
And far, in forest-deeps unseen,
The topmost elmtree gather'd green
   From draughts of balmy air.

Sometimes the linnet piped his song :
Sometimes the throstle whistled strong :
Sometimes the sparhawk, wheel'd along,
Hush'd all the groves from fear of wrong :
   By grassy capes with fuller sound
In curves the yellowing river ran,
And drooping chestnut-buds began
To spread into the perfect fan,
   Above the teeming ground.

Then, in the boyhood of the year,
Sir Launcelot and Queen Guinevere
Rode thro' the coverts of the deer,
With blissful treble ringing clear.
   She seem'd a part of joyous Spring :
A gown of grass-green silk she wore,
Buckled with golden clasps before ;
A light-green tuft of plumes she bore
   Closed in a golden ring.

Now on some twisted ivy-net,
Now by some tinkling rivulet,

In mosses mixt with violet
Her cream-white mule his pastern set:
And fleeter now she skimm'd the plains
Than she whose elfin prancer springs
By night to eery warblings,
When all the glimmering moorland rings
  With jingling bridle-reins.

As she fled fast thro' sun and shade,
The happy winds upon her play'd,
Blowing the ringlet from the braid:
She look'd so lovely, as she sway'd
The rein with dainty finger-tips,
A man had given all other bliss,
And all his worldly worth for this,
To waste his whole heart in one kiss
  Upon her perfect lips.

A FAREWELL.

Flow down, cold rivulet, to the sea,
  Thy tribute wave deliver:
No more by thee my steps shall be,
  For ever and for ever.

Flow, softly flow, by lawn and lea,
  A rivulet then a river:
No where by thee my steps shall be,
  For ever and for ever.

But here will sigh thine alder tree,
  And here thine aspen shiver;
And here by thee will hum the bee,
  For ever and for ever.

A thousand suns will stream on thee,
  A thousand moons will quiver;
But not by thee my steps shall be,
  For ever and for ever.

THE BEGGAR MAID.

Her arms across her breast she laid;
  She was more fair than words can say:
Bare-footed came the beggar maid
  Before the king Cophetua.
In robe and crown the king stept down,
  To meet and greet her on her way;
"It is no wonder," said the lords,
  "She is more beautiful than day."

As shines the moon in clouded skies,
  She in her poor attire was seen:
One praised her ankles, one her eyes,
  One her dark hair and lovesome mien.
So sweet a face, such angel grace,
  In all that land had never been:
Cophetua sware a royal oath:
  "This beggar maid shall be my queen!"

THE VISION OF SIN.

I.

I had a vision when the night was late:
A youth came riding toward a palace-gate.
He rode a horse with wings, that would have flown,
But that his heavy rider kept him down.
And from the palace came a child of sin,
And took him by the curls, and led him in,
Where sat a company with heated eyes,
Expecting when a fountain should arise:
A sleepy light upon their brows and lips—
As when the sun, a crescent of eclipse,
Dreams over lake and lawn, and isles and capes—
Suffused them, sitting, lying, languid shapes,
By heaps of gourds, and skins of wine, and piles of grapes.

II.

Then methought I heard a mellow sound,
Gathering up from all the lower ground;
Narrowing in to where they sat assembled
Low voluptuous music winding trembled,
Wov'n in circles: they that heard it sigh'd,
Panted hand in hand with faces pale,
Swung themselves, and in low tones replied;
Till the fountain spouted, showering wide
Sleet of diamond-drift and pearly hail;
Then the music touch'd the gates and died;
Rose again from where it seem'd to fail,
Storm'd in orbs of song, a growing gale;
Till thronging in and in, to where they waited,
As 't were a hundred-throated nightingale,
The strong tempestuous treble throbb'd and palpitated;
Ran into its giddiest whirl of sound,
Caught the sparkles, and in circles,
Purple gauzes, golden hazes, liquid mazes,
Flung the torrent rainbow round:
Then they started from their places,
Moved with violence, changed in hue,
Caught each other with wild grimaces,

*"In robe and crown the king stept down,
To meet and greet her on her way."*

Half-invisible to the view,
Wheeling with precipitate paces
To the melody, till they flew,
Hair, and eyes, and limbs, and faces,
Twisted hard in fierce embraces,
Like to Furies, like to Graces,
Dash'd together in blinding dew:
Till, kill'd with some luxurious agony,
The nerve-dissolving melody
Flutter'd headlong from the sky.

III.

And then I look'd up toward a mountain-tract,
That girt the region with high cliff and lawn:
I saw that every morning, far withdrawn
Beyond the darkness and the cataract,
God made himself an awful rose of dawn,
Unheeded: and detaching, fold by fold,
From those still heights, and, slowly drawing near,
A vapor heavy, hueless, formless, cold,
Came floating on for many a month and year,
Unheeded: and I thought I would have spoken,
And warn'd that madman ere it grew too late:
But, as in dreams, I could not. Mine was broken,
When that cold vapor touch'd the palace gate,
And link'd again. I saw within my head
A gray and gap-tooth'd man as lean as death,
Who slowly rode across a wither'd heath,
And lighted at a ruin'd inn, and said:

IV.

"Wrinkled ostler, grim and thin!
  Here is custom come your way;
Take my brute, and lead him in,
  Stuff his ribs with mouldy hay.

"Bitter barmaid, waning fast!
  See that sheets are on my bed;
What! the flower of life is past:
  It is long before you wed.

"Slip-shod waiter, lank and sour,
  At the Dragon on the heath!
Let us have a quiet hour,
  Let us hob-and-nob with Death.

"I am old, but let me drink;
  Bring me spices, bring me wine;
I remember, when I think,
  That my youth was half divine.

"Wine is good for shrivell'd lips,
  When a blanket wraps the day,
When the rotten woodland drips,
  And the leaf is stamp'd in clay.

"Sit thee down, and have no shame,
  Cheek by jowl, and knee by knee:
What care I for any name?
  What for order or degree?

"Let me screw thee up a peg:
  Let me loose thy tongue with wine:
Callest thou that thing a leg?
  Which is thinnest? thine or mine?

"Thou shalt not be saved by works:
  Thou hast been a sinner too:
Ruin'd trunks on wither'd forks,
  Empty scarecrows, I and you!

"Fill the cup, and fill the can:
  Have a rouse before the morn:
Every moment dies a man,
  Every moment one is born.

"We are men of ruin'd blood;
  Therefore comes it we are wise.
Fish are we that love the mud,
  Rising to no fancy-flies.

"Name and fame! to fly sublime
  Thro' the courts, the camps, the schools,
Is to be the ball of Time,
  Bandied by the hands of fools.

"Friendship! — to be two in one —
  Let the canting liar pack!

Well I know, when I am gone,
  How she mouths behind my back

"Virtue! — to be good and just —
  Every heart, when sifted well,
Is a clot of warmer dust,
  Mix'd with cunning sparks of hell.

"Oh! we two as well can look
  Whited thought and cleanly life
As the priest, above his book
  Leering at his neighbor's wife.

"Fill the cup, and fill the can:
  Have a rouse before the morn:
Every moment dies a man,
  Every moment one is born.

"Drink, and let the parties rave:
  They are fill'd with idle spleen;
Rising, falling, like a wave,
  For they know not what they mean.

"He that roars for liberty
  Faster binds a tyrant's power;
And the tyrant's cruel glee
  Forces on the freer hour.

"Fill the can, and fill the cup:
  All the windy ways of men
Are but dust that rises up,
  And is lightly laid again.

"Greet her with applausive breath,
  Freedom, gayly doth she tread;
In her right a civic wreath,
  In her left a human head.

"No, I love not what is new;
  She is of an ancient house:
And I think we know the hue
  Of that cap upon her brows.

"Let her go! her thirst she slakes
  Where the bloody conduit runs:
Then her sweetest meal she makes
  On the first-born of her sons.

"Drink to lofty hopes that cool —
  Visions of a perfect State:
Drink we, last, the public fool,
  Frantic love and frantic hate.

"Chant me now some wicked stave,
  Till thy drooping courage rise,
And the glow-worm of the grave
  Glimmer in thy rheumy eyes.

"Fear not thou to loose thy tongue;
  Set thy heary fancies free;
What is loathsome to the young
  Savors well to thee and me.

"Change, reverting to the years,
  When thy nerves could understand
What there is in loving tears,
  And the warmth of hand in hand.

"Tell me tales of thy first love —
  April hopes, the fools of chance;
Till the graves begin to move,
  And the dead begin to dance.

"Fill the can, and fill the cup:
  All the windy ways of men
Are but dust that rises up,
  And is lightly laid again.

"Trooping from their mouldy dens
  The chap-fallen circle spreads:
Welcome, fellow-citizens,
  Hollow hearts and empty heads!

"You are bones, and what of that?
  Every face, however full,
Padded round with flesh and fat,
  Is but modell'd on a skull.

"Death is king, and Vivat Rex!
  Tread a measure on the stones,
Madam — if I know your sex,
  From the fashion of your bones.

"No, I cannot praise the fire
  In your eye — nor yet your lip:
All the more do I admire
  Joints of cunning workmanship.

"Lo! God's likeness — the ground-plan —
  Neither modell'd, glazed, or framed:
Buss me, thou rough sketch of man,
  Far too naked to be shamed!

"Drink to Fortune, drink to Chance,
  While we keep a little breath!
Drink to heavy Ignorance!
  Hob-and-nob with brother Death!

"Thou art mazed, the night is long,
  And the longer night is near:
What! I am not all as wrong
  As a bitter jest is dear.

"Youthful hopes, by scores, to all,
  When the locks are crisp and curl'd;
Unto me my maudlin gall
  And my mockeries of the world.

"Fill the cup, and fill the can!
  Mingle madness, mingle scorn!
Dregs of life, and lees of man:
  Yet we will not die forlorn."

        v.

The voice grew faint: there came a further change:
Once more uprose the mystic mountain-range:
Below were men and horses pierced with worms,
And slowly quickening into lower forms;
By shards and scurf of salt, and scum of dross,
Old plash of rains, and refuse patch'd with moss.
Then some one spake: "Behold! it was a crime
Of sense avenged by sense that wore with time."
Another said: "The crime of sense became
The crime of malice, and is equal blame."
And one: "He had not wholly quench'd his power;
A little grain of conscience made him sour."
At last I heard a voice upon the slope
Cry to the summit, "Is there any hope?"
To which an answer peal'd from that high land,
But in a tongue no man could understand;
And on the glimmering limit far withdrawn
God made Himself an awful rose of dawn.

Come not, when I am dead,
  To drop thy foolish tears upon my grave,
To trample round my fallen head,
  And vex the unhappy dust thou wouldst not save.
There let the wind sweep and the plover cry;
  But thou, go by.

Child, if it were thine error or thy crime
  I care no longer, being all unblest:

"Break, break, break,
On thy cold gray stones, O Sea!"

Wed whom thou wilt, but I am sick of
    Time,
And I desire to rest.
Pass on, weak heart, and leave me where
    I lie:
    Go by, go by.

THE EAGLE.

FRAGMENT.

He clasps the crag with hooked hands;
Close to the sun in lonely lands,
Ring'd with the azure world, he stands.

The wrinkled sea beneath him crawls;
He watches from his mountain walls,
And like a thunderbolt he falls.

Move eastward, happy earth, and leave
    Yon orange sunset waning slow:
From fringes of the faded eve,
    O, happy planet, eastward go;
Till over thy dark shoulder glow
    Thy silver sister-world, and rise
To glass herself in dewy eyes
That watch me from the glen below.

Ah, bear me with thee, smoothly borne,
    Dip forward under starry light,
And move me to my marriage-morn,
    And round again to happy night.

Break, break, break,
    On thy cold gray stones, O Sea!
And I would that my tongue could utter
    The thoughts that arise in me.

O well for the fisherman's boy,
    That he shouts with his sister at play!
O well for the sailor lad,
    That he sings in his boat on the bay!

And the stately ships go on
    To their haven under the hill;
But O for the touch of a vanish'd hand,
    And the sound of a voice that is still!

Break, break, break,
    At the foot of thy crags, O Sea!
But the tender grace of a day that is dead
    Will never come back to me.

THE POET'S SONG.

The rain had fallen, the Poet arose,
    He pass'd by the town and out of the
        street,
A light wind blew from the gates of the
        sun,
    And waves of shadow went over the
        wheat,
And he sat him down in a lonely place,
    And chanted a melody loud and sweet,

That made the wild-swan pause in her
    cloud,
And the lark drop down at his feet.

The swallow stopt as he hunted the bee,
    The snake slipt under a spray,
The wild hawk stood with the down on
    ' his beak,
    And stared, with his foot on the prey,
And the nightingale thought, "I have
    sung many songs,
    But never a one so gay,
For he sings of what the world will be
    When the years have died away."

My life is full of weary days,
    But good things have not kept aloof,
Nor wandered into other ways:
, I have not lack'd thy mild reproof,
    Nor golden largess of thy praise.

And now shake hands across the brink
    Of that deep grave to which I go:
Shake hands once more: I cannot sink
    So far — far down, but I shall know
Thy voice, and answer from below.

THE CAPTAIN.

A LEGEND OF THE NAVY.

HE that only rules by terror
    Doeth grievous wrong.
Deep as Hell I count his error,
    Let him hear my song.
Brave the Captain was: the seamen
    Made a gallant crew,
Gallant sons of English freemen,
    Sailors bold and true.
But they hated his oppression,
    Stern he was and rash;
So for every light transgression
    Doom'd them to the lash.
Day by day more harsh and cruel
    Seem'd the Captain's mood.
Secret wrath like smother'd fuel
    Burnt in each man's blood.
Yet he hoped to purchase glory,
    Hoped to make the name
Of his vessel great in story,
    Wheresoe'er he came.
So they past by capes and islands,
    Many a harbor-mouth,
Sailing under palmy highlands
    Far within the South.

On a day when they were going
    O'er the lone expanse,
In the north, her canvas flowing,
    Rose a ship of France.
Then the Captain's color heighten'd,
    Joyful came his speech:
But a cloudy gladness lighten'd
    In the eyes of each.
"Chase," he said: the ship flew forward,
    And the wind did blow;
Stately, lightly, went she Norward,
    Till she near'd the foe.
Then they look'd at him they hated,
    Had what they desired:
Mute with folded arms they waited —
    Not a gun was fired.
But they heard the foeman's thunder
    Roaring out their doom;
All the air was torn in sunder,
    Crashing went the boom,
Spars were splinter'd, decks were shatter'd,
    Bullets fell like rain;
Over mast and deck were scatter'd
    Blood and brains of men.
Spars were splinter'd; decks were broken:
    Every mother's son —
Down they dropt — no word was spoken —
    Each beside his gun.
On the decks as they were lying,
    Were their faces grim.
In their blood, as they lay dying,
    Did they smile on him.
Those, in whom he had reliance
    For his noble name,
With one smile of still defiance
    Sold him unto shame.
Shame and wrath his heart confounded,
    Pale he turn'd and red,
Till himself was deadly wounded
    Falling on the dead.
Dismal error! fearful slaughter!
    Years have wander'd by,
Side by side beneath the water
    Crew and Captain lie;
There the sunlit ocean tosses
    O'er them mouldering,
And the lonely seabird crosses
    With one waft of the wing.

THREE SONNETS TO A COQUETTE.

I.

CARESS'D or chidden by the dainty hand,
    And singing airy trifles this or that,
Light Hope at Beauty's call would perch
    and stand,

And run thro' every change of sharp and flat;
And Fancy came and at her pillow sat,
When sleep had bound her in his rosy band,
And chased away the still-recurring gnat,
And woke her with a lay from fairy land.
But now they live with Beauty less and less,
For Hope is other Hope and wanders far,
Nor cares to lisp in love's delicious creeds;
And Fancy watches in the wilderness,
Poor Fancy sadder than a single star,
That sets at twilight in a land of reeds.

II.

The form, the form alone is eloquent!
A nobler yearning never broke her rest
Than but to dance and sing, be gayly drest,
And win all eyes with all accomplishment:
Yet in the waltzing-circle as we went,
My fancy made me for a moment blest
To find my heart so near the beauteous breast
That once had power to rob it of content.
A moment came the tenderness of tears,
The phantom of a wish that once could move,
A ghost of passion that no smiles restore —
For ah! the slight coquette, she cannot love,
And if you kiss'd her feet a thousand years,
She still would take the praise, and care no more.

III.

Wan Sculptor weepest thou to take the cast
Of those dead lineaments that near thee lie?
O sorrowest thou, pale Painter, for the past,
In painting some dead friend from memory?
Weep on: beyond his object Love can last:
His object lives: more cause to weep have I:
My tears, no tears of love, are flowing fast,
No tears of love, but tears that Love can die.

I pledge her not in any cheerful cup,
Nor care to sit beside her where she sits —
Ah pity — hint it not in human tones,
But breathe it into earth and close it up
With secret death for ever, in the pits
Which some green Christmas crams with weary bones.

SONG.

LADY, let the rolling drums
Beat to battle where thy warrior stands:
Now thy face across his fancy comes,
And gives the battle to his hands.

Lady, let the trumpets blow,
Clasp thy little babes about thy knee:
Now their warrior father meets the foe,
And strikes him dead for thine and thee.

SONG.

HOME they brought him slain with spears.
They brought him home at even-fall:
All alone she sits and hears
Echoes in his empty hall,
Sounding on the morrow.

The Sun peep'd in from open field,
The boy began to leap and prance,
Rode upon his father's lance,
Beat upon his father's shield —
"O hush, my joy, my sorrow."

ON A MOURNER.

I.

NATURE, so far as in her lies,
Imitates God, and turns her face
To every land beneath the skies,
Counts nothing that she meets with base,
But lives and loves in every place;

II.

Fills out the homely quickset-screens,
And makes the purple lilac ripe,
Steps from her airy hill, and greens
The swamp, where hums the dropping snipe,
With moss and braided marish-pipe;

III.

And on thy heart a finger lays,
Saying, "Beat quicker, for the time
Is pleasant, and the woods and ways

Are pleasant, and the beech and lime
 Put forth and feel a gladder clime."

IV.

And murmurs of a deeper voice,
 Going before to some far shrine,
Teach that sick heart the stronger choice,
 Till all thy life one way incline
 With one wide will that closes thine.

V.

And when the zoning eve has died
 Where yon dark valleys wind forlorn,
Come Hope and Memory, spouse and bride,
 From out the borders of the morn,
 With that fair child betwixt them born.

VI.

And when no mortal motion jars
 The blackness round the tombing sod,
Thro' silence and the trembling stars
 Comes Faith from tracts no feet have trod,
 And Virtue, like a household god

VII.

Promising empire; such as those
 That once at dead of night did greet
Troy's wandering prince, so that he rose
 With sacrifice, while all the fleet
 Had rest by stony hills of Crete.

MISCELLANEOUS.

(PUBLISHED IN 1869.)

NORTHERN FARMER.

NEW STYLE.

1.

Dosn't thou 'ear my 'erse's legs, as they
 canters awaäy?
Proputty, proputty, proputty — that 's
 what I 'ears 'em saäy.
Proputty, proputty, proputty — Sam,
 thou 's an ass for thy paaïns:
Theer 's moor sense i' one o' 'is legs nor
 in all thy braaïns.

II.

Woä — theer 's a craw to pluck wi' tha,
 Sam : yon 's parson's 'ouse —
Dosn't thou knaw that a man mun be
 eäther a man or a mouse?
Time to think on it then; for thou 'll be
 twenty to weeäk.*
Proputty, proputty — woä then woä —
 let ma 'ear mysén speäk.

III.

Me an' thy muther, Sammy, 'as beän
 a-talkin' o' thee;
Thou 's been talkin' to muther, an' she
 beän a tellin' it me.

 * This week.

Thou 'll not marry for munny — thou 's
 sweet upo' parson's lass —
Noä — thou 'll marry for luvv — an' we
 boäth on us thinks tha an ass.

IV.

Seeä'd her to-daäy goä by — Saäint's-
 daäy — they was ringing the bells.
She 's a beauty thou thinks — an' soä is
 scoors o' gells,
Them as 'as munny an' all — wot 's a
 beauty? — the flower as blaws.
But proputty, proputty sticks, an' pro-
 putty, proputty graws.

V.

Do'ant be stunt :* taäke time : I knaws
 what maäkes tha sa mad.
Warn't I craäzed fur the lasses mysén
 when I wur a lad?
But I knaw'd a Quaäker feller as often
 'as towd ma this :
"Doänt thou marry for munny, but goä
 wheer munny is!"

VI.

An' I went wheer munny war : an' thy
 mother coom to 'and,
Wi' lots o' munny laaïd by, an' a nicetish
 bit o' land.

 * Obstinate.

Maäybe she warn't a beauty : — I niver
  giv it a thowt —
But warn't she as good to cuddle an' kiss
  as a lass as 'ant nowt ?

VII.

Parson's lass 'ant nowt, an' she weänt 'a
  nowt when 'e's deäd,
Mun be a guvness, lad, or summut, and
  addle * her breäd :
Why ? fur 'e's nobbut a curate, an' weänt
  nivir git naw 'igher ;
An' 'e maäde the bed as 'e ligs on afoor
  'e coom'd to the shire.

VIII.

And thin 'e coom'd to the parish wi' lots
  o' 'Varsity debt,
Stook to his taäil they did, an' 'e 'ant
  got shut on 'em yet.
An' 'e ligs on 'is back i' the grip, wi'
  noän to lend 'im a shove,
Woorse nor a far-welter'd † yowe : fur,
  Sammy, 'e married fur luvv.

IX.

Luvv ? what's luvv ? thou can luvv thy
  lass an' 'er munny too,
Maakin' 'em goä togither as they 've good
  right to do.
Could'n I luvv thy muther by cause o'
  'er munny laaïd by ?
Naäy — fur I luvv'd 'er a vast sight moor
  fur it : reäson why.

X.

Ay an' thy muther says thou wants to
  marry the lass,
Cooms of a gentleman burn : an' we boäth
  on us thinks tha an ass.
Woä then, proputty, wiltha ? — an ass as
  near as mays nowt — ‡
Woä then, wiltha ? dangtha ! — the bees
  is as fell as owt. §

XI.

Breäk me a bit o' the esh for his 'eäd,
  lad, out o' the fence !
Gentleman burn ! what's gentleman
  burn ? is it shillins an' pence ?
Proputty, proputty's ivrything 'ere, an',
  Sammy, I 'm blest
If it is n't the saäme oop yonder, fur
  them as 'as it 's the best.

* Earn.
† Or fow-welter'd, — said of a sheep lying on its back
in the furrow.
‡ Makes nothing.
§ The flies are as fierce as anything.

XII.

Tis'n them as 'as munny as breäks into
  'ouses an' steäls,
Them as 'as coäts to their backs an' taäkes
  their regular meäls.
Noä, but it 's them as niver knaws wheer
  a meäl 's to be 'ad.
Taäke my word for it, Sammy, the poor
  in a loomp is bad.

XIII.

Them or thir feythers, tha sees, mun 'a
  beän a laäzy lot,
Fur work mun 'a gone to the gittin'
  whiniver munny was got.
Feyther 'ad ammost nowt ; leaästwaays
  'is munny was 'id.
But 'e tued an' moil'd 'issén deäd, an' 'e
  died a good un, 'e did.

XIV.

Loook thou theer wheer Wrigglesby beck
  comes out by the 'ill !
Feyther run up to the farm, an' I runs
  up to the mill ;
An' I 'll run up to the brig, an' that
  thou 'll live to see ;
And if thou marries a good un I 'll leäve
  the land to thee.

XV.

Thim's my noätions, Sammy, wheerby
  I means to stick ;
But if thou marries a bad un, I 'll leäve
  the land to Dick. —
Coom oop, proputty, proputty — that's
  what I 'ears 'im saäy —
Proputty, proputty, proputty — canter
  an' canter awaäy.

THE GOLDEN SUPPER.

[This poem is founded upon a story in Boccaccio.
A young lover, Julian, whose cousin and foster-sister,
Camilla, has been wedded to his friend and rival, Lionel,
endeavors to narrate the story of his own love for her
and the strange sequel of it. He speaks of having been
haunted in delirium by visions and the sound of bells,
sometimes tolling for a funeral, and at last ringing for a
marriage ; but he breaks away, overcome, as he ap-
proaches the Event, and a witness to it completes the
tale.]

HE flies the event : he leaves the event
  to me :
Poor Julian — how he rush'd away ; the
  bells,
Those marriage-bells, echoing in ear and
  heart —

But cast a parting glance at me, you saw,
As who should say "continue." Well, he had
One golden hour — of triumph shall I say?
Solace at least — before he left his home.

   Would you had seen him in that hour of his!
He moved thro' all of it majestically —
Restrain'd himself quite to the close — but now —

   Whether they *were* his lady's marriage-bells,
Or prophets of them in his fantasy,
I never ask'd: but Lionel and the girl
Were wedded, and our Julian came again
Back to his mother's house among the pines.
But these, their gloom, the mountains and the Bay,
The whole land weigh'd him down as Ætna does
The Giant of Mythology: he would go,
Would leave the land for ever, and had gone
Surely, but for a whisper "Go not yet,"
Some warning, and divinely as it seem'd
By that which follow'd — but of this I deem
As of the visions that he told — the event
Glanced back upon them in his after life,
And partly made them — tho' he knew it not.

   And thus he stay'd and would not look at her —
No, not for months: but, when the eleventh moon
After their marriage lit the lover's Bay,
Heard yet once more the tolling bell, and said,
Would you could toll me out of life, but found —
All softly as his mother broke it to him —
A crueller reason than a crazy ear,
For that low knell tolling his lady dead —
Dead — and had lain three days without a pulse:
All that look'd on her had pronounced her dead.
And so they bore her (for in Julian's land
They never nail a dumb head up in elm),
Bore her free-faced to the free airs of heaven,
And laid her in the vault of her own kin.

What did he then? not die: he is here and hale —
Not plunge headforemost from the mountain there,
And leave the name of Lover's Leap: not he:
He knew the meaning of the whisper now,
Thought that he knew it. "This, I stay'd for this;
O love, I have not seen you for so long.
Now, now, will I go down into the grave,
I will be all alone with all I love,
And kiss her on the lips. She is his no more:
The dead returns to me, and I go down
To kiss the dead."

        The fancy stirr'd him so
He rose and went, and entering the dim vault,
And, making there a sudden light, beheld
All round about him that which all will be.
The light was but a flash, and went again.
Then at the far end of the vault he saw
His lady with the moonlight on her face;
Her breast as in a shadow-prison, bars
Of black and bands of silver, which the moon
Struck from an open grating overhead
High in the wall, and all the rest of her
Drown'd in the gloom and horror of the vault.

   "It was my wish," he said, "to pass, to sleep,
To rest, to be with her — till the great day
Peal'd on us with that music which rights all,
And raised us hand in hand." And kneeling there
Down in the dreadful dust that once was man,
Dust, as he said, that once was loving hearts,
Hearts that had beat with such a love as mine —
Not such as mine, no, nor for such as her —
He softly put his arm about her neck
And kiss'd her more than once, till helpless death
And silence made him bold — nay, but I wrong him,
He reverenced his dear lady even in death;
But, placing his true hand upon her heart,
"O, you warm heart," he moan'd, "not even death

Can chill you all at once": then start-
ing, thought
His dreams had come again. "Do I
wake or sleep?
Or am I made immortal, or my love
Mortal once more?" It beat — the heart
— it beat:
Faint — but it beat: at which his own
began
To pulse with such a vehemence that it
drown'd
The feebler motion underneath his hand.
But when at last his doubts were satisfied,
He raised her softly from the sepulchre,
And, wrapping her all over with the cloak
He came in, and now striding fast, and now
Sitting awhile to rest, but evermore
Holding his golden burden in his arms,
So bore her thro' the solitary land
Back to the mother's house where she
was born.

There the good mother's kindly min-
istering,
With half a night's appliances, recall'd
Her fluttering life: she rais'd an eye that
ask'd
"Where?" till the things familiar to
her youth
Had made a silent answer: then she spoke,
"Here! and how came I here?" and
learning it
(They told her somewhat rashly as I think)
At once began to wander and to wail,
"Ay, but you know that you must give
me back:
Send! bid him come"; but Lionel was
away —
Stung by his loss had vanish'd, none
knew where.
"He casts me out," she wept, "and
goes" — a wail
That seeming something, yet was nothing,
born
Not from believing mind, but shatter'd
nerve,
Yet haunting Julian, as her own reproof
At some precipitance in her burial.
Then, when her own true spirit had re-
turn'd,
"O yes, and you," she said, "and none
but you.
For you have given me life and love again,
And none but you yourself shall tell him
of it,
And you shall give me back when he
returns."

"Stay then a little," answer'd Julian,
"here,
And keep yourself, none knowing, to
yourself;
And I will do your will. I may not stay,
No, not an hour; but send me notice of
him
When he returns, and then will I return,
And I will make a solemn offering of you
To him you love." And faintly she replied,
"And I will do *your* will, and none
shall know."

Not know? with such a secret to be
known.
But all their house was old and loved
them both,
And all the house had known the loves
of both;
Had died almost to serve them any way,
And all the land was waste and solitary:
And then he rode away; but after this,
An hour or two, Camilla's travail came
Upon her, and that day a boy was born,
Heir of his face and land, to Lionel.

And thus our lonely lover rode away,
And pausing at a hostel in a marsh,
There fever seized upon him: myself
was then
Travelling that land, and meant to rest
an hour;
And sitting down to such a base repast,
It makes me angry yet to speak of it —
I heard a groaning overhead, and climb'd
The moulder'd stairs (for everything was
vile)
And in a loft, with none to wait on him,
Found, as it seem'd, a skeleton alone,
Raving of dead men's dust and beating
hearts.

A dismal hostel in a dismal land,
A flat malarian world of reed and rush!
But there from fever and my care of him
Sprang up a friendship that may help us
yet.
For while we roam'd along the dreary
coast,
And waited for her message, piece by piece
I learnt the drearier story of his life;
And, tho' he loved and honor'd Lionel,
Found that the sudden wail his lady made
Dwelt in his fancy: did he know her worth,
Her beauty even? should he not be taught,
Ev'n by the price that others set upon it,
The value of that jewel he had to guard?

Suddenly came her notice and we past,
I with our lover to his native Bay.

   This love is of the brain, the mind,
     the soul :
That makes the sequel pure; tho' some of us
Beginning at the sequel know no more.
Not such am I : and yet I say, the bird
That will not hear my call, however sweet,
But if my neighbor whistle answers
     him —
What matter? there are others in the wood.
Yet when I saw her (and I thought him
     crazed,
Tho' not with such a craziness as needs
A cell and keeper), those dark eyes of
     hers —
Oh! such dark eyes! and not her eyes
     alone,
But all from these to where she touch'd
     on earth,
For such a craziness as Julian's seem'd
No less than one divine apology.

   So sweetly and so modestly she came
To greet us, her young hero in her arms!
"Kiss him," she said. "You gave me
     life again.
He, but for you, had never seen it once.
His other father you! Kiss him, and then
Forgive him, if his name be Julian too."

   Talk of lost hopes and broken heart!
     his own
Sent such a flame into his face, I knew
Some sudden vivid pleasure hit him there.

   But he was all the more resolved to go,
And sent at once to Lionel, praying him
By that great love they both had borne
     the dead,
To come and revel for one hour with him
Before he left the land for evermore ;
And then to friends — they were not
     many — who lived
Scatteringly about that lonely land of his,
And bade them to a banquet of farewells.

   And Julian made a solemn feast : I never
Sat at a costlier ; for all round his hall
From column on to column, as in a wood,
Not such as here — an equatorial one,
Great garlands swung and blossom'd ;
     and beneath,
Heirlooms, and ancient miracles of Art,
Chalice and salver, wines that, Heaven
     knows when,
Had suck'd the fire of some forgotten sun
And kept it thro' a hundred years of
     gloom,
Yet glowing in a heart of ruby — cups
Where nymph and god ran ever round
     in gold —
Others of glass as costly — some with gems
Movable and resettable at will,
And trebling all the rest in value — Ah
     heavens !
Why need I tell you all ? — suffice to say
That whatsoever such a house as his,
And his was old, has in it rare or fair
Was brought before the guest : and they,
     the guests,
Wonder'd at some strange light in Julian's
     eyes
(I told you that he had his golden hour),
And such a feast, ill-suited as it seem'd
To such a time, to Lionel's loss and his,
And that resolved self-exile from a land
He never would revisit, such a feast
So rich, so strange, and stranger ev'n
     than rich,
But rich as for the nuptials of a king.

   And stranger yet, at one end of the hall
Two great funereal curtains, looping down,
Parted a little ere they met the floor,
About a picture of his lady, taken
Some years before, and falling hid the
     frame.
And just above the parting was a lamp :
So the sweet figure folded round with night
Seem'd stepping out of darkness with a
     smile.

   Well then — our solemn feast — we ate
     and drank,
And might — the wines being of such
     nobleness —
Have jested also, but for Julian's eyes,
And something weird and wild about it
     all :
What was it ? for our lover seldom spoke,
Scarce touch'd the meats ; but ever and
     anon
A priceless goblet with a priceless wine
Arising, show'd he drank beyond his use ;
And when the feast was near an end, he
     said :

   "There is a custom in the Orient,
     friends —
I read of it in Persia — when a man
Will honor those who feast with him, he
     brings

And shows them whatsoever he accounts
Of all his treasures the most beautiful,
Gold, jewels, arms, whatever it may be.
This custom —"

    Pausing here a moment, all
The guests broke in upon him with meeting hands
And cries about the banquet:— "Beautiful!
Who could desire more beauty at a feast?"

 The lover answer'd, "There is more than one
Here sitting who desires it. Laud me not
Before my time, but hear me to the close.
This custom steps yet further when the guest
Is loved and honor'd to the uttermost.
For after he has shown him gems or gold,
He brings and sets before him in rich guise
That which is thrice as beautiful as these,
The beauty that is dearest to his heart —
'O my heart's lord, would I could show you,' he says,
'Ev'n my heart too.' And I propose to-night
To show you what is dearest to my heart,
And my heart too.

  "But solve me first a doubt.
I knew a man, nor many years ago;
He had a faithful servant, one who loved
His master more than all on earth beside.
He falling sick, and seeming close on death,
His master would not wait until he died,
But bade his menials bear him from the door,
And leave him in the public way to die.
I knew another, not so long ago,
Who found the dying servant, took him home,
And fed, and cherish'd him, and saved his life.
I ask you now, should this first master claim
His service, whom does it belong to? him
Who thrust him out, or him who saved his life?"

 This question, so flung down before the guests,
And balanced either way by each, at length
When some were doubtful how the law would hold,
Was handed over by consent of all
To one who had not spoken, Lionel.

Fair speech was his, and delicate of phrase.
And he beginning languidly — his loss
Weigh'd on him yet — but warming as he went,
Glanced at the point of law, to pass it by,
Affirming that as long as either lived,
By all the laws of love and gratefulness,
The service of the one so saved was due
All to the saver — adding, with a smile,
The first for many weeks — a semi-smile
As at a strong conclusion — "body and soul
And life and limbs, all his to work his will."

 Then Julian made a secret sign to me
To bring Camilla down before them all.
And crossing her own picture as she came,
And looking as much lovelier as herself
Is lovelier than all others — on her head
A diamond circlet, and from under this
A veil, that seem'd no more than gilded air,
Flying by each fine ear, an Eastern gauze
With seeds of gold — so, with that grace of hers,
Slow-moving as a wave against the wind,
That flings a mist behind it in the sun —
And bearing high in arms the mighty babe,
The younger Julian, who himself was crown'd
With roses, none so rosy as himself —
And over all her babe and her the jewels
Of many generations of his house
Sparkled and flash'd, for he had decked them out
As for a solemn sacrifice of love —
So she came in: — I am long in telling it.
I never yet beheld a thing so strange,
Sad, sweet, and strange together — floated in, —
While all the guests in mute amazement rose, —
And slowly pacing to the middle hall,
Before the board, there paused and stood, her breast
Hard-heaving, and her eyes upon her feet,
Not daring yet to glance at Lionel.
But him she carried, him nor lights nor feast
Dazed or amazed, nor eyes of men; who cared
Only to use his own, and staring wide
And hungering for the gilt and jewell'd world

About him, look'd, as he is like to prove,
When Julian goes, the lord of all he saw.

"My guests," said Julian: "you are honor'd now
Ev'n to the uttermost: in her behold
Of all my treasures the most beautiful,
Of all things upon earth the dearest to me."
Then waving us a sign to seat ourselves,
Led his dear lady to a chair of state.
And I, by Lionel sitting, saw his face
Fire, and dead ashes and all fire again
Thrice in a second, felt him tremble too,
And heard him muttering, "So like, so like;
She never had a sister. I knew none.
Some cousin of his and hers — O God, so like!"
And then he suddenly ask'd her if she were.
She shook, and cast her eyes down, and was dumb.
And then some other question'd if she came
From foreign lands, and still she did not speak.
Another, if the boy were hers: but she
To all their queries answer'd not a word,
Which made the amazement more, till one of them
Said, shuddering, "Her spectre!" But his friend
Replied, in half a whisper, "Not at least
The spectre that will speak if spoken to.
Terrible pity, if one so beautiful
Prove, as I almost dread to find her, dumb!"

But Julian, sitting by her, answer'd all:
"She is but dumb, because in her you see
That faithful servant whom we spoke about,
Obedient to her second master now;
Which will not last. I have here to-night a guest
So bound to me by common love and loss —
What! shall I bind him more? in his behalf,
Shall I exceed the Persian, giving him
That which of all things is the dearest to me,
Not only showing? and he himself pronounced
That my rich gift is wholly mine to give.

"Now all be dumb, and promise all of you
Not to break in on what I say by word
Or whisper, while I show you all my heart."
And then began the story of his love
As here to-day, but not so wordily —
The passionate moment would not suffer that —
Past thro' his visions to the burial; thence
Down to this last strange hour in his own hall;
And then rose up, and with him all his guests
Once more as by enchantment; all but he,
Lionel, who fain had risen, but fell again,
And sat as if in chains — to whom he said:

"Take my free gift, my cousin, for your wife;
And were it only for the giver's sake,
And tho' she seem so like the one you lost,
Yet cast her not away so suddenly,
Lest there be none left here to bring her back:
I leave this land for ever." Here he ceased.

Then taking his dear lady by one hand,
And bearing on one arm the noble babe,
He slowly brought them both to Lionel.
And there the widower husband and dead wife
Rush'd each at each with a cry, that rather seem'd
For some new death than for a life renew'd;
At this the very babe began to wail;
At once they turn'd, and caught and brought him in
To their charm'd circle, and, half-killing him
With kisses, round him closed and claspt again.
But Lionel, when at last he freed himself
From wife and child, and lifted up a face
All over glowing with the sun of life,
And love, and boundless thanks — the sight of this
So frighted our good friend, that turning to me
And saying, "It is over: let us go" —
There were our horses ready at the doors —
We bade them no farewell, but mounting these
He past for ever from his native land;
And I with him, my Julian, back to mine.

THE VICTIM.

I.

A PLAGUE upon the people fell,
 A famine after laid them low,
Then thorpe and byre arose in fire,
 For on them brake the sudden foe;
So thick they died the people cried
 "The Gods are moved against the land."
The Priest in horror about his altar
 To Thor and Odin lifted a hand:
  "Help us from famine
  And plague and strife!
  What would you have of us?
  Human life?
  Were it our nearest,
  Were it our dearest,
  (Answer, O answer)
  We give you his life."

II.

But still the foeman spoil'd and burn'd,
 And cattle died, and deer in wood,
And bird in air, and fishes turn'd
 And whiten'd all the rolling flood;
And dead men lay all over the way,
 Or down in a furrow scathed with flame:
And ever and aye the Priesthood moan'd
 Till at last it seem'd that an answer came:
  "The King is happy
  In child and wife;
  Take you his dearest,
  Give us a life."

III.

The Priest went out by heath and hill;
 The King was hunting in the wild;
They found the mother sitting still;
 She cast her arms about the child.
The child was only eight summers old,
 His beauty still with his years increased,
His face was ruddy, his hair was gold,
 He seem'd a victim due to the priest.
  The Priest beheld him,
  And cried with joy,
  "The Gods have answer'd:
  We give them the boy."

IV.

The King return'd from out the wild,
 He bore but little game in hand;
The mother said "They have taken the child
 To spill his blood and heal the land:

The land is sick, the people diseased,
 And blight and famine on all the lea:
The holy Gods, they must be appeased,
 So I pray you tell the truth to me.
  They have taken our son,
  They will have his life.
  Is *he* your dearest?
  Or I, the wife?"

V.

The King bent low, with hand on brow,
 He stay'd his arms upon his knee:
"O wife, what use to answer now?
 For now the Priest has judged for me."
The King was shaken with holy fear:
 "The Gods," he said, "would have chosen well;
Yet both are near, and both are dear,
 And which the dearest I cannot tell!"
  But the Priest was happy,
  His victim won:
  "We have his dearest,
  His only son!"

VI.

The rites prepared, the victim bared,
 The knife uprising toward the blow,
To the altar-stone she sprang alone,
 "Me, not my darling, no!"
He caught her away with a sudden cry;
 Suddenly from him brake his wife,
And shrieking "*I* am his dearest, I—
 I am his dearest!" rush'd on the knife.
  And the Priest was happy,
  "O, Father Odin,
  We give you a life.
  Which was his nearest?
  Who was his dearest?
  The Gods have answer'd;
  We give them the wife!"

WAGES.

GLORY of warrior, glory of orator, glory of song,
 Paid with a voice flying by to be lost on an endless sea —
Glory of Virtue, to fight, to struggle, to right the wrong —
 Nay, but she aim'd not at glory, no lover of glory she:
Give her the glory of going on, and still to be.
The wages of sin is death: if the wages of Virtue be dust,

Would she have heart to endure for
  the life of the worm and the fly?
She desires no isles of the blest, no quiet
  seats of the just,
To rest in a golden grove, or to bask
  in a summer sky:
Give her the wages of going on, and not
  to die.

THE HIGHER PANTHEISM.

The sun, the moon, the stars, the seas,
  the hills and the plains —
Are not these, O Soul, the Vision of Him
  who reigns?

Is not the Vision He? tho' He be not
  that which He seems?
Dreams are true while they last, and do
  we not live in dreams?

Earth, these solid stars, this weight of
  body and limb,
Are they not sign and symbol of thy division from Him?

Dark is the world to thee: thyself art the
  reason why;
For is He not all but thou, that hast
  power to feel "I am I"?

Glory about thee, without thee; and thou
  fulfillest thy doom,
Making Him broken gleams, and a stifled
  splendor and gloom.

Speak to Him thou for He hears, and
  Spirit with Spirit can meet —
Closer is He than breathing, and nearer
  than hands and feet.

God is law, say the wise; O Soul, and
  let us rejoice,
For if He thunder by law the thunder is
  yet His voice.

Law is God, say some: no God at all,
  says the fool;
For all we have power to see is a straight
  staff bent in a pool;

And the ear of man cannot hear, and the
  eye of man cannot see;
But if we could see and hear, this Vision —
  were it not He?

Flower in the crannied wall,
I pluck you out of the crannies; —
Hold you here, root and all, in my hand,
Little flower — but if I could understand
What you are, root and all, and all in all,
I should know what God and man is.

LUCRETIUS.

Lucilia, wedded to Lucretius, found
Her master cold; for when the morning
  flush
Of passion and the first embrace had died
Between them, tho' he loved her none the
  less,
Yet often when the woman heard his foot
Return from pacings in the field, and ran
To greet him with a kiss, the master took
Small notice, or austerely, for — his mind
Half buried in some weightier argument,
Or fancy-borne perhaps upon the rise
And long roll of the Hexameter — he past
To turn and ponder those three hundred
  scrolls
Left by the Teacher whom he held divine.
She brook'd it not; but wrathful, petulant,
Dreaming some rival, sought and found
  a witch
Who brew'd the philtre which had power,
  they said,
To lead an errant passion home again.
And this, at times, she mingled with his
  drink,
And this destroy'd him; for the wicked
  broth
Confused the chemic labor of the blood,
And tickling the brute brain within the
  man's
Made havoc among those tender cells,
  and check'd
His power to shape: he loathed himself;
  and once
After a tempest woke upon a morn
That mock'd him with returning calm,
  and cried;

"Storm in the night! for thrice I heard
  the rain
Rushing; and once the flash of a thunderbolt —
Methought I never saw so fierce a fork —
Struck out the streaming mountain-side,
  and show'd

A riotous confluence of watercourses
Blanching and billowing in a hollow of it,
Where all but yester-eve was dusty-dry.

"Storm, and what dreams, ye holy
    Gods, what dreams!
For thrice I waken'd after dreams. Per-
    chance
We do but recollect the dreams that come
Just ere the waking: terrible! for it
    seem'd
A void was made in Nature; all her bonds
Crack'd; and I saw the flaring atom-
    streams
And torrents of her myriad universe,
Ruining along the illimitable inane,
Fly on to clash together again, and make
Another and another frame of things
For ever: that was mine, my dream, I
    knew it —
Of and belonging to me, as the dog
With inward yelp and restless forefoot
    plies
His function of the woodland: but the
    next!
I thought that all the blood by Sylla shed
Came driving rainlike down again on
    earth,
And where it dash'd the reddening
    meadow, sprang
No dragon warriors from Cadmean teeth,
For these I thought my dream would
    show to me,
But girls, Hetairai, curious in their art,
Hired animalisms, vile as those that made
The mulberry-faced Dictator's orgies
    worse
Than aught they fable of the quiet Gods.
And hands they mixt, and yell'd and
    round me drove
In narrowing circles till I yell'd again
Half-suffocated, and sprang up, and
    saw —
Was it the first beam of my latest day?

"Then, then, from utter gloom stood
    out the breasts,
The breasts of Helen, and hoveringly a
    sword
Now over and now under, now direct,
Pointed itself to pierce, but sank down
    shamed
At all that beauty; and as I stared, a
    fire,
The fire that left a roofless Ilion,
Shot out of them, and scorch'd me that
    I woke.

"Is this thy vengeance, holy Venus,
    thine,
Because I would not one of thine own
    doves,
Not ev'n a rose, were offer'd to thee? thine,
Forgetful how my rich prooemion makes
Thy glory fly along the Italian field,
In lays that will outlast thy Deity?

"Deity? nay, thy worshippers. My
    tongue
Trips, or I speak profanely. Which of
    these
Angers thee most, or angers thee at all?
Not if thou be'st of those who, far aloof
From envy, hate and pity, and spite and
    scorn,
Live the great life which all our greatest
    fain
Would follow, centred in eternal calm.

"Nay, if thou canst, O Goddess, like
    ourselves
Touch, and be touch'd, then would I cry
    to thee
To kiss thy Mavors, roll thy tender arms
Round him, and keep him from the lust
    of blood
That makes a steaming slaughter-house
    of Rome.

"Ay, but I meant not thee; I meant
    not her,
Whom all the pines of Ida shook to see
Slide from that quiet heaven of hers, and
    tempt
The Trojan, while his neat-herds were
    abroad;
Nor her that o'er her wounded hunter
    wept
Her Deity false in human-amorous tears;
Nor whom her beardless apple-arbiter
Decided fairest. Rather, O ye Gods,
Poet-like, as the great Sicilian called
Calliope to grace his golden verse —
Ay, and this Kypris also — did I take
That popular name of thine to shadow forth
The all-generating powers and genial heat
Of Nature, when she strikes thro' the
    thick blood
Of cattle, and light is large, and lambs
    are glad
Nosing the mother's udder, and the bird
Makes his heart voice amid the blaze of
    flowers:
Which things appear the work of mighty
    Gods.

"The Gods! and if I go *my* work is left
Unfinish'd — *if* I go. The Gods, who haunt
The lucid interspace of world and world,
Where never creeps a cloud, or moves a wind,
Nor ever falls the least white star of snow,
Nor ever lowest roll of thunder moans,
Nor sound of human sorrow mounts to mar
Their sacred everlasting calm! and such,
Not all so fine, nor so divine a calm,
Not such, nor all unlike it, man may gain
Letting his own life go. The Gods, the Gods!
If all be atoms, how then should the Gods
Being atomic not be dissoluble,
Not follow the great law? My master held
That Gods there are, for all men so believe.
I prest my footsteps into his, and meant
Surely to lead my Memmius in a train
Of flowery clauses onward to the proof
That Gods there are, and deathless.
 Meant? I meant?
I have forgotten what I meant: my mind
Stumbles, and all my faculties are lamed.

"Look where another of our Gods, the Sun,
Apollo, Delius, or of older use
All-seeing Hyperion — what you will —
Has mounted yonder; since he never sware,
Except his wrath were wreak'd on wretched man,
That he would only shine among the dead
Hereafter; tales! for never yet on earth
Could dead flesh creep, or bits of roasting ox
Moan round the spit — nor knows he what he sees;
King of the East altho' he seem, and girt
With song and flame and fragrance, slowly lifts
His golden feet on those empurpled stairs
That climb into the windy halls of heaven:
And here he glances on an eye new-born,
And gets for greeting but a wail of pain;
And here he stays upon a freezing orb
That fain would gaze upon him to the last;
And here upon a yellow eyelid fall'n
And closed by those who mourn a friend in vain,
Not thankful that his troubles are no more.
And me, altho' his fire is on my face
Blinding, he sees not, nor at all can tell
Whether I mean this day to end myself,
Or lend an ear to Plato where he says,

That men like soldiers may not quit the post
Allotted by the Gods: but he that holds
The Gods are careless, wherefore need he care
Greatly for them, nor rather plunge at once,
Being troubled, wholly out of sight, and sink
Past earthquake — ay, and gout and stone, that break
Body toward death, and palsy, death-in-life,
And wretched age — and worst disease of all,
These prodigies of myriad nakednesses,
And twisted shapes of lust, unspeakable,
Abominable, strangers at my hearth
Not welcome, harpies miring every dish,
The phantom husks of something foully done,
And fleeting thro' the boundless universe,
And blasting the long quiet of my breast
With animal heat and dire insanity?

"How should the mind, except it loved them, clasp
These idols to herself? or do they fly
Now thinner, and now thicker, like the flakes
In a fall of snow, and so press in, perforce
Of multitude, as crowds that in an hour
Of civic tumult jam the doors, and bear
The keepers down, and throng, their rags and they,
The basest, far into that council-hall
Where sit the best and stateliest of the land?

"Can I not fling this horror off me again,
Seeing with how great ease Nature can smile,
Balmier and nobler from her bath of storm,
At random ravage? and how easily
The mountain there has cast his cloudy slough,
Now towering o'er him in serenest air,
A mountain o'er a mountain, — ay, and within
All hollow as the hopes and fears of men?

"But who was he, that in the garden snared
Picus and Faunus, rustic Gods? a tale
To laugh at — more to laugh at in myself —
For look! what is it? there? yon arbutus

LUCRETIUS.   127

Totters ; a noiseless riot underneath
Strikes through the wood, sets all the
   tops quivering —
The mountain quickens into Nymph and
   Faun ;
And here an Oread — how the sun delights
To glance and shift about her slippery
   sides,
And rosy knees and supple roundedness,
And budded bosom-peaks — who this
   way runs
Before the rest — A satyr, a satyr, see,
Follows ; but him I proved impossible ;
Twy-natured is no nature : yet he draws
Nearer and nearer, and I scan him now
Beastlier than any phantom of his kind
That ever butted his rough brother-brute
For lust or lusty blood or provender :
I hate, abhor, spit, sicken at him ; and she
Loathes him as well ; such a precipitate
   heel,
Fledged as it were with Mercury's ankle-
   wing,
Whirls her to me : but will she fling her-
   self,
Shameless upon me ? Catch her, goat-
   foot : nay,
Hide, hide them, million-myrtled wilder-
   ness,
And cavern-shadowing laurels, hide ! do
   I wish —
What ? — that the bush were leafless ?
   or to whelm
All of them in one massacre ? O ye Gods,
I know you careless, yet, behold, to you
From childly wont and ancient use I call —
I thought I lived securely as yourselves —
No lewdness, narrowing envy, monkey-
   spite,
No madness of ambition, avarice, none :
No larger feast than under plane or pine
With neighbors laid along the grass, to
   take
Only such cups as left us friendly-warm,
Affirming each his own philosophy —
Nothing to mar the sober majesties
Of settled, sweet, Epicurean life.
But now it seems some unseen monster
   lays
His vast and filthy hands upon my will,
Wrenching it backward into his ; and
   spoils
My bliss in being ; and it was not great ;
For save when shutting reasons up in
   rhythm,
Or Heliconian honey in living words,
To make a truth less harsh, I often grew

Tired of so much within our little life,
Or of so little in our little life —
Poor little life that toddles half an hour
Crown'd with a flower or two, and there
   an end —
And since the nobler pleasure seems to
   fade,
Why should I, beastlike as I find myself,
Not manlike end myself ? — our privi-
   lege —
What beast has heart to do it ? And
   what man,
What Roman would be dragg'd in tri-
   umph thus ?
Not I ; not he, who bears one name with
   her
Whose death-blow struck the dateless
   doom of kings,
When, brooking not the Tarquin in her
   veins,
She made her blood in sight of Collatine
And all his peers, flushing the guiltless air,
Spout from the maiden fountain in her
   heart.
And from it sprang the Commonwealth,
   which breaks
As I am breaking now !

      "And therefore now
Let her, that is the womb and tomb of all,
Great Nature, take, and forcing far apart
Those blind beginnings that have made
   me man
Dash them anew together at her will
Through all her cycles — into man once
   more,
Or beast or bird or fish, or opulent flower :
But till this cosmic order everywhere
Shatter'd into one earthquake in one day
Cracks all to pieces, — and that hour per-
   haps
Is not so far when momentary man
Shall seem no more a something to him-
   self,
But he, his hopes and hates, his homes
   and fanes,
And even his bones long laid within the
   grave,
The very sides of the grave itself shall pass,
Vanishing, atom and void, atom and void,
Into the unseen for ever, — till that hour,
My golden work in which I told a truth
That stays the rolling Ixionian wheel,
And numbs the Fury's ringlet-snake,
   and plucks
The mortal soul from out immortal hell,
Shall stand : ay, surely : then it fails at last

And perishes as I must; for O Thou,
Passionless bride, divine Tranquillity,
Yearn'd after by the wisest of the wise,
Who fail to find thee, being as thou art
Without one pleasure and without one pain,
Howbeit I know thou surely must be mine
Or soon or late, yet out of season, thus
I woo thee roughly, for thou carest not
How roughly men may woo thee so they win —
Thus — thus: the soul flies out and dies in the air."

With that he drove the knife into his side:
She heard him raging, heard him fall; ran in,
Beat breast, tore hair, cried out upon herself
As having fail'd in duty to him, shriek'd
That she but meant to win him back, fell on him,
Clasp'd, kiss'd him, wail'd: he answer'd,
"Care not thou!
Thy duty? What is duty? Fare thee well!"

IDYLLS OF THE KING.

"Flos Regum Arthurus."
JOSEPH OF EXETER.

DEDICATION.

THESE to His Memory — since he held them dear,
Perchance as finding there unconsciously
Some image of himself — I dedicate,
I dedicate, I consecrate with tears —
These Idylls.

   And indeed He seems to me
Scarce other than my own ideal knight,
"Who reverenced his conscience as his king;
Whose glory was, redressing human wrong;
Who spake no slander, no, nor listen'd to it;
Who loved one only and who clave to her —"
Her — over all whose realms to their last isle,
Commingled with the gloom of imminent war,
The shadow of His loss drew like eclipse,
Darkening the world. We have lost him: he is gone:
We know him now: all narrow jealousies
Are silent; and we see him as he moved,
How modest, kindly, all-accomplish'd, wise,
With what sublime repression of himself,
And in what limits, and how tenderly;
Not swaying to this faction or to that;
Not making his high place the lawless perch
Of wing'd ambitions, nor a vantage-ground
For pleasure; but thro' all this tract of years
Wearing the white flower of a blameless life,
Before a thousand peering littlenesses,
In that fierce light which beats upon a throne,
And blackens every blot: for where is he,
Who dares foreshadow for an only son
A lovelier life, a more unstain'd, than his?
Or how should England dreaming of *his* sons
Hope more for these than some inheritance
Of such a life, a heart, a mind as thine,
Thou noble Father of her Kings to be,
Laborious for her people and her poor —
Voice in the rich dawn of an ampler day —
Far-sighted summoner of War and Waste
To fruitful strifes and rivalries of peace —
Sweet nature gilded by the gracious gleam
Of letters, dear to Science, dear to Art,
Dear to thy land and ours, a Prince indeed,
Beyond all titles, and a household name,
Hereafter, thro' all times, Albert the Good.

  Break not, O woman's-heart, but still endure;
Break not, for thou art Royal, but endure,
Remembering all the beauty of that star

Which shone so close beside Thee, that
  ye made
One light together, but has past and leaves
The Crown a lonely splendor.

                May all love,
His love, unseen but felt, o'ershadow
  Thee,
The love of all Thy sons encompass Thee,
The love of all Thy daughters cherish
  Thee,
The love of all Thy people comfort Thee,
Till God's love set Thee at his side again!

THE COMING OF ARTHUR.

LEODOGRAN, the King of Cameliard,
Had one fair daughter, and none other
  child;
And she was fairest of all flesh on earth,
Guinevere, and in her his one delight.

For many a petty king ere Arthur came
Ruled in this isle, and ever waging war
Each upon other, wasted all the land;
And still from time to time the heathen
  host
Swarm'd overseas, and harried what was
  left.
And so there grew great tracts of wilder-
  ness,
Wherein the beast was ever more and
  more,
But man was less and less, till Arthur
  came.
For first Aurelius lived and fought and
  died,
And after him King Uther fought and
  died,
But either fail'd to make the kingdom one.
And after these King Arthur for a space,
And thro' the puissance of his Table
  Round,
Drew all their petty princedoms under
  him,
Their king and head, and made a realm,
  and reign'd.

    And thus the land of Cameliard was
  waste,
Thick with wet woods, and many a beast
  therein,
And none or few to scare or chase the
  beast;
So that wild dog, and wolf and boar and
  bear
Came night and day, and rooted in the
  fields,
And wallow'd in the gardens of the king.
And ever and anon the wolf would steal
The children and devour, but now and
  then,
Her own brood lost or dead, lent her fierce
  teat
To human sucklings; and the children,
  housed
In her foul den, there at their meat would
  growl,
And mock their foster-mother on four feet,
Till, straighten'd, they grew up to wolf-
  like men,
Worse than the wolves. And King Leodo-
  gran
Groan'd for the Roman legions here again,
And Cæsar's eagle: then his brother king,
Rience, assail'd him: last a heathen horde,
Reddening the sun with smoke and earth
  with blood,
And on the spike that split the mother's
  heart
Spitting the child, brake on him, till,
  amazed,
He knew not whither he should turn for
  aid.

    But — for he heard of Arthur newly
  crown'd,
Tho' not without an uproar made by those
Who cried, "He is not Uther's son" —
  the king
Sent to him, saying, "Arise, and help
  us thou!
For here between the man and beast we
  die."

    And Arthur yet had done no deed of
  arms,
But heard the call, and came: and Guin-
  evere
Stood by the castle walls to watch him
  pass;
But since he neither wore on helm or
  shield
The golden symbol of his kinglihood,
But rode a simple knight among his
  knights,
And many of these in richer arms than he,
She saw him not, or mark'd not, if she saw,
One among many, tho' his face was bare.
But Arthur, looking downward as he past,
Felt the light of her eyes into his life
Smite on the sudden, yet rode on, and
  pitch'd

His tents beside the forest. And he drave
The heathen, and he slew the beast, and
  fell'd
The forest, and let in the sun, and made
Broad pathways for the hunter and the
  knight;
And so return'd.

        For while he linger'd there,
A doubt that ever smoulder'd in the hearts
Of those great Lords and Barons of his
  realm
Flash'd forth and into war: for most of
  these
Made head against him, crying, "Who
  is he
That he should rule us? who hath proven
  him,
King Uther's son? for lo! we look at him
And find nor face nor bearing, limbs nor
  voice,
Are like to those of Uther whom we knew.
This is the son of Gorloïs, not the king;
This is the son of Anton, not the king."

       And Arthur, passing thence to battle,
  felt
Travail, and throes and agonies of the life,
Desiring to be join'd with Guinevere;
And thinking as he rode, "Her father
  said
That there between the man and beast
  they die.
Shall I not lift her from this land of beasts
Up to my throne, and side by side with
  me?
What happiness to reign a lonely king,
Vext — O ye stars that shudder over me,
O earth that soundest hollow under me,
Vext with waste dreams? for saving I be
  join'd
To her that is the fairest under heaven,
I seem as nothing in the mighty world,
And cannot will my will, nor work my
  work
Wholly, nor make myself in mine own
  realm
Victor and lord. But were I join'd with
  her,
Then might we live together as one life,
And reigning with one will in everything
Have power on this dark land to lighten it,
And power on this dead world to make it
  live."

       And Arthur from the field of battle sent
Ulfius, and Brastias, and Bedivere,
His new-made knights, to King Leodo-
  gran,
Saying, "If I in aught have served thee
  well,
Give me thy daughter Guinevere to wife."

       Whom when he heard, Leodogran in
  heart
Debating — "How should I that am a
  king,
However much he holp me at my need,
Give my one daughter saving to a king,
And a king's son" — lifted his voice, and
  call'd
A hoary man, his chamberlain, to whom
He trusted all things, and of him required
His counsel: "Knowest thou aught of
  Arthur's birth?"

       Then spake the hoary chamberlain and
  said,
"Sir king, there be but two old men that
  know:
And each is twice as old as I; and one
Is Merlin, the wise man that ever served
King Uther thro' his magic art; and one
Is Merlin's master (so they call him) Bleys,
Who taught him magic; but the scholar
  ran
Before the master, and so far, that Bleys
Laid magic by, and sat him down, and
  wrote
All things and whatsoever Merlin did
In one great annal-book, where after-years
Will learn the secret of our Arthur's
  birth."

       To whom the King Leodogran replied,
"O friend, had I been holpen half as well
By this King Arthur as by thee to-day,
Then beast and man had had their share
  of me:
But summon here before us yet once more
Ulfius, and Brastias, and Bedivere."

       Then, when they came before him, the
  king said,
"I have seen the cuckoo chased by lesser
  fowl,
And reason in the chase: but wherefore
  now
Do these your lords stir up the heat of
  war,
Some calling Arthur born of Gorloïs,
Others of Anton? Tell me, ye yourselves,
Hold ye this Arthur for King Uther's
  son?"

And Ulfius and Brastias answer'd,
"Ay."
Then Bedivere, the first of all his knights
Knighted by Arthur at his crowning,
spake —
For bold in heart and act and word was he,
Whenever slander breathed against the king —

"Sir, there be many rumors on this head :
For there be those who hate him in their hearts,
Call him baseborn, and since his ways are sweet,
And theirs are bestial, hold him less than man :
And there be those who deem him more than man,
And dream he dropt from heaven : but my belief
In all this matter — so ye care to learn —
Sir, for ye know that in King Uther's time
The prince and warrior Gorloïs, he that held
Tintagil castle by the Cornish sea,
Was wedded with a winsome wife, Ygerne :
And daughters had she borne him, — one whereof,
Lot's wife, the Queen of Orkney, Bellicent,
Hath ever like a loyal sister cleaved
To Arthur, — but a son she had not borne.
And Uther cast upon her eyes of love :
But she, a stainless wife to Gorloïs,
So loathed the bright dishonor of his love,
That Gorloïs and King Uther went to war :
And overthrown was Gorloïs and slain.
Then Uther in his wrath and heat besieged
Ygerne within Tintagil, where her men,
Seeing the mighty swarm about their walls,
Left her and fled, and Uther enter'd in,
And there was none to call to but himself.
So, compass'd by the power of the king,
Enforc'd she was to wed him in her tears,
And with a shameful swiftness ; afterward,
Not many moons, King Uther died himself,
Moaning and wailing for an heir to rule
After him, lest the realm should go to wrack.
And that same night, the night of the new year,
By reason of the bitterness and grief
That vext his mother, all before his time
Was Arthur born, and all as soon as born
Deliver'd at a secret postern gate
To Merlin, to be holden far apart
Until his hour should come ; because the lords
Of that fierce day were as the lords of this,
Wild beasts, and surely would have torn the child
Piecemeal among them, had they known ; for each
But sought to rule for his own self and hand,
And many hated Uther for the sake
Of Gorloïs. Wherefore Merlin took the child,
And gave him to Sir Anton, an old knight
And ancient friend of Uther ; and his wife
Nursed the young prince, and rear'd him with her own ;
And no man knew. And ever since the lords
Have foughten like wild beasts among themselves,
So that the realm has gone to wrack : but now,
This year, when Merlin (for his hour had come)
Brought Arthur forth, and set him in the hall,
Proclaiming, 'Here is Uther's heir, your king,'
A hundred voices cried, 'Away with him !
No king of ours ! a son of Gorloïs he,
Or else the child of Anton, and no king,
Or else baseborn.' Yet Merlin thro' his craft,
And while the people clamor'd for a king,
Had Arthur crown'd ; but after, the great lords
Banded, and so brake out in open war."

Then while the king debated with himself
If Arthur were the child of shamefulness,
Or born the son of Gorloïs, after death,
Or Uther's son, and born before his time,
Or whether there were truth in anything
Said by these three, there came to Cameliard,
With Gawain and young Modred, her two sons,
Lot's wife, the Queen of Orkney, Bellicent ;
Whom as he could, not as he would, the king
Made feast for, saying, as they sat at meat,

"A doubtful throne is ice on summer seas —

Ye come from Arthur's court : think ye
this king —
So few his knights, however brave they
be —
Hath body enow to beat his foemen
down?"

"O king," she cried, "and I will tell
thee : few,
Few, but all brave, all of one mind with
him ;
For I was near him when the savage yells
Of Uther's peerage died, and Arthur sat
Crown'd on the daïs, and his warriors
cried,
'Be thou the king, and we will work thy
will
Who love thee.' Then the king in low
deep tones,
And simple words of great authority,
Bound them by so strait vows to his own
self,
That when they rose, knighted from
kneeling, some
Were pale as at the passing of a ghost,
Some flush'd, and others dazed, as one
who wakes
Half-blinded at the coming of a light.

"But when he spake and cheer'd his
Table Round
With large divine and comfortable words
Beyond my tongue to tell thee — I beheld
From eye to eye thro' all their Order flash
A momentary likeness of the king :
And ere it left their faces, thro' the cross
And those around it and the Crucified,
Down from the casement over Arthur,
smote
Flame-color, vert and azure, in three rays,
One falling upon each of three fair queens,
Who stood in silence near his throne, the
friends
Of Arthur, gazing on him, tall, with bright
Sweet faces, who will help him at his need.

"And there I saw mage Merlin, whose
vast wit
And hundred winters are but as the hands
Of loyal vassals toiling for their liege.

"And near him stood the Lady of the
Lake,
Who knows a subtler magic than his
own —
Clothed in white samite, mystic, wonder-
ful.

She gave the king his huge cross-hilted
sword,
Whereby to drive the heathen out : a mist
Of incense curl'd about her, and her face
Wellnigh was hidden in the minster
gloom ;
But there was heard among the holy
hymns
A voice as of the waters, for she dwells
Down in a deep, calm, whatsoever storms
May shake the world, and when the sur-
face rolls,
Hath power to walk the waters like our
Lord.

"There likewise I beheld Excalibur
Before him at his crowning borne, the
sword
That rose from out the bosom of the lake,
And Arthur row'd across and took it —
rich
With jewels, elfin Urim, on the hilt,
Bewildering heart and eye — the blade
so bright
That men are blinded by it — on one side,
Graven in the oldest tongue of all this
world,
'Take me,' but turn the blade and you
shall see,
And written in the speech ye speak your-
self,
'Cast me away !' And sad was Arthur's
face
Taking it, but old Merlin counsell'd him,
'Take thou and strike ! the time to cast
away
Is yet far-off.' So this great brand the king
Took, and by this will beat his foemen
down."

Thereat Leodogran rejoiced, but
thought
To sift his doubtings to the last, and ask'd,
Fixing full eyes of question on her face,
"The swallow and the swift are near akin,
But thou art closer to this noble prince,
Being his own dear sister" ; and she said,
"Daughter of Gorloïs and Ygerne am
I" ;
"And therefore Arthur's sister," ask'd
the King.
She answer'd, "These be secret things,"
and sign'd
To those two sons to pass and let them be.
And Gawain went, and breaking into song
Sprang out, and follow'd by his flying
hair,

Ran like a colt, and leapt at all he saw:
But Modred laid his ear beside the doors,
And there half heard; the same that afterward
Struck for the throne, and striking found his doom.

And then the Queen made answer, "What know I?
For dark my mother was in eyes and hair,
And dark in hair and eyes am I; and dark
Was Gorloïs, yea and dark was Uther too,
Wellnigh to blackness; but this king is fair
Beyond the race of Britons and of men.
Moreover always in my mind I hear
A cry from out the dawning of my life,
A mother weeping, and I hear her say,
'O that ye had some brother, pretty one,
To guard thee on the rough ways of the world.'"

"Ay," said the King, "and hear ye such a cry?
But when did Arthur chance upon thee first?"

"O king!" she cried, "and I will tell thee true:
He found me first when yet a little maid:
Beaten I had been for a little fault
Whereof I was not guilty; and out I ran
And flung myself down on a bank of heath,
And hated this fair world and all therein,
And wept, and wish'd that I were dead; and he —
I know not whether of himself he came,
Or brought by Merlin, who, they say, can walk
Unseen at pleasure — he was at my side,
And spake sweet words, and comforted my heart,
And dried my tears, being a child with me.
And many a time he came, and evermore
As I grew greater grew with me; and sad
At times he seem'd, and sad with him was I,
Stern too at times, and then I loved him not,
But sweet again, and then I loved him well.
And now of late I see him less and less,
But those first days had golden hours for me,
For then I surely thought he would be king.

"But let me tell thee now another tale:
For Bleys, our Merlin's master, as they say,
Died but of late, and sent his cry to me,
To hear him speak before he left his life.
Shrunk like a fairy changeling lay the mage,
And when I enter'd told me that himself
And Merlin ever served about the king,
Uther, before he died, and on the night
When Uther in Tintagil past away
Moaning and wailing for an heir, the two
Left the still king, and passing forth to breathe,
Then from the castle gateway by the chasm
Descending thro' the dismal night — a night
In which the bounds of heaven and earth were lost —
Beheld, so high upon the dreary deeps
It seem'd in heaven, a ship, the shape thereof
A dragon wing'd, and all from stem to stern
Bright with a shining people on the decks,
And gone as soon as seen. And then the two
Dropt to the cove, and watch'd the great sea fall,
Wave after wave, each mightier than the last,
Till last, a ninth one, gathering half the deep
And full of voices, slowly rose and plunged
Roaring, and all the wave was in a flame:
And down the wave and in the flame was borne
A naked babe, and rode to Merlin's feet,
Who stoopt and caught the babe, and cried 'The King!
Here is an heir for Uther!' And the fringe
Of that great breaker, sweeping up the strand,
Lash'd at the wizard as he spake the word,
And all at once all round him rose in fire,
So that the child and he were clothed in fire.
And presently thereafter follow'd calm,
Free sky and stars: 'And this same child,' he said,
'Is he who reigns; nor could I part in peace
Till this were told.' And saying this the seer
Went thro' the strait and dreadful pass of death,
Not ever to be question'd any more
Save on the further side; but when I met

Merlin, and ask'd him if these things
   were truth —
The shining dragon and the naked child
Descending in the glory of the seas —
He laugh'd as is his wont, and answer'd me
In riddling triplets of old time, and said:

   "'Rain, rain, and sun! a rainbow in
      the sky!
A young man will be wiser by and by;
An old man's wit may wander ere he die.
   Rain, rain, and sun! a rainbow on the
      lea!
And truth is this to me, and that to thee;
And truth or clothed or naked let it be.
   Rain, sun, and rain! and the free blos-
      som blows:
Sun, rain, and sun! and where is he who
      knows?
From the great deep to the great deep he
      goes.'

"So Merlin riddling anger'd me; but
   thou
Fear not to give this king thine only child,
Guinevere: so great bards of him will sing
Hereafter; and dark sayings from of old
Ranging and ringing thro' the minds of
   men,
And echo'd by old folk beside their fires
For comfort after their wage-work is done,
Speak of the king; and Merlin in our time
Hath spoken also, not in jest, and sworn
Tho' men may wound him that he will
   not die,
But pass, again to come; and then or now
Utterly smite the heathen underfoot,
Till these and all men hail him for their
   king."

   She spake and King Leodogran rejoiced,
But musing "Shall I answer yea or nay?"
Doubted, and drowsed, nodded and slept,
   and saw,
Dreaming, a slope of land that ever grew,
Field after field, up to a height, the peak
Haze-hidden, and thereon a phantom
   king,
Now looming, and now lost; and on the
   slope
The sword rose, the hind fell, the herd
   was driven,
Fire glimpsed; and all the land from
   roof and rick,
In drifts of smoke before a rolling wind,
Stream'd to the peak, and mingled with
   the haze

And made it thicker; while the phantom
   king
Sent out at times a voice; and here or
   there
Stood one who pointed toward the voice,
   the rest
Slew on and burnt, crying, "No king of
   ours,
No son of Uther, and no king of ours";
Till with a wink his dream was changed,
   the haze
Descended, and the solid earth became
As nothing, and the king stood out in
   heaven,
Crown'd. And Leodogran awoke, and sent
Ulfius, and Brastias, and Bedivere,
Back to the court of Arthur answering yea.

   Then Arthur charged his warrior whom
   he loved
And honor'd most, Sir Lancelot, to ride
   forth
And bring the Queen; — and watch'd
   him from the gates:
And Lancelot past away among the
   flowers,
(For then was latter April) and return'd
Among the flowers, in May, with Guin-
   evere.
To whom arrived, by Dubric the high
   saint,
Chief of the church in Britain, and before
The stateliest of her altar-shrines, the king
That morn was married, while in stain-
   less white,
The fair beginners of a nobler time,
And glorying in their vows and him,
   his knights
Stood round him, and rejoicing in his
   joy.
And holy Dubric spread his hands and
   spake,
"Reign ye, and live and love, and make
   the world
Other, and may thy Queen be one with
   thee,
And all this Order of thy Table Round
Fulfil the boundless purpose of their
   king."

   Then at the marriage feast came in
   from Rome,
The slowly-fading mistress of the world,
Great lords, who claim'd the tribute as
   of yore.
But Arthur spake, "Behold, for these
   have sworn

To fight my wars, and worship me their king;
The old order changeth, yielding place to new ;
And we that fight for our fair father Christ,
Seeing that ye be grown too weak and old
To drive the heathen from your Roman wall,
No tribute will we pay " : so those great lords
Drew back in wrath, and Arthur strove with Rome.

And Arthur and his knighthood for a space
Were all one will, and thro' that strength the king
Drew in the petty princedoms under him,
Fought, and in twelve great battles overcame
The heathen hordes, and made a realm and reign'd.

GERAINT AND ENID.

The brave Geraint, a knight of Arthur's court,
A tributary prince of Devon, one
Of that great order of the Table Round,
Had married Enid, Yniol's only child,
And loved her, as he loved the light of Heaven.
And as the light of Heaven varies, now
At sunrise, now at sunset, now by night
With moon and trembling stars, so loved Geraint
To make her beauty vary day by day,
In crimsons and in purples and in gems.
And Enid, but to please her husband's eye,
Who first had found and loved her in a state
Of broken fortunes, daily fronted him
In some fresh splendor ; and the Queen herself,
Grateful to Prince Geraint for service done,
Loved her, and often with her own white hands
Array'd and deck'd her, as the loveliest,
Next after her own self, in all the court.
And Enid loved the Queen, and with true heart
Adored her, as the stateliest and the best
And loveliest of all women upon earth.
And seeing them so tender and so close,
Long in their common love rejoiced Geraint.
But when a rumor rose about the Queen,
Touching her guilty love for Lancelot,
Tho' yet there lived no proof, nor yet was heard
The world's loud whisper breaking into storm,
Not less Geraint believed it ; and there fell
A horror on him, lest his gentle wife,
Thro' that great tenderness for Guinevere,
Had suffer'd, or should suffer any taint
In nature : wherefore going to the king,
He made this pretext, that his princedom lay
Close on the borders of a territory,
Wherein were bandit earls, and caitiff knights,
Assassins, and all fliers from the hand
Of Justice, and whatever loathes a law :
And therefore, till the king himself should please
To cleanse this common sewer of all his realm,
He craved a fair permission to depart,
And there defend his marches ; and the king
Mused for a little on his plea, but, last,
Allowing it, the Prince and Enid rode,
And fifty knights rode with them, to the shores
Of Severn, and they past to their own land ;
Where, thinking, that if ever yet was wife
True to her lord, mine shall be so to me,
He compass'd her with sweet observances
And worship, never leaving her, and grew
Forgetful of his promise to the king,
Forgetful of the falcon and the hunt,
Forgetful of the tilt and tournament,
Forgetful of his glory and his name,
Forgetful of his princedom and its cares.
And this forgetfulness was hateful to her.
And by and by the people, when they met
In twos and threes, or fuller companies,
Began to scoff and jeer and babble of him
As of a prince whose manhood was all gone,
And molten down in mere uxoriousness.
And this she gather'd from the people's eyes :
This too the woman who attired her head,
To please her, dwelling on his boundless love,
Told Enid, and they sadden'd her the more :
And day by day she thought to tell Geraint,
But could not out of bashful delicacy ;

Enid.

While he that watch'd her sadden, was the more
Suspicious that her nature had a taint.

At last it chanced that on a summer morn
(They sleeping each by either) the new sun
Beat thro' the blindless casement of the room,
And heated the strong warrior in his dreams;
Who, moving, cast the coverlet aside,
And bared the knotted column of his throat,
The massive square of his heroic breast,
And arms on which the standing muscle sloped,
As slopes a wild brook o'er a little stone,
Running too vehemently to break upon it.
And Enid woke and sat beside the couch,
Admiring him, and thought within herself,
Was ever man so grandly made as he?
Then, like a shadow, past the people's talk
And accusation of uxoriousness
Across her mind, and bowing over him,
Low to her own heart piteously she said:

"O noble breast and all-puissant arms,
Am I the cause, I the poor cause that men
Reproach you, saying all your force is gone?
I *am* the cause because I dare not speak
And tell him what I think and what they say.
And yet I hate that he should linger here;
I cannot love my lord and not his name.
Far liever had I gird his harness on him,
And ride with him to battle and stand by,
And watch his mightful hand striking great blows
At caitiffs and at wrongers of the world.
Far better were I laid in the dark earth,
Not hearing any more his noble voice,
Not to be folded more in these dear arms,
And darken'd from the high light in his eyes,
Than that my lord thro' me should suffer shame.
Am I so bold, and could I so stand by,
And see my dear lord wounded in the strife,
Or maybe pierced to death before mine eyes,
And yet not dare to tell him what I think,
And how men slur him, saying all his force

Is melted into mere effeminacy ?
O me, I fear that I am no true wife."

Half inwardly, half audibly she spoke,
And the strong passion in her made her
   weep
True tears upon his broad and naked
   breast,
And these awoke him, and by great mis-
   chance
He heard but fragments of her later words,
And that she fear'd she was not a true wife.
And then he thought, "In spite of all my
   care,
For all my pains, poor man, for all my pains,
She is not faithful to me, and I see her
Weeping for some gay knight in Arthur's
   hall."
Then tho' he loved and reverenced her
   too much
To dream she could be guilty of foul act,
Right thro' his manful breast darted the
   pang
That makes a man, in the sweet face of her
Whom he loves most, lonely and misera-
   ble.
At this he hurl'd his huge limbs out of bed,
And shook his drowsy squire awake and
   cried,
"My charger and her palfrey," then to her,
"I will ride forth into the wilderness ;
For tho' it seems my spurs are yet to win,
I have not fall'n so low as some would wish.
And you, put on your worst and meanest
   dress
And ride with me." And Enid ask'd,
   amazed,
"If Enid errs, let Enid learn her fault."
But he, "I charge you, ask not but obey."
Then she bethought her of a faded silk,
A faded mantle and a faded veil,
And moving toward a cedarn cabinet,
Wherein she kept them folded reverently
With sprigs of summer laid between the
   folds,
She took them, and array'd herself therein,
Remembering when first he came on her
Drest in that dress, and how he loved
   her in it,
And all her foolish fears about the dress,
And all his journey to her, as himself
Had told her, and their coming to the
   court.

For Arthur on the Whitsuntide before
Held court at old Caerleon upon Usk.
There on a day, he sitting high in hall,
Before him came a forester of Dean,
Wet from the woods, with notice of a hart
Taller than all his fellows, milky-white,
First seen that day : these things he told
   the king.
Then the good king gave order to let blow
His horns for hunting on the morrow
   morn.
And when the Queen petition'd for his
   leave
To see the hunt, allow'd it easily.
So with the morning all the court were
   gone.
But Guinevere lay late into the morn,
Lost in sweet dreams, and dreaming of
   her love
For Lancelot, and forgetful of the hunt ;
But rose at last, a single maiden with her,
Took horse, and forded Usk, and gain'd
   the wood ;
There, on a little knoll beside it, stay'd
Waiting to hear the hounds ; but heard
   instead
A sudden sound of hoofs, for Prince
   Geraint,
Late also, wearing neither hunting-dress
Nor weapon, save a golden-hilted brand,
Came quickly flashing thro' the shallow
   ford
Behind them, and so gallop'd up the knoll.
A purple scarf, at either end whereof
There swung an apple of the purest gold,
Sway'd round about him, as he gallop'd up
To join them, glancing like a dragon-fly
In summer suit and silks of holiday.
Low bow'd the tributary Prince, and she,
Sweetly and statelily, and with all grace
Of womanhood and queenhood, answer'd
   him :
"Late, late, Sir Prince," she said, "later
   than we !"
"Yea, noble Queen," he answer'd, "and
   so late
That I but come like you to see the hunt,
Not join it." "Therefore wait with me,"
   she said ;
"For on this little knoll, if anywhere,
There is good chance that we shall hear
   the hounds :
Here often they break covert at our feet."

And while they listen'd for the distant
   hunt,
And chiefly for the baying of Cavall,
King Arthur's hound of deepest mouth,
   there rode
Full slowly by a knight, lady, and dwarf ;

Whereof the dwarf lagg'd latest, and the knight
Had visor up, and show'd a youthful face,
Imperious, and of haughtiest lineaments.
And Guinevere, not mindful of his face
In the king's hall, desired his name, and sent
Her maiden to demand it of the dwarf;
Who being vicious, old, and irritable,
And doubling all his master's vice of pride,
Made answer sharply that she should not know.
"Then will I ask it of himself," she said.
"Nay, by my faith, thou shalt not," cried the dwarf;
"Thou art not worthy ev'n to speak of him";
And when she put her horse toward the knight,
Struck at her with his whip, and she return'd
Indignant to the Queen; whereat Geraint
Exclaiming, "Surely I will learn the name,"
Made sharply to the dwarf, and ask'd it of him,
Who answer'd as before; and when the Prince
Had put his horse in motion toward the knight,
Struck at him with his whip, and cut his cheek.
The Prince's blood spirted upon the scarf,
Dyeing it; and his quick, instinctive hand
Caught at the hilt, as to abolish him:
But he, from his exceeding manfulness
And pure nobility of temperament,
Wroth to be wroth at such a worm, refrain'd
From ev'n a word, and so returning said:

"I will avenge this insult, noble Queen,
Done in your maiden's person to yourself:
And I will track this vermin to their earths:
For tho' I ride unarm'd, I do not doubt
To find, at some place I shall come at, arms
On loan, or else for pledge; and, being found,
Then will I fight him, and will break his pride,
And on the third day, will again be here,
So that I be not fall'n in fight. Farewell."

"Farewell, fair Prince," answer'd the stately Queen.
"Be prosperous in this journey, as in all;

And may ye light on all things that ye love,
And live to wed with her whom first ye love:
But ere ye wed with any, bring your bride,
And I, were she the daughter of a king,
Yea, tho' she were a beggar from the hedge,
Will clothe her for her bridals like the sun."

And Prince Geraint, now thinking that he heard
The noble hart at bay, now the far horn,
A little vext at losing of the hunt,
A little at the vile occasion, rode,
By ups and downs, thro' many a grassy glade
And valley, with fixt eye following the three.
At last they issued from the world of wood,
And climb'd upon a fair and even ridge,
And show'd themselves against the sky, and sank.
And thither came Geraint, and underneath
Beheld the long street of a little town
In a long valley, on one side whereof,
White from the mason's hand, a fortress rose;
And on one side a castle in decay,
Beyond a bridge that spann'd a dry ravine:
And out of town and valley came a noise
As of a broad brook o'er a shingly bed
Brawling, or like a clamor of the rooks
At distance, ere they settle for the night.

And onward to the fortress rode the three,
And enter'd, and were lost behind the walls.
"So," thought Geraint, "I have track'd him to his earth."
And down the long street riding wearily,
Found every hostel full, and everywhere
Was hammer laid to hoof, and the hot hiss
And bustling whistle of the youth who scour'd
His master's armor; and of such a one
He ask'd, "What means the tumult in the town?"
Who told him, scouring still "The sparrow-hawk!"
Then riding close behind an ancient churl,
Who, smitten by the dusty sloping beam,
Went sweating underneath a sack of corn,
Ask'd yet once more what meant the hubbub here?

GERAINT AND ENID.

*"Beheld the long street of a little town
In a long valley."*

Who answer'd gruffly, "Ugh! the sparrow-hawk."
Then riding further past an armorer's,
Who, with back turn'd, and bow'd above his work,
Sat riveting a helmet on his knee,
He put the self-same query, but the man
Not turning round, nor looking at him, said:
"Friend, ne that labors for the sparrow-hawk
Has little time for idle questioners."
Whereat Geraint flash'd into sudden spleen:
"A thousand pips eat up your sparrow-hawk!

Tits, wrens, and all wing'd nothings peck him dead!
Ye think the rustic cackle of your bourg
The murmur of the world! What is it to me?
O wretched set of sparrows, one and all,
Who pipe of nothing but of sparrow-hawks!
Speak, if ye be not like the rest, hawk-mad,
Where can I get me harborage for the night?
And arms, arms, arms to fight my enemy!
Speak!"
At this the armorer turning all amazed
And seeing one so gay in purple silks,

Came forward with the helmet yet in hand
And answer'd, "Pardon me, O stranger knight;
We hold a tourney here to-morrow morn,
And there isscantly time for half the work.
Arms? truth! I know not: all are wanted here.
Harborage? truth, good truth, I know not, save,
It may be, at Earl Yniol's, o'er the bridge
Yonder." He spoke and fell to work again.

Then rode Geraint, a little spleenful yet,
Across the bridge that spann'd the dry ravine.
There musing sat the hoary-headed Earl,
(His dress a suit of fray'd magnificence,
Once fit for feasts of ceremony) and said:
"Whither, fair son?" to whom Geraint replied,
"O friend, I seek a harborage for the night."
Then Yniol, "Enter therefore and partake
The slender entertainment of a house
Once rich, now poor, but ever open-door'd."
"Thanks, venerable friend," replied Geraint;
"So that ye do not serve me sparrowhawks
For supper, I will enter, I will eat
With all the passion of a twelve hours' fast."
Then sigh'd and smiled the hoary-headed Earl,
And answer'd, "Graver cause than yours is mine
To curse this hedgerow thief, the sparrowhawk:
But in, go in; for save yourself desire it,
We will not touch upon him ev'n in jest."

Then rode Geraint into the castle court,
His charger trampling many a prickly star
Of sprouted thistle on the broken stones.
He look'd and saw that all was ruinous.
Here stood a shatter'd archway plumed with fern;
And here had fall'n a great part of a tower,
Whole, like a crag that tumbles from the cliff,
And like a crag was gay with wilding flowers:
And high above a piece of turret stair,
Worn by the feet that now were silent, wound
Bare to the sun, and monstrous ivy-stems
Claspt the gray walls with hairy-fibred arms,
And suck'd the joining of the stones, and look'd
A knot, beneath, of snakes, aloft, a grove.

And while he waited in the castle court,
The voice of Enid, Yniol's daughter, rang
Clear thro' the open casement of the Hall,
Singing; and as the sweet voice of a bird,
Heard by the lander in a lonely isle,
Moves him to think what kind of bird it is
That sings so delicately clear, and make
Conjecture of the plumage and the form;
So the sweet voice of Enid moved Geraint;
And made him like a man abroad at morn
When first the liquid note beloved of men
Comes flying over many a windy wave
To Britain, and in April suddenly
Breaks from a coppice gemm'd with green and red,
And he suspends his converse with a friend,
Or it may be the labor of his hands,
To think or say, "there is the nightingale";
So fared it with Geraint, who thought and said,
"Here, by God's grace, is the one voice for me."

It chanced the song that Enid sang was one
Of Fortune and her wheel, and Enid sang:

"Turn, Fortune, turn thy wheel and lower the proud;
Turn thy wild wheel thro' sunshine, storm, and cloud;
Thy wheel and thee we neither love nor hate.

"Turn, Fortune, turn thy wheel with smile or frown;
With that wild wheel we go not up or down;
Our hoard is little, but our hearts are great.

"Smile and we smile, the lords of many lands;
Frown and we smile, the lords of our own hands;
For man is man and master of his fate.

GERAINT AND ENID. 141

"Turn, turn thy wheel above the staring crowd;
Thy wheel and thou are shadows in the cloud;
Thy wheel and thee we neither love nor hate."

"Hark, by the bird's song you may learn the nest"
Said Yniol; "Enter quickly." Entering then,
Right o'er a mount of newly-fallen stones,
The dusky-rafter'd many-cobweb'd Hall,
He found an ancient dame in dim brocade;
And near her, like a blossom vermeil-white,
That lightly breaks a faded flower-sheath,
Moved the fair Enid, all in faded silk,
Her daughter. In a moment thought Geraint,
"Here by God's rood is the one maid for me."
But none spake word except the hoary Earl:
"Enid, the good knight's horse stands in the court;
Take him to stall, and give him corn, and then
Go to the town and buy us flesh and wine;
And we will make us merry as we may.
Our hoard is little, but our hearts are great."

"In a moment thought Geraint,
'Here by God's rood is the one maid for me.'"

He spake: the Prince, as Enid past him, fain
To follow, strode astride, but Yniol caught
His purple scarf, and held, and said
"Forbear!
Rest! the good house, tho' ruin'd, O my Son,
Endures not that her guest should serve himself."
And reverencing the custom of the house
Geraint, from utter courtesy, forbore.

So Enid took his charger to the stall;
And after went her way across the bridge,
And reach'd the town, and while the Prince and Earl
Yet spoke together, came again with one,
A youth, that following with a costrel bore
The means of goodly welcome, flesh and wine.
And Enid brought sweet cakes to make them cheer,
And in her veil enfolded, manchet bread.
And then, because their hall must also serve
For kitchen, boil'd the flesh, and spread the board,
And stood behind, and waited on the three.
And seeing her so sweet and serviceable,
Geraint had longing in him evermore
To stoop and kiss the tender little thumb,
That crost the trencher as she laid it down:
But after all had eaten, then Geraint,
For now the wine made summer in his veins,
Let his eye rove in following, or rest
On Enid at her lowly handmaid-work,
Now here, now there, about the dusky hall;
Then suddenly addrest the hoary Earl:

"Fair Host and Earl, I pray your courtesy;
This sparrow-hawk, what is he, tell me of him.
His name? but no, good faith, I will not have it:
For if he be the knight whom late I saw
Ride into that new fortress by your town,
White from the mason's hand, then have I sworn
From his own lips to have it — I am Geraint
Of Devon — for this morning when the Queen
Sent her own maiden to demand the name,
His dwarf, a vicious under-shapen thing,
Struck at her with his whip, and she return'd
Indignant to the Queen; and then I swore
That I would track this caitiff to his hold,
And fight and break his pride, and have it of him.
And all unarm'd I rode, and thought to find
Arms in your town, where all the men are mad;
They take the rustic murmur of their bourg
For the great wave that echoes round the world;
They would not hear me speak: but if ye know
Where I can light on arms, or if yourself
Should have them, tell me, seeing I have sworn
That I will break his pride and learn his name,
Avenging this great insult done the Queen."

Then cried Earl Yniol. "Art thou he indeed,
Geraint, a name far-sounded among men
For noble deeds? and truly I, when first
I saw you moving by me on the bridge,
Felt you were somewhat, yea and by your state
And presence might have guess'd you one of those
That eat in Arthur's hall at Camelot.
Nor speak I now from foolish flattery;
For this dear child hath often heard me praise
Your feats of arms, and often when I paused
Hath ask'd again, and ever loved to hear;
So grateful is the noise of noble deeds
To noble hearts who see but acts of wrong:
O never yet had woman such a pair
Of suitors as this maiden; first Limours,
A creature wholly given to brawls and wine,
Drunk even when he woo'd; and be he dead
I know not, but he past to the wild land.
The second was your foe, the sparrow-hawk,
My curse, my nephew — I will not let his name
Slip from my lips if I can help it — he,
When I that knew him fierce and turbulent
Refused her to him, then his pride awoke;
And since the proud man often is the mean,
He sow'd a slander in the common ear,
Affirming that his father left him gold,

And in my charge, which was not ren-
    der'd to him;
Bribed with large promises the men who
    served
About my person, the more easily
Because my means were somewhat broken
    into
Thro' open doors and hospitality;
Raised my own town against me in the
    night
Before my Enid's birthday, sack'd my
    house;
From mine own earldom foully ousted me;
Built that new fort to overawe my friends,
For truly there are those who love me yet;
And keeps me in this ruinous castle here,
Where doubtless he would put me soon
    to death,
But that his pride too much despises me:
And I myself sometimes despise myself;
For I have let men be, and have their way;
Am much too gentle, have not used my
    power:
Nor know I whether I be very base
Or very manful, whether very wise
Or very foolish; only this I know,
That whatsoever evil happen to me,
I seem to suffer nothing heart or limb,
But can endure it all most patiently."

"Well said, true heart," replied Ge-
    raint, "but arms:
That if the sparrow-hawk, this nephew,
    fight,
In next day's tourney I may break his
    pride."

And Yniol answer'd "Arms, indeed,
    but old
And rusty, old and rusty, Prince Geraint,
Are mine, and therefore at your asking,
    yours.
But in this tournament can no man tilt,
Except the lady he loves best be there.
Two forks are fixt into the meadow ground,
And over these is laid a silver wand,
And over that is placed the sparrow-hawk,
The prize of beauty for the fairest there.
And this, what knight soever be in field
Lays claim to for the lady at his side,
And tilts with my good nephew thereupon,
Who being apt at arms and big of bone
Has ever won it for the lady with him,
And toppling over all antagonism
Has earn'd himself the name of sparrow-
    hawk.
But you, that have no lady, cannot fight."

To whom Geraint with eyes all bright
    replied,
Leaning a little toward him, "Your
    leave!
Let *me* lay lance in rest, O noble host,
For this dear child, because I never saw,
Tho' having seen all beauties of our time,
Nor can see elsewhere, anything so fair.
And if I fall her name will yet remain
Untarnish'd as before; but if I live,
So aid me Heaven when at mine utter-
    most,
As I will make her truly my true wife."

Then, howsoever patient, Yniol's heart
Danced in his bosom, seeing better days.
And looking round he saw not Enid there,
(Who hearing her own name had slipt
    away)
But that old dame, to whom full tenderly
And fondling all her hand in his he said,
"Mother, a maiden is a tender thing,
And best by her that bore her understood.
Go thou to rest, but ere thou go to rest
Tell her, and prove her heart toward the
    Prince."

So spake the kindly-hearted Earl, and
    she
With frequent smile and nod departing
    found,
Half disarray'd as to her rest, the girl;
Whom first she kiss'd on either cheek,
    and then
On either shining shoulder laid a hand,
And kept her off and gazed upon her face,
And told her all their converse in the
    hall,
Proving her heart: but never light and
    shade
Coursed one another more on open ground
Beneath a troubled heaven, than red and
    pale
Across the face of Enid hearing her;
While slowly falling as a scale that falls,
When weight is added only grain by grain,
Sank her sweet head upon her gentle
    breast;
Nor did she lift an eye nor speak a word,
Rapt in the fear and in the wonder of it;
So moving without answer to her rest
She found no rest, and ever fail'd to draw
The quiet night into her blood, but lay
Contemplating her own unworthiness;
And when the pale and bloodless east
    began
To quicken to the sun, arose, and raised

Her mother too, and hand in hand they moved
Down to the meadow where the jousts were held,
And waited there for Yniol and Geraint.

And thither came the twain, and when Geraint
Beheld her first in field, awaiting him,
He felt, were she the prize of bodily force,
Himself beyond the rest pushing could move
The chair of Idris. Yniol's rusted arms
Were on his princely person, but thro' these
Princelike his bearing shone; and errant knights
And ladies came, and by and by the town
Flow'd in, and settling circled all the lists.
And there they fixt the forks into the ground,
And over these they placed a silver wand
And over that a golden sparrow-hawk.
Then Yniol's nephew, after trumpet blown,
Spake to the lady with him and proclaim'd,
"Advance and take as fairest of the fair,
For I these two years past have won it for thee."
The prize of beauty." Loudly spake the Prince,
"Forbear: there is a worthier," and the knight
With some surprise and thrice as much disdain
Turn'd, and beheld the four, and all his face
Glow'd like the heart of a great fire at Yule,
So burnt he was with passion, crying out,
"Do battle for it then," no more; and thrice
They clash'd together, and thrice they brake their spears.
Then each, dishorsed and drawing, lash'd at each
So often and with such blows, that all the crowd
Wonder'd, and now and then from distant walls
There came a clapping as of phantom hands.
So twice they fought, and twice they breathed, and still
The dew of their great labor, and the blood
Of their strong bodies, flowing, drain'd their force.
But either's force was match'd till Yniol's cry,
"Remember that great insult done the Queen,"
Increased Geraint's, who heaved his blade aloft,
And crack'd the helmet thro', and bit the bone,
And fell'd him, and set foot upon his breast,
And said, "Thy name?" To whom the fallen man
Made answer, groaning, "Edyrn, son of Nudd!
Ashamed am I that I should tell it thee.
My pride is broken: men have seen my fall."
"Then, Edyrn, son of Nudd," replied Geraint,
"These two things shalt thou do, or else thou diest.
First, thou thyself, thy lady, and thy dwarf,
Shalt ride to Arthur's court, and being there,
Crave pardon for that insult done the Queen,
And shalt abide her judgment on it; next,
Thou shalt give back their earldom to thy kin.
These two things shalt thou do, or thou shalt die."
And Edyrn answer'd, "These things will I do,
For I have never yet been overthrown,
And thou hast overthrown me, and my pride
Is broken down, for Enid sees my fall!"
And rising up, he rode to Arthur's court,
And there the Queen forgave him easily.
And being young, he changed, and came to loathe
His crime of traitor, slowly drew himself
Bright from his old dark life, and fell at last
In the great battle fighting for the king.

But when the third day from the hunting-morn
Made a low splendor in the world, and wings
Moved in her ivy, Enid, for she lay
With her fair head in the dim-yellow light,
Among the dancing shadows of the birds,

GERAINT AND ENID.

Woke and bethought her of her promise
  given
No later than last eve to Prince Geraint—
So bent he seem'd on going the third day,
He would not leave her, till her promise
  given—
To ride with him this morning to the court,
And there be made known to the stately
  Queen,
And there be wedded with all ceremony.
At this she cast her eyes upon her dress,
And thought it never yet had look'd so
  mean.
For as a leaf in mid-November is
To what it was in mid-October, seem'd
The dress that now she look'd on to the
  dress
She look'd on ere the coming of Geraint.
And still she look'd, and still the terror
  grew
Of that strange bright and dreadful thing,
  a court,
All staring at her in her faded silk :
And softly to her own sweet heart she said :

"This noble prince who won our earl-
  dom back,
So splendid in his acts and his attire,
Sweet heaven, how much I shall discredit
  him !
Would he could tarry with us here awhile !
But being so beholden to the Prince,
It were but little grace in any of us,
Bent as he seem'd on going this third day,
To seek a second favor at his hands.
Yet if he could but tarry a day or two,
Myself would work eye dim, and finger
  lame,
Far liefer than so much discredit him."

And Enid fell in longing for a dress
All branch'd and flower'd with gold, a
  costly gift
Of her good mother, given her on the night
Before her birthday, three sad years ago,
That night of fire, when Edyrn sack'd
  their house,
And scatter'd all they had to all the winds :
For while the mother show'd it, and the
  two
Were turning and admiring it, the work
To both appear'd so costly, rose a cry
That Edyrn's men were on them, and
  they fled
With little save the jewels they had on,
Which being sold and sold had bought
  them bread :

And Edyrn's men had caught them in
  their flight,
And placed them in this ruin ; and she
  wish'd
The Prince had found her in her ancient
  home ;
Then let her fancy flit across the past,
And roam the goodly places that she knew ;
And last bethought her how she used to
  watch,
Near that old home, a pool of golden carp ;
And one was patch'd and blurr'd and
  lustreless
Among his burnish'd brethren of the pool ;
And half asleep she made comparison
Of that and these to her own faded self
And the gay court, and fell asleep again ;
And dreamt herself was such a faded form
Among her burnish'd sisters of the pool ;
But this was in the garden of a king ;
And tho' she lay dark in the pool, she knew
That all was bright ; that all about were
  birds
Of sunny plume in gilded trellis-work ;
That all the turf was rich in plots that
  look'd
Each like a garnet or a turkis in it ;
And lords and ladies of the high court
  went
In silver tissue talking things of state ;
And children of the king in cloth of gold
Glanced at the doors or gambol'd down
  the walks ;
And while she thought "they will not
  see me," came
A stately queen whose name was Guine-
  vere,
And all the children in their cloth of gold
Ran to her, crying, "if we have fish at all
Let them be gold ; and charge the gar-
  deners now
To pick the faded creature from the pool,
And cast it on the mixen that it die."
And therewithal one came and seized on
  her,
And Enid started waking, with her heart
All overshadow'd by the foolish dream,
And lo ! it was her mother grasping her
To get her well awake ; and in her hand
A suit of bright apparel, which she laid
Flat on the couch, and spoke exultingly :

"See here, my child, how fresh the
  colors look,
How fast they hold like colors of a shell
That keeps the wear and polish of the
  wave.

Why not ? it never yet was worn, I trow :
Look on it, child, and tell me if ye know
   it."

   And Enid look'd, but all confused at
      first,
Could scarce divide it from her foolish
   dream :
Then suddenly she knew it and rejoiced,
And answer'd, " Yea, I know it ; your
   good gift,
So sadly lost on that unhappy night ;
Your own good gift!" "Yea, surely,"
   said the dame,
"And gladly given again this happy morn.
For when the jousts were ended yesterday,
Went Yniol thro' the town, and every-
   where
He found the sack and plunder of our house
All scatter'd thro' the houses of the
   town ;
And gave command that all which once
   was ours,
Should now be ours again : and yester-eve,
While you were talking sweetly with your
   Prince
Came one with this and laid it in my hand,
For love or fear, or seeking favor of us,
Because we have our earldom back again.
And yester-eve I would not tell you of it,
But kept it for a sweet surprise at morn.
Yea, truly is it not a sweet surprise ?
For I myself unwillingly have worn
My faded suit, as you, my child, have yours,
And howsoever patient, Yniol his.
Ah, dear, he took me from a goodly house,
With store of rich apparel, sumptuous fare,
And page, and maid, and squire, and
   seneschal,
And pastime both of hawk and hound,
   and all
That appertains to noble maintenance.
Yea, and he brought me to a goodly house ;
But since our fortune slipt from sun to
   shade,
And all thro' that young traitor, cruel
   need
Constrain'd us, but a better time has come ;
So clothe yourself in this, that better fits
Our mended fortunes and a Prince's bride :
For tho' ye won the prize of fairest fair,
And tho' I heard him call you fairest fair,
Let never maiden think, however fair,
She is not fairer in new clothes than old.
And should some great court-lady say,
   the Prince
Hath pick'd a ragged-robin from the hedge,
And like a madman brought her to the
   court,
Then were ye shamed, and, worse, might
   shame the Prince
To whom we are beholden ; but I know,
When my dear child is set forth at her
   best,
That neither court nor country, tho' they
   sought
Thro' all the provinces like those of old
That lighted on Queen Esther, has her
   match."

   Here ceased the kindly mother out of
      breath ;
And Enid listen'd brightening as she lay ;
Then, as the white and glittering star of
   morn
Parts from a bank of snow, and by and by
Slips into golden cloud, the maiden rose,
And left her maiden couch, and robed
   herself,
Help'd by the mother's careful hand and
   eye,
Without a mirror, in the gorgeous gown ;
Who, after, turn'd her daughter round,
   and said,
She never yet had seen her half so fair ;
And call'd her like that maiden in the
   tale,
Whom Gwydion made by glamour out
   of flowers,
And sweeter than the bride of Cassivelaun,
Flur, for whose love the Roman Cæsar
   first
Invaded Britain, "but we beat him back,
As this great prince invaded us, and we,
Not beat him back, but welcomed him
   with joy.
And I can scarcely ride with you to court,
For old am I, and rough the ways and
   wild ;
But Yniol goes, and I full oft shall dream
I see my princess as I see her now,
Clothed with my gift, and gay among the
   gay."

   But while the women thus rejoiced,
      Geraint
Woke where he slept in the high hall,
   and call'd
For Enid, and when Yniol made report
Of that good mother making Enid gay
In such apparel as might well beseem
His princess, or indeed the stately queen,
He answer'd ; "Earl, entreat her by my
   love,

Albeit I give no reason but my wish,
That she ride with me in her faded silk."
Yniol with that hard message went ; it fell,
Like flaws in summer laying lusty corn :
For Enid all abash'd she knew not why,
Dared not to glance at her good mother's face,
But silently, in all obedience,
Her mother silent too, nor helping her,
Laid from her limbs the costly-broider'd gift,
And robed them in her ancient suit again,
And so descended. Never man rejoiced
More than Geraint to greet her thus attired ;
And glancing all at once as keenly at her,
As careful robins eye the delver's toil,
Made her cheek burn and either eyelid fall,
But rested with her sweet face satisfied ;
Then seeing cloud upon the mother's brow,
Her by both hands he caught, and sweetly said.

"O my new mother, be not wroth or grieved
At your new son, for my petition to her.
When late I left Caerleon, our great Queen,
In words whose echo lasts, they were so sweet,
Made promise, that whatever bride I brought,
Herself would clothe her like the sun in Heaven.
Thereafter, when I reach'd this ruin'd hold,
Beholding one so bright in dark estate,
I vow'd that could I gain her, our kind Queen,
No hand but hers, should make your Enid burst
Sunlike from cloud — and likewise thought perhaps,
That service done so graciously would bind
The two together ; for I wish the two
To love each other : how should Enid find
A nobler friend ? Another thought I had ;
I came among you here so suddenly,
That tho' her gentle presence at the lists
Might well have served for proof that I was loved,
I doubted whether filial tenderness,
Or easy nature, did not let itself
Be moulded by your wishes for her weal ;
Or whether some false sense in her own self
Of my contrasting brightness, overbore
Her fancy dwelling in this dusky hall ;
And such a sense might make her long for court
And all its dangerous glories : and I thought,
That could I someway prove such force in her
Link'd with such love for me, that at a word
(No reason given her) she could cast aside
A splendor dear to women, new to her,
And therefore dearer ; or if not so new,
Yet therefore tenfold dearer by the power
Of intermitted custom ; then I felt
That I could rest, a rock in ebbs and flows,
Fixt on her faith. Now, therefore, I do rest,
A prophet certain of my prophecy,
That never shadow of mistrust can cross
Between us. Grant me pardon for my thoughts :
And for my strange petition I will make
Amends hereafter by some gaudy-day,
When your fair child shall wear your costly gift
Beside your own warm hearth, with, on her knees,
Who knows ? another gift of the high God,
Which, maybe, shall have learn'd to lisp you thanks."

He spoke : the mother smiled, but half in tears,
Then brought a mantle down and wrapt her in it,
And claspt and kiss'd her, and they rode away.

Now thrice that morning Guinevere had climb'd
The giant tower, from whose high crest, they say,
Men saw the goodly hills of Somerset,
And white sails flying on the yellow sea ;
But not to goodly hill or yellow sea
Look'd the fair Queen, but up the vale of Usk,
By the flat meadow, till she saw them come ;
And then descending met them at the gates,
Embraced her with all welcome as a friend,
And did her honor as the Prince's bride,
And clothed her for her bridals like the sun ;

GERAINT AND ENID.

*"The giant tower, from whose high crest, they say,
Men saw the goodly hills of Somerset,
And white sails flying on the yellow sea."*

And all that week was old Caerleon gay,
For by the hands of Dubric, the high
    saint,
They twain were wedded with all cere-
    mony.

And this was on the last year's Whit-
    suntide.
But Enid ever kept the faded silk,
Remembering how first he came on her,
Drest in that dress, and how he loved
    her in it,
And all her foolish fears about the dress,
And all his journey toward her, as himself
Had told her, and their coming to the
    court.

And now this morning when he said
    to her,
"Put on your worst and meanest dress,"
    she found
And took it, and array'd herself therein.

O purblind race of miserable men,
How many among us at this very hour
Do forge a life-long trouble for ourselves,
By taking true for false, or false for
    true ;
Here, thro' the feeble twilight of this
    world
Groping, how many, until we pass and
    reach
That other, where we see as we are seen !

GERAINT AND ENID.   149

So fared it with Geraint, who issuing forth
That morning, when they both had got to horse,
Perhaps because he loved her passionately,
And felt that tempest brooding round his heart,
Which, if he spoke at all, would break perforce
Upon a head so dear in thunder, said:
"Not at my side. I charge you ride before,
Ever a good way on before; and this
I charge you, on your duty as a wife,
Whatever happens, not to speak to me,
No, not a word!" and Enid was aghast;
And forth they rode, but scarce three paces on,
When crying out "Effeminate as I am,
I will not fight my way with gilded arms,
All shall be iron"; he loosed a mighty purse,
Hung at his belt, and hurl'd it toward the squire.
So the last sight that Enid had of home
Was all the marble threshold flashing, strown
With gold and scatter'd coinage, and the squire
Chafing his shoulder: then he cried again,
"To the wilds!" and Enid leading down the tracks
Thro' which he bade her lead him on, they past
The marches, and by bandit-haunted holds,
Gray swamps and pools, waste places of the hern
And wildernesses, perilous paths, they rode:
Round was their pace at first, but slacken'd soon:
A stranger meeting them had surely thought
They rode so slowly and they look'd so pale,
That each had suffer'd some exceeding wrong.
For he was ever saying to himself
"O I that wasted time to tend upon her,
To compass her with sweet observances,
To dress her beautifully and keep her true" —
And there he broke the sentence in his heart
Abruptly, as a man upon his tongue

May break it, when his passion masters him.
And she was ever praying the sweet heavens
To save her dear lord whole from any wound.
And ever in her mind she cast about
For that unnoticed failing in herself,
Which made him look so cloudy and so cold;
Till the great plover's human whistle amazed
Her heart, and glancing round the waste she fear'd
In every wavering brake an ambuscade.
Then thought again "if there be such in me,
I might amend it by the grace of heaven,
If he would only speak and tell me of it."

But when the fourth part of the day was gone,
Then Enid was aware of three tall knights
On horseback, wholly arm'd, behind a rock
In shadow, waiting for them, caitiffs all;
And heard one crying to his fellow, "Look,
Here comes a laggard hanging down his head,
Who seems no bolder than a beaten hound;
Come, we will slay him and will have his horse
And armor, and his damsel shall be ours."

Then Enid ponder'd in her heart, and said;
"I will go back a little to my lord,
And I will tell him all their caitiff talk;
For, be he wroth even to slaying me,
Far liever by his dear hand had I die,
Than that my lord should suffer loss or shame."

Then she went back some paces of return,
Met his full frown timidly firm, and said:
"My lord, I saw three bandits by the rock
Waiting to fall on you, and heard them boast
That they would slay you, and possess your horse
And armor, and your damsel should be theirs."

He made a wrathful answer. "Did I
  wish
Your warning or your silence? one com-
  mand
I laid upon you, not to speak to me,
And thus you keep it! Well then, look
  — for now,
Whether you wish me victory or defeat,
Long for my life, or hunger for my death,
Yourself shall see my vigor is not lost."

Then Enid waited pale and sorrowful,
And down upon him bare the bandit
  three.
And at the midmost charging, Prince
  Geraint
Drave the long spear a cubit thro' his
  breast
And out beyond; and then against his
  brace
Of comrades, each of whom had broken
  on him
A lance that splinter'd like an icicle,
Swung from his brand a windy buffet out
Once, twice, to right, to left, and stunn'd
  the twain
Or slew them, and dismounting like a man
That skins the wild beast after slaying
  him,
Stript from the three dead wolves of
  woman born
The three gay suits of armor which they
  wore,
And let the bodies lie, but bound the
  suits
Of armor on their horses, each on each,
And tied the bridle-reins of all the three
Together, and said to her, "Drive them on
Before you"; and she drove them thro'
  the waste.

He follow'd nearer: ruth began to work
Against his anger in him, while he watch'd
The being he loved best in all the world,
With difficulty in mild obedience
Driving them on: he fain had spoken to
  her,
And loosed in words of sudden fire the
  wrath
And smoulder'd wrong that burnt him
  all within;
But evermore it seem'd an easier thing
At once without remorse to strike her
  dead,
Than to cry "Halt," and to her own
  bright face
Accuse her of the least immodesty:

And thus tongue-tied, it made him wroth
  the more
That she *could* speak whom his own ear
  had heard
Call herself false: and suffering thus he
  made
Minutes an age: but in scarce longer time
Than at Caerleon the full-tided Usk,
Before he turn to fall seaward again,
Pauses, did Enid, keeping watch, behold
In the first shallow shade of a deep wood,
Before a gloom of stubborn-shafted oaks,
Three other horsemen waiting, wholly
  arm'd,
Whereof one seem'd far larger than her
  lord,
And shook her pulses, crying, "Look, a
  prize!
Three horses and three goodly suits of
  arms,
And all in charge of whom? a girl: set on."
"Nay" said the second, "yonder comes
  a knight."
The third, "A craven; how he hangs his
  head."
The giant answer'd merrily, "Yea, but
  one?
Wait here, and when he passes fall upon
  him."

And Enid ponder'd in her heart and
  said,
"I will abide the coming of my lord,
And I will tell him all their villany.
My lord is weary with the fight before,
And they will fall upon him unawares.
I needs must disobey him for his good;
How should I dare obey him to his harm?
Needs must I speak, and tho' he kill me
  for it,
I save a life dearer to me than mine."

And she abode his coming, and said to
  him
With timid firmness, "Have I leave to
  speak?"
He said, "Ye take it, speaking," and
  she spoke.

"There lurk three villains yonder in
  the wood,
And each of them is wholly arm'd, and
  one
Is larger-limb'd than you are, and they
  say
That they will fall upon you while you
  pass."

GERAINT AND ENID. 151

To which he flung a wrathful answer back:
"And if there were an hundred in the wood,
And every man were larger-limb'd than I,
And all at once should sally out upon me,
I swear it would not ruffle me so much
As you that not obey me. Stand aside,
And if I fall, cleave to the better man."

And Enid stood aside to wait the event,
Not dare to watch the combat, only breathe
Short fits of prayer, at every stroke a breath.
And he, she dreaded most, bare down upon him.
Aim'd at the helm, his lance err'd ; but Geraint's,
A little in the late encounter strain'd,
Struck thro' the bulky bandit's corselet home,
And then brake short, and down his enemy roll'd,
And there lay still ; as he that tells the tale,
Saw once a great piece of a promontory,
That had a sapling growing on it, slip
From the long shore-cliff's windy walls to the beach,
And there lie still, and yet the sapling grew :
So lay the man transfixt. His craven pair
Of comrades, making slowlier at the Prince,
When now they saw their bulwark fallen, stood ;
On whom the victor, to confound them more,
Spurr'd with his terrible war-cry ; for as one,
That listens near a torrent mountain-brook,
All thro' the crash of the near cataract hears
The drumming thunder of the huger fall
At distance, were the soldiers wont to hear
His voice in battle, and be kindled by it,
And foemen scared, like that false pair who turn'd
Flying, but, overtaken, died the death
Themselves had wrought on many an innocent.

Thereon Geraint, dismounting, pick'd the lance
That pleased him best, and drew from those dead wolves

Their three gay suits of armor, each from each,
And bound them on their horses, each on each,
And tied the bridle-reins of all the three
Together, and said to her, "Drive them on
Before you," and she drove them thro' the wood.

He follow'd nearer still : the pain she had
To keep them in the wild ways of the wood,
Two sets of three laden with jingling arms,
Together, served a little to disedge
The sharpness of that pain about her heart :
And they themselves, like creatures gently born
But into bad hands fall'n, and now so long
By bandits groom'd, prick'd their light ears, and felt
Her low firm voice and tender government.

So thro' the green gloom of the wood they past,
And issuing under open heavens beheld
A little town with towers, upon a rock,
And close beneath, a meadow gemlike chased
In the brown wild, and mowers mowing in it :
And down a rocky pathway from the place
There came a fair-hair'd youth, that in his hand
Bare victual for the mowers : and Geraint
Had ruth again on Enid looking pale :
Then, moving downward to the meadow ground,
He, when the fair-hair'd youth came by him, said,
"Friend, let her eat ; the damsel is so faint."
"Yea, willingly," replied the youth ; "and you,
My lord, eat also, tho' the fare is coarse,
And only meet for mowers" ; then set down
His basket, and dismounting on the sward
They let the horses graze, and ate themselves.
And Enid took a little delicately,
Less having stomach for it than desire
To close with her lord's pleasure ; but Geraint
Ate all the mowers' victual unawares,
And when he found all empty, was amazed ;
And " Boy," said he, " I have eaten all, but take

A horse and arms for guerdon; choose
    the best."
He, reddening in extremity of delight,
"My lord, you overpay me fifty-fold."
"Ye will be all the wealthier," cried the
    Prince.
"I take it as free gift, then," said the boy,
"Not guerdon; for myself can easily,
While your good damsel rests, return,
    and fetch
Fresh victual for these mowers of our
    Earl;
For these are his, and all the field is his,
And I myself am his; and I will tell him
How great a man you are: he loves to know
When men of mark are in his territory:
And he will have you to his palace here,
And serve you costlier than with mowers'
    fare."

Then said Geraint, "I wish no better
    fare:
I never ate with angrier appetite
Than when I left your mowers dinnerless,
And into no Earl's palace will I go.
I know, God knows, too much of palaces!
And if he want me, let him come to me.
But hire us some fair chamber for the
    night,
And stalling for the horses, and return
With victual for these men, and let us
    know."

"Yea, my kind lord," said the glad
    youth, and went,
Held his head high, and thought him-
    self a knight,
And up the rocky pathway disappear'd,
Leading the horse, and they were left
    alone.

But when the Prince had brought his
    errant eyes
Home from the rock, sideways he let
    them glance
At Enid, where she droopt: his own
    false doom,
That shadow of mistrust should never cross
Betwixt them, came upon him, and he
    sigh'd;
Then with another humorous ruth re-
    mark'd
The lusty mowers laboring dinnerless,
And watch'd the sun blaze on the turn-
    ing scythe,
And after nodded sleepily in the heat.
But she, remembering her old ruin'd hall,

And all the windy clamor of the daws
About her hollow turret, pluck'd the grass
There growing longest by the meadow's
    edge,
And into many a listless annulet,
Now over, now beneath her marriage ring,
Wove and unwove it, till the boy return'd
And told them of a chamber, and they
    went;
Where, after saying to her, "If ye will,
Call for the woman of the house," to
    which
She answer'd, "Thanks, my lord"; the
    two remain'd
Apart by all the chamber's width, and
    mute
As creatures voiceless thro' the fault of
    birth,
Or two wild men supporters of a shield,
Painted, who stare at open space, nor
    glance
The one at other, parted by the shield.

On a sudden, many a voice along the
    street,
And heel against the pavement echoing,
    burst
Their drowse; and either started while
    the door,
Push'd from without, drave backward to
    the wall,
And midmost of a rout of roisterers,
Femininely fair and dissolutely pale,
Her suitor in old years before Geraint,
Enter'd, the wild lord of the place,
    Limours.
He moving up with pliant courtliness,
Greeted Geraint full face, but stealthily,
In the mid-warmth of welcome and
    graspt hand,
Found Enid with the corner of his eye,
And knew her sitting sad and solitary.
Then cried Geraint for wine and goodly
    cheer
To feed the sudden guest, and sumptu-
    ously
According to his fashion, bade the host
Call in what men soever were his friends,
And feast with these in honor of their earl;
"And care not for the cost; the cost is
    mine."

And wine and food were brought, and
    Earl Limours
Drank till he jested with all ease, and told
Free tales, and took the word and play'd
    upon it,

GERAINT AND ENID.

And made it of two colors; for his talk,
When wine and free companions kindled him,
Was wont to glance and sparkle like a gem
Of fifty facets; thus he moved the Prince
To laughter and his comrades to applause.
Then, when the Prince was merry, ask'd Limours,
"Your leave, my lord, to cross the room, and speak
To your good damsel there who sits apart,
And seems so lonely?" "My free leave" he said;
"Get her to speak: she does not speak to me."
Then rose Limours and looking at his feet,
Like him who tries the bridge he fears may fail,
Crost and came near, lifted adoring eyes,
Bow'd at her side and utter'd whisperingly:

"Enid, the pilot star of my lone life,
Enid my early and my only love,
Enid the loss of whom has turn'd me wild —
What chance is this? how is it I see you here?
You are in my power at last, are in my power.
Yet fear me not: I call mine own self wild,
But keep a touch of sweet civility
Here in the heart of waste and wilderness.
I thought, but that your father came between,
In former days you saw me favorably.
And if it were so do not keep it back:
Make me a little happier: let me know it:
Owe you me nothing for a life half-lost?
Yea, yea, the whole dear debt of all you are.
And, Enid, you and he, I see it with joy —
You sit apart, you do not speak to him,
You come with no attendance, page or maid,
To serve you — does he love you as of old?
For, call it lovers' quarrels, yet I know
Tho' men may bicker with the things they love,
They would not make them laughable in all eyes,
Not while they loved them; and your wretched dress,
A wretched insult on you, dumbly speaks
Your story, that this man loves you no more.
Your beauty is no beauty to him now:

A common chance — right well I know it — pall'd —
For I know men: nor will ye win him back,
For the man's love once gone never returns.
But here is one who loves you as of old;
With more exceeding passion than of old:
Good, speak the word: my followers ring him round:
He sits unarm'd; I hold a finger up;
They understand: no; I do not mean blood:
Nor need you look so scared at what I say:
My malice is no deeper than a moat,
No stronger than a wall: there is the keep;
He shall not cross us more; speak but the word:
Or speak it not; but then by Him that made me
The one true lover which you ever had,
I will make use of all the power I have.
O pardon me! the madness of that hour,
When first I parted from you, moves me yet."

At this the tender sound of his own voice
And sweet self-pity, or the fancy of it,
Made his eye moist; but Enid fear'd his eyes,
Moist as they were, wine-heated from the feast;
And answer'd with such craft as women use,
Guilty or guiltless, to stave off a chance
That breaks upon them perilously, and said:

"Earl, if you love me as in former years,
And do not practise on me, come with morn,
And snatch me from him as by violence;
Leave me to-night: I am weary to the death."

Low at leave-taking, with his brandish'd plume
Brushing his instep, bow'd the all-amorous Earl,
And the stout Prince bade him a loud good-night.
He moving homeward babbled to his men,
How Enid never loved a man but him,
Nor cared a broken egg-shell for her lord.

But Enid left alone with Prince Geraint,
Debating his command of silence given,

And that she now perforce must violate it,
Held commune with herself, and while
    she held
He fell asleep, and Enid had no heart
To wake him, but hung o'er him, wholly
    pleased
To find him yet unwounded after fight,
And hear him breathing low and equally.
Anon she rose, and stepping lightly,
    heap'd
The pieces of his armor in one place,
All to be there against a sudden need ;
Then dozed awhile herself, but overtoil'd
By that day's grief and travel, evermore
Seem'd catching at a rootless thorn, and
    then
Went slipping down horrible precipices,
And strongly striking out her limbs
    awoke ;
Then thought she heard the wild Earl at
    the door,
With all his rout of random followers,
Sound on a dreadful trumpet, summon-
    ing her ;
Which was the red cock shouting to the
    light,
As the gray dawn stole o'er the dewy
    world,
And glimmer'd on his armor in the room.
And once again she rose to look at it,
But touch'd it unawares: jangling, the
    casque
Fell, and he started up and stared at her.
Then breaking his command of silence
    given,
She told him all that Earl Limours had
    said,
Except the passage that he loved her
    not ;
Nor left untold the craft herself had used;
But ended with apology so sweet,
Low-spoken, and of so few words, and
    seem'd
So justified by that necessity,
That tho' he thought "was it for him
    she wept
In Devon?" he but gave a wrathful
    groan,
Saying "your sweet faces make good
    fellows fools
And traitors. Call the host and bid him
    bring
Charger and palfrey." So she glided out
Among the heavy breathings of the house,
And like a household Spirit at the walls
Beat, till she woke the sleepers, and re-
    turn'd :

Then tending her rough lord, tho' all un-
    ask'd,
In silence, did him service as a squire ;
Till issuing arm'd he found the host and
    cried,
"Thy reckoning, friend?" and ere he
    learnt it, "Take
Five horses and their armors" ; and the
    host,
Suddenly honest, answer'd in amaze,
"My lord, I scarce have spent the worth
    of one !"
"Ye will be all the wealthier," said the
    Prince,
And then to Enid, " Forward ! and to-day
I charge you, Enid, more especially,
What thing soever ye may hear, or see,
Or fancy (tho' I count it of small use
To charge you) that ye speak not but
    obey."

And Enid answer'd, "Yea, my lord, I
    know
Your wish, and would obey ; but riding
    first,
I hear the violent threats you do not hear,
I see the danger which you cannot see :
Then not to give you warning, that seems
    hard ;
Almost beyond me : yet I would obey."

"Yea so," said he, "do it : be not too
    wise ;
Seeing that ye are wedded to a man,
Not quite mismated with a yawning
    clown,
But one with arms to guard his head and
    yours,
With eyes to find you out however far,
And ears to hear you even in his dreams."

With that he turn'd and look'd as
    keenly at her
As careful robins eye the delver's toil ;
And that within her, which a wanton
    fool,
Or hasty judger would have call'd her
    guilt,
Made her cheek burn and either eyelid fall.
And Geraint look'd and was not satisfied.

Then forward by a way which, beaten
    broad,
Led from the territory of false Limours
To the waste earldom of another earl,
Doorm, whom his shaking vassals call'd
    the Bull,

Went Enid with her sullen follower on.
Once she look'd back, and when she saw him ride
More near by many a rood than yestermorn,
It wellnigh made her cheerful; till Geraint
Waving an angry hand as who should say
"Ye watch me," sadden'd all her heart again.
But while the sun yet beat a dewy blade,
The sound of many a heavily-galloping hoof
Smote on her ear, and turning round she saw
Dust, and the points of lances bicker in it.
Then not to disobey her lord's behest,
And yet to give him warning, for he rode
As if he heard not, moving back she held
Her finger up, and pointed to the dust.
At which the warrior in his obstinacy,
Because she kept the letter of his word
Was in a manner pleased, and turning, stood.
And in the moment after, wild Limours,
Borne on a black horse, like a thundercloud
Whose skirts are loosen'd by the breaking storm,
Half ridden off with by the thing he rode,
And all in passion uttering a dry shriek,
Dash'd on Geraint, who closed with him, and bore
Down by the length of lance and arm beyond
The crupper, and so left him stunn'd or dead,
And overthrew the next that follow'd him,
And blindly rush'd on all the rout behind.
But at the flash and motion of the man
They vanish'd panic-stricken, like a shoal
Of darting fish, that on a summer morn
Adown the crystal dykes at Camelot
Come slipping o'er their shadows on the sand,
But if a man who stands upon the brink
But lift a shining hand against the sun,
There is not left the twinkle of a fin
Betwixt the cressy islets white in flower,
So, scared but at the motion of the man,
Fled all the boon companions of the Earl,
And left him lying in the public way;
So vanish friendships only made in wine.

Then like a stormy sunlight smiled Geraint,
Who saw the chargers of the two that fell
Start from their fallen lords, and wildly fly,
Mixt with the fliers. "Horse and man," he said,
"All of one mind and all right-honest friends!
Not a hoof left: and I methinks till now
Was honest — paid with horses and with arms;
I cannot steal or plunder, no nor beg:
And so what say ye, shall we strip him there
Your lover? has your palfrey heart enough
To bear his armor? shall we fast, or dine?
No? — then do you, being right honest, pray
That we may meet the horsemen of Earl Doorm,
I too would still be honest." Thus he said:
And sadly gazing on her bridle-reins,
And answering not one word, she led the way.

But as a man to whom a dreadful loss
Falls in a far land and he knows it not,
But coming back he learns it, and the loss
So pains him that he sickens nigh to death;
So fared it with Geraint, who being prick'd
In combat with the follower of Limours,
Bled underneath his armor secretly,
And so rode on, nor told his gentle wife
What ail'd him, hardly knowing it himself,
Till his eye darken'd and his helmet wagg'd;
And at a sudden swerving of the road,
Tho' happily down on a bank of grass,
The Prince, without a word, from his horse fell.

And Enid heard the clashing of his fall,
Suddenly came, and at his side all pale
Dismounting, loosed the fastenings of his arms,
Nor let her true hand falter, nor blue eye
Moisten, till she had lighted on his wound,
And tearing off her veil of faded silk
Had bared her forehead to the blistering sun,
And swathed the hurt that drain'd her dear lord's life.
Then after all was done that hand could do,
She rested, and her desolation came
Upon her, and she wept beside the way.

And many past, but none regarded her,
For in that realm of lawless turbulence,
A woman weeping for her murder'd mate
Was cared as much for as a summer
    shower :
One took him for a victim of Earl Doorm,
Nor dared to waste a perilous pity on him :
Another hurrying past, a man-at-arms,
Rode on a mission to the bandit Earl ;
Half whistling and half singing a coarse
    song,
He drove the dust against her veilless eyes.
Another, flying from the wrath of Doorm
Before an ever-fancied arrow, made
The long way smoke beneath him in his
    fear ;
At which her palfrey whinnying lifted
    heel,
And scour'd into the coppices and was
    lost,
While the great charger stood, grieved
    like a man.

But at the point of noon the huge Earl
    Doorm,
Broad-faced with under-fringe of russet
    beard,
Bound on a foray, rolling eyes of prey,
Came riding with a hundred lances up ;
But ere he came, like one that hails a ship,
Cried out with a big voice, " What, is he
    dead ?"
"No, no, not dead !" she answer'd in all
    haste.
"Would some of your kind people take
    him up,
And bear him hence out of this cruel sun :
Most sure am I, quite sure, he is not dead."

Then said Earl Doorm ; "Well, if he
    be not dead,
Why wail ye for him thus ? ye seem a
    child.
And be he dead, I count you for a fool ;
Your wailing will not quicken him : dead
    or not,
Ye mar a comely face with idiot tears.
Yet, since the face *is* comely — some of
    you,
Here, take him up, and bear him to our
    hall :
An if he live, we will have him of our
    band ;
And if he die, why earth has earth enough
To hide him. See ye take the charger too,
A noble one."
        He spake, and past away,
But left two brawny spearmen, who ad-
    vanced,
Each growling like a dog, when his good
    bone
Seems to be pluck'd at by the village boys
Who love to vex him eating, and he fears
To lose his bone, and lays his foot upon it,
Gnawing and growling : so the ruffians
    growl'd,
Fearing to lose, and all for a dead man,
Their chance of booty from the morning's
    raid ;
Yet raised and laid him on a litter-bier,
Such as they brought upon their forays out
For those that might be wounded ; laid
    him on it
All in the hollow of his shield, and took
And bore him to the naked hall of Doorm,
(His gentle charger following him unled)
And cast him and the bier in which he lay
Down on an oaken settle in the hall,
And then departed, hot in haste to join
Their luckier mates, but growling as be-
    fore,
And cursing their lost time, and the dead
    man,
And their own Earl, and their own souls,
    and her.
They might as well have blest her : she
    was deaf
To blessing or to cursing save from one.

So for long hours sat Enid by her lord,
There in the naked hall, propping his head,
And chafing his pale hands, and calling
    to him.
And at the last he waken'd from his swoon,
And found his own dear bride propping
    his head,
And chafing his faint hands, and calling
    to him ;
And felt the warm tears falling on his face ;
And said to his own heart, "she weeps
    for me" :
And yet lay still, and feign'd himself as
    dead,
That he might prove her to the uttermost,
And say to his own heart "she weeps
    for me."

But in the falling afternoon return'd
The huge Earl Doorm with plunder to the
    hall.
His lusty spearmen follow'd him with
    noise :
Each hurling down a heap of things that
    rang

Against the pavement, cast his lance aside,
And doff'd his helm: and then there flutter'd in,
Half-bold, half-frighted, with dilated eyes,
A tribe of women, dress'd in many hues,
And mingled with the spearmen: and Earl Doorm
Struck with a knife's haft hard against the board,
And call'd for flesh and wine to feed his spears.
And men brought in whole hogs and quarter beeves,
And all the hall was dim with steam of flesh:
And none spake word, but all sat down at once,
And ate with tumult in the naked hall,
Feeding like horses when you hear them feed;
Till Enid shrank far back into herself,
To shun the wild ways of the lawless tribe.
But when Earl Doorm had eaten all he would,
He roll'd his eyes about the hall, and found
A damsel drooping in a corner of it.
Then he remember'd her, and how she wept;
And out of her there came a power upon him;
And rising on the sudden he said, "Eat!
I never yet beheld a thing so pale.
God's curse, it makes me mad to see you weep.
Eat! Look yourself. Good luck had your good man,
For were I dead who is it would weep for me?
Sweet lady, never since I first drew breath,
Have I beheld a lily like yourself.
And so there lived some color in your cheek,
There is not one among my gentlewomen
Were fit to wear your slipper for a glove.
But listen to me, and by me be ruled,
And I will do the thing I have not done,
For you shall share my earldom with me, girl,
And we will live like two birds in one nest,
And I will fetch you forage from all fields,
For I compel all creatures to my will."

He spoke: the brawny spearman let his cheek
Bulge with the unswallow'd piece, and turning stared;

While some, whose souls the old serpent long had drawn
Down, as the worm draws in the wither'd leaf
And makes it earth, hiss'd each at other's ear
What shall not be recorded—women they,
Women, or what had been those gracious things,
But now desired the humbling of their best,
Yea, would have helped him to it: and all at once
They hated her, who took no thought of them,
But answer'd in low voice, her meek head yet
Drooping, "I pray you of your courtesy,
He being as he is, to let me be."

She spake so low he hardly heard her speak,
But like a mighty patron, satisfied
With what himself had done so graciously,
Assumed that she had thanked him, adding, "yea,
Eat and be glad, for I account you mine."

She answer'd meekly, "How should I be glad
Henceforth in all the world at anything,
Until my lord arise and look upon me?"

Here the huge Earl cried out upon her talk,
As all but empty heart and weariness
And sickly nothing; suddenly seized on her,
And bare her by main violence to the board,
And thrust the dish before her, crying, "Eat."

"No, no," said Enid, vext, "I will not eat,
Till yonder man upon the bier arise,
And eat with me." "Drink, then," he answer'd. "Here!"
(And fill'd a horn with wine and held it to her,)
"Lo! I, myself, when flush'd with fight, or hot,
God's curse, with anger—often I myself,
Before I well have drunken, scarce can eat:
Drink therefore and the wine will change your will."

"Not so," she cried, "by Heaven, I will not drink,
Till my dear lord arise and bid me do it,
And drink with me; and if he rise no more,
I will not look at wine until I die."

At this he turn'd all red and paced his hall,
Now gnaw'd his under, now his upper lip,
And coming up close to her, said at last:
"Girl, for I see ye scorn my courtesies,
Take warning: yonder man is surely dead;
And I compel all creatures to my will.
Not eat nor drink? And wherefore wail for one,
Who put your beauty to this flout and scorn
By dressing it in rags? Amazed am I,
Beholding how ye butt against my wish,
That I forbear you thus: cross me no more.
At least put off to please me this poor gown,
This silken rag, this beggar-woman's weed:
I love that beauty should go beautifully:
For see ye not my gentlewomen here,
How gay, how suited to the house of one,
Who loves that beauty should go beautifully!
Rise therefore; robe yourself in this: obey."

He spoke, and one among his gentlewomen
Display'd a splendid silk of foreign loom,
Where like a shoaling sea the lovely blue
Play'd into green, and thicker down the front
With jewels than the sward with drops of dew,
When all night long a cloud clings to the hill,
And with the dawn ascending lets the day
Strike where it clung: so thickly shone the gems.

But Enid answer'd, harder to be moved
Than hardest tyrants in their day of power,
With life-long injuries burning unavenged,
And now their hour has come; and Enid said:

"In this poor gown my dear lord found me first,
And loved me serving in my father's hall:
In this poor gown I rode with him to court,
And there the Queen array'd me like the sun:
In this poor gown he bade me clothe myself,
When now we rode upon this fatal quest
Of honor, where no honor can be gain'd:
And this poor gown I will not cast aside
Until himself arise a living man,
And bid me cast it. I have griefs enough:
Pray you be gentle, pray you let me be:
I never loved, can never love but him:
Yea, God, I pray you of your gentleness,
He being as he is, to let me be."

Then strode the brute Earl up and down his hall,
And took his russet beard between his teeth;
Last, coming up quite close, and in his mood
Crying, "I count it of no more avail,
Dame, to be gentle than ungentle with you;
Take my salute," unknightly with flat hand,
However lightly, smote her on the cheek.

Then Enid, in her utter helplessness,
And since she thought, "he had not dared to do it,
Except he surely knew my lord was dead,"
Sent forth a sudden sharp and bitter cry,
As of a wild thing taken in the trap,
Which sees the trapper coming thro' the wood.

This heard Geraint, and grasping at his sword,
(It lay beside him in the hollow shield,)
Made but a single bound, and with a sweep of it
Shore thro' the swarthy neck, and like a ball
The russet-bearded head roll'd on the floor.
So died Earl Doorm by him he counted dead.
And all the men and women in the hall
Rose when they saw the dead man rise, and fled
Yelling as from a spectre, and the two
Were left alone together, and he said:

"Enid, I have used you worse than that dead man;
Done you more wrong: we both have undergone
That trouble which has left me thrice your own:

"The russet-bearded head roll'd on the floor.
So died Earl Doorm by him he counted dead."

Henceforward I will rather die th in doubt.
And here I lay this penance on myself,
Not, tho' mine own ears heard you yester-morn —
You thought me sleeping, but I heard you say,
I heard you say, that you were no true wife:
I swear I will not ask your meaning in it:
I do believe yourself against yourself,
And will henceforward rather die than doubt."

And Enid could not say one tender word,
She felt so blunt and stupid at the heart:
She only prayed him, "Fly, they will return
And slay you: fly, your charger is without,
My palfrey lost." "Then, Enid, shall you ride
Behind me." "Yea," said Enid, "let us go."
And moving out they found the stately horse,
Who now no more a vassal to the thief,
But free to stretch his limbs in lawful fight,
Neigh'd with all gladness as they came, and stoop'd
With a low whinny toward the pair: and she
Kiss'd the white star upon his noble front,
Glad also; then Geraint upon the horse

Mounted, and reach'd a hand, and on his foot
She set her own and climb'd; he turn'd his face
And kiss'd her climbing, and she cast her arms
About him, and at once they rode away.

And never yet, since high in Paradise
O'er the four rivers the first roses blew,
Came purer pleasure unto mortal kind
Than lived thro' her, who in that perilous hour
Put hand to hand beneath her husband's heart,
And felt him hers again: she did not weep,
But o'er her meek eyes came a happy mist
Like that which kept the heart of Eden green
Before the useful trouble of the rain:
Yet not so misty were her meek blue eyes
As not to see before them on the path,
Right in the gateway of the bandit hold,
A knight of Arthur's court, who laid his lance
In rest, and made as if to fall upon him.
Then, fearing for his hurt and loss of blood,
She, with her mind all full of what had chanced,
Shriek'd to the stranger, "Slay not a dead man!"

"The voice of Enid," said the knight;
  but she,
Beholding it was Edyrn, son of Nudd,
Was moved so much the more, and shriek'd
  again,
"O cousin, slay not him who gave you
  life."
And Edyrn moving frankly forward spake:
"My lord Geraint, I greet you with all
  love;
I took you for a bandit knight of Doorm;
And fear not, Enid, I should fall upon him,
Who love you, Prince, with something
  of the love
Wherewith we love the Heaven that
  chastens us.
For once, when I was up so high in pride
That I was halfway down the slope to
  Hell,
By overthrowing me you threw me higher.
Now, made a knight of Arthur's Table
  Round,
And since I knew this Earl, when I my-
  self
Was half a bandit in my lawless hour,
I come the mouthpiece of our King to
  Doorm
(The King is close behind me) bidding him
Disband himself, and scatter all his
  powers,
Submit, and hear the judgment of the
  King."

"He hears the judgment of the King
  of Kings,"
Cried the wan Prince; "and lo the
  powers of Doorm
Are scatter'd," and he pointed to the field,
Where, huddled here and there on mound
  and knoll,
Were men and women staring and aghast,
While some yet fled; and then he plain-
  lier told
How the huge Earl lay slain within his
  hall.
But when the knight besought him,
  "Follow me,
Prince, to the camp, and in the King's
  own ear
Speak what has chanced; ye surely have
  endured
Strange chances here alone"; that other
  flush'd,
And hung his head, and halted in reply,
Fearing the mild face of the blameless
  King,
And after madness acted question ask'd:

Till Edyrn crying, "If ye will not go
To Arthur, then will Arthur come to you,"
"Enough," he said, "I follow," and they
  went.
But Enid in their going had two fears,
One from the bandit scatter'd in the field,
And one from Edyrn. Every now and
  then,
When Edyrn rein'd his charger at her side,
She shrank a little. In a hollow land,
From which old fires have broken, men
  may fear
Fresh fire and ruin. He, perceiving, said:

"Fair and dear cousin, you that most
  had cause
To fear me, fear no longer, I am changed.
Yourself were first the blameless cause to
  make
My nature's prideful sparkle in the blood
Break into furious flame; being repulsed
By Yniol and yourself, I schemed and
  wrought
Until I overturn'd him; then set up
(With one main purpose ever at my heart)
My haughty jousts, and took a paramour;
Did her mock-honor as the fairest fair,
And, toppling over all antagonism,
So wax'd in pride, that I believed myself
Unconquerable, for I was wellnigh mad:
And, but for my main purpose in these
  jousts,
I should have slain your father, seized
  yourself.
I lived in hope that sometime you would
  come
To these my lists with him whom best
  you loved;
And there, poor cousin, with your meek
  blue eyes,
The truest eyes that ever answer'd heaven,
Behold me overturn and trample on him.
Then, had you cried, or knelt, or pray'd
  to me,
I should not less have kill'd him. And
  you came, —
But once you came, —and with your own
  true eyes
Beheld the man you loved (I speak as one
Speaks of a service done him) overthrow
My proud self, and my purpose three
  years old,
And set his foot upon me, and give me life.
There was I broken down; there was I
  saved;
Tho' thence I rode all-shamed, hating the
  life

He gave me, meaning to be rid of it.
And all the penance the Queen laid upon me
Was but to rest awhile within her court;
Where first as sullen as a beast new-caged,
And waiting to be treated like a wolf,
Because I knew my deeds were known, I found,
Instead of scornful pity or pure scorn,
Such fine reserve and noble reticence,
Manners so kind, yet stately, such a grace
Of tenderest courtesy, that I began
To glance behind me at my former life,
And find that it had been the wolf's indeed:
And oft I talk'd with Dubric, the high saint,
Who, with mild heat of holy oratory,
Subdued me somewhat to that gentleness,
Which, when it weds with manhood, makes a man.
And you were often there about the Queen,
But saw me not, or mark'd not if you saw;
Nor did I care or dare to speak with you,
But kept myself aloof till I was changed;
And fear not, cousin; I am changed indeed."

He spoke, and Enid easily believed,
Like simple noble natures, credulous
Of what they long for, good in friend or foe,
There most in those who most have done them ill.
And when they reach'd the camp the King himself
Advanced to greet them, and beholding her
Tho' pale, yet happy, ask'd her not a word,
But went apart with Edyrn, whom he held
In converse for a little, and return'd,
And, gravely smiling, lifted her from horse,
And kiss'd her with all pureness, brother-like,
And show'd an empty tent allotted her,
And glancing for a minute, till he saw her
Pass into it, turn'd to the Prince, and said:

"Prince, when of late ye pray'd me for my leave
To move to your own land, and there defend
Your marches, I was prick'd with some reproof,
As one that let foul wrong stagnate and be,
By having look'd too much thro' alien eyes,
And wrought too long with delegated hands,
Not used mine own: but now behold me come
To cleanse this common sewer of all my realm,
With Edyrn and with others: have ye look'd
At Edyrn? have ye seen how nobly changed?
This work of his is great and wonderful.
His very face with change of heart is changed.
The world will not believe a man repents:
And this wise world of ours is mainly right.
Full seldom *does* a man repent, or use
Both grace and will to pick the vicious quitch
Of blood and custom wholly out of him,
And make all clean, and plant himself afresh.
Edyrn has done it, weeding all his heart
As I will weed this land before I go.
I, therefore, made him of our Table Round,
Not rashly, but have proved him every way
One of our noblest, our most valorous,
Sanest and most obedient: and indeed
This work of Edyrn wrought upon himself
After a life of violence, seems to me
A thousand-fold more great and wonderful
Than if some knight of mine, risking his life,
My subject with my subjects under him,
Should make an onslaught single on a realm
Of robbers, tho' he slew them one by one,
And were himself nigh wounded to the death."

So spake the King; low bow'd the Prince, and felt
His work was neither great nor wonderful,
And past to Enid's tent; and thither came
The King's own leech to look into his hurt;
And Enid tended on him there; and there
Her constant motion round him, and the breath
Of her sweet tendance hovering over him,
Fill'd all the genial courses of his blood
With deeper and with ever deeper love,
As the south-west that blowing Bala lake
Fills all the sacred Dee. So past the days.

But while Geraint lay healing of his hurt,
The blameless King went forth and cast his eyes
On each of all whom Uther left in charge
Long since, to guard the justice of the King:
He look'd and found them wanting; and as now
Men weed the white horse on the Berkshire hills
To keep him bright and clean as heretofore,
He rooted out the slothful officer
Or guilty, which for bribe had wink'd at wrong,
And in their chairs set up a stronger race
With hearts and hands, and sent a thousand men
To till the wastes, and moving everywhere
Clear'd the dark places and let in the law,
And broke the bandit holds and cleansed the land.

Then, when Geraint was whole again, they past
With Arthur to Caer'eon upon Usk.
There the great Queen once more embraced her friend,
And clothed her in apparel like the day.
And tho' Geraint could never take again
That comfort from their converse which he took
Before the Queen's fair name was breathed upon,
He rested well content that all was well.
Thence after tarrying for a space they rode,
And fifty knights rode with them to the shores
Of Severn, and they past to their own land.
And there he kept the justice of the King
So vigorously yet mildly, that all hearts
Applauded, and the spiteful whisper died:
And being ever foremost in the chase,
And victor at the tilt and tournament,
They call'd him the great Prince and man of men.
But Enid, whom her ladies loved to call
Enid the Fair, a grateful people named
Enid the Good; and in their halls arose
The cry of children, Enids and Geraints
Of times to be; nor did he doubt her more
But rested in her fealty, till he crown'd
A happy life with a fair death, and fell
Against the heathen of the Northern Sea
In battle, fighting for the blameless King.

MERLIN AND VIVIEN.

A STORM was coming, but the winds were still,
And in the wild woods of Broceliande,
Before an oak, so hollow huge and old
It look'd a tower of ruin'd masonwork,
At Merlin's feet the wily Vivien lay.

The wily Vivien stole from Arthur's court:
She hated all the knights, and heard in thought
Their lavish comment when her name was named.
For once, when Arthur walking all alone,
Vext at a rumor rife about the Queen,
Had met her, Vivien, being greeted fair,
Would fain have wrought upon his cloudy mood
With reverent eyes mock-loyal, shaken voice,
And flutter'd adoration, and at last
With dark sweet hints of some who prized him more
Than who should prize him most; at which the King
Had gazed upon her blankly and gone by:
But one had watch'd, and had not held his peace:
It made the laughter of an afternoon
That Vivien should attempt the blameless King.
And after that, she set herself to gain
Him, the most famous man of all those times,
Merlin, who knew the range of all their arts,
Had built the King his havens, ships, and halls,
Was also Bard, and knew the starry heavens;
The people call'd him Wizard; whom at first
She play'd about with slight and sprightly talk,
And vivid smiles, and faintly-venom'd points
Of slander, glancing here and grazing there;
And yielding to his kindlier moods, the Seer
Would watch her at her petulance, and play,
Ev'n when they seem'd unlovable, and laugh

kitten ; thus he	Than hid her, clung about her lissome limbs,
ılf disdain'd, and	In color like the satin-shining palm On sallows in the windy gleams of March:
ıut half disdain'd, ts with graver fits,	And while she kiss'd them, crying, "Trample me,
l often when they	Dear feet, that I have follow'd thro' the world,
gaze upon him ion, that the old	And I will pay you worship ; tread me down
flattery, and at	And I will kiss you for it" ; he was mute : So dark a forethought roll'd about his brain,
ish in age for love, rue : for thus at	As on a dull day in an Ocean cave The blind wave feeling round his long sea-hall
:her clung to him, the seasons went.	In silence : wherefore, when she lifted up A face of sad appeal, and spake and said,
reat melancholy ; ıurt he gain'd the	"O Merlin, do ye love me?" and again, "O Merlin, do ye love me?" and once more,
at, and stept into	"Great Master, do ye love me?" he was mute.
ut he mark'd her	And lissome Vivien, holding by his heel, Writhed toward him, slided up his knee
he the sail ; the	and sat, Behind his ankle twined her hollow feet
wind across the	Together, curved an arm about his neck, Clung like a snake ; and letting her left
ands, they disem-	hand Droop from his mighty shoulder, as a leaf,
ferlin all the way, of Broceliande.	Made with her right a comb of pearl to part
ld her of a charm, ght on any one rith waving arms, ever seem'd to lie of a hollow tower, ape for evermore ; hat man for ever-	The lists of such a beard as youth gone out Had left in ashes : then he spoke and said, Not looking at her, "who are wise in love Love most, say least," and Vivien an- swer'd quick, "I saw the little elf-god eyeless once In Arthur's arras hall at Camelot : But neither eyes nor tongue — O stupid
ıim who wrought	child ! Yet you are wise who say it ; let me think
he lay as dead se and name and	Silence is wisdom : I am silent then And ask no kiss" ; then adding all at once,
to work the charm ıter of the Time, ıry would be great .tness whom she	"And lo, I clothe myself with wisdom," drew The vast and shaggy mantle of his beard Across her neck and bosom to her knee, And call'd herself a gilded summer fly Caught in a great old tyrant spider's web,
length and kiss'd	Who meant to eat her up in that wild wood Without one word. So Vivien call'd
ıce and in love. d her hair ; a robe that more exprest	herself, But rather seem'd a lovely baleful star Veil'd in gray vapor ; till he sadly smiled :

"Drew
The vast and shaggy mantle of his beard
Across her neck and bosom to her knee."

"To what request for what strange boon," he said,
"Are these your pretty tricks and fooleries,
O Vivien, the preamble? yet my thanks,
For these have broken up my melancholy."

And Vivien answer'd smiling saucily,
"What, O my Master, have ye found your voice?
I bid the stranger welcome. Thanks at last!
But yesterday you never open'd lip,
Except indeed to drink: no cup had we:
In mine own lady palms I cull'd the spring
That gather'd trickling dropwise from the cleft,
And made a pretty cup of both my hands
And offer'd you it kneeling: then ye drank
And knew no more, nor gave me one poor word;
O no more thanks than might a goat have given
With no more sign of reverence than a beard.
And when we halted at that other well,
And I was faint to swooning, and ye lay
Foot-gilt with all the blossom-dust of those

MERLIN AND VIVIEN.

Deep meadows we had traversed, did you know
That Vivien bathed your feet before her own?
And yet no thanks: and all thro' this wild wood
And all this morning when I fondled you:
Boon, yes, there was a boon, one not so strange —
How had I wrong'd you? surely you are wise,
But such a silence is more wise than kind."

And Merlin lock'd his hand in hers and said;
"O did you never lie upon the shore,
And watch the curl'd white of the coming wave
Glass'd in the slippery sand before it breaks?
Ev'n such a wave, but not so pleasurable,
Dark in the glass of some presageful mood,
Had I for three days seen, ready to fall.
And then I rose and fled from Arthur's court
To break the mood. You follow'd me unask'd;
And when I look'd, and saw you following still,
My mind involved yourself the nearest thing
In that mind-mist: for shall I tell you truth?
You seem'd that wave about to break upon me
And sweep me from my hold upon the world,
My use and name and fame. Your pardon, child.
Your pretty sports have brighten'd all again.
And ask your boon, for boon I owe you thrice,
Once for wrong done you by confusion, next
For thanks it seems till now neglected, last
For these your dainty gambols: wherefore ask;
And take this boon so strange and not so strange."

And Vivien answer'd smiling mournfully;
"O not so strange as my long asking it,
Nor yet so strange as you yourself are strange,
Nor half so strange as that dark mood of yours.
I ever fear'd ye were not wholly mine;
And see, yourself have own'd ye did me wrong.
The people call you prophet: let it be:
But not of those that can expound themselves.
Take Vivien for expounder: she will call
That three-days-long presageful gloom of yours
No presage, but the same mistrustful mood
That makes you seem less noble than yourself,
Whenever I have ask'd this very boon,
Now ask'd again: for see you not, dear love,
That such a mood as that, which lately gloom'd
Your fancy when you saw me following you,
Must make me fear still more you are not mine,
Must make me yearn still more to prove you mine,
And make me wish still more to learn this charm
Of woven paces and of waving hands,
As proof of trust. O Merlin, teach it me.
The charm so taught will charm us both to rest.
For, grant me some slight power upon your fate,
I, feeling that you felt me worthy trust,
Should rest and let you rest, knowing you mine.
And therefore be as great as you are named,
Not muffled round with selfish reticence.
How hard you look and how denyingly!
O, if you think this wickedness in me,
That I should prove it on you unawares,
To make you lose your use and name and fame,
That makes me most indignant; then our bond
Had best be loosed for ever: but think or not,
By Heaven that hears I tell you the clean truth,
As clean as blood of babes, as white as milk:
O Merlin, may this earth, if ever I,
If these unwitty wandering wits of mine,
Ev'n in the jumbled rubbish of a dream,
Have tript on such conjectural treachery—
May this hard earth cleave to the Nadir hell

Down, down, and close again, and nip
  me flat,
If I be such a traitress. Yield my boon,
Till which I scarce can yield you all I am;
And grant my re-reiterated wish,
The great proof of your love: because I
  think,
However wise, ye hardly know me yet."

And Merlin loosed his hand from hers
  and said,
" I never was less wise, however wise,
Too curious Vivien, tho' you talk of trust,
Than when I told you first of such a charm.
Yea, if ye talk of trust I tell you this,
Too much I trusted, when I told you that,
And stirr'd this vice in you which ruin'd
  man
Thro' woman the first hour; for howsoe'er
In children a great curiousness be well,
Who have to learn themselves and all the
  world,
In you, that are no child, for still I find
Your face is practised, when I spell the
  lines,
I call it,—well, I will not call it vice:
But since you name yourself the summer
  fly,
I well could wish a cobweb for the gnat,
That settles, beaten back, and beaten
  back
Settles, till one could yield for weariness:
But since I will not yield to give you power
Upon my life and use and name and fame,
Why will you never ask some other boon?
Yea, by God's rood, I trusted you too
  much."

And Vivien, like the tenderest-hearted
  maid
That ever bided tryst at village stile,
Made answer, either eyelid wet with tears.
"Nay, master, be not wrathful with your
  maid;
Caress her: let her feel herself forgiven
Who feels no heart to ask another boon.
I think you hardly know the tender rhyme
Of ' trust me not at all or all in all.'
I heard the great Sir Lancelot sing it
  once,
And it shall answer for me. Listen to it.

'In Love, if Love be Love, if Love be
  ours,
Faith and unfaith can ne'er be equal
  powers:
Unfaith in aught is want of faith in all.

' It is the little rift within the lute,
That by and by will make the music mute,
And ever widening slowly silence all.

' The little rift within the lover's lute
Or little pitted speck in garner'd fruit,
That rotting inward slowly moulders all.

'It is not worth the keeping: let it go:
But shall it? answer, darling, answer, no.
And trust me not at all or all in all.'

O master, do ye love my tender rhyme?"

And Merlin look'd and half believed
  her true,
So tender was her voice, so fair her face,
So sweetly gleam'd her eyes behind her
  tears
Like sunlight on the plain behind a
  shower:
And yet he answer'd half indignantly.

"Far other was the song that once I
  heard
By this huge oak, sung nearly where we
  sit:
For here we met, some ten or twelve of us,
To chase a creature that was current then
In these wild woods, the hart with golden
  horns.
It was the time when first the question rose
About the founding of a Table Round,
That was to be, for love of God and men
And noble deeds, the flower of all the
  world.
And each incited each to noble deeds.
And while we waited, one, the youngest
  of us,
We could not keep him silent, out he
  flash'd,
And into such a song, such fire for fame,
Such trumpet-blowings in it, coming down
To such a stern and iron-clashing close.
That when he stopt we long'd to hurl
  together,
And should have done it; but the beau-
  teous beast
Scared by the noise upstarted at our feet,
And like a silver shadow slipt away
Thro' the dim land; and all day long we
  rode
Thro' the dim land against a rushing
  wind,
That glorious roundel echoing in our ears,
And chased the flashes of his golden horns
Until they vanish'd by the fairy well

MERLIN AND VIVIEN.

That laughs at iron — as our warriors did —
Where children cast their pins and nails, and cry,
'Laugh, little well,' but touch it with a sword,
It buzzes wildly round the point; and there
We lost him: such a noble song was that.
But, Vivien, when you sang me that sweet rhyme,
I felt as tho' you knew this cursed charm,
Were proving it on me, and that I lay
And felt them slowly ebbing, name and fame."

And Vivien answer'd smiling mournfully;
"O mine have ebb'd away for evermore,
And all thro' following you to this wild wood,
Because I saw you sad, to comfort you.
Lo now, what hearts have men! they never mount
As high as woman in her selfless mood.
And touching fame, howe'er ye scorn my song,
Take one verse more — the lady speaks it — this:

'My name, once mine, now thine, is closelier mine,
For fame, could fame be mine, that fame were thine,
And shame, could shame be thine, that shame were mine.
So trust me not at all or all in all.'

"Says she not well? and there is more — this rhyme
Is like the fair pearl-necklace of the Queen,
That burst in dancing, and the pearls were spilt;
Some lost, some stolen, some as relics kept.
But nevermore the same two sister pearls
Ran down the silken thread to kiss each other
On her white neck — so is it with this rhyme:
It lives dispersedly in many hands,
And every minstrel sings it differently;
Yet is there one true line, the pearl of pearls;
'Man dreams of Fame while woman wakes to love.'
True: Love, tho' Love were of the grossest, carves
A portion from the solid present, eats

And uses, careless of the rest; but Fame,
The Fame that follows death is nothing to us;
And what is Fame in life but half-disfame,
And counterchanged with darkness? you yourself
Know well that Envy calls you Devil's son,
And since you seem the Master of all Art,
They fain would make you Master of all Vice."

And Merlin lock'd his hand in hers and said,
"I once was looking for a magic weed,
And found a fair young squire who sat alone,
Had carved himself a knightly shield of wood,
And then was painting on it fancied arms,
Azure, an Eagle rising or, the Sun
In dexter chief; the scroll 'I follow fame.'
And speaking not, but leaning over him,
I took his brush and blotted out the bird,
And made a Gardener putting in a graff,
With this for motto, 'Rather use than fame.'
You should have seen him blush; but afterwards
He made a stalwart knight. O Vivien,
For you, methinks you think you love me well;
For me, I love you somewhat; rest: and Love
Should have some rest and pleasure in himself,
Not ever be too curious for a boon,
Too prurient for a proof against the grain
Of him you say you love: but Fame with men,
Being but ampler means to serve mankind,
Should have small rest or pleasure in herself,
But work as vassal to the larger love,
That dwarfs the petty love of one to one.
Use gave me Fame at first, and Fame again
Increasing gave me use. Lo, there my boon!
What other? for men sought to prove me vile,
Because I wish'd to give them greater minds:
And then did Envy call me Devil's son:
The sick weak beast seeking to help herself

By striking at her better, miss'd, and
    brought
Her own claw back, and wounded her
    own heart.
Sweet were the days when I was all un-
    known,
But when my name was lifted up, the
    storm
Broke on the mountain and I cared not
    for it.
Right well know I that Fame is half-
    disfame,
Yet needs must work my work. That
    other fame,
To one at least, who hath not children,
    vague,
The cackle of the unborn about the grave,
I cared not for it: a single misty star,
Which is the second in a line of stars
That seem a sword beneath a belt of three,
I never gazed upon it but I dreamt
Of some vast charm concluded in that star
To make fame nothing. Wherefore, if I
    fear,
Giving you power upon me thro' this
    charm,
That you might play me falsely, having
    power,
However well you think you love me now
(As sons of kings loving in pupilage
Have turn'd to tyrants when they came
    to power)
I rather dread the loss of use than fame;
If you — and not so much from wicked-
    ness,
As some wild turn of anger, or a mood
Of overstrain'd affection, it may be,
To keep me all to your own self, or else
A sudden spurt of woman's jealousy, —
Should try this charm on whom you say
    you love."

    And Vivien answer'd smiling as in
        wrath.
"Have I not sworn? I am not trusted.
    Good!
Well, hide it, hide it; I shall find it out;
And being found take heed of Vivien.
A woman and not trusted, doubtless I
Might feel some sudden turn of anger born
Of your misfaith; and your fine epithet
Is accurate too, for this full love of mine
Without the full heart back may merit
    well
Your term of overstrain'd. So used as I,
My daily wonder is, I love at all.
And as to woman's jealousy, O why not?

O to what end, except a jealous one,
And one to make me jealous if I love,
Was this fair charm invented by yourself?
I well believe that all about this world
Ye cage a buxom captive here and there,
Closed in the four walls of a hollow tower
From which is no escape for evermore."

    Then the great Master merrily an-
        swer'd her.
"Full many a love in loving youth was
    mine,
I needed then no charm to keep them
    mine
But youth and love; and that full heart
    of yours
Whereof you prattle, may now assure you
    mine;
So live uncharm'd. For those who wrought
    it first,
The wrist is parted from the hand that
    waved,
The feet unmortised from their ankle-
    bones
Who paced it, ages back: but will ye
    hear
The legend as in guerdon for your rhyme?

    "There lived a king in the most East-
        ern East,
Less old than I, yet older, for my blood
Hath earnest in it of far springs to be.
A tawny pirate anchor'd in his port,
Whose bark had plunder'd twenty name-
    less isles;
And passing one, at the high peep of dawn,
He saw two cities in a thousand boats
All fighting for a woman on the sea.
And pushing his black craft among them
    all,
He lightly scatter'd theirs and brought
    her off,
With loss of half his people arrow-slain;
A maid so smooth, so white, so wonderful,
They said a light came from her when
    she moved:
And since the pirate would not yield her
    up,
The King impaled him for his piracy;
Then made her Queen: but those isle-
    nurtur'd eyes
Waged such unwilling tho' successful war
On all the youth, they sicken'd; coun-
    cils thinn'd,
And armies waned, for magnet-like she
    drew
The rustiest iron of old fighters' hearts;

MERLIN AND VIVIEN.   169

And beasts themselves would worship; camels knelt
Unbidden, and the brutes of mountain back
That carry kings in castles, bow'd black knees
Of homage, ringing with their serpent hands,
To make her smile, her golden ankle-bells.
What wonder, being jealous, that he sent
His horns of proclamation out thro' all
The hundred under-kingdoms that he sway'd
To find a wizard who might teach the King
Some charm, which being wrought upon the Queen
Might keep her all his own: to such a one
He promised more than ever king has given,
A league of mountain full of golden mines,
A province with a hundred miles of coast,
A palace and a princess, all for him:
But on all those who tried and fail'd, the King
Pronounced a dismal sentence, meaning by it
To keep the list low and pretenders back,
Or like a king, not to be trifled with—
Their heads should moulder on the city gates.
And many tried and fail'd, because the charm
Of nature in her overbore their own:
And many a wizard brow bleach'd on the walls:
And many weeks a troop of carrion crows
Hung like a cloud above the gateway towers."

And Vivien breaking in upon him, said:
" I sit and gather honey; yet, methinks,
Your tongue has tript a little: ask yourself.
The lady never made *unwilling* war
With those fine eyes: she had her pleasure in it,
And made her good man jealous with good cause.
And lived there neither dame nor damsel then
Wroth at a lover's loss? were all as tame,
I mean, as noble, as their Queen was fair?
Not one to flirt a venom at her eyes,
Or pinch a murderous dust into her drink,
Or make her paler with a poison'd rose?

Well, those were not our days: but did they find
A wizard? Tell me, was he like to thee?"

She ceased, and made her lithe arm round his neck
Tighten, and then drew back, and let her eyes
Speak for her, glowing on him, like a bride's
On her new lord, her own, the first of men.

He answer'd laughing, " Nay, not like to me.
At last they found — his foragers for charms —
A little glassy-headed hairless man,
Who lived alone in a great wild on grass;
Read but one book, and ever reading grew
So grated down and filed away with thought,
So lean his eyes were monstrous; while the skin
Clung but to crate and basket, ribs and spine.
And since he kept his mind on one sole aim,
Nor ever touch'd fierce wine, nor tasted flesh,
Nor own'd a sensual wish, to him the wall
That sunders ghosts and shadow-casting men
Became a crystal, and he saw them thro' it,
And heard their voices talk behind the wall,
And learnt their elemental secrets, powers
And forces; often o'er the sun's bright eye
Drew the vast eyelid of an inky cloud,
And lash'd it at the base with slanting storm;
Or in the noon of mist and driving rain,
When the lake whiten'd and the pinewood roar'd,
And the cairn'd mountain was a shadow, sunn'd
The world to peace again: here was the man.
And so by force they dragg'd him to the King.
And then he taught the King to charm the Queen
In such-wise, that no man could see her more,
Nor saw she save the King, who wrought the charm,
Coming and going, and she lay as dead,
And lost all use of life: but when the King

*"She ceased, and made her lithe arm round his neck
Tighten, and then drew back, and let her eyes
Speak for her."*

Made proffer of the league of golden mines,
The province with a hundred miles of
　coast,
The palace and the princess, that old man
Went back to his old wild, and lived on
　grass,
And vanish'd, and his book came down
　to me."

　And Vivien answer'd smiling saucily;
"You have the book: the charm is
　written in it:
Good: take my counsel: let me know
　it at once:
For keep it like a puzzle chest in chest,
With each chest lock'd and padlock'd
　thirty-fold,
And whelm all this beneath as vast a
　mound
As after furious battle turfs the slain
On some wild down above the windy deep,
I yet should strike upon a sudden means
To dig, pick, open, find and read the charm:
Then, if I tried it, who should blame me
　then?"

And smiling as a Master smiles at one
That is not of his school, nor any school
But that where blind and naked Ignorance
Delivers brawling judgments, unashamed,
On all things all day long; he answer'd
　her.

　"*You* read the book, my pretty Vivien!
O ay, it is but twenty pages long,
But every page having an ample marge,
And every marge enclosing in the midst
A square of text that looks a little blot,
The text no larger than the limbs of fleas:
And every square of text an awful charm,
Writ in a language that has long gone by.
So long, that mountains have arisen since
With cities on their flanks — *you* read
　the book!
And every margin scribbled, crost, and
　cramm'd
With comment, densest condensation,
　hard
To mind and eye; but the long sleepless
　nights
Of my long life have made it easy to me.

And none can read the text, not even I;
And none can read the comment but myself;
And in the comment did I find the charm.
O, the results are simple; a mere child
Might use it to the harm of any one,
And never could undo it: ask no more:
For tho' you should not prove it upon me,
But keep that oath you swore, you might, perchance,
Assay it on some one of the Table Round,
And all because you dream they babble of you."

And Vivien, frowning in true anger, said:
"What dare the full-fed liars say of me?
They ride abroad redressing human wrongs!
They sit with knife in meat and wine in horn.
They bound to holy vows of chastity!
Were I not woman, I could tell a tale.
But you are man, you well can understand
The shame that cannot be explain'd for shame.
Not one of all the drove should touch me: swine!"

Then answer'd Merlin careless of her words.
"Ye breathe but accusation vast and vague,
Spleen-born, I think, and proofless. If ye know,
Set up the charge ye know, to stand or fall!"

And Vivien answer'd frowning wrathfully.
"O ay, what say ye to Sir Valence, him
Whose kinsman left him watcher o'er his wife
And two fair babes, and went to distant lands;
Was one year gone, and on returning found
Not two but three: there lay the reckling, one
But one hour old! What said the happy sire?
A seven months' babe had been a truer gift.
Those twelve sweet moons confused his fatherhood."

Then answer'd Merlin "Nay, I know the tale.
Sir Valence wedded with an outland dame:
Some cause had kept him sunder'd from his wife:
One child they had: it lived with her: she died:
His kinsman travelling on his own affair
Was charged by Valence to bring home the child.
He brought, not found it therefore: take the truth."

"O ay," said Vivien, "overtrue a tale.
What say ye then to sweet Sir Sagramore,
That ardent man? 'to pluck the flower in season';
So says the song, 'I trow it is no treason.'
O Master, shall we call him overquick
To crop his own sweet rose before the hour?"

And Merlin answer'd "Overquick are you
To catch a lothly plume fall'n from the wing
Of that foul bird of rapine whose whole prey
Is man's good name: he never wrong'd his bride.
I know the tale. An angry gust of wind
Puff'd out his torch among the myriad-room'd
And many-corridor'd complexities
Of Arthur's palace: then he found a door
And darkling felt the sculptured ornament
That wreathen round it made it seem his own;
And wearied out made for the couch and slept,
A stainless man beside a stainless maid;
And either slept, nor knew of other there;
Till the high dawn piercing the royal rose
In Arthur's casement glimmer'd chastely down,
Blushing upon them blushing, and at once
He rose without a word and parted from her:
But when the thing was blazed about the court,
The brute world howling forced them into bonds,
And as it chanced they are happy, being pure."

"O ay," said Vivien, "that were likely too.
What say ye then to fair Sir Percivale

And of the horrid foulness that he wrought,
The saintly youth, the spotless lamb of Christ,
Or some black wether of St. Satan's fold,
What, in the precincts of the chapel-yard,
Among the knightly brasses of the graves,
And by the cold Hic Jacets of the dead!"

And Merlin answer'd careless of her charge,
"A sober man is Percivale and pure;
But once in life was fluster'd with new wine,
Then paced for coolness in the chapel-yard;
Where one of Satan's shepherdesses caught
And meant to stamp him with her master's mark;
And that he sinn'd, is not believable;
For, look upon his face!— but if he sinn'd,
The sin that practice burns into the blood,
And not the one dark hour which brings remorse,
Will brand us, after, of whose fold we be:
Or else were he, the holy king, whose hymns
Are chanted in the minster, worse than all.
But is your spleen froth'd out, or have ye more?"

And Vivien answer'd frowning yet in wrath;
"O ay; what say ye to Sir Lancelot, friend?
Traitor or true? that commerce with the Queen,
I ask you, is it clamor'd by the child,
Or whisper'd in the corner? do you know it?"

To which he answer'd sadly, "Yea, I know it.
Sir Lancelot went ambassador, at first,
To fetch her, and she took him for the King;
So fixt her fancy on him : let him be.
But have you no one word of loyal praise
For Arthur, blameless King and stainless man?"

She answer'd with a low and chuckling laugh;
"Him? is he man at all, who knows and winks?
Sees what his fair bride is and does, and winks?
By which the good king means to blind himself,
And blinds himself and all the Table Round
To all the foulness that they work. Myself
Could call him (were it not for womanhood)
The pretty, popular name such manhood earns,
Could call him the main cause of all their crime;
Yea, were he not crown'd king, coward, and fool."

Then Merlin to his own heart, loathing, said;
"O true and tender! O my liege and king!
O selfless man and stainless gentleman,
Who wouldst against thine own eye-witness fain
Have all men true and leal, all women pure;
How, in the mouths of base interpreters,
From over-fineness not intelligible
To things with every sense as false and foul
As the poach'd filth that floods the middle street,
Is thy white blamelessness accounted blame!"

But Vivien deeming Merlin overborne
By instance, recommenced, and let her tongue
Rage like a fire among the noblest names,
Polluting, and imputing her whole self,
Defaming and defacing, till she left
Not even Lancelot brave, nor Galahad clean.

Her words had issue other than she will'd.
He dragg'd his eyebrow bushes down, and made
A snowy penthouse for his hollow eyes,
And mutter'd in himself, "tell *her* the charm!
So, if she had it, would she rail on me
To snare the next, and if she have it not,
So will she rail. What did the wanton say?
'Not mount as high'; we scarce can sink as low:
For men at most differ as Heaven and earth,
But women, worst and best, as Heaven and Hell.
I know the Table Round, my friends of old;
All brave, and many generous, and some chaste.

I think she cloaks the wounds of loss with
    lies ;
I do believe she tempted them and fail'd,
She is so bitter: for fine plots may fail,
Tho' harlots paint their talk as well as face
With colors of the heart that are not theirs.
I will not let her know: nine tithes of
    times
Face-flatterers and backbiters are the
    same.
And they, sweet soul, that most impute
    a crime
Are pronest to it, and impute themselves,
Wanting the mental range ; or low desire
Not to feel lowest makes them level all ;
Yea, they would pare the mountain to
    the plain,
To leave an equal baseness ; and in this
Are harlots like the crowd, that if they find
Some stain or blemish in a name of note,
Not grieving that their greatest are so
    small,
Inflate themselves with some insane delight,
And judge all nature from her feet of clay,
Without the will to lift their eyes, and see
Her godlike head crown'd with spiritual
    fire,
And touching other worlds.   I am weary
    of her."

He spoke in words part heard, in whispers part,
Half-suffocated in the hoary fell
And many-winter'd fleece of throat and
    chin.
But Vivien, gathering somewhat of his
    mood,
And hearing "harlot" mutter'd twice or
    thrice,
Leapt from her session on his lap, and stood
Stiff as a viper frozen ; loathsome sight,
How from the rosy lips of life and love,
Flash'd the bare-grinning skeleton of
    death !
White was her cheek ; sharp breaths of
    anger puff'd
Her fairy nostril out ; her hand halfclench'd
Went faltering sideways downward to her
    belt,
And feeling ; had she found a dagger there
(For in a wink the false love turns to hate)
She would have stabb'd him ; but she
    found it not :
His eye was calm, and suddenly she took
To bitter weeping like a beaten child,

A long, long weeping, not consolable.
Then her false voice made way broken
    with sobs.

"O crueller than was ever told in tale,
Or sung in song ! O vainly lavish'd love !
O cruel, there was nothing wild or strange,
Or seeming shameful, for what shame in
    love,
So love be true, and not as yours is —
    nothing
Poor Vivien had not done to win his trust
Who call'd her what he call'd her — all
    her crime,
All — all — the wish to prove him wholly
    hers."

She mused a little, and then clapt her
    hands
Together with a wailing shriek, and said :
"Stabb'd through the heart's affections
    to the heart !
Seethed like the kid in its own mother's
    milk !
Kill'd with a word worse than a life of
    blows !
I thought that he was gentle, being great :
O God, that I had loved a smaller man !
I should have found in him a greater heart.
O, I, that flattering my true passion, saw
The knights, the court, the king, dark
    in your light,
Who love to make men darker than they
    are,
Because of that high pleasure which I had
To seat you sole upon my pedestal
Of worship — I am answer'd, and henceforth
The course of life that seem'd so flowery
    to me
With you for guide and master, only you,
Becomes the sea-cliff pathway broken
    short,
And ending in a ruin — nothing left,
But into some low cave to crawl, and there,
If the wolf spare me, weep my life away,
Kill'd with inutterable unkindliness."

She paused, she turn'd away, she hung
    her head,
The snake of gold slid from her hair, the
    braid
Slipt and uncoil'd itself, she wept afresh,
And the dark wood grew darker toward
    the storm
In silence, while his anger slowly died
Within him, till he let his wisdom go

MERLIN AND VIVIEN.

"Leapt from her session on his lap, and stood
Stiff as a viper frozen."

For ease of heart, and half believed her true:
Call'd her to shelter in the hollow oak,
"Come from the storm" and having no reply,
Gazed at the heaving shoulder, and the face
Hand-hidden, as for utmost grief or shame;
Then thrice essay'd, by tenderest-touching terms
To sleek her ruffled peace of mind, in vain.
At last she let herself be conquer'd by him,
And as the cageling newly flown returns,
The seeming-injured simple-hearted thing
Came to her old perch back, and settled there.

There while she sat, half-falling from his knees,
Half-nestled at his heart, and since he saw
The slow tear creep from her closed eye-lid yet,
About her, more in kindness than in love,
The gentle wizard cast a shielding arm.
But she dislink'd herself at once and rose,
Her arms upon her breast across, and stood
A virtuous gentlewoman deeply wrong'd,
Upright and flush'd before him: then she said:

"There must be now no passages of love
Betwixt us twain henceforward evermore.
Since, if I be what I am grossly call'd,

What should be granted which your own
   gross heart
Would reckon worth the taking? I will go.
In truth, but one thing now — better have
   died
Thrice than have ask'd it once — could
   make me stay —
That proof of trust — so often asked in
   vain !
How justly, after that vile term of yours,
I find with grief ! I might believe you
   then,
Who knows? once more. O, what was
   once to me
Mere matter of the fancy, now has grown
The vast necessity of heart and life.
Farewell ; think kindly of me, for I fear
My fate or fault, omitting gayer youth
For one so old, must be to love you still.
But ere I leave you let me swear once
   more
That if I schemed against your peace in
   this,
May yon just heaven, that darkens o'er
   me, send
One flash, that, missing all things else,
   may make
My scheming brain a cinder, if I lie."

   Scarce had she ceased, when out of
   heaven a bolt
(For now the storm was close above them)
   struck,
Furrowing a giant oak, and javelining
With darted spikes and splinters of the
   wood
The dark earth round. He raised his eyes
   and saw
The tree that shone white-listed thro' the
   gloom.
But Vivien, fearing heaven had heard her
   oath,
And dazzled by the livid-flickering fork,
And deafen'd with the stammering cracks
   and claps
That follow'd, flying back and crying out,
" O Merlin, tho' you do not love me, save,
Yet save me !" clung to him and hugg'd
   him close ;
And call'd him dear protector in her fright,
Nor yet forgot her practice in her fright,
But wrought upon his mood and hugg'd
   him close.
The pale blood of the wizard at her touch
Took gayer colors, like an opal warm'd.
She blamed herself for telling hearsay
   tales :

She shook from fear, and for her fault she
   wept
Of petulancy ; she call'd him lord and
   liege,
Her seer, her bard, her silver star of eve,
Her God, her Merlin, the one passionate
   love
Of her whole life ; and ever overhead
Bellow'd the tempest, and the rotten
   branch
Snapt in the rushing of the river rain
Above them ; and in change of glare and
   gloom
Her eyes and neck glittering went and
   came ;
Till now the storm, its burst of passion
   spent,
Moaning and calling out of other lands,
Had left the ravaged woodland yet once
   more
To peace ; and what should not have
   been had been,
For Merlin, overtalk'd and overworn,
Had yielded, told her all the charm, and
   slept.

   Then, in one moment, she put forth
   the charm
Of woven paces and of waving hands,
And in the hollow oak he lay as dead,
And lost to life and use and name and
   fame.

   Then crying " I have made his glory
   mine,"
And shrieking out " O fool !" the harlot
   leapt
Adown the forest, and the thicket closed
Behind her, and the forest echo'd "fool."

LANCELOT AND ELAINE.

ELAINE the fair, Elaine the lovable,
Elaine, the lily maid of Astolat,
High in her chamber up a tower to the
   east
Guarded the sacred shield of Lancelot ;
Which first she placed where morning's
   earliest ray
Might strike it, and awake her with the
   gleam ;
Then fearing rust or soilure fashion'd for it
A case of silk, and braided thereupon
All the devices blazon'd on the shield
In their own tinct, and added, of her wit,
A border fantasy of branch and flower,

And yellow-throated nestling in the nest.
Nor rested thus content, but day by day
Leaving her household and good father climb'd
That eastern tower, and entering barr'd her door,
Stript off the case, and read the naked shield,
Now guess'd a hidden meaning in his arms,
Now made a pretty history to herself
Of every dint a sword had beaten in it,
And every scratch a lance had made upon it,
Conjecturing when and where: this cut is fresh ;
That ten years back ; this dealt him at Caerlyle ;
That at Caerleon ; this at Camelot :
And ah God's mercy what a stroke was there !
And here a thrust that might have kill'd, but God
Broke the strong lance, and roll'd his enemy down,
And saved him : so she lived in fantasy.

How came the lily maid by that good shield
Of Lancelot, she that knew not ev'n his name ?
He left it with her, when he rode to tilt
For the great diamond in the diamond jousts,
Which Arthur had ordain'd, and by that name
Had named them, since a diamond was the prize.

For Arthur long before they crown'd him king,
Roving the trackless realms of Lyonnesse,
Had found a glen, gray boulder and black tarn.
A horror lived about the tarn, and clave
Like its own mists to all the mountain side :
For here two brothers, one a king, had met
And fought together ; but their names were lost.
And each had slain his brother at a blow,
And down they fell and made the glen abhorr'd :
And there they lay till all their bones were bleach'd,
And lichen'd into color with the crags :
And he, that once was king, had on a crown
Of diamonds, one in front, and four aside.
And Arthur came, and laboring up the pass
All in a misty moonshine, unawares
Had trodden that crown'd skeleton, and the skull
Brake from the nape, and from the skull the crown
Roll'd into light, and turning on its rims
Fled like a glittering rivulet to the tarn :
And down the shingly scaur he plunged, and caught,
And set it on his head, and in his heart
Heard murmurs "lo, thou likewise shalt be king."

Thereafter, when a king, he had the gems
Pluck'd from the crown, and show'd them to his knights,
Saying "these jewels, whereupon I chanced
Divinely, are the kingdom's not the king's —
For public use : henceforward let there be,
Once every year, a joust for one of these :
For so by nine years' proof we needs must learn
Which is our mightiest, and ourselves shall grow
In use of arms and manhood, till we drive
The Heathen, who, some say, shall rule the land
Hereafter, which God hinder." Thus he spoke :
And eight years past, eight jousts had been, and still
Had Lancelot won the diamond of the year,
With purpose to present them to the Queen,
When all were won ; but meaning all at once
To snare her royal fancy with a boon
Worth half her realm, had never spoken word.

Now for the central diamond and the last
And largest, Arthur, holding then his court
Hard on the river nigh the place which now
Is this world's hugest, let proclaim a joust

At Camelot, and when the time drew nigh
Spake (for she had been sick) to Guinevere
"Are you so sick, my Queen, you cannot move
To these fair jousts?" "Yea, lord," she said, "ye know it."
"Then will ye miss," he answer'd, "the great deeds
Of Lancelot, and his prowess in the lists,
A sight ye love to look on." And the Queen
Lifted her eyes, and they dwelt languidly
On Lancelot, where he stood beside the King.
He thinking that he read her meaning there,
"Stay with me, I am sick; my love is more
Than many diamonds," yielded, and a heart,
Love-loyal to the least wish of the Queen
(However much he yearn'd to make complete
The tale of diamonds for his destined boon)
Urged him to speak against the truth, and say,
"Sir King, mine ancient wound is hardly whole,
And lets me from the saddle"; and the King
Glanced first at him, then her, and went his way.
No sooner gone than suddenly she began.

"To blame, my lord Sir Lancelot, much to blame.
Why go ye not to these fair jousts? the knights
Are half of them our enemies, and the crowd
Will murmur, lo the shameless ones, who take
Their pastime now the trustful king is gone!"
Then Lancelot vext at having lied in vain:
"Are ye so wise? ye were not once so wise,
My Queen, that summer, when ye loved me first.
Then of the crowd ye took no more account
Than of the myriad cricket of the mead,
When its own voice clings to each blade of grass,
And every voice is nothing. As to knights,
Them surely can I silence with all ease.

But now my loyal worship is allow'd
Of all men: many a bard, without offence,
Has link'd our names together in his lay,
Lancelot, the flower of bravery, Guinevere,
The pearl of beauty: and our knights at feast
Have pledged us in this union, while the king
Would listen smiling. How then? is there more?
Has Arthur spoken aught? or would yourself,
Now weary of my service and devoir,
Henceforth be truer to your faultless lord?"

She broke into a little scornful laugh.
"Arthur, my lord, Arthur, the faultless King,
That passionate perfection, my good lord —
But who can gaze upon the Sun in heaven?
He never spake word of reproach to me,
He never had a glimpse of mine untruth,
He cares not for me: only here to-day
There gleam'd a vague suspicion in his eyes:
Some meddling rogue has tamper'd with him — else
Rapt in this fancy of his Table Round,
And swearing men to vows impossible,
To make them like himself: but, friend, to me
He is all fault who hath no fault at all:
For who loves me must have a touch of earth;
The low sun makes the color: I am yours,
Not Arthur's, as ye know, save by the bond.
And therefore hear my words: go to the jousts:
The tiny-trumpeting gnat can break our dream
When sweetest; and the vermin voices here
May buzz so loud — we scorn them, but they sting."

Then answer'd Lancelot, the chief of knights.
"And with what face, after my pretext made,
Shall I appear, O Queen, at Camelot, I
Before a king who honors his own word,
As if it were his God's?"
"Yea," said the Queen,
"A moral child without the craft to rule,

Else had he not lost me : but listen to me,
If I must find you wit : we hear it said
That men go down before your spear at a touch
But knowing you are Lancelot; your great name,
This conquers : hide it therefore ; go unknown :
Win! by this kiss you will : and our true king
Will then allow your pretext, O my knight,
As all for glory ; for to speak him true,
Ye know right well, how meek soe'er he seem,
No keener hunter after glory breathes.
He loves it in his knights more than himself :
They prove to him his work : win and return."

Then got Sir Lancelot suddenly to horse,
Wroth at himself: not willing to be known,
He left the barren-beaten thoroughfare,
Chose the green path that show'd the rarer foot,
And there among the solitary downs,
Full often lost in fancy, lost his way ;
Till as he traced a faintly-shadow'd track,
That all in loops and links among the dales
Ran to the Castle of Astolat, he saw
Fired from the west, far on a hill, the towers.
Thither he made and wound the gateway horn.
Then came an old, dumb, myriad-wrinkled man,
Who let him into lodging and disarm'd.
And Lancelot marvell'd at the wordless man ;
And issuing found the Lord of Astolat
With two strong sons, Sir Torre and Sir Lavaine,
Moving to meet him in the castle court ;
And close behind them stept the lily maid
Elaine, his daughter : mother of the house
There was not : some light jest among them rose
With laughter dying down as the great knight
Approach'd them : then the Lord of Astolat.

"Then came an old, dumb, myriad-wrinkled man,
Who let him into lodging and disarm'd."

"Whence comest thou, my guest, and by what name
Livest between the lips? for by thy state
And presence I might guess thee chief of those,
After the king, who eat in Arthur's halls.
Him have I seen: the rest, his Table Round,
Known as they are, to me they are unknown."

Then answer'd Lancelot, the chief of knights.
"Known am I, and of Arthur's hall, and known,
What I by mere mischance have brought, my shield.
But since I go to joust as one unknown
At Camelot for the diamond, ask me not,
Hereafter you shall know me — and the shield —
I pray you lend me one, if such you have,
Blank, or at least with some device not mine."

Then said the Lord of Astolat, "Here is Torre's:
Hurt in his first tilt was my son, Sir Torre.
And so, God wot, his shield is blank enough.
His ye can have." Then added plain Sir Torre,
"Yea since I cannot use it, ye may have it."
Here laugh'd the father saying "Fie, Sir Churl,
Is that an answer for a noble knight?
Allow him: but Lavaine, my younger here,
He is so full of lustihood, he will ride,
Joust for it, and win, and bring it in an hour
And set it in this damsel's golden hair,
To make her thrice as wilful as before."

"Nay, father, nay good father, shame me not
Before this noble knight" said young Lavaine
"For nothing. Surely I but play'd on Torre:
He seem'd so sullen, vex the could not go:
A jest, no more: for, knight, the maiden dream,
That some one put this diamond in her hand,
And that it was too slippery to be held,
And slipt and fell into some pool or stream,
The castle-well, belike; and then I said
That *if* I went and *if* I fought and won it
(But all was jest and joke among ourselves)
Then must she keep it safelier. All was jest.
But father give me leave, an if he will,
To ride to Camelot with this noble knight:
Win shall I not, but do my best to win:
Young as I am, yet would I do my best."

"So ye will grace me," answer'd Lancelot,
Smiling a moment, "with your fellowship
O'er these waste downs whereon I lost myself,
Then were I glad of you as guide and friend;
And you shall win this diamond — as I hear,
It is a fair large diamond, — if ye may,
And yield it to this maiden, if ye will."
"A fair large diamond," added plain Sir Torre,
"Such be for Queens and not for simple maids."
Then she, who held her eyes upon the ground,
Elaine, and heard her name so tost about,
Flush'd slightly at the slight disparagement
Before the stranger knight, who, looking at her,
Full courtly, yet not falsely, thus return'd.
"If what is fair be but for what is fair,
And only Queens are to be counted so,
Rash were my judgment then, who deem this maid
Might wear as fair a jewel as is on earth,
Not violating the bond of like to like."

He spoke and ceased: the lily maid Elaine,
Won by the mellow voice before she look'd,
Lifted her eyes, and read his lineaments.
The great and guilty love he bare the Queen,
In battle with the love he bare his lord,
Had marr'd his face, and mark'd it ere his time.
Another sinning on such heights with one,
The flower of all the west and all the world,
Had been the sleeker for it: but in him
His mood was often like a fiend, and rose
And drove him into wastes and solitudes

"Lifted her eyes, and read his lineaments."

For agony, who was yet a living soul.
Marr'd as he was, he seem'd the goodliest
    man,
That ever among ladies ate in Hall,
And noblest, when she lifted up her eyes.
However marr'd, of more than twice her
    years,
Seam'd with an ancient swordcut on the
    cheek,
And bruised and bronzed, she lifted up
    her eyes
And loved him, with that love which was
    her doom.

  Then the great knight, the darling of
    the court,
Loved of the loveliest, into that rude hall
Stept with all grace, and not with half
    disdain
Hid under grace, as in a smaller time,
But kindly man moving among his kind:
Whom they with meats and vintage of
    their best
And talk and minstrel melody entertain'd.
And much they ask'd of court and Table
    Round,
And ever well and readily answer'd he:
But Lancelot, when they glanced at
    Guinevere,
Suddenly speaking of the wordless man,
Heard from the Baron that, ten years
    before,
The heathen caught and reft him of his
    tongue.

"He learnt and warn'd me of their fierce
 design
Against my house, and him they caught
 and maim'd;
But I my sons and little daughter fled
From bonds or death, and dwelt among
 the woods
By the great river in a boatman's hut.
Dull days were those, till our good Arthur
 broke
The Pagan yet once more on Badon hill."

"O there, great Lord, doubtless,"
 Lavaine said, rapt
By all the sweet and sudden passion of
 youth
Toward greatness in its elder, "you have
 fought.
O tell us — for we live apart — you know
Of Arthur's glorious wars." And Lan-
 celot spoke
And answer'd him at full, as having been
With Arthur in the fight which all day long
Rang by the white mouth of the violent
 Glem;
And in the four wild battles by the shore
Of Duglas; that on Bassa; then the war
That thunder'd in and out the gloomy
 skirts
Of Celidon the forest; and again
By castle Gurnion where the glorious King
Had on his cuirass worn our Lady's Head,
Carved of one emerald, center'd in a sun
Of silver rays, that lighten'd as he
 breathed;
And at Caerleon had he help'd his lord,
When the strong neighings of the wild
 white Horse
Set every gilded parapet shuddering;
And up in Agned Cathregonion too,
And down the waste sand-shores of Trath
 Treroit,
Where many a heathen fell; "and on
 the mount
Of Badon I myself beheld the King
Charge at the head of all his Table Round,
And all his legions crying Christ and him,
And break them; and I saw him, after,
 stand
High on a heap of slain, from spur to plume
Red as the rising sun with heathen blood,
And seeing me, with a great voice he cried
'They are broken, they are broken' for
 the King,
However mild he seems at home, nor cares
For triumph in our mimic wars, the
 jousts —

For if his own knight cast him down, he
 laughs
Saying, his knights are better men than
 he —
Yet in this heathen war the fire of God
Fills him: I never saw his like: there lives
No greater leader."
 While he utter'd this,
Low to her own heart said the lily maid
"Save your great self, fair lord"; and
 when he fell
From talk of war to traits of pleasantry —
Being mirthful he but in a stately kind —
She still took note that when the living
 smile
Died from his lips, across him came a cloud
Of melancholy severe, from which again,
Whenever in her hovering to and fro
The lily maid had striven to make him
 cheer,
There brake a sudden-beaming tender-
 ness
Of manners and of nature: and she thought
That all was nature, all, perchance, for her.
And all night long his face before her lived,
As when a painter, poring on a face,
Divinely thro' all hindrance finds the man
Behind it, and so paints him that his face,
The shape and color of a mind and life,
Lives for his children, ever at its best
And fullest; so the face before her lived,
Dark-splendid, speaking in the silence,
 full
Of noble things, and held her from her
 sleep.
Till rathe she rose, half-cheated in the
 thought
She needs must bid farewell to sweet
 Lavaine.
First as in fear, step after step, she stole
Down the long tower-stairs, hesitating:
Anon, she heard Sir Lancelot cry in the
 court,
"This shield, my friend, where is it?"
 and Lavaine
Past inward, as she came from out the
 tower.
There to his proud horse Lancelot turn'd,
 and smooth'd
The glossy shoulder, humming to himself.
Half-envious of the flattering hand, she
 drew
Nearer and stood. He look'd, and more
 amazed
Than if seven men had set upon him, saw
The maiden standing in the dewy light.
He had not dream'd she was so beautiful.

Then came on him a sort of sacred fear,
For silent, tho' he greeted her, she stood
Rapt on his face as if it were a God's.
Suddenly flash'd on her a wild desire,
That he should wear her favor at the tilt.
She braved a riotous heart in asking for it.
" Fair lord, whose name I know not —
   noble it is,
I well believe, the noblest — will you wear
My favor at this tourney ?" "Nay,"
   said he,
"Fair lady, since I never yet have worn
Favor of any lady in the lists.
Such is my wont, as those, who know me,
   know."
" Yea, so," she answer'd ; " then in wear-
   ing mine
Needs must be lesser likelihood, noble
   lord,
That those who know should know you."
   And he turn'd
Her counsel up and down within his mind,
And found it true, and answer'd, " true,
   my child.
Well, I will wear it : fetch it out to me :
What is it ?" and she told him "a red
   sleeve
Broider'd with pearls," and brought it :
   then he bound
Her token on his helmet, with a smile
Saying, " I never yet have done so much
For any maiden living," and the blood
Sprang to her face and fill'd her with de-
   light ;
But left her all the paler, when Lavaine
Returning brought the yet-unblazon'd
   shield,
His brother's ; which he gave to Lancelot,
Who parted with his own to fair Elaine ;
" Do me this grace, my child, to have my
   shield
In keeping till I come." "A grace to
   me,"
She answer'd, "twice to-day. I am your
   Squire."
Whereat Lavaine said, laughing, " Lily
   maid,
For fear our people call you lily maid
In earnest, let me bring your color back ;
Once, twice, and thrice : now get you
   hence to bed" :
So kiss'd her, and Sir Lancelot his own
   hand,
And thus they moved away : she stay'd
   a minute,
Then made a sudden step to the gate,
   and there —

Her bright hair blown about the serious
   face
Yet rosy-kindled with her brother's kiss —
Paused in the gateway, standing by the
   shield
In silence, while she watch'd their arms
   far-off
Sparkle, until they dipt below the downs.
Then to her tower she climb'd, and took
   the shield,
There kept it, and so lived in fantasy.

   Meanwhile the new companions past
      away
Far o'er the long backs of the bushless
   downs,
To where Sir Lancelot knew there lived
   a knight
Not far from Camelot, now for forty years
A hermit, who had pray'd, labor'd and
   pray'd
And ever laboring had scoop'd himself
In the white rock a chapel and a hall
On massive columns, like a shorecliff
   cave,
And cells and chambers : all were fair
   and dry ;
The green light from the meadows under-
   neath
Struck up and lived along the milky
   roofs ;
And in the meadows tremulous aspen-
   trees
And poplars made a noise of falling
   showers.
And thither wending there that night
   they bode.

   But when the next day broke from un-
      derground,
And shot red fire and shadows thro' the
   cave,
They rose, heard mass, broke fast, and
   rode away :
Then Lancelot saying, "hear, but hold
   my name
Hidden, you ride with Lancelot of the
   Lake,"
Abash'd Lavaine, whose instant rever-
   ence,
Dearer to true young hearts than their
   own praise,
But left him leave to stammer, "is it
   indeed ?"
And after muttering "the great Lancelot"
At last he got his breath and answer'd
   "One,

"Then to her tower she climb'd, and took the shield,
There kept it, and so lived in fantasy."

One have I seen — that other, our liege
    lord,
The dread Pendragon, Britain's king of
    kings,
Of whom the people talk mysteriously,
He will be there — then were I stricken
    blind
That minute, I might say that I had seen."

  So spake Lavaine, and when they
    reach'd the lists
By Camelot in the meadow, let his eyes
Run thro' the peopled gallery which half
    round
Lay like a rainbow fall'n upon the grass,
Until they found the clear-faced King,
    who sat
Robed in red samite, easily to be known,
Since to his crown the golden dragon
    clung,
And down his robe the dragon writhed
    in gold,
And from the carven-work behind him
    crept
Two dragons gilded, sloping down to make
Arms for his chair, while all the rest of
    them
Thro' knots and loops and folds innumer-
    able
Fled ever thro' the woodwork, till they
    found
The new design wherein they lost them-
    selves,
Yet with all ease, so tender was the work:

And, in the costly canopy o'er him set,
Blazed the last diamond of the nameless king.
Then Lancelot answer'd young Lavaine and said,
"Me you call great : mine is the firmer seat,
The truer lance : but there is many a youth
Now crescent, who will come to all I am
And overcome it ; and in me there dwells
No greatness, save it be some far-off touch
Of greatness to know well I am not great :
There is the man." And Lavaine gaped upon him
As on a thing miraculous, and anon
The trumpets blew ; and then did either side,
They that assail'd, and they that held the lists,
Set lance in rest, strike spur, suddenly move,
Meet in the midst, and there so furiously
Shock, that a man far-off might well perceive,
If any man that day were left afield,
The hard earth shake, and a low thunder of arms.
And Lancelot bode a little, till he saw
Which were the weaker ; then he hurl'd into it
Against the stronger : little need to speak
Of Lancelot in his glory : King, duke, earl,
Count, baron — whom he smote, he overthrew.

But in the field were Lancelot's kith and kin,
Ranged with the Table Round that held the lists,
Strong men, and wrathful that a stranger knight
Should do and almost overdo the deeds
Of Lancelot ; and one said to the other "Lo !
What is he ? I do not mean the force alone,
The grace and versatility of the man —
Is it not Lancelot !" "When has Lancelot worn
Favor of any lady in the lists ?
Not such his wont, as we, that know him, know."
"How then ? who then ?" a fury seized on them,
A fiery family passion for the name
Of Lancelot, and a glory one with theirs.

They couch'd their spears and prick'd their steeds and thus,
Their plumes driv'n backward by the wind they made
In moving, all together down upon him
Bare, as a wild wave in the wide North-sea,
Green-glimmering toward the summit, bears, with all
Its stormy crests that smoke against the skies,
Down on a bark, and overbears the bark,
And him that helms it, so they overbore
Sir Lancelot and his charger, and a spear
Down-glancing, lamed the charger, and a spear
Prick'd sharply his own cuirass, and the head
Pierced thro' his side, and there snapt, and remain'd.

Then Sir Lavaine did well and worshipfully ;
He bore a knight of old repute to the earth,
And brought his horse to Lancelot where he lay.
He up the side, sweating with agony, got,
But thought to do while he might yet endure,
And being lustily holpen by the rest,
His party, — tho' it seemed half-miracle
To those he fought with — drave his kith and kin,
And all the Table Round that held the lists,
Back to the barrier ; then the heralds blew
Proclaiming his the prize, who wore the sleeve
Of scarlet, and the pearls ; and all the knights,
His party, cried "Advance, and take your prize
The diamond" ; but he answer'd, "diamond me
No diamonds ! for God's love, a little air !
Prize me no prizes, for my prize is death !
Hence will I and I charge you, follow me not."

He spoke, and vanish'd suddenly from the field
With young Lavaine into the poplar grove.
There from his charger down he slid, and sat,
Gasping to Sir Lavaine, "draw the lancehead" :

"Ah my sweet lord Sir Lancelot," said
  Lavaine,
"I dread me, if I draw it, ye will die."
But he "I die already with it: draw —
Draw," — and Lavaine drew, and that
  other gave
A marvellous great shriek and ghastly
  groan,
And half his blood burst forth, and down
  he sank
For the pure pain, and wholly swoon'd
  away.
Then came the hermit out and bare him in,
There stanch'd his wound; and there, in
  daily doubt
Whether to live or die, for many a week
Hid from the wide world's rumor by the
  grove
Of poplars with their noise of falling
  showers,
And ever-tremulous aspen-trees, he lay.

But on that day when Lancelot fled
  the lists,
His party, knights of utmost North and
  West,
Lords of waste marches, kings of desolate
  isles,
Came round their great Pendragon, say-
  ing to him
"Lo, Sire, our knight thro' whom we
  won the day
Hath gone sore wounded, and hath left
  his prize
Untaken, crying that his prize is death."
"Heaven hinder," said the King, "that
  such an one,
So great a knight as we have seen to-
  day —
He seem'd to me another Lancelot —
Yea, twenty times I thought him Lance-
  lot —
He must not pass uncared for. Wherefore
  rise,
O Gawain, and ride forth and find the
  knight.
Wounded and wearied needs must he be
  near.
I charge you that you get at once to horse.
And, knights and kings, there breathes
  not one of you
Will deem this prize of ours is rashly
  given:
His prowess was too wondrous. We will
  do him
No customary honor: since the knight
Came not to us, of us to claim the prize,
Ourselves will send it after. Rise and
  take
This diamond, and deliver it, and return,
And bring us where he is and how he fares,
And cease not from your quest, until you
  find."

So saying from the carven flower above,
To which it made a restless heart, he took,
And gave, the diamond: then from where
  he sat
At Arthur's right, with smiling face arose,
With smiling face and frowning heart, a
  Prince
In the mid might and flourish of his May,
Gawain, surnamed The Courteous, fair
  and strong,
And after Lancelot, Tristram, and Geraint
And Lamorack, a good knight, but there-
  withal
Sir Modred's brother, of a crafty house,
Nor often loyal to his word, and now
Wroth that the king's command to sally
  forth
In quest of whom he knew not, made him
  leave
The banquet, and concourse of knights
  and kings.

So all in wrath he got to horse and went;
While Arthur to the banquet, dark in
  mood,
Past, thinking "is it Lancelot who has
  come
Despite the wound he spake of, all for gain
Of glory, and has added wound to wound,
And ridd'n away to die?" So fear'd the
  King,
And, after two days' tarriance there, re-
  turn'd.
Then when he saw the Queen, embracing
  ask'd,
"Love, are you yet so sick?" "Nay,
  lord," she said.
"And where is Lancelot?" Then the
  Queen amazed
"Was he not with you? won he not your
  prize?"
"Nay, but one like him." "Why that
  like was he."
And when the King demanded how she
  knew,
Said "Lord, no sooner had ye parted
  from us,
Than Lancelot told me of a common talk
That men went down before his spear at
  a touch,

But knowing he was Lancelot; his great
name
Conquer'd; and therefore would he hide
his name
From all men, ev'n the king, and to this end
Had made the pretext of a hindering
wound,
That he might joust unknown of all, and
learn
If his old prowess were in aught decay'd:
And added, 'our true Arthur, when he
learns,
Will well allow my pretext, as for gain
Of purer glory.'"
              Then replied the King:
"Far lovelier in our Lancelot had it been,
In lieu of idly dallying with the truth,
To have trusted me as he has trusted you.
Surely his king and most familiar friend
Might well have kept his secret. True,
indeed,
Albeit I know my knights fantastical,
So fine a fear in our large Lancelot
Must needs have moved my laughter:
now remains
But little cause for laughter: his own
kin—
Ill news, my Queen, for all who love him,
these!
His kith and kin, not knowing, set upon
him;
So that he went sore wounded from the
field:
Yet good news too: for goodly hopes are
mine
That Lancelot is no more a lonely heart.
He wore, against his wont, upon his helm
A sleeve of scarlet, broider'd with great
pearls,
Some gentle maiden's gift."

              "Yea, lord," she said,
"Your hopes are mine," and saying that
she choked,
And sharply turn'd about to hide her face,
Past to her chamber, and there flung
herself
Down on the great King's couch, and
writhed upon it,
And clench'd her fingers till they bit the
palm,
And shriek'd out "traitor" to the un-
hearing wall,
Then flash'd into wild tears, and rose
again,
And moved about her palace, proud and
pale.

Gawain the while thro' all the region
round
Rode with his diamond, wearied of the
quest,
Touch'd at all points, except the poplar
grove,
And came at last, tho' late, to Astolat:
Whom glittering in enamell'd arms the
maid
Glanced at, and cried "What news from
Camelot, lord?
What of the knight with the red sleeve?"
"He won."
"I knew it," she said. "But parted
from the jousts
Hurt in the side," whereat she caught
her breath;
Thro' her own side she felt the sharp lance
go;
Thereon she smote her hand: wellnigh
she swoon'd:
And, while he gazed wonderingly at her,
came
The lord of Astolat out, to whom the
Prince
Reported who he was, and on what quest
Sent, that he bore the prize and could not
find
The victor, but had ridden wildly round
To seek him, and was wearied of the search.
To whom the lord of Astolat "Bide with
us,
And ride no longer wildly, noble Prince!
Here was the knight, and here he left a
shield;
This will he send or come for: further-
more
Our son is with him; we shall hear anon,
Needs must we hear." To this the cour-
teous Prince
Accorded with his wonted courtesy,
Courtesy with a touch of traitor in it,
And stay'd; and cast his eyes on fair
Elaine:
Where could be found face daintier?
then her shape
From forehead down to foot perfect—
again
From foot to forehead exquisitely turn'd:
"Well—if I bide, lo! this wild flower
for me!"
And oft they met among the garden yews,
And there he set himself to play upon
her
With sallying wit, free flashes from a
height
Above her, graces of the court, and songs,

Sighs, and slow smiles, and golden eloquence.
And amorous adulation, till the maid
Rebell'd against it, saying to him, "Prince,
O loyal nephew of our noble King,
Why ask you not to see the shield he left,
Whence you might learn his name?
Why slight your King,
And lose the quest he sent you on, and prove
No surer than our falcon yesterday,
Who lost the hern we slipt him at, and went
To all the winds?" "Nay, by mine head," said he,
"I lose it, as we lose the lark in heaven,
O damsel, in the light of your blue eyes:
But an ye will it let me see the shield."
And when the shield was brought, and Gawain saw
Sir Lancelot's azure lions, crown'd with gold,
Ramp in the field, he smote his thigh, and mock'd;
"Right was the King! our Lancelot! that true man!"
"And right was I," she answer'd merrily, "I,
Who dream'd my knight the greatest knight of all."
"And if *I* dream'd," said Gawain, "that you love
This greatest knight, your pardon! lo, you know it!
Speak therefore: shall I waste myself in vain?"
Full simple was her answer "What know I?
My brethren have been all my fellowship,
And I, when often they have talk'd of love,
Wish'd it had been my mother, for they talk'd,
Meseem'd, of what they knew not; so myself—
I know not if I know what true love is,
But if I know, then, if I love not him,
Methinks there is none other I can love."
"Yea, by God's death," said he, "ye love him well,
But would not, knew ye what all others know,
And whom he loves." "So be it," cried Elaine,
And lifted her fair face and moved away:
But he pursued her calling "Stay a little!
One golden minute's grace: he wore your sleeve:
Would he break faith with one I may not name?
Must our true man change like a leaf at last?
Nay—like enough: why then, far be it from me
To cross our mighty Lancelot in his loves!
And, damsel, for I deem you know full well
Where your great knight is hidden, let me leave
My quest with you; the diamond also:
For if you love, it will be sweet to give it;
And if he love, it will be sweet to have it
From your own hand; and whether he love or not,
A diamond is a diamond. Fare you well
A thousand times!—a thousand times farewell!
Yet, if he love, and his love hold, we two
May meet at court hereafter: there, I think,
So you will learn the courtesies of the court,
We two shall know each other."
            Then he gave,
And slightly kiss'd the hand to which he gave,
The diamond, and all wearied of the quest
Leapt on his horse, and carolling as he went
A true-love ballad, lightly rode away.

Thence to the court he past; there told the King
What the King knew "Sir Lancelot is the knight"
And added "Sire, my liege, so much I learnt;
But fail'd to find him tho' I rode all round
The region: but I lighted on the maid,
Whose sleeve he wore; she loves him; and to her,
Deeming our courtesy is the truest law,
I gave the diamond: she will render it;
For by mine head she knows his hiding-place."

The seldom-frowning King frown'd, and replied,
"Too courteous truly! ye shall go no more
On quest of mine, seeing that ye forget
Obedience is the courtesy due to kings."

He spake and parted. Wroth but all
   in awe,
For twenty strokes of the blood, without
   a word,
Linger'd that other, staring after him ;
Then shook his hair, strode off, and
   buzz'd abroad
About the maid of Astolat, and her love.
All ears were prick'd at once, all tongues
   were loosed :
"The maid of Astolat loves Sir Lancelot,
Sir Lancelot loves the maid of Astolat."
Some read the King's face, some the
   Queen's, and all
Had marvel what the maid might be, but
   most
Predoom'd her as unworthy. One old
   dame
Came suddenly on the Queen with the
   sharp news.
She, that had heard the noise of it before,
But sorrowing Lancelot should have
   stoop'd so low,
Marr'd her friend's point with pale tran-
   quillity.
So ran the tale like fire about the court,
Fire in dry stubble a nine days' wonder
   flared :
Till ev'n the knights at banquet twice or
   thrice
Forgot to drink to Lancelot and the
   Queen,
And pledging Lancelot and the lily maid
Smiled at each other, while the Queen
   who sat
With lips severely placid felt the knot
Climb in her throat, and with her feet
   unseen
Crush'd the wild passion out against the
   floor
Beneath the banquet, where the meats
   became
As wormwood, and she hated all who
   pledged.

But far away the maid in Astolat,
Her guiltless rival, she that ever kept
The one-day-seen Sir Lancelot in her
   heart,
Crept to her father, while he mused alone,
Sat on his knee, stroked his gray face and
   said,
"Father, you call me wilful, and the
   fault
Is yours who let me have my will, and now,
Sweet father, will you let me lose my
   wits ?"

"Nay," said he,
   fore, let m[e]
She answer'd, "[
   Lavaine."
"Ye will not lo[
   Lavaine :
Bide," answer'd
   hear anon
Of him, and of th[
   said,
"And of that othe[
And find that oth[
And with mine ow[n
   to him,
Lest I be found a[
As yon proud Pr[
   to me.
Sweet father, I be[
Gaunt as it were [
Death-pale, for lac[
The gentler-born
   bound,
My father, to be [
To noble knights [
When these have
   me hence
I pray you." T[
   said,
"Ay, ay, the dia[r
   child,
Right fain were
   were whol[e
Being our greate[
   give it —
And sure I think t[he
For any mouth to g[
Nay, I mean not[
   gone,
Being so very wil[

Lightly, her sui[
And while she ma[
Her father's latest [
"Being so very w[
And changed its[
   heart,
"Being so very w[
But she was happy
As we shake off th[
And in her heart s[
"What matter, s[
   life ?"
Then far away with[
Rode o'er the lon[g
   downs
To Camelot, and
Came on her brot[

Making a roan horse caper and curvet
For pleasure all about a field of flowers :
Whom when she saw, "Lavaine," she cried, "Lavaine,
How fares my lord Sir Lancelot?" He amazed,
"Torre and Elaine! why here? Sir Lancelot!
How know ye my lord's name is Lancelot?"
But when the maid had told him all her tale,
Then turn'd Sir Torre, and being in his moods
Left them, and under the strange-statued gate,
Where Arthur's wars were render'd mystically,
Past up the still rich city to his kin,
His own far blood, which dwelt at Camelot ;
And her, Lavaine across the poplar grove
Led to the caves : there first she saw the casque
Of Lancelot on the wall : her scarlet sleeve,
Tho' carved and cut, and half the pearls away,
Stream'd from it still ; and in her heart she laugh'd,
Because he had not loosed it from his helm,
But meant once more perchance to tourney in it.
And when they gain'd the cell in which he slept,
His battle-writhen arms and mighty hands
Lay naked on the wolfskin, and a dream
Of dragging down his enemy made them move.
Then she that saw him lying unsleek, unshorn,
Gaunt as it were the skeleton of himself,
Utter'd a little tender dolorous cry.
The sound not wonted in a place so still
Woke the sick knight, and while he roll'd his eyes
Yet blank from sleep, she started to him, saying
"Your prize the diamond sent you by the King" :
His eyes glisten'd : she fancied "is it for me?"
And when the maid had told him all the tale
Of King and Prince, the diamond sent, the quest
Assign'd to her not worthy of it, she knelt
Full lowly by the corners of his bed,
And laid the diamond in his open hand.
Her face was near, and as we kiss the child
That does the task assign'd, he kiss'd her face.
At once she slipt like water to the floor.
"Alas," he said, "your ride has wearied you.
Rest must you have." "No rest for me," she said ;
"Nay, for near you, fair lord, I am at rest."
What might she mean by that? his large black eyes,
Yet larger thro' his leanness, dwelt upon her,
Till all her heart's sad secret blazed itself
In the heart's colors on her simple face ;
And Lancelot look'd and was perplext in mind,
And being weak in body said no more ;
But did not love the color ; woman's love,
Save one, he not regarded, and so turn'd
Sighing, and feign'd a sleep until he slept.

Then rose Elaine and glided thro' the fields,
And past beneath the wildly-sculptured gates
Far up the dim rich city to her kin ;
There bode the night : but woke with dawn, and past
Down thro' the dim rich city to the fields,
Thence to the cave : so day by day she past
In either twilight ghost-like to and fro
Gliding, and every day she tended him,
And likewise many a night : and Lancelot
Would, tho' he call'd his wound a little hurt
Whereof he should be quickly whole, at times
Brain-feverous in his heat and agony, seem
Uncourteous, even he : but the meek maid
Sweetly forebore him ever, being to him
Meeker than any child to a rough nurse,
Milder than any mother to a sick child,
And never woman yet, since man's first fall,
Did kindlier unto man, but her deep love
Upbore her ; till the hermit, skill'd in all
The simples and the science of that time,
Told him that her fine care had saved his life.
And the sick man forgot her simple blush,
Would call her friend and sister, sweet Elaine,
Would listen for her coming and regret
Her parting step, and held her tenderly,

"She knelt
Full lowly by the corners of his bed."

And loved her with all love except the love
Of man and woman when they love their
   best
Closest and sweetest, and had died the
   death
In any knightly fashion for her sake.
And peradventure had he seen her first
She might have made this and that other
   world
Another world for the sick man; but now
The shackles of an old love straiten'd
   him,
His honor rooted in dishonor stood,
And faith unfaithful kept him falsely true.

   Yet the great knight in his mid-sick-
     ness made
Full many a holy vow and pure resolve.
These, as but born of sickness, could not
   live :
For when the blood ran lustier in him
   again,
Full often the sweet image of one face,
Making a treacherous quiet in his heart,
Dispersed his resolution like a cloud.

Then if the maiden, while that ghostly
   grace
Beam'd on his fancy, spoke, he answer'd
   not,
Or short and coldly, and she knew right
   well
What the rough sickness meant, but what
   this meant
She knew not, and the sorrow dimm'd
   her sight,
And drave her ere her time across the fields
Far into the rich city, where alone
She murmur'd "vain, in vain : it can-
   not be.
He will not love me : how then ? must
   I die."
Then as a little helpless innocent bird,
That has but one plain passage of few notes,
Will sing the simple passage o'er and o'er
For all an April morning, till the ear
Wearies to hear it, so the simple maid
Went half the night repeating, "must
   I die ?"
And now to right she turn'd, and now
   to left,

And found no ease in turning or in rest;
And "him or death" she mutter'd,
    "death or him,"
Again and like a burthen, "him or death."

But when Sir Lancelot's deadly hurt
    was whole,
To Astolat returning rode the three.
There morn by morn, arraying her sweet
    self
In that wherein she deem'd she look'd
    her best,
She came before Sir Lancelot, for she
    thought
"If I be loved, these are my festal robes,
If not, the victim's flowers before he fall."
And Lancelot ever prest upon the maid
That she should ask some goodly gift of
    him
For her own self or hers; "and do not shun
To speak the wish most dear to your
    true heart;
Such service have ye done me, that I
    make
My will of yours, and Prince and Lord am I
In mine own land, and what I will I can."
Then like a ghost she lifted up her face,
But like a ghost without the power to
    speak.
And Lancelot saw that she withheld her
    wish,
And bode among them yet a little space
Till he should learn it; and one morn
    it chanced
He found her in among the garden yews,
And said, "Delay no longer, speak your
    wish,
Seeing I must go to-day": then out she
    brake;
"Going? and we shall never see you more.
And I must die for want of one bold word."
"Speak: that I live to hear," he said,
    "is yours."
Then suddenly and passionately she
    spoke:
"I have gone mad. I love you: let
    me die."
"Ah, sister," answer'd Lancelot, "what
    is this?"
And innocently extending her white arms,
"Your love," she said, "your love — to
    be your wife."
And Lancelot answer'd, "Had I chos'n
    to wed,

Then suddenly and passionately she spoke.

I had been wedded earlier, sweet Elaine:
But now there never will be wife of mine."
"No, no," she cried, "I care not to be wife,
But to be with you still, to see your face,
To serve you, and to follow you thro' the world."
And Lancelot answer'd, "Nay, the world, the world,
All ear and eye, with such a stupid heart
To interpret ear and eye, and such a tongue
To blare its own interpretation — nay,
Full ill then should I quit your brother's love,
And your good father's kindness." And she said
"Not to be with you, not to see your face —
Alas for me then, my good days are done."
"Nay, noble maid," he answer'd, "ten times nay!
This is not love: but love's first flash in youth,
Most common: yea I know it of mine own self:
And you yourself will smile at your own self
Hereafter, when you yield your flower of life
To one more fitly yours, not thrice your age:
And then will I, for true you are and sweet
Beyond mine old belief in womanhood,
More specially should your good knight be poor,
Endow you with broad land and territory
Even to the half my realm beyond the seas,
So that would make you happy: furthermore,
Ev'n to the death, as tho' ye were my blood,
In all your quarrels will I be your knight.
This will I do, dear damsel, for your sake,
And more than this I cannot."
        While he spoke
She neither blush'd nor shook, but deathly-pale
Stood grasping what was nearest, then replied:
"Of all this will I nothing"; and so fell,
And thus they bore her swooning to her tower.

    Then spake, to whom thro' those black walls of yew
Their talk had pierced, her father. "Ay, a flash,

I fear me, that will strike my blossom dead.
Too courteous are you, fair Lord Lancelot.
I pray you, use some rough discourtesy
To blunt or break her passion."
            Lancelot said,
"That were against me: what I can I will";
And there that day remain'd, and toward even
Sent for his shield: full meekly rose the maid,
Stript off the case, and gave the naked shield;
Then, when she heard his horse upon the stones,
Unclasping flung the casement back, and look'd
Down on his helm, from which her sleeve had gone.
And Lancelot knew the little clinking sound;
And she by tact of love was well aware
That Lancelot knew that she was looking at him.
And yet he glanced not up, nor waved his hand,
Nor bade farewell, but sadly rode away.
This was the one discourtesy that he used.

    So in her tower alone the maiden sat:
His very shield was gone; only the case,
Her own poor work, her empty labor, left.
But still she heard him, still his picture form'd
And grew between her and the pictured wall.
Then came her father, saying in low tones
"Have comfort," whom she greeted quietly.
Then came her brethren saying, "Peace to thee
Sweet sister," whom she answer'd with all calm.
But when they left her to herself again,
Death, like a friend's voice from a distant field
Approaching thro' the darkness, call'd; the owls
Wailing had power upon her, and she mixt
Her fancies with the sallow-rifted glooms
Of evening, and the moanings of the wind.

    And in those days she made a little song,
And call'd her song "The Song of Love and Death,"
And sang it: sweetly could she make and sing.

LANCELOT AND ELAINE.

"Sweet is true love tho' given in vain,
    in vain ;
And sweet is death who puts an end to pain:
I know not which is sweeter, no, not I.

"Love, art thou sweet? then bitter
    death must be :
Love, thou art bitter; sweet is death to me.
O Love, if death be sweeter, let me die.

"Sweet love, that seems not made to
    fade away,
Sweet death, that seems to make us love-
    less clay,
I know not which is sweeter, no, not I.

"I fain would follow love, if that could
    be ;
I needs must follow death, who calls for
    me ;
Call and I follow, I follow ! let me die."

  High with the last line scaled her voice,
    and this,
All in a fiery dawning wild with wind
That shook her tower, the brothers heard,
    and thought
With shuddering " Hark the Phantom
    of the house
That ever shrieks before a death," and
    call'd
The father, and all three in hurry and fear
Ran to her, and lo ! the blood-red light of
    dawn
Flared on her face, she shrilling "Let
    me die ! "

  As when we dwell upon a word we
    know
Repeating, till the word we know so well
Becomes a wonder and we know not why,
So dwelt the father on her face and thought
" Is this Elaine ? " till back the maiden
    fell,
Then gave a languid hand to each, and lay,
Speaking a still good-morrow with her
    eyes.
At last she said " Sweet brothers, yester-
    night
I seem'd a curious little maid again,
As happy as when we dwelt among the
    woods,
And when ye used to take me with the
    flood
Up the great river in the boatman's boat.
Only ye would not pass beyond the cape
That has the poplar on it : there ye fixt
Your limit, oft returning with the tide.
And yet I cried because ye would not pass
Beyond it, and far up the shining flood
Until we found the palace of the king.
And yet ye would not ; but this night
    I dream'd
That I was all alone upon the flood,
And then I said " Now shall I have my
    will " :
And there I woke, but still the wish re-
    main'd.
So let me hence that I may pass at last
Beyond the poplar and far up the flood,
Until I find the palace of the king.
There will I enter in among them all,
And no man there will dare to mock at me ;
But there the fine Gawain will wonder at
    me,
And there the great Sir Lancelot muse at
    me ;
Gawain, who bade a thousand farewells
    to me,
Lancelot, who coldly went nor bade me
    one :
And there the King will know me and
    my love,
And there the Queen herself will pity me,
And all the gentle court will welcome me,
And after my long voyage I shall rest ! "

  "Peace," said her father, " O my child,
    ye seem
Light-headed, for what force is yours to go,
So far, being sick ? and wherefore would
    ye look
On this proud fellow again, who scorns us
    all ? "

  Then the rough Torre began to heave
    and move,
And bluster into stormy sobs and say
" I never loved him : an I meet with him,
I care not howsoever great he be.
Then will I strike at him and strike him
    down,
Give me good fortune, I will strike him
    dead,
For this discomfort he hath done the
    house."

  To which the gentle sister made reply,
" Fret not yourself, dear brother, nor be
    wroth,
Seeing it is no more Sir Lancelot's fault
Not to love me, than it is mine to love
Him of all men who seems to me the
    highest."

"Highest?" the Father answer'd,
 echoing "highest?"
(He meant to break the passion in her)
 "nay,
Daughter, I know not what you call the
 highest;
But this I know, for all the people know it,
He loves the Queen, and in an open shame:
And she returns his love in open shame.
If this be high, what is it to be low?"

Then spake the lily maid of Astolat;
"Sweet father, all too faint and sick am I
For anger: these are slanders: never yet
Was noble man but made ignoble talk.
He makes no friend who never made a
 foe.
But now it is my glory to have loved
One peerless, without stain: so let me
 pass,
My father, howsoe'er I seem to you,
Not all unhappy, having loved God's best
And greatest, tho' my love had no return:
Yet, seeing ye desire your child to live,
Thanks, but ye work against your own
 desire;
For if I could believe the things ye say
I should but die the sooner; wherefore
 cease,
Sweet father, and bid call the ghostly man
Hither, and let me shrive me clean, and
 die."

So when the ghostly man had come
 and gone,
She with a face, bright as for sin forgiven,
Besought Lavaine to write as she devised
A letter, word for word; and when he
 ask'd
"Is it for Lancelot, is it for my dear lord?
Then will I bear it gladly"; she replied,
"For Lancelot and the Queen and all
 the world,
But I myself must bear it." Then he
 wrote
The letter she devised; which being writ
And folded, "O sweet father, tender and
 true,
Deny me not," she said — "ye never yet
Denied my fancies — this, however
 strange,
My latest: lay the letter in my hand
A little ere I die, and close the hand
Upon it; I shall guard it even in death.
And when the heat is gone from out my
 heart,
Then take the little bed on which I died

For Lancelot's love, and deck it like the
 Queen's
For richness, and me also like the Queen
In all I have of rich, and lay me on it.
And let there be prepared a chariot-bier
To take me to the river, and a barge
Be ready on the river, clothed in black.
I go in state to court, to meet the Queen.
There surely I shall speak for mine own
 self,
And none of you can speak for me so well.
And therefore let our dumb old man alone
Go with me, he can steer and row, and he
Will guide me to that palace, to the
 doors."

She ceased: her father promised;
 whereupon
She grew so cheerful that they deem'd
 her death
Was rather in the fantasy than the blood.
But ten slow mornings past, and on the
 eleventh
Her father laid the letter in her hand,
And closed the hand upon it, and she died.
So that day there was dole in Astolat.

But when the next sun brake from
 underground,
Then, those two brethren slowly with
 bent brows
Accompanying, the sad chariot-bier
Past like a shadow thro' the field, that
 shone
Full-summer, to that stream whereon the
 barge,
Pall'd all its length in blackest samite,
 lay.
There sat the lifelong creature of the
 house,
Loyal, the dumb old servitor, on deck,
Winking his eyes, and twisted all his face.
So those two brethren from the chariot
 took
And on the black decks laid her in her
 bed,
Set in her hand a lily, o'er her hung
The silken case with braided blazonings,
And kiss'd her quiet brows, and saying
 to her
"Sister, farewell for ever," and again
"Farewell, sweet sister," parted all in
 tears.
Then rose the dumb old servitor, and the
 dead
Steer'd by the dumb went upward with
 the flood —

*"Then rose the dumb old servitor, and the dead
Steer'd by the dumb went upward with the flood."*

In her right hand the lily, in her left
The letter — all her bright hair stream-
    ing down —
And all the coverlid was cloth of gold
Drawn to her waist, and she herself in
    white
All but her face, and that clear-featured
    face
Was lovely, for she did not seem as dead
But fast asleep, and lay as tho' she smiled.

    That day Sir Lancelot at the palace
      craved
Audience of Guinevere, to give at last
The price of half a realm, his costly gift,
Hard-won and hardly won with bruise
    and blow,
With deaths of others, and almost his
    own,
The nine-years-fought-for diamonds: for
    he saw
One of her house, and sent him to the Queen
Bearing his wish, whereto the Queen
    agreed
With such and so unmoved a majesty
She might have seem'd her statue, but
    that he,
Low-drooping till he wellnigh kiss'd her
    feet
For loyal awe, saw with a sidelong eye
The shadow of a piece of pointed lace,
In the Queen's shadow, vibrate on the
    walls,
And parted, laughing in his courtly
    heart.

    All in an oriel on the summer side,
Vine-clad, of Arthur's palace toward the
    stream,
They met, and Lancelot kneeling utter'd,
    "Queen,
Lady, my liege, in whom I have my joy,
Take, what I had not won except for you,
These jewels, and make me happy, making
    them
An armlet for the roundest arm on earth,
Or necklace for a neck to which the swan's
Is tawnier than her cygnet's: these are
    words:
Your beauty is your beauty, and I sin
In speaking, yet O grant my worship of it
Words, as we grant grief tears. Such sin
    in words
Perchance, we both can pardon: but, my
    Queen,
I hear of rumors flying thro' your court.
Our bond, as not the bond of man and wife,
Should have in it an absoluter trust
To make up that defect: let rumors be:
When did not rumors fly? these, as I trust
That you trust me in your own nobleness,
I may not well believe that you believe."

    While thus he spoke, half turn'd away,
      the Queen
Brake from the vast oriel-embowering vine
Leaf after leaf, and tore, and cast them off,
Till all the place whereon she stood was
    green;
Then, when he ceased, in one cold pas-
    sive hand

Received at once and laid aside the gems
There on a table near her, and replied.

"It may be, I am quicker of belief
Than you believe me, Lancelot of the Lake.
Our bond is not the bond of man and wife.
This good is in it, whatsoe'er of ill,
It can be broken easier. I for you
This many a year have done despite and
  wrong
To one whom ever in my heart of hearts
I did acknowledge nobler. What are
  these ?
Diamonds for me! they had been thrice
  their worth
Being your gift, had you not lost your own.
To loyal hearts the value of all gifts
Must vary as the giver's. Not for me!
For her! for your new fancy. Only this
Grant me, I pray you: have your joys
  apart.
I doubt not that however changed, you
  keep
So much of what is graceful: and myself
Would shun to break those bounds of
  courtesy
In which as Arthur's queen I move and
  rule :
So cannot speak my mind. An end to this!
A strange one ! yet I take it with Amen.
So pray you, add my diamonds to her
  pearls ;
Deck her with these ; tell her she shines
  me down :
An armlet for an arm to which the Queen's
Is haggard, or a necklace for a neck
O as much fairer — as a faith once fair
Was richer than these diamonds — hers
  not mine —
Nay, by the mother of our Lord himself,
Or hers or mine, mine now to work my
  will —
She shall not have them."
                Saying which she seized,
And, thro' the casement standing wide
  for heat,
Flung them, and down they flash'd, and
  smote the stream.
Then from the smitten surface flash'd, as
  it were,
Diamonds to meet them, and they past
  away.
Then while Sir Lancelot leant, in half
  disgust
At love, life, all things, on the window
  ledge,
Close underneath his eyes, and right across

Where these had fallen, slowly past the
  barge
Whereon the lily maid of Astolat
Lay smiling, like a star in blackest night.

But the wild Queen, who saw not, burst
  away
To weep and wail in secret ; and the barge,
On to the palace-doorway sliding, paused.
There two stood arm'd, and kept the
  door ; to whom,
All up the marble stair, tier over tier,
Were added mouths that gaped, and eyes
  that ask'd
"What is it ?" but that oarsman's hag-
  gard face,
As hard and still as is the face that men
Shape to their fancy's eye from broken
  rocks
On some cliff-side, appall'd them, and
  they said,
"He is enchanted, cannot speak — and
  she,
Look how she sleeps — the Fairy Queen,
  so fair !
Yea, but how pale ! what are they ?
  flesh and blood ?
Or come to take the King to fairy land ?
For some do hold our Arthur cannot die,
But that he passes into fairy land."

While thus they babbled of the King,
  the King
Came girt with knights : then turn'd
  the tongueless man
From the half-face to the full eye, and rose
And pointed to the damsel, and the doors.
So Arthur bade the meek Sir Percivale
And pure Sir Galahad to uplift the maid ;
And reverently they bore her into hall.
Then came the fine Gawain and wonder'd
  at her,
And Lancelot later came and mused at her,
And last the Queen herself and pitied her :
But Arthur spied the letter in her hand,
Stoopt, took, brake seal, and read it ;
  this was all.

"Most noble lord, Sir Lancelot of the
  Lake,
I, sometime call'd the maid of Astolat,
Come, for you left me taking no farewell,
Hither, to take my last farewell of you.
I loved you, and my love had no return,
And therefore my true love has been my
  death.
And therefore to our lady Guinevere,

And to all other ladies, I make moan.
Pray for my soul, and yield me burial.
Pray for my soul thou too, Sir Lancelot,
As thou art a knight peerless."

      Thus he read,
And ever in the reading, lords and dames
Wept, looking often from his face who read
To hers which lay so silent, and at times,
So touch'd were they, half-thinking that her lips,
Who had devised the letter, moved again.

  Then freely spoke Sir Lancelot to them all;
"My lord liege Arthur, and all ye that hear,
Know that for this most gentle maiden's death
Right heavy am I; for good she was and true,
But loved me with a love beyond all love
In women, whomsoever I have known.
Yet to be loved makes not to love again;
Not at my years, however it hold in youth.
I swear by truth and knighthood that I gave
No cause, not willingly, for such a love:
To this I call my friends in testimony,
Her brethren, and her father, who himself
Besought me to be plain and blunt, and use,
To break her passion, some discourtesy
Against my nature: what I could, I did.
I left her and I bade her no farewell.
Tho', had I dreamt the damsel would have died,
I might have put my wits to some rough use,
And help'd her from herself."

      Then said the Queen
(Sea was her wrath, yet working after storm)
"Ye might at least have done her so much grace,
Fair lord, as would have help'd her from her death."
He raised his head, their eyes met and hers fell,
He adding,
  "Queen, she would not be content
Save that I wedded her, which could not be.
Then might she follow me thro' the world, she ask'd;

It could not be. I told her that her love
Was but the flash of youth, would darken down
To rise hereafter in a stiller flame
Toward one more worthy of her — then would I,
More specially were he, she wedded, poor,
Estate them with large land and territory
In mine own realm beyond the narrow seas,
To keep them in all joyance: more than this
I could not; this she would not, and she died."

He pausing, Arthur answer'd, "O my knight,
It will be to thy worship, as my knight,
And mine, as head of all our Table Round,
To see that she be buried worshipfully."

So toward that shrine which then in all the realm
Was richest, Arthur leading, slowly went
The marshall'd order of their Table Round,
And Lancelot sad beyond his wont, to see
The maiden buried, not as one unknown,
Nor meanly, but with gorgeous obsequies,
And mass, and rolling music, like a Queen.
And when the knights had laid her comely head
Low in the dust of half-forgotten kings,
Then Arthur spake among them, "Let her tomb
Be costly, and her image thereupon.
And let the shield of Lancelot at her feet
Be carven, and her lily in her hand.
And let the story of her dolorous voyage
For all true hearts be blazon'd on her tomb
In letters gold and azure!" which was wrought
Thereafter; but when now the lords and dames
And people, from the high door streaming, brake
Disorderly, as homeward each, the Queen,
Who mark'd Sir Lancelot where he moved apart,
Drew near, and sigh'd in passing "Lancelot,
Forgive me; mine was jealousy in love."
He answer'd with his eyes upon the ground,
"That is love's curse; pass on, my Queen, forgiven."
But Arthur who beheld his cloudy brows

Approach'd him, and with full affection flung
One arm about his neck, and spake and said.

"Lancelot, my Lancelot, thou in whom I have
Most love and most affiance, for I know
What thou hast been in battle by my side,
And many a time have watched thee at the tilt
Strike down the lusty and long-practised knight,
And let the younger and unskill'd go by
To win his honor and to make his name,
And loved thy courtesies and thee, a man
Made to be loved; but now I would to God,
For the wild people say wild things of thee,
Thou couldst have loved this maiden, shaped, it seems,
By God for thee alone, and from her face,
If one may judge the living by the dead,
Delicately pure and marvellously fair,
Who might have brought thee, now a lonely man
Wifeless and heirless, noble issue, sons
Born to the glory of thy name and fame,
My knight, the great Sir Lancelot of the Lake."

Then answer'd Lancelot, "Fair she was, my King,
Pure, as you ever wish your knights to be.
To doubt her fairness were to want an eye,
To doubt her pureness were to want a heart —
Yea, to be loved, if what is worthy love
Could bind him, but free love will not be bound."

"Free love, so bound, were freëst," said the King.
"Let love be free; free love is for the best:
And, after heaven, on our dull side of death,
What should be best, if not so pure a love
Clothed in so pure a loveliness? yet thee
She fail'd to bind, tho' being, as I think,
Unbound as yet, and gentle, as I know."

And Lancelot answer'd nothing, but he went,
And at the inrunning of a little brook
Sat by the river in a cove, and watch'd
The high-reed wave, and lifted up his eyes
And saw the barge that brought her moving down,
Far-off, a blot upon the stream, and said
Low in himself "Ah simple heart and sweet,
Ye loved me, damsel, surely with a love
Far tenderer than my Queen's. Pray for thy soul?
Ay, that will I. Farewell too — now at last —
Farewell, fair lily. 'Jealousy in love'?
Not rather dead love's harsh heir, jealous pride?
Queen, if I grant the jealousy as of love,
May not your crescent fear for name and fame
Speak, as it waxes, of a love that wanes?
Why did the King dwell on my name to me?
Mine own name shames me, seeming a reproach,
Lancelot, whom the Lady of the Lake
Stole from his mother — as the story runs —
She chanted snatches of mysterious song
Heard on the winding waters, eve and morn
She kiss'd me saying thou art fair, my child,
As a king's son, and often in her arms
She bare me, pacing on the dusky mere.
Would she had drown'd me in it, where'er it be!
For what am I? what profits me my name
Of greatest knight? I fought for it, and have it:
Pleasure to have it, none; to lose it, pain;
Now grown a part of me: but what use in it?
To make men worse by making my sin known?
Or sin seem less, the sinner seeming great?
Alas for Arthur's greatest knight, a man
Not after Arthur's heart! I needs must break
These bonds that so defame me: not without
She wills it: would I, if she will'd it? nay,
Who knows? but if I would not, then may God,
I pray him, send a sudden Angel down
To seize me by the hair and bear me far,
And fling me deep in that forgotten mere,
Among the tumbled fragments of the hills."

So groan'd Sir Lancelot in remorseful pain,
Not knowing he should die a holy man.

THE HOLY GRAIL.

From noiseful arms, and acts of prowess done
In tournament or tilt, Sir Percivale,
Whom Arthur and his knighthood call'd
    The Pure,
Had pass'd into the silent life of prayer,
Praise, fast, and alms; and leaving for the cowl
The helmet in an abbey far away
From Camelot, there, and not long after, died.

And one, a fellow-monk among the rest,
Ambrosius, loved him much beyond the rest,
And honor'd him, and wrought into his heart
A way by love that waken'd love within,
To answer that which came: and as they sat
Beneath a world-old yew-tree, darkening half
The cloisters, on a gustful April morn
That puff'd the swaying branches into smoke
Above them, ere the summer when he died,
The monk Ambrosius question'd Percivale:

"O brother, I have seen this yew-tree smoke,
Spring after spring, for half a hundred years:
For never have I known the world without,
Nor ever stray'd beyond the pale: but thee,
When first thou camest — such a courtesy
Spake thro' the limbs and in the voice — I knew
For one of those who eat in Arthur's hall;
For good ye are and bad, and like to coins,
Some true, some light, but every one of you
Stamp'd with the image of the King; and now
Tell me, what drove thee from the Table Round,
My brother? was it earthly passion crost?"

"Nay," said the knight; "for no such passion mine.
But the sweet vision of the Holy Grail
Drove me from all vainglories, rivalries,
And earthly heats that spring and sparkle out
Among us in the jousts, while women watch
Who wins, who falls; and waste the spiritual strength
Within us, better offer'd up to Heaven."

To whom the monk: "The Holy Grail! — I trust
We are green in Heaven's eyes; but here too much
We moulder — as to things without I mean —
Yet one of your own knights, a guest of ours,
Told us of this in our refectory,
But spake with such a sadness and so low
We heard not half of what he said. What is it?
The phantom of a cup that comes and goes?"

"Nay, monk! what phantom?" answer'd Percivale.
"The cup, the cup itself, from which our Lord
Drank at the last sad supper with his own.
This, from the blessed land of Aromat —
After the day of darkness, when the dead
Went wandering o'er Moriah — the good saint,
Arimathæan Joseph, journeying brought
To Glastonbury, where the winter thorn
Blossoms at Christmas, mindful of our Lord.
And there awhile it bode; and if a man
Could touch or see it, he was heal'd at once,
By faith, of all his ills. But then the times
Grew to such evil that the holy cup
Was caught away to Heaven, and disappear'd."

To whom the monk: "From our old books I know
That Joseph came of old to Glastonbury,
And there the heathen Prince, Arviragus,
Gave him an isle of marsh whereon to build;
And there he built with wattles from the marsh
A little lonely church in days of yore,
For so they say, these books of ours, but seem
Mute of this miracle, far as I have read.
But who first saw the holy thing to-day?"

"A woman," answer'd Percivale, "a nun,
And one no further off in blood from me
Than sister ; and if ever holy maid
With knees of adoration wore the stone,
A holy maid ; tho' never maiden glow'd,
But that was in her earlier maidenhood,
With such a fervent flame of human love,
Which being rudely blunted, glanced and shot
Only to holy things ; to prayer and praise
She gave herself, to fast and alms. And yet,
Nun as she was, the scandal of the Court,
Sin against Arthur and the Table Round,
And the strange sound of an adulterous race,
Across the iron grating of her cell
Beat, and she pray'd and fasted all the more.

"And he to whom she told her sins, or what
Her all but utter whiteness held for sin,
A man wellnigh a hundred winters old,
Spake often with her of the Holy Grail,
A legend handed down thro' five or six,
And each of these a hundred winters old,
From our Lord's time. And when King Arthur made
His Table Round, and all men's hearts became
Clean for a season, surely he had thought
That now the Holy Grail would come again ;
But sin broke out. Ah, Christ, that it would come,
And heal the world of all their wickedness !
'O Father !' asked the maiden, 'might it come
To me by prayer and fasting ?' 'Nay,' said he,
'I know not, for thy heart is pure as snow.'
And so she pray'd and fasted, till the sun
Shone, and the wind blew, thro' her, and I thought
She might have risen and floated when I saw her.

"For on a day she sent to speak with me.
And when she came to speak, behold her eyes
Beyond my knowing of them, beautiful,
Beyond all knowing of them, wonderful,
Beautiful in the light of holiness.
And 'O my brother, Percivale,' she said,
'Sweet brother, I have seen the Holy Grail :
For, waked at dead of night, I heard a sound
As of a silver horn from o'er the hills
Blown, and I thought, "It is not Arthur's use
To hunt by moonlight" ; and the slender sound
As from a distance beyond distance grew
Coming upon me — O never harp nor horn,
Nor aught we blow with breath, or touch with hand,
Was like that music as it came ; and then
Stream'd thro' my cell a cold and silver beam,
And down the long beam stole the Holy Grail,
Rose-red with beatings in it, as if alive,
Till all the white walls of my cell were dyed
With rosy colors leaping on the wall ;
And then the music faded, and the Grail
Pass'd, and the beam decay'd, and from the walls
The rosy quiverings died into the night.
So now the Holy Thing is here again
Among us, brother, fast thou too and pray,
And tell thy brother knights to fast and pray,
That so perchance the vision may be seen
By thee and those, and all the world be heal'd.'

"Then leaving the pale nun, I spake of this
To all men ; and myself fasted and pray'd
Always, and many among us many a week
Fasted and pray'd even to the uttermost,
Expectant of the wonder that would be.

"And one there was among us, ever moved
Among us in white armor, Galahad.
'God make thee good as thou art beautiful,'
Said Arthur, when he dubb'd him knight ;
and none,
In so young youth, was ever made a knight
Till Galahad ; and this Galahad, when he heard
My sister's vision, fill'd me with amaze ;
His eyes became so like her own, they seem'd
Hers, and himself her brother more than I.

"Sister or brother none had he; but some
Call'd him a son of Lancelot, and some said
Begotten by enchantment — chatterers they,
Like birds of passage piping up and down,
That gape for flies — we know not whence they come;
For when was Lancelot wanderingly lewd?

"But she, the wan sweet maiden shore away
Clean from her forehead all that wealth of hair
Which made a silken mat-work for her feet;
And out of this she plaited broad and long
A strong sword-belt, and wove with silver thread
And crimson in the belt a strange device,
A crimson grail within a silver beam;
And saw the bright boy-knight, and bound it on him,
Saying, 'My knight, my love, my knight of heaven,
O thou, my love, whose love is one with mine,
I, maiden, round thee, maiden, bind my belt.
Go forth, for thou shalt see what I have seen,
And break thro' all, till one will crown thee king
Far in the spiritual city': and as she spake
She sent the deathless passion in her eyes
Thro' him, and made him hers, and laid her mind
On him, and he believed in her belief.

"Then came a year of miracle: O brother,
In our great hall there stood a vacant chair,
Fashion'd by Merlin ere he past away,
And carven with strange figures; and in and out
The figures, like a serpent, ran a scroll
Of letters in a tongue no man could read.
And Merlin call'd it 'The Siege perilous,'
Perilous for good and ill; 'for there,' he said,
'No man could sit but he should lose himself':
And once by misadvertence Merlin sat
In his own chair, and so was lost; but he,
Galahad, when he heard of Merlin's doom,
Cried, 'If I lose myself I save myself!'

"Then on a summer night it came to pass,
While the great banquet lay along the hall,
That Galahad would sit down in Merlin's chair.

"And all at once, as there we sat, we heard
A cracking and a riving of the roofs,
And rending, and a blast, and overhead
Thunder, and in the thunder was a cry.
And in the blast there smote along the hall
A beam of light seven times more clear than day:
And down the long beam stole the Holy Grail
All over cover'd with a luminous cloud,
And none might see who bare it, and it past.
But every knight beheld his fellow's face
As in a glory, and all the knights arose,
And staring each at other like dumb men
Stood, till I found a voice and sware a vow.

"I sware a vow before them all, that I,
Because I had not seen the Grail, would ride
A twelvemonth and a day in quest of it,
Until I found and saw it, as the nun
My sister saw it; and Galahad sware the vow,
And good Sir Bors, our Lancelot's cousin, sware,
And Lancelot sware, and many among the knights,
And Gawain sware, and louder than the rest."

Then spake the monk Ambrosius, asking him,
"What said the King? Did Arthur take the vow?"

"Nay, for my lord," said Percivale, "the king,
Was not in hall: for early that same day,
Scaped thro' a cavern from a bandit hold,
An outraged maiden sprang into the hall
Crying on help: for all her shining hair
Was smear'd with earth, and either milky arm
Red-rent with hooks of bramble, and all she wore
Torn as a sail that leaves the rope is torn
In tempest: so the king arose and went

To smoke the scandalous hive of those
    wild bees
That made such honey in his realm.
    Howbeit
Some little of this marvel he too saw,
Returning o'er the plain that then began
To darken under Camelot; whence the
    king
Look'd up, calling aloud, 'Lo there! the
    roofs
Of our great hall are rolled in thunder-
    smoke!
Pray Heaven, they be not smitten by
    the bolt.'
For dear to Arthur was that hall of ours,
As having there so oft with all his knights
Feasted, and as the stateliest under
    heaven.

"O brother, had you known our mighty
    hall,
Which Merlin built for Arthur long ago!
For all the sacred mount of Camelot,
And all the dim rich city, roof by roof,
Tower after tower, spire beyond spire,
By grove, and garden-lawn, and rushing
    brook,
Climbs to the mighty hall that Merlin
    built.
And four great zones of sculpture, set
    betwixt
With many a mystic symbol, gird the
    hall:
And in the lowest beasts are slaying men,
And in the second men are slaying beasts,
And on the third are warriors, perfect men,
And on the fourth are men with growing
    wings,
And over all one statue in the mould
Of Arthur, made by Merlin, with a crown,
And peak'd wings pointed to the Northern
    Star.
And eastward fronts the statue, and the
    crown
And both the wings are made of gold,
    and flame
At sunrise till the people in far fields,
Wasted so often by the heathen hordes,
Behold it, crying, 'We have still a king.'

"And, brother, had you known our
    hall within,
Broader and higher than any in all the
    lands!
Where twelve great windows blazon
    Arthur's wars,
And all the light that falls upon the board
Streams thro' the twelve great battles of
    our King.
Nay, one there is, and at the eastern
    end,
Wealthy with wandering lines of mount
    and mere,
Where Arthur finds the brand, Excalibur.
And also one to the west, and counter
    to it,
And blank: and who shall blazon it?
    when and how?—
O there, perchance, when all our wars
    are done,
The brand Excalibur will be cast away.

"So to this hall full quickly rode the
    King,
In horror lest the work by Merlin wrought,
Dreamlike, should on the sudden vanish,
    wrapt
In unremorseful folds of rolling fire.
And in he rode, and up I glanced, and saw
The golden dragon sparkling over all:
And many of those who burnt the hold,
    their arms
Hack'd, and their foreheads grimed with
    smoke, and sear'd,
Follow'd, and in among bright faces, ours,
Full of the vision, prest: and then the
    King
Spake to me, being nearest, 'Percivale,'
(Because the hall was all in tumult—some
Vowing, and some protesting), 'what is
    this?'

"O brother, when I told him what
    had chanced,
My sister's vision, and the rest, his face
Darken'd, as I have seen it more than
    once,
When some brave deed seem'd to be done
    in vain,
Darken; and 'Woe is me, my knights,'
    he cried,
'Had I been here, ye had not sworn the
    vow.'
Bold was mine answer, 'Had thyself
    been here,
My King, thou wouldst have sworn.'
    'Yea, yea,' said he,
'Art thou so bold and hast not seen the
    Grail?'

"'Nay, Lord, I heard the sound, I
    saw the light,
But since I did not see the Holy Thing,
I sware a vow to follow it till I saw.'

"Then when he asked us, knight by knight, if any
Had seen it, all their answers were as one:
'Nay, Lord, and therefore have we sworn our vows.'

"'Lo now,' said Arthur, 'have ye seen a cloud?
What go ye into the wilderness to see?'

"Then Galahad on the sudden, and in a voice
Shrilling along the hall to Arthur, call'd,
'But I, Sir Arthur, saw the Holy Grail,
I saw the Holy Grail and heard a cry—
O Galahad, and O Galahad, follow me.'

"'Ah, Galahad, Galahad,' said the King, 'for such
As thou art is the vision, not for these.
Thy holy nun and thou have seen a sign—
Holier is none, my Percivale, than she—
A sign to maim this Order which I made.
But you, that follow but the leader's bell'
(Brother, the King was hard upon his knights)
'Taliessin is our fullest throat of song,
And one hath sung and all the dumb will sing.
Lancelot is Lancelot, and hath overborne
Five knights at once, and every younger knight,
Unproven, holds himself as Lancelot,
Till overborne by one, he learns—and ye,
What are ye? Galahads?—no, nor Percivales'
(For thus it pleased the King to range me close
After Sir Galahad); 'nay,' said he, 'but men
With strength and will to right the wrong'd, of power
To lay the sudden heads of violence flat,
Knights that in twelve great battles splash'd and dyed
The strong White Horse in his own heathen blood—
But one hath seen, and all the blind will see.
Go, since your vows are sacred, being made:
Yet—for ye know the cries of all my realm
Pass thro' this hall—how often, O my knights,
Your places being vacant at my side,
This chance of noble deeds will come and go
Unchallenged, while you follow wandering fires
Lost in the quagmire? Many of you, yea most,
Return no more: ye think I show myself
Too dark a prophet: come now, let us meet
The morrow morn once more in one full field
Of gracious pastime, that once more the King,
Before you leave him for this Quest, may count
The yet-unbroken strength of all his knights,
Rejoicing in that Order which he made.'

"So when the sun broke next from under ground,
All the great table of our Arthur closed
And clash'd in such a tourney and so full,
So many lances broken—never yet
Had Camelot seen the like, since Arthur came.
And I myself and Galahad, for a strength
Was in us from the vision, overthrew
So many knights that all the people cried,
And almost burst the barriers in their heat,
Shouting 'Sir Galahad and Sir Percivale!'

"But when the next day brake from under ground—
O brother, had you known our Camelot,
Built by old kings, age after age, so old
The King himself had fears that it would fall,
So strange, and rich, and dim; for where the roofs
Totter'd toward each other in the sky,
Met foreheads all along the street of those
Who watch'd us pass; and lower, and where the long
Rich galleries, lady-laden, weigh'd the necks
Of dragons clinging to the crazy walls,
Thicker than drops from thunder, showers of flowers
Fell as we past; and men and boys astride
On wyvern, lion, dragon, griffin, swan,
At all the corners, named us each by name,
Calling 'God speed!' but in the street below
The knights and ladies wept, and rich and poor
Wept, and the King himself could hardly speak

For grief, and in the middle street the
  Queen,
Who rode by Lancelot, wail'd and shriek'd
  aloud,
'This madness has come on us for our
  sins.'
And then we reach'd the weirdly-sculp-
  tured gate,
Where Arthur's wars were render'd mys-
  tically,
And thence departed every one his way.

"And I was lifted up in heart, and
  thought
Of all my late-shown prowess in the lists,
How my strong lance had beaten down
  the knights,
So many and famous names; and never yet
Had heaven appear'd so blue, nor earth
  so green,
For all my blood danced in me, and I knew
That I should light upon the Holy Grail.

"Thereafter, the dark warning of our
  King,
That most of us would follow wandering
  fires,
Came like a driving gloom across my
  mind.
Then every evil word I had spoken once,
And every evil thought I had thought
  of old,
And every evil deed I ever did,
Awoke and cried, 'This Quest is not for
  thee.'
And lifting up mine eyes, I found myself
Alone, and in a land of sand and thorns,
And I was thirsty even unto death;
And I, too, cried, 'This Quest is not for
  thee.'

"And on I rode, and when I thought
  my thirst
Would slay me, saw deep lawns, and then
  a brook,
With one sharp rapid, where the crisp-
  ing white
Play'd ever back upon the sloping wave,
And took both ear and eye; and o'er the
  brook
Were apple-trees, and apples by the brook
Fallen, and on the lawns. 'I will rest
  here,'
I said, 'I am not worthy of the Quest';
But even while I drank the brook, and
  ate
The goodly apples, all these things at once

Fell into dust, an
And thirsting, in a

"And then bel
Spinning; and f
  she sat,
And kind the wom
And all her bear
  rose
Opening her arm
  should say
'Rest here'; but
  lo! she, t
Fell into dust
  house
Became no better
And in it a dead
Fell into dust, ar

"And on I roc
  thirst.
Then flash'd a y
  world,
And where it smot
  field,
The ploughman
  fell down
Before it; where
The milkmaid le
  down
Before it, and I kn
'The sun is rising
Then was I ware
In golden armor
About a casque a
In golden armor
And on the sple
  blind;
And seem'd to r
  world,
Being so huge.
  meant
To crush me, mov
Opened his arm
  came,
And up I went a
  too,
Fell into dust, a
And wearying in a

"And I rode
  hill,
And on the top,
Prick'd with in
  heaven.
And by the gatev
  these

THE HOLY GRAIL.

Cried to me climbing, 'Welcome, Percivale!
Thou mightiest and thou purest among men!'
And glad was I and clomb, but found at top
No man, nor any voice. And thence I past
Far thro' a ruinous city, and I saw
That man had once dwelt there; but there I found
Only one man of an exceeding age.
'Where is that goodly company,' said I,
'That so cried out upon me?' and he had
Scarce any voice to answer, and yet gasp'd
'Whence and what art thou?' and even as he spoke
Fell into dust, and disappear'd, and I
Was left alone once more, and cried in grief,
'Lo, if I find the Holy Grail itself
And touch it, it will crumble into dust.'

"And thence I dropt into a lowly vale,
Low as the hill was high, and where the vale
Was lowest, found a chapel and thereby
A holy hermit in a hermitage,
To whom I told my phantoms, and he said:

"'O son, thou hast not true humility,
The highest virtue, mother of them all;
For when the Lord of all things made Himself
Naked of glory for His mortal change,
"Take thou my robe," she said, "for all is thine,"
And all her form shone forth with sudden light
So that the angels were amazed, and she
Follow'd him down, and like a flying star
Led on the gray-hair'd wisdom of the east;
But her thou hast not known: for what is this
Thou thoughtest of thy prowess and thy sins?
Thou hast not lost thyself to save thyself
As Galahad.' When the hermit made an end,
In silver armor suddenly Galahad shone
Before us, and against the chapel door
Laid lance, and enter'd, and we knelt in prayer.
And there the hermit slaked my burning thirst
And at the sacring of the mass I saw
The holy elements alone; but he:

'Saw ye no more? I, Galahad, saw the Grail,
The Holy Grail, descend upon the shrine:
I saw the fiery face as of a child
That smote itself into the bread, and went;
And hither am I come; and never yet
Hath what thy sister taught me first to see,
This Holy Thing, fail'd from my side, nor come
Cover'd, but moving with me night and day,
Fainter by day, but always in the night
Blood-red, and sliding down the blacken'd marsh
Blood-red, and on the naked mountain top
Blood-red, and in the sleeping mere below
Blood-red. And in the strength of this I rode,
Shattering all evil customs everywhere,
And past thro' Pagan realms, and made them mine,
And clash'd with Pagan hordes, and bore them down,
And broke thro' all, and in the strength of this
Come victor. But my time is hard at hand,
And hence I go; and one will crown me king
Far in the spiritual city; and come thou, too,
For thou shalt see the vision when I go.'

"While thus he spake, his eye, dwelling on mine,
Drew me, with power upon me, till I grew
One with him, to believe as he believed.
Then, when the day began to wane, we went.

"There rose a hill that none but man could climb,
Scarr'd with a hundred wintry watercourses —
Storm at the top, and when we gain'd it, storm
Round us and death; for every moment glanced
His silver arms and gloom'd: so quick and thick
The lightnings here and there to left and right
Struck, till the dry old trunks about us, dead,
Yea, rotten with a hundred years of death,
Sprang into fire: and at the base we found
On either hand, as far as eye could see,
A great black swamp and of an evil smell,

Part black, part whiten'd with the bones
  of men,
Not to be crost, save that some ancient king
Had built a way, where, link'd with
  many a bridge,
A thousand piers ran into the great sea.
And Galahad fled along them bridge by
  bridge,
And every bridge as quickly as he crost
Sprang into fire and vanish'd, tho' I
  yearn'd
To follow; and thrice above him all the
  heavens
Open'd and blazed with thunder such as
  seem'd
Shoutings of all the sons of God: and first
At once I saw him far on the great sea,
In silver-shining armor starry-clear;
And o'er his head the holy vessel hung
Clothed in white samite or a luminous
  cloud.
And with exceeding swiftness ran the boat
If boat it were — I saw not whence it came.
And when the heavens open'd and blazed
  again
Roaring, I saw him like a silver star —
And had he set the sail, or had the boat
Become a living creature clad with wings?
And o'er his head the holy vessel hung
Redder than any rose, a joy to me,
For now I knew the veil had been with-
  drawn.
Then in a moment when they blazed again
Opening, I saw the least of little stars
Down on the waste, and straight beyond
  the star
I saw the spiritual city and all her spires
And gateways in a glory like one pearl —
No larger, tho' the goal of all the saints —
Strike from the sea; and from the star
  there shot
A rose-red sparkle to the city, and there
Dwelt, and I knew it was the Holy Grail,
Which never eyes on earth again shall
  see.
Then fell the floods of heaven drowning
  the deep.
And how my feet recross'd the deathful
  ridge
No memory in me lives; but that I touch'd
The chapel-doors at dawn I know; and
  thence
Taking my war-horse from the holy man,
Glad that no phantom vext me more,
  return'd
To whence I came, the gate of Arthur's
  wars."

"O brother," ask'd Ambr
  in sooth
These ancient books — and
  win thee — teem,
Only I find not there this I
With miracles and marvels
Not all unlike; which ofte
Who read but on my brevia
Till my head swims; and t
  and pass
Down to the little thorpe tha
And almost plaster'd like a
To these old walls — and
  our folk;
And knowing every honest
As well as ever shepherd kn
And every homely secret in
Delight myself with gossip a
And ills and aches, and teetl
  in,
And mirthful sayings, ch
  place,
That have no meaning half a
Or lulling random squabble
  rise,
Chafferings and chatterings
  ket-cross,
Rejoice, small man, in this
  of mine,
Yea, even in their hens and in
O brother, saving this Sir (
Came ye on none but phan
  quest,
No man, no woman?"

Then, S
"All men, to one so bound b
And women were as phant
  brother,
Why wilt thou shame me to (
How far I falter'd from my qu
For after I had lain so man
A bedmate of the snail and (
In grass and burdock, I w;
  wan
And meagre, and the vision I
And then I chanced upon a
With one great dwelling in t
  it;
Thither I made, and there w
By maidens each as fair as
But when they led me into
The Princess of that castle
Brother, and that one only,
Made my heart leap; for w
  of old
A slender page about her fa

And she a slender maiden, all my heart
Went after her with longing: yet we twain
Had never kiss'd a kiss, or vow'd a vow.
And now I came upon her once again,
And one had wedded her, and he was dead,
And all his land and wealth and state were hers.
And while I tarried, every day she set
A banquet richer than the day before
By me; for all her longing and her will
Was toward me as of old; till one fair morn,
I walking to and fro beside a stream
That flash'd across her orchard underneath
Her castle-walls, she stole upon my walk,
And calling me the greatest of all knights,
Embraced me, and so kiss'd me the first time,
And gave herself and all her wealth to me.
Then I remember'd Arthur's warning word,
That most of us would follow wandering fires,
And the Quest faded in my heart. Anon,
The heads of all her people drew to me,
With supplication both of knees and tongue:
'We have heard of thee: thou art our greatest knight,
Our Lady says it, and we well believe:
Wed thou our Lady, and rule over us,
And thou shalt be as Arthur in our land.'
O me, my brother! but one night my vow
Burnt me within, so that I rose and fled,
But wail'd and wept, and hated mine own self,
And ev'n the Holy Quest, and all but her;
Then after I was join'd with Galahad
Cared not for her, nor anything upon earth."

Then said the monk, "Poor men, when yule is cold,
Must be content to sit by little fires.
And this am I, so that ye care for me
Ever so little; yea, and blest be Heaven
That brought thee here to this poor house of ours,
Where all the brethren are so hard, to warm
My cold heart with a friend: but O the pity
To find thine own first love once more — to hold,
Hold her a wealthy bride within thine arms,

Or all but hold, and then — cast her aside,
Foregoing all her sweetness, like a weed.
For we that want the warmth of double life,
We that are plagued with dreams of something sweet
Beyond all sweetness in a life so rich, —
Ah, blessed Lord, I speak too earthly wise,
Seeing I never stray'd beyond the cell,
But live like an old badger in his earth,
With earth about him everywhere, despite
All fast and penance. Saw ye none beside,
None of your knights?"

"Yea so," said Percivale:
"One night my pathway swerving east, I saw
The pelican on the casque of our Sir Bors
All in the middle of the rising moon:
And toward him spurr'd and hail'd him, and he me,
And each made joy of either; then he ask'd,
'Where is he? hast thou seen him — Lancelot?' 'Once,'
Said good Sir Bors, 'he dash'd across me — mad,
And maddening what he rode: and when I cried,
"Ridest thou then so hotly on a quest So holy?" Lancelot shouted, "Stay me not!
I have been the sluggard, and I ride apace,
For now there is a lion in the way."
So vanish'd.'

"Then Sir Bors had ridden on
Softly, and sorrowing for our Lancelot,
Because his former madness, once the talk
And scandal of our table, had return'd;
For Lancelot's kith and kin so worship him
That ill to him is ill to them; to Bors
Beyond the rest: he well had been content
Not to have seen, so Lancelot might have seen,
The Holy Cup of healing; and, indeed,
Being so clouded with his grief and love,
Small heart was his after the Holy Quest:
If God would send the vision, well: if not,
The Quest and he were in the hands of heaven.

"And then, with small adventure met, Sir Bors
Rode to the lonest tract of all the realm,

And found a people there among their
 crags,
Our race and blood, a remnant that were
 left
Paynim amid their circles, and the stones
They pitch up straight to heaven : and
 their wise men
Were strong in that old magic which can
 trace
The wandering of the stars, and scoff'd
 at him
And this high Quest as at a simple thing :
Told him he follow'd — almost Arthur's
 words —
A mocking fire : 'what other fire than he,
Whereby the blood beats, and the blossom
 blows,
And the sea rolls, and all the world is
 warm'd ?'
And when his answer chafed them, the
 rough crowd,
Hearing he had a difference with their
 priests,
Seized him, and bound and plunged him
 into a cell
Of great piled stones ; and lying bounden
 there
In darkness thro' innumerable hours
He heard the hollow-ringing heavens
 sweep
Over him, till by miracle — what else ? —
Heavy as it was, a great stone slipt and fell,
Such as no wind could move : and thro'
 the gap
Glimmer'd the streaming scud : then
 came a night
Still as the day was loud ; and thro' the gap
The seven clear stars of Arthur's Table
 Round —
For, brother, so one night, because they
 roll
Thro' such a round in heaven, we named
 the stars,
Rejoicing in ourselves and in our king —
And these, like bright eyes of familiar
 friends,
In on him shone, 'And then to me, to
 me,'
Said good Sir Bors, 'beyond all hopes
 of mine,
Who scarce had pray'd or ask'd it for
 myself —
Across the seven clear stars — O grace to
 me —
In color like the fingers of a hand
Before a burning taper, the sweet Grail
Glided and past, and close upon it peal'd

A sharp quick thunder.' Afterwards a
 maid,
Who kept our holy faith among her kin
In secret, entering, loosed and let him go."

To whom the monk : "And I remem-
 ber now
That pelican on the casque. Sir Bors it was
Who spake so low and sadly at our board ;
And mighty reverent at our grace was he :
A square-set man and honest ; and his
 eyes,
An out-door sign of all the warmth within.
Smiled with his lips — a smile beneath
 a cloud,
But heaven had meant it for a sunny one :
Ay, ay, Sir Bors, who else ? But when
 ye reach'd
The city, found ye all your knights re-
 turn'd,
Or was there sooth in Arthur's prophecy,
Tell me, and what said each, and what
 the King ?"

Then answer'd Percivale : "And that
 can I,
Brother, and truly ; since the living words
Of so great men as Lancelot and our King
Pass not from door to door and out again,
But sit within the house. O, when we
 reach'd
The city, our horses stumbling as they
 trode
On heaps of ruin, hornless unicorns,
Crack'd basilisks, and splinter'd cock-
 atrices,
And shatter'd talbots, which had left the
 stones
Raw, that they fell from, brought us to
 the hall.

"And there sat Arthur on the daïs-
 throne,
And those that had gone out upon the
 Quest,
Wasted and worn, and but a tithe of them,
And those that had not, stood before the
 King.
Who, when he saw me, rose, and bade
 me hail,
Saying, 'A welfare in thine eye reproves
Our fear of some disastrous chance for thee
On hill, or plain, at sea, or flooding ford.
So fierce a gale made havoc here of late
Among the strange devices of our kings ;
Yea, shook this newer, stronger hall of
 ours,

And from the statue Merlin moulded for us
Half-wrench'd a golden wing; but now — the quest,
This vision — hast thou seen the Holy Cup,
That Joseph brought of old to Glastonbury?'

"So when I told him all thyself hast heard,
Ambrosius, and my fresh but fixt resolve
To pass away into the quiet life,
He answer'd not, but, sharply turning, ask'd
Of Gawain, 'Gawain, was this Quest for thee?'

"'Nay, lord,' said Gawain, 'not for such as I.
Therefore I communed with a saintly man,
Who made me sure the Quest was not for me;
For I was much awearied of the Quest:
But found a silk pavilion in a field,
And merry maidens in it; and then this gale
Tore my pavilion from the tenting-pin,
And blew my merry maidens all about
With all discomfort; yea, and but for this,
My twelvemonth and a day were pleasant to me.'

"He ceased; and Arthur turn'd to whom at first
He saw not, for Sir Bors, on entering, push'd
Athwart the throng to Lancelot, caught his hand,
Held it, and there, half-hidden by him, stood,
Until the King espied him, saying to him,
'Hail, Bors! if ever loyal man and true
Could see it, thou hast seen the Grail'; and Bors,
'Ask me not, for I may not speak of it, I saw it': and the tears were in his eyes.

"Then there remain'd but Lancelot, for the rest
Spake but of sundry perils in the storm;
Perhaps, like him of Cana in Holy Writ,
Our Arthur kept his best until the last;
'Thou, too, my Lancelot,' ask'd the King, 'my friend,
Our mightiest, hath this Quest avail'd for thee?'

"'Our mightiest!' answer'd Lancelot, with a groan;
'O King!' — and when he paused, methought I spied
A dying fire of madness in his eyes —
'O King, my friend, if friend of thine I be,
Happier are those that welter in their sin,
Swine in the mud, that cannot see for slime,
Slime of the ditch: but in me lived a sin
So strange, of such a kind, that all of pure,
Noble, and knightly in me twined and clung
Round that one sin, until the wholesome flower
And poisonous grew together, each as each,
Not to be pluck'd asunder; and when thy knights
Sware, I sware with them only in the hope
That could I touch or see the Holy Grail
They might be pluck'd asunder. Then I spake
To one most holy saint, who wept and said,
That save they could be pluck'd asunder, all
My quest were but in vain; to whom I vow'd
That I would work according as he will'd.
And forth I went, and while I yearn'd and strove
To tear the twain asunder in my heart,
My madness came upon me as of old,
And whipt me into waste fields far away;
There was I beaten down by little men,
Mean knights, to whom the moving of my sword
And shadow of my spear had been enow
To scare them from me once; and then I came
All in my folly to the naked shore,
Wide flats, where nothing but coarse grasses grew;
But such a blast, my King, began to blow,
So loud a blast along the shore and sea,
Ye could not hear the waters for the blast,
Tho' heapt in mounds and ridges all the sea
Drove like a cataract, and all the sand
Swept like a river, and the clouded heavens
Were shaken with the motion and the sound.
And blackening in the sea-foam sway'd a boat,
Half-swallow'd in it, anchor'd with a chain;
And in my madness to myself I said,
"I will embark and I will lose myself,
And in the great sea wash away my sin."

I burst the chain, I sprang into the boat.
Seven days I drove along the dreary deep,
And with me drove the moon and all the
 stars ;
And the wind fell, and on the seventh
 night
I heard the shingle grinding in the surge,
And felt the boat shock earth, and look-
 ing up,
Behold, the enchanted towers of Carbonek,
A castle like a rock upon a rock,
With chasm-like portals open to the sea,
And steps that met the breaker ! there
 was none
Stood near it but a lion on each side
That kept the entry, and the moon was full.
Then from the boat I leapt, and up the
 stairs.
There drew my sword. With sudden-
 flaring manes
Those two great beasts rose upright like
 a man,
Each gript a shoulder, and I stood be-
 tween ;
And, when I would have smitten them,
 heard a voice,
" Doubt not, go forward ; if thou doubt,
 the beasts
Will tear thee piecemeal." Then with
 violence
The sword was dash'd from out my hand,
 and fell.
And up into the sounding hall I past ;
But nothing in the sounding hall I saw
No bench nor table, painting on the wall
Or shield of knight ; only the rounded
 moon
Thro' the tall oriel on the rolling sea.
But always in the quiet house I heard,
Clear as a lark, high o'er me as a lark,
A sweet voice singing in the topmost tower
To the eastward : up I climb'd a thou-
 sand steps
With pain : as in a dream I seem'd to
 climb
For ever : at the last I reach'd a door,
A light was in the crannies, and I heard,
" Glory and joy and honor to our Lord
And to the Holy Vessel of the Grail."
Then in my madness I essay'd the door ;
It gave ; and thro' a stormy glare, a heat
As from a seventimes-heated furnace, I,
Blasted and burnt, and blinded as I was,
With such a fierceness that I swoon'd
 away —
O, yet methought I saw the Holy Grail,
All pall'd in crimson samite, and around

Great angels, awful shapes, and wings
 and eyes.
And but for all my madness and my sin,
And then my swooning, I had sworn I saw
That which I saw ; but what I saw was
 veil'd
And cover'd ; and this quest was not for
 me.'

"So speaking, and here ceasing,
 Lancelot left
The hall long silent, till Sir Gawain —
 nay,
Brother, I need not tell thee foolish
 words, —
A reckless and irreverent knight was he,
Now bolden'd by the silence of his King, —
Well, I will tell thee : 'O king, my
 liege,' he said,
' Hath Gawain fail'd in any quest of thine ?
When have I stinted stroke in foughten
 field ?
But as for thine, my good friend, Percivale,
Thy holy nun and thou have driven
 men mad,
Yea, made our mightiest madder than
 our least.
But by mine eyes and by mine ears I swear,
I will be deafer than the blue-eyed cat,
And thrice as blind as any noonday owl,
To holy virgins in their ecstasies,
Henceforward.'

"'Deafer,' said the blameless King,
'Gawain, and blinder unto holy things
Hope not to make thyself by idle vows,
Being too blind to have desire to see.
But if indeed there came a sign from
 heaven,
Blessed are Bors, Lancelot, and Percivale,
For these have seen according to their
 sight.
For every fiery prophet in old times,
And all the sacred madness of the bard,
When God made music thro' them, could
 but speak
His music by the framework and the
 chord ;
And as ye saw it ye have spoken truth.

"'Nay — but thou errest, Lancelot :
 never yet
Could all of true and noble in knight
 and man
Twine round one sin, whatever it might be,
With such a closeness, but apart there
 grew,

Save that he were the swine thou spakest of,
Some root of knighthood and pure nobleness;
Whereto see thou, that it may bear its flower.

"'And spake I not too truly, O my knights?
Was I too dark a prophet when I said
To those who went upon the Holy Quest,
That most of them would follow wandering fires,
Lost in the quagmire?—lost to me and gone,
And left me gazing at a barren board,
And a lean Order—scarce return'd a tithe—
And out of those to whom the vision came
My greatest hardly will believe he saw;
Another hath beheld it afar off,
And leaving human wrongs to right themselves,
Cares but to pass into the silent life.
And one hath had the vision face to face,
And now his chair desires him here in vain,
However they may crown him otherwhere.

"'And some among you held, that if the King
Had seen the sight he would have sworn the vow:
Not easily, seeing that the King must guard
That which he rules, and is but as the hind
To whom a space of land is given to plough,
Who may not wander from the allotted field,
Before his work be done; but, being done,
Let visions of the night or of the day
Come, as they will; and many a time they come,
Until this earth he walks on seems not earth,
This light that strikes his eyeball is not light,
This air that smites his forehead is not air
But vision—yea, his very hand and foot—
In moments when he feels he cannot die,
And knows himself no vision to himself,
Nor the high God a vision, nor that One
Who rose again: ye have seen what ye have seen.'

"So spake the king: I knew not all he meant."

PELLEAS AND ETTARRE.

KING ARTHUR made new knights to fill the gap
Left by the Holy Quest; and as he sat
In hall at old Caerleon, the high doors
Were softly sunder'd, and thro' these a youth,
Pelleas, and the sweet smell of the fields
Past, and the sunshine came along with him.

"Make me thy knight, because I know, Sir King,
All that belongs to knighthood, and I love,"
Such was his cry; for having heard the King
Had let proclaim a tournament—the prize
A golden circlet and a knightly sword,
Full fain had Pelleas for his lady won
The golden circlet, for himself the sword:
And there were those who knew him near the King
And promised for him: and Arthur made him knight.

And this new knight, Sir Pelleas of the isles—
But lately come to his inheritance,
And lord of many a barren isle was he—
Riding at noon, a day or twain before,
Across the forest call'd of Dean, to find
Caerleon and the King, had felt the sun
Beat like a strong knight on his helm, and reel'd
Almost to falling from his horse; but saw
Near him a mound of even-sloping side,
Whereon a hundred stately beeches grew,
And here and there great hollies under them.
But for a mile all round was open space,
And fern and heath: and slowly Pelleas drew
To that dim day, then binding his good horse
To a tree, cast himself down; and as he lay
At random looking over the brown earth
Thro' that green-glooming twilight of the grove,
It seem'd to Pelleas that the fern without
Burnt as a living fire of emeralds,
So that his eyes were dazzled looking at it.
Then o'er it crost the dimness of a cloud
Floating, and once the shadow of a bird

Flying, and then a fawn; and his eyes
　　closed.
And since he loved all maidens, but no
　　maid
In special, half-awake he whisper'd,
　　"Where?
O where? I love thee, tho' I know thee
　　not.
For fair thou art and pure as Guinevere,
And I will make thee with my spear and
　　sword
As famous — O my queen, my Guinevere,
For I will be thine Arthur when we meet."

　　Suddenly waken'd with a sound of talk
And laughter at the limit of the wood,
And glancing thro' the hoary boles, he
　　saw,
Strange as to some old prophet might
　　have seem'd
A vision hovering on a sea of fire,
Damsels in divers colors like the cloud
Of sunset and sunrise, and all of them
On horses, and the horses richly trapt
Breast-high in that bright line of bracken
　　stood :
And all the damsels talk'd confusedly,
And one was pointing this way, and one
　　that,
Because the way was lost.

　　　　　　　　　　And Pelleas rose,
And loosed his horse, and led him to the
　　light.
There she that seem'd the chief among
　　them said,
"In happy time behold our pilot-star!
Youth, we are damsels-errant, and we
　　ride,
Arm'd as ye see, to tilt against the knights
There at Caerleon, but have lost our way :
To right? to left? straight forward? back
　　again?
Which? tell us quickly."

　　　　　　　　And Pelleas gazing thought,
"Is Guinevere herself so beautiful?"
For large her violet eyes look'd, and her
　　bloom
A rosy dawn kindled in stainless heavens,
And round her limbs, mature in woman-
　　hood,
And slender was her hand and small her
　　shape,
And but for those large eyes, the haunts
　　of scorn,
She might have seem'd a toy to trifle with,
And pass and care no more. But while
　　he gazed
The beauty of her flesh abash'd the boy,
As tho' it were the beauty of her soul :
For as the base man, judging of the good,
Puts his own baseness in him by default
Of will and nature, so did Pelleas lend
All the young beauty of his own soul to
　　hers,
Believing her; and when she spake to him,
Stammer'd, and could not make her a
　　reply.
For out of the waste islands had he come,
Where saving his own sisters he had known
Scarce any but the women of his isles,
Rough wives, that laugh'd and scream'd
　　against the gulls,
Makers of nets, and living from the sea.

Then with a slow smile turn'd the lady
　　round
And look'd upon her people; and as when
A stone is flung into some sleeping tarn,
The circle widens till it lip the marge,
Spread the slow smile thro' all her com-
　　pany.
Three knights were there among; and
　　they too smiled,
Scorning him; for the lady was Ettarre,
And she was a great lady in her land.

Again she said, "O wild and of the
　　woods,
Knowest thou not the fashion of our
　　speech?
Or have the Heavens but given thee a
　　fair face,
Lacking a tongue?"

　　　　　　　　"O damsel," answer'd he,
"I woke from dreams; and coming out
　　of gloom
Was dazzled by the sudden light, and
　　crave
Pardon : but will ye to Caerleon? I
Go likewise : shall I lead you to the King?"

"Lead then," she said; and thro' the
　　woods they went.
And while they rode, the meaning in his
　　eyes,
His tenderness of manner, and chaste
　　awe,
His broken utterances and bashfulness,
Were all a burthen to her, and in her
　　heart
She mutter'd, "I have lighted on a fool,

Raw, yet so stale!" But since her mind was bent
On hearing, after trumpet blown, her name
And title, "Queen of Beauty," in the lists
Cried — and beholding him so strong, she thought
That peradventure he will fight for me,
And win the circlet: therefore flatter'd him,
Being so gracious, that he wellnigh deem'd
His wish by hers was echo'd; and her knights
And all her damsels too were gracious to him,
For she was a great lady.

     And when they reach'd
Caerleon, ere they past to lodging, she,
Taking his hand, "O the strong hand," she said,
"See! look at mine! but wilt thou fight for me,
And win me this fine circlet, Pelleas,
That I may love thee?"

     Then his helpless heart
Leapt, and he cried "Ay! wilt thou if I win?"
"Ay, that will I," she answer'd, and she laugh'd,
And straitly nipt the hand, and flung it from her;
Then glanced askew at those three knights of hers,
Till all her ladies laugh'd along with her.

"O happy world," thought Pelleas, "all, meseems,
Are happy; I the happiest of them all."
Nor slept that night for pleasure in his blood,
And green wood-ways, and eyes among the leaves;
Then being on the morrow knighted, sware
To love one only. And as he came away,
The men who met him rounded on their heels
And wonder'd after him, because his face
Shone like the countenance of a priest of old
Against the flame about a sacrifice
Kindled by fire from heaven: so glad was he.

  Then Arthur made vast banquets, and strange knights
From the four winds came in: and each one sat,
Tho' served with choice from air, land, stream, and sea,
Oft in mid-banquet measuring with his eyes
His neighbor's make and might: and Pelleas look'd
Noble among the noble, for he dream'd
His lady loved him, and he knew himself
Loved of the King: and him his new-made knight
Worshipt, whose lightest whisper moved him more
Than all the ranged reasons of the world.

  Then blush'd and brake the morning of the jousts,
And this was call'd "The Tournament of Youth":
For Arthur, loving his young knight, withheld
His older and his mightier from the lists,
That Pelleas might obtain his lady's love,
According to her promise, and remain
Lord of the tourney. And Arthur had the jousts
Down in the flat field by the shore of Usk
Holden: the gilded parapets were crown'd
With faces, and the great tower fill'd with eyes
Up to the summit, and the trumpets blew.
There all day long Sir Pelleas kept the field
With honor: so by that strong hand of his
The sword and golden circlet were achieved.

  Then rang the shout his lady loved: the heat
Of pride and glory fired her face; her eye
Sparkled; she caught the circlet from his lance,
And there before the people crown'd herself.
So for the last time she was gracious to him.

  Then at Caerleon for a space — her look
Bright for all others, cloudier on her knight —
Linger'd Ettarre: and seeing Pelleas droop,
Said Guinevere, "We marvel at thee much,
O damsel, wearing this unsunny face
To him who won thee glory!" And she said,

"Had ye not held your Lancelot in your bower,
My Queen, he had not won." Whereat the Queen,
As one whose foot is bitten by an ant,
Glanced down upon her, turn'd and went her way.

But after, when her damsels, and herself,
And those three knights all set their faces home,
Sir Pelleas follow'd. She that saw him cried,
"Damsels — and yet I should be shamed to say it —
I cannot bide Sir Baby. Keep him back
Among yourselves. Would rather that we had
Some rough old knight who knew the worldly way,
Albeit grizzlier than a bear, to ride
And jest with: take him to you, keep him off,
And pamper him with papmeat, if ye will,
Old milky fables of the wolf and sheep,
Such as the wholesome mothers tell their boys.
Nay, should ye try him with a merry one
To find his mettle, good: and if he fly us,
Small matter! let him." This her damsels heard,
And mindful of her small and cruel hand,
They, closing round him thro' the journey home,
Acted her hest, and always from her side
Restrain'd him with all manner of device,
So that he could not come to speech with her.
And when she gain'd her castle, upsprang the bridge,
Down rang the grate of iron thro' the groove,
And he was left alone in open field.

"These be the ways of ladies," Pelleas thought,
"To those who love them, trials of our faith.
Yea, let her prove me to the uttermost,
For loyal to the uttermost am I."
So made his moan; and, darkness falling, sought
A priory not far off, there lodged, but rose
With morning every day, and, moist or dry,

Full-arm'd upon his charger all day long
Sat by the walls, and no one open'd to him.

And this persistence turn'd her scorn to wrath.
Then calling her three knights, she charged them, "Out!
And drive him from the walls." And out they came,
But Pelleas overthrew them as they dash'd
Against him one by one; and these return'd,
But still he kept his watch beneath the wall.

Thereon her wrath became a hate;
and once,
A week beyond, while walking on the walls
With her three knights, she pointed downward, "Look,
He haunts me — I cannot breathe — besieges me;
Down! strike him! put my hate into your strokes,
And drive him from my walls." And down they went,
And Pelleas overthrew them one by one;
And from the tower above him cried Ettarre,
"Bind him, and bring him in."

He heard her voice;
Then let the strong hand, which had overthrown
Her minion-knights, by those he overthrew
Be bounden straight, and so they brought him in.

Then when he came before Ettarre, the sight
Of her rich beauty made him at one glance
More bondsman in his heart than in his bonds.
Yet with good cheer he spake, "Behold me, Lady,
A prisoner, and the vassal of thy will;
And if thou keep me in thy donjon here,
Content am I so that I see thy face
But once a day: for I have sworn my vows,
And thou hast given thy promise, and I know
That all these pains are trials of my faith,
And that thyself when thou hast seen me strain'd

And sifted to the utmost, wilt at length
Yield me thy love and know me for thy
   knight."

Then she began to rail so bitterly,
With all her damsels, he was stricken
   mute;
But when she mock'd his vows and the
   great King,
Lighted on words: "For pity of thine
   own self,
Peace, Lady, peace: is he not thine and
   mine?"
"Thou fool," she said, "I never heard
   his voice
But long'd to break away. Unbind him
   now,
And thrust him out of doors; for save
   he be
Fool to the midmost marrow of his bones,
He will return no more." And those,
   her three,
Laugh'd, and unbound, and thrust him
   from the gate.

And after this, a week beyond, again
She call'd them, saying, "There he
   watches yet,
There like a dog before his master's door!
Kick'd, he returns: do ye not hate him,
   ye?
Ye know yourselves: how can ye bide
   at peace,
Affronted with his fulsome innocence?
Are ye but creatures of the board and bed,
No men to strike? Fall on him all at once,
And if ye slay him I reck not: if ye fail,
Give ye the slave mine order to be bound,
Bind him as heretofore, and bring him in:
It may be ye shall slay him in his bonds."

She spake; and at her will they
   couch'd their spears,
Three against one: and Gawain passing by,
Bound upon solitary adventure, saw
Low down beneath the shadow of those
   towers
A villany, three to one: and thro' his heart
The fire of honor and all noble deeds
Flash'd, and he call'd, "I strike upon
   thy side —
The caitiffs!" "Nay," said Pelleas,
   "but forbear;
He needs no aid who doth his lady's will."

So Gawain, looking at the villany done,
Forebore, but in his heat and eagerness
Trembled and quiver'd, as the dog, with-
   held
A moment from the vermin that he sees
Before him, shivers, ere he springs and
   kills.

And Pelleas overthrew them, one to
   three;
And they rose up, and bound, and brought
   him in.
Then first her anger, leaving Pelleas,
   burn'd
Full on her knights in many an evil name
Of craven, weakling, and thrice-beaten
   hound:
"Yet, take him, ye that scarce are fit to
   touch,
Far less to bind, your victor, and thrust
   him out,
And let who will release him from his
   bonds.
And if he comes again"—there she brake
   short;
And Pelleas answer'd, "Lady, for indeed
I loved you and I deem'd you beautiful,
I cannot brook to see your beauty marr'd
Thro' evil spite: and if ye love me not,
I cannot bear to dream you so forsworn:
I had liefer ye were worthy of my love,
Than to be loved again of you — farewell;
And tho' ye kill my hope, not yet my love,
Vex not yourself: ye will not see me more."

While thus he spake, she gazed upon
   the man
Of princely bearing, tho' in bonds, and
   thought,
"Why have I push'd him from me? this
   man loves,
If love there be: yet him I loved not.
   Why?
I deem'd him fool? yea, so? or that in him
A something — was it nobler than my-
   self? —
Seem'd my reproach? He is not of my
   kind.
He could not love me, did he know me well.
Nay, let him go — and quickly." And
   her knights
Laugh'd not, but thrust him bounden
   out of door.

Forth sprang Gawain, and loosed him
   from his bonds,
And flung them o'er the walls; and after-
   ward,
Shaking his hands, as from a lazar's rag,

"Faith of my body," he said, "and art
 thou not —
Yea thou art he, whom late our Arthur
 made
Knight of his table ; yea, and he that won
The circlet ? wherefore hast thou so de-
 famed
Thy brotherhood in me and all the rest,
As let these caitiffs on thee work their
 will ?"

And Pelleas answer'd, "O, their wills
 are hers
For whom I won the circlet ; and mine,
 hers,
Thus to be bounden, so to see her face,
Marr'd tho' it be with spite and mockery
 now,
Other than when I found her in the woods ;
And tho' she hath me bounden but in spite,
And all to flout me, when they bring me in,
Let me be bounden, I shall see her face ;
Else must I die thro' mine unhappiness."

And Gawain answer'd kindly tho' in
 scorn,
"Why, let my lady bind me if she will,
And let my lady beat me if she will :
But an she send her delegate to thrall
These fighting hands of mine — Christ
 kill me then
But I will slice him handless by the wrist,
And let my lady sear the stump for him,
Howl as he may. But hold me for your
 friend :
Come, ye know nothing : here I pledge
 my troth,
Yea, by the honor of the Table Round,
I will be leal to thee and work thy work,
And tame thy jailing princess to thine
 hand.
Lend me thine horse and arms, and I
 will say
That I have slain thee. She will let me in
To hear the manner of thy fight and fall ;
Then, when I come within her counsels,
 then
From prime to vespers will I chant thy
 praise
As prowest knight and truest lover, more
Than any have sung thee living, till she
 long
To have thee back in lusty life again,
Not to be bound, save by white bonds
 and warm,
Dearer than freedom. Wherefore now
 thy horse
And armor : let me go : be comforted :
Give me three days to melt her fancy,
 and hope
The third night hence will bring thee news
 of gold."

Then Pelleas lent his horse and all his
 arms,
Saving the goodly sword, his prize, and
 took
Gawain's, and said, " Betray me not, but
 help —
Art thou not he whom men call light-of-
 love ?"

"Ay," said Gawain, "for women be
 so light."
Then bounded forward to the castle walls,
And raised a bugle hanging from his neck,
And winded it, and that so musically
That all the old echoes hidden in the wall
Rang out like hollow woods at hunting-
 tide.

Up ran a score of damsels to the tower ;
"Avaunt," they cried, "our lady loves
 thee not."
But Gawain lifting up his visor said,
Gawain am I, Gawain of Arthur's court,
And I have slain this Pelleas whom ye
 hate :
Behold his horse and armor. Open gate,
And I will make you merry."

                        And down they ran,
Her damsels, crying to their lady, "Lo !
Pelleas is dead — he told us — he that hath
His horse and armor : will ye let him in ?
He slew him ! Gawain, Gawain of the
 court,
Sir Gawain — there he waits below the
 wall,
Blowing his bugle as who should say him
 nay."

And so, leave given, straight on thro'
 open door
Rode Gawain, whom she greeted cour-
 teously.
"Dead, is it so ?" she ask'd. "Ay, ay,"
 said he,
"And oft in dying cried upon your name."
"Pity on him," she answer'd, "a good
 knight,
But never let me bide one hour at peace."
"Ay," thought Gawain, "and ye be fair
 enow :

But I to your dead man have given my troth,
That whom ye loathe him will I make you love."

So those three days, aimless about the land,
Lost in a doubt, Pelleas wandering
Waited, until the third night brought a moon
With promise of large light on woods and ways.

The night was hot: he could not rest, but rode
Ere midnight to her walls, and bound his horse
Hard by the gates. Wide open were the gates,
And no watch kept; and in thro' these he past,
And heard but his own steps, and his own heart
Beating, for nothing moved but his own self,
And his own shadow. Then he crost the court,
And saw the postern portal also wide
Yawning; and up a slope of garden, all
Of roses white and red, and wild ones mixt
And overgrowing them, went on, and found,
Here too, all hush'd below the mellow moon,
Save that one rivulet from a tiny cave
Came lightening downward, and so spilt itself
Among the roses, and was lost again.

Then was he ware that white pavilions rose,
Three from the bushes, gilden-peakt: in one,
Red after revel, droned her lurdane knights
Slumbering, and their three squires across their feet:
In one, their malice on the placid lip
Froz'n by sweet sleep, four of her damsels lay:
And in the third, the circlet of the jousts
Bound on her brow, were Gawain and Ettarre.

Back, as a hand that pushes thro' the leaf
To find a nest and feels a snake, he drew
Back, as a coward slinks from what he fears
To cope with, or a traitor proven, or bound,
Beaten, did Pelleas in an utter shame
Creep with his shadow thro' the court again,
Fingering at his sword-handle until he stood
There on the castle-bridge once more, and thought,
"I will go back, and slay them where they lie."

And so went back and seeing them yet in sleep
Said, "Ye, that so dishallow the holy sleep,
Your sleep is death," and drew the sword, and thought,
"What! slay a sleeping knight? the King hath bound
And sworn me to this brotherhood"; again,
"Alas that ever a knight should be so false."
Then turn'd, and so return'd, and groaning laid
The naked sword athwart their naked throats,
There left it, and them sleeping; and she lay,
The circlet of the tourney round her brows,
And the sword of the tourney across her throat.

And forth he past, and mounting on his horse
Stared at her towers that, larger than themselves
In their own darkness, throng'd into the moon.
Then crush'd the saddle with his thighs, and clench'd
His hands, and madden'd with himself and moan'd:

"Would they have risen against me in their blood
At the last day? I might have answer'd them
Even before high God. O towers so strong,
Huge, solid, would that even while I gaze
The crack of earthquake shivering to your base

Split you, and Hell burst up your harlot
  roofs
Bellowing, and charr'd you thro' and
  thro' within,
Black as the harlot's heart — hollow as
  a skull !
Let the fierce east scream thro' your eye-
  let-holes,
And whirl the dust of harlots round and
  round
In dung and nettles ! hiss, snake — I
  saw him there —
Let the fox bark, let the wolf yell.   Who
  yells
Here in the still sweet summer night,
  but I —
I, the poor Pelleas whom she call'd her
  fool ?
Fool, beast — he, she, or I ? myself most
  fool ;
Beast too, as lacking human wit — dis-
  graced,
Dishonor'd all for trial of true love —
Love ? — we be all alike : only the king
Hath made us fools and liars.   O noble
  vows !
O great and sane and simple race of brutes
That own no lust because they have no
  law !
For why should I have loved her to my
  shame ?
I loathe her, as I loved her to my shame.
I never loved her, I but lusted for her —
Away — "

    He dash'd the rowel into his horse,
And bounded forth and vanish'd thro'
  the night.

    Then she, that felt the cold touch on
  her throat,
Awaking knew the sword, and turn'd
  herself
To Gawain : "Liar, for thou hast not
  slain
This Pelleas ! here he stood and might
  have slain
Me and thyself."   And he that tells the
  tale
Says that her ever-veering fancy turn'd
To Pelleas, as the one true knight on earth,
And only lover ; and thro' her love her life
Wasted and pined, desiring him in vain.

    But he by wild and way, for half the
  night,
And over hard and soft, striking the sod

From out the soft
  hard,
Rode till the star a
Beside that towe
  cowl'd,
Glanced from th
  dawn.
For so the word
  heart
He knew not wh
  sweet star,
Pure on the virgi
And there he wo
  his eyes
Harder and drier
In summer : thitl
And linger'd talk
  more
Till the sweet hea
  the height
Again with livin
Of seasons : har
  heart
Seem'd ; but so
  that he,
Gasping, "Of A
  here,
Here let me rest
  down,
And gulph'd his
  so lay,
Till shaken by a d
The hall of Merli
Reel'd in the sn
  and fell.

    He woke, and
  nigh,
Sent hands upon
  crying
"False ! and I h
  evere."

    But Percivale
  plied,
"Am I but false
Or art thou maze
  one
Of our free-spoke
That Lancelot " -
  self and pa

    Then fared it w
  one
Who gets a wound
That made it pl
  again,

PELLEAS AND ETTARRE.

And pricks it deeper: and he shrank and wail'd,
"Is the Queen false?" and Percivale was mute.
"Have any of our Round Table held their vows?"
And Percivale made answer not a word.
"Is the king true?" "The king!" said Percivale.
"Why then let men couple at once with wolves.
What! art thou mad?"

But Pelleas, leaping up,
Ran thro' the doors and vaulted on his horse
And fled: small pity upon his horse had he,
Or on himself, or any, and when he met
A cripple, one that held a hand for alms —
Hunch'd as he was, and like an old dwarf-elm
That turns its back on the salt blast, the boy
Paused not but overrode him, shouting "False,
And false with Gawain!" and so left him bruised.
And batter'd, and fled on, and hill and wood
Went ever streaming by him till the gloom
That follows on the turning of the world,
Darken'd the common path: he twitch'd the reins,
And made his beast that better knew it, swerve
Now off it and now on; but when he saw
High up in heaven the hall that Merlin built,
Blackening against the dead-green stripes of even,
"Black nest of rats," he groan'd, "ye build too high."

Not long thereafter from the city gates
Issued Sir Lancelot riding airily,
Warm with a gracious parting from the Queen,
Peace at his heart, and gazing at a star
And marvelling what it was: on whom the boy,
Across the silent seeded meadow-grass
Borne, clash'd: and Lancelot, saying,
"What name hast thou
That ridest here so blindly and so hard?"

"I have no name," he shouted, "a scourge am I,
To lash the treasons of the Table Round."
"Yea, but thy name?" "I have many names," he cried:
"I am wrath and shame and hate and evil fame,
And like a poisonous wind I pass to blast
And blaze the crime of Lancelot and the Queen."
"First over me," said Lancelot, "shalt thou pass."
"Fight therefore," yell'd the other, and either knight
Drew back a space, and when they closed, at once
The weary steed of Pelleas floundering flung
His rider, who called out from the dark field,
"Thou art false as Hell: slay me: I have no sword."
Then Lancelot, "Yea, between thy lips — and sharp;
But here will I disedge it by thy death."
"Slay then," he shriek'd, "my will is to be slain."
And Lancelot, with his heel upon the fall'n,
Rolling his eyes, a moment stood, then spake:
"Rise, weakling; I am Lancelot; say thy say."

And Lancelot slowly rode his war-horse back
To Camelot, and Sir Pelleas in brief while
Caught his unbroken limbs from the dark field,
And follow'd to the city. It chanced that both
Brake into hall together, worn and pale.
There with her knights and dames was Guinevere.
Full wonderingly she gazed on Lancelot
So soon return'd, and then on Pelleas, him
Who had not greeted her, but cast himself
Down on a bench, hard-breathing. "Have ye fought?"
She ask'd of Lancelot. "Ay, my Queen," he said.
"And thou hast overthrown him?"
"Ay, my Queen."
Then she, turning to Pelleas, "O young knight,
Hath the great heart of knighthood in thee fail'd

So far thou canst not bide, unfrowardly,
A fall from him?" Then, for he answer'd
    not,
"Or hast thou other griefs? If I, the
    Queen,
May help them, loose thy tongue, and
    let me know."
But Pelleas lifted up an eye so fierce
She quail'd; and he, hissing "I have no
    sword,"

Sprang from the door into the d
    Queen
Look'd hard upon her lover, h
And each foresaw the dolorou
    be:
And all talk died, as in a grov
Beneath the shadow of some bir
Then a long silence came upon
And Modred thought, "The tir
    at hand."

GUINEVERE.

Queen Guinevere had fled the court,
    and sat
There in the holy house at Almesbury
Weeping, none with her save a little maid,
A novice: one low light betwixt them
    burn'd
Blurr'd by the creeping mist, for all
    abroad,
Beneath a moon unseen albeit at full,
The white mist, like a face-cloth to the
    face,
Clung to the dead earth, and the land
    was still.

For hither had she fled, he
    flight
Sir Modred; he that like a su
Lay couchant with his eyes
    throne,
Ready to spring, waiting a ch
    this,
He chill'd the popular prais
    King
With silent smiles of slow
    ment;
And tamper'd with the Lords of
    Horse,

Heathen, the brood by Hengist left ; and
  sought
To make disruption in the Table Round
Of Arthur, and to splinter it into feuds
Serving his traitorous end ; and all his
  aims
Were sharpen'd by strong hate for Lance-
  lot.

For thus it chanced one morn when all
  the court,
Green-suited, but with plumes that
  mock'd the may,
Had been, their wont, a-maying and re-
  turn'd,
That Modred still in green, all ear and
  eye,
Climb'd to the high top of the garden-wall
To spy some secret scandal if he might,
And saw the Queen who sat betwixt her
  best
Enid, and lissome Vivien, of her court
The wiliest and the worst ; and more than
  this
He saw not, for Sir Lancelot passing by
Spied where he couch'd, and as the gar-
  dener's hand
Picks from the colewort a green caterpillar,
So from the high wall and the flowering
  grove
Of grass s Lancelot pluck'd him by the
  heel,
And cast him as a worm upon the way ;
But when he knew the Prince tho' marr'd
  with dust,
He, reverencing king's blood in a bad man,
Made such excuses as he might, and these
Full knightly without scorn ; for in those
  days
No knight of Arthur's noblest dealt in
  scorn ;
But, if a man were halt or hunch'd, in
  him
By those whom God had made full-limb'd
  and tall,
Scorn was allow'd as part of his defect,
And he was answer'd softly by the King
And all his Table. So Sir Lancelot holp
To raise the Prince, who rising twice or
  thrice
Full sharply smote his knees, and smiled,
  and went :
But, ever after, the small violence done
Rankled in him and ruffled all his heart,
As the sharp wind that ruffles all day long
A little bitter pool about a stone
On the bare coast.

But when Sir Lancelot told
This matter to the Queen, at first she
  laugh'd
Lightly, to think of Modred's dusty fall,
Then shudder'd, as the village wife who
  cries
"I shudder, some one steps across my
  grave" ;
Then laugh'd again, but faintlier, for in-
  deed
She half-foresaw that he, the subtle beast,
Would track her guilt until he found,
  and hers
Would be for evermore a name of scorn.
Henceforward rarely could she front in
  Hall,
Or elsewhere, Modred's narrow foxy face,
Heart-hiding smile, and gray persistent
  eye :
Henceforward too, the Powers that tend
  the soul,
To help it from the death that cannot die,
And save it even in extremes, began
To vex and plague her. Many a time
  for hours,
Beside the placid breathings of the King,
In the dead night, grim faces came and
  went
Before her, or a vague spiritual fear—
Like to some doubtful noise of creaking
  doors,
Heard by the watcher in a haunted house,
That keeps the rust of murder on the
  walls—
Held her awake : or if she slept, she
  dream'd
An awful dream ; for then she seem'd to
  stand
On some vast plain before a setting sun,
And from the sun there swiftly made at her
A ghastly something, and its shadow flew
Before it, till it touch'd her, and she
  turn'd—
When lo ! her own, that broadening from
  her feet,
And blackening, swallow'd all the land,
  and in it
Far cities burnt, and with a cry she woke.
And all this trouble did not pass but grew ;
Till ev'n the clear face of the guileless
  King,
And trustful courtesies of household life,
Became her bane ; and at the last she said,
"O Lancelot, get thee hence to thine own
  land,
For if thou tarry we shall meet again,
And if we meet again, some evil chance

Will make the smouldering scandal break
 and blaze
Before the people, and our lord the King."
And Lancelot ever promised, but re-
 main'd,
And still they met and met. Again she
 said,
"O Lancelot, if thou love me get thee
 hence."
And then they were agreed upon a night
(When the good King should not be there)
 to meet
And part for ever. Passion-pale they met
And greeted: hands in hands, and eye
 to eye,
Low on the border of her couch they sat
Stammering and staring: it was their last
 hour,
A madness of farewells. And Modred
 brought
His creatures to the basement of the tower
For testimony; and crying with full voice
"Traitor, come out, ye are trapt at last,"
 aroused
Lancelot, who rushing outward lionlike
Leapt on him, and hurl'd him headlong,
 and he fell
Stunn'd, and his creatures took and bare
 him off
And all was still: then she, "the end is
 come
And I am shamed for ever"; and he said
"Mine be the shame; mine was the sin:
 but rise,
And fly to my strong castle overseas:
There will I hide thee, till my life shall end,
There hold thee with my life against the
 world."
She answer'd "Lancelot, wilt thou hold
 me so?
Nay friend, for we have taken our fare-
 wells.
Would God, that thou couldst hide me
 from myself!
Mine is the shame, for I was wife, and thou
Unwedded: yet rise now, and let us fly,
For I will draw me into sanctuary,
And bide my doom." So Lancelot got
 her horse,
Set her thereon, and mounted on his own,
And then they rode to the divided way,
There kiss'd, and parted weeping: for he
 past,
Love-loyal to the least wish of the Queen,
Back to his land; but she to Almesbury
Fled all night long by glimmering waste
 and weald,

And heard the Spirits of the waste and
 weald
Moan as she fled, or thought she heard
 them moan:
And in herself she moan'd "too late, too
 late!"
Till in the cold wind that foreruns the
 morn,
A blot in heaven, the Raven, flying high,
Croak'd, and she thought "he spies a
 field of death;
For now the Heathen of the Northern Sea,
Lured by the crimes and frailties of the
 court,
Begin to slay the folk, and spoil the land."

And when she came to Almesbury she
 spake
There to the nuns, and said, "mine
 enemies
Pursue me, but, O peaceful Sisterhood,
Receive, and yield me sanctuary, nor ask
Her name, to whom ye yield it, till her
 time
To tell you": and her beauty, grace, and
 power
Wrought as a charm upon them, and they
 spared
To ask it.

So the stately Queen abode
For many a week, unknown, among the
 nuns;
Nor with them mix'd, nor told her name,
 nor sought,
Wrapt in her grief, for housel or for shrift,
But communed only with the little maid,
Who pleased her with a babbling heed-
 lessness
Which often lured her from herself; but
 now,
This night, a rumor wildly blown about
Came, that Sir Modred had usurped the
 realm,
And leagued him with the heathen, while
 the King
Was waging war on Lancelot: then she
 thought,
"With what a hate the people and the
 King
Must hate me," and bow'd down upon
 her hands
Silent, until the little maid, who brook'd
No silence, brake it, uttering "late! so
 late!
What hour, I wonder, now?" and when
 she drew
No answer, by and by began to hum

An air the nuns had taught her; "late, so late!"
Which when she heard, the Queen look'd up, and said,
"O maiden, if indeed ye list to sing,
Sing, and unbind my heart that I may weep."
Whereat full willingly sang the little maid.

"Late, late, so late! and dark the night and chill!
Late, late, so late! but we can enter still.
Too late, too late! ye cannot enter now.

"No light had we: for that we do repent;
And learning this, the bridegroom will relent.
Too late, too late! ye cannot enter now.

"No light: so late! and dark and chill the night!
O let us in, that we may find the light!
Too late, too late: ye cannot enter now.

"Have we not heard the bridegroom is so sweet?
O let us in, tho' late, to kiss his feet!
No, no, too late! ye cannot enter now."

So sang the novice, while full passionately,
Her head upon her hands, remembering
Her thought when first she came, wept the sad Queen.
Then said the little novice prattling to her.

"O pray you, noble lady, weep no more;
But let my words, the words of one so small,
Who knowing nothing knows but to obey,
And if I do not there is penance given —
Comfort your sorrows; for they do not flow
From evil done; right sure am I of that,
Who see your tender grace and stateliness.
But weigh your sorrows with our lord the King's,
And weighing find them less; for gone is he
To wage grim war against Sir Lancelot there,
Round that strong castle where he holds the Queen;
And Modred whom he left in charge of all,
The traitor — Ah sweet lady, the King's grief
For his own self, and his own Queen, and realm,
Must needs be thrice as great as any of ours.
For me, I thank the saints, I am not great.
For if there ever come a grief to me
I cry my cry in silence, and have done:
None knows it, and my tears have brought me good:
But even were the griefs of little ones
As great as those of great ones, yet this grief
Is added to the griefs the great must bear,
That howsoever much they may desire
Silence, they cannot weep behind a cloud:
As even here they talk at Almesbury
About the good King and his wicked Queen,
And were I such a King with such a Queen,
Well might I wish to veil her wickedness,
But were I such a King, it could not be."

Then to her own sad heart mutter'd the Queen.
"Will the child kill me with her innocent talk?"
But openly she answer'd "must not I,
If this false traitor have displaced his lord,
Grieve with the common grief of all the realm?"

"Yea," said the maid, "this is all woman's grief,
That *she* is woman, whose disloyal life
Hath wrought confusion in the Table Round
Which good King Arthur founded, years ago,
With signs and miracles and wonders, there
At Camelot, ere the coming of the Queen."

Then thought the Queen within herself again;
"Will the child kill me with her foolish prate?"
But openly she spake and said to her;
"O little maid, shut in by nunnery walls,
What canst thou know of Kings and Tables Round,
Or what of signs and wonders, but the signs
And simple miracles of thy nunnery?"

To whom the little novice garrulously.
"Yea, but I know: the land was full of
    signs
And wonders ere the coming of the Queen.
So said my father, and himself was knight
Of the great Table — at the founding of it;
And rode thereto from Lyonnesse, and
    he said
That as he rode, an hour or maybe twain
After the sunset, down the coast, he heard
Strange music, and he paused and turn-
    ing — there,
All down the lonely coast of Lyonnesse,
Each with a beacon-star upon his head,
And with a wild sea-light about his feet,
He saw them — headland after headland
    flame
Far on into the rich heart of the west:
And in the light the white mermaiden
    swam,
And strong man-breasted things stood
    from the sea,
And sent a deep sea-voice thro' all the land,
To which the little elves of chasm and
    cleft
Made answer, sounding like a distant horn.
So said my father — yea, and furthermore,
Next morning, while he past the dim-lit
    woods,
Himself beheld three spirits mad with joy
Come dashing down on a tall wayside
    flower,
That shook beneath them, as the thistle
    shakes
When three gray linnets wrangle for the
    seed:
And still at evenings on before his horse
The flickering fairy-circle wheel'd and
    broke
Flying, and link'd again, and wheel'd
    and broke
Flying, for all the land was full of life.
And when at last he came to Camelot,
A wreath of airy dancers hand-in-hand
Swung round the lighted lantern of the
    hall;
And in the hall itself was such a feast
As never man had dream'd; for every
    knight
Had whatsoever meat he long'd for served
By hands unseen; and even as he said
Down in the cellars merry bloated things
Shoulder'd the spigot, straddling on the
    butts
While the wine ran: so glad were spirits
    and men
Before the coming of the sinful Queen."

Then spake the Queen and somewhat
    bitterly.
"Were they so glad? ill prophets were
    they all,
Spirits and men: could none of them
    foresee,
Not even thy wise father with his signs
And wonders, what has fall'n upon the
    realm?"

To whom the novice garrulously again.
"Yea, one, a bard; of whom my father
    said,
Full many a noble war-song had he sung,
Ev'n in the presence of an enemy's fleet,
Between the steep cliff and the coming
    wave;
And many a mystic lay of life and death
Had chanted on the smoky mountain-
    tops,
When round him bent the spirits of the
    hills
With all their dewy hair blown back
    like flame:
So said my father — and that night the
    bard
Sang Arthur's glorious wars, and sang
    the King
As wellnigh more than man, and rail'd
    at those
Who call'd him the false son of Gorloïs:
For there was no man knew from whence
    he came;
But after tempest, when the long wave
    broke
All down the thundering shores of Bude
    and Bos,
There came a day as still as heaven, and
    then
They found a naked child upon the sands
Of dark Tintagil by the Cornish sea;
And that was Arthur; and they foster'd
    him
Till he by miracle was approven king:
And that his grave should be a mystery
From all men, like his birth; and could
    he find
A woman in her womanhood as great
As he was in his manhood, then, he sang,
The twain together well might change
    the world.
But even in the middle of his song
He falter'd, and his hand fell from the harp,
And pale he turn'd, and reel'd, and
    would have fall'n,
But that they stay'd him up; nor would
    he tell

"The sands
Of dark Tintagil by the Cornish sea."

His vision; but what doubt that he foresaw
This evil work of Lancelot and the Queen?"

Then thought the Queen "lo! they have set her on,
Our simple-seeming Abbess and her nuns,
To play upon me," and bow'd her head nor spake.
Whereat the novice crying, with clasp'd hands,
Shame on her own garrulity garrulously,
Said the good nuns would check her gadding tongue
Full often, "and, sweet lady, if I seem
To vex an ear too sad to listen to me,
Unmannerly, with prattling and the tales
Which my good father told, check me too:
Nor let me shame my father's memory, one
Of noblest manners, tho' himself would say
Sir Lancelot had the noblest; and he died,
Kill'd in a tilt, come next, five summers back,
And left me; but of others who remain,
And of the two first-famed for courtesy—
And pray you check me if I ask amiss—
But pray you, which had noblest, while you moved
Among them, Lancelot or our lord the King?"

Then the pale Queen look'd up and answer'd her.
"Sir Lancelot, as became a noble knight,
Was gracious to all ladies, and the same
In open battle or the tilting-field
Forbore his own advantage, and the King
In open battle or the tilting-field
Forbore his own advantage, and these two
Were the most nobly-mannered men of all;
For manners are not idle, but the fruit
Of loyal nature, and of noble mind."

"Yea," said the maid, "be manners such fair fruit?
Then Lancelot's needs must be a thousand-fold
Less noble, being, as all rumor runs,
The most disloyal friend in all the world."

To which a mournful answer made the Queen.
"O closed about by narrowing nunnery-walls,
What knowest thou of the world, and all its lights
And shadows, all the wealth and all the woe?
If ever Lancelot, that most noble knight,
Were for one hour less noble than himself,

Pray for him that he scape the doom of
   fire,
And weep for her, who drew him to his
   doom."

   "Yea," said the little novice, "I pray
      for both ;
But I should all as soon believe that his,
Sir Lancelot's, were as noble as the King's,
As I could think, sweet lady, yours
   would be
Such as they are, were you the sinful
   Queen."

   So she, like many another babbler, hurt
Whom she would soothe, and harm'd
   where she would heal ;
For here a sudden flush of wrathful heat
Fired all the pale face of the Queen, who
   cried,
"Such as thou art be never maiden more
For ever! thou their tool, set on to plague
And play upon, and harry me, petty spy
And traitress." When that storm of
   anger brake
From Guinevere, aghast the maiden rose,
White as her veil, and stood before the
   Queen
As tremulously as foam upon the beach
Stands in a wind, ready to break and
   fly,
And when the Queen had added "get
   thee hence"
Fled frighted. Then that other left alone
Sigh'd, and began to gather heart again,
Saying in herself "the simple, fearful
   child
Meant nothing, but my own too-fearful
   guilt
Simpler than any child, betrays itself.
But help me, heaven, for surely I repent.
For what is true repentance but in
   thought —
Not ev'n in inmost thought to think again
The sins that made the past so pleasant
   to us :
And I have sworn never to see him more,
To see him more."

         And ev'n in saying this,
Her memory from old habit of the mind
Went slipping back upon the golden days
In which she saw him first, when Lance-
   lot came,
Reputed the best knight and goodliest
   man,
Ambassador, to lead her to his lord
Arthur, and led her forth, and far ahead
Of his and her retinue moving, they,
Rapt in sweet talk or lively, all on love
And sport and tilts and pleasure, (for
   the time
Was maytime, and as yet no sin was
   dream'd,)
Rode under groves that look'd a paradise
Of blossom, over sheets of hyacinth
That seem'd the heavens upbreaking thro'
   the earth,
And on from hill to hill, and every day
Beheld at noon in some delicious dale
The silk pavilions of King Arthur raised
For brief repast or afternoon repose
By couriers gone before ; and on again,
Till yet once more ere set of sun they
   saw
The Dragon of the great Pendragonship,
That crown'd the state pavilion of the
   King,
Blaze by the rushing brook or silent well.

   But when the Queen immersed in such
      a trance,
And moving thro' the past unconsciously,
Came to that point where first she saw
   the King
Ride toward her from the city, sigh'd to
   find
Her journey done, glanced at him,
   thought him cold,
High, self-contain'd, and passionless, not
   like him,
"Not like my Lancelot" — while she
   brooded thus
And grew half-guilty in her thoughts
   again,
There rode an armed warrior to the doors.
A murmuring whisper thro' the nunnery
   ran,
Then on a sudden a cry, "the King."
   She sat
Stiff-stricken, listening ; but when armed
   feet
Thro' the long gallery from the outer doors
Rang coming, prone from off her seat she
   fell,
And grovell'd with her face against the
   floor :
There with her milkwhite arms and shad-
   owy hair
She made her face a darkness from the
   King :
And in the darkness heard his armed feet
Pause by her ; then came silence, then
   a voice,

Monotonous and hollow like a Ghost's
Denouncing judgment, but tho' changed
    the King's.

"Liest thou here so low, the child of
    one
I honor'd, happy, dead before thy shame?
Well is it that no child is born of thee.
The children born of thee are sword and
    fire,
Red ruin, and the breaking up of laws,
The craft of kindred and the Godless hosts
Of heathen swarming o'er the Northern
    Sea.
Whom I, while yet Sir Lancelot, my
    right arm,
The mightiest of my knights, abode with
    me,
Have everywhere about this land of Christ
In twelve great battles ruining over-
    thrown.
And knowest thou now from whence I
    come — from him,
From waging bitter war with him: and he,
That did not shun to smite me in worse
    way,
Had yet that grace of courtesy in him left,
He spared to lift his hand against the King
Who made him knight: but many a
    knight was slain;
And many more, and all his kith and kin
Clave to him, and abode in his own land.
And many more when Modred raised re-
    volt,
Forgetful of their troth and fealty, clave
To Modred, and a remnant stays with me.
And of this remnant will I leave a part,
True men who love me still, for whom I
    live,
To guard thee in the wild hour coming on,
Lest but a hair of this low head be harm'd.
Fear not: thou shalt be guarded till my
    death.
Howbeit I know, if ancient prophecies
Have err'd not, that I march to meet my
    doom.
Thou hast not made my life so sweet to me,
That I the King should greatly care to live;
For thou hast spoilt the purpose of my life.
Bear with me for the last time while I show,
Ev'n for thy sake, the sin which thou hast
    sinn'd.
For when the Roman left us, and their law
Relax'd its hold upon us, and the ways
Were fill'd with rapine, here and there a
    deed
Of prowess done redress'd a random wrong.
But I was first of all the kings who drew
The knighthood-errant of this realm and
    all
The realms together under me, their Head,
In that fair order of my Table Round,
A glorious company, the flower of men,
To serve as model for the mighty world,
And be the fair beginning of a time.
I made them lay their hands in mine and
    swear
To reverence the King, as if he were
Their conscience, and their conscience as
    their King,
To break the heathen and uphold the
    Christ,
To ride abroad redressing human wrongs,
To speak no slander, no, nor listen to it,
To lead sweet lives in purest chastity,
To love one maiden only, cleave to her,
And worship her by years of noble deeds,
Until they won her; for indeed I knew
Of no more subtle master under heaven
Than is the maiden passion for a maid,
Not only to keep down the base in man,
But teach high thought, and amiable
    words
And courtliness, and the desire of fame,
And love of truth, and all that makes a
    man.
And all this throve until I wedded thee!
Believing, 'lo mine helpmate, one to feel
My purpose and rejoicing in my joy.'
Then came thy shameful sin with Lance-
    lot;
Then came the sin of Tristram and Isolt;
Then others, following these my mightiest
    knights,
And drawing foul ensample from fair
    names,
Sinn'd also, till the loathsome opposite
Of all my heart had destined did obtain,
And all thro' thee! so that this life of
    mine
I guard as God's high gift from scathe
    and wrong,
Not greatly care to lose; but rather think
How sad it were for Arthur, should he live,
To sit once more within his lonely hall,
And miss the wonted number of my
    knights,
And miss to hear high talk of noble deeds
As in the golden days before thy sin.
For which of us, who might be left, could
    speak
Of the pure heart, nor seem to glance at
    thee?
And in thy bowers of Camelot or of Usk

Thy shadow still would glide from room
    to room,
And I should evermore be vext with thee
In hanging robe or vacant ornament,
Or ghostly footfall echoing on the stair.
For think not, tho' thou wouldst not
    love thy lord,
Thy lord has wholly lost his love for thee.
I am not made of so slight elements.
Yet must I leave thee, woman, to thy
    shame.
I hold that man the worst of public foes
Who either for his own or children's sake,
To save his blood from scandal, lets the
    wife
Whom he knows false, abide and rule the
    house :
For being thro' his cowardice allow'd
Her station, taken everywhere for pure,
She like a new disease, unknown to men,
Creeps, no precaution used, among the
    crowd,
Makes wicked lightnings of her eyes, and
    saps
The fealty of our friends, and stirs the
    pulse
With devil's leaps, and poisons half the
    young.
Worst of the worst were that man he that
    reigns !
Better the King's waste hearth and aching
    heart
Than thou reseated in thy place of light,
The mockery of my people, and their
    bane."

    He paused, and in the pause she crept
    an inch
Nearer, and laid her hands about his feet.
Far off a solitary trumpet blew.
Then waiting by the doors the warhorse
    neigh'd
As at a friend's voice, and he spake again.

    "Yet think not that I come to urge
    thy crimes,
I did not come to curse thee, Guinevere,
I, whose vast pity almost makes me die
To see thee, laying there thy golden head,
My pride in happier summers, at my feet.
The wrath which forced my thoughts on
    that fierce law,
The doom of treason and the flaming death,
(When first I learnt thee hidden here) is
    past.
The pang — which while I weigh'd thy
    heart with one
Too wholly true to dream untruth in thee,
Made my tears burn — is also past, in part.
And all is past, the sin is sinn'd, and I,
Lo ! I forgive thee, as Eternal God
Forgives : do thou for thine own soul the
    rest.
But how to take last leave of all I loved ?
O golden hair, with which I used to play
Not knowing ! O imperial-moulded form,
And beauty such as never woman wore,
Until it came a kingdom's curse with
    thee —
I cannot touch thy lips, they are not mine,
But Lancelot's : nay, they never were
    the King's.
I cannot take thy hand ; that too is flesh,
And in the flesh thou hast sinn'd ; and
    mine own flesh,
Here looking down on thine polluted, cries
'I loathe thee' : yet not less, O Guinevere,
For I was ever virgin save for thee,
My love thro' flesh hath wrought into
    my life
So far, that my doom is, I love thee still.
Let no man dream but that I love thee still.
Perchance, and so thou purify thy soul,
And so thou lean on our fair father Christ,
Hereafter in that world where all are pure
We two may meet before high God, and
    thou
Wilt spring to me, and claim me thine,
    and know
I am thine husband — not a smaller soul,
Nor Lancelot, nor another. Leave me
    that,
I charge thee, my last hope. Now must
    I hence.
Thro' the thick night I hear the trumpet
    blow :
They summon me their King to lead mine
    hosts
Far down to that great battle in the west,
Where I must strike against the man
    they call
My sister's son — no kin of mine, who
    leagues
With lords of the White Horse, heathen,
    and knights —
Traitors — and strike him dead, and meet
    myself
Death, or I know not what mysterious
    doom.
And thou remaining here wilt learn the
    event ;
But hither shall I never come again,
Never lie by thy side, see thee no more,
Farewell !"

"And lo, he sat on horseback at the door!
And near him the sad nuns with each a light
Stood, and he gave them charge about the Queen."

And while she grovell'd at his feet,
She felt the King's breath wander o'er
    her neck,
And in the darkness o'er her fallen head,
Perceived the waving of his hands that
    blest.

  Then, listening till those armed steps
    were gone,
Rose the pale Queen, and in her anguish
    found
The casement: "peradventure" so she
    thought,
"If I might see his face, and not be seen."
And lo, he sat on horseback at the door!
And near him the sad nuns with each a
    light
Stood, and he gave them charge about
    the Queen,
To guard and foster her for evermore.
And while he spake to these his helm was
    lower'd,
To which for crest the golden dragon clung
Of Britain; so she did not see the face,
Which then was as an angel's, but she saw,
Wet with the mists and smitten by the
    lights,
The Dragon of the great Pendragonship
Blaze, making all the night a steam of
    fire.

And even then he turn'd; and more and
    more
The moony vapor rolling round the King,
Who seem'd the phantom of a Giant in it,
Enwound him fold by fold, and made him
    gray
And grayer, till himself became as mist
Before her, moving ghostlike to his doom.

    Then she stretch'd out her arms and
      cried aloud
"O Arthur!" there her voice brake sud-
    denly,
Then — as a stream that spouting from a
    cliff
Fails in mid air, but gathering at the base
Re-makes itself, and flashes down the
    vale —
Went on in passionate utterance.

            "Gone — my lord!
Gone thro' my sin to slay and to be slain!
And he forgave me, and I could not speak.
Farewell? I should have answer'd his
    farewell.
His mercy choked me. Gone, my lord
    the King,
My own true lord! how dare I call him
    mine?
The shadow of another cleaves to me,
And makes me one pollution: he, the
    King,
Call'd me polluted: shall I kill myself?
What help in that? I cannot kill my
    sin,
If soul be soul; nor can I kill my shame;
No, nor by living can I live it down.
The days will grow to weeks, the weeks
    to months,
The months will add themselves and make
    the years,
The years will roll into the centuries,
And mine will ever be a name of scorn.
I must not dwell on that defeat of fame.
Let the world be; that is but of the
    world.
What else? what hope? I think there
    was a hope,
Except he mock'd me when he spake of
    hope;
His hope he call'd it; but he never mocks,
For mockery is the fume of little hearts.
And blessed be the King, who hath for-
    given
My wickedness to him, and left me hope
That in mine own heart I can live down
    sin

And be his mate hereafter in the heavens
Before high God. Ah great and gentle
    lord,
Who wast, as is the conscience of a saint
Among his warring senses, to thy
    knights —
To whom my false voluptuous pride, that
    took
Full easily all impressions from below,
Would not look up, or half-despised the
    height
To which I would not or I could not
    climb —
I thought I could not breathe in that fine
    air
That pure severity of perfect light —
I wanted warmth and color which I found
In Lancelot — now I see thee what thou
    art,
Thou art the highest and most human
    too,
Not Lancelot, nor another. Is there none
Will tell the King I love him tho' so
    late?
Now — ere he goes to the great Battle?
    none:
Myself must tell him in that purer life,
But now it were too daring. Ah my God,
What might I not have made of thy fair
    world,
Had I but loved thy highest creature
    here?
It was my duty to have loved the highest:
It surely was my profit had I known:
It would have been my pleasure had I
    seen.
We needs must love the highest when
    we see it,
Not Lancelot, nor another."

                    Here her hand
Grasp'd, made her veil her eyes: she
    look'd and saw
The novice, weeping, suppliant, and said
    to her
"Yea, little maid, for am *I* not forgiven?"
Then glancing up beheld the holy nuns
All round her, weeping; and her heart
    was loosed
Within her, and she wept with these and
    said.

    "Ye know me then, that wicked one,
      who broke
The vast design and purpose of the King.
O shut me round with narrowing nun-
    nery-walls,

Meek maidens, from the voices crying
  'shame.'
I must not scorn myself: he loves me
  still.
Let no one dream but that he loves me
  still.
So let me, if you do not shudder at me
Nor shun to call me sister, dwell with
  you;
Wear black and white, and be a nun like
  you;
Fast with your fasts, not feasting with
  your feasts;
Grieve with your griefs, not grieving at
  your joys,
But not rejoicing; mingle with your rites;
Pray and be pray'd for; lie before your
  shrines;
Do each low office of your holy house;
Walk your dim cloister, and distribute
  dole
To poor sick people, richer in his eyes
Who ransom'd us, and haler too than I;
And treat their loathsome hurts and heal
  mine own;
And so wear out in almsdeed and in prayer
The sombre close of that voluptuous day,
Which wrought the ruin of my lord the
  King."

She said: they took her to themselves;
  and she
Still hoping, fearing "is it yet too late?"
Dwelt with them, till in time their Ab-
  bess died.
Then she, for her good deeds and her pure
  life,
And for the power of ministration in her,
And likewise for the high rank she had
  borne,
Was chosen Abbess, there, an Abbess,
  lived
For three brief years, and there, an Ab-
  bess, past
To where beyond these voices there is
  peace.

THE PASSING OF ARTHUR.

THAT story which the bold Sir Bedivere,
First made and latest left of all the knights,
Told, when the man was no more than a
  voice
In the white winter of his age, to those
With whom he dwelt, new faces, other
  minds.

Before that last weird battle in the west
There came on Arthur sleeping, Gawain
  kill'd
In Lancelot's war, the ghost of Gawain
  blown
Along a wandering wind, and past his ear
Went shrilling "Hollow, hollow all de-
  light!
Hail, king! to-morrow thou shalt pass
  away.
Farewell! there is an isle of rest for thee.
And I am blown along a wandering wind,
And hollow, hollow, hollow all delight."
And fainter onward, like wild birds that
  change
Their season in the night and wail their
  way
From cloud to cloud, down the long wind
  the dream
Shrill'd; but in going mingled with dim
  cries
Far in the moonlit haze among the hills,
As of some lonely city sack'd by night,
When all is lost, and wife and child
  with wail
Pass to new lords; and Arthur woke
  and call'd,
"Who spake? A dream. O light upon
  the wind.
Thine, Gawain, was the voice — are
  these dim cries
Thine? or doth all that haunts the
  waste and wild
Mourn, knowing it will go along with
  me?"

This heard the bold Sir Bedivere and
  spake:
"O me, my king, let pass whatever will,
Elves, and the harmless glamour of the
  field;
But in their stead thy name and glory
  cling
To all high places like a golden cloud
For ever: but as yet thou shalt not pass.
Light was Gawain in life, and light in
  death
Is Gawain, for the ghost is as the man;
And care not thou for dreams from him,
  but rise —
I hear the steps of Modred in the west,
And with him many of thy people and
  knights
Once thine, whom thou hast loved, but
  grosser grown
Than heathen, spitting at their vows
  and thee.

Right well in heart they know thee for the king.
Arise, go forth and conquer as of old."

Then spake King Arthur to Sir Bedivere :
"Far other is this battle in the west
Whereto we move, than when we strove in youth,
And thrust the heathen from the Roman wall,
And shook him thro' the north. Ill doom is mine
To war against my people and my knights.
The king who fights his people fights himself.
And they my knights, who loved me once, the stroke
That strikes them dead is as my death to me.
Yet let us hence, and find or feel a way
Thro' this blind haze, which ever since I saw
One lying in the dust at Almesbury,
Hath folded in the passes of the world."

Then rose the king and moved his host by night,
And ever push'd Sir Modred, league by league,
Back to the sunset bound of Lyonnesse —
A land of old upheaven from the abyss
By fire, to sink into the abyss again ;
Where fragments of forgotten peoples dwelt,
And the long mountains ended in a coast
Of ever-shifting sand, and far away
The phantom circle of a moaning sea.
There the pursuer could pursue no more,
And he that fled no further fly the king ;
And there, that day when the great light of heaven
Burn'd at his lowest in the rolling year,
On the waste sand by the waste sea they closed.
Nor ever yet had Arthur fought a fight
Like this last, dim, weird battle of the west.
A deathwhite mist slept over sand and sea :
Whereof the chill, to him who breathed it, drew
Down with his blood, till all his heart was cold
With formless fear : and ev'n on Arthur fell
Confusion, since he saw not whom he fought,
For friend and foe were shadows in the mist,
And friend slew friend not knowing whom he slew ;
And some had visions out of golden youth,
And some beheld the faces of old ghosts
Look in upon the battle ; and in the mist
Was many a noble deed, many a base,
And chance and craft and strength in single fights,
And ever and anon with host to host
Shocks, and the splintering spear, the hard mail hewn,
Shield-breakings, and the clash of brands, the crash
Of battle-axes on shatter'd helms, and shrieks
After the Christ, of those who falling down
Looked up for heaven, and only saw the mist ;
And shouts of heathen and the traitor knights,
Oaths, insult, filth, and monstrous blasphemies,
Sweat, writhings, anguish, laboring of the lungs
In that close mist, and cryings for the light,
Moans of the dying, and voices of the dead.

Last, as by some one deathbed after wail
Of suffering, silence follows, or thro' death
Or deathlike swoon, thus over all that shore,
Save for some whisper of the seething seas,
A dead hush fell ; but when the dolorous day
Grew drearier toward twilight falling, came
A bitter wind, clear from the North, and blew
The mist aside, and with that wind the tide
Rose, and the pale king glanced across the field
Of battle : but no man was moving there ;
Nor any cry of Christian heard thereon,
Nor yet of heathen ; only the wan wave
Brake in among dead faces, to and fro
Swaying the helpless hands, and up and down
Tumbling the hollow helmets, of the fallen,
And shiver'd brands that once had fought with Rome,
And rolling far along the gloomy shores
The voice of days of old and days to be.

THE PASSING OF ARTHUR.

Then spake King Arthur to Sir Bedi-
vere,
And whiter than the mist that all day long
Had held the field of battle was the King:

"Hearest thou this great voice that
shakes the world,
And wastes the narrow realm whereon
we move,
And beats upon the faces of the dead,
My dead, as tho' they had not died for
me?—
O Bedivere, for on my heart hath fall'n
Confusion, till I know not what I am,
Nor whence I am, nor whether I be king.
Behold, I seem but king among the dead."

Then spake the bold Sir Bedivere:
"My King,
King everywhere! and so the dead have
kings,
There also will I worship thee as king.
Yet still thy life is whole, and still I live
Who love thee; but who hates thee, he
that brought
The heathen back among us, yonder
stands,
Modred, unharm'd, the traitor of thine
house."

Then spake the King: "My house hath
been my doom.
But call not thou this traitor of my house
Who hath but dwelt beneath one roof
with me.
My house are rather they who sware my
vows,
Yea, even while they brake them, own'd
me king.
And well for thee, saying in my dark hour,
When all the purport of my throne hath
fail'd,
That quick or dead thou holdest me for
king.
King am I, whatsoever be their cry;
And one last act of kinghood shalt thou see
Yet, ere I pass." And uttering this the
king
Made at the man: then Modred smote
his liege
Hard on that helm which many a heathen
sword
Had beaten thin; while Arthur at one
blow,
Striking the last stroke with Excalibur,
Slew him, and all but slain himself, he
fell.

So all day long the noise of battle roll'd
Among the mountains by the winter sea;
Until King Arthur's Table, man by man,
Had fall'n in Lyonnesse about their lord,
King Arthur. Then, because his wound
was deep,
The bold Sir Bedivere uplifted him,
And bore him to a chapel nigh the field,
A broken chancel with a broken cross,
That stood on a dark strait of barren land:
On one side lay the Ocean, and on one
Lay a great water, and the moon was full.

Then spake King Arthur to Sir Bedi-
vere:
"The sequel of to-day unsolders all
The goodliest fellowship of famous knights
Whereof this world holds record. Such
a sleep
They sleep—the men I loved. I think
that we
Shall never more, at any future time,
Delight our souls with talk of knightly
deeds,
Walking about the gardens and the halls
Of Camelot, as in the days that were.
I perish by this people which I made,—
Tho' Merlin sware that I should come again
To rule once more; but let what will be,
be.
I am so deeply smitten thro' the helm
That without help I cannot last till morn.
Thou therefore take my brand Excalibur,
Which was my pride: for thou remem-
berest how
In those old days, one summer noon, an
arm
Rose up from out the bosom of the lake,
Clothed in white samite, mystic, wonder-
ful,
Holding the sword—and how I row'd
across
And took it, and have worn it, like a
king;
And, wheresoever I am sung or told
In aftertime, this also shall be known:
But now delay not: take Excalibur,
And fling him far into the middle mere:
Watch what thou seëst, and lightly bring
me word."

To him replied the bold Sir Bedivere:
"It is not meet, Sir King, to leave thee
thus,
Aidless, alone, and smitten thro' the
helm—
A little thing may harm a wounded man;

Yet I thy hest will all perform at full,
Watch what I see, and lightly bring thee
  word."

  So saying, from the ruin'd shrine he
    stept,
And in the moon athwart the place of
  tombs,
Where lay the mighty bones of ancient
  men,
Old knights, and over them the sea-wind
  sang
Shrill, chill, with flakes of foam. He,
    stepping down
By zigzag paths, and juts of pointed rock,
Came on the shining levels of the lake.

  There drew he forth the brand Excali-
    bur,
And o'er him, drawing it, the winter moon,
Brightening the skirts of a long cloud,
  ran forth
And sparkled keen with frost against
  the hilt:
For all the haft twinkled with diamond
  sparks,
Myriads of topaz-lights, and jacinth-work
Of subtlest jewelry. He gazed so long
That both his eyes were dazzled as he stood,
This way and that dividing the swift mind,
In act to throw: but at the last it seem'd
Better to leave Excalibur conceal'd
There in the many-knotted waterflags,
That whistled stiff and dry about the
  marge.
So strode he back slow to the wounded
  King.

  Then spake King Arthur to Sir Bedi-
    vere:
"Hast thou perform'd my mission which
  I gave?
What is it thou hast seen? or what hast
  heard?"

  And answer made the bold Sir Bedi-
    vere:
"I heard the ripple washing in the reeds,
And the wild water lapping on the crag."

  To whom replied King Arthur, faint
    and pale:
"Thou hast betray'd thy nature and thy
  name,
Not rendering true answer, as beseem'd
Thy fëalty, nor like a noble knight:
For surer sign had follow'd, either hand,
Or voice, or else a motion of the mere.
This is a shameful thing for men to lie.
Yet now, I charge thee, quickly go again,
As thou art lief and dear, and do the thing
I bade thee, watch, and lightly bring me
  word."

  Then went Sir Bedivere the second time
Across the ridge, and paced beside the
  mere,
Counting the dewy pebbles, fix'd in
  thought;
But when he saw the wonder of the hilt,
How curiously and strangely chased, he
  smote
His palms together, and he cried aloud:

  "And if indeed I cast the brand away,
Surely a precious thing, one worthy note,
Should thus be lost for ever from the
  earth,
Which might have pleased the eyes of
  many men.
What good should follow this, if this
  were done?
What harm, undone? Deep harm to
  disobey,
Seeing obedience is the bond of rule.
Were it well to obey then, if a king demand
An act unprofitable, against himself?
The King is sick, and knows not what
  he does.
What record, or what relic of my lord
Should be to aftertime, but empty breath
And rumors of a doubt? But were this
  kept,
Stored in some treasure-house of mighty
  kings,
Some one might show it at a joust of
  arms,
Saying, 'King Arthur's sword, Excalibur,
Wrought by the lonely maiden of the
  Lake.
Nine years she wrought it, sitting in the
  deeps
Upon the hidden bases of the hills.'
So might some old man speak in the
  aftertime
To all the people, winning reverence.
But now much honor and much fame
  were lost."

  So spake he, clouded with his own
    conceit,
And hid Excalibur the second time,
And so strode back slow to the wounded
  King.

Then spoke King Arthur, breathing heavily:
"What is it thou hast seen? or what hast heard?"

And answer made the bold Sir Bedivere:
"I heard the water lapping on the crag,
And the long ripple washing in the reeds."

To whom replied King Arthur, much in wrath:
"Ah, miserable and unkind, untrue,
Unknightly, traitor-hearted! Woe is me!
Authority forgets a dying king,
Laid widow'd of the power in his eye
That bow'd the will. I see thee what thou art,
For thou, the latest-left of all my knights
In whom should meet the offices of all,
Thou wouldst betray me for the precious hilt;
Either from lust of gold, or like a girl
Valuing the giddy pleasure of the eyes.
Yet, for a man may fail in duty twice,
And the third time may prosper, get thee hence:
But, if thou spare to fling Excalibur,
I will arise and slay thee with my hands."

Then quickly rose Sir Bedivere, and ran,
And, leaping down the ridges lightly, plunged
Among the bulrush-beds, and clutch'd the sword,
And strongly wheel'd and threw it. The great brand
Made lightnings in the splendor of the moon,
And flashing round and round, and whirl'd in an arch,
Shot like a streamer of the northern morn,
Seen where the moving isles of winter shock
By night, with noises of the northern sea.
So flash'd and fell the brand Excalibur:
But ere he dipt the surface, rose an arm
Clothed in white samite, mystic, wonderful,
And caught him by the hilt, and brandish'd him
Three times, and drew him under in the mere.
And lightly went the other to the King.

Then spoke King Arthur, drawing thicker breath:
"Now see I by thine eyes that this is done.
Speak out: what is it thou hast heard, or seen?"

And answer made the bold Sir Bedivere:
"Sir King, I closed mine eyelids, lest the gems
Should blind my purpose, for I never saw,
Nor shall see, here or elsewhere, till I die,
Not tho' I live three lives of mortal men,
So great a miracle as yonder hilt.
Then with both hands I flung him, wheeling him;
But when I look'd again, behold an arm,
Clothed in white samite, mystic, wonderful,
That caught him by the hilt, and brandish'd him
Three times, and drew him under in the mere."

And answer made King Arthur, breathing hard:
"My end draws nigh; 't is time that I were gone.
Make broad thy shoulders to receive my weight,
And bear me to the margin; yet I fear
My wound hath taken cold, and I shall die."

So saying, from the pavement he half rose,
Slowly, with pain, reclining on his arm,
And looking wistfully with wide blue eyes
As in a picture. Him Sir Bedivere
Remorsefully regarded thro' his tears,
And would have spoken, but he found not words;
Then took with care, and kneeling on one knee,
O'er both his shoulders drew the languid hands,
And rising bore him thro' the place of tombs.

But, as he walk'd, King Arthur panted hard,
Like one that feels a nightmare on his bed
When all the house is mute. So sigh'd the King,
Muttering and murmuring at his ear
"Quick, quick!
I fear it is too late, and I shall die."
But the other swiftly strode from ridge to ridge,

Cloth'd with his breath, and looking, as he walk'd,
Larger than human on the frozen hills.
He heard the deep behind him, and a cry
Before. His own thought drove him like a goad.
Dry clash'd his harness in the icy caves
And barren chasms, and all to left and right
The bare black cliff clang'd round him, as he based
His feet on juts of slippery crag that rang
Sharp-smitten with the dint of armed heels —
And on a sudden, lo! the level lake,
And the long glories of the winter moon.

Then saw they how there hove a dusky barge,
Dark as a funeral scarf from stem to stern,
Beneath them; and descending they were ware
That all the decks were dense with stately forms,
Black-stoled, black-hooded, like a dream
— by these
Three Queens with crowns of gold: and from them rose
A cry that shiver'd to the tingling stars,
And, as it were one voice, an agony
Of lamentation, like a wind that shrills
All night in a waste land, where no one comes,
Or hath come, since the making of the world.

Then murmur'd Arthur, "Place me in the barge";
So to the barge they came. There those three Queens
Put forth their hands, and took the King, and wept.
But she, that rose the tallest of them all
And fairest, laid his head upon her lap,
And loosed the shatter'd casque, and chafed his hands,
And call'd him by his name, complaining loud,
And dropping bitter tears against his brow
Striped with dark blood: for all his face was white
And colorless, and like the wither'd moon
Smote by the fresh beam of the springing east;
And all his greaves and cuisses dash'd with drops
Of onset; and the light and lustrous curls —
That made his forehead like a rising sun
High from the daïs-throne — were parch'd with dust;
Or, clotted into points and hanging loose,
Mix'd with the knightly growth that fringed his lips.
So like a shatter'd column lay the King;
Not like that Arthur who, with lance in rest,
From spur to plume a star of tournament,
Shot thro' the lists at Camelot, and charged
Before the eyes of ladies and of kings.

Then loudly cried the bold Sir Bedivere:
"Ah! my Lord Arthur, whither shall I go?
Where shall I hide my forehead and my eyes?
For now I see the true old times are dead,
When every morning brought a noble chance,
And every chance brought out a noble knight.
Such times have been not since the light that led
The holy Elders with the gift of myrrh.
But now the whole Round Table is dissolved
Which was an image of the mighty world;
And I, the last, go forth companionless,
And the days darken round me, and the years,
Among new men, strange faces, other minds."

And slowly answered Arthur from the barge:
"The old order changeth, yielding place to new,
And God fulfils himself in many ways,
Lest one good custom should corrupt the world.
Comfort thyself: what comfort is in me?
I have lived my life, and that which I have done
May He within himself make pure! but thou,
If thou shouldst never see my face again,
Pray for my soul. More things are wrought by prayer
Than this world dreams of. Wherefore, let thy voice
Rise like a fountain for me night and day.

For what are men better than sheep or
  goats
That nourish a blind life within the
  brain,
If, knowing God, they lift not hands of
  prayer
Both for themselves and those who call
  them friend?
For so the whole round earth is every
  way
Bound by gold chains about the feet of
  God.
But now farewell. I am going a long
  way
With these thou seëst — if indeed I go
(For all my mind is clouded with a
  doubt) —
To the island-valley of Avilion;
Where falls not hail, or rain, or any snow,
Nor ever wind blows loudly; but it lies
Deep-meadow'd, happy, fair with orchard-
  lawns
And bowery hollows crown'd with sum-
  mer sea,
Where I will heal me of my grievous
  wound."

So said he, and the barge with oar and
  sail
Moved from the brink, like some full-
  breasted swan
That, fluting a wild carol ere her death,
Ruffles her pure cold plume, and takes
  the flood
With swarthy webs. Long stood Sir
  Bedivere
Revolving many memories, till the hull
Look'd one black dot against the verge
  of dawn,
And on the mere the wailing died away.

At length he groan'd, and turning
  slowly clomb
The last hard footstep of that iron crag;
Thence mark'd the black hull moving
  yet, and cried,
"He passes to be king among the dead,
And after healing of his grievous wound
He comes again; but — if he come no
  more —
O me, be yon dark Queens in yon black
  boat,
Who shriek'd and wail'd, the three whereat
  we gazed
On that high day, when, clothed with
  living light,
They stood before his throne in silence,
  friends
Of Arthur, who should help him at his
  need?"

Then from the dawn it seem'd there
  came, but faint
As, from beyond the limit of the world,
Like the last echo born of a great cry,
Sounds, as if some fair city were one
  voice
Around a king returning from his wars.

Thereat once more he moved about,
  and clomb
E'en to the highest he could climb, and
  saw,
Straining his eyes beneath an arch of hand,
Or thought he saw, the speck that bare
  the king,
Down that long water opening on the deep
Somewhere far off, pass on and on, and go
From less to less and vanish into light.
And the new sun rose bringing the new
  year.

THE PRINCESS: A MEDLEY.

TO

HENRY LUSHINGTON

THIS VOLUME IS INSCRIBED BY HIS FRIEND

A. TENNYSON.

PROLOGUE.

SIR WALTER VIVIAN all a summer's day
Gave his broad lawns until the set of sun
Up to the people : thither flock'd at noon
His tenants, wife and child, and thither half
The neighboring borough with their Institute
Of which he was the patron. I was there
From college, visiting the son, — the son
A Walter too, — with others of our set,
Five others : we were seven at Vivian-place.

And me that morning Walter show'd the house,
Greek, set with busts : from vases in the hall
Flowers of all heavens, and lovelier than their names,
Grew side by side ; and on the pavement lay
Carved stones of the Abbey-ruin in the park,
Huge Ammonites, and the first bones of Time :
And on the tables every clime and age
Jumbled together ; celts and calumets,
Claymore and snowshoe, toys in lava, fans
Of sandal, amber, ancient rosaries,
Laborious orient ivory sphere in sphere,
The cursed Malayan crease, and battle-clubs
From the isles of palm : and higher on the walls,
Betwixt the monstrous horns of elk and deer,
His own forefathers' arms and armor hung.

And "this" he said "was Hugh's at Agincourt ;
And that was old Sir Ralph's at Ascalon :
A good knight he ! we keep a chronicle
With all about him" — which he brought,
and I
Dived in a hoard of tales that dealt with knights
Half-legend, half-historic, counts and kings
Who laid about them at their wills and died ;
And mixt with these, a lady, one that arm'd
Her own fair head, and sallying thro' the gate,
Had beat her foes with slaughter from her walls.

"O miracle of women," said the book,
"O noble heart who, being strait-besieged
By this wild king to force her to his wish,
Nor bent, nor broke, nor shunn'd a soldier's death,
But now when all was lost or seem'd as lost —
Her stature more than mortal in the burst
Of sunrise, her arm lifted, eyes on fire —
Brake with a blast of trumpets from the gate,
And, falling on them like a thunderbolt,
She trampled some beneath her horses' heels,
And some were whelm'd with missiles of the wall,
And some were push'd with lances from the rock,
And part were drown'd within the whirling brook :
O miracle of noble womanhood ! "

So sang the gallant glorious chronicle;
And, I all rapt in this, "Come out," he said,
"To the Abbey : there is Aunt Elizabeth
And sister Lilia with the rest." We went

(I kept the book and had my finger in it)
Down thro' the park: strange was the
   sight to me;
For all the sloping pasture murmur'd,
   sown
With happy faces and with holiday.
There moved the multitude, a thousand
   heads:
The patient leaders of their Institute
Taught them with facts. One rear'd a
   font of stone
And drew, from butts of water on the slope,
The fountain of the moment, playing now
A twisted snake, and now a rain of pearls,
Or steep-up spout whereon the gilded ball
Danced like a wisp: and somewhat low-
   er down
A man with knobs and wires and vials
   fired
A cannon: Echo answer'd in her sleep
From hollow fields: and here were tele-
   scopes
For azure views; and there a group of
   girls
In circle waited, whom the electric shock
Dislink'd with shrieks and laughter:
   round the lake
A little clock-work steamer paddling plied
And shook the lilies: perch'd about the
   knolls
A dozen angry models jetted steam:
A petty railway ran: a fire-balloon
Rose gem-like up before the dusky groves
And dropt a fairy parachute and past:
Aud there thro' twenty posts of telegraph
They flash'd a saucy message to and fro
Between the mimic stations; so that sport
Went hand in hand with Science; other-
   where
Pure sport: a herd of boys with clamor
   bowl'd
And stump'd the wicket; babies roll'd
   about
Like tumbled fruit in grass; and men
   and maids
Arranged a country dance, and flew thro'
   light
And shadow, while the twangling violin
Struck up with Soldier-laddie, and over-
   head
The broad ambrosial aisles of lofty lime
Made noise with bees and breeze from
   end to end.

   Strange was the sight and smacking of
      the time;
And long we gazed, but satiated at length

Came to the ruins. High-arch'd and ivy-
   claspt,
Of finest Gothic lighter than a fire,
Thro' one wide chasm of time and frost
   they gave
The park, the crowd, the house; but all
   within
The sward was trim as any garden lawn:
And here we lit on Aunt Elizabeth,
And Lilia with the rest, and lady friends
From neighbor seats: and there was
   Ralph himself,
A broken statue propt against the wall,
As gay as any. Lilia, wild with sport,
Half child half woman as she was, had
   wound
A scarf of orange round the stony helm,
And robed the shoulders in a rosy silk,
That made the old warrior from his ivied
   nook
Glow like a sunbeam: near his tomb a
   feast
Shone, silver-set; about it lay the guests,
And there we join'd them: then the
   maiden Aunt
Took this fair day for text, and from it
   preach'd
An universal culture for the crowd,
And all things great; but we, unwor-
   thier, told
Of college: he had climb'd across the
   spikes,
And he had squeezed himself betwixt
   the bars,
And he had breath'd the Proctor's dogs;
   and one
Discuss'd his tutor, rough to common
   men,
But honeying at the whisper of a lord;
And one the Master, as a rogue in grain
Veneer'd with sanctimonious theory.

   But while they talk'd, above their
      heads I saw
The feudal warrior lady-clad; which
   brought
My book to mind: and opening this I
   read
Of old Sir Ralph a page or two that rang
With tilt and tourney; then the tale of her
That drove her foes with slaughter from
   her walls,
And much I praised her nobleness, and
   "Where,"
Ask'd Walter, patting Lilia's head (she lay
Beside him) "lives there such a woman
   now?"

Quick answer'd Lilia "There are thousands now
Such women, but convention beats them down :
It is but bringing up; no more than that:
You men have done it: how I hate you all!
Ah, were I something great! I wish I were
Some mighty poetess, I would shame you then,
That love to keep us children! O I wish
That I were some great princess, I would build
Far off from men a college like a man's,
And I would teach them all that men are taught ;
We are twice as quick!" And here she shook aside
The hand that play'd the patron with her curls.

And one said smiling "Pretty were the sight
If our old halls could change their sex, and flaunt
With prudes for proctors, dowagers for deans,
And sweet girl-graduates in their golden hair.
I think they should not wear our rusty gowns,
But move as rich as Emperor-moths, or Ralph
Who shines so in the corner ; yet I fear,
If there were many Lilias in the brood,
However deep you might embower the nest,
Some boy would spy it."
    At this upon the sward
She tapt her tiny silken-sandal'd foot :
"That's your light way ; but I would make it death
For any male thing but to peep at us."

Petulant she spoke, and at herself she laugh'd ;
A rosebud set with little wilful thorns,
And sweet as English air could make her, she :
But Walter hail'd a score of names upon her,
And "petty Ogress," and "ungrateful Puss,"
And swore he long'd at college, only long'd,
All else was well, for she-society.
They boated and they cricketed ; they talk'd

At wine, in clubs, of art, of politics ;
They lost their weeks ; they vext the souls of deans ;
They rode ; they betted ; made a hundred friends,
And caught the blossom of the flying terms,
But miss'd the mignonette of Vivian-place,
The little hearth-flower Lilia. Thus he spoke,
Part banter, part affection.
    "True," she said,
"We doubt not that. O yes, you miss'd us much.
I'll stake my ruby ring upon it you did."

She held it out ; and as a parrot turns
Up thro' gilt wires a crafty loving eye,
And takes a lady's finger with all care,
And bites it for true heart and not for harm,
So he with Lilia's. Daintily she shriek'd
And wrung it. "Doubt my word again!" he said.
"Come, listen ! here is proof that you were miss'd :
We seven stay'd at Christmas up to read ;
And there we took one tutor as to read :
The hard-grain'd Muses of the cube and square
Were out of season : never man, I think,
So moulder'd in a sinecure as he :
For while our cloisters echo'd frosty feet,
And our long walks were stript as bare as brooms,
We did but talk you over, pledge you all
In wassail ; often, like as many girls —
Sick for the hollies and the yews of home —
As many little trifling Lilias — play'd
Charades and riddles as at Christmas here,
And *what's my thought* and *when* and *where* and *how*,
And often told a tale from mouth to mouth
As here at Christmas."
    She remember'd that :
A pleasant game, she thought : she liked it more
Than magic music, forfeits, all the rest.
But these — what kind of tales did men tell men,
She wonder'd, by themselves ?
    A half-disdain
Perch'd on the pouted blossom of her lips :
And Walter nodded at me ; "*He* began,

The rest would follow, each in turn; and so
We forged a sevenfold story. Kind?
    what kind?
Chimeras, crotchets, Christmas solecisms,
Seven-headed monsters only made to kill
Time by the fire in winter."
              "Kill him now,
The tyrant! kill him in the summer too,"
Said Lilia; "Why not now," the maiden Aunt.
"Why not a summer's as a winter's tale?
A tale for summer as befits the time,
And something it should be to suit the place
Heroic, for a hero lies beneath,
Grave, solemn!"
        Walter warp'd his mouth at this
To something so mock-solemn, that I laugh'd
And Lilia woke with sudden-shrilling mirth
An echo like a ghostly woodpecker,
Hid in the ruins; till the maiden Aunt
(A little sense of wrong had touch'd her face
With color) turn'd to me with "As you will;
Heroic if you will, or what you will,
Or be yourself your hero if you will."
"Take Lilia, then, for heroine" clamor'd he,
"And make her some great Princess, six feet high,
Grand, epic, homicidal; and be you
The Prince to win her!"
        "Then follow me, the Prince,"
I answer'd, "each be hero in his turn!
Seven and yet one, like shadows in a dream. —
Heroic seems our Princess as required —
But something made to suit with Time and place,
A Gothic ruin and a Grecian house,
A talk of college and of ladies' rights,
A feudal knight in silken masquerade,
And, yonder, shrieks and strange experiments
For which the good Sir Ralph had burnt them all —
This *were* a medley! we should have him back
Who told the 'Winter's tale' to do it for us.
No matter: we will say whatever comes.
And let the ladies sing us, if they will,
From time to time, some ballad or a song
To give us breathing-space."
                So I began,
And the rest follow'd: and the women sang
Between the rougher voices of the men,
Like linnets in the pauses of the wind:
And here I give the story and the songs.

I.

A PRINCE I was, blue-eyed, and fair in face,
Of temper amorous, as the first of May,
With lengths of yellow ringlets, like a girl,
For on my cradle shone the Northern star.

There lived an ancient legend in our house.
Some sorcerer, whom a far-off grandsire burnt.
Because he cast no shadow, had foretold,
Dying, that none of all our blood should know
The shadow from the substance, and that one
Should come to fight with shadows and to fall.
For so, my mother said, the story ran.
And, truly, waking dreams were, more or less,
An old and strange affection of the house.
Myself too had weird seizures, Heaven knows what:
On a sudden in the midst of men and day,
And while I walk'd and talk'd as heretofore,
I seem'd to move among a world of ghosts,
And feel myself the shadow of a dream.
Our great court-Galen poised his gilt-head cane,
And paw'd his beard, and mutter'd "catalepsy."
My mother pitying made a thousand prayers;
My mother was as mild as any saint,
Half-canonized by all that look'd on her,
So gracious was her tact and tenderness:
But my good father thought a king a king;
He cared not for the affection of the house;
He held his sceptre like a pedant's wand
To lash offence, and with long arms and hands
Reach'd out, and pick'd offenders from the mass
For judgment.

Now it chanced that I had been,
While life was yet in bud and blade, be-
troth'd
To one, a neighboring Princess: she to me
Was proxy-wedded with a bootless calf
At eight years old; and still from time
to time
Came murmurs of her beauty from the
South,
And of her brethren, youths of puissance;
And still I wore her picture by my heart,
And one dark tress; and all around them
both
Sweet thoughts would swarm as bees about
their queen.

But when the days drew nigh that I
should wed,
My father sent ambassadors with furs
And jewels, gifts, to fetch her: these
brought back
A present, a great labor of the loom;
And therewithal an answer vague as
wind:
Besides, they saw the king; he took the
gifts;
He said there was a compact; that was
true:
But then she had a will; was he to blame?
And maiden fancies; loved to live alone
Among her women; certain, would not
wed.

That morning in the presence room I
stood
With Cyril and with Florian, my two
friends:
The first, a gentleman of broken means
(His father's fault) but given to starts
and bursts
Of revel; and the last, my other heart,
And almost my half-self, for still we moved
Together, twinn'd as horse's ear and eye.

Now, while they spake, I saw my
father's face
Grow long and troubled like a rising moon,
Inflamed with wrath; he started on his
feet,
Tore the king's letter, snow'd it down,
and rent
The wonder of the loom thro' warp and
woof
From skirt to skirt; and at the last he
sware
That he would send a hundred thousand
men,
And bring her in a whirlwind. then he
chew'd
The thrice-turn'd cud of wrath, and
cook'd his spleen,
Communing with his captains of the war.

At last I spoke. "My father, let me
go.
It cannot be but some gross error lies
In this report, this answer of a king,
Whom all men rate as kind and hospi-
table:
Or, maybe, I myself, my bride once seen,
Whate'er my grief to find her less than
fame,
May rue the bargain made." And Flo-
rian said:
"I have a sister at the foreign court,
Who moves about the Princess; she,
you know,
Who wedded with a nobleman from
thence:
He, dying lately, left her, as I hear,
The lady of three castles in that land:
Thro' her this matter might be sifted
clean."
And Cyril whisper'd: "Take me with
you too."
Then laughing "what, if these weird
seizures come
Upon you in those lands, and no one near
To point you out the shadow from the
truth!
Take me: I'll serve you better in a strait;
I grate on rusty hinges here": but
"No!"
Roar'd the rough king, "you shall not;
we ourself
Will crush her pretty maiden fancies dead
In iron gauntlets: break the council up."

But when the council broke, I rose and
past
Thro' the wild woods that hung about the
town;
Found a still place, and pluck'd her like-
ness out;
Laid it on flowers, and watch'd it lying
bathed
In the green gleam of dewy-tassell'd trees:
What were those fancies? wherefore break
her troth?
Proud look'd the lips: but while I medi-
tated
A wind arose and rush'd upon the South,
And shook the songs, the whispers, and
the shrieks

Of the wild woods together; and a Voice
Went with it, "Follow, follow, thou shalt
    win."

Then, ere the silver sickle of that month
Became her golden shield, I stole from
    court
With Cyril and with Florian, unperceived,
Cat-footed thro' the town and half in
    dread
To hear my father's clamor at our backs
With Ho! from some bay-window shake
    the night;
But all was quiet: from the bastion'd
    walls
Like threaded spiders, one by one, we
    dropt,
And flying reach'd the frontier: then we
    crost
To a livelier land; and so by tilth and
    grange,
And vines, and blowing bosks of wilder-
    ness,
We gain'd the mother-city thick with
    towers,
And in the imperial palace found the king.

His name was Gama; crack'd and small
    his voice,
But bland the smile that like a wrink-
    ling wind
On glassy water drove his cheek in lines;
A little dry old man, without a star,
Not like a king: three days he feasted us,
And on the fourth I spake of why we
    came,
And my betroth'd. "You do us, Prince,"
    he said,
Airing a snowy hand and signet gem,
"All honor. We remember love ourselves
In our sweet youth: there did a com-
    pact pass
Long summers back, a kind of cere-
    mony —
I think the year in which our olives fail'd.
I would you had her, Prince, with all
    my heart,
With my full heart: but there were
    widows here,
Two widows, Lady Psyche, Lady Blanche;
They fed her theories, in and out of place
Maintaining that with equal husbandry
The woman were an equal to the man.
They harp'd on this; with this our ban-
    quets rang;
Our dances broke and buzz'd in knots of
    talk;

Nothing but this; my very ears were hot
To hear them: knowledge, so my daugh-
    ter held,
Was all in all: they had but been, she
    thought,
As children; they must lose the child,
    assume
The woman: then, Sir, awful odes she
    wrote,
Too awful, sure, for what they treated of,
But all she is and does is awful; odes
About this losing of the child; and rhymes
And dismal lyrics, prophesying change
Beyond all reason: these the women sang;
And they that know such things — I
    sought but peace;
No critic I — would call them master-
    pieces:
They master'd me. At last she begg'd a
    boon
A certain summer-palace which I have
Hard by your father's frontier: I said no,
Yet being an easy man, gave it: and there,
All wild to found an University
For maidens, on the spur she fled; and
    more
We know not, — only this: they see no
    men,
Not ev'n her brother Arac, nor the twins
Her brethren, tho' they love her, look
    upon her
As on a kind of paragon; and I
(Pardon me saying it) were much loath
    to breed
Dispute betwixt myself and mine: but
    since
(And I confess with right) you think me
    bound
In some sort, I can give you letters to her;
And yet, to speak the truth, I rate your
    chance
Almost at naked nothing."
                                Thus the king;
And I, tho' nettled that he seem'd to slur
With garrulous ease and oily courtesies
Our formal compact, yet, not less (all
    frets
But chafing me on fire to find my bride)
Went forth again with both my friends.
    We rode
Many a long league back to the North.
    At last
From hills, that look'd across a land of
    hope,
We dropt with evening on a rustic town
Set in a gleaming river's crescent-curve,
Close at the boundary of the liberties;

There, enter'd an old hostel, call'd mine host
To council, plied him with his richest wines,
And show'd the late-writ letters of the king.

He with a long low sibilation, stared
As blank as death in marble; then exclaim'd
Averring it was clear against all rules
For any man to go: but as his brain
Began to mellow, "If the king," he said,
"Had given us letters, was he bound to speak?
The king would bear him out"; and at the last —
The summer of the vine in all his veins —
"No doubt that we might make it worth his while.
She once had past that way; he heard her speak;
She scared him; life! he never saw the like;
She look'd as grand as doomsday and as grave:
And he, he reverenced his liege-lady there;
He always made a point to post with mares;
His daughter and his housemaid were the boys:
The land, he understood, for miles about
Was till'd by women; all the swine were sows,
And all the dogs" —
 But while he jested thus,
A thought flash'd thro' me which I clothed in act,
Remembering how we three presented Maid
Or Nymph, or Goddess, at high tide of feast,
In masque or pageant at my father's court.
We sent mine host to purchase female gear;
He brought it, and himself, a sight to shake
The midriff of despair with laughter, holp
To lace us up, till, each, in maiden plumes
We rustled: him we gave a costly bribe
To guerdon silence, mounted our good steeds,
And boldly ventured on the liberties.

We follow'd up the river as we rode,
And rode till midnight when the college lights
Began to glitter firefly-like in copse
And linden alley: then we past an arch,
Whereon a woman-statue rose with wings
From four wing'd horses dark against the stars;
And some inscription ran along the front,
But deep in shadow: further on we gain'd
A little street half garden and half house;
But scarce could hear each other speak for noise
Of clocks and chimes, like silver hammers falling
On silver anvils, and the splash and stir
Of fountains spouted up and showering down
In meshes of the jasmine and the rose:
And all about us peal'd the nightingale,
Rapt in her song, and careless of the snare.

There stood a bust of Pallas for a sign,
By two sphere lamps blazon'd like Heaven and Earth
With constellation and with continent,
Above an entry: riding in, we call'd;
A plump-arm'd Ostleress and a stable wench
Came running at the call, and help'd us down.
Then stept a buxom hostess forth, and sail'd,
Full-blown, before us into rooms which gave
Upon a pillar'd porch, the bases lost
In laurel: her we ask'd of that and this,
And who were tutors. "Lady Blanche" she said,
"And Lady Psyche." "Which was prettiest,
Best-natured?" "Lady Psyche." "Hers are we,"
One voice, we cried; and I sat down and wrote,
In such a hand as when a field of corn
Bows all its ears before the roaring East;

"Three ladies of the Northern empire pray
Your Highness would enroll them with your own,
As Lady Psyche's pupils."
 This I seal'd:
The seal was Cupid bent above a scroll,
And o'er his head Uranian Venus hung,
And raised the blinding bandage from his eyes:
I gave the letter to be sent with dawn;
And then to bed, where half in doze I seem'd
To float about a glimmering night, and watch

A full sea glazed with muffled moonlight, swell
On some dark shore just seen that it was rich.

As thro' the land at eve we went,
  And pluck'd the ripen'd ears,
We fell out, my wife and I,
  O we fell out I know not why,
And kiss'd again with tears.
And blessings on the falling out
  That all the more endears,
When we fall out with those we love
  And kiss again with tears!
For when we came where lies the child
  We lost in other years,
There above the little grave,
  O there above the little grave,
We kiss'd again with tears.

II.

At break of day the College Portress came:
She brought us Academic silks, in hue
The lilac, with a silken hood to each,
And zoned with gold; and now when these were on,
And we as rich as moths from dusk cocoons,
She, curtseying her obeisance, let us know
The Princess Ida waited: out we paced,
I first, and following thro' the porch that sang
All round with laurel, issued in a court
Compact with lucid marbles, boss'd with lengths
Of classic frieze, with ample awnings gay
Betwixt the pillars, and with great urns of flowers.
The Muses and the Graces, group'd in threes,
Enring'd a billowing fountain in the midst;
And here and there on lattice edges lay
Or book or lute; but hastily we past,
And up a flight of stairs into the hall.

There at a board by tome and paper sat,
With two tame leopards couch'd beside her throne
All beauty compass'd in a female form,
The Princess; liker to the inhabitant
Of some clear planet close upon the Sun,
Than our man's earth; such eyes were in her head,
And so much grace and power, breathing down
From over her arch'd brows, with every turn
Lived thro' her to the tips of her long hands,
And to her feet. She rose her height, and said:

"We give you welcome: not without redound
Of use and glory to yourselves ye come,
The first-fruits of the stranger: aftertime,
And that full voice which circles round the grave,
Will rank you nobly, mingled up with me.
What! are the ladies of your land so tall?"
"We of the court" said Cyril. "From the court"
She answer'd, "then ye know the Prince?" and he:
"The climax of his age! as tho' there were
One rose in all the world, your Highness that,
He worships your ideal": she replied:
"We scarcely thought in our own hall to hear
This barren verbiage, current among men,
Light coin, the tinsel clink of compliment.
Your flight from out your bookless wilds would seem
As arguing love of knowledge and of power;
Your language proves you still the child.
Indeed,
We dream not of him: when we set our hand
To this great work, we purposed with ourself
Never to wed. You likewise will do well,
Ladies, in entering here, to cast and fling
The tricks, which make us toys of men,
that so,
Some future time, if so indeed you will,
You may with those self-styled our lords ally
Your fortunes, justlier balanced, scale with scale."

At those high words, we conscious of ourselves,
Perused the matting; then an officer
Rose up, and read the statutes, such as these:
Not for three years to correspond with home;
Not for three years to cross the liberties;
Not for three years to speak with any men;

And many more, which hastily subscribed,
We enter'd on the boards: and "Now" she cried
"Ye are green wood, see ye warp not.
Look, our hall!
Our statues!—not of those that men desire,
Sleek Odalisques, or oracles of mode,
Nor stunted squaws of West or East; but she
That taught the Sabine how to rule, and she
The foundress of the Babylonian wall,
The Carian Artemisia strong in war,
The Rhodope, that built the pyramid,
Clelia, Cornelia, with the Palmyrene
That fought Aurelian, and the Roman brows
Of Agrippina. Dwell with these, and lose
Convention, since to look on noble forms
Makes noble thro' the sensuous organism
That which is higher. O lift your natures up:
Embrace our aims: work out your freedom. Girls,
Knowledge is now no more a fountain seal'd:
Drink deep, until the habits of the slave,
The sins of emptiness, gossip and spite
And slander, die. Better not be at all
Than not be noble. Leave us: you may go:
To-day the Lady Psyche will harangue
The fresh arrivals of the week before;
For they press in from all the provinces,
And fill the hive."
  She spoke, and bowing waved
Dismissal: back again we crost the court
To Lady Psyche's: as we enter'd in,
There sat along the forms, like morning doves
That sun their milky bosoms on the thatch,
A patient range of pupils; she herself
Erect behind a desk of satin-wood,
A quick brunette, well-moulded, falcon-eyed,
And on the hither side, or so she look'd,
Of twenty summers. At her left, a child,
In shining draperies, headed like a star,
Her maiden babe, a double April old,
Aglaïa slept. We sat: the Lady glanced:
Then Florian, but no livelier than the dame
That whisper'd "Asses' ears" among the sedge,

"My sister." "Comely too by all that's fair"
Said Cyril. "O hush, hush!" and she began.

"This world was once a fluid haze of light,
Till toward the centre set the starry tides,
And eddied into suns, that wheeling cast
The planets: then the monster, then the man;
Tattoo'd or woaded, winter-clad in skins,
Raw from the prime, and crushing down his mate;
As yet we find in barbarous isles, and here
Among the lowest."
  Thereupon she took
A bird's-eye-view of all the ungracious past;
Glanced at the legendary Amazon
As emblematic of a nobler age;
Appraised the Lycian custom, spoke of those
That lay at wine with Lar and Lucumo;
Ran down the Persian, Grecian, Roman lines
Of empire, and the woman's state in each,
How far from just; till warming with her theme
She fulmined out her scorn of laws Salique
And little-footed China, touch'd on Mahomet
With much contempt, and came to chivalry:
When some respect, however slight, was paid
To woman, superstition all awry:
However then commenced the dawn: a beam
Had slanted forward, falling in a land
Of promise; fruit would follow. Deep, indeed,
Their debt of thanks to her who first had dared
To leap the rotten pales of prejudice,
Disyoke their necks from custom, and assert
None lordlier than themselves but that which made
Woman and man. She had founded; they must build.
Here might they learn whatever men were taught:
Let them not fear: some said their heads were less:
Some men's were small; not they the least of men;

For often fineness compensated size:
Besides the brain was like the hand, and grew
With using; thence the man's, if more was more;
He took advantage of his strength to be
First in the field: some ages had been lost;
But woman ripen'd earlier, and her life
Was longer; and albeit their glorious names
Were fewer, scatter'd stars, yet since in truth
The highest is the measure of the man,
And not the Kaffir, Hottentot, Malay,
Nor those horn-handed breakers of the glebe,
But Homer, Plato, Verulam; even so
With woman: and in arts of government
Elizabeth and others; arts of war
The peasant Joan and others; arts of grace
Sappho and others vied with any man:
And, last not least, she who had left her place,
And bow'd her state to them, that they might grow
To use and power on this Oasis, lapt
In the arms of leisure, sacred from the blight
Of ancient influence and scorn.
                        At last
She rose upon a wind of prophecy
Dilating on the future; "everywhere
Two heads in council, two beside the hearth,
Two in the tangled business of the world,
Two in the liberal offices of life,
Two plummets dropt for one to sound the abyss
Of science, and the secrets of the mind:
Musician, painter, sculptor, critic, more:
And everywhere the broad and bounteous Earth
Should bear a double growth of those rare souls,
Poets, whose thoughts enrich the blood of the world."

    She ended here, and beckon'd us: the rest
Parted; and, glowing full-faced welcome, she
Began to address us, and was moving on
In gratulation, till as when a boat.
Tacks, and the slacken'd sail flaps, all her voice
Faltering and fluttering in her throat, she cried

"My brother!" "Well, my sister." "O" she said
"What do you here? and in this dress? and these?
Why who are these? a wolf within the fold!
A pack of wolves! the Lord be gracious to me!
A plot, a plot, a plot, to ruin all!"
"No plot, no plot," he answer'd.
       "Wretched boy,
How saw you not the inscription on the gate,
LET NO MAN ENTER IN ON PAIN OF DEATH?"
"And if I had" he answer'd "who could think
The softer Adams of your Academe,
O sister, Sirens tho' they be, were such
As chanted on the blanching bones of men?"
"But you will find it otherwise" she said.
"You jest: ill jesting with edge-tools!
my vow
Binds me to speak, and O that iron will,
That axelike edge unturnable, our Head,
The Princess." "Well then, Psyche, take my life,
And nail me like a weasel on a grange
For warning: bury me beside the gate,
And cut this epitaph above my bones;
*Here lies a brother by a sister slain,
All for the common good of womankind."*
"Let me die too" said Cyril "having seen
And heard the Lady Psyche."
                        I struck in:
"Albeit so mask'd, Madam, I love the truth;
Receive it; and in me behold the Prince
Your countryman, affianced years ago
To the Lady Ida: here, for here she was,
And thus (what other way was left) I came."
"O Sir, O Prince, I have no country; none;
If any, this; but none. Whate'er I was
Disrooted, what I am is grafted here.
Affianced, Sir? love-whispers may not breathe
Within this vestal limit, and how should I,
Who am not mine, say, live: the thunderbolt
Hangs silent; but prepare: I speak; it falls."
"Yet pause," I said: "for that inscription there,
I think no more of deadly lurks therein,

Than in a clapper clapping in a garth,
To scare the fowl from fruit: if more
 there be,
If more and acted on, what follows? war;
Your own work marr'd: for this your
 Academe,
Whichever side be Victor, in the halloo
Will topple to the trumpet down, and pass
With all fair theories only made to gild
A stormless summer." "Let the Princess
 judge
Of that" she said: "farewell Sir,— and
 to you.
I shudder at the sequel, but I go."

"Are you that Lady Psyche" I rejoin'd,
"The fifth in line from that old Florian,
Yet hangs his portrait in my father's hall
(The gaunt old Baron with his beetle brow
Sun-shaded in the heat of dusty fights)
As he bestrode my Grandsire, when he
 fell,
And all else fled: we point to it, and we
 say,
The loyal warmth of Florian is not cold,
But branches current yet in kindred
 veins."
"Are you that Psyche" Florian added
 "she
With whom I sang about the morning
 hills,
Flung ball, flew kite, and raced the purple
 fly,
And snared the squirrel of the glen? are
 you
That Psyche, wont to bind my throbbing
 brow,
To smooth my pillow, mix the foaming
 draught
Of fever, tell me pleasant tales, and read
My sickness down to happy dreams? are
 you
That brother-sister Psyche, both in one?
You were that Psyche, but what are you
 now?"
"You are that Psyche," Cyril said, "for
 whom
I would be that for ever which I seem,
Woman, if I might sit beside your feet,
And glean your scatter'd sapience."
             Then once more,
"Are you that Lady Psyche" I began,
"That on her bridal morn before she past
From all her old companions, when the
 king
Kiss'd her pale cheek, declared that an-
 cient ties

Would still be dear beyond the southern
 hills;
That were there any of our people there
In want or peril, there was one to hear
And help them: look! for such are these
 and I."
"Are you that Psyche" Florian ask'd
 "to whom,
In gentler days, your arrow-wounded fawn
Came flying while you sat beside the well?
The creature laid his muzzle on your lap,
And sobb'd, and you sobb'd with it, and
 the blood
Was sprinkled on your kirtle, and you
 wept.
That was fawn's blood, not brother's, yet
 you wept.
O by the bright head of my little niece,
You were that Psyche, and what are you
 now?"
"You are that Psyche" Cyril said again,
"The mother of the sweetest little maid,
That ever crow'd for kisses."
                "Out upon it!"
She answer'd, "peace! and why should
 I not play
The Spartan Mother with emotion, be
The Lucius Junius Brutus of my kind?
Him you call great: he for the common
 weal,
The fading politics of mortal Rome,
As I might slay this child, if good need
 were,
Slew both his sons: and I, shall I, on
 whom
The secular emancipation turns
Of half this world, be swerved from right
 to save
A prince, a brother? a little will I yield.
Best so, perchance, for us, and well for
 you.
O hard, when love and duty clash! I fear
My conscience will not count me fleck-
 less; yet—
Hear my conditions: promise (otherwise
You perish) as you came, to slip away,
To-day, to-morrow, soon: it shall be said,
These women were too barbarous, would
 not learn;
They fled, who might have shamed us:
 promise, all."

What could we else, we promised each;
 and she,
Like some wild creature newly-caged,
 commenced
A to-and-fro, so pacing till she paused

By Florian ; holding out her lily arms
Took both his hands, and smiling faintly said :
"I knew you at the first : tho' you have grown
You scarce have alter'd : I am sad and glad
To see you, Florian. *I* give thee to death
My brother ! it was duty spoke, not I.
My needful seeming harshness, pardon it.
Our mother, is she well ?"
      With that she kiss'd
His forehead, then, a moment after, clung
About him, and betwixt them blossom'd up
From out a common vein of memory
Sweet household talk, and phrases of the hearth,
And far allusion, till the gracious dews
Began to glisten and to fall : and while
They stood, so rapt, we gazing, came a voice,
"I brought a message here from Lady Blanche."
Back started she, and turning round we saw
The Lady Blanche's daughter where she stood,
Melissa, with her hand upon the lock,
A rosy blonde, and in a college gown,
That clad her like an April daffodilly
(Her mother's color) with her lips apart,
And all her thoughts as fair within her eyes,
As bottom agates seen to wave and float
In crystal currents of clear morning seas.

 So stood that same fair creature at the door.
Then Lady Psyche "Ah — Melissa — you !
You heard us ?" and Melissa, "O pardon me ;
I heard, I could not help it, did not wish :
But, dearest Lady, pray you fear me not,
Nor think I bear that heart within my breast,
To give three gallant gentlemen to death."
"I trust you" said the other "for we two
Were always friends, none closer, elm and vine :
But yet your mother's jealous temperament —
Let not your prudence, dearest, drowse, or prove
The Danaid of a leaky vase, for fear
This whole foundation ruin, and I lose
My honor, these their lives." "Ah, fear me not"
Replied Melissa "no — I would not tell,
No, not for all Aspasia's cleverness,
No, not to answer, Madam, all those hard things
That Sheba came to ask of Solomon."
"Be it so" the other "that we still may lead
The new light up, and culminate in peace,
For Solomon may come to Sheba yet."
Said Cyril "Madam, he the wisest man
Feasted the woman wisest then, in halls
Of Lebanonian cedar : nor should you
(Tho' madam *you* should answer, *we* would ask)
Less welcome find among us, if you came
Among us, debtors for our lives to you,
Myself for something more." He said not what,
But "Thanks," she answer'd "go : we have been too long
Together : keep your hoods about the face ;
They do so that affect abstraction here.
Speak little ; mix not with the rest ; and hold
Your promise : all, I trust, may yet be well."

 We turn'd to go, but Cyril took the child,
And held her round the knees against his waist,
And blew the swoll'n cheek of a trumpeter,
While Psyche watch'd them, smiling, and the child
Push'd her flat hand against his face and laugh'd ;
And thus our conference closed.
      And then we stroll'd
For half the day thro' stately theatres
Bench'd crescent-wise. In each we sat, we heard
The grave Professor. On the lecture slate
The circle rounded under female hands
With flawless demonstration : follow'd then
A classic lecture, rich in sentiment,
With scraps of thundrous Epic lilted out
By violet-hooded Doctors, elegies
And quoted odes, and jewels five-words-long
That on the stretch'd forefinger of all Time
Sparkle for ever : then we dipt in all
That treats of whatsoever is, the state,

The total chronicles of man, the mind,
The morals, something of the frame, the rock,
The star, the bird, the fish, the shell, the flower,
Electric, chemic laws, and all the rest,
And whatsoever can be taught and known;
Till like three horses that have broken fence,
And glutted all night long breast-deep in corn,
We issued gorged with knowledge, and I spoke:
"Why, Sirs, they do all this as well as we."
"They hunt old trails" said Cyril "very well;
But when did woman ever yet invent?"
"Ungracious!" answer'd Florian, "have you learnt
No more from Psyche's lecture, you that talk'd
The trash that made me sick, and almost sad?"
"O trash" he said "but with a kernel in it.
Should I not call her wise, who made me wise?
And learnt? I learnt more from her in a flash,
Than if my brainpan were an empty hull,
And every Muse tumbled a science in.
A thousand hearts lie fallow in these halls,
And round these halls a thousand baby loves
Fly twanging headless arrows at the hearts,
Whence follows many a vacant pang; but O
With me, Sir, enter'd in the bigger boy,
The Head of all the golden-shafted firm,
The long-limb'd lad that had a Psyche too;
He cleft me thro' the stomacher; and now
What think you of it, Florian? do I chase
The substance or the shadow? will it hold?
I have no sorcerer's malison on me,
No ghostly hauntings like his Highness. I
Flatter myself that always everywhere
I know the substance when I see it. Well,
Are castles shadows? Three of them? Is she
The sweet proprietress a shadow? If not,
Shall those three castles patch my tatter'd coat?
For dear are those three castles to my wants,
And dear is sister Psyche to my heart,
And two dear things are one of double worth,
And much I might have said, but that my zone
Unmann'd me: then the Doctors! O to hear
The Doctors! O to watch the thirsty plants
Imbibing! once or twice I thought to roar,
To break my chain, to shake my mane: but thou,
Modulate me, Soul of mincing mimicry!
Make liquid treble of that bassoon, my throat;
Abase those eyes that ever loved to meet
Star-sisters answering under crescent brows;
Abate the stride, which speaks of man, and loose
A flying charm of blushes o'er this cheek,
Where they like swallows coming out of time
Will wonder why they came: but hark the bell
For dinner, let us go!"
     And in we stream'd
Among the columns, pacing staid and still
By twos and threes, till all from end to end
With beauties every shade of brown and fair
In colors gayer than the morning mist,
The long hall glitter'd like a bed of flowers.
How might a man not wander from his wits
Pierced thro' with eyes, but that I kept mine own
Intent on her, who rapt in glorious dreams,
The second-sight of some Astræan age,
Sat compass'd with professors: they, the while,
Discuss'd a doubt and tost it to and fro:
A clamor thicken'd, mixt with inmost terms
Of art and science: Lady Blanche alone
Of faded form and haughtiest lineaments,
With all her autumn tresses falsely brown,
Shot sidelong daggers at us, a tiger-cat
In act to spring.
    At last a solemn grace
Concluded, and we sought the gardens: there
One walk'd reciting by herself, and one
In this hand held a volume as to read,
And smoothed a petted peacock down with that:
Some to a low song oar'd a shallop by,

Or under arches of the marble bridge
Hung, shadow'd from the heat; some
   hid and sought
In the orange thickets: others tost a
   ball
Above the fountain-jets, and back again
With laughter: others lay about the
   lawns,
Of the older sort, and murmur'd that
   their May
Was passing: what was learning unto
   them?
They wish'd to marry; they could rule
   a house;
Men hated learned women: but we three
Sat muffled like the Fates; and often
   came
Melissa hitting all we saw with shafts
Of gentle satire, kin to charity,
That harm'd not: then day droopt; the
   chapel bells
Call'd us: we left the walks; we mixt
   with those
Six hundred maidens clad in purest white,
Before two streams of light from wall to
   wall,
While the great organ almost burst his
   pipes,
Groaning for power, and rolling thro'
   the court
A long melodious thunder to the sound
Of solemn psalms, and silver litanies,
The work of Ida, to call down from
   Heaven
A blessing on her labors for the world.

Sweet and low, sweet and low,
   Wind of the western sea,
Low, low, breathe and blow,
   Wind of the western sea!
Over the rolling waters go,
Come from the dying moon, and blow,
   Blow him again to me;
While my little one, while my pretty one,
   sleeps.

Sleep and rest, sleep and rest,
   Father will come to thee soon;
Rest, rest, on mother's breast,
   Father will come to thee soon;
Father will come to his babe in the nest,
Silver sails all out of the west
   Under the silver moon:
Sleep, my little one, sleep, my pretty
   one, sleep.

III.

Morn in the white wake of the morning
   star
Came furrowing all the orient into gold.
We rose, and each by other drest with care
Descended to the courts that lay three parts
In shadow, but the Muses' heads were
   touch'd
Above the darkness from their native
   East.

There while we stood beside the fount,
   and watch'd
Or seem'd to watch the dancing bubble,
   approach'd
Melissa, tinged with wan from lack of
   sleep,
Or grief, and glowing round her dewy eyes
The circled Iris of a night of tears;
"And fly" she cried, "O fly, while yet
   you may!
My mother knows": and when I ask'd
   her "how"
"My fault" she wept "my fault! and
   yet not mine;
Yet mine in part. O hear me, pardon me.
My mother, 't is her wont from night to
   night
To rail at Lady Psyche and her side.
She says the Princess should have been
   the Head,
Herself and Lady Psyche the two arms;
And so it was agreed when first they came;
But Lady Psyche was the right hand now,
And she the left, or not, or seldom used;
Hers more than half the students, all
   the love.
And so last night she fell to canvass you:
Her countrywomen! she did not envy her.
'Who ever saw such wild barbarians?
Girls?—more like men!' and at these
   words the snake,
My secret, seem'd to stir within my breast;
And oh, Sirs, could I help it, but my
   cheek
Began to burn and burn, and her lynx eye
To fix and make me hotter, till she
   laugh'd:
'O marvellously modest maiden, you!
Men! girls, like men! why, if they had
   been men
You need not set your thoughts in rubric
   thus
For wholesale comment.' Pardon, I am
   shamed
That I must needs repeat for my excuse

What looks so little graceful : 'men'
  (for still
My mother went revolving on the word)
'And so they are,—very like men in-
    deed—
And with that woman closeted for hours!'
Then came these dreadful words out one
    by one,
'Why — these — are — men': I shud-
    der'd : 'and you know it.'
'O ask me nothing,' I said : 'And she
    knows too,
And she conceals it.' So my mother
    clutch'd
The truth at once, but with no word
    from me ;
And now thus early risen she goes to in-
    form
The Princess: Lady Psyche will be crush'd;
But you may yet be saved, and therefore
    fly :
But heal me with your pardon ere you go."

"What pardon, sweet Melissa, for a
    blush?"
Said Cyril : "Pale one, blush again :
    than wear
Those lilies, better blush our lives away.
Yet let us breathe for one hour more in
    Heaven"
He added, "lest some classic Angel speak
In scorn of us, 'they mounted, Gany-
    medes,
To tumble, Vulcans, on the second morn.'
But I will melt this marble into wax
To yield us farther furlough" : and he
    went.

Melissa shook her doubtful curls, and
    thought
He scarce would prosper. "Tell us,"
    Florian ask'd,
"How grew this feud betwixt the right
    and left."
"O long ago," she said, "betwixt these
    two
Division smoulders hidden ; 'tis my
    mother,
Too jealous, often fretful as the wind
Pent in a crevice : much I bear with her:
I never knew my father, but she says
(God help her) she was wedded to a fool ;
And still she rail'd against the state of
    things.
She had the care of Lady Ida's youth,
And from the Queen's decease she brought
    her up.

But when your sister came she won the
    heart
Of Ida : they were still together, grew
(For so they said themselves) inosculated ;
Consonant chords that shiver to one note ;
One mind in all things : yet my mother
    still
Affirms your Psyche thieved her theories,
And angled with them for her pupil's love :
She calls her plagiarist ; I know not what :
But I must go : I dare not tarry" and
    light,
As flies the shadow of a bird, she fled.

Then murmur'd Florian gazing after
    her.
"An open-hearted maiden, true and pure.
If I could love, why this were she : how
    pretty
Her blushing was, and how she blush'd
    again,
As if to close with Cyril's random wish :
Not like your Princess cramm'd with
    erring pride,
Nor like poor Psyche whom she drags
    in tow."

"The crane," I said, "may chatter of
    the crane,
The dove may murmur of the dove, but I
An eagle clang an eagle to the sphere.
My princess, O my princess! true she
    errs,
But in her own grand way : being herself
Three times more noble than threescore
    of men,
She sees herself in every woman else,
And so she wears her error like a crown
To blind the truth and me : for her, and
    her,
Hebes are they to hand ambrosia, mix
The nectar ; but — ah she — whene'er
    she moves
The Samian Herè rises and she speaks
A Memnon smitten with the morning
    Sun."

So saying from the court we paced,
    and gain'd
The terrace ranged along the Northern
    front,
And leaning there on those balusters, high
Above the empurpled champaign, drank
    the gale
That blown about the foliage underneath,
And sated with the innumerable rose,
Beat balm upon our eyelids. Hither came

Cyril, and yawning "O hard task," he cried;
"No fighting shadows here! I forced a way
Thro' solid opposition crabb'd and gnarl'd.
Better to clear prime forests, heave and thump
A league of street in summer solstice down,
Than hammer at this reverend gentlewoman.
I knock'd and, bidden, enter'd; found her there
At point to move, and settled in her eyes
The green malignant light of coming storm.
Sir, I was courteous, every phrase well-oil'd,
As man's could be; yet maiden-meek I pray'd
Concealment: she demanded who we were,
And why we came? I fabled nothing fair,
But, your example pilot, told her all.
Up went the hush'd amaze of hand and eye.
But when I dwelt upon your old affiance,
She answer'd sharply that I talk'd astray.
I urged the fierce inscription on the gate,
And our three lives. True — we had limed ourselves
With open eyes, and we must take the chance.
But such extremes, I told her, well might harm
The woman's cause. 'Not more than now,' she said,
'So puddled as it is with favoritism.'
I tried the mother's heart. Shame might befall
Melissa, knowing, saying not she knew:
Her answer was 'Leave me to deal with that.'
I spoke of war to come and many deaths,
And she replied, her duty was to speak,
And duty duty, clear of consequences.
I grew discouraged, Sir; but since I knew
No rock so hard but that a little wave
May beat admission in a thousand years,
I recommenced; 'Decide not ere you pause.
I find you here but in the second place,
Some say the third — the authentic foundress you.
I offer boldly: we will seat you highest:
Wink at our advent: help my prince to gain
His rightful bride, and here I promise you

Some palace in our land, where you shall reign
The head and heart of all our fair she-world,
And your great name flow on with broadening time
For ever.' Well, she balanced this a little,
And told me she would answer us to-day,
Meantime be mute: thus much, nor more I gain'd."

He ceasing, came a message from the Head.
"That afternoon the Princess rode to take
The dip of certain strata to the North.
Would we go with her? we should find the land
Worth seeing; and the river made a fall
Out yonder": then she pointed on to where
A double hill ran up his furrowy forks
Beyond the thick-leaved platans of the vale.

Agreed to, this, the day fled on thro' all
Its range of duties to the appointed hour.
Then summon'd to the porch we went.
She stood
Among her maidens, higher by the head,
Her back against a pillar, her foot on one
Of those tame leopards. Kittenlike he roll'd
And paw'd about her sandal. I drew near;
I gazed. On a sudden my strange seizure came
Upon me, the weird vision of our house:
The Princess Ida seem'd a hollow show,
Her gay-furr'd cats a painted fantasy,
Her college and her maidens, empty masks,
And I myself the shadow of a dream,
For all things were and were not. Yet I felt
My heart beat thick with passion and with awe;
Then from my breast the involuntary sigh
Brake, as she smote me with the light of eyes
That lent my knee desire to kneel, and shook
My pulses, till to horse we got, and so
Went forth in long retinue following up
The river as it narrow'd to the hills.

I rode beside her and to me she said:
"O friend, we trust that you esteem'd us not

Too harsh to your companion yestermorn;
Unwillingly we spake.". "No — not to her,"
I answer'd, "but to one of whom we spake
Your Highness might have seem'd the thing you say."
"Again?" she cried, "are you ambassadresses
From him to me? we give you, being strange,
A license: speak, and let the topic die."

I stammer'd that I knew him — could have wish'd —
"Our king expects — was there no pre-contract?
There is no truer-hearted — ah, you seem
All he prefigured, and he could not see
The bird of passage flying south but long'd
To follow: surely, if your Highness keep
Your purport, you will shock him ev'n to death,
Or baser courses, children of despair."

"Poor boy" she said "can he not read — no books?
Quoit, tennis, ball — no games? nor deals in that
Which men delight in, martial exercise?
To nurse a blind ideal like a girl,
Methinks he seems no better than a girl;
As girls were once, as we ourself have been:
We had our dreams; perhaps he mixt with them:
We touch on our dead self, nor shun to do it,
Being other — since we learnt our meaning here,
To lift the woman's fall'n divinity
Upon an even pedestal with man."

She paused, and added with a haughtier smile
"And as to precontracts, we move, my friend,
At no man's beck, but know ourself and thee,
O Vashti, noble Vashti! Summon'd out
She kept her state, and left the drunken king
To brawl at Shushan underneath the palms."

"Alas your Highness breathes full East," I said,
"On that which leans to you. I know the Prince,
I prize his truth: and then how vast a work
To assail this gray pre-eminence of man!
You grant me license; might I use it? think,
Ere half be done perchance your life may fail;
Then comes the feebler heiress of your plan,
And takes and ruins all; and thus your pains
May only make that footprint upon sand
Which old-recurring waves of prejudice
Resmooth to nothing: might I dread that you,
With only Fame for spouse and your great deeds
For issue, yet may live in vain, and miss,
Meanwhile, what every woman counts her due,
Love, children, happiness?"
  And she exclaim'd,
"Peace, you young savage of the Northern wild!
What! tho' your Prince's love were like a God's,
Have we not made ourself the sacrifice?
You are bold indeed: we are not talk'd to thus:
Yet will we say for children, would they grew
Like field-flowers everywhere! we like them well:
But children die; and let me tell you, girl,
Howe'er you babble, great deeds cannot die;
They with the sun and moon renew their light
Forever, blessing those that look on them.
Children — that men may pluck them from our hearts,
Kill us with pity, break us with ourselves —
O — children — there is nothing upon earth
More miserable than she that has a son
And sees him err: nor would we work for fame;
Tho' she perhaps might reap the applause of Great,
Who learns the one POU STO whence after-hands

May move the world, tho' she herself effect
But little: wherefore up and act, nor shrink
For fear our solid aim be dissipated
By frail successors. Would, indeed, we had been,
In lieu of many mortal flies, a race
Of giants living, each, a thousand years,
That we might see our own work out, and watch
The sandy footprint harden into stone."

I answer'd nothing, doubtful in myself
If that strange Poet-princess with her grand
Imaginatious might at all be won.
And she broke out interpreting my thoughts:

"No doubt we seem a kind of monster to you;
We are used to that: for women, up till this
Cramp'd under worse than South-sea-isle taboo,
Dwarfs of the gynæceum, fail so far
In high desire, they know not, cannot guess
How much their welfare is a passion to us.
If we could give them surer, quicker proof—
Oh if our end were less achievable
By slow approaches, than by single act
Of immolation, any phase of death,
We were as prompt to spring against the pikes,
Or down the fiery gulf as talk of it,
To compass our dear sisters' liberties."

She bow'd as if to veil a noble tear;
And up we came to where the river sloped
To plunge in cataract, shattering on black blocks
A breadth of thunder. O'er it shook the woods,
And danced the color, and, below, stuck out
The bones of some vast bulk that lived and roar'd
Before man was. She gazed awhile and said,
"As these rude bones to us, are we to her
That will be." "Dare we dream of that," I ask'd,

"Which wrought us, as the workman and his work,
That practice betters?" "How," she cried, "you love
The metaphysics! read and earn our prize,
A golden broach: beneath an emerald plane
Sits Diotima, teaching him that died
Of hemlock; our device; wrought to the life;
She rapt upon her subject, he on her:
For there are schools for all." "And yet" I said
"Methinks I have not found among them all
One anatomic." "Nay, we thought of that,"
She answer'd, "but it pleased us not: in truth
We shudder but to dream our maids should ape
Those monstrous males that carve the living hound,
And cram him with the fragments of the grave,
Or in the dark dissolving human heart,
And holy secrets of this microcosm,
Dabbling a shameless hand with shameful jest,
Encarnalize their spirits: yet we know
Knowledge is knowledge, and this matter hangs:
Howbeit ourself, foreseeing casualty,
Nor willing men should come among us, learnt,
For many weary moons before we came,
This craft of healing. Were you sick, ourself
Would tend upon you. To your question now,
Which touches on the workman and his work.
Let there be light and there was light: 't is so:
For was, and is, and will be, are but is;
And all creation is one act at once,
The birth of light: but we that are not all,
As parts, can see but parts, now this, now that,
And live, perforce, from thought to thought, and make
One act a phantom of succession: thus
Our weakness somehow shapes the shadow, Time;
But in the shadow will we work, and mould
The woman to the fuller day."

"The splendor falls on castle walls
And snowy summits old in story."

She spake
With kindled eyes: we rode a league beyond,
And, o'er a bridge of pinewood crossing, came
On flowery levels underneath the crag,
Full of all beauty. "O how sweet" I said
(For I was half-oblivious of my mask)
"To linger here with one that loved us."
"Yea"
She answer'd "or with fair philosophies
That lift the fancy; for indeed these fields
Are lovely, lovelier not the Elysian lawns,
Where paced the Demigods of old, and saw
The soft white vapor streak the crowned towers

Built to the Sun": then, turning to her maids,
"Pitch our pavilion here upon the sward;
Lay out the viands." At the word, they raised
A tent of satin, elaborately wrought
With fair Corinna's triumph; here she stood,
Engirt with many a florid maiden-cheek,
The woman-conqueror; woman-conquer'd there
The bearded Victor of ten-thousand hymns,
And all the men mourn'd at his side:
but we
Set forth to climb; then, climbing, Cyril kept

With Psyche, with Melissa Florian, I
With mine affianced. Many a little hand
Glanced like a touch of sunshine on the
    rocks,
Many a light foot shone like a jewel set
In the dark crag: and then we turn'd,
    we wound
About the cliffs, the copses, out and in,
Hammering and clinking, chattering
    stony names
Of shale and hornblende, rag and trap
    and tuff,
Amygdaloid and trachyte, till the Sun
Grew broader toward his death and fell,
    and all
The rosy heights came out above the lawns.

The splendor falls on castle walls
    And snowy summits old in story:
The long light shakes across the lakes,
    And the wild cataract leaps in glory.
Blow, bugle, blow, set the wild echoes
    flying,
Blow, bugle; answer, echoes, dying, dy-
    ing, dying.

O hark, O hear! how thin and clear,
    And thinner, clearer, farther going!
O sweet and far from cliff and scar
    The horns of Elfland faintly blowing!
Blow, let us hear the purple glens replying:
Blow, bugle; answer, echoes, dying, dy-
    ing, dying.

O love, they die in yon rich sky,
    They faint on hill or field or river:
Our echoes roll from soul to soul,
    And grow for ever and for ever.
Blow, bugle, blow, set the wild echoes
    flying,
And answer, echoes, answer, dying, dy-
    ing, dying.

IV.

"THERE sinks the nebulous star we call
    the Sun,
If that hypothesis of theirs be sound"
Said Ida; "let us down and rest"; and
    we
Down from the lean and wrinkled preci-
    pices,
By every coppice-feather'd chasm and
    cleft,
Dropt thro' the ambrosial gloom to where
    below
No bigger than a glow-worm shone the
    tent
Lamp-lit from the inner. Once she lean'd
    on me,
Descending; once or twice she lent her
    hand,
And blissful palpitations in the blood,
Stirring a sudden transport rose and fell.

But when we planted level feet, and dipt
Beneath the satin dome and enter'd in,
There leaning deep in broider'd down we
    sank
Our elbows: on a tripod in the midst
A fragrant flame rose, and before us glow'd
Fruit, blossom, viand, amber wine, and
    gold.

Then she "Let some one sing to us:
    lightlier move
The minutes fledged with music": and
    a maid,
Of those beside her, smote her harp, and
    sang.

"Tears, idle tears, I know not what
    they mean,
Tears from the depth of some divine de-
    spair
Rise in the heart, and gather to the eyes,
In looking on the happy Autumn-fields,
And thinking of the days that are no more.

"Fresh as the first beam glittering on
    a sail,
That brings our friends up from the un-
    derworld,
Sad as the last which reddens over one
That sinks with all we love below the
    verge;
So sad, so fresh, the days that are no more.

"Ah, sad and strange as in dark sum-
    mer dawns
The earliest pipe of half-awaken'd birds
To dying ears, when unto dying eyes
The casement slowly grows a glimmering
    square;
So sad, so strange, the days that are no
    more.

"Dear as remember'd kisses after death,
And sweet as those by hopeless fancy
    feign'd
On lips that are for others; deep as love,

*'In looking on the happy Autumn-fields,
And thinking of the days that are no more.'*

Deep as first love, and wild with all regret;
O Death in Life, the days that are no more."

    She ended with such passion that the tear,
She sang of, shook and fell, an erring pearl
Lost in her bosom: but with some disdain
Answer'd the Princess "If indeed there haunt
About the moulder'd lodges of the Past
So sweet a voice and vague, fatal to men,
Well needs it we should cram our ears with wool
And so pace by: but thine are fancies hatch'd
In silken-folded idleness; nor is it
Wiser to weep a true occasion lost,
But trim our sails, and let old bygones be,
While down the streams that float us each and all
To the issue, goes, like glittering bergs of ice,
Throne after throne, and molten on the waste
Becomes a cloud: for all things serve their time
Toward that great year of equal mights and rights,
Nor would I fight with iron laws, in the end
Found golden: let the past be past; let be

Their cancell'd Babels: tho' the rough kex break
The starr'd mosaic, and the beard-blown goat
Hang on the shaft, and the wild figtree split
Their monstrous idols, care not while we hear
A trumpet in the distance pealing news
Of better, and Hope, a poising eagle, burns
Above the unrisen morrow": then to me;
"Know you no song of your own land," she said,
"Not such as moans about the retrospect,
But deals with the other distance and the hues
Of promise; not a death's-head at the wine."

Then I remember'd one myself had made,
What time I watch'd the swallow winging south
From mine own land, part made long since, and part
Now while I sang, and maidenlike as far
As I could ape their treble, did I sing.

"O Swallow, Swallow, flying, flying South,
Fly to her, and fall upon her gilded eaves,
And tell her, tell her, what I tell to thee.

"O tell her, Swallow, thou that knowest each,
That bright and fierce and fickle is the South,
And dark and true and tender is the North.

"O Swallow, Swallow, if I could follow, and light
Upon her lattice, I would pipe and trill,
And cheep and twitter twenty million loves.

"O were I thou that she might take me in,
And lay me on her bosom, and her heart
Would rock the snowy cradle till I died.

"Why lingereth she to clothe her heart with love,
Delaying as the tender ash delays
To clothe herself, when all the woods are green?

"O tell her, Swallow, that thy brood is flown:

Say to her, I do but wanton in the South,
But in the North long since my nest is made.

"O tell her, brief is life but love is long,
And brief the sun of summer in the North,
And brief the moon of beauty in the South.

"O Swallow, flying from the golden woods,
Fly to her, and pipe and woo her, and make her mine,
And tell her, tell her, that I follow thee."

I ceased, and all the ladies, each at each,
Like the Ithacensian suitors in old time,
Stared with great eyes, and laugh'd with alien lips,
And knew not what they meant; for still my voice
Rang false: but smiling "Not for thee," she said,
"O Bulbul, any rose of Gulistan
Shall burst her veil: marsh-divers, rather, maid,
Shall croak thee sister, or the meadow-crake
Grate her harsh kindred in the grass: and this
A mere love-poem! O for such, my friend,
We hold them slight: they mind us of the time
When we made bricks in Egypt. Knaves are men,
That lute and flute fantastic tenderness,
And dress the victim to the offering up,
And paint the gates of Hell with Paradise,
And play the slave to gain the tyranny.
Poor soul! I had a maid of honor once;
She wept her true eyes blind for such a one,
A rogue of canzonets and serenades.
I loved her. Peace be with her. She is dead.
So they blaspheme the muse! but great is song
Used to great ends: ourself have often tried
Valkyrian hymns, or into rhythm have dash'd
The passion of the prophetess; for song
Is duer unto freedom, force and growth
Of spirit than to junketing and love.
Love is it? Would this same mock-love, and this
Mock-Hymen were laid up like winter bats,
Till all men grew to rate us at our worth,

Not vassals to be beat, nor petty babes
To be dandled, no, but living wills, and
  sphered
Whole in ourselves and owed to none.
  Enough!
But now to leaven play with profit, you,
Know you no song, the true growth of
  your soil,
That gives the manners of your country-
  women?"

    She spoke and turn'd her sumptuous
  head with eyes
Of shining expectation fixt on mine.
Then while I dragg'd my brains for such
  a song,
Cyril, with whom the bell-mouth'd glass
  had wrought,
Or master'd by the sense of sport, began
To troll a careless, careless tavern-catch
Of Moll and Meg, and strange experiences
Unmeet for ladies. Florian nodded at
  him,
I frowning; Psyche flush'd and wann'd
  and shook;
The lilylike Melissa droop'd her brows;
"Forbear" the Princess cried; "For-
  bear, Sir" I;
And heated thro' and thro' with wrath
  and love,
I smote him on the breast; he started up;
There rose a shriek as of a city sack'd;
Melissa clamor'd "Flee the death";
  "To horse"
Said Ida; "home! to horse!" and fled,
  as flies
A troop of snowy doves athwart the dusk,
When some one batters at the dovecote-
  doors,
Disorderly the women. Alone I stood
With Florian, cursing Cyril, vext at
  heart,
In the pavilion: there like parting hopes
I heard them passing from me: hoof by
  hoof,
And every hoof a knell to my desires,
Clang'd on the bridge; and then another
  shriek,
"The Head, the Head, the Princess, O'
  the Head!"
For blind with rage she miss'd the plank,
  and roll'd
In the river. Out I sprang from glow to
  gloom:
There whirl'd her white robe like a blos-
  som'd branch
Rapt to the horrible fall: a glance I gave,

No more; but woman-vested as I was
Plunged; and the flood drew; yet I
  caught her; then
Oaring one arm, and bearing in my left
The weight of all the hopes of half the
  world,
Strove to buffet to land in vain. A tree
Was half-disrooted from his place and
  stoop'd
To drench his dark locks in the gurgling
  wave
Mid-channel. Right on this we drove
  and caught,
And grasping down the boughs I gain'd
  the shore.

    There stood her maidens glimmeringly
  group'd
In the hollow bank. One reaching for-
  ward drew
My burden from mine arms; they cried
  "she lives":
They bore her back into the tent: but I,
So much a kind of shame within me
  wrought,
Not yet endured to meet her opening eyes,
Nor found my friends; but push'd alone
  on foot
(For since her horse was lost I left her mine)
Across the woods, and less from Indian
  craft
Than beelike instinct hiveward, found
  at length
The garden portals. Two great statues,
  Art
And Science, Caryatids, lifted up
A weight of emblem, and betwixt were
  valves
Of open-work in which the hunter rued
His rash intrusion, manlike, but his
  brows
Had sprouted, and the branches thereupon
Spread out at top, and grimly spiked the
  gates.

    A little space was left between the horns,
Thro' which I clamber'd o'er at top with
  pain,
Dropt on the sward, and up the linden
  walks,
And, tost on thoughts that changed from
  hue to hue,
Now poring on the glowworm, now the
  star,
I paced the terrace, till the Bear had
  wheel'd
Thro' a great arc his seven slow suns.

A step
Of lightest echo, then a loftier form
Than female, moving thro' the uncertain
  gloom,
Disturb'd me with the doubt "if this
  were she"
But it was Florian. "Hist O Hist," he
  said,
"They seek us : out so late is out of rules.
Moreover ' seize the strangers ' is the cry.
How came you here ?" I told him : " I "
  said he,
" Last of the train, a moral leper, I,
To whom none spake, half-sick at heart,
  return'd.
Arriving all confused among the rest
With hooded brows I crept into the hall,
And, couch'd behind a Judith, under-
  neath
The head of Holofernes peep'd and saw.
Girl after girl was call'd to trial : each
Disclaim'd all knowledge of us : last of all,
Melissa : trust me, Sir, I pitied her.
She, question'd if she knew us men, at
  first
Was silent ; closer prest, denied it not :
And then, demanded if her mother knew,
Or Psyche, she affirm'd not, or denied :
From whence the Royal mind, familiar
  with her,
Easily gather'd either guilt. She sent
For Psyche, but she was not there ; she
  call'd
For Psyche's child to cast it from the
  doors ;
She sent for Blanche to accuse her face
  to face ;
And I slipt out : but whither will you now ?
And where are Psyche, Cyril? both are fled :
What, if together ? that were not so well.
Would rather we had never come ! I dread
His wildness, and the chances of the dark."

"And yet," I said, "you wrong him
  more than I
That struck him : this is proper to the
  clown,
Tho' smock'd, or furr'd and purpled,
  still the clown,
To harm the thing that trusts him, and
  to shame
That which he says he loves : for Cyril,
  howe'er
He deal in frolic, as to-night — the song
Might have been worse and sinn'd in
  grosser lips
Beyond all pardon — as it is, I hold

These flashes on the surface are not he.
He has a solid base of temperament :
But as the waterlily starts and slides
Upon the level in little puffs of wind
Tho' anchor'd to the bottom, such is he."

Scarce had I ceased when from a tam-
  arisk near
Two Proctors leapt upon us, crying,
  " Names " :
He, standing still, was clutch'd ; but I
  began
To thrid the musky-circled mazes, wind
And double in and out the boles, and race
By all the fountains : fleet I was of foot :
Before me shower'd the rose in flakes ;
  behind
I heard the puff'd pursuer ; at mine ear
Bubbled the nightingale and heeded not,
And secret laughter tickled all my soul.
At last I hook'd my ankle in a vine,
That claspt the feet of a Mnemosyne,
And falling on my face was caught and
  known.

They haled us to the Princess where
  she sat
High in the hall : above her droop'd a
  lamp,
And made the single jewel on her brow
Burn like the mystic fire on a mast-head,
Prophet of storm : a handmaid on each side
Bow'd toward her, combing out her long
  black hair
Damp from the river; and close behind
  her stood
Eight daughters of the plough, stronger
  than men,
Huge women blowzed with health, and
  wind, and rain,
And labor. Each was like a Druid rock ;
Or like a spire of land that stands apart
Cleft from the main, and wail'd about
  with mews.

Then, as we came, the crowd dividing
  clove
An advent to the throne : and there beside,
Half-naked as if caught at once from bed
And tumbled on the purple footcloth, lay
The lily-shining child ; and on the left,
Bow'd on her palms and folded up from
  wrong,
Her round white shoulder shaken with
  her sobs,
Melissa knelt ; but Lady Blanche erect
Stood up and spake, an affluent orator.

"It was not thus, O Princess, in old days:
You prized my counsel, lived upon my lips:
I led you then to all the Castalies;
I fed you with the milk of every Muse;
I loved you like this kneeler, and you me
Your second mother: those were gracious times.
Then came your new friend: you began to change —
I saw it and grieved — to slacken and to cool;
Till taken with her seeming openness
You turn'd your warmer currents all to her,
To me you froze: this was my meed for all.
Yet I bore up in part from ancient love,
And partly that I hoped to win you back,
And partly conscious of my own deserts,
And partly that you were my civil head,
And chiefly you were born for something great,
In which I might your fellow-worker be,
When time should serve; and thus a noble scheme
Grew up from seed we two long since had sown;
In us true growth, in her a Jonah's gourd,
Up in one night and due to sudden sun:
We took this palace; but even from the first
You stood in your own light and darken'd mine.
What student came but that you planed her path
To Lady Psyche, younger, not so wise,
A foreigner, and I your countrywoman,
I your old friend and tried, she new in all?
But still her lists were swell'd and mine were lean;
Yet I bore up in hope she would be known:
Then came these wolves: *they* knew her: *they* endured,
Long-closeted with her the yestermorn,
To tell her what they were, and she to hear:
And me none told: not less to an eye like mine,
A lidless watcher of the public weal,
Last night, their mask was patent, and my foot
Was to you: but I thought again: I fear'd
To meet a cold 'We thank you, we shall hear of it
From Lady Psyche': you had gone to her,
She told, perforce; and winning easy grace,
No doubt, for slight delay, remain'd among us
In our young nursery still unknown, the stem
Less grain than touchwood, while my honest heat
Were all miscounted as malignant haste
To push my rival out of place and power.
But public use required she should be known;
And since my oath was ta'en for public use,
I broke the letter of it to keep the sense.
I spoke not then at first, but watch'd them well,
Saw that they kept apart, no mischief done;
And yet this day (tho' you should hate me for it)
I came to tell you; found that you had gone,
Ridd'n to the hills, she likewise: now, I thought,
That surely she will speak; if not, then I:
Did she? These monsters blazon'd what they were,
According to the coarseness of their kind,
For thus I hear; and known at last (my work)
And full of cowardice and guilty shame,
I grant in her some sense of shame, she flies;
And I remain on whom to wreak your rage,
I, that have lent my life to build up yours,
I that have wasted here health, wealth, and time,
And talents, I — you know it — I will not boast:
Dismiss me, and I prophesy your plan,
Divorced from my experience, will be chaff
For every gust of chance, and men will say
We did not know the real light, but chased
The wisp that flickers where no foot can tread."

She ceased: the Princess answer'd coldly "Good:
Your oath is broken: we dismiss you: go.
For this lost lamb (she pointed to the child)
Our mind is changed: we take it to ourself."

Thereat the Lady stretch'd a vulture throat,
And shot from crooked lips a haggard smile.
"The plan was mine. I built the nest" she said
"To hatch the cuckoo. Rise!" and stoop'd to updrag
Melissa: she, half on her mother propt,
Half-drooping from her, turn'd her face, and cast
A liquid look on Ida, full of prayer,
Which melted Florian's fancy as she hung,
A Niobëan daughter, one arm out,
Appealing to the bolts of Heaven; and while
We gazed upon her came a little stir
About the doors, and on a sudden rush'd
Among us, out of breath, as one pursued,
A woman-post in flying raiment. Fear
Stared in her eyes, and chalk'd her face, and wing'd
Her transit to the throne, whereby she fell
Delivering seal'd despatches which the Head
Took half-amazed, and in her lion's mood
Tore open, silent we with blind surmise
Regarding, while she read, till over brow
And cheek and bosom brake the wrathful bloom
As of some fire against a stormy cloud,
When the wild peasant rights himself, the rick
Flames, and his anger reddens in the heavens;
For anger most it seem'd, while now her breast,
Beaten with some great passion at her heart,
Palpitated, her hand shook, and we heard
In the dead hush the papers that she held
Rustle: at once the lost lamb at her feet
Sent out a bitter bleating for its dam;
The plaintive cry jarr'd on her ire; she crush'd
The scrolls together, made a sudden turn
As if to speak, but, utterance failing her,
She whirl'd them on to me, as who should say
"Read," and I read — two letters — one her sire's.

"Fair daughter, when we sent the Prince your way
We knew not your ungracious laws, which learnt,
We, conscious of what temper you are built,
Came all in haste to hinder wrong, but fell
Into his father's hands, who has this night,
You lying close upon his territory,
Slipt round and in the dark invested you,
And here he keeps me hostage for his son."

The second was my father's running thus:
"You have our son: touch not a hair of his head:
Render him up unscathed: give him your hand:
Cleave to your contract: tho' indeed we hear
You hold the woman is the better man;
A rampant heresy, such as if it spread
Would make all women kick against their Lords
Thro' all the world, and which might well deserve
That we this night should pluck your palace down;
And we will do it, unless you send us back
Our son, on the instant, whole."
So far I read;
And then stood up and spoke impetuously.

"O not to pry and peer on your reserve,
But led by golden wishes, and a hope
The child of regal compact, did I break
Your precinct; not a scorner of your sex
But venerator, zealous it should be
All that it might be: hear me, for I bear,
Tho' man, yet human, whatsoe'er your wrongs,
From the flaxen curl to the gray lock a life
Less mine than yours: my nurse would tell me of you;
I babbled for you, as babies for the moon,
Vague brightness; when a boy, you stoop'd to me
From all high places, lived in all fair lights,
Came in long breezes rapt from inmost south
And blown to inmost north; at eve and dawn
With Ida, Ida, Ida, rang the woods;
The leader wildswan in among the stars
Would clang it, and lapt in wreaths of glowworm light
The mellow breaker murmur'd Ida. Now,
Because I would have reach'd you, had you been

Sphered up with Cassiopëia, or the en-
throned
Persephone in Hades, now at length,
Those winters of abeyance all worn out,
A man I came to see you : but, indeed,
Not in this frequence can I lend full
tongue,
O noble Ida, to those thoughts that wait
On you, their centre : let me say but this,
That many a famous man and woman,
town
And landskip, have I heard of, after seen
The dwarfs of presage ; tho' when
known, there grew
Another kind of beauty in detail
Made them worth knowing : but in you
I found
My boyish dream involved and dazzled
down
And master'd, while that after-beauty
makes
Such head from act to act, from hour to
hour,
Within me, that except you slay me
here,
According to your bitter statute-book,
I cannot cease to follow you, as they say
The seal does music ; who desire you more
Than growing boys their manhood ; dy-
ing lips,
With many thousand matters left to do,
The breath of life ; O more than poor
men wealth,
Than sick men health — yours, yours,
not mine — but half
Without you; with you, whole ; and of
those halves
You worthiest ; and howe'er you block
and bar
Your heart with system out from mine,
I hold
That it becomes no man to nurse despair,
But in the teeth of clench'd antagonisms
To follow up the worthiest till he die :
Yet that I came not all unauthorized
Behold your father's letter."
On one knee
Kneeling, I gave it, which she caught,
and dash'd
Unopen'd at her feet : a tide of fierce
Invective seem'd to wait behind her lips,
As waits a river level with the dam
Ready to burst and flood the world with
foam :
And so she would have spoken, but there
rose
A hubbub in the court of half the maids

Gather'd together : from the illumined
hall
Long lanes of splendor slanted o'er a press
Of snowy shoulders, thick as herded ewes,
And rainbow robes, and gems and gemlike
eyes,
And gold and golden heads ; they to and
fro
Fluctuated, as flowers in storm, some
red, some pale,
All open-mouth'd, all gazing to the light,
Some crying there was an army in the
land,
And some that men were in the very walls,
And some they cared not ; till a clamor
grew
As of a new-world Babel, woman-built,
And worse-confounded : high above them
stood
The placid marble Muses, looking peace.

Not peace she look'd, the Head : but
rising up
Robed in the long night of her deep hair, so
To the open window moved, remaining
there
Fixt like a beacon-tower above the waves
Of tempest, when the crimson-rolling eye
Glares ruin, and the wild birds on the
light
Dash themselves dead. She stretch'd
her arms and call'd
Across the tumult and the tumult fell.

"What fear ye brawlers? am not I
your Head ?
On me, me, me, the storm first breaks :
I dare
All these male thunderbolts : what is it
ye fear ?
Peace ! there are those to avenge us and
they come :
If not, — myself were like enough, O girls,
To unfurl the maiden banner of our rights,
And clad in iron burst the ranks of war,
Or, falling, protomartyr of our cause,
Die : yet I blame you not so much for fear ;
Six thousand years of fear have made you
that
From which I would redeem you ; but for
those
That stir this hubbub — you and you —
I know
Your faces there in the crowd — to-
morrow morn
We hold a great convention : then shall
they

That love their voices more than duty,
  learn
With whom they deal, dismiss'd in shame
  to live
No wiser than their mothers, household
  stuff,
Live chattels, mincers of each other's fame,
Full of weak poison, turnspits for the
  clown,
The drunkard's football, laughing-stocks
  of Time,
Whose brains are in their hands and in
  their heels,
But fit to flaunt, to dress, to dance, to
  thrum,
To tramp, to scream, to burnish, and to
  scour,
For ever slaves at home and fools abroad."

She, ending, waved her hands: thereat
  the crowd
Muttering, dissolved: then with a smile,
  that look'd
A stroke of cruel sunshine on the cliff,
When all the glens are drown'd in azure
  gloom
Of thunder-shower, she floated to us and
  said:

"You have done well and like a gen-
  tleman,
And like a prince: you have our thanks
  for all:
And you look well too in your woman's
  dress:
Well have you done and like a gentleman.
You saved our life: we owe you bitter
  thanks:
Better have died and spilt our bones in
  the flood —
Then men had said — but now — What
  hinders me
To take such bloody vengeance on you
  both? —
Yet since our father — Wasps in our good
  hive,
You would-be quenchers of the light to be,
Barbarians, grosser than your native
  bears —
O would I had his sceptre for one hour!
You that have dared to break our bound,
  and gull'd
Our servants, wrong'd and lied and
  thwarted us —
I wed with thee! *I* bound by precontract
Your bride, your bondslave! not tho' all
  the gold

That veins the world were pack'd to make
  your crown,
And every spoken tongue should lord
  you. Sir,
Your falsehood and yourself are hateful
  to us:
I trample on your offers and on you:
Begone: we will not look upon you more.
Here, push them out at gates."
                In wrath she spake.
Then those eight mighty daughters of
  the plough
Bent their broad faces toward us and
  address'd
Their motion: twice I sought to plead
  my cause,
But on my shoulder hung their heavy
  hands,
The weight of destiny: so from her face
They push'd us, down the steps, and
  thro' the court,
And with grim laughter thrust us out at
  gates.

We cross'd the street and gain'd a petty
  mound
Beyond it, whence we saw the lights and
  heard
The voices murmuring. While I listen'd,
  came
On a sudden the weird seizure and the
  doubt:
I seem'd to move among a world of ghosts;
The Princess with her monstrous woman-
  guard,
The jest and earnest working side by side,
The cataract and the tumult and the kings
Were shadows; and the long fantastic
  night
With all its doings had and had not been,
And all things were and were not.
              This went by
As strangely as it came, and on my spirits
Settled a gentle cloud of melancholy;
Not long; I shook it off; for spite of
  doubts
And sudden ghostly shadowings I was one
To whom the touch of all mischance but
  came
As night to him that sitting on a hill
Sees the midsummer, midnight, Norway
  sun
Set into sunrise; then we moved away.

———

Thy voice is heard thro' rolling drums,
  That beat to battle where he stands;

Thy face across his fancy comes,
  And gives the battle to his hands :
A moment, while the trumpets blow,
  He sees his brood about thy knee ;
The next, like fire he meets the foe,
  And strikes him dead for thine and thee.

So Lilia sang: we thought her half-possess'd,
She struck such warbling fury thro' the words ;
And, after, feigning pique at what she call'd
The raillery, or grotesque, or false sublime —
Like one that wishes at a dance to change
The music — clapt her hands and cried for war,
Or some grand fight to kill and make an end :
And he that next inherited the tale
Half turning to the broken statue, said,
"Sir Ralph has got your colors : if I prove
Your knight, and fight your battle, what for me ?"
It chanced, her empty glove upon the tomb
Lay by her like a model of her hand.
She took it and she flung it. "Fight" she said,
"And make us all we would be, great and good."
He knightlike in his cap instead of casque,
A cap of Tyrol borrow'd from the hall,
Arranged the favor, and assumed the Prince.

V.

Now, scarce three paces measured from the mound,
We stumbled on a stationary voice,
And "Stand, who goes ?" "Two from the palace " I.
"The second two : they wait," he said, "pass on ;
His Highness wakes": and one, that clash'd in arms,
By glimmering lanes and walls of canvas, led
Threading the soldier-city, till we heard
The drowsy folds of our great ensign shake
From blazon'd lions o'er the imperial tent
Whispers of war.
         Entering, the sudden light
Dazed me half-blind : I stood and seem'd to hear,
As in a poplar grove when a light wind wakes
A lisping of the innumerous leaf and dies,
Each hissing in his neighbor's ear ; and then
A strangled titter, out of which there brake
On all sides, clamoring etiquette to death,
Unmeasured mirth ; while now the two old kings
Began to wag their baldness up and down,
The fresh young captains flash'd their glittering teeth,
The huge bush-bearded Barons heaved and blew,
And slain with laughter roll'd the gilded Squire.

At length my Sire, his rough cheek wet with tears,
Panted from weary sides "King, you are free !
We did but keep you surety for our son,
If this be he, — or a draggled mawkin, thou,
That tends her bristled grunters in the sludge " :
For I was drench'd with ooze, and torn with briers,
More crumpled than a poppy from the sheath,
And all one rag, disprinced from head to heel.
Then some one sent beneath his vaulted palm
A whisper'd jest to some one near him "Look,
He has been among his shadows." "Satan take
The old women and their shadows ! (thus the King
Roar'd) make yourself a man to fight with men.
Go : Cyril told us all."
         As boys that slink
From ferule and the trespass-chiding eye,
Away we stole, and transient in a trice
From what was left of faded woman-slough
To sheathing splendors and the golden scale
Of harness, issued in the sun, that now
Leapt from the dewy shoulders of the Earth,
And hit the Northern hills. Here Cyril met us,
A little shy at first, but by and by

We twain, with mutual pardon ask'd and
    given
For stroke and song, resolder'd peace,
    whereon
Follow'd his tale. Amazed he fled away
Thro' the dark land, and later in the night
Had come on Psyche weeping: "then we
    fell
Into your father's hand, and there she lies,
But will not speak, nor stir."
                 He show'd a tent
A stone-shot off: we enter'd in, and there
Among piled arms and rough accoutre-
    ments,
Pitiful sight, wrapp'd in a soldier's cloak,
Like some sweet sculpture draped from
    head to foot,
And push'd by rude hands from its ped-
    estal,
All her fair length upon the ground she lay:
And at her head a follower of the camp,
A charr'd and wrinkled piece of woman-
    hood,
Sat watching like a watcher by the dead.

    Then Florian knelt, and "Come" he
    whisper'd to her,
" Lift up your head, sweet sister: lie not
    thus.
What have you done but right? you
    could not slay
Me, nor your prince: look up: be com-
    forted:
Sweet is it to have done the thing one
    ought,
When fall'n in darker ways." And like-
    wise I:
" Be comforted: have I not lost her too,
In whose least act abides the nameless
    charm
That none has else for me?" She heard,
    she moved,
She moan'd, a folded voice; and up she
    sat,
And raised the cloak from brows as pale
    and smooth
As those that mourn half-shrouded over
    death
In deathless marble. "Her" she said
    " my friend —
Parted from her — betray'd her cause and
    mine —
Where shall I breathe ? why kept ye not
    your faith ?
O base and bad ! what comfort ? none for
    me !"
To whom remorseful Cyril " Yet I pray

Take comfort: live, dear lady, for your
    child !"
At which she lifted up her voice and cried.

    "Ah me, my babe, my blossom, ah my
    child,
My one sweet child, whom I shall see no
    more !
For now will cruel Ida keep her back;
And either she will die from want of care,
Or sicken with ill-usage, when they say
The child is hers — for every little fault,
The child is hers; and they will beat my
    girl
Remembering her mother: O my flower !
Or they will take her, they will make
    her hard,
And she will pass me by in after-life
With some cold reverence worse than
    were she dead.
Ill mother that I was to leave her there,
To lag behind, scared by the cry they
    made,
The horror of the shame among them all:
But I will go and sit beside the doors,
And make a wild petition night and day,
Until they hate to hear me like a wind
Wailing for ever, till they open to me,
And lay my little blossom at my feet,
My babe, my sweet Aglaïa, my one child:
And I will take her up and go my way,
And satisfy my soul with kissing her :
Ah ! what might that man not deserve
    of me,
Who gave me back my child?" "Be
    comforted "
Said Cyril "you shall have it" : but again
She veil'd her brows, and prone she sank,
    and so
Like tender things that being caught
    feign death,
Spoke not, nor stirr'd.
                 By this a murmur ran
Thro' all the camp and inward raced the
    scouts
With rumor of Prince Arac hard at hand.
We left her by the woman, and without
Found the gray kings at parle: and
    " Look you " cried
My father " that our compact be fulfill'd:
You have spoilt this child; she laughs
    at you and man:
She wrongs herself, her sex, and me, and
    him:
But red-faced war has rods of steel and fire;
She yields, or war."
                 Then Gama turn'd to me:

"We fear, indeed, you spent a stormy time
With our strange girl : and yet they say
  that still
You love her. Give us, then, your mind
  at large :
How say you, war or not ?"
            "Not war, if possible,
O king," I said, "lest from the abuse of
  war,
The desecrated shrine, the trampled year,
The smouldering homestead, and the
  household flower
Torn from the lintel — all the common
  wrong —
A smoke go up thro' which I loom to her
Three times a monster : now she lightens
  scorn
At him that mars her plan, but then
  would hate
(And every voice she talk'd with ratify it,
And every face she look'd on justify it)
The general foe. More soluble is this knot,
By gentleness than war. I want her love.
What were I nigher this altho' we dash'd
Your cities into shards with catapults,
She would not love ; — or brought her
  chain'd, a slave,
The lifting of whose eyelash is my lord,
Not ever would she love ; but brooding
  turn
The book of scorn, till all my flitting chance
Were caught within the record of her
  wrongs,
And crush'd to death : and rather, Sire,
  than this
I would the old God of war himself were
  dead,
Forgotten, rusting on his iron hills,
Rotting on some wild shore with ribs of
  wreck,
Or like an old-world mammoth bulk'd
  in ice,
Not to be molten out."
              And roughly spake
My father, "Tut, you know them not,
  the girls.
Boy, when I hear you prate I almost think
That idiot legend credible. Look you, Sir !
Man is the hunter ; woman is his game :
The sleek and shining creatures of the
  chase,
We hunt them for the beauty of their skins;
They love us for it, and we ride them down.
Wheedling and siding with them ! Out !
  for shame !
Boy, there 's no rose that 's half so dear
  to them

As he that does the thing they dare not do,
Breathing and sounding beauteous battle,
  comes
With the air of the trumpet round him,
  and leaps in
Among the women, snares them by the
  score
Flatter'd and fluster'd, wins, tho' dash'd
  with death
He reddens what he kisses : thus I won
Your mother, a good mother, a good wife,
Worth winning ; but this firebrand —
  gentleness
To such as her ! if Cyril spake her true,
To catch a dragon in a cherry net,
To trip a tigress with a gossamer,
Were wisdom to it."
            "Yea but Sire," I cried,
"Wild natures need wise curbs. The
  soldier ? No :
What dares not Ida do that she should
  prize
The soldier ? I beheld her, when she rose
The yesternight, and storming in extremes
Stood for her cause, and flung defiance
  down
Gagelike to man, and had not shunn'd
  the death,
No, not the soldier's : yet I hold her, king,
True woman : but you clash them all in
  one,
That have as many differences as we.
The violet varies from the lily as far
As oak from elm : one loves the soldier,
  one
The silken priest of peace, one this, one
  that,
And some unworthily ; their sinless faith,
A maiden moon that sparkles on a sty,
Glorifying clown and satyr ; whence they
  need
More breadth of culture : is not Ida right ?
They worth it ? truer to the law within ?
Severer in the logic of a life ?
Twice as magnetic to sweet influences
Of earth and heaven ? and she of whom
  you speak,
My mother, looks as whole as some serene
Creation minted in the golden moods
Of sovereign artists ; not a thought, a
  touch,
But pure as lines of green that streak the
  white
Of the first snowdrop's inner leaves ; I say,
Not like the piebald miscellany, man,
Bursts of great heart and slips in sensual
  mire,

But whole and one : and take them all-
   in-all,
Were we ourselves but half as good, as
   kind,
As truthful, much that Ida claims as right
Had ne'er been mooted, but as frankly
   theirs
As dues of Nature. To our point : not
   war :
Lest I lose all."
"Nay, nay, you spake but sense"
Said Gama. "We remember love our-
   self
In our sweet youth; we did not rate him
   then
This red-hot iron to be shaped with blows.
You talk almost like Ida : *she* can talk ;
And there is something in it as you say :
But you talk kindlier : we esteem you
   for it. —
He seems a gracious and a gallant Prince,
I would he had our daughter : for the rest,
Our own detention, why, the causes
   weigh'd,
Fatherly fears — you used us courteous-
   ly —
We would do much to gratify your
   Prince —
We pardon it ; and for your ingress here
Upon the skirt and fringe of our fair land,
You did but come as goblins in the night,
Nor in the furrow broke the ploughman's
   head,
Nor burnt the grange, nor buss'd the
   milking-maid,
Nor robb'd the farmer of his bowl of cream :
But let your Prince (our royal word upon it,
He comes back safe) ride with us to our
   lines,
And speak with Arac : Arac's word is
   thrice
As ours with Ida : something may be
   done —
I know not what — and ours shall see us
   friends.
You, likewise, our late guests, if so you
   will,
Follow us : who knows ? we four may
   build some plan
Foursquare to opposition."
               Here he reach'd
White hands of farewell to my sire, who
   growl'd
An answer which, half-muffled in his
   beard,
Let so much out as gave us leave to go.

Then rode we with the old king across
   the lawns
Beneath huge trees, a thousand rings of
   Spring
In every bole, a song on every spray
Of birds that piped their Valentines, and
   woke
Desire in me to infuse my tale of love
In the old king's ears, who promised help,
   and oozed
All o'er with honey'd answer as we rode ;
And blossom-fragrant slipt the heavy dews
Gather'd by night and peace, with each
   light air
On our mail'd heads : but other thoughts
   than Peace
Burnt in us, when we saw the embattled
   squares,
And squadrons of the Prince, trampling
   the flowers
With clamor : for among them rose a cry
As if to greet the king ; they made a halt ;
The horses yell'd ; they clash'd their
   arms ; the drum
Beat ; merrily-blowing shrill'd the mar-
   tial fife ;
And in the blast and bray of the long horn
And serpent-throated bugle, undulated
The banner : anon to meet us lightly
   pranced
Three captains out ; nor ever had I seen
Such thews of men : the midmost and the
   highest
Was Arac : all about his motion clung
The shadow of his sister, as the beam
Of the East, that play'd upon them, made
   them glance
Like those three stars of the airy Giant's
   zone,
That glitter burnish'd by the frosty dark ;
And as the fiery Sirius alters hue,
And bickers into red and emerald, shone
Their morions, wash'd with morning, as
   they came.

And I that prated peace, when first I
   heard
War-music, felt the blind wildbeast of
   force,
Whose home is in the sinews of a man,
Stir in me as to strike : then took the king
His three broad sons ; with now a wan-
   dering hand
And now a pointed finger, told them all :
A common light of smiles at our disguise
Broke from their lips, and, ere the windy
   jest

Had labor'd down within his ample lungs,
The genial giant, Arac, roll'd himself
Thrice in the saddle, then burst out in
  words.

"Our land invaded, 'sdeath! and he
  himself
Your captive, yet my father wills not war:
And, 'sdeath! myself, what care I, war
  or no?
But then this question of your troth re-
  mains:
And there's a downright honest mean-
  ing in her;
She flies too high, she flies too high! and
  yet
She ask'd but space and fairplay for her
  scheme;
She prest and prest it on me — I myself,
What know I of these things? but, life
  and soul!
I thought her half-right talking of her
  wrongs;
I say she flies too high, 'sdeath! what
  of that?
I take her for the flower of womankind,
And so I often told her, right or wrong,
And, Prince, she can be sweet to those
  she loves,
And, right or wrong, I care not: this is all,
I stand upon her side: she made me
  swear it —
'Sdeath — and with solemn rites by can-
  dle-light —
Swear by St. something — I forget her
  name —
Her that talk'd down the fifty wisest men;
She was a princess too; and so I swore.
Come, this is all; she will not: waive
  your claim:
If not, the foughten field, what else, at
  once
Decides it, 'sdeath! against my father's
  will."

I lagg'd in answer loath to render up
My precontract, and loath by brainless war
To cleave the rift of difference deeper
  yet;
Till one of those two brothers, half aside
And fingering at the hair about his lip,
To prick us on to combat "Like to like!
The woman's garment hid the woman's
  heart."
A taunt that clench'd his purpose like a
  blow!
For fiery-short was Cyril's counter-scoff,
And sharp I answer'd, touch'd upon the
  point
Where idle boys are cowards to their
  shame,
"Decide it here: why not? we are three
  to three."

Then spake the third "But three to
  three? no more?
No more, and in our noble sister's cause?
More, more, for honor: every captain
  waits
Hungry for honor, angry for his king.
More, more, some fifty on a side, that
  each
May breathe himself, and quick! by
  overthrow
Of these or those, the question settled die."

"Yea" answer'd I "for this wild
  wreath of air,
This flake of rainbow flying on the highest
Foam of men's deeds — this honor, if ye
  will.
It needs must be for honor if at all:
Since, what decision? if we fail, we fail,
And if we win, we fail: she would not
  keep
Her compact." "'Sdeath! but we will
  send to her,"
Said Arac, "worthy reasons why she
  should
Bide by this issue: let our missive thro',
And you shall have her answer by the
  word."

"Boys!" shriek'd the old king, but
  vainlier than a hen
To her false daughters in the pool; for
  none
Regarded; neither seem'd there more to
  say:
Back rode we to my father's camp, and
  found
He thrice had sent a herald to the gates,
To learn if Ida yet would cede our claim,
Or by denial flush her babbling wells
With her own people's life: three times
  he went:
The first, he blew and blew, but none
  appear'd:
He batter'd at the doors; none came:
  the next,
An awful voice within had warn'd him
  thence:
The third, and those eight daughters of
  the plough

Came sallying thro' the gates, and caught his hair,
And so belabor'd him on rib and cheek
They made him wild: not less one glance he caught
Thro' open doors of Ida station'd there
Unshaken, clinging to her purpose, firm
Tho' compass'd by two armies and the noise
Of arms; and standing like a stately Pine
Set in a cataract on an island-crag,
When storm is on the heights, and right and left
Suck'd from the dark heart of the long hills roll
The torrents, dash'd to the vale: and yet her will
Bred will in me to overcome it or fall.

But when I told the king that I was pledged
To fight in tourney for my bride, he clash'd
His iron palms together with a cry;
Himself would tilt it out among the lads:
But overborne by all his bearded lords
With reasons drawn from age and state, perforce
He yielded, wroth and red, with fierce demur:
And many a bold knight started up in heat,
And sware to combat for my claim till death.

All on this side the palace ran the field
Flat to the garden-wall: and likewise here,
Above the garden's glowing blossom-belts,
A column'd entry shone and marble stairs,
And great bronze valves, emboss'd with Tomyris
And what she did to Cyrus after fight,
But now fast barr'd: so hereupon the flat
All that long morn the lists were hammer'd up,
And all that morn the heralds to and fro,
With message and defiance, went and came;
Last, Ida's answer, in a royal hand,
But shaken here and there, and rolling words
Oration-like. I kiss'd it and I read.

  " O brother, you have known the pangs we felt,
What heats of indignation when we heard
Of those that iron-cramp'd their women's feet;
Of lands in which at the altar the poor bride
Gives her harsh groom for bridal-gift a scourge;
Of living hearts that crack within the fire
Where smoulder their dead despots; and of those, —
Mothers, — that, all prophetic pity, fling
Their pretty maids in the running flood, and swoops
The vulture, beak and talon, at the heart
Made for all noble motion: and I saw
That equal baseness lived in sleeker times
With smoother men: the old leaven leaven'd all:
Millions of throats would bawl for civil rights,
No woman named: therefore I set my face
Against all men, and lived but for mine own.
Far off from men I built a fold for them:
I stored it full of rich memorial:
I fenced it round with gallant institutes,
And biting laws to scare the beasts of prey,
And prosper'd; till a rout of saucy boys
Brake on us at our books, and marr'd our peace,
Mask'd like our maids, blustering I know not what
Of insolence and love, some pretext held
Of baby troth, invalid, since my will
Seal'd not the bond — the striplings! — for their sport! —
I tamed my leopards: shall I not tame these?
Or you? or I? for since you think me touch'd
In honor — what, I would not aught of false —
Is not our cause pure? and whereas I know
Your prowess, Arac, and what mother's blood
You draw from, fight; you failing, I abide
What end soever: fail you will not. Still
Take not his life: he risk'd it for my own;
His mother lives: yet whatsoe'er you do,
Fight and fight well; strike and strike home. O dear
Brothers, the woman's Angel guards you, you
The sole men to be mingled with our cause,
The sole men we shall prize in the after-time,

Your very armor hallow'd, and your statues
Rear'd, sung to, when, this gad-fly brush'd aside,
We plant a solid foot into the Time,
And mould a generation strong to move
With claim on claim from right to right, till she
Whose name is yoked with children's, know herself;
And Knowledge in our own land make her free,
And, ever following those two crowned twins,
Commerce and conquest, shower the fiery grain
Of freedom broadcast over all that orbs
Between the Northern and the Southern morn."

Then came a postscript dash'd across the rest.
"See that there be no traitors in your camp:
We seem a nest of traitors — none to trust
Since our arms fail'd — this Egypt-plague of men !
Almost our maids were better at their homes,
Than thus man-girdled here: indeed I think
Our chiefest comfort is the little child
Of one unworthy mother; which she left:
She shall not have it back: the child shall grow
To prize the authentic mother of her mind.
I took it for an hour in mine own bed
This morning: there the tender orphan hands
Felt at my heart, and seem'd to charm from thence
The wrath I nursed against the world: farewell."

I ceased; he said: "Stubborn, but she may sit
Upon a king's right hand in thunder-storms,
And breed up warriors! See now, tho' yourself
Be dazzled by the wildfire Love to sloughs
That swallow common sense, the spindling king,
This Gama swamp'd in lazy tolerance.
When the man wants weight, the woman takes it up,
And topples down the scales; but this is fixt
As are the roots of earth and base of all,
Man for the field and woman for the hearth:
Man for the sword and for the needle she:
Man with the head and woman with the heart:
Man to command and woman to obey;
All else confusion. Look you ! the gray mare
Is ill to live with, when her whinny shrills
From tile to scullery, and her small good-man
Shrinks in his arm-chair while the fires of Hell
Mix with his hearth: but you — she 's yet a colt —
Take, break her: strongly groom'd and straitly curb'd
She might not rank with those detestable
That let the bantling scald at home, and brawl
Their rights or wrongs like potherbs in the street.
They say she 's comely; there's the fairer chance:
I like her none the less for rating at her !
Besides, the woman wed is not as we,
But suffers change of frame. A lusty brace
Of twins may weed her of her folly. Boy,
The bearing and the training of a child
Is woman's wisdom."

Thus the hard old king:
I took my leave, for it was nearly noon:
I pored upon her letter which I held,
And on the little clause "take not his life":
I mused on that wild morning in the woods,
And on the "Follow, follow, thou shalt win":
I thought on all the wrathful king had said,
And how the strange betrothment was to end:
Then I remember'd that burnt sorcerer's curse
That one should fight with shadows and should fall;
And like a flash the weird affection came:
King, camp, and college turn'd to hollow shows;
I seem'd to move in old memorial tilts,
And doing battle with forgotten ghosts,
To dream myself the shadow of a dream:

And ere I woke it was the point of noon,
The lists were ready. Empanoplied and
    plumed
We enter'd in, and waited, fifty there
Opposed to fifty, till the trumpet blared
At the barrier like a wild horn in a land
Of echoes, and a moment, and once more
The trumpet, and again : at which the
    storm
Of galloping hoofs bare on the ridge of
    spears
And riders front to front, until they closed
In conflict with the crash of shivering
    points,
And thunder. Yet it seem'd a dream,
    I dream'd
Of fighting. On his haunches rose the
    steed,
And into fiery splinters leapt the lance,
And out of stricken helmets sprang the
    fire.
Part sat like rocks : part reel'd but kept
    their seats :
Part roll'd on the earth and rose again
    and drew :
Part stumbled mixt with floundering
    horses. Down
From those two bulks at Arac's side, and
    down
From Arac's arm, as from a giant's flail,
The large blows rain'd, as here and every-
    where
He rode the mellay, lord of the ringing
    lists,
And all the plain, — brand, mace, and
    shaft, and shield —
Shock'd, like an iron-clanging anvil bang'd
With hammers ; till I thought, can this
    be he
From Gama's dwarfish loins ? if this be
    so,
The mother makes us most — and in my
    dream
I glanced aside, and saw the palace-front
Alive with fluttering scarfs and ladies'
    eyes,
And highest, among the statues, statue-
    like,
Between a cymbal'd Miriam and a Jael,
With Psyche's babe, was Ida watching us,
A single band of gold about her hair,
Like a Saint's glory up in heaven : but
    she
No saint — inexorable — no tenderness —
Too hard, too cruel : yet she sees me fight,
Yea, let her see me fall ! with that I
    drave

Among the thickest and bore down a
    Prince,
And Cyril, one. Yea, let me make my
    dream
All that I would. But that large-mould-
    ed man,
His visage all agrin as at a wake,
Made at me thro' the press, and, stagger-
    ing back
With stroke on stroke the horse and
    horseman, came
As comes a pillar of electric cloud,
Flaying the roofs and sucking up the
    drains,
And shadowing down the champaign till
    it strikes
On a wood, and takes, and breaks, and
    cracks, and splits,
And twists the grain with such a roar
    that Earth
Reels, and the herdsmen cry ; for every-
    thing
Gave way before him : only Florian, he
That loved me closer than his own right
    eye,
Thrust in between ; but Arac rode him
    down :
And Cyril seeing it, push'd against the
    Prince,
With Psyche's color round his helmet,
    tough,
Strong, supple, sinew-corded, apt at
    arms ;
But tougher, heavier, stronger, he that
    smote
And threw him : last I spurr'd ; I felt
    my veins
Stretch with fierce heat ; a moment hand
    to hand,
And sword to sword, and horse to horse
    we hung,
Till I struck out and shouted ; the blade
    glanced ;
I did but shear a feather, and dream and
    truth
Flow'd from me ; darkness closed me ;
    and I fell.

———

Home they brought her warrior dead :
    She nor swoon'd, nor utter'd cry :
All her maidens, watching, said,
    "She must weep or she will die."

Then they praised him, soft and low,
    Call'd him worthy to be loved,

"Like summer tempest came her tears—
'Sweet my child, I live for thee.'"

Truest friend and noblest foe;
  Yet she neither spoke nor moved.

Stole a maiden from her place,
  Lightly to the warrior stept,
Took the face-cloth from the face;
  Yet she neither moved nor wept.

Rose a nurse of ninety years,
  Set his child upon her knee —
Like summer tempest came her tears —
  "Sweet my child, I live for thee."

VI.

My dream had never died or lived again.
As in some mystic middle state I lay;
Seeing I saw not, hearing not I heard:
Tho', if I saw not, yet they told me
    all
So often that I speak as having seen.

  For so it seem'd, or so they said to me,
That all things grew more tragic and
    more strange;

That when our side was vanquish'd and my cause
For ever lost, there went up a great cry,
The Prince is slain. My father heard and ran
In on the lists, and there unlaced my casque
And grovell'd on my body, and after him
Came Psyche, sorrowing for Aglaïa.

But high upon the palace Ida stood
With Psyche's babe in arm: there on the roofs
Like that great dame of Lapidoth she sang.

"Our enemies have fall'n, have fall'n: the seed,
The little seed they laugh'd at in the dark,
Has risen and cleft the soil, and grown a bulk
Of spanless girth, that lays on every side
A thousand arms and rushes to the Sun.

"Our enemies have fall'n, have fall'n: they came;
The leaves were wet with women's tears: they heard
A noise of songs they would not understand:
They mark'd it with the red cross to the fall,
And would have strown it, and are fall'n themselves.

"Our enemies have fall'n, have fall'n: they came,
The woodmen with their axes: lo the tree!
But we will make it fagots for the hearth,
And shape it plank and beam for roof and floor,
And boats and bridges for the use of men.

"Our enemies have fall'n, have fall'n: they struck;
With their own blows they hurt themselves, nor knew
There dwelt an iron nature in the grain:
The glittering axe was broken in their arms,
Their arms were shatter'd to the shoulder blade.

"Our enemies have fall'n, but this shall grow
A night of Summer from the heat, a breadth
Of Autumn, dropping fruits of power; and roll'd
With music in the growing breeze of Time,
The tops shall strike from star to star, the fangs
Shall move the stony bases of the world.

"And now, O maids, behold our sanctuary
Is violate, our laws broken: fear we not
To break them more in their behoof, whose arms
Champion'd our cause and won it with a day
Blanch'd in our annals, and perpetual feast,
When dames and heroines of the golden year
Shall strip a hundred hollows bare of Spring,
To rain an April of ovation round
Their statues, borne aloft, the three: but come,
We will be liberal, since our rights are won.
Let them not lie in the tents with coarse mankind,
Ill nurses; but descend, and proffer these
The brethren of our blood and cause, that there
Lie bruised and maim'd, the tender ministries
Of female hands and hospitality."

She spoke, and with the babe yet in her arms,
Descending, burst the great bronze valves, and led
A hundred maids in train across the Park.
Some cowl'd, and some bare-headed, on they came,
Their feet in flowers, her loveliest: by them went
The enamor'd air sighing, and on their curls
From the high tree the blossom wavering fell,
And over them the tremulous isles of light
Slided, they moving under shade: but Blanche
At distance follow'd: so they came: anon
Thro' open field into the lists they wound
Timorously; and as the leader of the herd
That holds a stately fretwork to the Sun,
And follow'd up by a hundred airy does,
Steps with a tender foot, light as on air,
The lovely, lordly creature floated on
To where her wounded brethren lay; there stay'd;

Knelt on one knee, — the child on one, — and prest
Their hands, and call'd them dear deliverers,
And happy warriors, and immortal names,
And said "You shall not lie in the tents
　but here,
And nursed by those for whom you
　fought, and served
With female hands and hospitality."

Then, whether moved by this, or was
　it chance,
She past my way.　Up started from my
　side
The old lion, glaring with his whelpless
　eye,
Silent; but when she saw me lying stark,
Dishelm'd and mute, and motionlessly
　pale,
Cold ev'n to her, she sigh'd; and when
　she saw
The haggard father's face and reverend
　beard
Of grisly twine, all dabbled with the blood
Of his own son, shudder'd, a twitch of pain
Tortured her mouth, and o'er her forehead past
A shadow, and her hue changed, and she
　said:
"He saved my life: my brother slew
　him for it."
No more: at which the king in bitter
　scorn
Drew from my neck the painting and
　the tress,
And held them up: she saw them, and a
　day
Rose from the distance on her memory,
When the good Queen, her mother, shore
　the tress
With kisses, ere the days of Lady Blanche:
And then once more she look'd at my
　pale face:
Till understanding all the foolish work
Of Fancy, and the bitter close of all,
Her iron will was broken in her mind;
Her noble heart was molten in her breast;
She bow'd, she set the child on the earth;
　she laid
A feeling finger on my brows, and presently
"O Sire," she said, "he lives: he is
　not dead:
O let me have him with my brethren here
In our own palace: we will tend on him
Like one of these; if so, by any means,

To lighten this great clog of thanks, that
　make
Our progress falter to the woman's goal."

She said: but at the happy word "he
　lives"
My father stoop'd, re-father'd o'er my
　wounds.
So those two foes above my fallen life,
With brow to brow like night and evening mixt
Their dark and gray, while Psyche ever
　stole
A little nearer, till the babe that by us,
Half-lapt in glowing gauze and golden
　brede,
Lay like a new-fall'n meteor on the grass,
Uncared for, spied its mother and began
A blind and babbling laughter, and to
　dance
Its body, and reach its fatling innocent
　arms
And lazy lingering fingers. She the appeal
Brook'd not, but clamoring out, "Mine—
　mine — not yours,
It is not yours, but mine: give me the
　child"
Ceased all on tremble: piteous was the cry:
So stood the unhappy mother openmouth'd,
And turn'd each face her way: wan was
　her cheek
With hollow watch, her blooming mantle torn,
Red grief and mother's hunger in her eye,
And down dead-heavy sank her curls,
　and half
The sacred mother's bosom, panting, burst
The laces toward her babe; but she nor
　cared
Nor knew it, clamoring on, till Ida heard,
Look'd up, and rising slowly from me,
　stood
Erect and silent, striking with her glance
The mother, me, the child; but he that lay
Beside us, Cyril, batter'd as he was,
Trail'd himself up on one knee; then he
　drew
Her robe to meet his lips, and down she
　look'd
At the arm'd man sideways, pitying as it
　seem'd,
Or self-involved; but when she learnt his
　face,
Remembering his ill-omen'd song, arose
Once more thro' all her height, and o'er
　him grew

Tall as a figure lengthen'd on the sand
When the tide ebbs in sunshine, and he
 said :

"O fair and strong and terrible ! Lioness
That with your long locks play the Lion's
 mane !
But Love and Nature, these are two more
 terrible
And stronger. See, your foot is on our
 necks,
We vanquish'd, you the Victor of your
 will.
What would you more? give her the child !
 remain
Orb'd in your isolation : he is dead,
Or all as dead : henceforth we let you be :
Win you the hearts of women ; and beware
Lest, where you seek the common love
 of these,
The common hate with the revolving
 wheel
Should drag you down, and some great
 Nemesis
Break from a darken'd future, crown'd
 with fire,
And tread you out forever : but howsoe'er
Fix'd in yourself, never in your own arms
To hold your own, deny not hers to her,
Give her the child ! O if, I say, you keep
One pulse that beats true woman, if you
 loved
The breast that fed or arm that dandled
 you,
Or own one part of sense not flint to prayer,
Give her the child ! or if you scorn to
 lay it,
Yourself, in hands so lately claspt with
 yours,
Or speak to her, your dearest, her one fault
The tenderness, not yours, that could
 not kill,
Give *me* it : *I* will give it her."
  He said :
At first her eye with slow dilation roll'd
Dry flame, she listening ; after sank and
 sank
And, into mournful twilight mellowing,
 dwelt
Full on the child ; she took it : " Pretty
 bud !
Lily of the vale ! half open'd bell of the
 woods !
Sole comfort of my dark hour, when a world
Of traitorous friend and broken system
 made
No purple in the distance, mystery,

Pledge of a love not to be mine, farewell ;
These men are hard upon us as of old,
We two must part : and yet how fain was I
To dream thy cause embraced in mine,
 to think
I might be something to thee, when I felt
Thy helpless warmth about my barren
 breast
In the dead prime : but may thy mother
 prove
As true to thee as false, false, false to me !
And, if thou needs must bear the yoke,
 I wish it
Gentle as freedom"—here she kiss'd it :
 then—
"All good go with thee ! take it Sir"
 and so
Laid the soft babe in his hard-mailed
 hands,
Who turn'd half-round to Psyche as she
 sprang
To meet it, with an eye that swum in
 thanks ;
Then felt it sound and whole from head
 to foot,
And hugg'd and never hugg'd it close
 enough,
And in her hunger mouth'd and mum-
 bled it,
And hid her bosom with it ; after that
Put on more calm and added suppliantly ;

"We two were friends : I go to mine
 own land
For ever : find some other : as for me
I scarce am fit for your great plans : yet
 speak to me,
Say one soft word and let me part
 forgiven."

But Ida spoke not, rapt upon the child.
Then Arac. "Ida—'sdeath ! you blame
 the man ;
You wrong yourselves — the woman is
 so hard
Upon the woman. Come, a grace to me !
I am your warrior : I and mine have fought
Your battle : kiss her ; take her hand,
 she weeps :
'Sdeath ! I would sooner fight thrice o'er
 than see it."

But Ida spoke not, gazing on the ground,
And reddening in the furrows of his
 chin,
And moved beyond his custom, Gama
 said :

"I've heard that there is iron in the blood,
And I believe it. Not one word? not one?
Whence drew you this steel temper? not from me,
Not from your mother now a saint with saints.
She said you had a heart—I heard her say it—
'Our Ida has a heart'—just ere she died—
'But see that some one with authority
Be near her still' and I—I sought for one—
All people said she had authority—
The Lady Blanche: much profit! Not one word;
No! tho' your father sues: see how you stand
Stiff as Lot's wife, and all the good knights maim'd,
I trust that there is no one hurt to death,
For your wild whim: and was it then for this,
Was it for this we gave our palace up,
Where we withdrew from summer heats and state,
And had our wine and chess beneath the planes,
And many a pleasant hour with her that's gone,
Ere you were born to vex us? Is it kind?
Speak to her I say: is this not she of whom,
When first she came, all flush'd you said to me
Now had you got a friend of your own age,
Now could you share your thought; now should men see
Two women faster welded in one love
Than pairs of wedlock; she you walk'd with, she
You talk'd with, whole nights long, up in the tower,
Of sine and arc, spheroïd and azimuth,
And right ascension, Heaven knows what; and now
A word, but one, one little kindly word,
Not one to spare her: out upon you, flint!
You love nor her, nor me, nor any; nay,
You shame your mother's judgment too. Not one?
You will not? well—no heart have you, or such
As fancies like the vermin in a nut
Have fretted all to dust and bitterness."
So said the small king moved beyond his wont.

But Ida stood nor spoke, drain'd of her force
By many a varying influence and so long.
Down thro' her limbs a drooping languor wept:
Her head a little bent; and on her mouth
A doubtful smile dwelt like a clouded moon
In a still water: then brake out my sire
Lifting his grim head from my wounds.
"O you,
Woman, whom we thought woman even now,
And were half fool'd to let you tend our son,
Because he might have wish'd it—but we see
The accomplice of your madness unforgiven,
And think that you might mix his draught with death,
When your skies change again: the rougher hand
Is safer: on to the tents: take up the Prince."

He rose, and while each ear was prick'd to attend
A tempest, thro' the cloud that dimm'd her broke
A genial warmth and light once more, and shone
Thro' glittering drops on her sad friend.
"Come hither.
O Psyche," she cried out, "embrace me, come,
Quick while I melt; make reconcilement sure
With one that cannot keep her mind an hour:
Come to the hollow heart they slander so!
Kiss and be friends, like children being chid!
I seem no more: *I* want forgiveness too:
I should have had to do with none but maids,
That have no links with men. Ah false but dear,
Dear traitor, too much loved, why?—why?—Yet see,
Before these kings we embrace you yet once more
With all forgiveness, all oblivion,
And trust, not love, you less.
And now, O sire,
Grant me your son, to nurse, to wait upon him,

Like mine own brother. For my debt to him,
This nightmare weight of gratitude, I know it;
Taunt me no more: yourself and yours shall have
Free adit; we will scatter all our maids
Till happier times each to her proper hearth:
What use to keep them here — now? grant my prayer.
Help, father, brother, help; speak to the king:
Thaw this male nature to some touch of that
Which kills me with myself, and drags me down
From my fixt height to mob me up with all
The soft and milky rabble of womankind,
Poor weakling ev'n as they are."
            Passionate tears
Follow'd: the king replied not: Cyril said:
"Your brother, Lady, — Florian, — ask for him
Of your great head — for he is wounded too —
That you may tend upon him with the prince."
"Ay so," said Ida with a bitter smile,
"Our laws are broken: let him enter too."
Then Violet, she that sang the mournful song,
And had a cousin tumbled on the plain,
Petition'd too for him. "Ay so," she said,
"I stagger in the stream: I cannot keep
My heart an eddy from the brawling hour:
We break our laws with ease, but let it be."
"Ay so?" said Blanche: "Amazed am I to hear
Your Highness: but your Highness breaks with ease
The law your Highness did not make: 't was I.
I had been wedded wife, I knew mankind,
And block'd them out; but these men came to woo
Your Highness — verily I think to win."

  So she, and turn'd askance a wintry eye:
But Ida with a voice, that like a bell
Toll'd by an earthquake in a trembling tower,
Rang ruin, answer'd full of grief and scorn.

"Fling our doors wide! all, all, not one, but all,
Not only he, but by my mother's soul,
Whatever man lies wounded, friend or foe,
Shall enter, if he will. Let our girls flit,
Till the storm die! but had you stood by us,
The roar that breaks the Pharos from his base
Had left us rock. She fain would sting us too,
But shall not. Pass, and mingle with your likes.
We brook no further insult but are gone."

  She turn'd; the very nape of her white neck
Was rosed with indignation: but the Prince
Her brother came; the king her father charm'd
Her wounded soul with words: nor did mine own
Refuse her proffer, lastly gave his hand.
Then us they lifted up, dead weights, and bare
Straight to the doors: to them the doors gave way
Groaning, and in the Vestal entry shriek'd
The virgin marble under iron heels:
And on they moved and gain'd the hall, and there
Rested: but great the crush was, and each base,
To left and right, of those tall columns drown'd
In silken fluctuation and the swarm
Of female whisperers: at the further end
Was Ida by the throne, the two great cats
Close by her, like supporters on a shield,
Bow-back'd with fear: but in the centre stood
The common men with rolling eyes; amazed
They glared upon the women, and aghast
The women stared at these, all silent, save
When armor clash'd or jingled, while the day,
Descending, struck athwart the hall, and shot
A flying splendor out of brass and steel,
That o'er the statues leapt from head to head,
Now fired an angry Pallas on the helm,
Now set a wrathful Dian's moon on flame,
And now and then an echo started up,

And shuddering fled from room to room,
 and died
Of fright in far apartments.
 Then the voice
Of Ida sounded, issuing ordinance:
And me they bore up the broad stairs,
 and thro'
The long-laid galleries past a hundred
 doors
To one deep chamber shut from sound,
 and due
To languid limbs and sickness; left me
 in it;
And others otherwhere they laid; and all
That afternoon a sound arose of hoof
And chariot, many a maiden passing home
Till happier times; but some were left
 of those
Held sagest, and the great lords out and in,
From those two hosts that lay beside the
 walls,
Walk'd at their will, and everything was
 changed.

Ask me no more: the moon may draw
 the sea;
 The cloud may stoop from heaven and
 take the shape,
 With fold to fold, of mountain or of cape;
But O too fond, when have I answer'd thee?
 Ask me no more.

Ask me no more: what answer should I
 give?
 I love not hollow cheek or faded eye:
 Yet, O my friend, I will not have thee
 die!
Ask me no more, lest I should bid thee live;
 Ask me no more.

Ask me no more: thy fate and mine are
 seal'd:
 I strove against the stream and all in
 vain:
 Let the great river take me to the
 main:
No more, dear love, for at a touch I yield;
 Ask me no more.

VII.

So was their sanctuary violated,
So their fair college turn'd to hospital;
At first with all confusion: by and by
Sweet order lived again with other laws:

A kindlier influence reign'd; and every-
 where
Low voices with the ministering hand
Hung round the sick: the maidens came,
 they talk'd,
They sang, they read: till she not fair,
 began
To gather light, and she that was, became
Her former beauty treble, and to and fro
With books, with flowers, with Angel of-
 fices,
Like creatures native unto gracious act,
And in their own clear element, they
 moved.

But sadness on the soul of Ida fell,
And hatred of her weakness, blent with
 shame.
Old studies fail'd; seldom she spoke;
 but oft
Clomb to the roofs, and gazed alone for
 hours
On that disastrous leaguer, swarms of men
Darkening her female field: void was
 her use,
And she as one that climbs a peak to gaze
O'er land and main, and sees a great black
 cloud
Drag inward from the deeps, a wall of
 night,
Blot out the slope of sea from verge to
 shore,
And suck the blinding splendor from the
 sand,
And quenching lake by lake and tarn by
 tarn
Expunge the world: so fared she gazing
 there;
So blacken'd all her world in secret, blank
And waste it seem'd and vain; till down
 she came,
And found fair peace once more among
 the sick.

And twilight dawn'd; and morn by
 morn the lark
Shot up and shrill'd in flickering gyres,
 but I
Lay silent in the muffled cage of life:
And twilight gloom'd; and broader-
 grown the bowers
Drew the great night into themselves,
 and Heaven,
Star after star, arose and fell; but I,
Deeper than those weird doubts could
 reach me, lay
Quite sunder'd from the moving Universe,

Nor knew what eye was on me, nor the hand
That nursed me, more than infants in their sleep.

But Psyche tended Florian: with her oft,
Melissa came; for Blanche had gone, but left
Her child among us, willing she should keep
Court-favor: here and there the small bright head,
A light of healing, glanced about the couch,
Or thro' the parted silks the tender face
Peep'd, shining in upon the wounded man
With blush and smile, a medicine in themselves
To wile the length from languorous hours, and draw
The sting from pain; nor seem'd it strange that soon
He rose up whole, and those fair charities
Join'd at her side; nor stranger seem'd that hearts
So gentle, so employ'd, should close in love,
Than when two dewdrops on the petal shake
To the same sweet air, and tremble deeper down,
And slip at once all-fragrant into one.

Less prosperously the second suit obtain'd
At first with Psyche. Not tho' Blanche had sworn
That after that dark night among the fields,
She needs must wed him for her own good name;
Not tho' he built upon the babe restored;
Nor tho' she liked him, yielded she, but fear'd
To incense the Head once more; till on a day
When Cyril pleaded, Ida came behind
Seen but of Psyche: on her foot she hung
A moment, and she heard, at which her face
A little flush'd, and she past on; but each
Assumed from thence a half-consent involved
In stillness, plighted troth, and were at peace.

Nor only these: Love in the sacred halls
Held carnival at will, and flying struck
With showers of random sweet on maid and man.
Nor did her father cease to press my claim,
Nor did mine own now reconciled; nor yet
Did those twin brothers, risen again and whole;
Nor Arac, satiate with his victory.

But I lay still, and with me oft she sat:
Then came a change; for sometimes I would catch
Her hand in wild delirium, gripe it hard,
And fling it like a viper off, and shriek
"You are not Ida"; clasp it once again,
And call her Ida, tho' I knew her not,
And call her sweet, as if in irony,
And call her hard and cold which seem'd a truth:
And still she fear'd that I should lose my mind,
And often she believed that I should die:
Till out of long frustration of her care,
And pensive tendance in the all-weary noons,
And watches in the dead, the dark, when clocks
Throbb'd thunder thro' the palace floors, or call'd
On flying Time from all their silver tongues —
And out of memories of her kindlier days,
And sidelong glances at my father's grief,
And at the happy lovers heart in heart —
And out of hauntings of my spoken love,
And lonely listenings to my mutter'd dream,
And often feeling of the helpless hands,
And wordless broodings on the wasted cheek —
From all a closer interest flourish'd up,
Tenderness touch by touch, and last, to these,
Love, like an Alpine harebell hung with tears
By some cold morning glacier; frail at first
And feeble, all unconscious of itself,
But such as gather'd color day by day.

Last I woke sane, but wellnigh close to death
For weakness: it was evening: silent light

Slept on the painted walls, wherein were wrought
Two grand designs; for on one side arose
The women up in wild revolt, and storm'd
At the Oppian law. Titanic shapes, they cramm'd
The forum, and half-crush'd among the rest
A dwarf-like Cato cower'd. On the other side
Hortensia spoke against the tax; behind,
A train of dames: by axe and eagle sat,
With all their foreheads drawn in Roman scowls,
And half the wolf's-milk curdled in their veins,
The fierce triumvirs; and before them paused
Hortensia, pleading: angry was her face.

I saw the forms: I knew not where I was:
They did but look like hollow shows; nor more
Sweet Ida: palm to palm she sat: the dew
Dwelt in her eyes, and softer all her shape
And rounder seem'd: I moved: I sigh'd: a touch
Came round my wrist, and tears upon my hand:
Then all for languor and self-pity ran
Mine down my face, and with what life I had,
And like a flower that cannot all unfold,
So drench'd it is with tempest, to the sun,
Yet, as it may, turns toward him, I on her
Fixt my faint eyes, and utter'd whisperingly:

"If you be, what I think you, some sweet dream,
I would but ask you to fulfil yourself:
But if you be that Ida whom I knew,
I ask you nothing: only, if a dream,
Sweet dream, be perfect. I shall die to-night.
Stoop down and seem to kiss me ere I die."

I could no more, but lay like one in trance,
That hears his burial talk'd of by his friends,
And cannot speak, nor move, nor make one sign,
But lies and dreads his doom. She turn'd; she paused;
She stoop'd; and out of languor leapt a cry;

Leapt fiery Passion from the brinks of death;
And I believed that in the living world
My spirit closed with Ida's at the lips;
Till back I fell, and from mine arms she rose
Glowing all over noble shame; and all
Her falser self slipt from her like a robe,
And left her woman, lovelier in her mood
Than in her mould that other, when she came
From barren deeps to conquer all with love;
And down the streaming crystal dropt; and she
Far-fleeted by the purple island-sides,
Naked, a double light in air and wave,
To meet her Graces, where they deck'd her out
For worship without end; nor end of mine,
Stateliest, for thee! but mute she glided forth,
Nor glanced behind her, and I sank and slept,
Fill'd thro' and thro' with Love, a happy sleep.

Deep in the night I woke: she, near me, held
A volume of the Poets of her land:
There to herself, all in low tones, she read.

"Now sleeps the crimson petal, now the white;
Nor waves the cypress in the palace walk;
Nor winks the gold fin in the porphyry font:
The fire-fly wakens: waken thou with me.

"Now droops the milkwhite peacock like a ghost,
And like a ghost she glimmers on to me.

"Now lies the Earth all Danaë to the stars,
And all thy heart lies open unto me.

"Now slides the silent meteor on, and leaves
A shining furrow, as thy thoughts in me.

"Now folds the lily all her sweetness up,
And slips into the bosom of the lake:
So fold thyself, my dearest, thou, and slip
Into my bosom and be lost in me."

> "Come down, O maid, from yonder mountain height:
> What pleasure lives in height (the shepherd sang)
> In height and cold, the splendor of the hills?"

I heard her turn the page; she found a small
Sweet Idyl, and once more, as low, she read:

"Come down, O maid, from yonder mountain height:
What pleasure lives in height (the shepherd sang)
In height and cold, the splendor of the hills?
But cease to move so near the Heavens, and cease
To glide a sunbeam by the blasted Pine,
To sit a star upon the sparkling spire;
And come, for Love is of the valley, come,
For Love is of the valley, come thou down
And find him; by the happy threshold, he,
Or hand in hand with Plenty in the maize,
Or red with spirted purple of the vats,
Or foxlike in the vine; nor cares to walk
With Death and Morning on the silver horns,
Nor wilt thou snare him in the white ravine,
Nor find him dropt upon the firths of ice,
That huddling slant in furrow-cloven falls
To roll the torrent out of dusky doors:
But follow; let the torrent dance thee down
To find him in the valley; let the wild
Lean-headed Eagles yelp alone, and leave
The monstrous ledges there to slope, and spill
Their thousand wreaths of dangling water-smoke,
That like a broken purpose waste in air:
So waste not thou; but come; for all the vales

Await thee, azure pillars of the hearth
Arise to thee; the children call, and I
Thy shepherd pipe, and sweet is every sound,
Sweeter thy voice, but every sound is sweet;
Myriads of rivulets hurrying thro' the lawn,
The moan of doves in immemorial elms,
And murmuring of innumerable bees."

So she low-toned; while with shut eyes I lay
Listening; then look'd. Pale was the perfect face;
The bosom with long sighs labor'd; and meek
Seem'd the full lips, and mild the luminous eyes,
And the voice trembled and the hand. She said
Brokenly, that she knew it, she had fail'd
In sweet humility; had fail'd in all;
That all her labor was but as a block
Left in the quarry; but she still were loath,
She still were loath to yield herself to one,
That wholly scorn'd to help their equal rights
Against the sons of men, and barbarous laws.
She pray'd me not to judge their cause from her
That wrong'd it, sought far less for truth than power
In knowledge: something wild within her breast,
A greater than all knowledge, beat her down.
And she had nursed me there from week to week:
Much had she learnt in little time. In part
It was ill counsel had misled the girl
To vex true hearts: yet was she but a girl—
"Ah fool, and made myself a Queen of farce!
When comes another such? never, I think,
Till the Sun drop dead from the signs."
Her voice
Choked, and her forehead sank upon her hands,
And her great heart thro' all the faultful Past
Went sorrowing in a pause I dared not break;
Till notice of a change in the dark world
Was lispt about the acacias, and a bird,
That early woke to feed her little ones,
Sent from a dewy breast a cry for light:
She moved, and at her feet the volume fell.

"Blame not thyself too much," I said,
"nor blame
Too much the sons of men and barbarous laws;
These were the rough ways of the world till now.
Henceforth thou hast a helper, me, that know
The woman's cause is man's: they rise or sink
Together, dwarf'd or godlike, bond or free:
For she that out of Lethe scales with man
The shining steps of Nature, shares with man
His nights, his days, moves with him to one goal,
Stays all the fair young planet in her hands—
If she be small, slight-natured, miserable,
How shall men grow? but work no more alone!
Our place is much: as far as in us lies
We two will serve them both in aiding her—
Will clear away the parasitic forms
That seem to keep her up but drag her down—
Will leave her space to burgeon out of all
Within her—let her make herself her own
To give or keep, to live and learn and be
All that not harms distinctive womanhood.
For woman is not undevelopt man,
But diverse: could we make her as the man,
Sweet Love were slain: his dearest bond is this,
Not like to like, but like in difference.
Yet in the long years liker must they grow;
The man be more of woman, she of man;
He gain in sweetness and in moral height,
Nor lose the wrestling thews that throw the world;
She mental breadth, nor fail in childward care,
Nor lose the childlike in the larger mind;
Till at the last she set herself to man,
Like perfect music unto noble words;
And so these twain, upon the skirts of Time,
Sit side by side, full-summ'd in all their powers,
Dispensing harvest, sowing the To-be,

Self-reverent each and reverencing each,
Distinct in individualities,
But like each other ev'n as those who love.
Then comes the statelier Eden back to
  men:
Then reign the world's great bridals,
  chaste and calm:
Then springs the crowning race of hu-
  mankind.
May these things be!"
            Sighing she spoke "I fear
They will not."
    "Dear, but let us type them now
In our own lives, and this proud watch-
  word rest
Of equal; seeing either sex alone
Is half itself, and in true marriage lies
Nor equal, nor unequal: each fulfils
Defect in each, and always thought in
  thought,
Purpose in purpose, will in will, they grow,
The single pure and perfect animal,
The two-cell'd heart beating, with one
  full stroke,
Life."
    And again sighing she spoke: "A dream
That once was mine! what woman taught
  you this?"

"Alone" I said "from earlier than I
  know,
Immersed in rich foreshadowings of the
  world,
I loved the woman: he, that doth not, lives
A drowning life, besotted in sweet self,
Or pines in sad experience worse than
  death,
Or keeps his wing'd affections clipt with
  crime:
Yet was there one thro' whom I loved
  her, one
Not learned, save in gracious household
  ways,
Not perfect, nay, but full of tender wants,
No Angel, but a dearer being, all dipt
In Angel instincts, breathing Paradise,
Interpreter between the Gods and men,
Who look'd all native to her place, and yet
On tiptoe seem'd to touch upon a sphere
Too gross to tread, and all male minds
  perforce
Sway'd to her from their orbits as they
  moved,
And girdled her with music Happy he
With such a mother! faith in womankind
Beats with his blood, and trust in all
  things high

Comes easy to him, and tho' he trip and
  fall .
He shall not blind his soul with clay."
                              "But I,"
Said Ida, tremulously, "so all unlike—
It seems you love to cheat yourself with
  words:
This mother is your model. I have heard
Of your strange doubts: they well might
  be: I seem
A mockery to my own self. Never, Prince;
You cannot love me."
            "Nay but thee" I said
"From yearlong poring on thy pictured
  eyes,
Ere seen I loved, and loved thee seen,
  and saw
Thee woman thro' the crust of iron moods
That mask'd thee from men's reverence
  up, and forced
Sweet love on pranks of saucy boyhood:
  now,
Giv'n back to life, to life indeed, thro'
  thee,
Indeed I love: the new day comes, the
  light
Dearer for night, as dearer thou for faults
Lived over: lift thine eyes; my doubts
  are dead,
My haunting sense of hollow shows: the
  change,
This truthful change in thee has kill'd it.
  Dear,
Look up, and let thy nature strike on mine,
Like yonder morning on the blind half-
  world;
Approach and fear not; breathe upon my
  brows;
In that fine air I tremble, all the past
Melts mist-like into this bright hour, and
  this
Is morn to more, and all the rich to-come
Reels, as the golden Autumn woodland
  reels
Athwart the smoke of burning weeds.
  Forgive me,
I waste my heart in signs: let be. My
  bride,
My wife, my life. O we will walk this
  world,
Yoked in all exercise of noble end,
And so thro' those dark gates across the
  wild
That no man knows. Indeed I love thee:
  come,
Yield thyself up: my hopes and thine
  are one:

Accomplish thou my manhood and thyself;
Lay thy sweet hands in mine and trust to me."

CONCLUSION.

So closed our tale, of which I give you all
The random scheme as wildly as it rose:
The words are mostly mine; for when we ceased
There came a minute's pause, and Walter said,
"I wish she had not yielded!" then to me,
"What, if you drest it up poetically!"
So pray'd the men, the women: I gave assent:
Yet how to bind the scattered scheme of seven
Together in one sheaf? What style could suit?
The men required that I should give throughout
The sort of mock-heroic gigantesque,
With which we banter'd little Lilia first:
The women — and perhaps they felt their power,
For something in the ballads which they sang,
Or in their silent influence as they sat,
Had ever seem'd to wrestle with burlesque,
And drove us, last, to quite a solemn close —
They hated banter, wish'd for something real,
A gallant fight, a noble princess — why
Not make her true-heroic — true-sublime?
Or all, they said, as earnest as the close?
Which yet with such a framework scarce could be.
Then rose a little feud betwixt the two,
Betwixt the mockers and the realists:
And I, betwixt them both, to please them both,
And yet to give the story as it rose,
I moved as in a strange diagonal,
And maybe neither pleased myself nor them.

But Lilia pleased me, for she took no part
In our dispute: the sequel of the tale
Had touch'd her; and she sat, she pluck'd the grass,
She flung it from her, thinking: last, she fixt

A showery glance upon her aunt, and said,
"You — tell us what we are" who might have told,
For she was cramm'd with theories out of books,
But that there rose a shout: the gates were closed
At sunset, and the crowd were swarming now,
To take their leave, about the garden rails.

So I and some went out to these: we climb'd
The slope to Vivian-place, and turning saw
The happy valleys, half in light, and half
Far-shadowing from the west, a land of peace;
Gray halls alone among their massive groves;
Trim hamlets; here and there a rustic tower
Half-lost in belts of hop and breadths of wheat;
The shimmering glimpses of a stream; the seas;
A red sail, or a white; and far beyond,
Imagined more than seen, the skirts of France.

"Look there, a garden!" said my college friend,
The Tory member's elder son "and there!
God bless the narrow sea which keeps her off,
And keeps our Britain, whole within herself,
A nation yet, the rulers and the ruled —
Some sense of duty, something of a faith,
Some reverence for the laws ourselves have made,
Some patient force to change them when we will,
Some civic manhood firm against the crowd —
But yonder, whiff! there comes a sudden heat,
The gravest citizen seems to lose his head,
The king is scared, the soldier will not fight,
The little boys begin to shoot and stab,
A kingdom topples over with a shriek
Like an old woman, and down rolls the world
In mock heroics stranger than our own;
Revolts, republics, revolutions, most
No graver than a schoolboys' barring out;
Too comic for the solemn things they are,

Too solemn for the comic touches in them,
Like our wild Princess with as wise a dream
As some of theirs — God bless the narrow
    seas !
I wish they were a whole Atlantic broad."

"Have patience," I replied, "ourselves
    are full
Of social wrong; and maybe wildest
    dreams
Are but the needful preludes of the truth :
For me, the genial day, the happy crowd,
The sport half-science, fill me with a faith,
This fine old world of ours is but a child
Yet in the go-cart. Patience ! Give it
    time
To learn its limbs : there is a hand that
    guides."

In such discourse we gain'd the gar-
    den rails,
And there we saw Sir Walter where he
    stood,
Before a tower of crimson holly-oaks,
Among six boys, head under head, and
    look'd
No little lily-handed Baronet he,
A great broad-shoulder'd genial English-
    man,
A lord of fat prize-oxen and of sheep,
A raiser of huge melons and of pine,
A patron of some thirty charities,
A pamphleteer on guano and on grain,
A quarter-sessions chairman, abler none ;
Fair-hair'd and redder than a windy morn ;
Now shaking hands with him, now him,
    of those
That stood the nearest — now address'd
    to speech —
Who spoke few words and pithy, such
    as closed

Welcome, farewell, and welcome for the
    year
To follow : a shout rose again, and made
The long line of the approaching rook-
    ery swerve
From the elms, and shook the branches
    of the deer
From slope to slope thro' distant ferns,
    and rang
Beyond the bourn of sunset ; O, a shout
More joyful than the city-roar that hails
Premier or king ! Why should not these
    great Sirs
Give up their parks some dozen times a
    year
To let the people breathe ? So thrice they
    cried,
I likewise, and in groups they stream'd
    away.

But we went back to the Abbey, and
    sat on,
So much the gathering darkness charm'd :
    we sat
But spoke not, rapt in nameless revery,
Perchance upon the future man : the walls
Blacken'd about us, bats wheel'd, and owls
    whoop'd,
And gradually the powers of the night,
That range above the region of the wind,
Deepening the courts of twilight broke
    them up
Thro' all the silent spaces of the worlds,
Beyond all thought into the Heaven of
    Heavens.

Last little Lilia, rising quietly,
Disrobed the glimmering statue of Sir
    Ralph
From those rich silks, and home well-
    pleased we went.

IN MEMORIAM.

STRONG Son of God, immortal Love,
  Whom we, that have not seen thy face,
  By faith, and faith alone, embrace,
Believing where we cannot prove;

Thine are these orbs of light and shade;
  Thou madest Life in man and brute;
  Thou madest Death; and lo, thy foot
Is on the skull which thou hast made.

Thou wilt not leave us in the dust:
  Thou madest man, he knows not why;
  He thinks he was not made to die;
And thou hast made him: thou art just.

Thou seemest human and divine,
  The highest, holiest manhood, thou:
  Our wills are ours, we know not how;
Our wills are ours, to make them thine.

Our little systems have their day;
  They have their day and cease to be:
  They are but broken lights of thee,
And thou, O Lord, art more than they.

We have but faith: we cannot know;
  For knowledge is of things we see;
  And yet we trust it comes from thee,
A beam in darkness: let it grow.

Let knowledge grow from more to more,
  But more of reverence in us dwell;
  That mind and soul, according well,
May make one music as before,

But vaster. We are fools and slight;
  We mock thee when we do not fear:
  But help thy foolish ones to bear;
Help thy vain worlds to bear thy light.

Forgive what seem'd my sin in me;
  What seem'd my worth since I began;
  For merit lives from man to man,
And not from man, O Lord, to thee.

Forgive my grief for one removed,
  Thy creature, whom I found so fair.
  I trust he lives in thee, and there
I find him worthier to be loved.

Forgive these wild and wandering cries,
  Confusions of a wasted youth;
  Forgive them where they fail in truth,
And in thy wisdom make me wise.

IN MEMORIAM.
A. H. H.
OBIIT MDCCCXXXIII.

I.

I HELD it truth, with him who sings
  To one clear harp in divers tones,
  That men may rise on stepping-stones
Of their dead selves to higher things.

But who shall so forecast the years
  And find in loss a gain to match?
  Or reach a hand thro' time to catch
The far-off interest of tears?

Let Love clasp Grief lest both be drown'd,
  Let darkness keep her raven gloss:
  Ah, sweeter to be drunk with loss,
To dance with death, to beat the ground,

Than that the victor Hours should scorn
  The long result of love, and boast,
  "Behold the man that loved and lost,
But all he was is overworn."

II.

OLD Yew, which graspest at the stones
  That name the under-lying dead,
  Thy fibres net the dreamless head,
Thy roots are wrapt about the bones.

The seasons bring the flower again,
  And bring the firstling to the flock;
  And in the dusk of thee, the clock
Beats out the little lives of men.

O not for thee the glow, the bloom,
  Who changest not in any gale,
  Nor branding summer suns avail
To touch thy thousand years of gloom:

And gazing on thee, sullen tree,
  Sick for thy stubborn hardihood,
  I seem to fail from out my blood
And grow incorporate into thee.

III.

O SORROW, cruel fellowship,
  O Priestess in the vaults of Death,
  O sweet and bitter in a breath,
What whispers from thy lying lip?

"The stars," she whispers, "blindly run;
  A web is wov'n across the sky;
  From out waste places comes a cry,
And murmurs from the dying sun:

"And all the phantom, Nature, stands—
  With all the music in her tone,
  A hollow echo of my own,—
A hollow form with empty hands."

And shall I take a thing so blind,
  Embrace her as my natural good;
  Or crush her, like a vice of blood,
Upon the threshold of the mind?

IV.

To Sleep I give my powers away;
  My will is bondsman to the dark;
  I sit within a helmless bark,
And with my heart I muse and say:

O heart, how fares it with thee now,
  That thou shouldst fail from thy desire,
  Who scarcely darest to inquire,
"What is it makes me beat so low?"

Something it is which thou hast lost,
  Some pleasure from thine early years.
  Break, thou deep vase of chilling tears,
That grief hath shaken into frost!

Such clouds of nameless trouble cross
  All night below the darken'd eyes;
  With morning wakes the will, and cries,
"Thou shalt not be the fool of loss."

V.

I SOMETIMES hold it half a sin
  To put in words the grief I feel;
  For words, like Nature, half reveal
And half conceal the Soul within.

But, for the unquiet heart and brain,
  A use in measured language lies;
  The sad mechanic exercise,
Like dull narcotics, numbing pain.

In words, like weeds, I'll wrap me o'er,
  Like coarsest clothes against the cold;
  But that large grief which these enfold
Is given in outline and no more.

VI.

ONE writes, that "Other friends remain,"
  That "Loss is common to the race"—
  And common is the commonplace,
And vacant chaff well meant for grain.

That loss is common would not make
  My own less bitter, rather more:
  Too common! Never morning wore
To evening, but some heart did break.

O father, wheresoe'er thou be,
  Who pledgest now thy gallant son;
  A shot, ere half thy draught be done,
Hath still'd the life that beat from thee.

O mother, praying God will save
  Thy sailor,—while thy head is bow'd,
  His heavy-shotted hammock-shroud
Drops in his vast and wandering grave.

Ye know no more than I who wrought
  At that last hour to please him well;
  Who mused on all I had to tell,
And something written, something thought;

Expecting still his advent home;
  And ever met him on his way
  With wishes, thinking, here to-day,
Or here to-morrow will he come.

O somewhere, meek unconscious dove,
  That sittest ranging golden hair;
  And glad to find thyself so fair,
Poor child, that waitest for thy love!

For now her father's chimney glows
  In expectation of a guest;
  And thinking "this will please him best,"
She takes a riband or a rose;

For he will see them on to-night;
  And with the thought her color burns;
  And, having left the glass, she turns
Once more to set a ringlet right;

And, even when she turn'd, the curse
  Had fallen, and her future Lord
  Was drown'd in passing thro' the ford,
Or kill'd in falling from his horse.

O what to her shall be the end?
  And what to me remains of good?
  To her, perpetual maidenhood,
And unto me no second friend.

VII.

DARK house, by which once more I stand
  Here in the long unlovely street,
  Doors, where my heart was used to beat
So quickly, waiting for a hand,

A hand that can be clasp'd no more, —
  Behold me, for I cannot sleep,
  And like a guilty thing I creep
At earliest morning to the door.

He is not here ; but far away
  The noise of life begins again,
  And ghastly thro' the drizzling rain
On the bald street breaks the blank day.

VIII.

A HAPPY lover who has come
  To look on her that loves him well,
  Who 'lights and rings the gateway bell,
And learns her gone and far from home ;

He saddens, all the magic light
  Dies off at once from bower and hall,
  And all the place is dark, and all
The chambers emptied of delight :

So find I every pleasant spot
  In which we two were wont to meet,
  The field, the chamber, and the street,
For all is dark where thou art not.

Yet as that other, wandering there
  In those deserted walks, may find
  A flower beat with rain and wind,
Which once she foster'd up with care ;

So seems it in my deep regret,
  O my forsaken heart, with thee
  And this poor flower of poesy
Which little cared for fades not yet.

But since it pleased a vanish'd eye,
  I go to plant it on his tomb,
  That if it can it there may bloom,
Or dying, there at least may die.

IX.

FAIR ship, that from the Italian shore
  Sailest the placid ocean-plains
  With my lost Arthur's loved remains,
Spread thy full wings, and waft him o'er.

So draw him home to those that mourn
  In vain ; a favorable speed
  Ruffle thy mirror'd mast, and lead
Thro' prosperous floods his holy urn.

All night no ruder air perplex
  Thy sliding keel, till Phosphor, bright
  As our pure love, thro' early light
Shall glimmer on the dewy decks.

Sphere all your lights around, above ;
  Sleep, gentle heavens, before the prow ;
  Sleep, gentle winds, as he sleeps now,
My friend, the brother of my love ;

My Arthur, whom I shall not see
  Till all my widow'd race be run ;
  Dear as the mother to the son,
More than my brothers are to me.

X.

I HEAR the noise about thy keel ;
  I hear the bell struck in the night ;
  I see the cabin-window bright ;
I see the sailor at the wheel.

Thou bringest the sailor to his wife,
  And travell'd men from foreign lands ;
  And letters unto trembling hands ;
And, thy dark freight, a vanish'd life.

So bring him : we have idle dreams :
  This look of quiet flatters thus
  Our home-bred fancies : O to us,
The fools of habit, sweeter seems

To rest beneath the clover sod,
  That takes the sunshine and the rains,
  Or where the kneeling hamlet drains
The chalice of the grapes of God ;

Than if with thee the roaring wells
  Should gulf him fathom-deep in brine ;
  And hands so often clasp'd in mine,
Should toss with tangle and with shells.

XI.

CALM is the morn without a sound,
  Calm as to suit a calmer grief,
  And only thro' the faded leaf
The chestnut pattering to the ground :

Calm and deep peace on this 'high wold,
  And on these dews that drench the furze,
  And all the silvery gossamers
That twinkle into green and gold :

Calm and still light on yon great plain
  That sweeps with all its autumn bowers,
  And crowded farms and lessening
    towers,
To mingle with the bounding main :

Calm and deep peace in this wide air,
  These leaves that redden to the fall ;
  And in my heart, if calm at all,
If any calm, a calm despair :

*"Fair ship, that from the Italian shore
Sailest the placid ocean-plains."*

Calm on the seas, and silver sleep,
  And waves that sway themselves in rest,
  And dead calm in that noble breast
Which heaves but with the heaving deep.

XII.

Lo, as a dove when up she springs
  To bear thro' Heaven a tale of woe,
  Some dolorous message knit below
The wild pulsation of her wings;

Like her I go; I cannot stay;
  I leave this mortal ark behind,
  A weight of nerves without a mind,
And leave the cliffs, and haste away

O'er ocean-mirrors rounded large,
  And reach the glow of southern skies,
  And see the sails at distance rise,
And linger weeping on the marge,

And saying; "Comes he thus, my friend?
  Is this the end of all my care?"
  And circle moaning in the air:
"Is this the end? Is this the end?"

And forward dart again, and play
  About the prow, and back return
  To where the body sits, and learn,
That I have been an hour away.

XIII.

TEARS of the widower, when he sees
  A late-lost form that sleep reveals,
  And moves his doubtful arms, and feels
Her place is empty, fall like these;

Which weep a loss for ever new,
  A void where heart on heart reposed;
  And, where warm hands have prest and
    closed,
Silence, till I be silent too.

Which weep the comrade of my choice,
  An awful thought, a life removed,
  The human-hearted man I loved,
A Spirit, not a breathing voice.

Come Time, and teach me, many years,
  I do not suffer in a dream;

For now so strange do these things seem,
Mine eyes have leisure for their tears;

My fancies time to rise on wing,
  And glance about the approaching sails,
  As tho' they brought but merchants' bales,
And not the burden that they bring.

XIV.

If one should bring me this report,
  That thou hadst touch'd the land to-day,
  And I went down unto the quay,
And found thee lying in the port;

And standing, muffled round with woe,
  Should see thy passengers in rank
  Come stepping lightly down the plank,
And beckoning unto those they know;

And if along with these should come
  The man I held as half-divine;
  Should strike a sudden hand in mine,
And ask a thousand things of home;

And I should tell him all my pain,
  And how my life had droop'd of late,
  And he should sorrow o'er my state
And marvel what possess'd my brain;

And I perceived no touch of change,
  No hint of death in all his frame,
  But found him all in all the same,
I should not feel it to be strange.

XV.

To-night the winds begin to rise
  And roar from yonder dropping day:
  The last red leaf is whirl'd away,
The rooks are blown about the skies;

The forest crack'd, the waters curl'd,
  The cattle huddled on the lea;
  And wildly dash'd on tower and tree
The sunbeam strikes along the world:

And but for fancies, which aver
  That all thy motions gently pass
  Athwart a plane of molten glass,
I scarce could brook the strain and stir

That makes the barren branches loud;
  And but for fear it is not so,
  The wild unrest that lives in woe
Would dote and pore on yonder cloud

That rises upward always higher,
  And onward drags a laboring breast,
  And topples round the dreary west,
A looming bastion fringed with fire.

XVI.

What words are these have fall'n from me?
  Can calm despair and wild unrest
  Be tenants of a single breast,
Or sorrow such a changeling be?

Or doth she only seem to take
  The touch of change in calm or storm;
  But knows no more of transient form
In her deep self, than some dead lake

That holds the shadow of a lark
  Hung in the shadow of a heaven?
  Or has the shock, so harshly given,
Confused me like the unhappy bark

That strikes by night a craggy shelf,
  And staggers blindly ere she sink?
  And stunn'd me from my power to think
And all my knowledge of myself;

And made me that delirious man
  Whose fancy fuses old and new,
  And flashes into false and true,
And mingles all without a plan?

XVII.

Thou comest, much wept for: such a breeze
  Compell'd thy canvas, and my prayer
  Was as the whisper of an air
To breathe thee over lonely seas.

For I in spirit saw thee move
  Thro' circles of the bounding sky,
  Week after week: the days go by:
Come quick, thou bringest all I love.

Henceforth, wherever thou mayst roam,
  My blessing, like a line of light,
  Is on the waters day and night,
And like a beacon guards thee home.

So may whatever tempest mars
  Mid-ocean, spare thee, sacred bark;
  And balmy drops in summer dark
Slide from the bosom of the stars.

So kind an office hath been done,
  Such precious relics brought by thee;
  The dust of him I shall not see
Till all my widow'd race be run.

XVIII.

'T is well; 't is something; we may stand
  Where he in English earth is laid,
  And from his ashes may be made
The violet of his native land.

'T is little; but it looks in truth
  As if the quiet bones were blest
  Among familiar names to rest
And in the places of his youth.

Come then, pure hands, and bear the head
  That sleeps or wears the mask of sleep,
  And come, whatever loves to weep,
And hear the ritual of the dead.

Ah yet, ev'n yet, if this might be,
  I, falling on his faithful heart,
  Would breathing thro' his lips impart
The life that almost dies in me;

That dies not, but endures with pain,
  And slowly forms the firmer mind,
  Treasuring the look it cannot find,
The words that are not heard again.

XIX.

The Danube to the Severn gave
  The darken'd heart that beat no more;
  They laid him by the pleasant shore,
And in the hearing of the wave.

There twice a day the Severn fills;
  The salt sea-water passes by,
  And hushes half the babbling Wye,
And makes a silence in the hills.

The Wye is hush'd nor moved along,
  And hush'd my deepest grief of all,
  When fill'd with tears that cannot fall,
I brim with sorrow drowning song.

The tide flows down, the wave again
  Is vocal in its wooded walls;
  My deeper anguish also falls,
And I can speak a little then.

XX.

The lesser griefs that may be said,
  That breathe a thousand tender vows,
  Are but as servants in a house
Where lies the master newly dead;

Who speak their feeling as it is,
  And weep the fulness from the mind:
  "It will be hard," they say, "to find
Another service such as this."

My lighter moods are like to these,
  That out of words a comfort win;
  But there are other griefs within,
And tears that at their fountain freeze;

For by the hearth the children sit
  Cold in that atmosphere of Death,
  And scarce endure to draw the breath,
Or like to noiseless phantoms flit:

But open converse is there none,
  So much the vital spirits sink
  To see the vacant chair, and think,
"How good! how kind! and he is gone."

XXI.

I sing to him that rests below,
  And, since the grasses round me wave,
  I take the grasses of the grave,
And make them pipes whereon to blow.

The traveller hears me now and then,
  And sometimes harshly will he speak;
  "This fellow would make weakness weak,
And melt the waxen hearts of men."

Another answers, "Let him be,
  He loves to make parade of pain,
  That with his piping he may gain
The praise that comes to constancy."

A third is wroth, "Is this an hour
  For private sorrow's barren song,
  When more and more the people throng
The chairs and thrones of civil power?

"A time to sicken and to swoon,
  When Science reaches forth her arms
  To feel from world to world, and charms
Her secret from the latest moon?"

Behold, ye speak an idle thing:
  Ye never knew the sacred dust:
  I do but sing because I must,
And pipe but as the linnets sing:

And one is glad; her note is gay,
  For now her little ones have ranged;
  And one is sad; her note is changed,
Because her brood is stol'n away.

XXII.

The path by which we twain did go,
  Which led by tracts that pleased us well,
  Thro' four sweet years arose and fell,
From flower to flower, from snow to snow:

And we with singing cheer'd the way,
  And, crown'd with all the season lent,
  From April on to April went,
And glad at heart from May to May:

But where the path we walk'd began
  To slant the fifth autumnal slope,
  As we descended following Hope,
There sat the Shadow fear'd of man;

Who broke our fair companionship,
  And spread his mantle dark and cold,
  And wrapt thee formless in the fold,
And dull'd the murmur on thy lip,

And bore thee where I could not see
  Nor follow, tho' I walk in haste,
  And think that somewhere in the waste
The Shadow sits and waits for me.

XXIII.

Now, sometimes in my sorrow shut,
  Or breaking into song by fits,
  Alone, alone, to where he sits,
The Shadow cloak'd from head to foot,

Who keeps the keys of all the creeds,
  I wander, often falling lame,
  And looking back to whence I came,
Or on to where the pathway leads;

And crying, How changed from where
    it ran
  Thro' lands where not a leaf was dumb;
  But all the lavish hills would hum
The murmur of a happy Pan:

When each by turns was guide to each,
  And Fancy light from Fancy caught,
  And Thought leapt out to wed with
    Thought
Ere Thought could wed itself with Speech;

And all we met was fair and good,
  And all was good that Time could bring,
  And all the secret of the Spring
Moved in the chambers of the blood;

And many an old philosophy
  On Argive heights divinely sang,
  And round us all the thicket rang
To many a flute of Arcady.

XXIV.

AND was the day of my delight
  As pure and perfect as I say?
  The very source and fount of Day
Is dash'd with wandering isles of night.

If all was good and fair we met,
  This earth had been the Paradise
  It never look'd to human eyes
Since Adam left his garden yet.

And is it that the haze of grief
  Makes former gladness loom so great?
  The lowness of the present state,
That sets the past in this relief?

Or that the past will always win
  A glory from its being far;
  And orb into the perfect star
We saw not, when we moved therein?

XXV.

I KNOW that this was Life,—the track
  Whereon with equal feet we fared;
  And then, as now, the day prepared
The daily burden for the back.

But this it was that made me move
  As light as carrier-birds in air;
  I loved the weight I had to bear,
Because it needed help of Love:

Nor could I weary, heart or limb,
  When mighty Love would cleave in
    twain
  The lading of a single pain,
And part it, giving half to him.

XXVI.

STILL onward winds the dreary way;
  I with it; for I long to prove
  No lapse of moons can canker Love,
Whatever fickle tongues may say.

And if that eye which watches guilt
  And goodness, and hath power to see
  Within the green the moulder'd tree,
And towers fall'n as soon as built—

O, if indeed that eye foresee
  Or see (in Him is no before)
  In more of life true life no more
And Love the indifference to be,

Then might I find, ere yet the morn
  Breaks hither over Indian seas,
  That Shadow waiting with the keys,
To shroud me from my proper scorn.

XXVII.

I ENVY not in any moods
  The captive void of noble rage,
  The linnet born within the cage,
That never knew the summer woods:

I envy not the beast that takes
  His license in the field of time,
  Unfetter'd by the sense of crime,
To whom a conscience never wakes ;

Nor, what may count itself as blest,
  The heart that never plighted troth,
  But stagnates in the weeds of sloth ;
Nor any want-begotten rest.

I hold it true, whate'er befall ;
  I feel it, when I sorrow most ;
  'T is better to have loved and lost
Than never to have loved at all.

XXVIII.

The time draws near the birth of Christ :
  The moon is hid ; the night is still ;
  The Christmas bells from hill to hill
Answer each other in the mist.

Four voices of four hamlets round,
  From far and near, on mead and moor,
  Swell out and fail, as if a door
Were shut between me and the sound :

Each voice four changes on the wind,
  That now dilate, and now decrease,
  Peace and goodwill, goodwill and peace,
Peace and goodwill, to all mankind.

This year I slept and woke with pain,
  I almost wish'd no more to wake,
  And that my hold on life would break
Before I heard those bells again :

But they my troubled spirit rule,
  For they controll'd me when a boy ;
  They bring me sorrow touch'd with joy,
The merry merry bells of Yule.

XXIX.

With such compelling cause to grieve
  As daily vexes household peace,
  And chains regret to his decease,
How dare we keep our Christmas-eve ;

Which brings no more a welcome guest
  To enrich the threshold of the night
  With shower'd largess of delight,
In dance and song and game and jest.

Yet go, and while the holly boughs
  Entwine the cold baptismal font,
  Make one wreath more for Use and
      Wont,
That guard the portals of the house ;

Old sisters of a day gone by,
  Gray nurses, loving nothing new ;
  Why should they miss their yearly due
Before their time ? They too will die.

XXX.

With trembling fingers did we weave
  The holly round the Christmas hearth ;
  A rainy cloud possess'd the earth,
And sadly fell our Christmas-eve.

At our old pastimes in the hall
  We gamboll'd, making vain pretence
  Of gladness, with an awful sense
Of one mute Shadow watching all.

We paused : the winds were in the beech :
  We heard them sweep the winter land ;
  And in a circle hand-in-hand
Sat silent, looking each at each.

Then echo-like our voices rang ;
  We sung, tho' every eye was dim,
  A merry song we sang with him
Last year : impetuously we sang :

We ceased : a gentler feeling crept
  Upon us : surely rest is meet :
  "They rest," we said, "their sleep is
      sweet,"
And silence follow'd, and we wept.

Our voices took a higher range ;
  Once more we sang : "They do not die
  Nor lose their mortal sympathy,
Nor change to us, although they change ;

"Rapt from the fickle and the frail
  With gather'd power, yet the same,
  Pierces the keen seraphic flame
From orb to orb, from veil to veil."

Rise, happy morn, rise, holy morn,
  Draw forth the cheerful day from night :
  O Father, touch the east, and light
The light that shone when Hope was born.

XXXI.

When Lazarus left his charnel-cave,
  And home to Mary's house return'd,
  Was this demanded — if he yearn'd
To hear her weeping by his grave ?

"Where wert thou, brother, those four
      days ?"
  There lives no record of reply,
  Which telling what it is to die
Had surely added praise to praise.

From every house the neighbors met,
　The streets were fill'd with joyful sound,
　A solemn gladness even crown'd
The purple brows of Olivet.

Behold a man raised up by Christ!
　The rest remaineth unreveal'd;
　He told it not; or something seal'd
The lips of that Evangelist.

XXXII.

Her eyes are homes of silent prayer,
　Nor other thought her mind admits
　But, he was dead, and there he sits,
And he that brought him back is there.

Then one deep love doth supersede
　All other, when her ardent gaze
　Roves from the living brother's face,
And rests upon the Life indeed.

All subtle thought, all curious fears,
　Borne down by gladness so complete,
　She bows, she bathes the Saviour's feet
With costly spikenard and with tears.

Thrice blest whose lives are faithful prayers,
　Whose loves in higher love endure;
　What souls possess themselves so pure,
Or is there blessedness like theirs?

XXXIII.

O thou that after toil and storm
　Mayst seem to have reach'd a purer air,
　Whose faith hath centre everywhere,
Nor cares to fix itself to form,

Leave thou thy sister when she prays,
　Her early Heaven, her happy views;
　Nor thou with shadow'd hint confuse
A life that leads melodious days.

Her faith thro' form is pure as thine,
　Her hands are quicker unto good:
　O, sacred be the flesh and blood
To which she links a truth divine!

See thou, that countest reason ripe
　In holding by the law within,
　Thou fail not in a world of sin,
And ev'n for want of such a type.

XXXIV.

My own dim life should teach me this,
　That life shall live for evermore,
　Else earth is darkness at the core,
And dust and ashes all that is;

This round of green, this orb of flame,
　Fantastic beauty; such as lurks
　In some wild Poet, when he works
Without a conscience or an aim.

What then were God to such as I?
　'Twere hardly worth my while to choose
　Of things all mortal, or to use
A little patience ere I die;

'T were best at once to sink to peace,
　Like birds the charming serpent draws,
　To drop head-foremost in the jaws
Of vacant darkness and to cease.

XXXV.

Yet if some voice that man could trust
　Should murmur from the narrow house,
　"The cheeks drop in; the body bows;
Man dies: nor is there hope in dust":

Might I not say, "Yet even here,
　But for one hour, O Love, I strive
　To keep so sweet a thing alive"?
But I should turn mine ears and hear

The moanings of the homeless sea,
　The sound of streams that swift or slow
　Draw down Æonian hills, and sow
The dust of continents to be;

And Love would answer with a sigh,
　"The sound of that forgetful shore
　Will change my sweetness more and more,
Half-dead to know that I shall die."

O me, what profits it to put
　An idle case! If Death were seen
　At first as Death, Love had not been,
Or been in narrowest working shut,

Mere fellowship of sluggish moods,
　Or in his coarsest Satyr-shape
　Had bruised the herb and crush'd the grape,
And bask'd and batten'd in the woods.

XXXVI.

Tho' truths in manhood darkly join,
　Deep-seated in our mystic frame,
　We yield all blessing to the name
Of Him that made them current coin;

For Wisdom dealt with mortal powers,
　Where truth in closest words shall fail,
　When truth embodied in a tale
Shall enter in at lowly doors.

And so the Word had breath, and wrought
  With human hands the creed of creeds
  In loveliness of perfect deeds,
More strong than all poetic thought;

Which he may read that binds the sheaf,
  Or builds the house, or digs the grave,
  And those wild eyes that watch the wave
In roarings round the coral reef.

XXXVII.

URANIA speaks with darken'd brow:
  "Thou pratest here where thou art least;
  This faith has many a purer priest,
And many an abler voice than thou.

"Go down beside thy native rill,
  On thy Parnassus set thy feet,
  And hear thy laurel whisper sweet
About the ledges of the hill."

And my Melpomene replies,
  A touch of shame upon her cheek:
  "I am not worthy ev'n to speak
Of thy prevailing mysteries;

"For I am but an earthly Muse,
  And owning but a little art
  To lull with song an aching heart,
And render human love his dues;

"But brooding on the dear one dead,
  And all he said of things divine,
  (And dear to me as sacred wine
To dying lips is all he said,)

"I murmur'd, as I came along,
  Of comfort clasp'd in truth reveal'd;
  And loiter'd in the master's field,
And darken'd sanctities with song."

XXXVIII.

WITH weary steps I loiter on,
  Tho' always under alter'd skies
  The purple from the distance dies,
My prospect and horizon gone.

No joy the blowing season gives,
  The herald melodies of spring,
  But in the songs I love to sing
A doubtful gleam of solace lives.

If any care for what is here
  Survive in spirits render'd free,
  Then are these songs I sing of thee
Not all ungrateful to thine ear.

XXXIX.

OLD warder of these buried bones,
  And answering now my random stroke
  With fruitful cloud and living smoke,
Dark yew, that graspest at the stones

And dippest toward the dreamless head,
  To thee too comes the golden hour
  When flower is feeling after flower;
But Sorrow fixt upon the dead,

And darkening the dark graves of men,
  What whisper'd from her lying lips?
  Thy gloom is kindled at the tips,
And passes into gloom again.

XL.

COULD we forget the widow'd hour
  And look on Spirits breathed away,
  As on a maiden in the day
When first she wears her orange-flower!

When crown'd with blessing she doth rise
  To take her latest leave of home,
  And hopes and light regrets that come
Make April of her tender eyes;

And doubtful joys the father move,
  And tears are on the mother's face,
  As parting with a long embrace
She enters other realms of love;

Her office there to rear, to teach,
  Becoming as is meet and fit
  A link among the days, to knit
The generations each with each;

And, doubtless, unto thee is given
  A life that bears immortal fruit
  In such great offices as suit
The full-grown energies of heaven.

Ay me, the difference I discern!
  How often shall her old fireside
  Be cheer'd with tidings of the bride,
How often she herself return,

And tell them all they would have told,
  And bring her babe, and make her boast,
  Till even those that miss'd her most,
Shall count new things as dear as old:

But thou and I have shaken hands,
  Till growing winters lay me low;
  My paths are in the fields I know,
And thine in undiscover'd lands.

XLI.

Thy spirit ere our fatal loss
  Did ever rise from high to higher;
  As mounts the heavenward altar-fire,
As flies the lighter thro' the gross.

But thou art turn'd to something strange,
  And I have lost the links that bound
  Thy changes; here upon the ground,
No more partaker of thy change.

Deep folly! yet that this could be,—
  That I could wing my will with might
  To leap the grades of life and light,
And flash at once, my friend, to thee:

For tho' my nature rarely yields
  To that vague fear implied in death;
  Nor shudders at the gulfs beneath,
The howlings from forgotten fields;

Yet oft when sundown skirts the moor
  An inner trouble I behold,
  A spectral doubt which makes me cold,
That I shall be thy mate no more,

Tho' following with an upward mind
  The wonders that have come to thee,
  Thro' all the secular to-be,
But evermore a life behind.

XLII.

I vex my heart with fancies dim:
  He still outstript me in the race;
  It was but unity of place
That made me dream I rank'd with him.

And so may Place retain us still,
  And he the much-beloved again,
  A lord of large experience, train
To riper growth the mind and will:

And what delights can equal those
  That stir the spirit's inner deeps,
  When one that loves but knows not, reaps
A truth from one that loves and knows?

XLIII.

If Sleep and Death be truly one,
  And every spirit's folded bloom
  Thro' all its intervital gloom
In some long trance should slumber on;

Unconscious of the sliding hour,
  Bare of the body, might it last,
  And silent traces of the past
Be all the color of the flower:

So then were nothing lost to man;
  So that still garden of the souls
  In many a figured leaf enrolls
The total world since life began;

And love will last as pure and whole
  As when he loved me here in Time,
  And at the spiritual prime
Rewaken with the dawning soul.

XLIV.

How fares it with the happy dead?
  For here the man is more and more;
  But he forgets the days before
God shut the doorways of his head.

The days have vanish'd, tone and tint,
  And yet perhaps the hoarding sense
  Gives out at times (he knows not whence)
A little flash, a mystic hint;

And in the long harmonious years
  (If Death so taste Lethean springs)
  May some dim touch of earthly things
Surprise thee ranging with thy peers.

If such a dreamy touch should fall,
  O turn thee round, resolve the doubt;
  My guardian angel will speak out
In that high place, and tell thee all.

XLV.

The baby new to earth and sky,
  What time his tender palm is prest
  Against the circle of the breast,
Has never thought that "this is I":

But as he grows he gathers much,
  And learns the use of "I," and "me,"
  And finds "I am not what I see,
And other than the things I touch."

So rounds he to a separate mind
  From whence clear memory may begin,
  As thro' the frame that binds him in
His isolation grows defined.

This use may lie in blood and breath,
  Which else were fruitless of their due,
  Had man to learn himself anew
Beyond the second birth of Death.

XLVI.

We ranging down this lower track,
  The path we came by, thorn and flower,
  Is shadow'd by the growing hour,
Lest life should fail in looking back.

So be it: there no shade can last
　In that deep dawn behind the tomb,
　But clear from marge to marge shall
　　bloom
The eternal landscape of the past;

A lifelong tract of time reveal'd;
　The fruitful hours of still increase;
　Days order'd in a wealthy peace,
And those five years its richest field.

O Love, thy province were not large,
　A bounded field, nor stretching far;
　Look also, Love, a brooding star,
A rosy warmth from marge to marge.

XLVII.

That each, who seems a separate whole,
　Should move his rounds, and fusing all
　The skirts of self again, should fall
Remerging in the general Soul,

Is faith as vague as all unsweet:
　Eternal form shall still divide
　The eternal soul from all beside;
And I shall know him when we meet:

And we shall sit at endless feast,
　Enjoying each the other's good:
　What vaster dream can hit the mood
Of Love on earth? He seeks at least

Upon the last and sharpest height,
　Before the spirits fade away,
　Some landing-place, to clasp and say,
"Farewell! We lose ourselves in light."

XLVIII.

If these brief lays, of Sorrow born,
　Were taken to be such as closed
　Grave doubts and answers here pro-
　　posed,
Then these were such as men might scorn:

Her care is not to part and prove;
　She takes, when harsher moods remit,
　What slender shade of doubt may flit,
And makes it vassal unto love:

And hence, indeed, she sports with words,
　But better serves a wholesome law,
　And holds it sin and shame to draw
The deepest measure from the chords:

Nor dare she trust a larger lay,
　But rather loosens from the lip
　Short swallow-flights of song, that dip
Their wings in tears, and skim away.

XLIX.

From art, from nature, from the schools,
　Let random influences glance,
　Like light in many a shiver'd lance
That breaks about the dappled pools:

The lightest wave of thought shall lisp,
　The fancy's tenderest eddy wreathe,
　The slightest air of song shall breathe
To make the sullen surface crisp.

And look thy look, and go thy way,
　But blame not thou the winds that
　　make
　The seeming-wanton ripple break,
The tender-pencil'd shadow play.

Beneath all fancied hopes and fears
　Ay me! the sorrow deepens down,
　Whose muffled motions blindly drown
The bases of my life in tears.

L.

Be near me when my light is low,
　When the blood creeps, and the nerves
　　prick
And tingle; and the heart is sick,
And all the wheels of Being slow.

Be near me when the sensuous frame
　Is rack'd with pangs that conquer trust;
　And Time, a maniac scattering dust,
And Life, a Fury slinging flame.

Be near me when my faith is dry,
　And men the flies of latter spring,
　That lay their eggs, and sting and sing,
And weave their petty cells and die.

Be near me when I fade away,
　To point the term of human strife,
　And on the low dark verge of life
The twilight of eternal day.

LI.

Do we indeed desire the dead
　Should still be near us at our side?
　Is there no baseness we would hide?
No inner vileness that we dread?

Shall he for whose applause I strove,
　I had such reverence for his blame,
　See with clear eye some hidden shame
And I be lessen'd in his love?

I wrong the grave with fears untrue:
　Shall love be blamed for want of faith?

There must be wisdom with great
    Death :
The dead shall look me thro' and thro'.

Be near us when we climb or fall :
    Ye watch, like God, the rolling hours
    With larger other eyes than ours,
To make allowance for us all.

LII.

I CANNOT love thee as I ought,
    For love reflects the thing beloved ;
    My words are only words, and moved
Upon the topmost froth of thought.

"Yet blame not thou thy plaintive song,"
    The Spirit of true love replied ;
    "Thou canst not move me from thy side,
Nor human frailty do me wrong.

"What keeps a spirit wholly true
    To that ideal which he bears ?
    What record ? not the sinless years
That breathed beneath the Syrian blue :

"So fret not, like an idle girl,
    That life is dash'd with flecks of sin.
    Abide : thy wealth is gather'd in,
When Time hath sunder'd shell from
    pearl."

LIII.

How many a father have I seen,
    A sober man, among his boys,
    Whose youth was full of foolish noise,
Who wears his manhood hale and green :

And dare we to this fancy give,
    That had the wild oat not been sown,
    The soil, left barren, scarce had grown
The grain by which a man may live ?

O, if we held the doctrine sound
    For life outliving heats of youth,
    Yet who would preach it as a truth
To those that eddy round and round ?

Hold thou the good : define it well :
    For fear divine Philosophy
    Should push beyond her mark, and be
Procuress to the Lords of Hell.

LIV.

O YET we trust that somehow good
    Will be the final goal of ill,
    To pangs of nature, sins of will,
Defects of doubt, and taints of blood ;

That nothing walks with aimless feet ;
    That not one life shall be destroy'd,
    Or cast as rubbish to the void,
When God hath made the pile complete ;

That not a worm is cloven in vain ;
    That not a moth with vain desire
    Is shrivel'd in a fruitless fire,
Or but subserves another's gain.

Behold, we know not anything ;
    I can but trust that good shall fall
    At last — far off — at last, to all,
And every winter change to spring.

So runs my dream : but what am I ?
    An infant crying in the night :
    An infant crying for the light :
And with no language but a cry.

LV.

THE wish, that of the living whole
    No life may fail beyond the grave,
    Derives it not from what we have
The likest God within the soul ?

Are God and Nature then at strife,
    That Nature lends such evil dreams ?
    So careful of the type she seems,
So careless of the single life ;

That I, considering everywhere
    Her secret meaning in her deeds,
    And finding that of fifty seeds
She often brings but one to bear,

I falter where I firmly trod,
    And falling with my weight of cares
    Upon the great world's altar-stairs
That slope thro' darkness up to God,

I stretch lame hands of faith, and grope,
    And gather dust and chaff, and call
    To what I feel is Lord of all,
And faintly trust the larger hope.

LVI.

"So careful of the type ?" but no.
    From scarped cliff and quarried stone
    She cries, "A thousand types are gone :
I care for nothing, all shall go.

"Thou makest thine appeal to me :
    I bring to life, I bring to death :
    The spirit does but mean the breath :
I know no more." And he, shall he,

Man, her last work, who seem'd so fair,
  Such splendid purpose in his eyes,
  Who roll'd the psalm to wintry skies,
Who built him fanes of fruitless prayer,

Who trusted God was love indeed
  And love Creation's final law —
  Tho' Nature, red in tooth and claw
With ravine, shriek'd against his creed —

Who loved, who suffer'd countless ills,
  Who battled for the True, the Just,
  Be blown about the desert dust,
Or seal'd within the iron hills?

No more? A monster then, a dream,
  A discord. Dragons of the prime,
  That tare each other in their slime,
Were mellow music match'd with him.

O life as futile, then, as frail!
  O for thy voice to soothe and bless!
  What hope of answer, or redress?
Behind the veil, behind the veil.

LVII.

Peace; come away: the song of woe
  Is after all an earthly song:
  Peace; come away: we do him wrong
To sing so wildly: let us go.

Come; let us go: your cheeks are pale;
  But half my life I leave behind:
  Methinks my friend is richly shrined;
But I shall pass; my work will fail.

Yet in these ears, till hearing dies,
  One set slow bell will seem to toll
  The passing of the sweetest soul
That ever look'd with human eyes.

I hear it now, and o'er and o'er,
  Eternal greetings to the dead;
  And "Ave, Ave, Ave," said,
"Adieu, adieu" for evermore.

LVIII.

In those sad words I took farewell:
  Like echoes in sepulchral halls,
  As drop by drop the water falls
In vaults and catacombs, they fell;

And, falling, idly broke the peace
  Of hearts that beat from day to day,
  Half-conscious of their dying clay,
And those cold crypts where they shall
  cease.

The high Muse answer'd: "Wherefore
    grieve
  Thy brethren with a fruitless tear?
  Abide a little longer here,
And thou shalt take a nobler leave."

LIX.

O Sorrow, wilt thou live with me,
  No casual mistress, but a wife,
  My bosom-friend and half of life;
As I confess it needs must be;

O Sorrow, wilt thou rule my blood,
  Be sometimes lovely like a bride,
  And put thy harsher moods aside,
If thou wilt have me wise and good.

My centred passion cannot move,
  Nor will it lessen from to-day;
  But I'll have leave at times to play
As with the creature of my love;

And set thee forth, for thou art mine,
  With so much hope for years to come,
  That, howsoe'er I know thee, some
Could hardly tell what name were thine.

LX.

He past; a soul of nobler tone:
  My spirit loved and loves him yet,
  Like some poor girl whose heart is set
On one whose rank exceeds her own.

He mixing with his proper sphere,
  She finds the baseness of her lot,
  Half jealous of she knows not what,
And envying all that meet him there.

The little village looks forlorn;
  She sighs amid her narrow days,
  Moving about the household ways,
In that dark house where she was born.

The foolish neighbors come and go,
  And tease her till the day draws by:
  At night she weeps, "How vain am I!
How should he love a thing so low?"

LXI.

If, in thy second state sublime,
  Thy ransom'd reason change replies
  With all the circle of the wise,
The perfect flower of human time;

And if thou cast thine eyes below,
  How dimly character'd and slight,

How dwarf'd a growth of cold and night,
How blanch'd with darkness must I grow!

Yet turn thee to the doubtful shore,
  Where thy first form was made a man;
  I loved thee, Spirit, and love, nor can
The soul of Shakespeare love thee more.

LXII.

Tho' if an eye that's downward cast
  Could make thee somewhat blench or fail,
  Then be my love an idle tale,
And fading legend of the past;

And thou, as one that once declined,
  When he was little more than boy,
  On some unworthy heart with joy,
But lives to wed an equal mind;

And breathes a novel world, the while
  His other passion wholly dies,
  Or in the light of deeper eyes
Is matter for a flying smile.

LXIII.

Yet pity for a horse o'er-driven,
  And love in which my hound has part,
  Can hang no weight upon my heart
In its assumptions up to heaven;

And I am so much more than these,
  As thou, perchance, art more than I,
  And yet I spare them sympathy
And I would set their pains at ease.

So mayst thou watch me where I weep,
  As, unto vaster motions bound,
  The circuits of thine orbit round
A higher height, a deeper deep.

LXIV.

Dost thou look back on what hath been,
  As some divinely gifted man,
  Whose life in low estate began
And on a simple village green;

Who breaks his birth's invidious bar,
  And grasps the skirts of happy chance,
  And breasts the blows of circumstance,
And grapples with his evil star;

Who makes by force his merit known
  And lives to clutch the golden keys,
  To mould a mighty state's decrees,
And shape the whisper of the throne;

And moving up from high to higher,
  Becomes on Fortune's crowning slope
  The pillar of a people's hope,
The centre of a world's desire;

Yet feels, as in a pensive dream,
  When all his active powers are still,
  A distant dearness in the hill,
A secret sweetness in the stream,

The limit of his narrower fate,
  While yet beside its vocal springs
  He play'd at counsellors and kings,
With one that was his earliest mate;

Who ploughs with pain his native lea
  And reaps the labor of his hands,
  Or in the furrow musing stands;
"Does my old friend remember me?"

LXV.

Sweet soul, do with me as thou wilt;
  I lull a fancy trouble-tost
  With "Love's too precious to be lost,
A little grain shall not be spilt."

And in that solace can I sing,
  Till out of painful phases wrought
  There flutters up a happy thought,
Self-balanced on a lightsome wing:

Since we deserved the name of friends,
  And thine effect so lives in me,
  A part of mine may live in thee
And move thee on to noble ends.

LXVI.

You thought my heart too far diseased;
  You wonder when my fancies play
  To find me gay among the gay,
Like one with any trifle pleased.

The shade by which my life was crost,
  Which makes a desert in the mind,
  Has made me kindly with my kind,
And like to him whose sight is lost;

Whose feet are guided thro' the land,
  Whose jest among his friends is free,
  Who takes the children on his knee,
And winds their curls about his hand:

He plays with threads, he beats his chair
  For pastime, dreaming of the sky;
  His inner day can never die,
His night of loss is always there.

LXVII.

When on my bed the moonlight falls,
  I know that in thy place of rest,
  By that broad water of the west,
There comes a glory on the walls:

Thy marble bright in dark appears,
  As slowly steals a silver flame
  Along the letters of thy name,
And o'er the number of thy years.

The mystic glory swims away;
  From off my bed the moonlight dies;
  And closing eaves of wearied eyes
I sleep till dusk is dipt in gray:

And then I know the mist is drawn
  A lucid veil from coast to coast,
  And in the dark church like a ghost
Thy tablet glimmers to the dawn.

LXVIII.

When in the down I sink my head,
  Sleep, Death's twin-brother, times my breath;
  Sleep, Death's twin-brother, knows not Death,
Nor can I dream of thee as dead:

I walk as ere I walk'd forlorn,
  When all our path was fresh with dew,
  And all the bugle breezes blew
Reveillée to the breaking morn.

But what is this? I turn about,
  I find a trouble in thine eye,
  Which makes me sad I know not why,
Nor can my dream resolve the doubt:

But ere the lark hath left the lea
  I wake, and I discern the truth;
  It is the trouble of my youth
That foolish sleep transfers to thee.

LXIX.

I dream'd there would be Spring no more,
  That Nature's ancient power was lost:
  The streets were black with smoke and frost,
They chatter'd trifles at the door:

I wander'd from the noisy town,
  I found a wood with thorny boughs:
  I took the thorns to bind my brows,
I wore them like a civic crown:

I met with scoffs, I met with scorns
  From youth and babe and hoary hairs:
  They call'd me in the public squares
The fool that wears a crown of thorns:

They call'd me fool, they call'd me child:
  I found an angel of the night;
  The voice was low, the look was bright;
He look'd upon my crown and smiled:

He reach'd the glory of a hand,
  That seem'd to touch it into leaf:
  The voice was not the voice of grief,
The words were hard to understand.

LXX.

I cannot see the features right,
  When on the gloom I strive to paint
  The face I know; the hues are faint
And mix with hollow masks of night;

Cloud-towers by ghostly masons wrought,
  A gulf that ever shuts and gapes,
  A hand that points, and palled shapes
In shadowy thoroughfares of thought;

And crowds that stream from yawning doors,
  And shoals of pucker'd faces drive;
  Dark bulks that tumble half alive,
And lazy lengths on boundless shores;

Till all at once beyond the will
  I hear a wizard music roll,
  And thro' a lattice on the soul
Looks thy fair face and makes it still.

LXXI.

Sleep, kinsman thou to death and trance
  And madness, thou hast forged at last
  A night-long Present of the Past
In which we went thro' summer France.

Hadst thou such credit with the soul?
  Then bring an opiate trebly strong,
  Drug down the blindfold sense of wrong
That so my pleasure may be whole;

While now we talk as once we talk'd
  Of men and minds, the dust of change,
  The days that grow to something strange,
In walking as of old we walk'd

Beside the river's wooded reach,
  The fortress, and the mountain ridge,
  The cataract flashing from the bridge,
The breaker breaking on the beach.

"I found a wood with thorny boughs."

LXXII.

Risest thou thus, dim dawn, again,
  And howlest, issuing out of night,
    With blasts that blow the poplar white,
And lash with storm the streaming pane?

Day, when my crown'd estate begun
  To pine in that reverse of doom,
    Which sicken'd every living bloom,
And blurr'd the splendor of the sun;

Who usherest in the dolorous hour
  With thy quick tears that make the rose
    Pull sideways, and the daisy close
Her crimson fringes to the shower;

Who mightst have heaved a windless flame
  Up the deep East, or, whispering, play'd
    A checker-work of beam and shade
Along the hills, yet look'd the same,

As wan, as chill, as wild as now;
  Day, mark'd as with some hideous crime,
    When the dark hand struck down thro' time,
And cancell'd nature's best: but thou,

Lift as thou mayst thy burden'd brows
  Thro' clouds that drench the morning star,
    And whirl the ungarner'd sheaf afar,
And sow the sky with flying boughs,

And up thy vault with roaring sound
  Climb thy thick noon, disastrous day;

Touch thy dull goal of joyless gray,
And hide thy shame beneath the ground.

LXXIII.

So many worlds, so much to do,
  So little done, such things to be,
  How know I what had need of thee,
For thou wert strong as thou wert true?

The fame is quench'd that I foresaw,
  The head hath miss'd an earthly wreath:
  I curse not nature, no, nor death;
For nothing is that errs from law.

We pass; the path that each man trod
  Is dim, or will be dim, with weeds:
  What fame is left for human deeds
In endless age? It rests with God.

O hollow wraith of dying fame,
  Fade wholly, while the soul exults,
  And self-infolds the large results
Of force that would have forged a name.

LXXIV.

As sometimes in a dead man's face,
  To those that watch it more and more,
  A likeness, hardly seen before,
Comes out — to some one of his race:

So, dearest, now thy brows are cold,
  I see thee what thou art, and know
  Thy likeness to the wise below,
Thy kindred with the great of old.

But there is more than I can see,
  And what I see I leave unsaid,
  Nor speak it, knowing Death has made
His darkness beautiful with thee.

LXXV.

I LEAVE thy praises unexpress'd
  In verse that brings myself relief,
  And by the measure of my grief
I leave thy greatness to be guess'd;

What practice howsoe'er expert
  In fitting aptest words to things,
  Or voice the richest-toned that sings,
Hath power to give thee as thou wert?

I care not in these fading days
  To raise a cry that lasts not long,
  And round thee with the breeze of song
To stir a little dust of praise.

Thy leaf has perish'd in the green,
  And, while we breathe beneath the sun,
  The world which credits what is done
Is cold to all that might have been.

So here shall silence guard thy fame;
  But somewhere, out of human view,
  Whate'er thy hands are set to do
Is wrought with tumult of acclaim.

LXXVI.

TAKE wings of fancy, and ascend,
  And in a moment set thy face
  Where all the starry heavens of space
Are sharpen'd to a needle's end;

Take wings of foresight; lighten thro'
  The secular abyss to come,
  And lo, thy deepest lays are dumb
Before the mouldering of a yew;

And if the matin songs, that woke
  The darkness of our planet, last,
  Thine own shall wither in the vast,
Ere half the lifetime of an oak.

Ere these have clothed their branchy bowers
  With fifty Mays, thy songs are vain;
  And what are they when these remain
The ruin'd shells of hollow towers?

LXXVII.

WHAT hope is here for modern rhyme
  To him, who turns a musing eye
  On songs, and deeds, and lives, that lie
Foreshorten'd in the tract of time?

These mortal lullabies of pain
  May bind a book, may line a box,
  May serve to curl a maiden's locks;
Or when a thousand moons shall wane

A man upon a stall may find,
  And, passing, turn the page that tells
  A grief, then changed to something else,
Sung by a long-forgotten mind.

But what of that? My darken'd ways
  Shall ring with music all the same;
  To breathe my loss is more than fame,
To utter love more sweet than praise.

LXXVIII.

AGAIN at Christmas did we weave
  The holly round the Christmas hearth;
  The silent snow possess'd the earth,
And calmly fell our Christmas-eve:

The yule-clog sparkled keen with frost,
  No wing of wind the region swept,
  But over all things brooding slept
The quiet sense of something lost.

As in the winters left behind,
  Again our ancient games had place,
  The mimic picture's breathing grace,
And dance and song and hoodman-blind.

Who show'd a token of distress?
  No single tear, no mark of pain:
  O sorrow, then can sorrow wane?
O grief, can grief be changed to less?

O last regret, regret can die!
  No— mixt with all this mystic frame,
  Her deep relations are the same,
But with long use her tears are dry.

LXXIX.

"More than my brothers are to me"—
  Let this not vex thee, noble heart!
  I know thee of what force thou art
To hold the costliest love in fee.

But thou and I are one in kind,
  As moulded like in nature's mint;
  And hill and wood and field did print
The same sweet forms in either mind.

For us the same cold streamlet curl'd
  Thro' all his eddying coves; the same
  All winds that roam the twilight came
In whispers of the beauteous world.

At one dear knee we proffer'd vows,
  One lesson from one book we learn'd,
  Ere childhood's flaxen ringlet turn'd
To black and brown on kindred brows.

And so my wealth resembles thine,
  But he was rich where I was poor,
  And he supplied my want the more
As his unlikeness fitted mine.

LXXX.

If any vague desire should rise,
  That holy Death ere Arthur died
  Had moved me kindly from his side,
And dropt the dust on tearless eyes;

Then fancy shapes, as fancy can,
  The grief my loss in him had wrought,
  A grief as deep as life or thought,
But stay'd in peace with God and man.

I make a picture in the brain;
  I hear the sentence that he speaks;
  He bears the burden of the weeks;
But turns his burden into gain.

His credit thus shall set me free;
  And, influence-rich to soothe and save,
  Unused example from the grave
Reach out dead hands to comfort me.

LXXXI.

Could I have said while he was here,
  "My love shall now no further range;
  There cannot come a mellower change,
For now is love mature in ear."

Love, then, had hope of richer store:
  What end is here to my complaint?
  This haunting whisper makes me faint,
"More years had made me love thee more."

But Death returns an answer sweet:
  "My sudden frost was sudden gain,
  And gave all ripeness to the grain,
It might have drawn from after-heat."

LXXXII.

I wage not any feud with Death
  For changes wrought on form and face;
  No lower life that earth's embrace
May breed with him, can fright my faith.

Eternal process moving on,
  From state to state the spirit walks;
  And these are but the shatter'd stalks,
Or ruin'd chrysalis of one.

Nor blame I Death, because he bare
  The use of virtue out of earth:
  I know transplanted human worth
Will bloom to profit, otherwhere.

For this alone on Death I wreak
  The wrath that garners in my heart;
  He put our lives so far apart
We cannot hear each other speak.

LXXXIII.

Dip down upon the northern shore,
  O sweet new-year delaying long;
  Thou doest expectant nature wrong;
Delaying long, delay no more.

What stays thee from the clouded noons,
  Thy sweetness from its proper place?
  Can trouble live with April days,
Or sadness in the summer moons?

Bring orchis, bring the foxglove spire,
  The little speedwell's darling blue,
  Deep tulips dash'd with fiery dew,
Laburnums, dropping-wells of fire.

O thou, new-year, delaying long,
  Delayest the sorrow in my blood,
  That longs to burst a frozen bud,
And flood a fresher throat with song.

LXXXIV.

When I contemplate all alone
  The life that had been thine below,
  And fix my thoughts on all the glow
To which thy crescent would have grown;

I see thee sitting crown'd with good,
  A central warmth diffusing bliss
  In glance and smile, and clasp and kiss,
On all the branches of thy blood;

Thy blood, my friend, and partly mine;
  For now the day was drawing on,
  When thou shouldst link thy life with one
Of mine own house, and boys of thine

Had babbled "Uncle" on my knee;
  But that remorseless iron hour
  Made cypress of her orange flower,
Despair of Hope, and earth of thee.

I seem to meet their least desire,
  To clap their cheeks, to call them mine.
  I see their unborn faces shine
Beside the never-lighted fire.

I see myself an honor'd guest,
  Thy partner in the flowery walk
  Of letters, genial table-talk,
Or deep dispute, and graceful jest;

While now thy prosperous labor fills
  The lips of men with honest praise,
  And sun by sun the happy days
Descend below the golden hills

With promise of a morn as fair;
  And all the train of bounteous hours
  Conduct by paths of growing powers
To reverence and the silver hair;

Till slowly worn her earthly robe,
  Her lavish mission richly wrought,
  Leaving great legacies of thought,
Thy spirit should fail from off the globe;

What time mine own might also flee,
  As link'd with thine in love and fate,
  And, hovering o'er the dolorous strait
To the other shore, involved in thee,

Arrive at last the blessed goal,
  And He that died in Holy Land
  Would reach us out the shining hand,
And take us as a single soul.

What reed was that on which I leant?
  Ah, backward fancy, wherefore wake
  The old bitterness again, and break
The low beginnings of content.

LXXXV.

This truth came borne with bier and pall,
  I felt it, when I sorrow'd most,
  'T is better to have loved and lost,
Than never to have loved at all —

O true in word, and tried in deed,
  Demanding, so to bring relief
  To this which is our common grief,
What kind of life is that I lead;

And whether trust in things above
  Be dimm'd of sorrow, or sustain'd;
  And whether love for him have drain'd
My capabilities of love;

Your words have virtue such as draws
  A faithful answer from the breast,
  Thro' light reproaches, half exprest,
And loyal unto kindly laws.

My blood an even tenor kept,
  Till on mine ear this message falls,
  That in Vienna's fatal walls
God's finger touch'd him, and he slept.

The great Intelligences fair
  That range above our mortal state,
  In circle round the blessed gate,
Received and gave him welcome there;

And led him thro' the blissful climes,
  And show'd him in the fountain fresh
  All knowledge that the sons of flesh
Shall gather in the cycled times.

But I remain'd, whose hopes were dim,
  Whose life, whose thoughts were little worth,
  To wander on a darken'd earth,
Where all things round me breathed of him.

O friendship, equal-poised control,
  O heart, with kindliest motion warm,
  O sacred essence, other form,
O solemn ghost, O crowned soul!

Yet none could better know than I,
  How much of act at human hands
  The sense of human will demands
By which we dare to live or die.

Whatever way my days decline,
  I felt and feel, tho' left alone,
  His being working in mine own,
The footsteps of his life in mine;

A life that all the Muses deck'd
  With gifts of grace, that might express
  All-comprehensive tenderness,
All-subtilizing intellect:

And so my passion hath not swerved
  To works of weakness, but I find
  An image comforting the mind,
And in my grief a strength reserved.

Likewise the imaginative woe,
  That loved to handle spiritual strife,
  Diffused the shock thro' all my life,
But in the present broke the blow.

My pulses therefore beat again
  For other friends that once I met;
  Nor can it suit me to forget
The mighty hopes that make us men.

I woo your love: I count it crime
  To mourn for any overmuch;
  I, the divided half of such
A friendship as had master'd Time;

Which masters Time indeed, and is
  Eternal, separate from fears:
  The all-assuming months and years
Can take no part away from this:

But Summer on the steaming floods,
  And Spring that swells the narrow brooks,
  And Autumn, with a noise of rooks,
That gather in the waning woods,

And every pulse of wind and wave
  Recalls, in change of light or gloom,
  My old affection of the tomb,
And my prime passion in the grave:

My old affection of the tomb,
  A part of stillness, yearns to speak:

"Arise, and get thee forth and seek
A friendship for the years to come.

"I watch thee from the quiet shore;
  Thy spirit up to mine can reach;
  But in dear words of human speech
We two communicate no more."

And I, "Can clouds of nature stain
  The starry clearness of the free?
  How is it? Canst thou feel for me
Some painless sympathy with pain?"

And lightly does the whisper fall;
  "'T is hard for thee to fathom this;
  I triumph in conclusive bliss,
And that serene result of all."

So hold I commerce with the dead;
  Or so methinks the dead would say;
  Or so shall grief with symbols play,
And pining life be fancy-fed.

Now looking to some settled end,
  That these things pass, and I shall prove
  A meeting somewhere, love with love,
I crave your pardon, O my friend;

If not so fresh, with love as true,
  I, clasping brother-hands, aver
  I could not, if I would, transfer
The whole I felt for him to you.

For which be they that hold apart
  The promise of the golden hours?
  First love, first friendship, equal powers,
That marry with the virgin heart.

Still mine, that cannot but deplore,
  That beats within a lonely place,
  That yet remembers his embrace,
But at his footstep leaps no more,

My heart, tho' widow'd, may not rest
  Quite in the love of what is gone,
  But seeks to beat in time with one
That warms another living breast.

Ah, take the imperfect gift I bring,
  Knowing the primrose yet is dear,
  The primrose of the later year,
As not unlike to that of Spring.

LXXXVI.

Sweet after showers, ambrosial air,
  That rollest from the gorgeous gloom
  Of evening over brake and bloom
And meadow, slowly breathing bare

The round of space, and rapt below
  Thro' all the dewy-tassell'd wood,
  And shadowing down the horned flood
In ripples, fan my brows and blow

The fever from my cheek, and sigh
  The full new life that feeds thy breath
  Throughout my frame, till Doubt and Death,
Ill brethren, let the fancy fly

From belt to belt of crimson seas
  On leagues of odor streaming far,
  To where in yonder orient star
A hundred spirits whisper "Peace."

LXXXVII.

I PAST beside the reverend walls
  In which of old I wore the gown;
  I roved at random thro' the town,
And saw the tumult of the halls;

And heard once more in college fanes
  The storm their high-built organs make,
  And thunder-music, rolling, shake
The prophets blazon'd on the panes;

And caught once more the distant shout,
  The measured pulse of racing oars
  Among the willows; paced the shores
And many a bridge, and all about

The same gray flats again, and felt
  The same, but not the same; and last
  Up that long walk of limes I past
To see the rooms in which he dwelt.

Another name was on the door:
  I linger'd; all within was noise
  Of songs, and clapping hands, and boys
That crash'd the glass and beat the floor;

Where once we held debate, a band
  Of youthful friends, on mind and art,
  And labor, and the changing mart,
And all the framework of the land;

When one would aim an arrow fair,
  But send it slackly from the string;
  And one would pierce an outer ring,
And one an inner, here and there;

And last the master-bowman, he,
  Would cleave the mark. A willing ear
  We lent him. Who, but hung to hear
The rapt oration flowing free

From point to point, with power and grace
  And music in the bounds of law,
  To those conclusions when we saw
The God within him light his face,

And seem to lift the form, and glow
  In azure orbits heavenly-wise;
  And over those ethereal eyes
The bar of Michael Angelo.

LXXXVIII.

WILD bird, whose warble, liquid sweet,
  Rings Eden thro' the budded quicks,
  O tell me where the senses mix,
O tell me where the passions meet,

Whence radiate: fierce extremes employ
  Thy spirits in the darkening leaf,
  And in the midmost heart of grief
Thy passion clasps a secret joy:

And I — my harp would prelude woe —
  I cannot all command the strings;
  The glory of the sum of things
Will flash along the chords and go.

LXXXIX.

WITCH-ELMS that counterchange the floor
  Of this flat lawn with dusk and bright;
  And thou, with all thy breadth and height
Of foliage, towering sycamore;

How often, hither wandering down,
  My Arthur found your shadows fair,
  And shook to all the liberal air
The dust and din and steam of town:

He brought an eye for all he saw;
  He mixt in all our simple sports;
  They pleased him, fresh from brawling courts
And dusty purlieus of the law.

O joy to him in this retreat,
  Immantled in ambrosial dark,
  To drink the cooler air, and mark
The landscape winking thro' the heat:

O sound to rout the brood of cares,
  The sweep of scythe in morning dew,
  The gust that round the garden flew,
And tumbled half the mellowing pears!

O bliss, when all in circle drawn
  About him, heart and ear were fed
  To hear him, as he lay and read
The Tuscan poets on the lawn:

Or in the all-golden afternoon
　　　A guest, or happy sister, sung,
　　　Or here she brought the harp and flung
　　A ballad to the brightening moon :

　　Nor less it pleased in livelier moods,
　　　Beyond the bounding hill to stray,
　　　And break the livelong summer day
　　With banquet in the distant woods ;

　　Whereat we glanced from theme to theme,
　　　Discuss'd the books to love or hate,
　　　Or touch'd the changes of the state,
　　Or threaded some Socratic dream ;

　　But if I praised the busy town,
　　　He loved to rail against it still,
　　　For " ground in yonder social mill
　　We rub each other's angles down,

　　"And merge " he said " in form and gloss
　　　The picturesque of man and man."
　　We talk'd : the stream beneath us ran,
　　The wine-flask lying couch'd in moss,

　　Or cool'd within the glooming wave ;
　　　And last, returning from afar,
　　　Before the crimson-circled star
　　Had fall'n into her father's grave,

　　And brushing ankle-deep in flowers,
　　　We heard behind the woodbine veil
　　　The milk that bubbled in the pail,
　　And buzzings of the honeyed hours.

　　　　　　　xc.

　　He tasted love with half his mind,
　　　Nor ever drank the inviolate spring
　　　Where nighest heaven, who first could fling
　　This bitter seed among mankind ;

　　That could the dead, whose dying eyes
　　　Were closed with wail, resume their life,
　　　They would but find in child and wife
　　An iron welcome when they rise :

　　'T was well, indeed, when warm with wine,
　　　To pledge them with a kindly tear,
　　　To talk them o'er, to wish them here,
　　To count their memories half divine ;

　　But if they came who past away,
　　　Behold their brides in other hands ;
　　　The hard heir strides about their lands,
　　And will not yield them for a day.

　　Yea, tho' their sons were none of these,
　　　Not less the yet-loved sire would make
　　　Confusion worse than death, and shake
　　The pillars of domestic peace.

　　Ah dear, but come thou back to me :
　　　Whatever change the years have wrought,
　　　I find not yet one lonely thought
　　That cries against my wish for thee.

　　　　　　　xci.

　　When rosy plumelets tuft the larch,
　　　And rarely pipes the mounted thrush ;
　　　Or underneath the barren bush
　　Flits by the sea-blue bird of March ;

　　Come, wear the form by which I know
　　　Thy spirit in time among thy peers ;
　　　The hope of unaccomplish'd years
　　Be large and lucid round thy brow.

　　When summer's hourly-mellowing change
　　　May breathe, with many roses sweet,
　　　Upon the thousand waves of wheat,
　　That ripple round the lonely grange ;

　　Come : not in watches of the night,
　　　But where the sunbeam broodeth warm,
　　　Come, beauteous in thine after form,
　　And like a finer light in light.

　　　　　　　xcii.

　　If any vision should reveal
　　　Thy likeness, I might count it vain
　　　As but the canker of the brain ;
　　Yea, tho' it spake and made appeal

　　To chances where our lots were cast
　　　Together in the days behind,
　　　I might but say, I hear a wind
　　Of memory murmuring the past.

　　Yea, tho' it spake and bared to view
　　　A fact within the coming year ;
　　　And tho' the months, revolving near,
　　Should prove the phantom-warning true,

　　They might not seem thy prophecies,
　　　But spiritual presentiments,
　　　And such refraction of events
　　As often rises ere they rise.

　　　　　　　xciii.

　　I shall not see thee.　Dare I say
　　　No spirit ever brake the band

That stays him from the native land,
Where first he walk'd when claspt in
   clay ?

No visual shade of some one lost,
   But he, the Spirit himself, may come
Where all the nerve of sense is numb;
Spirit to Spirit, Ghost to Ghost.

O, therefore from thy sightless range
   With gods in unconjectured bliss,
   O, from the distance of the abyss
Of tenfold-complicated change,

Descend, and touch, and enter; hear
   The wish too strong for words to name;
   That in this blindness of the frame
My Ghost may feel that thine is near.

XCIV.

How pure at heart and sound in head,
   With what divine affections bold
   Should be the man whose thought would hold
An hour's communion with the dead.

In vain shalt thou, or any, call
   The spirits from their golden day,
   Except, like them, thou too canst say,
My spirit is at peace with all.

They haunt the silence of the breast,
   Imaginations calm and fair,
   The memory like a cloudless air,
The conscience as a sea at rest:

But when the heart is full of din,
   And doubt beside the portal waits,
   They can but listen at the gates,
And hear the household jar within.

XCV.

By night we linger'd on the lawn,
   For underfoot the herb was dry;
   And genial warmth; and o'er the sky
The silvery haze of summer drawn;

And calm that let the tapers burn
   Unwavering: not a cricket chirr'd:
   The brook alone far-off was heard,
And on the board the fluttering urn :

And bats went round in fragrant skies,
   And wheel'd or lit the filmy shapes
   That haunt the dusk, with ermine capes
And woolly breasts and beaded eyes;

While now we sang old songs that peal'd
   From knoll to knoll, where, couch'd at ease,
   The white kine glimmer'd, and the trees
Laid their dark arms about the field.

But when those others, one by one,
   Withdrew themselves from me and night,
   And in the house light after light
Went out, and I was all alone,

A hunger seized my heart; I read
   Of that glad year which once had been,
   In those fall'n leaves which kept their green,
The noble letters of the dead:

And strangely on the silence broke
   The silent-speaking words, and strange
   Was love's dumb cry defying change
To test his worth; and strangely spoke

The faith, the vigor, bold to dwell
   On doubts that drive the coward back,
   And keen thro' wordy snares to track
Suggestion to her inmost cell.

So word by word, and line by line,
   The dead man touch'd me from the past,
   And all at once it seem'd at last
His living soul was flash'd on mine,

And mine in his was wound, and whirl'd
   About empyreal heights of thought,
   And came on that which is, and caught
The deep pulsations of the world,

Æonian music measuring out
   The steps of Time — the shocks of Chance —
   The blows of Death. At length my trance
Was cancell'd, stricken thro' with doubt.

Vague words! but ah, how hard to frame
   In matter-moulded forms of speech,
   Or ev'n for intellect to reach
Thro' memory that which I became:

Till now the doubtful dusk reveal'd
   The knolls once more where, couch'd at ease,
   The white kine glimmer'd, and the trees
Laid their dark arms about the field :

And suck'd from out the distant gloom
   A breeze began to tremble o'er

The large leaves of the sycamore,
  And fluctuate all the still perfume,

And gathering freshlier overhead,
  Rock'd the full-foliaged elms, and swung
The heavy-folded rose, and flung
The lilies to and fro, and said

"The dawn, the dawn," and died away;
  And East and West, without a breath,
  Mixt their dim lights, like life and death,
To broaden into boundless day.

XCVI.

You say, but with no touch of scorn,
  Sweet-hearted, you, whose light-blue eyes
  Are tender over drowning flies,
You tell me, doubt is Devil-born.

I know not: one indeed I knew
  In many a subtle question versed,
  Who touch'd a jarring lyre at first,
But ever strove to make it true:

Perplext in faith, but pure in deeds,
  At last he beat his music out.
  There lives more faith in honest doubt,
Believe me, than in half the creeds.

He fought his doubts and gather'd strength,
  He would not make his judgment blind,
  He faced the spectres of the mind
And laid them: thus he came at length

To find a stronger faith his own;
  And Power was with him in the night,
  Which makes the darkness and the light,
And dwells not in the light alone,

But in the darkness and the cloud,
  As over Sinaï's peaks of old,
  While Israel made their gods of gold,
Altho' the trumpet blew so loud.

XCVII.

My love has talk'd with rocks and trees;
  He finds on misty mountain-ground
  His own vast shadow glory-crown'd;
He sees himself in all he sees.

Two partners of a married life —
  I look'd on these and thought of thee
In vastness and in mystery,
  And of my spirit as of a wife.

These two — they dwelt with eye on eye,
  Their hearts of old have beat in tune,
  Their meetings made December June,
Their every parting was to die.

Their love has never past away;
  The days she never can forget
  Are earnest that he loves her yet,
Whate'er the faithless people say.

Her life is lone, he sits apart,
  He loves her yet, she will not weep,
  Tho' rapt in matters dark and deep
He seems to slight her simple heart.

He thrids the labyrinth of the mind,
  He reads the secret of the star,
  He seems so near and yet so far,
He looks so cold: she thinks him kind.

She keeps the gift of years before,
  A wither'd violet is her bliss:
  She knows not what his greatness is;
For that, for all, she loves him more.

For him she plays, to him she sings
  Of early faith and plighted vows;
  She knows but matters of the house,
And he, he knows a thousand things.

Her faith is fixt and cannot move,
  She darkly feels him great and wise,
  She dwells on him with faithful eyes,
"I cannot understand: I love."

XCVIII.

You leave us: you will see the Rhine,
  And those fair hills I sail'd below,
  When I was there with him; and go
By summer belts of wheat and vine

To where he breathed his latest breath,
  That City. All her splendor seems
  No livelier than the wisp that gleams
On Lethe in the eyes of Death.

Let her great Danube rolling fair
  Enwind her isles, unmark'd of me:
  I have not seen, I will not see
Vienna; rather dream that there,

A treble darkness, Evil haunts
  The birth, the bridal; friend from friend
  Is oftener parted, fathers bend
Above more graves, a thousand wants

Gnarr at the heels of men, and prey
  By each cold hearth, and sadness flings
  Her shadow on the blaze of kings :
And yet myself have heard him say,

That not in any mother town
  With statelier progress to and fro
  The double tides of chariots flow
By park and suburb under brown

Of lustier leaves ; nor more content,
  He told me, lives in any crowd,
  When all is gay with lamps, and loud
With sport and song, in booth and tent,

Imperial halls, or open plain ;
  And wheels the circled dance, and breaks
  The rocket molten into flakes
Of crimson or in emerald rain.

XCIX.

RISEST thou thus, dim dawn, again,
  So loud with voices of the birds,
  So thick with lowings of the herds,
Day, when I lost the flower of men ;

Who tremblest thro' thy darkling red
  On yon swoll'n brook that bubbles fast
  By meadows breathing of the past,
And woodlands holy to the dead ;

Who murmurest in the foliaged eaves
  A song that slights the coming care,
  And Autumn laying here and there
A fiery finger on the leaves :

Who wakenest with thy balmy breath
  To myriads on the genial earth,
  Memories of bridal, or of birth,
And unto myriads more, of death.

O, wheresoever those may be,
  Betwixt the slumber of the poles,
  To-day they count as kindred souls ;
They know me not, but mourn with me.

C.

I CLIMB the hill : from end to end
  Of all the landscape underneath,
  I find no place that does not breathe
Some gracious memory of my friend ;

No gray old grange, or lonely fold,
  Or low morass and whispering reed,
  Or simple stile from mead to mead,
Or sheepwalk up the windy wold ;

Nor hoary knoll of ash and haw
  That hears the latest linnet trill,
  Nor quarry trench'd along the hill,
And haunted by the wrangling daw ;

Nor runlet tinkling from the rock ;
  Nor pastoral rivulet that swerves
  To left and right thro' meadowy curves,
That feed the mothers of the flock ;.

But each has pleased a kindred eye,
  And each reflects a kindlier day ;
  And, leaving these, to pass away,
I think once more he seems to die.

CI.

UNWATCH'D, the garden bough shall sway,
  The tender blossom flutter down,
  Unloved, that beech will gather brown,
This maple burn itself away ;

Unloved, the sun-flower, shining fair,
  Ray round with flames her disk of seed,
  And many a rose-carnation feed
With summer spice the humming air ;

Unloved, by many a sandy bar,
  The brook shall babble down the plain,
  At noon or when the lesser wain
Is twisting round the polar star ;

Uncared for, gird the windy grove,
  And flood the haunts of hern and crake ;
  Or into silver arrows break
The sailing moon in creek and cove ;

Till from the garden and the wild
  A fresh association blow,
  And year by year the landscape grow
Familiar to the stranger's child ;

As year by year the laborer tills
  His wonted glebe, or lops the glades ;
  And year by year our memory fades
From all the circle of the hills.

CII.

WE leave the well-beloved place
  Where first we gazed upon the sky ;
  The roofs, that heard our earliest cry,
Will shelter one of stranger race.

We go, but ere we go from home,
  As down the garden-walks I move,
  Two spirits of a diverse love
Contend for loving masterdom.

One whispers, here thy boyhood sung
  Long since its matin song, and heard
  The low love-language of the bird
In native hazels tassel-hung.

The other answers, "Yea, but here
  Thy feet have stray'd in after hours
  With thy lost friend among the bowers,
And this hath made them trebly dear."

These two have striven half the day,
  And each prefers his separate claim,
  Poor rivals in a losing game,
That will not yield each other way.

I turn to go: my feet are set
  To leave the pleasant fields and farms;
  They mix in one another's arms
To one pure image of regret.

CIII.

On that last night before we went
  From out the doors where I was bred,
  I dream'd a vision of the dead,
Which left my after-morn content.

Methought I dwelt within a hall,
  And maidens with me: distant hills
  From hidden summits fed with rills
A river sliding by the wall.

The hall with harp and carol rang.
  They sang of what is wise and good
  And graceful. In the centre stood
A statue veil'd, to which they sang;

And which, tho' veil'd, was known to me,
  The shape of him I loved, and love
  For ever: then flew in a dove
And brought a summons from the sea:

And when they learnt that I must go
  They wept and wail'd, but led the way
  To where a little shallop lay
At anchor in the flood below;

And on by many a level mead,
  And shadowing bluff that made the banks,
  We glided winding under ranks
Of iris, and the golden reed;

And still as vaster grew the shore,
  And roll'd the floods in grander space,
  The maidens gather'd strength and grace
And presence, lordlier than before;

And I myself, who sat apart
  And watch'd them, wax'd in every limb;
  I felt the thews of Anakim,
The pulses of a Titan's heart;

As one would sing the death of war,
  And one would chant the history
  Of that great race, which is to be,
And one the shaping of a star;

Until the forward-creeping tides
  Began to foam, and we to draw
  From deep to deep, to where we saw
A great ship lift her shining sides.

The man we loved was there on deck,
  But thrice as large as man he bent
  To greet us. Up the side I went,
And fell in silence on his neck:

Whereat those maidens with one mind
  Bewail'd their lot; I did them wrong:
  "We served thee here," they said, "so long,
And wilt thou leave us now behind?"

So rapt I was, they could not win
  An answer from my lips, but he
  Replying, "Enter likewise ye
And go with us": they enter'd in.

And while the wind began to sweep
  A music out of sheet and shroud,
  We steer'd her toward a crimson cloud
That landlike slept along the deep.

CIV.

The time draws near the birth of Christ;
  The moon is hid, the night is still;
  A single church below the hill
Is pealing, folded in the mist.

A single peal of bells below,
  That wakens at this hour of rest
  A single murmur in the breast,
That these are not the bells I know.

Like strangers' voices here they sound,
  In lands where not a memory strays,
  Nor landmark breathes of other days,
But all is new unhallow'd ground.

CV.

To-night, ungather'd, let us leave
  This laurel, let this holly stand:
  We live within the stranger's land,
And strangely falls our Christmas eve.

Our father's dust is left alone
  And silent under other snows :
  There in due time the woodbine blows,
The violet comes, but we are gone.

No more shall wayward grief abuse
  The genial hour with mask and mime ;
  For change of place, like growth of time,
Has broke the bond of dying use.

Let cares that petty shadows cast,
  By which our lives are chiefly proved,
  A little spare the night I loved,
And hold it solemn to the past.

But let no footstep beat the floor,
  Nor bowl of wassail mantle warm ;
  For who would keep an ancient form
Thro' which the spirit breathes no more ?

Be neither song, nor game, nor feast ;
  Nor harp be touch'd, nor flute be blown ;
  No dance, no motion, save alone
What lightens in the lucid east

Of rising worlds by yonder wood.
  Long sleeps the summer in the seed ;
  Run out your measured arcs, and lead
The closing cycle rich in good.

CVI.

Ring out, wild bells, to the wild sky,
  The flying cloud, the frosty light :
  The year is dying in the night ;
Ring out, wild bells, and let him die.

Ring out the old, ring in the new,
  Ring, happy bells, across the snow :
  The year is going, let him go ;
Ring out the false, ring in the true.

Ring out the grief that saps the mind,
  For those that here we see no more ;
  Ring out the feud of rich and poor,
Ring in redress to all mankind.

Ring out a slowly dying cause,
  And ancient forms of party strife ;
  Ring in the nobler modes of life,
With sweeter manners, purer laws.

Ring out the want, the care, the sin,
  The faithless coldness of the times ;
  Ring out, ring out my mournful rhymes,
But ring the fuller minstrel in.

Ring out false pride in place and blood,
  The civic slander and the spite ;
  Ring in the love of truth and right,
Ring in the common love of good.

Ring out old shapes of foul disease ;
  Ring out the narrowing lust of gold ;
  Ring out the thousand wars of old,
Ring in the thousand years of peace.

Ring in the valiant man and free,
  The larger heart, the kindlier hand ;
  Ring out the darkness of the land,
Ring in the Christ that is to be.

CVII.

It is the day when he was born,
  A bitter day that early sank
  Behind a purple-frosty bank
Of vapor, leaving night forlorn.

The time admits not flowers or leaves
  To deck the banquet. Fiercely flies
  The blast of North and East, and ice
Makes daggers at the sharpen'd eaves,

And bristles all the brakes and thorns
  To yon hard crescent, as she hangs
  Above the wood which grides and clangs
Its leafless ribs and iron horns

Together, in the drifts that pass
  To darken on the rolling brine
  That breaks the coast. But fetch the wine,
Arrange the board and brim the glass ;

Bring in great logs and let them lie,
  To make a solid core of heat ;
  Be cheerful-minded, talk and treat
Of all things ev'n as he were by ;

We keep the day. With festal cheer,
  With books and music, surely we
  Will drink to him, whate'er he be,
And sing the songs he loved to hear.

CVIII.

I will not shut me from my kind,
  And, lest I stiffen into stone,
  I will not eat my heart alone,
Nor feed with sighs a passing wind :

What profit lies in barren faith,
  And vacant yearning, tho' with might
  To scale the heaven's highest height,
Or dive below the wells of Death ?

"Ring out, wild bells, to the wild sky."

What find I in the highest place,
   But mine own phantom chanting hymns!
   And on the depths of death there swims
The reflex of a human face.

I'll rather take what fruit may be
   Of sorrow under human skies:
   'T is held that sorrow makes us wise,
Whatever wisdom sleep with thee.

CIX.

HEART-AFFLUENCE in discursive talk
   From household fountains never dry;
   The critic clearness of an eye,
That saw thro' all the Muses' walk;

Seraphic intellect and force
   To seize and throw the doubts of man;
   Impassion'd logic, which outran
The hearer in its fiery course;

High nature amorous of the good,
   But touch'd with no ascetic gloom;
   And passion pure in snowy bloom
Thro' all the years of April blood;

A love of freedom rarely felt,
   Of freedom in her regal seat
   Of England; not the schoolboy heat,
The blind hysterics of the Celt;

And manhood fused with female grace
   In such a sort, the child would twine
   A trustful hand, unasked, in thine,
And find his comfort in thy face;

All these have been, and thee mine eyes
   Have look'd on: if they look'd in vain,

My shame is greater who remain,
Nor let thy wisdom make me wise.

CX.

Thy converse drew us with delight,
The men of rathe and riper years:
The feeble soul, a haunt of fears,
Forgot his weakness in thy sight.

On thee the loyal-hearted hung,
The proud was half disarm'd of pride,
Nor cared the serpent at thy side
To flicker with his double tongue.

The stern were mild when thou wert by,
The flippant put himself to school
And heard thee, and the brazen fool
Was soften'd, and he knew not why;

While I, thy dearest, sat apart,
And felt thy triumph was as mine;
And loved them more, that they were thine,
The graceful tact, the Christian art;

Nor mine the sweetness or the skill,
But mine the love that will not tire,
And, born of love, the vague desire
That spurs an imitative will.

CXI.

The churl in spirit, up or down
Along the scale of ranks, thro' all,
To him who grasps a golden ball,
By blood a king, at heart a clown;

The churl in spirit, howe'er he veil
His want in forms for fashion's sake,
Will let his coltish nature break
At seasons thro' the gilded pale:

For who can always act? but he,
To whom a thousand memories call,
Not being less but more than all
The gentleness he seem'd to be,

Best seem'd the thing he was, and join'd
Each office of the social hour
To noble manners, as the flower
And native growth of noble mind;

Nor ever narrowness or spite,
Or villain fancy fleeting by,
Drew in the expression of an eye,
Where God and Nature met in light;

And thus he bore without abuse
The grand old name of gentleman,
Defamed by every charlatan,
And soil'd with all ignoble use.

CXII.

High wisdom holds my wisdom less,
That I, who gaze with temperate eyes
On glorious insufficiencies,
Set light by narrower perfectness.

But thou, that fillest all the room
Of all my love, art reason why
I seem to cast a careless eye
On souls, the lesser lords of doom.

For what wert thou? some novel power
Sprang up for ever at a touch,
And hope could never hope too much,
In watching thee from hour to hour,

Large elements in order brought,
And tracts of calm from tempest made,
And world-wide fluctuation sway'd,
In vassal tides that follow'd thought.

CXIII.

'Tis held that sorrow makes us wise;
Yet how much wisdom sleeps with thee
Which not alone had guided me,
But served the seasons that may rise;

For can I doubt, who knew thee keen
In intellect, with force and skill
To strive, to fashion, to fulfil —
I doubt not what thou wouldst have been:

A life in civic action warm,
A soul on highest mission sent,
A potent voice of Parliament,
A pillar steadfast in the storm,

Should licensed boldness gather force,
Becoming, when the time has birth,
A lever to uplift the earth
And roll it in another course,

With thousand shocks that come and go,
With agonies, with energies,
With overthrowings, and with cries,
And undulations to and fro.

CXIV.

Who loves not Knowledge? Who shall rail
Against her beauty? May she mix

With men and prosper ! Who shall fix
Her pillars ? Let her work prevail.

But on her forehead sits a fire :
  She sets her forward countenance
  And leaps into the future chance,
Submitting all things to desire.

Half-grown as yet, a child, and vain —
  She cannot fight the fear of death.
  What is she, cut from love and faith,
But some wild Pallas from the brain

Of Demons ? fiery-hot to burst
  All barriers in her onward race
  For power. Let her know her place ;
She is the second, not the first.

A higher hand must make her mild,
  If all be not in vain ; and guide
  Her footsteps, moving side by side
With wisdom, like the younger child :

For she is earthly of the mind,
  But Wisdom heavenly of the soul.
  O, friend, who camest to thy goal
So early, leaving me behind,

I would the great world grew like thee,
  Who grewest not alone in power
  And knowledge, but by year and hour
In reverence and in charity.

CXV.

Now fades the last long streak of snow,
  Now bourgeons every maze of quick
  About the flowering squares, and thick
By ashen roots the violets blow.

Now rings the woodland loud and long,
  The distance takes a lovelier hue,
  And drown'd in yonder living blue
The lark becomes a sightless song.

Now dance the lights on lawn and lea,
  The flocks are whiter down the vale,
  And milkier every milky sail
On winding stream or distant sea ;

Where now the seamew pipes, or dives
  In yonder greening gleam, and fly
  The happy birds, that change their sky
To build and brood ; that live their lives

From land to land ; and in my breast
  Spring wakens too ; and my regret
Becomes an April violet,
And buds and blossoms like the rest.

CXVI.

Is it, then, regret for buried time
  That keenlier in sweet April wakes,
  And meets the year, and gives and takes
The colors of the crescent prime ?

Not all : the songs, the stirring air,
  The life re-orient out of dust,
  Cry thro' the sense to hearten trust
In that which made the world so fair.

Not all regret : the face will shine
  Upon me, while I muse alone ;
  And that dear voice, I once have known,
Still speak to me of me and mine :

Yet less of sorrow lives in me
  For days of happy commune dead ;
  Less yearning for the friendship fled,
Than some strong bond which is to be.

CXVII.

O DAYS and hours, your work is this,
  To hold me from my proper place,
  A little while from his embrace,
For fuller gain of after bliss :

That out of distance might ensue
  Desire of nearness doubly sweet ;
  And unto meeting when we meet,
Delight a hundredfold accrue,

For every grain of sand that runs,
  And every span of shade that steals,
  And every kiss of toothed wheels,
And all the courses of the suns.

CXVIII.

CONTEMPLATE all this work of Time,
  The giant laboring in his youth ;
  Nor dream of human love and truth,
As dying Nature's earth and lime ;

But trust that those we call the dead
  Are breathers of an ampler day
  For ever nobler ends. They say,
The solid earth whereon we tread

In tracts of fluent heat began,
  And grew to seeming-random forms,
  The seeming prey of cyclic storms,
Till at the last arose the man ;

Who throve and branch'd from clime to
    clime,
  The herald of a higher race,
  And of himself in higher place
If so he type this work of time

Within himself, from more to more ;
  Or, crown'd with attributes of woe
  Like glories, move his course, and show
That life is not as idle ore,

But iron dug from central gloom,
  And heated hot with burning fears,
  And dipt in baths of hissing tears,
And batter'd with the shocks of doom

To shape and use. Arise and fly
  The reeling Faun, the sensual feast ;
  Move upward, working out the beast,
And let the ape and tiger die.

CXIX.

Doors, where my heart was used to beat
  So quickly, not as one that weeps
  I come once more ; the city sleeps ;
I smell the meadow in the street ;

I hear a chirp of birds ; I see
  Betwixt the black fronts long-withdrawn
  A light-blue lane of early dawn,
And think of early days and thee,

And bless thee, for thy lips are bland
  And bright the friendship of thine eye ;
  And in my thoughts with scarce a sigh
I take the pressure of thine hand.

CXX.

I TRUST I have not wasted breath :
  I think we are not wholly brain,
  Magnetic mockeries ; not in vain,
Like Paul with beasts, I fought with
    Death ;

Not only cunning casts in clay :
  Let Science prove we are, and then
  What matters Science unto men,
At least to me ? I would not stay.

Let him, the wiser man who springs
  Hereafter, up from childhood shape
  His action like the greater ape,
But I was born to other things.

CXXI.

SAD Hesper o'er the buried sun
  And ready, thou, to die with him,
Thou watchest all things ever dim
And dimmer, and a glory done :

The team is loosen'd from the wain,
  The boat is drawn upon the shore ;
  Thou listenest to the closing door,
And life is darken'd in the brain.

Bright Phosphor, fresher for the night,
  By thee the world's great work is heard
  Beginning, and the wakeful bird ;
Behind thee comes the greater light :

The market boat is on the stream,
  And voices hail it from the brink ;
  Thou hear'st the village hammer clink,
And see'st the moving of the team.

Sweet Hesper-Phosphor, double name
  For what is one, the first, the last,
  Thou, like my present and my past,
Thy place is changed ; thou art the same.

CXXII.

O, WAST thou with me, dearest, then,
  While I rose up against my doom,
  And yearn'd to burst the folded gloom,
To bare the eternal Heavens again,

To feel once more, in placid awe,
  The strong imagination roll
  A sphere of stars about my soul,
In all her motion one with law ;

If thou wert with me, and the grave
  Divide us not, be with me now,
  And enter in at breast and brow,
Till all my blood, a fuller wave,

Be quicken'd with a livelier breath,
  And like an inconsiderate boy,
  As in the former flash of joy,
I slip the thoughts of life and death ;

And all the breeze of Fancy blows,
  And every dew-drop paints a bow,
  The wizard lightnings deeply glow,
And every thought breaks out a rose.

CXXIII.

THERE rolls the deep where grew the tree.
  O earth, what changes hast thou seen !
  There where the long street roars, hath been
The stillness of the central sea.

The hills are shadows, and they flow
  From form to form, and nothing stands ;

They melt like mist, the solid lands,
Like clouds they shape themselves and go.

But in my spirit will I dwell,
 And dream my dream, and hold it true;
 For tho' my lips may breathe adieu,
I cannot think the thing farewell.

CXXIV.

THAT which we dare invoke to bless;
 Our dearest faith; our ghastliest doubt;
 He, They, One, All; within, without;
The Power in darkness whom we guess;

I found Him not in world or sun,
 Or eagle's wing, or insect's eye;
 Nor thro' the questions men may try,
The petty cobwebs we have spun:

If e'er when faith had fall'n asleep,
 I heard a voice "believe no more"
 And heard an ever-breaking shore
That tumbled in the Godless deep;

A warmth within the breast would melt
 The freezing reason's colder part,
 And like a man in wrath the heart
Stood up and answer'd "I have felt."

No, like a child in doubt and fear:
 But that blind clamor made me wise;
 Then was I as a child that cries,
But, crying, knows his father near;

And what I am behold again
 What is, and no man understands;
 And out of darkness came the hands
That reach thro' nature, moulding men.

CXXV.

WHATEVER I have said or sung,
 Some bitter notes my harp would give,
 Yea, tho' there often seem'd to live
A contradiction on the tongue,

Yet Hope had never lost her youth;
 She did but look through dimmer eyes;
 Or Love but play'd with gracious lies,
Because he felt so fix'd in truth:

And if the song were full of care,
 He breathed the spirit of the song;
 And if the words were sweet and strong,
He set his royal signet there;

Abiding with me till I sail
 To seek thee on the mystic deeps,
 And this electric force, that keeps
A thousand pulses dancing, fail.

CXXVI.

LOVE is and was my Lord and King,
 And in his presence I attend
 To hear the tidings of my friend,
Which every hour his couriers bring.

Love is and was my King and Lord,
 And will be, tho' as yet I keep
 Within his court on earth, and sleep
Encompass'd by his faithful guard,

And hear at times a sentinel
 Who moves about from place to place,
 And whispers to the worlds of space,
In the deep night, that all is well.

CXXVII.

AND all is well, tho' faith and form
 Be sunder'd in the night of fear;
 Well roars the storm to those that hear
A deeper voice across the storm,

Proclaiming social truth shall spread,
 And justice, ev'n tho' thrice again
 The red fool-fury of the Seine
Should pile her barricades with dead.

But ill for him that wears a crown,
 And him, the lazar, in his rags:
 They tremble, the sustaining crags;
The spires of ice are toppled down,

And molten up, and roar in flood;
 The fortress crashes from on high,
 The brute earth lightens to the sky,
And the great Æon sinks in blood,

And compass'd by the fires of Hell;
 While thou, dear spirit, happy star,
 O'erlook'st the tumult from afar,
And smilest, knowing all is well.

CXXVIII.

THE love that rose on stronger wings,
 Unpalsied when he met with Death,
 Is comrade of the lesser faith
That sees the course of human things.

No doubt vast eddies in the flood
 Of onward time shall yet be made,
 And throned races may degrade;
Yet, O ye mysteries of good,

Wild Hours that fly with Hope and Fear,
 If all your office had to do
 With old results that look like new;
If this were all your mission here,

To draw, to sheathe a useless sword,
 To fool the crowd with glorious lies,
 To cleave a creed in sects and cries,
To change the bearing of a word,

To shift an arbitrary power,
 To cramp the student at his desk,
 To make old bareness picturesque
And tuft with grass a feudal tower;

Why then my scorn might well descend
 On you and yours. I see in part
 That all, as in some piece of art,
Is toil cöoperant to an end.

CXXIX.

Dear friend, far off, my lost desire,
 So far, so near in woe and weal;
 O loved the most, when most I feel
There is a lower and a higher;

Known and unknown; human, divine;
 Sweet human hand and lips and eye;
 Dear heavenly friend that canst not die,
Mine, mine, for ever, ever mine;

Strange friend, past, present, and to be;
 Love deeplier, darklier understood;
 Behold, I dream a dream of good,
And mingle all the world with thee.

CXXX.

Thy voice is on the rolling air;
 I hear thee where the waters run;
 Thou standest in the rising sun,
And in the setting thou art fair.

What art thou then? I cannot guess;
 But tho' I seem in star and flower
 To feel thee some diffusive power,
I do not therefore love thee less:

My love involves the love before;
 My love is vaster passion now;
 Tho' mix'd with God and Nature thou,
I seem to love thee more and more.

Far off thou art, but ever nigh;
 I have thee still, and I rejoice;
 I prosper, circled with thy voice;
I shall not lose thee tho' I die.

CXXXI.

O living will that shalt endure
 When all that seems shall suffer shock,
 Rise in the spiritual rock,
Flow thro' our deeds and make them pure,

That we may lift from out of dust
 A voice as unto him that hears,
 A cry above the conquer'd years
To one that with us works, and trust,

With faith that comes of self-control,
 The truths that never can be proved
 Until we close with all we loved,
And all we flow from, soul in soul.

O true and tried, so well and long,
 Demand not thou a marriage lay;
 In that it is thy marriage day
Is music more than any song.

Nor have I felt so much of bliss
 Since first he told me that he loved
 A daughter of our house; nor proved
Since that dark day a day like this;

Tho' I since then have number'd o'er
 Some thrice three years: they went and came,
 Remade the blood and changed the frame,
And yet is love not less, but more;

No longer caring to embalm
 In dying songs a dead regret,
 But like a statue solid-set,
And moulded in colossal calm.

Regret is dead, but love is more
 Than in the summers that are flown,
 For I myself with these have grown
To something greater than before;

Which makes appear the songs I made
 As echoes out of weaker times,
 As half but idle brawling rhymes,
The sport of random sun and shade.

But where is she, the bridal flower,
 That must be made a wife ere noon?
 She enters, glowing like the moon
Of Eden on its bridal bower:

On me she bends her blissful eyes
 And then on thee; they meet thy look

And brighten like the star that shook
Betwixt the palms of paradise.

O when her life was yet in bud,
  He too foretold the perfect rose.
For thee she grew, for thee she grows
For ever, and as fair as good.

And thou art worthy; full of power;
  As gentle; liberal-minded, great,
  Consistent; wearing all that weight
Of learning lightly like a flower.

But now set out: the noon is near,
  And I must give away the bride;
  She fears not, or with thee beside
And me behind her, will not fear:

For I that danced her on my knee,
  That watch'd her on her nurse's arm,
  That shielded all her life from harm,
At last must part with her to thee;

Now waiting to be made a wife,
  Her feet, my darling, on the dead;
  Their pensive tablets round her head,
And the most living words of life

Breathed in her ear. The ring is on,
  The "wilt thou" answer'd, and again
  The "wilt thou" ask'd, till out of twain
Her sweet "I will" has made ye one.

Now sign your names, which shall be read,
  Mute symbols of a joyful morn,
  By village eyes as yet unborn;
The names are sign'd, and overhead

Begins the clash and clang that tells
  The joy to every wandering breeze;
  The blind wall rocks, and on the trees
The dead leaf trembles to the bells.

O happy hour, and happier hours
  Await them. Many a merry face
  Salutes them — maidens of the place,
That pelt us in the porch with flowers.

O happy hour, behold the bride
  With him to whom her hand I gave.
  They leave the porch, they pass the grave
That has to-day its sunny side.

To-day the grave is bright for me,
  For them the light of life increased,
  Who stay to share the morning feast,
Who rest to-night beside the sea.

Let all my genial spirits advance
  To meet and greet a whiter sun;
  My drooping memory will not shun
The foaming grape of eastern France.

It circles round, and fancy plays,
  And hearts are warm'd, and faces bloom,
  As drinking health to bride and groom
We wish them store of happy days.

Nor count me all to blame if I
  Conjecture of a stiller guest,
  Perchance, perchance, among the rest,
And, tho' in silence, wishing joy.

But they must go, the time draws on,
  And those white-favor'd horses wait;
  They rise, but linger; it is late;
Farewell, we kiss, and they are gone.

A shade falls on us like the dark
  From little cloudlets on the grass,
  But sweeps away as out we pass
To range the woods, to roam the park,

Discussing how their courtship grew,
  And talk of others that are wed,
  And how she look'd, and what he said,
And back we come at fall of dew.

Again the feast, the speech, the glee,
  The shade of passing thought, the wealth
  Of words and wit, the double health,
The crowning cup, the three-times-three,

And last the dance;—till I retire:
  Dumb is that tower which spake so loud,
  And high in heaven the streaming cloud,
And on the downs a rising fire:

And rise, O moon, from yonder down
  Till over down and over dale
  All night the shining vapor sail
And pass the silent-lighted town,

The white-faced halls, the glancing rills,
  And catch at every mountain head,
  And o'er the friths that branch and spread
Their sleeping silver thro' the hills;

And touch with shade the bridal doors,
  With tender gloom the roof, the wall;
  And breaking let the splendor fall
To spangle all the happy shores

By which they rest, and ocean sounds,
 And, star and system rolling past,
 A soul shall draw from out the vast
And strike his being into bounds,

And, moved thro' life of lower phase,
 Result in man, be born and think,
 And act and love, a closer link
Betwixt us and the crowning race

Of those that, eye to eye, shall look
 On knowledge; under whose command
 Is Earth and Earth's, and in their hand
Is Nature like an open book;

No longer half-akin to brute,
 For all we thought and loved and did,
 And hoped, and suffer'd, is but seed
Of what in them is flower and fruit;

Whereof the man, that with me trod
 This planet, was a noble type
 Appearing ere the times were ripe,
That friend of mine who lives in God,

That God, which ever lives and loves,
 One God, one law, one element,
 And one far-off divine event,
To which the whole creation moves.

MAUD,

AND OTHER POEMS.

MAUD.

I.

I.

I HATE the dreadful hollow behind the little wood,
Its lips in the field above are dabbled with blood-red heath,
The red-ribb'd ledges drip with a silent horror of blood,
And Echo there, whatever is ask'd her, answers "Death."

II.

For there in the ghastly pit long since a body was found,
His who had given me life — O father! O God! was it well? —
Mangled, and flatten'd, and crush'd, and dinted into the ground:
There yet lies the rock that fell with him when he fell.

III.

Did he fling himself down? who knows? for a vast speculation had fail'd,
And ever he mutter'd and madden'd, and ever wann'd with despair,
And out he walk'd when the wind like a broken worldling wail'd,
And the flying gold of the ruin'd woodlands drove thro' the air.

IV.

I remember the time, for the roots of my hair were stirr'd
By a shuffled step, by a dead weight trail'd, by a whisper'd fright,
And my pulses closed their gates with a shock on my heart as I heard
The shrill-edged shriek of a mother divide the shuddering night.

V.

Villany somewhere! whose? One says, we are villains all.
Not he: his honest fame should at least by me be maintained:
But that old man, now lord of the broad estate and the Hall,
Dropt off gorged from a scheme that had left us flaccid and drain'd.

VI.

Why do they prate of the blessings of Peace? we have made them a curse,
Pickpockets, each hand lusting for all that is not its own;
And lust of gain, in the spirit of Cain, is it better or worse
Than the heart of the citizen hissing in war on his own hearthstone?

"I hate the dreadful hollow behind the little wood."

VII.

But these are the days of advance, the
    works of the men of mind,
When who but a fool would have faith in
    a tradesman's ware or his word?
Is it peace or war? Civil war, as I think,
    and that of a kind
The viler, as underhand, not openly bear-
    ing the sword.

VIII.

Sooner or later I too may passively take
    the print
Of the golden age — why not? I have
    neither hope nor trust;
May make my heart as a millstone, set
    my face as a flint,
Cheat and be cheated, and die : who
    knows? we are ashes and dust.

IX.

Peace sitting under her olive, and slur-
    ring the days gone by,
When the poor are hovell'd and hustled
    together, each sex, like swine,
When only the ledger lives, and when
    only not all men lie;
Peace in her vineyard — yes! — but a
    company forges the wine.

X.

And the vitriol madness flushes up in
    the ruffian's head,

Till the filthy by-lane rings to the yell
  of the trampled wife,
And chalk and alum and plaster are sold
  to the poor for bread,
And the spirit of murder works in the
  very means of life,

XI.

And Sleep must lie down arm'd, for the
  villanous centre-bits
Grind on the wakeful ear in the hush of
  the moonless nights,
While another is cheating the sick of a
  few last gasps, as he sits
To pestle a poison'd poison behind his
  crimson lights.

XII.

When a Mammonite mother kills her
  babe for a burial fee,
And Timour-Mammon grins on a pile of
  children's bones,
Is it peace or war? better, war! loud
  war by land and by sea,
War with a thousand battles, and shaking a hundred thrones.

XIII.

For I trust if an enemy's fleet came yonder round by the hill,
And the rushing battle-bolt sang from
  the three-decker out of the foam,
That the smooth-faced snubnosed rogue
  would leap from his counter and
  till,
And strike, if he could, were it but with
  his cheating yardwand, home.—

XIV.

What! am I raging alone as my father
  raged in his mood?
Must *I* too creep to the hollow and dash
  myself down and die
Rather than hold by the law that I made,
  nevermore to brood
On a horror of shatter'd limbs and a
  wretched swindler's lie?

XV.

Would there be sorrow for *me?* there was
  love in the passionate shriek,
Love for the silent thing that had made
  false haste to the grave—
Wrapt in a cloak, as I saw him, and
  thought he would rise and speak
And rave at the lie and the liar, ah God,
  as he used to rave.

XVI.

I am sick of the Hall and the hill, I am
  sick of the moor and the main.
Why should I stay? can a sweeter chance
  ever come to me here?
O, having the nerves of motion as well
  as the nerves of pain,
Were it not wise if I fled from the place
  and the pit and the fear?

XVII.

Workmen up at the Hall!—they are
  coming back from abroad;
The dark old place will be gilt by the
  touch of a millionnaire:
I have heard, I know not whence, of the
  singular beauty of Maud;
I play'd with the girl when a child; she
  promised then to be fair.

XVIII.

Maud with her venturous climbings and
  tumbles and childish escapes,
Maud the delight of the village, the ringing joy of the Hall,
Maud with her sweet purse-mouth when
  my father dangled the grapes,
Maud the beloved of my mother, the
  moon-faced darling of all,—

XIX.

What is she now? My dreams are bad.
  She may bring me a curse.
No, there is fatter game on the moor;
  she will let me alone.
Thanks, for the fiend best knows whether
  woman or man be the worse.
I will bury myself in myself, and the
  Devil may pipe to his own.

II.

LONG have I sigh'd for a calm: God
  grant I may find it at last!
It will never be broken by Maud, she
  has neither savor nor salt,
But a cold and clear-cut face, as I found
  when her carriage past,
Perfectly beautiful: let it be granted her:
  where is the fault?

All that I saw (for her eyes were down-
cast, not to be seen)
Faultily faultless, icily regular, splen-
didly null,
Dead perfection, no more; nothing more,
if it had not been
For a chance of travel, a paleness, an
hour's defect of the rose,
Or an underlip, you may call it a little
too ripe, too full,
Or the least little delicate aquiline curve
in a sensitive nose,
From which I escaped heart-free, with
the least little touch of spleen.

III.

COLD and clear-cut face, why come you
so cruelly meek,
Breaking a slumber in which all spleenful
folly was drown'd,
Pale with the golden beam of an eyelash
dead on the cheek,
Passionless, pale, cold face, star-sweet on
a gloom profound ;
Womanlike, taking revenge too deep for
a transient wrong
Done but in thought to your beauty, and
ever as pale as before
Growing and fading and growing upon
me without a sound,
Luminous, gemlike, ghostlike, deathlike,
half the night long
Growing and fading and growing, till I
could bear it no more,
But arose, and all by myself in my own
dark garden ground,
Listening now to the tide in its broad-
flung shipwrecking roar,
Now to the scream of a madden'd beach
dragg'd down by the wave,
Walk'd in a wintry wind by a ghastly
glimmer, and found
The shining daffodil dead, and Orion low
in his grave.

IV.

I.

A MILLION emeralds break from the ruby-
budded lime
In the little grove where I sit — ah,
wherefore cannot I be
Like things of the season gay, like the
bountiful season bland,

When the far-off sail is blown by the
breeze of a softer clime,
Half-lost in the liquid azure bloom of a
crescent of sea,
The silent sapphire-spangled marriage
ring of the land ?

II.

Below me, there, is the village, and looks
how quiet and small !
And yet bubbles o'er like a city, with
gossip, scandal, and spite ;
And Jack on his alehouse bench has as
many lies as a Czar ;
And here on the landward side, by a red
rock, glimmers the Hall ;
And up in the high Hall-garden I see
her pass like a light ;
But sorrow seize me if ever that light be
my leading star !

III.

When have I bow'd to her father, the
wrinkled head of the race ?
I met her to-day with her brother, but
not to her brother I bow'd :
I bow'd to his lady-sister as she rode by
on the moor ;
But the fire of a foolish pride flash'd
over her beautiful face.
O child, you wrong your beauty, believe
it, in being so proud ;
Your father has wealth well-gotten, and
I am nameless and poor.

IV.

I keep but a man and a maid, ever ready
to slander and steal ;
I know it, and smile a hard-set smile,
like a stoic, or like
A wiser epicurean, and let the world
have its way :
For nature is one with rapine, a harm
no preacher can heal ;
The Mayfly is torn by the swallow, the
sparrow spear'd by the shrike,
And the whole little wood where I sit is
a world of plunder and prey.

V.

We are puppets, Man in his pride, and
Beauty fair in her flower ;
Do we move ourselves, or are moved by
an unseen hand at a game

That pushes us off from the board, and
 others ever succeed?
Ah yet, we cannot be kind to each other
 here for an hour;
We whisper, and hint, and chuckle, and
 grin at a brother's shame;
However we brave it out, we men are a
 little breed.

VI.

A monstrous eft was of old the Lord and
 Master of Earth,
For him did his high sun flame, and his
 river billowing ran,
And he felt himself in his force to be
 Nature's crowning race.
As nine months go to the shaping an
 infant ripe for his birth,
So many a million of ages have gone to
 the making of man:
He now is first, but is he the last? is he
 not too base?

VII.

The man of science himself is fonder of
 glory, and vain,
An eye well-practised in nature, a spirit
 bounded and poor;
The passionate heart of the poet is whirl'd
 into folly and vice.
I would not marvel at either, but keep
 a temperate brain;
For not to desire or admire, if a man
 could learn it, were more
Than to walk all day like the sultan of
 old in a garden of spice.

VIII.

For the drift of the Maker is dark, an
 Isis hid by the veil.
Who knows the ways of the world, how
 God will bring them about?
Our planet is one, the suns are many,
 the world is wide.
Shall I weep if a Poland fall? shall I
 shriek if a Hungary fail?
Or an infant civilization be ruled with
 rod or with knout?
I have not made the world, and He that
 made it will guide.

IX.

Be mine a philosopher's life in the quiet
 woodland ways,
Where if I cannot be gay let a passion-
 less peace be my lot,
Far-off from the clamor of liars belied
 in the hubbub of lies;
From the long-neck'd geese of the world
 that are ever hissing dispraise
Because their natures are little, and,
 whether he heed it or not,
Where each man walks with his head in
 a cloud of poisonous flies.

X.

And most of all would I flee from the
 cruel madness of love,
The honey of poison-flowers and all the
 measureless ill.
Ah Maud, you milkwhite fawn, you are
 all unmeet for a wife.
Your mother is mute in her grave as her
 image in marble above;
Your father is ever in London, you wan-
 der about at your will;
You have but fed on the roses, and lain
 in the lilies of life.

V.

I.

A VOICE by the cedar tree,
In the meadow under the Hall!
She is singing an air that is known to me,
A passionate ballad gallant and gay,
A martial song like a trumpet's call!
Singing alone in the morning of life,
In the happy morning of life and of May,
Singing of men that in battle array,
Ready in heart and ready in hand,
March with banner and bugle and fife
To the death, for their native land.

II.

Maud with her exquisite face,
And wild voice pealing up to the sunny
 sky,
And feet like sunny gems on an English
 green,
Maud in the light of her youth and her
 grace,
Singing of Death, and of Honor that
 cannot die,
Till I well could weep for a time so sor-
 did and mean,
And myself so languid and base.

III.

Silence, beautiful voice
Be still, for you only trouble the mind

With a joy in which I cannot rejoice,
A glory I shall not find.
Still! I will hear you no more,
For your sweetness hardly leaves me a
    choice
But to move to the meadow and fall
    before
Her feet on the meadow grass, and
    adore,
Not her, who is neither courtly nor
    kind,
Not her, not her, but a voice.

VI.

I.

MORNING arises stormy and pale,
No sun, but a wannish glare
In fold upon fold of hueless cloud,
And the budded peaks of the wood are
    bow'd
Caught and cuff'd by the gale:
I had fancied it would be fair.

II.

Whom but Maud should I meet
Last night, when the sunset burn'd
On the blossom'd gable-ends
At the head of the village street,
Whom but Maud should I meet?
And she touch'd my hand with a smile
    so sweet
She made me divine amends
For a courtesy not return'd.

III.

And thus a delicate spark
Of glowing and growing light
Thro' the livelong hours of the dark
Kept itself warm in the heart of my
    dreams,
Ready to burst in a color'd flame;
Till at last when the morning came
In a cloud, it faded, and seems
But an ashen-gray delight.

IV.

What if with her sunny hair,
And smile as sunny as cold,
She meant to weave me a snare
Of some coquettish deceit,
Cleopatra-like as of old
To entangle me when we met,
To have her lion roll in a silken net
And fawn at a victor's feet.

V.

Ah, what shall I be at fifty
Should Nature keep me alive,
If I find the world so bitter
When I am but twenty-five?
Yet, if she were not a cheat,
If Maud were all that she seem'd,
And her smile were all that I dream'd,
Then the world were not so bitter
But a smile could make it sweet.

VI.

What if tho' her eye seem'd full
Of a kind intent to me,
What if that dandy-despot, he,
That jewell'd mass of millinery,
That oil'd and curl'd Assyrian Bull
Smelling of musk and of insolence,
Her brother, from whom I keep aloof,
Who wants the finer politic sense
To mask, tho' but in his own behoof,
With a glassy smile his brutal scorn —
What if he had told her yestermorn
How prettily for his own sweet sake
A face of tenderness might be feign'd,
And a moist mirage in desert eyes,
That so, when the rotten hustings shake
In another month to his brazen lies,
A wretched vote may be gain'd.

VII.

For a raven ever croaks, at my side,
Keep watch and ward, keep watch and
    ward,
Or thou wilt prove their tool.
Yea too, myself from myself I guard,
For often a man's own angry pride
Is cap and bells for a fool.

VIII.

Perhaps the smile and tender tone
Came out of her pitying womanhood,
For am I not, am I not, here alone
So many a summer since she died,
My mother, who was so gentle and good!
Living alone in an empty house,
Here half-hid in the gleaming wood,
Where I hear the dead at midday moan,
And the shrieking rush of the wainscot
    mouse,
And my own sad name in corners cried,
When the shiver of dancing leaves is
    thrown

About its echoing chambers wide,
Till a morbid hate and horror have grown
Of a world in which I have hardly mixt,
And a morbid eating lichen fixt
On a heart half-turn'd to stone.

IX.

O heart of stone, are you flesh, and caught
By that you swore to withstand?
For what was it else within me wrought
But, I fear, the new strong wine of love,
That made my tongue so stammer and trip
When I saw the treasured splendor, her hand,
Come sliding out of her sacred glove,
And the sunlight broke from her lip?

X.

I have play'd with her when a child;
She remembers it now we meet.
Ah well, well, well, I *may* be beguiled
By some coquettish deceit.
Yet, if she were not a cheat,
If Maud were all that she seem'd,
And her smile had all that I dream'd,
Then the world were not so bitter
But a smile could make it sweet.

VII.

I.

Did I hear it half in a doze
 Long since, I know not where?
Did I dream it an hour ago,
 When asleep in this arm-chair?

II.

Men were drinking together,
 Drinking and talking of me;
"Well, if it prove a girl, the boy
 Will have plenty: so let it be."

III.

Is it an echo of something
 Read with a boy's delight,
Viziers nodding together
 In some Arabian night?

IV.

Strange, that I hear two men,
 Somewhere, talking of me;
"Well, if it prove a girl, my boy
 Will have plenty: so let it be."

VIII.

She came to the village church,
And sat by a pillar alone;
An angel watching an urn
Wept over her, carved in stone;
And once, but once, she lifted her eyes,
And suddenly, sweetly, strangely blush'd
To find they were met by my own;
And suddenly, sweetly, my heart beat stronger
And thicker, until I heard no longer
The snowy-banded, dilettante,
Delicate-handed priest intone;
And thought, is it pride, and mused and sigh'd
"No surely, now it cannot be pride."

IX.

I was walking a mile,
More than a mile from the shore,
The sun look'd out with a smile
Betwixt the cloud and the moor,
And riding at set of day
Over the dark moor land;
Rapidly riding far away,
She waved to me with her hand.
There were two at her side,
Something flash'd in the sun,
Down by the hill I saw them ride,
In a moment they were gone:
Like a sudden spark
Struck vainly in the night,
Then returns the dark
With no more hope of light.

X.

I.

Sick, am I sick of a jealous dread?
Was not one of the two at her side
This new-made lord, whose splendor plucks
The slavish hat from the villager's head?
Whose old grandfather has lately died,
Gone to a blacker pit, for whom
Grimy nakedness dragging his trucks
And laying his trams in a poison'd gloom
Wrought, till he crept from a gutted mine
Master of half a servile shire,
And left his coal all turn'd into gold
To a grandson, first of his noble line,
Rich in the grace all women desire,

*"She came to the village church,
And sat by a pillar alone."*

Strong in the power that all men adore,
And simper and set their voices lower,
And soften as if to a girl, and hold
Awe-stricken breaths at a work divine,
Seeing his gewgaw castle shine,
New as his title, built last year,
There amid perky larches and pine,
And over the sullen-purple moor
(Look at it) pricking a cockney ear.

II.

What, has he found my jewel out?
For one of the two that rode at her side
Bound for the Hall, I am sure was he:
Bound for the Hall, and I think for a
    bride.

Blithe would her brother's acceptance be.
Maud could be gracious too, no doubt,
To a lord, a captain, a padded shape,
A bought commission, a waxen face,
A rabbit mouth that is ever agape —
Bought? what is it he cannot buy?
And therefore splenetic, personal, base,
A wounded thing with a rancorous cry,
At war with myself and a wretched
    race,
Sick, sick to the heart of life, am I.

III.

Last week came one to the county town,
To preach our poor little army down,
And play the game of the despot kings,

Tho' the state has done it and thrice as well:
This broad-brimm'd hawker of holy things,
Whose ear is cramm'd with his cotton, and rings
Even in dreams to the chink of his pence,
This huckster put down war! can he tell
Whether war be a cause or a consequence?
Put down the passions that make earth Hell!
Down with ambition, avarice, pride,
Jealousy, down! cut off from the mind
The bitter springs of anger and fear;
Down too, down at your own fireside,
With the evil tongue and the evil ear,
For each is at war with mankind.

IV.

I wish I could hear again
The chivalrous battle-song
That she warbled alone in her joy!
I might persuade myself then
She would not do herself this great wrong,
To take a wanton dissolute boy
For a man and leader of men.

V.

Ah God, for a man with heart, head, hand,
Like some of the simple great ones gone
For ever and ever by,
One still strong man in a blatant land,
Whatever they call him, what care I,
Aristocrat, democrat, autocrat, — one
Who can rule and dare not lie.

VI.

And ah for a man to arise in me,
That the man I am may cease to be!

XI.

I.

O LET the solid ground
  Not fail beneath my feet
Before my life has found
  What some have found so sweet;
Then let come what come may,
What matter if I go mad,
I shall have had my day.

II.

Let the sweet heavens endure,
  Not close and darken above me
Before I am quite quite sure
  That there is one to love me;
Then let come what come may
To a life that has been so sad,
I shall have had my day.

XII.

I.

BIRDS in the high Hall-garden
  When twilight was falling,
Maud, Maud, Maud, Maud,
  They were crying and calling.

II.

Where was Maud? in our wood;
  And I, who else, was with her,
Gathering woodland lilies,
  Myriads blow together.

III.

Birds in our wood sang
  Ringing thro' the valleys,
Maud is here, here, here
  In among the lilies.

IV.

I kiss'd her slender hand,
  She took the kiss sedately;
Maud is not seventeen,
  But she is tall and stately.

V.

I to cry out on pride
  Who have won her favor!
O Maud were sure of Heaven
  If lowliness could save her.

VI.

I know the way she went
  Home with her maiden posy,
For her feet have touch'd the meadows
  And left the daisies rosy.

VII.

Birds in the high Hall-garden
  Were crying and calling to her,
Where is Maud, Maud, Maud,
  One is come to woo her.

VIII.

Look, a horse at the door,
  And little King Charley snarling,
Go back, my lord, across the moor,
  You are not her darling.

XIII.

I.

Scorn'd, to be scorn'd by one that I scorn,
Is that a matter to make me fret?
That a calamity hard to be borne?
Well, he may live to hate me yet.
Fool that I am to be vext with his pride!
I past him, I was crossing his lands;
He stood on the path a little aside;
His face, as I grant, in spite of spite,
Has a broad-blown comeliness, red and
    white,
And six feet two, as I think, he stands;
But his essences turn'd the live air sick,
And barbarous opulence jewel-thick
Sunn'd itself on his breast and his hands.

II.

Who shall call me ungentle, unfair,
I long'd so heartily then and there
To give him the grasp of fellowship;
But while I past he was humming an
    air,
Stopt, and then with a riding whip
Leisurely tapping a glossy boot,
And curving a contumelious lip,
Gorgonized me from head to foot
With a stony British stare.

III.

Why sits he here in his father's chair?
That old man never comes to his place:
Shall I believe him ashamed to be seen?
For only once, in the village-street,
Last year, I caught a glimpse of his face,
A gray old wolf and a lean.
Scarcely, now, would I call him a cheat;
For then, perhaps, as a child of deceit,
She might by a true descent be untrue;
And Maud is as true as Maud is sweet:
Tho' I fancy her sweetness only due
To the sweeter blood by the other side;
Her mother has been a thing complete,
However she came to be so allied.
And fair without, faithful within,
Maud to him is nothing akin:
Some peculiar mystic grace
Made her only the child of her mother,
And heap'd the whole inherited sin
On that huge scapegoat of the race,
All, all upon the brother.

IV.

Peace, angry spirit, and let him be!
Has not his sister smiled on me?

XIV.

I.

Maud has a garden of roses
And lilies fair on a lawn;
There she walks in her state
And tends upon bed and bower,
And thither I climb'd at dawn
And stood by her garden-gate;
A lion ramps at the top,
He is claspt by a passion-flower.

II.

Maud's own little oak-room
(Which Maud, like a precious stone
Set in the heart of the carven gloom,
Lights with herself, when alone
She sits by her music and books,
And her brother lingers late
With a roystering company)looks
Upon Maud's own garden-gate:
And I thought as I stood, if a hand, as
    white
As ocean-foam in the moon, were laid
On the hasp of the window, and my Delight
Had a sudden desire, like a glorious
    ghost, to glide,
Like a beam of the seventh Heaven,
    down to my side,
There were but a step to be made.

III.

The fancy flatter'd my mind,
And again seem'd overbold;
Now I thought that she cared for me,
Now I thought she was kind
Only because she was cold.

IV.

I heard no sound where I stood
But the rivulet on from the lawn
Running down to my own dark wood;
Or the voice of the long sea-wave as it
    swell'd
Now and then in the dim-gray dawn;
But I look'd, and round, all round the
    house I beheld
The death-white curtain drawn;
Felt a horror over me creep,
Prickle my skin and catch my breath,
Knew that the death-white curtain meant
    but sleep,
Yet I shudder'd and thought like a fool
    of the sleep of death.

XV.

So dark a mind within me dwells,
  And I make myself such evil cheer,
That if *I* be dear to some one else,
  Then some one else may have much
      to fear ;
But if *I* be dear to some one else,
  Then I should be to myself more dear.
Shall I not take care of all that I think,
Yea ev'n of wretched meat and drink,
  If I be dear,
  If I be dear to some one else ?

XVI.

I.

This lump of earth has left his estate
The lighter by the loss of his weight ;
And so that he find what he went to
    seek,
And fulsome Pleasure clog him, and drown
His heart in the gross mud-honey of town,
He may stay for a year who has gone for
    a week :
But this is the day when I must speak,
And I see my Oread coming down,
O this is the day !
O beautiful creature, what am I
That I dare to look her way ;
Think I may hold dominion sweet,
Lord of the pulse that is lord of her breast,
And dream of her beauty with tender
    dread,
From the delicate Arab arch of her feet
To the grace that, bright and light as
    the crest
Of a peacock, sits on her shining head,
And she knows it not : O, if she knew it,
To know her beauty might half undo it.
I know it the one bright thing to save
My yet young life in the wilds of Time,
Perhaps from madness, perhaps from
    crime,
Perhaps from a selfish grave.

II.

What, if she be fasten'd to this fool
    lord,
Dare I bid her abide by her word ?
Should I love her so well if she
Had given her word to a thing so low ?
Shall I love her as well if she
Can break her word were it even for me ?
I trust that it is not so.

III.

Catch not my breath, O clamorous heart,
Let not my tongue be a thrall to my eye,
For I must tell her before we part,
I must tell her, or die.

XVII.

Go not, happy day,
  From the shining fields,
Go not, happy day,
  Till the maiden yields.
Rosy is the West,
  Rosy is the South,
Roses are her cheeks,
  And a rose her mouth.
When the happy Yes
  Falters from her lips,
Pass and blush the news
  O'er the blowing ships.
Over blowing seas,
  Over seas at rest,
Pass the happy news,
  Blush it thro' the West ;
Till the red man dance
  By his red cedar tree,
And the red man's babe
  Leap, beyond the sea.
Blush from West to East,
  Blush from East to West,
Till the West is East,
  Blush it thro' the West.
Rosy is the West,
  Rosy is the South,
Roses are her cheeks,
  And a rose her mouth.

XVIII.

I.

I have led her home, my love, my only
    friend.
There is none like her, none.
And never yet so warmly ran my blood
And sweetly, on and on
Calming itself to the long-wish'd-for end,
Full to the banks, close on the promised
    good.

II.

None like her, none.
Just now the dry-tongued laurels' patter-
    ing talk
Seem'd her light foot along the garden
    walk,

And shook my heart to think she comes
    once more;
But even then I heard her close the door,
The gates of Heaven are closed, and she
    is gone.

III.

There is none like her, none.
Nor will be when our summers have de-
    ceased.
O, art thou sighing for Lebanon
In the long breeze that streams to thy
    delicious East,
Sighing for Lebanon,
Dark cedar, tho' thy limbs have here in-
    creased,
Upon a pastoral slope as fair,
And looking to the South, and fed
With honey'd rain and delicate air,
And haunted by the starry head
Of her whose gentle will has changed my
    fate,
And made my life a perfumed altar-flame;
And over whom thy darkness must have
    spread
With such delight as theirs of old, thy great
Forefathers of the thornless garden, there
Shadowing the snow-limb'd Eve from
    whom she came.

IV.

Here will I lie, while these long branches
    sway,
And you fair stars that crown a happy
    day
Go in and out as if at merry play,
Who am no more so all forlorn,
As when it seem'd far better to be born
To labor and the mattock-harden'd hand,
Than nursed at ease and brought to un-
    derstand
A sad astrology, the boundless plan
That makes you tyrants in your iron skies,
Innumerable, pitiless, passionless eyes,
Cold fires, yet with power to burn and
    brand
His nothingness into man.

V.

But now shine on, and what care I,
Who in this stormy gulf have found a
    pearl
The countercharm of space and hollow sky,
And do accept my madness, and would
    die
To save from some slight shame one sim-
    ple girl.

VI.

Would die; for sullen-seeming Death
    may give
More life to Love than is or ever was
In our low world, where yet 't is sweet
    to live.
Let no one ask me how it came to pass;
It seems that I am happy, that to me
A livelier emerald twinkles in the grass,
A purer sapphire melts into the sea.

VII.

Not die; but live a life of truest breath,
And teach true life to fight with mortal
    wrongs.
O, why should Love, like men in drink-
    ing-songs,
Spice his fair banquet with the dust of
    death?
Make answer, Maud my bliss,
Maud made my Maud by that long lover's
    kiss,
Life of my life, wilt thou not answer this?
"The dusky strand of Death inwoven
    here
With dear Love's tie, makes Love him-
    self more dear."

VIII.

Is that enchanted moan only the swell
Of the long waves that roll in yonder bay?
And hark the clock within, the silver knell
Of twelve sweet hours that past in bridal
    white,
And died to live, long as my pulses play;
But now by this my love has closed her
    sight
And given false death her hand, and
    stol'n away
To dreamful wastes where footless fancies
    dwell
Among the fragments of the golden day.
May nothing there her maiden grace
    affright!
Dear heart, I feel with thee the drowsy
    spell.
My bride to be, my evermore delight,
My own heart's heart and ownest own
    farewell;
It is but for a little space I go:
And ye meanwhile far over moor and fell
Beat to the noiseless music of the night!
Has our whole earth gone nearer to the
    glow
Of your soft splendors that you look so
    bright?

I have climb'd nearer out of lonely Hell.
Beat, happy stars, timing with things below,
Beat with my heart more blest than heart can tell,
Blest, but for some dark undercurrent woe
That seems to draw — but it shall not be so:
Let all be well, be well.

XIX.

I.

Her brother is coming back to-night,
Breaking up my dream of delight.

II.

My dream? do I dream of bliss?
I have walk'd awake with Truth.
O when did a morning shine
So rich in atonement as this
For my dark-dawning youth,
Darken'd watching a mother decline
And that dead man at her heart and mine:
For who was left to watch her but I?
Yet so did I let my freshness die.

III.

I trust that I did not talk
To gentle Maud in our walk
(For often in lonely wanderings
I have cursed him even to lifeless things)
But I trust that I did not talk,
Not touch on her father's sin:
I am sure I did but speak
Of my mother's faded cheek
When it slowly grew so thin,
That I felt she was slowly dying
Vext with lawyers and harass'd with debt:
For how often I caught her with eyes all wet,
Shaking her head at her son and sighing
A world of trouble within!

IV.

And Maud too, Maud was moved
To speak of the mother she loved
As one scarce less forlorn,
Dying abroad and it seems apart
From him who had ceased to share her heart,
And ever mourning over the feud,
The household Fury sprinkled with blood
By which our houses are torn:
How strange was what she said,
When only Maud and the brother
Hung over her dying bed —
That Maud's dark father and mine
Had bound us one to the other,
Betrothed us over their wine,
On the day when Maud was born;
Seal'd her mine from her first sweet breath.
Mine, mine by a right, from birth till death,
Mine, mine — our fathers have sworn.

V.

But the true blood spilt had in it a heat
To dissolve the precious seal on a bond,
That, if left uncancell'd, had been so sweet:
And none of us thought of a something beyond,
A desire that awoke in the heart of the child,
As it were a duty done to the tomb,
To be friends for her sake, to be reconciled;
And I was cursing them and my doom,
And letting a dangerous thought run wild
While often abroad in the fragrant gloom
Of foreign churches — I see her there,
Bright English lily, breathing a prayer
To be friends, to be reconciled!

VI.

But then what a flint is he!
Abroad, at Florence, at Rome,
I find whenever she touch'd on me
This brother had laugh'd her down,
And at last, when each came home,
He had darken'd into a frown,
Chid her, and forbid her to speak
To me, her friend of the years before;
And this was what had redden'd her cheek
When I bow'd to her on the moor.

VII.

Yet Maud, altho' not blind
To the faults of his heart and mind,
I see she cannot but love him,
And says he is rough but kind,
And wishes me to approve him,
And tells me, when she lay
Sick once, with a fear of worse,
That he left his wine and horses and play,
Sat with her, read to her, night and day,
And tended her like a nurse.

VIII.

Kind? but the deathbed desire
Spurn'd by this heir of the liar —

Rough but kind — yet I know
He has plotted against me in this,
That he plots against me still.
Kind to Maud? that were not amiss.
Well, rough but kind; why let it be so:
For shall not Maud have her will?

IX.

For, Maud, so tender and true,
As long as my life endures
I feel I shall owe you a debt,
That I never can hope to pay;
And if ever I should forget
That I owe this debt to you
And for your sweet sake to yours;
O then, what then shall I say? —
If ever I *should* forget,
May God make me more wretched
Then ever I have been yet!

X.

So now I have sworn to bury
All this dead body of hate,
I feel so free and so clear
By the loss of that dead weight,
That I should grow light-headed, I fear,
Fantastically merry;
But that her brother comes, like a blight
On my fresh hope, to the Hall to-night.

XX.

I.

STRANGE, that I felt so gay,
Strange that *I* tried to-day
To beguile her melancholy;
The Sultan, as we name him, —
She did not wish to blame him —
But he vext her and perplext her
With his worldly talk and folly:
Was it gentle to reprove her
For stealing out of view
From a little lazy lover
Who but claims her as his due?
Or for chilling his caresses
By the coldness of her manners,
Nay, the plainness of her dresses?
Now I know her but in two,
Nor can pronounce upon it
If one should ask me whether
The habit, hat, and feather,
Or the frock and gypsy bonnet
Be the neater and completer;
For nothing can be sweeter
Than maiden Maud in either.

II.

But to-morrow, if we live,
Our ponderous squire will give
A grand political dinner
To half the squirelings near;
And Maud will wear her jewels,
And the bird of prey will hover,
And the titmouse hope to win her
With his chirrup at her ear.

III.

A grand political dinner
To the men of many acres,
A gathering of the Tory,
A dinner and then a dance
For the maids and marriage-makers,
And every eye but mine will glance
At Maud in all her glory.

IV.

For I am not invited,
But, with the Sultan's pardon,
I am all as well delighted,
For I know her own rose-garden,
And mean to linger in it
Till the dancing will be over;
And then, O then, come out to me
For a minute, but for a minute,
Come out to your own true lover,
That your true lover may see
Your glory also, and render
All homage to his own darling,
Queen Maud in all her splendor.

XXI.

RIVULET crossing my ground,
And bringing me down from the Hall
This garden-rose that I found,
Forgetful of Maud and me,
And lost in trouble and moving round
Here at the head of a tinkling fall,
And trying to pass to the sea;
O Rivulet, born at the Hall,
My Maud has sent it by thee
(If I read her sweet will right)
On a blushing mission to me,
Saying in odor and color, "Ah, be
Among the roses to-night."

XXII.

I.

COME into the garden, Maud,
  For the black bat, night, has flown,

"Come into the garden, Maud."

Come into the garden, Maud,
  I am here at the gate alone ;
And the woodbine spices are wafted
    abroad,
  And the musk of the roses blown.

II.

For a breeze of morning moves,
  And the planet of Love is on high,
Beginning to faint in the light that she
    loves
  On a bed of daffodil sky,
To faint in the light of the sun she loves,
  To faint in his light, and to die.

III.

All night have the roses heard
  The flute, violin, bassoon ;
All night has the casement jessamine
    stirr'd
  To the dancers dancing in tune ;
Till a silence fell with the waking bird,
  And a hush with the setting moon.

IV.

I said to the lily, "There is but one
  With whom she has heart to be gay.
When will the dancers leave her alone ?
  She is weary of dance and play."
Now half to the setting moon are gone,
  And half to the rising day ;
Low on the sand and loud on the stone
  The last wheel echoes away.

V.

I said to the rose, "The brief night goes
  In babble and revel and wine.
O young lord-lover, what sighs are those,
  For one that will never be thine ?
But mine, but mine," so I sware to the
    rose,
  "For ever and ever, mine."

VI.

And the soul of the rose went into my
    blood,
  As the music clash'd in the hall ;

And long by the garden lake I stood,
  For l heard your rivulet fall
From the lake to the meadow and on to
    the wood,
  Our wood, that is dearer than all ;

VII.

From the meadow your walks have left
    so sweet
That whenever a March-wind sighs
He sets the jewel-print of your feet
  In violets blue as your eyes,
To the woody hollows in which we meet
  And the valleys of Paradise.

VIII.

The slender acacia would not shake
  One long milk-bloom on the tree;
The white lake-blossom fell into the lake
  As the pimpernel dozed on the lea ;
But the rose was awake all night for your
    sake,
  Knowing your promise to me ;
The lilies and roses were all awake,
  They sigh'd for the dawn and thee.

IX.

Queen rose of the rosebud garden of girls,
  Come hither, the dances are done,
In gloss of satin and glimmer of pearls,
  Queen lily and rose in one ;
Shine out, little head, sunning over with
    curls,
  To the flowers, and be their sun.

X.

There has fallen a splendid tear
  From the passion-flower at the gate.
She is coming, my dove, my dear ;
  She is coming, my life, my fate ;
The red rose cries, "She is near, she is
    near" ;
  And the white rose weeps, "She is
    late" ;
The larkspur listens, "I hear, I hear";
  And the lily whispers, "I wait."

XI.

She is coming, my own, my sweet ;
  Were it ever so airy a tread,
My heart would hear her and beat,
  Were it earth in an earthy bed ;
My dust would hear her and beat,
  Had I lain for a century dead ;
Would start and tremble under her feet,
  And blossom in purple and red.

XXIII.

I.

"THE fault was mine, the fault was
    mine" —
Why am I sitting here so stunn'd and still,
Plucking the harmless wild-flower on the
    hill ? —
It is this guilty hand ! —
And there rises ever a passionate cry
From underneath in the darkening land —
What is it, that has been done ?
O dawn of Eden bright over earth and sky,
The fires of Hell brake out of thy rising
    sun,
The fires of Hell and of Hate ;
For she, sweet soul, had hardly spoken a
    word,
When her brother ran in his rage to the
    gate,
He came with the babe-faced lord ;
Heap'd on her terms of disgrace,
And while she wept, and l strove to be cool,
He fiercely gave me the lie,
Till I with as fierce an anger spoke,
And he struck me, madman, over the face,
Struck me before the languid fool,
Who was gaping and grinning by :
Struck for himself an evil stroke ;
Wrought for his house an irredeemable
    woe ;
For front to front in an hour we stood,
And a million horrible bellowing echoes
    broke
From the red-ribb'd hollow behind the
    wood,
And thunder'd up into Heaven the
    Christless code,
That must have life for a blow.
Ever and ever afresh they seem'd to grow.
Was it he lay there with a fading eye ?
"The fault was mine," he whisper'd,
    "fly !"
Then glided out of the joyous wood
The ghastly Wraith of one that I know ;
And there rang on a sudden a passionate
    cry,
A cry for a brother's blood :
It will ring in my heart and my ears, till
    I die, till I die.

II.

Is it gone ? my pulses beat —
What was it ? a lying trick of the brain ?
Yet I thought I saw her stand,
A shadow there at my feet,
High over the shadowy land.

It is gone; and the heavens fall in a
    gentle rain,
When they should burst and drown with
    deluging storms
The feeble vassals of wine and anger and
    lust,
The little hearts that know not how to
    forgive:
Arise, my God, and strike, for we hold
    Thee just,
Strike dead the whole weak race of ven-
    omous worms,
That sting each other here in the dust;
We are not worthy to live.

XXIV.

I.

SEE what a lovely shell,
Small and pure as a pearl,
Lying close to my foot,
Frail, but a work divine,
Made so fairily well
With delicate spire and whorl,
How exquisitely minute,
A miracle of design!

II.

What is it? a learned man
Could give it a clumsy name.
Let him name it who can,
The beauty would be the same.

III.

The tiny cell is forlorn,
Void of the little living will
That made it stir on the shore.
Did he stand at the diamond door
Of his house in a rainbow frill?
Did he push, when he was uncurl'd,
A golden foot or a fairy horn
Thro' his dim water-world?

IV.

Slight, to be crush'd with a tap
Of my finger-nail on the sand,
Small, but a work divine,
Frail, but of force to withstand,
Year upon year, the shock
Of cataract seas that snap
The three decker's oaken spine
Athwart the ledges of rock,
Here on the Breton strand!

V.

Breton, not Briton; here
Like a shipwreck'd man on a coast
Of ancient fable and fear —
Plagued with a flitting to and fro,
A disease, a hard mechanic ghost
That never came from on high
Nor ever arose from below,
But only moves with the moving eye,
Flying along the land and the main —
Why should it look like Maud?
Am I to be overawed
By what I cannot but know
Is a juggle born of the brain?

VI.

Back from the Breton coast,
Sick of a nameless fear,
Back to the dark sea-line
Looking, thinking of all I have lost;
An old song vexes my ear;
But that of Lamech is mine.

VII.

For years, a measureless ill,
For years, for ever, to part —
But she, she would love me still;
And as long, O God, as she
Have a grain of love for me,
So long, no doubt, no doubt,
Shall I nurse in my dark heart,
However weary, a spark of will
Not to be trampled out.

VIII.

Strange, that the mind, when fraught
With a passion so intense
One would think that it well
Might drown all life in the eye, —
That it should, by being so overwrought,
Suddenly strike on a sharper sense
For a shell, or a flower, little things
Which else would have been past by!
And now I remember, I,
When he lay dying there,
I noticed one of his many rings
(For he had many, poor worm) and thought
It is his mother's hair.

IX.

Who knows if he be dead?
Whether I need have fled?
Am I guilty of blood?
However this may be,
Comfort her, comfort her, all things good,
While I am over the sea!

Let me and my passionate love go by,
But speak to her all things holy and
   high,
Whatever happen to me !
Me and my harmful love go by ;
But come to her waking, find her asleep,
Powers of the height, Powers of the deep,
And comfort her tho' I die.

XXV.

COURAGE, poor heart of stone !
I will not ask thee why
Thou canst not understand
That thou art left for ever alone :
Courage, poor stupid heart of stone. —
Or if I ask thee why,
Care not thou to reply :
She is but dead, and the time is at hand
When thou shalt more than die.

XXVI.

I.

O THAT 't were possible
After long grief and pain
To find the arms of my true love
Round me once again !

II.

When I was wont to meet her
In the silent woody places
By the home that gave me birth,
We stood tranced in long embraces
Mixt with kisses sweeter sweeter
Than anything on earth.

III.

A shadow flits before me,
Not thou, but like to thee ;
Ah Christ, that it were possible
For one short hour to see
The souls we loved, that they might tell
   us
What and where they be.

IV.

It leads me forth at evening,
It lightly winds and steals
In a cold white robe before me,
When all my spirit reels
At the shouts, the leagues of lights,
And the roaring of the wheels.

V.

Half the night I waste in sighs,
Half in dreams I sorrow after
The delight of early skies ;
In a wakeful doze I sorrow
For the hand, the lips, the eyes,
For the meeting of the morrow,
The delight of happy laughter,
The delight of low replies.

VI.

'T is a morning pure and sweet,
And a dewy splendor falls
On the little flower that clings
To the turrets and the walls ;
'T is a morning pure and sweet,
And the light and shadow fleet ;
She is walking in the meadow,
And the woodland echo rings ;
In a moment we shall meet ;
She is singing in the meadow,
And the rivulet at her feet
Ripples on in light and shadow
To the ballad that she sings.

VII.

Do I hear her sing as of old,
My bird with the shining head,
My own dove with the tender eye ?
But there rings on a sudden a passionate
   cry,
There is some one dying or dead,
And a sullen thunder is roll'd ;
For a tumult shakes the city,
And I wake, my dream is fled ;
In the shuddering dawn, behold,
Without knowledge, without pity,
By the curtains of my bed
That abiding phantom cold.

VIII.

Get thee hence, nor come again,
Mix not memory with doubt,
Pass, thou deathlike type of pain,
Pass and cease to move about !
'T is the blot upon the brain
That *will* show itself without.

IX.

Then I rise, the eavedrops fall,
And the yellow vapors choke
The great city sounding wide ;
The day comes, a dull red ball
Wrapt in drifts of lurid smoke
On the misty river-tide.

X.

Thro' the hubbub of the market
I steal, a wasted frame,
It crosses here, it crosses there,
Thro' all that crowd confused and loud,
The shadow still the same;
And on my heavy eyelids
My anguish hangs like shame.

XI.

Alas for her that met me,
That heard me softly call,
Came glimmering thro' the laurels
At the quiet evenfall,
In the garden by the turrets
Of the old manorial hall.

XII.

Would the happy spirit descend,
From the realms of light and song,
In the chamber or the street,
As she looks among the blest,
Should I fear to greet my friend
Or to say "forgive the wrong,"
Or to ask her, "take me, sweet,
To the regions of thy rest"?

XIII.

But the broad light glares and beats,
And the shadow flits and fleets
And will not let me be;
And I loathe the squares and streets,
And the faces that one meets,
Hearts with no love for me:
Always I long to creep
Into some still cavern deep,
There to weep, and weep, and weep
My whole soul out to thee.

XXVII.

I.

Dead, long dead,
Long dead!
And my heart is a handful of dust,
And the wheels go over my head,
And my bones are shaken with pain,
For into a shallow grave they are thrust,
Only a yard beneath the street,
And the hoofs of the horses beat, beat,
The hoofs of the horses beat,
Beat into my scalp and my brain,
With never an end to the stream of passing feet,
Driving, hurrying, marrying, burying,
Clamor and rumble, and ringing and clatter,
And here beneath it is all as bad,
For I thought the dead had peace, but it is not so;
To have no peace in the grave, is that not sad?
But up and down and to and fro,
Ever about me the dead men go;
And then to hear a dead man chatter
Is enough to drive one mad.

II.

Wretchedest age, since Time began,
They cannot even bury a man;
And tho' we paid our tithes in the days that are gone,
Not a bell was rung, not a prayer was read;
It is that which makes us loud in the world of the dead;
There is none that does his work, not one;
A touch of their office might have sufficed,
But the churchmen fain would kill their church,
As the churches have kill'd their Christ.

III.

See, there is one of us sobbing,
No limit to his distress;
And another, a lord of all things, praying
To his own great self, as I guess;
And another, a statesman there, betraying
His party-secret, fool, to the press;
And yonder a vile physician, blabbing
The case of his patient — all for what?
To tickle the maggot born in an empty head,
And wheedle a world that loves him not,
For it is but a world of the dead.

IV.

Nothing but idiot gabble!
For the prophecy given of old
And then not understood,
Has come to pass as foretold;
Not let any man think for the public good,
But babble, merely for babble.
For I never whisper'd a private affair
Within the hearing of cat or mouse,
No, not to myself in the closet alone,
But I heard it shouted at once from the top of the house;
Everything came to be known:
Who told *him* we were there?

V.

Not that gray old wolf, for he came not back
From the wilderness, full of wolves,
  where he used to lie;
He has gather'd the bones for his o'er-
  grown whelp to crack;
Crack them now for yourself, and howl,
  and die.

VI.

Prophet, curse me the blabbing lip,
And curse me the British vermin, the rat;
I know not whether he came in the
  Hanover ship,
But I know that he lies and listens mute
In an ancient mansion's crannies and
  holes:
Arsenic, arsenic, sure, would do it,
Except that now we poison our babes,
  poor souls!
It is all used up for that.

VII.

Tell him now: she is standing here at
  my head;
Not beautiful now, not even kind;
He may take her now; for she never
  speaks her mind,
But is ever the one thing silent here.
She is not of us, as I divine;
She comes from another stiller world of
  the dead,
Stiller, not fairer than mine.

VIII.

But I know where a garden grows,
Fairer than aught in the world beside,
All made up of the lily and rose
That blow by night, when the season is
  good,
To the sound of dancing music and flutes:
It is only flowers, they had no fruits,
And I almost fear they are not roses, but
  blood;
For the keeper was one, so full of pride,
He linkt a dead man there to a spectral
  bride;
For he, if he had not been a Sultan of
  brutes,
Would he have that hole in his side?

IX.

But what will the old man say?
He laid a cruel snare in a pit
To catch a friend of mine one stormy day;
Yet now I could even weep to think of it;
For what will the old man say
When he comes to the second corpse in
  the pit?

X.

Friend, to be struck by the public foe,
Then to strike him and lay him low,
That were a public merit, far,
Whatever the Quaker holds, from sin;
But the red life spilt for a private blow—
I swear to you, lawful and lawless war
Are scarcely even akin.

XI.

O me, why have they not buried me deep
  enough?
Is it kind to have made me a grave so
  rough,
Me, that was never a quiet sleeper?
Maybe still I am but half-dead;
Then I cannot be wholly dumb;
I will cry to the steps above my head,
And somebody, surely, some kind heart
  will come
To bury me, bury me
Deeper, ever so little deeper.

XXVIII.

I.

My life has crept so long on a broken wing
Thro' cells of madness, haunts of horror
  and fear,
That I come to be grateful at last for a
  little thing:
My mood is changed, for it fell at a time
  of year
When the face of night is fair on the
  dewy downs,
And the shining daffodil dies, and the
  Charioteer
And starry Gemini hang like glorious
  crowns
Over Orion's grave low down in the west,
That like a silent lightning under the stars
She seem'd to divide in a dream from a
  band of the blest,
And spoke of a hope for the world in the
  coming wars—
"And in that hope, dear soul, let trouble
  have rest,
Knowing I tarry for thee," and pointed
  to Mars
As he glow'd like a ruddy shield on the
  Lion's breast.

THE BROOK.

II.

And it was but a dream, yet it yielded a dear delight
To have look'd, tho' but in a dream, upon eyes so fair,
That had been in a weary world my one thing bright;
And it was but a dream, yet it lighten'd my despair
When I thought that a war would arise in defence of the right,
That an iron tyranny now should bend or cease,
The glory of manhood stand on his ancient height,
Nor Britain's one sole God be the millionnaire:
No more shall commerce be all in all, and Peace
Pipe on her pastoral hillock a languid note,
And watch her harvest ripen, her herd increase,
Nor the cannon-bullet rust on a slothful shore,
And the cobweb woven across the cannon's throat
Shall shake its threaded tears in the wind no more.

III.

And as months ran on and rumor of battle grew,
"It is time, it is time, O passionate heart," said I
(For I cleaved to a cause that I felt to be pure and true),
"It is time, O passionate heart and morbid eye,
That old hysterical mock-disease should die."
And I stood on a giant deck and mix'd my breath
With a loyal people shouting a battle cry,
Till I saw the dreary phantom arise and fly
Far into the North, and battle, and seas of death.

IV.

Let it go or stay, so I wake to the higher aims
Of a land that has lost for a little her lust of gold,
And love of a peace that was full of wrongs and shames,
Horrible, hateful, monstrous, not to be told;
And hail once more to the banner of battle unroll'd !
Tho' many a light shall darken, and many shall weep
For those that are crush'd in the clash of jarring claims,
Yet God's just wrath shall be wreak'd on a giant liar;
And many a darkness into the light shall leap,
And shine in the sudden making of splendid names,
And noble thought be freër under the sun,
And the heart of a people beat with one desire;
For the peace, that I deem'd no peace, is over and done,
And now by the side of the Black and the Baltic deep,
And deathful-grinning mouths of the fortress, flames
The blood-red blossom of war with a heart of fire.

V.

Let it flame or fade, and the war roll down like a wind,
We have proved we have hearts in a cause, we are noble still,
And myself have awaked, as it seems, to the better mind;
It is better to fight for the good, than to rail at the ill;
I have felt with my native land, I am one with my kind,
I embrace the purpose of God and the doom assign'd.

THE BROOK;

AN IDYL.

"HERE, by this brook, we parted; I to the East
And he for Italy — too late — too late:
One whom the strong sons of the world despise;
For lucky rhymes to him were scrip and share,
And mellow metres more than cent for cent;
Nor could he understand how money breeds,
Thought it a dead thing; yet himself could make
The thing that is not as the thing that is.

O had he lived! In our schoolbooks
  we say,
Of those that held their heads above the
  crowd,
They flourish'd then or then; but life in
  him
Could scarce be said to flourish, only
  touch'd
On such a time as goes before the leaf,
When all the wood stands in a mist of
  green,
And nothing perfect: yet the brook he
  loved,
For which, in branding summers of
  Bengal,
Or ev'n the sweet half-English Neilgherry
  air
I panted, seems, as I re-listen to it,
Prattling the primrose fancies of the boy,
To me that loved him; for 'O brook,'
  he says,
'O babbling brook,' says Edmund in
  his rhyme,
'Whence come you?' and the brook,
  why not? replies.

I come from haunts of coot and hern,
  I make a sudden sally
And sparkle out among the fern,
  To bicker down a valley.

By thirty hills I hurry down,
  Or slip between the ridges,
By twenty thorps, a little town,
  And half a hundred bridges.

Till last by Philip's farm I flow
  To join the brimming river,
For men may come and men may go,
  But I go on for ever.

"Poor lad, he died at Florence, quite
  worn out,
Travelling to Naples. There is Darnley
  bridge,
It has more ivy; there the river; and there
Stands Philip's farm where brook and
  river meet.

I chatter over stony ways,
  In little sharps and trebles,
I bubble into eddying bays,
  I babble on the pebbles.

With many a curve my banks I fret
  By many a field and fallow,
And many a fairy foreland set
  With willow-weed and mallow.

I chatter, chatter, as I flow
  To join the brimming river,
For men may come and men may go,
  But I go on for ever.

"But Philip chatter'd more than brook
  or bird;
Old Philip; all about the fields you caught
His weary daylong chirping, like the dry
High-elbow'd grigs that leap in summer
  grass.

I wind about, and in and out,
  With here a blossom sailing,
And here and there a lusty trout,
  And here and there a grayling,

And here and there a foamy flake
  Upon me, as I travel
With many a silvery waterbreak
  Above the golden gravel,

And draw them all along, and flow
  To join the brimming river,
For men may come and men may go,
  But I go on for ever.

"O darling Katie Willows, his one
  child!
A maiden of our century, yet most meek;
A daughter of our meadows, yet not coarse;
Straight, but as lissome as a hazel wand;
Her eyes a bashful azure, and her hair
In gloss and hue the chestnut, when the
  shell
Divides threefold to show the fruit
  within.

"Sweet Katie, once I did her a good turn,
Her and her far-off cousin and be-
  trothed,
James Willows, of one name and heart
  with her.
For here I came, twenty years back —
  the week
Before I parted with poor Edmund; crost
By that old bridge which, half in ruins
  then,
Still makes a hoary eyebrow for the gleam
Beyond it, where the waters marry —
  crost,
Whistling a random bar of Bonny Doon,
And push'd at Philip's garden-gate. The
  gate,

"I come from haunts of coot and hern,
I make a sudden sally
And sparkle out among the fern."

Half-parted from a weak and scolding
  hinge,
Stuck; and he clamor'd from a case-
  ment, 'run'
To Katie somewhere in the walks below,
'Run, Katie!' Katie never ran: she
  moved
To meet me, winding under woodbine
  bowers,
A little flutter'd, with her eyelids down,
Fresh apple-blossom, blushing for a boon.

"What was it? less of sentiment than
  sense
Had Katie; not illiterate; nor of those
Who dabbling in the fount of fictive
  tears,
And nursed by mealy-mouth'd philan-
  thropies,
Divorce the Feeling from her mate the
  Deed.

"She told me. She and James had
  quarrell'd. Why?
What cause of quarrel? None, she said,
  no cause;
James had no cause: but when I prest
  the cause,
I learnt that James had flickering jeal-
  ousies
Which anger'd her. Who anger'd James?
  I said.
But Katie snatch'd her eyes at once from
  mine,
And sketching with her slender pointed
  foot
Some figure like a wizard's pentagram
On garden gravel, let my query pass
Unclaim'd, in flushing silence, till I
  ask'd
If James were coming. 'Coming every day,'
She answer'd, 'ever longing to explain,
But evermore her father came across

With some long-winded tale, and broke
  him short;
And James departed vext with him and
  her.'
How could I help her? 'Would I — was
  it wrong?'
(Claspt hands and that petitionary grace
Of sweet seventeen subdued me ere she
  spoke)
'O would I take her father for one hour,
For one half-hour, and let him talk to
  me!'
And even while she spoke, I saw where
  James
Made toward us, like a wader in the
  surf,
Beyond the brook, waist-deep in meadow-
  sweet.

"O Katie, what I suffer'd for your sake!
For in I went, and call'd old Philip out
To show the farm: full willingly he rose:
He led me thro' the short sweet-smelling
  lanes
Of his wheat suburb, babbling as he went.
He praised his land, his horses, his
  machines;
He praised his ploughs, his cows, his
  hogs, his dogs;
He praised his hens, his geese, his guinea-
  hens;
His pigeons, who in session on their roofs
Approved him, bowing at their own de-
  serts:
Then from the plaintive mother's teat he
  took
Her blind and shuddering puppies, nam-
  ing each,
And naming those, his friends, for whom
  they were:
Then crost the common into Darnley
  chase
To show Sir Arthur's deer. In copse and
  fern
Twinkled the innumerable ear and tail.
Then, seated on a serpent-rooted beech,
He pointed out a pasturing colt, and said:
'That was the four-year-old I sold the
  Squire.'
And there he told a long long-winded tale
Of how the Squire had seen the colt at
  grass,
And how it was the thing his daughter
  wish'd,
And how he sent the bailiff to the farm
To learn the price, and what the price
  he ask'd,

And how the bailiff swore that he was mad,
But he stood firm; and so the matter
  hung;
He gave them line: and five days after
  that
He met the bailiff at the Golden Fleece,
Who then and there had offer'd some-
  thing more,
But he stood firm; and so the matter
  hung;
He knew the man; the colt would fetch
  its price;
He gave them line: and how by chance
  at last
(It might be May or April, he forgot,
The last of April or the first of May)
He found the bailiff riding by the farm,
And, talking from the point, he drew him
  in,
And there he mellow'd all his heart with
  ale,
Until they closed a bargain, hand in hand.

'Then, while I breathed in sight of
  haven, he,
Poor fellow, could he help it? recom-
  menced,
And ran thro' all the coltish chronicle,
Wild Will, Black Bess, Tantivy, Tallyho,
Reform, White Rose, Bellerophon, the
  Jilt,
Arbaces, and Phenomenon, and the rest,
Till, not to die a listener, I arose,
And with me Philip, talking still; and so
We turn'd our foreheads from the falling
  sun,
And following our own shadows thrice as
  long
As when they follow'd us from Philip's
  door,
Arrived, and found the sun of sweet con-
  tent
Re-risen in Katie's eyes, and all things
  well.

I steal by lawns and grassy plots,
  I slide by hazel covers;
I move the sweet forget-me-nots
  That grow for happy lovers.

I slip, I slide, I gloom, I glance,
  Among my skimming swallows;
I make the netted sunbeam dance
  Against my sandy shallows.

I murmur under moon and stars
  In brambly wildernesses;

"I make the netted sunbeam dance
Against my sandy shallows."

I linger by my shingly bars;
  I loiter round my cresses;

And out again I curve and flow
  To join the brimming river,
For men may come and men may go,
  But I go on for ever.

Yes, men may come and go; and these are gone,
All gone. My dearest brother, Edmund, sleeps,
Not by the well-known stream and rustic spire,
But unfamiliar Arno, and the dome
Of Brunelleschi; sleeps in peace: and he,
Poor Philip, of all his lavish waste of words
Remains the lean P. W. on his tomb:
I scraped the lichen from it: Katie walks
By the long wash of Australasian seas
Far off, and holds her head to other stars,
And breathes in converse seasons. All are gone."

So Lawrence Aylmer, seated on a stile
In the long hedge, and rolling in his mind
Old waifs of rhyme, and bowing o'er the brook
A tonsured head in middle age forlorn,
Mused, and was mute. On a sudden a low breath
Of tender air made tremble in the hedge
The fragile bindweed-bells and briony rings;
And he look'd up. There stood a maiden near,
Waiting to pass. In much amaze he stared
On eyes a bashful azure, and on hair
In gloss and hue the chestnut, when the shell

Divides threefold to show the fruit within:
Then, wondering, ask'd her "Are you
  from the farm?"
"Yes" answer'd she. "Pray stay a
  little: pardon me;
What do they call you?" "Katie."
  "That were strange.
What surname?" "Willows." "No!"
  "That is my name."
"Indeed!" and here he look'd so self-
  perplext,
That Katie laugh'd, and laughing blush'd,
  till he
Laugh'd also, but as one before he wakes,
Who feels a glimmering strangeness in
  his dream.
Then looking at her; "Too happy, fresh
  and fair,
Too fresh and fair in our sad world's best
  bloom,
To be the ghost of one who bore your
  name
About these meadows, twenty years ago."

"Have you not heard?" said Katie,
  "we came back.
We bought the farm we tenanted before.
Am I so like her? so they said on board.
Sir, if you knew her in her English days,
My mother, as it seems you did, the
  days
That most she loves to talk of, come with
  me.
My brother James is in the harvest-field:
But she — you will be welcome — O,
  come in!"

THE LETTERS.

I.

STILL on the tower stood the vane,
  A black yew gloom'd the stagnant air,
I peer'd athwart the chancel pane
  And saw the altar cold and bare.
A clog of lead was round my feet,
  A band of pain across my brow;
"Cold altar, Heaven and earth shall meet
  Before you hear my marriage vow."

II.

I turn'd and humm'd a bitter song
  That mock'd the wholesome human
    heart,
And then we met in wrath and wrong,
  We met, but only meant to part.

Full cold my greeting was and dry;
  She faintly smiled, she hardly moved;
I saw with half-unconscious eye
  She wore the colors I approved.

III.

She took the little ivory chest,
  With half a sigh she turn'd the key,
Then raised her head with lips comprest,
  And gave my letters back to me.
And gave the trinkets and the rings,
  My gifts, when gifts of mine could
    please;
As looks a father on the things
  Of his dead son, I look'd on these.

IV.

She told me all her friends had said;
  I raged against the public liar;
She talk'd as if her love were dead,
  But in my words were seeds of fire.
"No more of love; your sex is known:
  I never will be twice deceived.
Henceforth I trust the man alone,
  The woman cannot be believed.

V.

"Thro' slander, meanest spawn of Hell
  (And women's slander is the worst),
And you, whom once I loved so well,
  Thro' you, my life will be accurst."
I spoke with heart, and heat and force,
  I shook her breast with vague alarms—
Like torrents from a mountain source
  We rush'd into each other's arms.

VI.

We parted: sweetly gleam'd the stars,
  And sweet the vapor-braided blue,
Low breezes fann'd the belfry bars,
  As homeward by the church I drew.
The very graves appear'd to smile,
  So fresh they rose in shadow'd swells;
"Dark porch," I said, "and silent aisle,
  There comes a sound of marriage bells."

ODE ON THE DEATH OF THE DUKE OF WELLINGTON.

I.

BURY the Great Duke
  With an empire's lamentation,
Let us bury the Great Duke
  To the noise of the mourning of a
    mighty nation,

Mourning when their leaders fall,
Warriors carry the warrior's pall,
And sorrow darkens hamlet and hall.

II.
Where shall we lay the man whom we deplore?
Here, in streaming London's central roar.
Let the sound of those he wrought for,
And the feet of those he fought for,
Echo round his bones for evermore.

III.
Lead out the pageant: sad and slow,
As fits an universal woe,
Let the long long procession go,
And let the sorrowing crowd about it grow,
And let the mournful martial music blow;
The last great Englishman is low.

IV.
Mourn, for to us he seems the last,
Remembering all his greatness in the Past.
No more in soldier fashion will he greet
With lifted hand the gazer in the street.
O friends, our chief state-oracle is mute:
Mourn for the man of long-enduring blood,
The statesman-warrior, moderate, resolute,
Whole in himself, a common good.
Mourn for the man of amplest influence,
Yet clearest of ambitious crime,
Our greatest yet with least pretence,
Great in council and great in war,
Foremost captain of his time,
Rich in saving common-sense,
And, as the greatest only are,
In his simplicity sublime.
O good gray head which all men knew,
O voice from which their omens all men drew,
O iron nerve to true occasion true,
O fall'n at length that tower of strength
Which stood four-square to all the winds that blew!
Such was he whom we deplore.
The long self-sacrifice of life is o'er.
The great World-victor's victor will be seen no more.

V.
All is over and done:
Render thanks to the Giver,
England, for thy son.
Let the bell be toll'd.
Render thanks to the Giver,
And render him to the mould.
Under the cross of gold
That shines over city and river,
There he shall rest for ever
Among the wise and the bold.
Let the bell be toll'd:
And a reverent people behold
The towering car, the sable steeds:
Bright let it be with its blazon'd deeds,
Dark in its funeral fold.
Let the bell be toll'd:
And a deeper knell in the heart be knoll'd;
And the sound of the sorrowing anthem roll'd
Thro' the dome of the golden cross;
And the volleying cannon thunder his loss;
He knew their voices of old.
For many a time in many a clime
His captain's-ear has heard them boom
Bellowing victory, bellowing doom:
When he with those deep voices wrought,
Guarding realms and kings from shame;
With those deep voices our dead captain taught
The tyrant, and asserts his claim
In that dread sound to the great name,
Which he has worn so pure of blame,
In praise and in dispraise the same,
A man of well-attemper'd frame.
O civic muse, to such a name,
To such a name for ages long,
To such a name,
Preserve a broad approach of fame,
And ever-echoing avenues of song.

VI.
Who is he that cometh, like an honor'd guest,
With banner and with music, with soldier and with priest,
With a nation weeping, and breaking on my rest?
Mighty Seaman, this is he
Was great by land as thou by sea.
Thine island loves thee well, thou famous man,
The greatest sailor since our world began.
Now, to the roll of muffled drums,
To thee the greatest soldier comes;
For this is he
Was great by land as thou by sea;
His foes were thine; he kept us free;
O give him welcome, this is he
Worthy of our gorgeous rites,
And worthy to be laid by thee;

For this is England's greatest son,
He that gain'd a hundred fights,
Nor ever lost an English gun;
This is he that far away
Against the myriads of Assaye
Clash'd with his fiery few and won;
And underneath another sun,
Warring on a later day,
Round affrighted Lisbon drew
The treble works, the vast designs
Of his labor'd rampart-lines,
Where he greatly stood at bay,
Whence he issued forth anew,
And ever great and greater grew,
Beating from the wasted vines
Back to France her banded swarms,
Back to France with countless blows,
Till o'er the hills her eagles flew
Beyond the Pyrenean pines,
Follow'd up in valley and glen
With blare of bugle, clamor of men,
Roll of cannon and clash of arms,
And England pouring on her foes.
Such a war had such a close.
Again their ravening eagle rose
In anger, wheel'd on Europe-shadowing wings,
And barking for the thrones of kings;
Till one that sought but Duty's iron crown
On that loud sabbath shook the spoiler down;
A day of onsets of despair!
Dash'd on every rocky square
Their surging charges foam'd themselves away;
Last, the Prussian trumpet blew;
Thro' the long-tormented air
Heaven flash'd a sudden jubilant ray,
And down we swept and charged and overthrew.
So great a soldier taught us there,
What long-enduring hearts could do
In that world's-earthquake, Waterloo!
Mighty Seaman, tender and true,
And pure as he from taint of craven guile,
O saviour of the silver-coasted isle,
O shaker of the Baltic and the Nile,
If aught of things that here befall
Touch a spirit among things divine,
If love of country move thee there at all,
Be glad, because his bones are laid by thine!
And thro' the centuries let a people's voice
In full acclaim,
A people's voice,
The proof and echo of all human fame,
A people's voice, when they rejoice
At civic revel and pomp and game,
Attest their great commander's claim
With honor, honor, honor, honor to him,
Eternal honor to his name.

VII.

A people's voice! we are a people yet.
Tho' all men else their nobler dreams forget,
Confused by brainless mobs and lawless Powers;
Thank Him who isled us here, and roughly set
His Briton in blown seas and storming showers,
We have a voice, with which to pay the debt
Of boundless love and reverence and regret
To those great men who fought, and kept it ours,
And keep it ours, O God, from brute control;
O Statesmen, guard us, guard the eye, the soul
Of Europe, keep our noble England whole,
And save the one true seed of freedom sown
Betwixt a people and their ancient throne,
That sober freedom out of which there springs
Our loyal passion for our temperate kings;
For, saving that, ye help to save mankind
Till public wrong be crumbled into dust,
And drill the raw world for the march of mind,
Till crowds at length be sane and crowns be just.
But wink no more in slothful overtrust.
Remember him who led your hosts;
He bade you guard the sacred coasts.
Your cannons moulder on the seaward wall;
His voice is silent in your council-hall
For ever; and whatever tempests lower
For ever silent; even if they broke
In thunder, silent; yet remember all
He spoke among you, and the Man who spoke;
Who never sold the truth to serve the hour,
Nor palter'd with Eternal God for power;
Who let the turbid streams of rumor flow
Thro' either babbling world of high and low;
Whose life was work, whose language rife
With rugged maxims hewn from life;
Who never spoke against a foe;

Whose eighty winters freeze with one rebuke
All great self-seekers trampling on the right :
Truth-teller was our England's Alfred named ;
Truth-lover was our English Duke ;
Whatever record leap to light
He never shall be shamed.

VIII.

Lo, the leader in these glorious wars
Now to glorious burial slowly borne,
Follow'd by the brave of other lands,
He, on whom from both her open hands
Lavish Honor shower'd all her stars,
And affluent Fortune emptied all her horn.
Yea, let all good things await
Him who cares not to be great,
But as he saves or serves the state.
Not once or twice in our rough island-story,
The path of duty was the way to glory :
He that walks it, only thirsting
For the right, and learns to deaden
Love of self, before his journey closes,
He shall find the stubborn thistle bursting
Into glossy purples, which outredden
All voluptuous garden-roses.
Not once or twice in our fair island-story,
The path of duty was the way to glory :
He, that ever following her commands,
On with toil of heart and knees and hands,
Thro' the long gorge to the far light has won
His path upward, and prevail'd,
Shall find the toppling crags of Duty scaled
Are close upon the shining table-lands
To which our God Himself is moon and sun.
Such was he : his work is done,
But while the races of mankind endure,
Let his great example stand
Colossal, seen of every land,
And keep the soldier firm, the statesman pure :
Till in all lands and thro' all human story
The path of duty be the way to glory :
And let the land whose hearths he saved from shame
For many and many an age proclaim
At civic revel and pomp and game,
And when the long-illumined cities flame,
Their ever-loyal iron leader's fame,
With honor, honor, honor, honor to him,
Eternal honor to his name.

IX.

Peace, his triumph will be sung
By some yet unmoulded tongue
Far on in summers that we shall not see :
Peace, it is a day of pain
For one about whose patriarchal knee
Late the little children clung :
O peace, it is a day of pain
For one, upon whose hand and heart and brain
Once the weight and fate of Europe hung.
Ours the pain, be his the gain !
More than is of man's degree
Must be with us, watching here
At this, our great solemnity.
Whom we see not we revere,
We revere, and we refrain
From talk of battles loud and vain,
And brawling memories all too free
For such a wise humility
As befits a solemn fane :
We revere, and while we hear
The tides of Music's golden sea
Setting toward eternity,
Uplifted high in heart and hope are we,
Until we doubt not that for one so true
There must be other nobler work to do
Than when he fought at Waterloo,
And Victor he must ever be.
For tho' the Giant Ages heave the hill
And break the shore, and evermore
Make and break, and work their will ;
Tho' world on world in myriad myriads roll
Round us, each with different powers,
And other forms of life than ours,
What know we greater than the soul ?
On God and Godlike men we build our trust.
Hush, the Dead March wails in the people's ears :
The dark crowd moves, and there are sobs and tears :
The black earth yawns : the mortal disappears ;
Ashes to ashes, dust to dust ;
He is gone who seem'd so great. —
Gone ; but nothing can bereave him
Of the force he made his own
Being here, and we believe him
Something far advanced in State,
And that he wears a truer crown
Than any wreath that man can weave him.
Speak no more of his renown,
Lay your earthly fancies down,
And in the vast cathedral leave him.
God accept him, Christ receive him.

1852.

THE DAISY.

WRITTEN AT EDINBURGH.

O LOVE, what hours were thine and mine
In lands of palm and southern pine ;
   In lands of palm, of orange-blossom,
Of olive, aloe, and maize and vine.

What Roman strength Turbia show'd
In ruin, by the mountain road ;
   How like a gem, beneath, the city
Of little Monaco, basking, glow'd.

How richly down the rocky dell
The torrent vineyard streaming fell
   To meet the sun and sunny waters,
That only heaved with a summer swell.

What slender campanili grew
By bays, the peacock's neck in hue ;
   Where, here and there, on sandy beaches
A milky-bell'd amaryllis blew.

How young Columbus seem'd to rove,
Yet present in his natal grove,
   Now watching high on mountain cornice,
And steering, now, from a purple cove,

Now pacing mute by ocean's rim
Till, in a narrow street and dim,
   I stay'd the wheels at Cogoletto,
And drank, and loyally drank to him.

Nor knew we well what pleased us most,
Not the clipt palm of which they boast ;
   But distant color, happy hamlet,
A moulder'd citadel on the coast,

Or tower, or high hill-convent, seen
A light amid its olives green ;
   Or olive-hoary cape in ocean ;
Or rosy blossom in hot ravine,

Where oleanders flush'd the bed
Of silent torrents, gravel-spread ;
   And, crossing, oft we saw the glisten
Of ice, far up on a mountain head.

We loved that hall, tho' white and cold,
Those niched shapes of noble mould,
   A princely people's awful princes,
The grave, severe Genovese of old.

At Florence too what golden hours,
In those long galleries, were ours ;
   What drives about the fresh Cascinè,
Or walks in Boboli's ducal bowers.

In bright vignettes, and each complete,
Of tower or duomo, sunny-sweet,
   Or palace, how the city glitter'd,
Thro' cypress avenues, at our feet.

But when we crost the Lombard plain
Remember what a plague of rain ;
   Of rain at Reggio, rain at Parma ;
At Lodi, rain, Piacenza, rain.

And stern and sad (so rare the smiles
Of sunlight) look'd the Lombard piles ;
   Porch-pillars on the lion resting,
And sombre, old, colonnaded aisles.

O Milan, O the chanting quires,
The giant windows' blazon'd fires,
   The height, the space, the gloom, the glory !
A mount of marble, a hundred spires !

I climb'd the roofs at break of day ;
Sun-smitten Alps before me lay.
   I stood among the silent statues,
And statued pinnacles, mute as they.

How faintly-flushed, how phantom-fair,
Was Monte Rosa hanging there
   A thousand shadowy-pencill'd valleys
And snowy dells in a golden air.

Remember how we came at last
To Como ; shower and storm and blast
   Had blown the lake beyond his limit,
And all was flooded ; and how we past

From Como, when the light was gray,
And in my head, for half the day,
   The rich Virgilian rustic measure
Of Lari Maxume, all the way,

Like ballad-burden music, kept,
As on The Lariano crept
   To that fair port below the castle
Of Queen Theodolind, where we slept ;

Or hardly slept, but watch'd awake
A cypress in the moonlight shake,
   The moonlight touching o'er a terrace
One tall Agavè above the lake.

What more ? we took our last adieu,
And up the snowy Splugen drew,
   But ere we reach'd the highest summit
I pluck'd a daisy, I gave it you.

It told of England then to me,
And now it tells of Italy.
   O love, we two shall go no longer
To lands of summer across the sea ;

So dear a life your arms enfold
Whose crying is a cry for gold:
   Yet here to-night in this dark city,
When ill and weary, alone and cold,

I found, tho' crush'd to hard and dry,
This nursling of another sky
   Still in the little book you lent me,
And where you tenderly laid it by:

And I forgot the clouded Forth,
The gloom that saddens Heaven and
   Earth,
   The bitter east, the misty summer
And gray metropolis of the North.

Perchance, to lull the throbs of pain,
Perchance, to charm a vacant brain,
   Perchance, to dream you still beside me,
My fancy fled to the South again.

TO THE REV. F. D. MAURICE.

COME, when no graver cares employ,
God-father, come and see your boy:
   Your presence will be sun in winter,
Making the little one leap for joy.

For, being of that honest few,
Who give the Fiend himself his due,
   Should eighty-thousand college-councils
Thunder "Anathema," friend, at you;

Should all our churchmen foam in spite
At you, so careful of the right,
   Yet one lay-hearth would give you welcome
(Take it and come) to the Isle of Wight;

Where, far from noise and smoke of town,
I watch the twilight falling brown
   All round a careless-order'd garden
Close to the ridge of a noble down.

You 'll have no scandal while you dine,
But honest talk and wholesome wine,
   And only hear the magpie gossip
Garrulous under a roof of pine:

For groves of pine on either hand,
To break the blast of winter, stand;
   And further on, the hoary Channel
Tumbles a breaker on chalk and sand;

Where, if below the milky steep
Some ship of battle slowly creep,
   And on thro' zones of light and shadow
Glimmer away to the lonely deep,

We might discuss the Northern sin
Which made a selfish war begin;
   Dispute the claims, arrange the chances;
Emperor, Ottoman, which shall win:

Or whether war's avenging rod
Shall lash all Europe into blood;
   Till you should turn to dearer matters,
Dear to the man that is dear to God;

How best to help the slender store,
How mend the dwellings, of the poor;
   How gain in life, as life advances,
Valor and charity more and more.

Come, Maurice, come: the lawn as yet
Is hoar with rime, or spongy-wet;
   But when the wreath of March has blossom'd,
Crocus, anemone, violet,

Or later, pay one visit here,
For those are few we hold as dear;
   Nor pay but one, but come for many,
Many and many a happy year.

January, 1854.

WILL.

I.

O WELL for him whose will is strong!
He suffers, but he will not suffer long;
He suffers, but he cannot suffer wrong:
For him nor moves the loud world's random mock,
Nor all Calamity's hugest waves confound,
Who seems a promontory of rock,
That, compass'd round with turbulent sound,
In middle ocean meets the surging shock,
Tempest-buffeted, citadel-crown'd.

II.

But ill for him who, bettering not with time,
Corrupts the strength of heaven-descended Will,
And ever weaker grows thro' acted crime,
Or seeming-genial venial fault,
Recurring and suggesting still!
He seems as one whose footsteps halt,
Toiling in immeasurable sand,
And o'er a weary, sultry land,
Far beneath a blazing vault,
Sown in a wrinkle of the monstrous hill,
The city sparkles like a grain of salt.

"O the wild charge they made!
All the world wondered.

THE CHARGE OF THE LIGHT BRIGADE.

I.

Half a league, half a league,
Half a league onward,
All in the valley of Death
  Rode the six hundred.
"Forward, the Light Brigade!
Charge for the guns!" he said:
Into the valley of Death
  Rode the six hundred.

II.

"Forward, the Light Brigade!"
Was there a man dismay'd?
Not tho' the soldier knew
  Some one had blunder'd:
Theirs not to make reply.
Theirs not to reason why,
Theirs but to do and die:
Into the valley of Death
  Rode the six hundred.

III.

Cannon to right of them,
Cannon to left of them,
Cannon in front of them
  Volley'd and thunder'd;
Storm'd at with shot and shell,
Boldly they rode and well,
Into the jaws of Death,
Into the mouth of Hell
  Rode the six hundred.

IV.

Flash'd all their sabres bare,
Flash'd as they turn'd in air
Sabring the gunners there,
Charging an army, while

All the world wonder'd :
Plunged in the battery-smoke,
Right thro' the line they broke ;
Cossack and Russian
Reel'd from the sabre-stroke
Shatter'd and sunder'd.
Then they rode back, but not
Not the six hundred.

V.

Cannon to right of them,
Cannon to left of them,
Cannon behind them
 Volley'd and thunder'd ;
Storm'd at with shot and shell,
While horse and hero fell,
They that had fought so well
Came thro' the jaws of Death
Back from the mouth of Hell,
All that was left of them,
 Left of six hundred.

VI.

When can their glory fade ?
O the wild charge they made !
 All the world wonder'd.
Honor the charge they made !
Honor the Light Brigade,
 Noble six hundred !

ENOCH ARDEN,

AND OTHER POEMS.

ENOCH ARDEN.

Long lines of cliff breaking have left a
 chasm ;
And in the chasm are foam and yellow
 sands ;
Beyond, red roofs about a narrow wharf
In cluster ; then a moulder'd church ;
 and higher
A long street climbs to one tall-tower'd
 mill ;
And high in heaven behind it a gray down
With Danish barrows ; and a hazelwood,
By autumn nutters haunted, flourishes
Green in a cuplike hollow of the down.

Here on this beach a hundred years ago,
Three children of three houses, Annie Lee,
The prettiest little damsel in the port,
And Philip Ray the miller's only son,
And Enoch Arden, a rough sailor's lad
Made orphan by a winter shipwreck,
 play'd
Among the waste and lumber of the shore,
Hard coils of cordage, swarthy fishing-
 nets,
Anchors of rusty fluke, and boats up-
 drawn ;
And built their castles of dissolving sand
To watch them overflow'd, or following
 up
And flying the white breaker, daily left
The little footprint daily wash'd away.

A narrow cave ran in beneath the cliff :
In this the children play'd at keeping
 house.
Enoch was host one day, Philip the next,
While Annie still was mistress ; but at
 times
Enoch would hold possession for a week :
"This is my house and this my little wife."
"Mine too" said Philip "turn and turn
 about" :
When, if they quarrell'd, Enoch stron-
 ger-made
Was master : then would Philip, his
 blue eyes
All flooded with the helpless wrath of tears,
Shriek out "I hate you, Enoch," and at
 this
The little wife would weep for company,
And pray them not to quarrel for her sake,
And say she would be little wife to both.

But when the dawn of rosy childhood
 past,
And the new warmth of life's ascending
 sun
Was felt by either, either fixt his heart
On that one girl ; and Enoch spoke his love,
But Philip loved in silence ; and the girl
Seem'd kinder unto Philip than to him ;
But she loved Enoch ; tho' she knew it not,
And would if ask'd deny it. Enoch set
A purpose evermore before his eyes,
To hoard all savings to the uttermost,

To purchase his own boat, and make a home
For Annie: and so prosper'd that at last
A luckier or a bolder fisherman;
A carefuller in peril, did not breathe
For leagues along that breaker-beaten coast
Than Enoch. Likewise had he served a year
On board a merchantman, and made himself
Full sailor; and he thrice had pluck'd a life
From the dread sweep of the down-streaming seas:
And all men look'd upon him favorably:
And ere he touch'd his one-and-twentieth May
He purchased his own boat, and made a home
For Annie, neat and nestlike, halfway up
The narrow street that clamber'd toward the mill.

Then, on a golden autumn eventide,
The younger people making holiday,
With bag and sack and basket, great and small,
Went nutting to the hazels. Philip stay'd
(His father lying sick and needing him)
An hour behind; but as he climb'd the hill,
Just where the prone edge of the wood began
To feather toward the hollow, saw the pair,
Enoch and Annie, sitting hand-in-hand,
His large gray eyes and weather-beaten face
All-kindled by a still and sacred fire,
That burn'd as on an altar. Philip look'd,
And in their eyes and faces read his doom;
Then, as their faces drew together, groan'd,
And slipt aside, and like a wounded life
Crept down into the hollows of the wood;
There, while the rest were loud in merry-making,
Had his dark hour unseen, and rose and past
Bearing a lifelong hunger in his heart.

So these were wed, and merrily rang the bells,
And merrily ran the years, seven happy years,
Seven happy years of health and competence,
And mutual love and honorable toil;

With children; first a daughter. In him woke,
With his first babe's first cry, the noble wish
To save all earnings to the uttermost,
And give his child a better bringing-up
Than his had been, or hers; a wish renew'd,
When two years after came a boy to be
The rosy idol of her solitudes,
While Enoch was abroad on wrathful seas,
Or often journeying landward; for in truth
Enoch's white horse, and Enoch's ocean-spoil
In ocean-smelling osier, and his face,
Rough-redden'd with a thousand winter gales,
Not only to the market-cross were known,
But in the leafy lanes behind the down,
Far as the portal-warding lion-whelp,
And peacock-yewtree of the lonely Hall,
Whose Friday fare was Enoch's ministering.

Then came a change, as all things human change.
Ten miles to northward of the narrow port
Open'd a larger haven: thither used
Enoch at times to go by land or sea;
And once when there, and clambering on a mast
In harbor, by mischance he slipt and fell:
A limb was broken when they lifted him;
And while he lay recovering there, his wife
Bore him another son, a sickly one:
Another hand crept too across his trade
Taking her bread and theirs: and on him fell,
Altho' a grave and staid God-fearing man,
Yet lying thus inactive, doubt and gloom.
He seem'd, as in a nightmare of the night,
To see his children leading evermore
Low miserable lives of hand-to-mouth,
And her, he loved, a beggar: then he pray'd
"Save them from this, whatever comes to me."
And while he pray'd, the master of that ship
Enoch had served in, hearing his mischance,
Came, for he knew the man and valued him,
Reporting of his vessel China bound,
And wanting yet a boatswain. Would he go?

There yet were many weeks before she sail'd,
Sail'd from this port. Would Enoch have the place?
And Enoch all at once assented to it,
Rejoicing at that answer to his prayer.

So now that shadow of mischance appear'd
No graver than as when some little cloud
Cuts off the fiery highway of the sun,
And isles a light in the offing: yet the wife —
When he was gone — the children — what to do?
Then Enoch lay long-pondering on his plans;
To sell the boat — and yet he loved her well —
How many a rough sea had he weather'd in her!
He knew her, as a horseman knows his horse —
And yet to sell her — then with what she brought
Buy goods and stores — set Annie forth in trade
With all that seamen needed or their wives —
So might she keep the house while he was gone.
Should he not trade himself out yonder? go
This voyage more than once? yea twice or thrice —
As oft as needed — last, returning rich,
Become the master of a larger craft,
With fuller profits lead an easier life,
Have all his pretty young ones educated,
And pass his days in peace among his own.

Thus Enoch in his heart determined all:
Then moving homeward came on Annie pale,
Nursing the sickly babe, her latest-born.
Forward she started with a happy cry,
And laid the feeble infant in his arms;
Whom Enoch took, and handled all his limbs,
Appraised his weight and fondled father-like,
But had no heart to break his purposes
To Annie, till the morrow, when he spoke.

Then first since Enoch's golden ring had girt
Her finger, Annie fought against his will:
Yet not with brawling opposition she,
But manifold entreaties, many a tear,
Many a sad kiss by day by night renew'd
(Sure that all evil would come out of it)
Besought him, supplicating, if he cared
For her or his dear children, not to go.
He not for his own self caring but her,
Her and her children, let her plead in vain;
So grieving held his will, and bore it thro'.

For Enoch parted with his old sea-friend,
Bought Annie goods and stores, and set his hand
To fit their little streetward sitting-room
With shelf and corner for the goods and stores.
So all day long till Enoch's last at home,
Shaking their pretty cabin, hammer and axe,
Auger and saw, while Annie seem'd to hear
Her own death-scaffold raising, shrill'd and rang,
Till this was ended, and his careful hand, —
The space was narrow, — having order'd all
Almost as neat and close as Nature packs
Her blossom or her seedling, paused; and he,
Who needs would work for Annie to the last,
Ascending tired, heavily slept till morn.

And Enoch faced this morning of farewell
Brightly and boldly. All his Annie's fears,
Save, as his Annie's, were a laughter to him.
Yet Enoch as a brave God-fearing man
Bow'd himself down, and in that mystery
Where God-in-man is one with man-in-God,
Pray'd for a blessing on his wife and babes
Whatever came to him: and then he said
"Annie, this voyage by the grace of God
Will bring fair weather yet to all of us.
Keep a clean hearth and a clear fire for me,
For I 'll be back, my girl, before you know it."
Then lightly rocking baby's cradle "and he,
This pretty, puny, weakly little one, —
Nay — for I love him all the better for it —

*"Forward she started with a happy cry,
And laid the feeble infant in his arms."*

God bless him, he shall sit upon my
 knees
And I will tell him tales of foreign
 parts,
And make him merry, when I come home
 again.
Come Annie, come, cheer up before I go."

Him running on thus hopefully she
 heard,
And almost hoped herself; but when he
 turn'd
The current of his talk to graver things
In sailor fashion roughly sermonizing
On providence and trust in Heaven, she
 heard,
Heard and not heard him; as the village
 girl,
Who sets her pitcher underneath the
 spring,
Musing on him that used to fill it for
 her,
Hears and not hears, and lets it overflow.

At length she spoke "O Enoch, you
 are wise;
And yet for all your wisdom well know I
That I shall look upon your face no more."

"Well then," said Enoch, "I shall
 look on yours.
Annie, the ship I sail in passes here

(He named the day); get you a seaman's glass,
Spy out my face, and laugh at all your fears."

But when the last of those last moments came,
"Annie, my girl, cheer up, be comforted,
Look to the babes, and till I come again,
Keep everything shipshape, for I must go.
And fear no more for me; or if you fear
Cast all your cares on God; that anchor holds.
Is He not yonder in those uttermost
Parts of the morning? if I flee to these
Can I go from Him? and the sea is His,
The sea is His: He made it."

Enoch rose,
Cast his strong arms about his drooping wife,
And kiss'd his wonder-stricken little ones;
But for the third, the sickly one, who slept
After a night of feverous wakefulness,
When Annie would have raised him Enoch said
"Wake him not; let him sleep; how should the child
Remember this?" and kiss'd him in his cot.
But Annie from her baby's forehead clipt
A tiny curl, and gave it: this he kept
Thro' all his future; but now hastily caught
His bundle, waved his hand, and went his way.

She when the day, that Enoch mention'd, came,
Borrow'd a glass, but all in vain: perhaps
She could not fix the glass to suit her eye;
Perhaps her eye was dim, hand tremulous;
She saw him not: and while he stood on deck
Waving, the moment and the vessel past.

Ev'n to the last dip of the vanishing sail
She watch'd it, and departed weeping for him;
Then, tho' she mourn'd his absence as his grave,
Set her sad will no less to chime with his,
But throve not in her trade, not being bred
To barter, nor compensating the want
By shrewdness, neither capable of lies,
Nor asking overmuch and taking less,
And still foreboding "what would Enoch say?"
For more than once, in days of difficulty
And pressure, had she sold her wares for less
Than what she gave in buying what she sold:
She fail'd and sadden'd knowing it; and thus,
Expectant of that news which never came,
Gain'd for her own a scanty sustenance,
And lived a life of silent melancholy.

Now the third child was sickly-born and grew
Yet sicklier, tho' the mother cared for it
With all a mother's care: nevertheless,
Whether her business often call'd her from it,
Or thro' the want of what it needed most,
Or means to pay the voice who best could tell
What most it needed — howsoe'er it was,
After a lingering, — ere she was aware, —
Like the caged bird escaping suddenly,
The little innocent soul flitted away.

In that same week when Annie buried it,
Philip's true heart, which hunger'd for her peace
(Since Enoch left he had not look'd upon her),
Smote him, as having kept aloof so long.
"Surely" said Philip "I may see her now,
May be some little comfort"; therefore went,
Past thro' the solitary room in front,
Paused for a moment at an inner door,
Then struck it thrice, and, no one opening,
Enter'd; but Annie, seated with her grief,
Fresh from the burial of her little one,
Cared not to look on any human face,
But turn'd her own toward the wall and wept.
Then Philip standing up said falteringly
"Annie, I came to ask a favor of you."

He spoke; the passion in her moan'd reply
"Favor from one so sad and so forlorn
As I am!" half abash'd him; yet unask'd,
His bashfulness and tenderness at war,
He set himself beside her, saying to her:

"I came to speak to you of what he wish'd,
Enoch, your husband: I have ever said
You chose the best among us — a strong man :
For where he fixt his heart he set his hand
To do the thing he will'd, and bore it thro'.
And wherefore did he go this weary way,
And leave you lonely? not to see the world —
For pleasure? — nay, but for the wherewithal
To give his babes a better bringing-up
Than his had been or yours: that was his wish.
And if he come again, vext will he be
To find the precious morning hours were lost.
And it would vex him even in his grave,
If he could know his babes were running wild
Like colts about the waste. So, Annie, now —
Have we not known each other all our lives?
I do beseech you by the love you bear
Him and his children not to say me nay —
For, if you will, when Enoch comes again
Why then he shall repay me — if you will,
Annie — for I am rich and well-to-do.
Now let me put the boy and girl to school :
This is the favor that I came to ask."

Then Annie with her brows against the wall
Answer'd "I cannot look you in the face ;
I seem so foolish and so broken down.
When you came in my sorrow broke me down ;
And now I think your kindness breaks me down ;
But Enoch lives; that is borne in on me :
He will repay you : money can be repaid ;
Not kindness such as yours."

And Philip ask'd
"Then you will let me, Annie?"

There she turn'd,
She rose, and fixt her swimming eyes upon him,
And dwelt a moment on his kindly face,
Then calling down a blessing on his head
Caught at his hand, and wrung it passionately,
And past into the little garth beyond.
So lifted up in spirit he moved away.

Then Philip put the boy and girl to school,
And bought them needful books, and everyway,
Like one who does his duty by his own,
Made himself theirs; and tho' for Annie's sake,
Fearing the lazy gossip of the port,
He oft denied his heart his dearest wish,
And seldom crost her threshold, yet he sent
Gifts by the children, garden-herbs and fruit,
The late and early roses from his wall,
Or conies from the down, and now and then,
With some pretext of fineness in the meal
To save the offence of charitable, flour
From his tall mill that whistled on the waste.

But Philip did not fathom Annie's mind :
Scarce could the woman when he came upon her,
Out of full heart and boundless gratitude
Light on a broken word to thank him with.
But Philip was her children's all-in-all ;
From distant corners of the street they ran
To greet his hearty welcome heartily ;
Lords of his house and of his mill were they;
Worried his passive ear with petty wrongs
Or pleasures, hung upon him, play'd with him
And call'd him Father Philip. Philip gain'd
As Enoch lost ; for Enoch seem'd to them
Uncertain as a vision or a dream,
Faint as a figure seen in early dawn
Down at the far end of an avenue,
Going we know not where : and so ten years,
Since Enoch left his hearth and native land,
Fled forward, and no news of Enoch came.

It chanced one evening Annie's children long'd
To go with others, nutting to the wood,
And Annie would go with them ; then they begg'd
For Father Philip (as they call'd him) too :
Him, like the working bee in blossom-dust,
Blanch'd with his mill, they found ; and saying to him
"Come with us Father Philip" he denied;

Then Philip put the boy and girl to school,
And bought them needful books.

But when the children pluck'd at him to go,
He laugh'd, and yielded readily to their wish,
For was not Annie with them? and they went.

But after scaling half the weary down,
Just where the prone edge of the wood began
To feather toward the hollow, all her force
Fail'd her; and sighing "let me rest" she said:
So Philip rested with her well-content;
While all the younger ones with jubilant cries
Broke from their elders, and tumultuously
Down thro' the whitening hazels made a plunge
To the bottom, and dispersed, and bent or broke
The lithe reluctant boughs to tear away
Their tawny clusters, crying to each other
And calling, here and there, about the wood.

But Philip sitting at her side forgot
Her presence, and remember'd one dark hour
Here in this wood, when like a wounded life
He crept into the shadow: at last he said

Lifting his honest forehead "Listen, Annie,
How merry they are down yonder in the wood.
Tired, Annie?" for she did not speak a word.
"Tired?" but her face had fall'n upon her hands;
At which, as with a kind of anger in him,
"The ship was lost" he said "the ship was lost!
No more of that! why should you kill yourself
And make them orphans quite?" And Annie said
"I thought not of it: but — I know not why —
Their voices make me feel so solitary."

    Then Philip coming somewhat closer spoke.
"Annie, there is a thing upon my mind,
And it has been upon my mind so long,
That tho' I know not when it first came there,
I know that it will out at last. O Annie,
It is beyond all hope, against all chance,
That he who left you ten long years ago
Should still be living; well then — let me speak:
I grieve to see you poor and wanting help:
I cannot help you as I wish to do
Unless — they say that women are so quick —
Perhaps you know what I would have you know —
I wish you for my wife. I fain would prove
A father to your children: I do think
They love me as a father: I am sure
That I love them as if they were mine own;
And I believe, if you were fast my wife,
That after all these sad uncertain years,
We might be still as happy as God grants
To any of His creatures. Think upon it:
For I am well-to-do — no kin, no care,
No burden, save my care for you and yours:
And we have known each other all our lives,
And I have loved you longer than you know."

    Then answer'd Annie; tenderly she spoke:
"You have been as God's good angel in our house.
God bless you for it, God reward you for it,
Philip, with something happier than myself.
Can once love twice? can you be ever loved
As Enoch was? what is it that you ask?"
"I am content" he answer'd "to be loved
A little after Enoch." "O" she cried
Scared as it were "dear Philip, wait a while:
If Enoch comes — but Enoch will not come —
Yet wait a year, a year is not so long:
Surely I shall be wiser in a year:
O wait a little!" Philip sadly said
"Annie, as I have waited all my life
I well may wait a little." "Nay" she cried
"I am bound: you have my promise — in a year:
Will you not bide your year as I bide mine?"
And Philip answer'd "I will bide my year."

    Here both were mute, till Philip glancing up
Beheld the dead flame of the fallen day
Pass from the Danish barrow overhead;
Then fearing night and chill for Annie rose,
And sent his voice beneath him thro' the wood.
Up came the children laden with their spoil;
Then all descended to the port, and there
At Annie's door he paused and gave his hand,
Saying gently "Annie, when I spoke to you,
That was your hour of weakness. I was wrong.
I am always bound to you, but you are free."
Then Annie weeping answer'd "I am bound."

    She spoke; and in one moment as it were,
While yet she went about her household ways,
Ev'n as she dwelt upon his latest words,
That he had loved her longer than she knew,
That autumn into autumn flash'd again,
And there he stood once more before her face,
Claiming her promise. "Is it a year?" she ask'd.

"Yes, if the nuts" he said "be ripe again:
Come out and see." But she — she put
 him off —
So much to look to — such a change — a
 month —
Give her a month — she knew that she
 was bound —
A month — no more. Then Philip with
 his eyes
Full of that lifelong hunger, and his voice
Shaking a little like a drunkard's hand,
"Take your own time, Annie, take your
 own time."
And Annie could have wept for pity of
 him;
And yet she held him on delayingly
With many a scarce-believable excuse,
Trying his truth and his long-sufferance,
Till half-another year had slipt away.

By this the lazy gossips of the port,
Abhorrent of a calculation crost,
Began to chafe as at a personal wrong.
Some thought that Philip did but trifle
 with her;
Some that she but held off to draw him on;
And others laugh'd at her and Philip too,
As simple folk that knew not their own
 minds;
And one, in whom all evil fancies clung
Like serpent eggs together, laughingly
Would hint at worse in either. Her own
 son
Was silent, tho' he often look'd his wish;
But evermore the daughter prest upon
 her
To wed the man so dear to all of them
And lift the household out of poverty;
And Philip's rosy face contracting grew
Careworn and wan; and all these things
 fell on her
Sharp as reproach.

 At last one night it chanced
That Annie could not sleep, but earnestly
Pray'd for a sign "my Enoch is he gone?"
Then compass'd round by the blind wall
 of night
Brook'd not the expectant terror of her
 heart,
Started from bed, and struck herself a
 light,
Then desperately seized the holy Book,
Suddenly set it wide to find a sign,
Suddenly put her finger on the text,
"Under the palm-tree." That was noth-
 ing to her:

No meaning there: she closed the Book
 and slept:
When lo! her Enoch sitting on a height,
Under a palm-tree, over him the Sun:
"He is gone" she thought "he is happy,
 he is singing
Hosanna in the highest: yonder shines
The Sun of Righteousness, and these be
 palms
Whereof the happy people strewing cried
'Hosanna in the highest!'" Here she
 woke,
Resolved, sent for him and said wildly
 to him
"There is no reason why we should not
 wed."
"Then for God's sake," he answer'd,
 "both our sakes,
So you will wed me, let it be at once."

So these were wed and merrily rang
 the bells,
Merrily rang the bells and they were wed.
But never merrily beat Annie's heart.
A footstep seem'd to fall beside her path,
She knew not whence; a whisper on her
 ear,
She knew not what; nor loved she to be
 left
Alone at home, nor ventured out alone.
What ail'd her then, that ere she enter'd,
 often
Her hand dwelt lingeringly on the latch,
Fearing to enter: Philip thought he
 knew:
Such doubts and fears were common to
 her state,
Being with child: but when her child
 was born,
Then her new child was as herself renew'd,
Then the new mother came about her
 heart,
Then her good Philip was her all-in-all,
And that mysterious instinct wholly died.

And where was Enoch? prosperously
 sail'd
The ship "Good Fortune," tho' at set-
 ting forth
The Biscay, roughly ridging eastward,
 shook
And almost overwhelm'd her, yet unvext
She slipt across the summer of the world,
Then after a long tumble about the Cape
And frequent interchange of foul and fair,
She passing thro' the summer world again,
The breath of heaven came continually

"By this the lazy gossips of the port,
Abhorrent of a calculation crost,
Began to chafe as at a personal wrong."

And sent her sweetly by the golden isles,
Till silent in her oriental haven.

   There Enoch traded for himself, and bought
Quaint monsters for the market of those times,
A gilded dragon, also, for the babes.

   Less lucky her home-voyage: at first indeed
Thro' many a fair sea-circle, day by day,
Scarce-rocking, her full-busted figure-head
Stared o'er the ripple feathering from her bows:
Then follow'd calms, and then winds variable,
Then baffling, a long course of them; and last
Storm, such as drove her under moonless heavens
Till hard upon the cry of "breakers" came
The crash of ruin, and the loss of all
But Enoch and two others. Half the night,
Buoy'd upon floating tackle and broken spars,

These drifted, stranding on an isle at morn
Rich, but the loneliest in a lonely sea.

No want was there of human sustenance
Soft fruitage, mighty nuts, and nourishing roots;
Nor save for pity was it hard to take
The helpless life so wild that it was tame.
There in a seaward-gazing mountain-gorge
They built, and thatch'd with leaves of palm, a hut,
Half hut, half native cavern. So the three,
Set in this Eden of all plenteousness,
Dwelt with eternal summer, ill-content.

For one, the youngest, hardly more than boy,
Hurt in that night of sudden ruin and wreck,
Lay lingering out a five-years' death-in-life.
They could not leave him. After he was gone,
The two remaining found a fallen stem;
And Enoch's comrade, careless of himself,
Fire-hollowing this in Indian fashion, fell
Sun-stricken, and that other lived alone.
In those two deaths he read God's warning "wait."

The mountain wooded to the peak, the lawns
And winding glades high up like ways to Heaven,
The slender coco's drooping crown of plumes,
The lightning flash of insect and of bird,
The lustre of the long convolvuluses
That coil'd around the stately stems, and ran
Ev'n to the limit of the land, the glows
And glories of the broad belt of the world,
All these he saw; but what he fain had seen
He could not see, the kindly human face,
Nor ever hear a kindly voice, but heard
The myriad shriek of wheeling ocean-fowl,
The league-long roller thundering on the reef,
The moving whisper of huge trees that branch'd
And blossom'd in the zenith, or the sweep
Of some precipitous rivulet to the wave,
As down the shore he ranged, or all day long
Sat often in the seaward-gazing gorge,
A shipwreck'd sailor, waiting for a sail:
No sail from day to day, but every day
The sunrise broken into scarlet shafts
Among the palms and ferns and precipices;
The blaze upon the waters to the east;
The blaze upon his island overhead;
The blaze upon the waters to the west;
Then the great stars that globed themselves in Heaven,
The hollower-bellowing ocean, and again
The scarlet shafts of sunrise — but no sail.

There often as he watch'd or seem'd to watch,
So still, the golden lizard on him paused,
A phantom made of many phantoms moved
Before him haunting him, or he himself
Moved haunting people, things and places, known
Far in a darker isle beyond the line;
The babes, their babble, Annie, the small house,
The climbing street, the mill, the leafy lanes,
The peacock-yewtree and the lonely Hall,
The horse he drove, the boat he sold, the chill
November dawns and dewy-glooming downs,
The gentle shower, the smell of dying leaves,
And the low moan of leaden-color'd seas.

Once likewise, in the ringing of his ears,
Tho' faintly, merrily — far and far away —
He heard the pealing of his parish bells;
Then, tho' he knew not wherefore, started up
Shuddering, and when the beauteous hateful isle
Return'd upon him, had not his poor heart
Spoken with That, which being everywhere
Lets none, who speaks with Him, seem all alone,
Surely the man had died of solitude.

Thus over Enoch's early-silvering head
The sunny and rainy seasons came and went
Year after year. His hopes to see his own,

And pace the sacred old familiar fields,
Not yet had perish'd, when his lonely
  doom
Came suddenly to an end. Another ship
(She wanted water) blown by baffling
  winds,
Like the Good Fortune, from her destined
  course,
Stay'd by this isle, not knowing where
  she lay:
For since the mate had seen at early dawn
Across a break on the mist-wreathen isle
The silent water slipping from the hills,
They sent a crew that landing burst away
In search of stream or fount, and fill'd
  the shores
With clamor. Downward from his
  mountain gorge
Stept the long-hair'd long-bearded soli-
  tary,
Brown, looking hardly human, strangely
  clad,
Muttering and mumbling, idiotlike it
  seem'd,
With inarticulate rage, and making signs
They knew not what: and yet he led
  the way
To where the rivulets of sweet water ran:
And ever as he mingled with the crew,
And heard them talking, his long-bounden
  tongue
Was loosen'd, till he made them under-
  stand;
Whom, when their casks were fill'd they
  took aboard:
And there the tale he utter'd brokenly,
Scarce-credited at first but more and more,
Amazed and melted all who listen'd to it:
And clothes they gave him and free pas-
  sage home;
But oft he work'd among the rest and shook
His isolation from him. None of these
Came from his county, or could answer
  him,
If question'd, aught of what he cared to
  know.
And dull the voyage was with long delays,
The vessel scarce sea-worthy; but ever-
  more
His fancy fled before the lazy wind
Returning, till beneath a clouded moon
He like a lover down thro' all his blood
Drew in the dewy meadowy morning-
  breath
Of England, blown across her ghostly wall:
And that same morning officers and men
Levied a kindly tax upon themselves,
Pitying the lonely man, and gave him it:
Then moving up the coast they landed
  him,
Ev'n in that harbor whence he sail'd be-
  fore.

  There Enoch spoke no word to anyone,
But homeward — home — what home?
  had he a home?
His home, he walk'd. Bright was that
  afternoon,
Sunny but chill; till drawn thro' either
  chasm,
Where either haven open'd on the deeps,
Roll'd a sea-haze and whelm'd the world
  in gray;
Cut off the length of highway on before,
And left but narrow breadth to left and
  right
Of wither'd holt or tilth or pasturage.
On the nigh-naked tree the Robin piped
Disconsolate, and thro' the dripping haze
The dead weight of the dead leaf bore it
  down:
Thicker the drizzle grew, deeper the gloom;
Last, as it seem'd, a great mist-blotted
  light
Flared on him, and he came upon the
  place.

  Then down the long street having
  slowly stolen,
His heart foreshadowing all calamity,
His eyes upon the stones, he reach'd the
  home
Where Annie lived and loved him, and
  his babes
In those far-off seven happy years were
  born;
But finding neither light nor murmur
  there
(A bill of sale gleam'd thro' the drizzle)
  crept
Still downward thinking "dead or dead
  to me!"

  Down to the pool and narrow wharf
  he went,
Seeking a tavern which of old he knew,
A front of timber-crost antiquity,
So propt, worm-eaten, ruinously old,
He thought it must have gone; but he
  was gone
Who kept it; and his widow, Miriam
  Lane,
With daily-dwindling profits held the
  house;

A haunt of brawling seamen once, but now
Stiller, with yet a bed for wandering men.
There Enoch rested silent many days.

But Miriam Lane was good and garrulous,
Nor let him be, but often breaking in,
Told him, with other annals of the port,
Not knowing — Enoch was so brown, so bow'd,
So broken — all the story of his house.
His baby's death, her growing poverty,
How Philip put her little ones to school,
And kept them in it, his long wooing her,
Her slow consent, and marriage, and the birth
Of Philip's child : and o'er his countenance
No shadow past, nor motion : anyone,
Regarding, well had deem'd he felt the tale
Less than the teller : only when she closed
" Enoch, poor man, was cast away and lost "
He, shaking his gray head pathetically,
Repeated muttering " cast away and lost " ;
Again in deeper inward whispers "lost !"

But Enoch yearn'd to see her face again ;
" If I might look on her sweet face again
And know that she is happy." So the thought
Haunted and harass'd him, and drove him forth,
At evening when the dull November day
Was growing duller twilight, to the hill.
There he sat down gazing on all below ;
There did a thousand memories roll upon him,
Unspeakable for sadness. By and by
The ruddy square of comfortable light,
Far-blazing from the rear of Philip's house,
Allured him, as the beacon-blaze allures
The bird of passage, till he madly strikes
Against it, and beats out his weary life.

For Philip's dwelling fronted on the street,
The latest house to landward ; but behind,
With one small gate that open'd on the waste,
Flourish'd a little garden square and wall'd :
And in it throve an ancient evergreen,
A yewtree, an I all round it ran a walk
Of shingle, and a walk divided it :

But Enoch shunn'd the middle walk and stole
Up by the wall, behind the yew ; and thence
That which he better might have shunn'd, if griefs
Like his have worse or better, Enoch saw.

For cups and silver on the burnish'd board
Sparkled and shone ; so genial was the hearth :
And on the right hand of the hearth he saw
Philip, the slighted suitor of old times,
Stout, rosy, with his babe across his knees ;
And o'er her second father stoopt a girl,
A later but a loftier Annie Lee,
Fair-hair'd and tall, and from her lifted hand
Dangled a length of ribbon and a ring
To tempt the babe, who rear'd his creasy arms,
Caught at and ever miss'd it, and they laugh'd :
And on the left hand of the hearth he saw
The mother glancing often toward her babe,
But turning now and then to speak with him,
Her son, who stood beside her tall and strong,
And saying that which pleased him, for he smiled.

Now when the dead man come to life beheld
His wife his wife no more, and saw the babe
Hers, yet not his, upon the father's knee,
And all the warmth, the peace, the happiness,
And his own children tall and beautiful,
And him, that other, reigning in his place,
Lord of his rights and of his children's love, —
Then he, tho' Miriam Lane had told him all,
Because things seen are mightier than things heard,
Stagger'd and shook, holding the branch, and fear'd
To send abroad a shrill and terrible cry,
Which in one moment, like the blast of doom,
Would shatter all the happiness of the hearth.

He therefore turning softly like a thief,
Lest the harsh shingle should grate underfoot,
And feeling all along the garden-wall,
Lest he should swoon and tumble and be found,
Crept to the gate, and open'd it, and closed,
As lightly as a sick man's chamber-door,
Behind him, and came out upon the waste.

And there he would have knelt, but that his knees
Were feeble, so that falling prone he dug
His fingers into the wet earth, and pray'd.

"Too hard to bear! why did they take me thence?
O God Almighty, blessed Saviour, Thou
That didst uphold me on my lonely isle,
Uphold me, Father, in my loneliness
A little longer! aid me, give me strength
Not to tell her, never to let her know.
Help me not to break in upon her peace.
My children too! must I not speak to these?
They know me not. I should betray myself.
Never: no father's kiss for me—the girl
So like her mother, and the boy, my son."

There speech and thought and nature fail'd a little,
And he lay tranced; but when he rose and paced
Back toward his solitary home again,
All down the long and narrow street he went
Beating it in upon his weary brain,
As tho' it were the burden of a song,
"Not to tell her, never to let her know."

He was not all unhappy. His resolve
Upbore him, and firm faith, and evermore
Prayer from a living source within the will,
And beating up thro' all the bitter world,
Like fountains of sweet water in the sea,
Kept him a living soul. "This miller's wife"
He said to Miriam "that you told me of,
Has she no fear that her first husband lives?"
"Ay, ay, poor soul" said Miriam, "fear enow!
If you could tell her you had seen him dead,
Why, that would be her comfort"; and he thought

"After the Lord has call'd me she shall know,
I wait His time" and Enoch set himself,
Scorning an alms, to work whereby to live.
Almost to all things could he turn his hand.
Cooper he was and carpenter, and wrought
To make the boatmen fishing-nets, or help'd
At lading and unlading the tall barks,
That brought the stinted commerce of those days;
Thus earn'd a scanty living for himself:
Yet since he did but labor for himself,
Work without hope, there was not life in it
Whereby the man could live; and as the year
Roll'd itself round again to meet the day
When Enoch had return'd, a languor came
Upon him, gentle sickness, gradually
Weakening the man, till he could do no more,
But kept the house, his chair, and last his bed.
And Enoch bore his weakness cheerfully.
For sure no gladlier does the stranded wreck
See thro' the gray skirts of a lifting squall
The boat that bears the hope of life approach
To save the life despair'd of, than he saw
Death dawning on him, and the close of all.

For thro' that dawning gleam'd a kindlier hope
On Enoch thinking "after I am gone,
Then may she learn I loved her to the last."
He call'd aloud for Miriam Lane and said
"Woman, I have a secret—only swear,
Before I tell you—swear upon the book
Not to reveal it, till you see me dead."
"Dead" clamor'd the good woman "hear him talk!
I warrant, man, that we shall bring you round."
"Swear" added Enoch sternly "on the book."
And on the book, half-frighted, Miriam swore.
Then Enoch rolling his gray eyes upon her,
"Did you know Enoch Arden of this town?"
"Know him?" she said "I knew him far away.
Ay, ay, I mind him coming down the street;

"Beating it in upon his weary brain,
As tho' it were the burden of a song,
'Not to tell her, never to let her know.'"

Held his head high, and cared for no man, he."
Slowly and sadly Enoch answer'd her;
"His head is low, and no man cares for him.
I think I have not three days more to live;
I am the man." At which the woman gave
A half-incredulous, half-hysterical cry.
"You Arden, you! nay, — sure he was a foot
Higher than you be." Enoch said again
"My God has bow'd me down to what I am;
My grief and solitude have broken me;
Nevertheless, know you that I am he
Who married — but that name has twice been changed —
I married her who married Philip Ray.
Sit, listen." Then he told her of his voyage,
His wreck, his lonely life, his coming back,
His gazing in on Annie, his resolve,
And how he kept it. As the woman heard,
Fast flow'd the current of her easy tears,
While in her heart she yearn'd incessantly
To rush abroad all round the little haven,
Proclaiming Enoch Arden and his woes;
But awed and promise-bounden she forbore,

Saying only "See your bairns before you go!
Eh, let me fetch 'em, Arden," and arose
Eager to bring them down, for Enoch hung
A moment on her words, but then replied.

"Woman, disturb me not now at the last,
But let me hold my purpose till I die.
Sit down again; mark me and understand,
While I have power to speak. I charge you now,
When you shall see her, tell her that I died
Blessing her, praying for her, loving her;
Save for the bar between us, loving her
As when she laid her head beside my own.
And tell my daughter Annie, whom I saw
So like her mother, that my latest breath
Was spent in blessing her and praying for her.
And tell my son that I died blessing him.
And say to Philip that I blest him too;
He never meant us anything but good.
But if my children care to see me dead,
Who hardly knew me living, let them come,
I am their father; but she must not come,
For my dead face would vex her after-life.
And now there is but one of all my blood,
Who will embrace me in the world-to-be:
This hair is his: she cut it off and gave it,
And I have borne it with me all these years,
And thought to bear it with me to my grave;
But now my mind is changed, for I shall see him,
My babe in bliss: wherefore when I am gone,
Take, give her this, for it may comfort her:
It will moreover be a token to her,
That I am he."

He ceased; and Miriam Lane
Made such a voluble answer promising all,
That once again he roll'd his eyes upon her
Repeating all he wish'd, and once again
She promised.

Then the third night after this,
While Enoch slumber'd motionless and pale,
And Miriam watch'd and dozed at intervals,
There came so loud a calling of the sea,
That all the houses in the haven rang.
He woke, he rose, he spread his arms abroad
Crying with a loud voice "a sail! a sail!
I am saved"; and so fell back and spoke no more.

So past the strong heroic soul away.
And when they buried him the little port
Had seldom seen a costlier funeral.

AYLMER'S FIELD.
1793.

Dust are our frames; and, gilded dust, our pride
Looks only for a moment whole and sound;
Like that long-buried body of the king,
Found lying with his urns and ornaments,
Which at a touch of light, an air of heaven,
Slipt into ashes and was found no more.

Here is a story which in rougher shape
Came from a grizzled cripple, whom I saw
Sunning himself in a waste field alone —
Old, and a mine of memories — who had served,
Long since, a bygone Rector of the place,
And been himself a part of what he told.

Sir Aylmer Aylmer that almighty man,
The county God — in whose capacious hall,
Hung with a hundred shields, the family tree
Sprang from the midriff of a prostrate king —
Whose blazing wyvern weathercock'd the spire,
Stood from his walls and wing'd his entry-gates
And swang besides on many a windy sign —
Whose eyes from under a pyramidal head
Saw from his windows nothing save his own —
What lovelier of his own had he than her,
His only child, his Edith, whom he loved
As heiress and not heir regretfully?
But "he that marries her marries her name"

Aylmer Hall.

This fiat somewhat soothed himself and
    wife,
His wife a faded beauty of the Baths,
Insipid as the Queen upon a card ;
Her all of thought and bearing hardly
    more
Than his own shadow in a sickly sun.

    A land of hops and poppy-mingled corn,
Little about it stirring save a brook !
A sleepy land where under the same wheel
The same old rut would deepen year by
    year ;
Where almost all the village had one
    name ;
Where Aylmer follow'd Aylmer at the
    Hall
And Averill Averill at the Rectory
Thrice over ; so that Rectory and Hall,
Bound in an immemorial intimacy,
Were open to each other ; tho' to dream
That Love could bind them closer well
    had made
The hoar hair of the Baronet bristle up
With horror, worse than had he heard
    his priest
Preach an inverted scripture, sons of men
Daughters of God ; so sleepy was the
    land.

    And might not Averill, had he will'd
    it so,
Somewhere beneath his own low range
    of roofs,
Have also set his many-shielded tree ?
There was an Aylmer-Averill marriage
    once,
When the red rose was redder than itself,
And York's white rose as red as Lancas-
    ter's,

With wounded peace which each had
  prick'd to death.
"Not proven" Averill said, or laughingly
"Some other race of Averills" — prov'n
  or no,
What cared he? what, if other or the
  same?
He lean'd not on his fathers but himself.
But Leolin, his brother, living oft
With Averill, and a year or two before
Call'd to the bar, but ever call'd away
By one low voice to one dear neighbor-
  hood,
Would often, in his walks with Edith,
  claim
A distant kinship to the gracious blood
That shook the heart of Edith hearing him.

Sanguine he was : a but less vivid hue
Than of that islet in the chestnut-bloom
Flamed in his cheek ; and eager eyes, that
  still
Took joyful note of all things joyful,
  beam'd,
Beneath a manelike mass of rolling gold,
Their best and brightest, when they dwelt
  on hers,
Edith, whose pensive beauty, perfect else,
But subject to the season or the mood,
Shone like a mystic star between the less
And greater glory varying to and fro,
We know not wherefore ; bounteously
  made,
And yet so finely, that a troublous touch
Thinn'd, or would seem to thin her in a
  day,
A joyous to dilate, as toward the light.
And these had been together from the
  first.
Leolin's first nurse was, five years after,
  hers :
So much the boy foreran ; but when his
  date
Doubled her own, for want of playmates,
  he
(Since Averill was a decade and a half
His elder, and their parents underground)
Had tost his ball and flown his kite, and
  roll'd
His hoop to pleasure Edith, with her dipt
Against the rush of the air in the prone
  swing.
Made blossom-ball or daisy-chain, ar-
  ranged
Her garden, sow'd her name and kept it
  green
In living letters, told her fairy-tales,

Show'd her the fairy footings on the
  grass,
The little dells of cowslip, fairy palms,
The petty marestail forest, fairy pines,
Or from the tiny pitted target blew
What look'd a flight of fairy arrows aim'd
All at one mark, all hitting : make-
  believes
For Edith and himself : or else he forged,
But that was later, boyish histories
Of battle, bold adventure, dungeon, wreck,
Flights, terrors, sudden rescues, and true
  love
Crown'd after trial; sketches rude and
  faint,
But where a passion yet unborn perhaps
Lay hidden as the music of the moon
Sleeps in the plain eggs of the nightin-
  gale.
And thus together, save for college-times
Or Temple-eaten terms, a couple, fair
As ever painter painted, poet sang,
Or Heav'n in lavish bounty moulded,
  grew.
And more and more, the maiden woman-
  grown,
He wasted hours with Averill ; there,
  when first
The tented winter-field was broken up
Into that phalanx of the summer spears
That soon should wear the garland ;
  there again
When burr and bine were gather'd ;
  lastly there
At Christmas ; ever welcome at the Hall,
On whose dull sameness his full tide of
  youth
Broke with a phosphorescence cheering
  even
My lady ; and the Baronet yet had laid
No bar between them : dull and self-
  involved,
Tall and erect, but bending from his height
With half-allowing smiles for all the
  world,
And mighty courteous in the main — his
  pride
Lay deeper than to wear it as his ring —
He, like an Aylmer in his Aylmerism,
Would care no more for Leolin's walking
  with her
Than for his old Newfoundland's, when
  they ran
To loose him at the stables, for he rose
Twofooted at the limit of his chain,
Roaring to make a third : and how should
  Love,

AYLMER'S FIELD. 373

Whom the cross-lightnings of four chance-
    met eyes
Flash into fiery life from nothing, follow
Such dear familiarities of dawn?
Seldom, but when he does, Master of all.

  So these young hearts not knowing
    that they loved,
Not she at least, nor conscious of a bar
Between them, nor by plight or broken
    ring
Bound, but an immemorial intimacy,
Wander'd at will, but oft accompanied
By Averill: his, a brother's love, that
    hung
With wings of brooding shelter o'er her
    peace,
Might have been other, save for Leolin's —
Who knows? but so they wander'd, hour
    by hour
Gather'd the blossom that rebloom'd, and
    drank
The magic cup that fill'd itself anew.

  A whisper half reveal'd her to herself.
For out beyond her lodges, where the
    brook
Vocal, with here and there a silence, ran
By sallowy rims, arose the laborers' homes,
A frequent haunt of Edith, on low knolls
That dimpling died into each other, huts
At random scatter'd, each a nest in bloom.
Her art, her hand, her counsel all had
    wrought
About them : here was one that, sum-
    mer-blanch'd,
Was parcel-bearded with the traveller's-
    joy
In Autumn, parcel ivy-clad; and here
The warm-blue breathings of a hidden
    hearth
Broke from a bower of vine and honey-
    suckle:
One look'd all rosetree, and another wore
A close-set robe of jasmine sown with stars:
This had a rosy sea of gillyflowers
About it; this, a milky-way on earth,
Like visions in the Northern dreamer's
    heavens,
A lily-avenue climbing to the doors;
One, almost to the martin-haunted eaves
A summer burial deep in hollyhocks;
Each, its own charm; and Edith's
    everywhere;
And Edith ever visitant with him,
He but less loved than Edith, of her poor:
For she — so lowly-lovely and so loving,
Queenly responsive when the loyal hand
Rose from the clay it work'd in as she past,
Not sowing hedgerow texts and passing
    by,
Nor dealing goodly counsel from a height
That makes the lowest hate it, but a voice
Of comfort and an open hand of help,
A splendid presence flattering the poor
    roofs
Revered as theirs, but kindlier than
    themselves
To ailing wife or wailing infancy
Or old bedridden palsy, — was adored;
He, loved for her and for himself. A grasp
Having the warmth and muscle of the
    heart,
A childly way with children, and a laugh
Ringing like proven golden coinage true,
Were no false passport to that easy realm,
Where once with Leolin at her side, the
    girl,
Nursing a child, and turning to the
    warmth
The tender pink five-beaded baby-soles,
Heard the good mother softly whisper
    "Bless,
God bless 'em : marriages are made in
    Heaven."

  A flash of semi-jealousy clear'd it to
    her.
My lady's Indian kinsman unannounced
With half a score of swarthy faces came.
His own, tho' keen and bold and soldierly,
Sear'd by the close ecliptic, was not fair;
Fairer his talk, a tongue that ruled the
    hour,
Tho' seeming boastful: so when first he
    dash'd
Into the chronicle of a deedful day,
Sir Aylmer half forgot his lazy smile
Of patron "Good! my lady's kinsman!
    good!"
My lady with her fingers interlock'd,
And rotatory thumbs on silken knees,
Call'd all her vital spirits into each ear
To listen: unawares they flitted off,
Busying themselves about the flowerage
That stood from out a stiff brocade in
    which,
The meteor of a splendid season, she,
Once with this kinsman, ah so long ago,
Stept thro' the stately minuet of those
    days:
But Edith's eager fancy hurried with him
Snatch'd thro' the perilous passes of his
    life:

Till Leolin ever watchful of her eye
Hated him with a momentary hate.
Wife-hunting, as the rumor ran, was he:
I know not, for he spoke not, only shower'd
His oriental gifts on every one
And most on Edith : like a storm he came,
And shook the house, and like a storm
he went.

Among the gifts he left her (possibly
He flow'd and ebb'd uncertain, to return
When others had been tested) there was
one,
A dagger, in rich sheath with jewels on it
Sprinkled about in gold that branch'd
itself
Fine as ice-ferns on January panes
Made by a breath. I know not whence
at first,
Nor of what race, the work ; but as he told
The story, storming a hill-fort of thieves
He got it ; for their captain after fight,
His comrades having fought their last
below,
Was climbing up the valley ; at whom
he shot —
Down from the beetling crag to which
he clung
Tumbled the tawny rascal at his feet,
This dagger with him, which when now
admired
By Edith whom his pleasure was to please,
At once the costly Sahib yielded to her.

And Leolin, coming after he was gone,
Tost over all her presents petulantly :
And when she show'd the wealthy scabbard, saying
"Look what a lovely piece of workmanship !"
Slight was his answer "Well — I care
not for it" ;
Then playing with the blade he prick'd
his hand,
"A gracious gift to give a lady, this !"
"But would it be more gracious" ask'd
the girl
"Were I to give this gift of his to one
That is no lady?" "Gracious? No"
said he.
"Me ? — but I cared not for it. O pardon me,
I seem to be ungraciousness itself."
"Take it" she added sweetly "tho' his
gift ;
For I am more ungracious ev'n than you,
I care not for it either" ; and he said

"Why then I love it" : but Sir Aylmer
past,
And neither loved nor liked the thing he
heard.

The next day came a neighbor. Blues
and reds
They talk'd of : blues were sure of it, he
thought :
Then of the latest fox — where started —
kill'd
In such a bottom : "Peter had the brush,
My Peter, first" : and did Sir Aylmer know
That great pock-pitten fellow had been
caught ?
Then made his pleasure echo, hand to
hand,
And rolling as it were the substance of it
Between his palms a moment up and
down —
"The birds were warm, the birds were
warm upon him ;
We have him now" : and had Sir Aylmer heard —
Nay, but he must — the land was ringing of it —
This blacksmith-border marriage — one
they knew —
Raw from the nursery — who could trust
a child ?
That cursed France with her egalities !
And did Sir Aylmer (deferentially
With nearing chair and lower'd accent)
think —
For people talk'd — that it was wholly
wise
To let that handsome fellow Averill walk
So freely with his daughter? people
talk'd —
The boy might get a notion into him ;
The girl might be entangled ere she knew.
Sir Aylmer Aylmer slowly stiffening
spoke :
"The girl and boy, Sir, know their differences !"
"Good" said his friend "but watch !"
and he "enough,
More than enough, Sir ! I can guard
my own."
They parted, and Sir Aylmer Aylmer
watch'd.

Pale, for on her the thunders of the house
Had fallen first, was Edith that same
night ;
Pale as the Jephtha's daughter, a rough
piece

AYLMER'S FIELD.

Of early rigid color, under which
Withdrawing by the counter door to that
Which Leolin open'd, she cast back upon
  him
A piteous glance, and vanish'd. He, as one
Caught in a burst of unexpected storm,
And pelted with outrageous epithets,
Turning beheld the Powers of the House
On either side the hearth, indignant; her,
Cooling her false cheek with a featherfan,
Him glaring, by his own stale devil
  spurr'd,
And, like a beast hard-ridden, breathing
  hard.
"Ungenerous, dishonorable, base,
Presumptuous! trusted as he was with
  her,
The sole succeeder to their wealth, their
  lands,
The last remaining pillar of their house,
The one transmitter of their ancient name,
Their child." "Our child!" "Our
  heiress!" "Ours!" for still,
Like echoes from beyond a hollow, came
Her sicklier iteration. Last he said
"Boy, mark me! for your fortunes are
  to make.
I swear you shall not make them out of
  mine.
Now inasmuch as you have practised on
  her,
Perplext her, made her half forget herself,
Swerve from her duty to herself and us —
Things in an Aylmer deem'd impossible,
Far as we track ourselves — I say that
  this —
Else I withdraw favor and countenance
From you and yours for ever — shall you
  do.
Sir, when you see her — but you shall
  not see her —
No, you shall write, and not to her, but
  me:
And you shall say that having spoken
  with me,
And after look'd into yourself, you find
That you meant nothing — as indeed
  you know
That you meant nothing. Such a match
  as this!
Impossible, prodigious!" These were
  words,
As meted by his measure of himself,
Arguing boundless forbearance: after
  which,
And Leolin's horror-stricken answer, "I
So foul a traitor to myself and her,
Never O never," for about as long
As the wind-hover hangs in balance,
  paused
Sir Aylmer reddening from the storm
  within,
Then broke all bonds of courtesy, and
  crying
"Boy, should I find you by my doors
  again,
My men shall lash you from them like a
  dog;
Hence!" with a sudden execration drove
The footstool from before him, and arose;
So, stammering "scoundrel" out of
  teeth that ground
As in a dreadful dream, while Leolin still
Retreated half-aghast, the fierce old man
Follow'd, and under his own lintel stood
Storming with lifted hands, a hoary face
Meet for the reverence of the hearth,
  but now,
Beneath a pale and unimpassion'd moon,
Vext with unworthy madness, and de-
  form'd.

Slowly and conscious of the rageful eye
That watch'd him, till he heard the pon-
  derous door
Close, crashing with long echoes thro'
  the land,
Went Leolin; then, his passions all in flood
And masters of his motion, furiously
Down thro' the bright lawns to his
  brother's ran,
And foam'd away his heart at Averill's
  ear:
Whom Averill solaced as he might,
  amazed:
The man was his, had been his father's,
  friend:
He must have seen, himself had seen it
  long;
He must have known, himself had
  known: besides,
He never yet had set his daughter forth
Here in the woman-markets of the west,
Where our Caucasians let themselves be
  sold.
Some one, he thought, had slander'd
  Leolin to him.
"Brother, for I have loved you more as son
Than brother, let me tell you: I myself —
What is their pretty saying? jilted, is it?
Jilted I was: I say it for your peace.
Pain'd, and, as bearing in myself the shame
The woman should have borne, humili-
  ated,

I lived for years a stunted sunless life;
Till after our good parents past away
Watching your growth, I seem'd again
  to grow.
Leolin, I almost sin in envying you:
The very whitest lamb in all my fold
Loves you: I know her: the worst
  thought she has
Is whiter even than her pretty hand:
She must prove true: for, brother, where
  two fight
The strongest wins, and truth and love
  are strength,
And you are happy: let her parents be."

　But Leolin cried out the more upon
  them —
Insolent, brainless, heartless! heiress,
  wealth,
Their wealth, their heiress! wealth
  enough was theirs
For twenty matches. Were he lord of this,
Why twenty boys and girls should marry
  on it,
And forty blest ones bless him, and him-
  self
Be wealthy still, ay wealthier. He be-
  lieved
This filthy marriage-hindering Mammon
  made
The harlot of the cities: nature crost
Was mother of the foul adulteries
That saturate soul with body. Name,
  too! name,
Their ancient name! they *might* be
  proud; its worth
Was being Edith's. Ah how pale she
  had look'd
Darling, to-night! they must have rated
  her
Beyond all tolerance. These old pheas-
  ant-lords,
These partridge-breeders of a thousand
  years,
Who had mildew'd in their thousands,
  doing nothing
Since Egbert — why, the greater their
  disgrace!
Fall back upon a name! rest, rot in that!
Not *keep* it noble, make it nobler? fools,
With such a vantage-ground for noble-
  ness!
He had known a man, a quintessence of
  man,
The life of all — who madly loved — and
  he,
Thwarted by one of these old father-fools,

Had rioted his life out, and made an end.
He would not do it! her sweet face and
  faith
Held him from that: but he had powers,
  he knew it:
Back would he to his studies, make a name,
Name, fortune too: the world should ring
  of him
To shame these mouldy Aylmers in their
  graves:
Chancellor, or what is greatest would he
  be —
"O brother, I am grieved to learn your
  grief —
Give me my fling, and let me say my
  say."

　At which, like one that sees his own
  excess,
And easily forgives it as his own,
He laugh'd; and then was mute; but
  presently
Wept like a storm: and honest Averill
  seeing
How low his brother's mood had fallen,
  fetch'd
His richest beeswing from a binn reserved
For banquets, praised the waning red,
  and told
The vintage — when *this* Aylmer came
  of age —
Then drank and past it; till at length
  the two,
Tho' Leolin flamed and fell again, agreed
That much allowance must be made for
  men.
After an angry dream this kindlier glow
Faded with morning, but his purpose held.

　Yet once by night again the lovers
  met,
A perilous meeting under the tall pines
That darken'd all the northward of her
  Hall.
Him, to her meek and modest bosom
  prest
In agony, she promised that no force,
Persuasion, no, nor death could alter her:
He, passionately hopefuller, would go,
Labor for his own Edith, and return
In such a sunlight of prosperity
He should not be rejected. "Write to
  me!
They loved me, and because I love their
  child
They hate me: there is war between us,
  dear,

Which breaks all bonds but ours; we
    must remain
Sacred to one another." So they talk'd,
Poor children, for their comfort: the wind
    blew;
The rain of heaven, and their own bitter
    tears,
Tears, and the careless rain of heaven,
    mixt
Upon their faces, as they kiss'd each other
In darkness, and above them roar'd the
    pine.

    So Leolin went; and as we task our-
    selves
To learn a language known but smatter-
    ingly
In phrases here and there at random, toil'd
Mastering the lawless science of our law,
That codeless myriad of precedent,
That wilderness of single instances,
Thro' which a few, by wit or fortune led,
May beat a pathway out to wealth and
    fame.
The jests, that flash'd about the pleader's
    room,
Lightning of the hour, the pun, the
    scurrilous tale, —
Old scandals buried now seven decades
    deep
In other scandals that have lived and died,
And left the living scandal that shall
    die —
Were dead to him already; bent as he was
To make disproof of scorn, and strong in
    hopes,
And prodigal of all brain-labor he,
Charier of sleep, and wine, and exercise,
Except when for a breathing-while at eve,
Some niggard fraction of an hour, he ran
Beside the river-bank: and then indeed
Harder the times were, and the hands
    of power
Were bloodier, and the according hearts
    of men
Seem'd harder too; but the soft river-
    breeze,
Which fann'd the gardens of that rival
    rose
Yet fragrant in a heart remembering
His former talks with Edith, on him
    breathed
Far purelier in his rushings to and fro,
After his books, to flush his blood with air,
Then to his books again. My lady's
    cousin,
Half-sickening of his pension'd afternoon,
Drove in upon the student once or twice,
Ran a Malayan muck against the times,
Had golden hopes for France and all
    mankind,
Answer'd all queries touching those at
    home
With a heaved shoulder and a saucy smile,
And fain had haled him out into the world,
And air'd him there: his nearer friend
    would say
"Screw not the chord too sharply lest it
    snap."
Then left alone he pluck'd her dagger forth
From where his worldless heart had kept
    it warm,
Kissing his vows upon it like a knight.
And wrinkled benchers often talk'd of
    him
Approvingly, and prophesied his rise:
For heart, I think, help'd head: her let-
    ters too,
Tho' far between, and coming fitfully
Like broken music, written as she found
Or made occasion, being strictly watch'd,
Charm'd him thro' every labyrinth till
    he saw
An end, a hope, a light breaking upon him.

    But they that cast her spirit into flesh,
Her worldly-wise begetters, plagued them-
    selves
To sell her, those good parents, for her
    good.
Whatever eldest-born of rank or wealth
Might lie within their compass, him they
    lured
Into their net made pleasant by the baits
Of gold and beauty, wooing him to woo.
So month by month the noise about their
    doors,
And distant blaze of those dull banquets,
    made
The nightly wirer of their innocent hare
Falter before he took it. All in vain.
Sullen, defiant, pitying, wroth, return'd
Leolin's rejected rivals from their suit
So often, that the folly taking wings
Slipt o'er those lazy limits down the wind
With rumor, and became in other fields
A mockery to the yeomen over ale,
And laughter to their lords: but those
    at home,
As hunters round a hunted creature draw
The cordon close and closer toward the
    death,
Narrow'd her goings out and comings in;
Forbade her first the house of Averill,

Then closed her access to the wealthier
  farms,
Last from her own home-circle of the poor
They barr'd her: yet she bore it: yet
  her cheek
Kept color: wondrous! but, O mystery!
What amulet drew her down to that old
  oak,
So old, that twenty years before, a part
Falling had let appear the brand of
  John —
Once grovelike, each huge arm a tree,
  but now
The broken base of a black tower, a cave
Of touchwood, with a single flourishing
  spray.
There the manorial lord too curiously
Raking in that millennial touchwood-dust
Found for himself a bitter treasure-trove;
Burst his own wyvern on the seal, and
  read
Writhing a letter from his child, for which
Came at the moment Leolin's emissary,
A crippled lad, and coming turn'd to fly,
But scared with threats of jail and halter
  gave
To him that fluster'd his poor parish wits
The letter which he brought, and swore
  besides
To play their go-between as heretofore
Nor let them know themselves betray'd;
  and then,
Soul-stricken at their kindness to him,
  went
Hating his own lean heart and miserable.

    Thenceforward oft from out a despot
      dream
The father panting woke, and oft, as dawn
Aroused the black republic on his elms,
Sweeping the frothfly from the fescue
  brush'd
Thro' the dim meadow toward his treas-
  ure-trove,
Seized it, took home, and to my lady, —
  who made
A downward crescent of her minion mouth,
Listless in all despondence, — read; and
  tore,
As if the living passion symbol'd there
Were living nerves to feel the rent; and
  burnt,
Now chafing at his own great self defied,
Now striking on huge stumbling-blocks
  of scorn
In babyisms, and dear diminutives
Scatter'd all over the vocabulary

Of such a love as like a chidden child,
After much wailing, hush'd itself at last
Hopeless of answer: then tho' Averill
  wrote
And bade him with good heart sustain
  himself —
All would be well — the lover heeded not,
But passionately restless came and went,
And rustling once at night about the place,
There by a keeper shot at, slightly hurt,
Raging return'd: nor was it well for her
Kept to the garden now, and grove of
  pines,
Watch'd even there; and one was set to
  watch
The watcher, and Sir Aylmer watch'd
  them all,
Yet bitterer from his readings: once
  indeed,
Warm'd with his wines, or taking pride
  in her,
She look'd so sweet, he kiss'd her tenderly
Not knowing what possess'd him: that
  one kiss
Was Leolin's one strong rival upon earth;
Seconded, for my lady follow'd suit,
Seem'd hope's returning rose: and then
  ensued
A Martin's summer of his faded love,
Or ordeal by kindness; after this
He seldom crost his child without a sneer;
The mother flow'd in shallower acrimo-
  nies:
Never one kindly smile, one kindly word:
So that the gentle creature shut from all
Her charitable use, and face to face
With twenty months of silence, slowly
  lost
Nor greatly cared to lose, her hold on life.
Last, some low fever ranging round to spy
The weakness of a people or a house,
Like flies that haunt a wound, or deer,
  or men,
Or almost all that is, hurting the hurt —
Save Christ as we believe him — found
  the girl
And flung her down upon a couch of fire,
Where careless of the household faces near,
And crying upon the name of Leolin,
She, and with her the race of Aylmer,
  past.

    Star to star vibrates light: may soul
      to soul
Strike thro' a finer element of her own?
So, — from afar, — touch as at once? or
  why

That night, that moment, when she named his name,
Did the keen shriek "yes love, yes Edith, yes,"
Shrill, till the comrade of his chambers woke,
And came upon him half-arisen from sleep,
With a weird bright eye, sweating and trembling,
His hair as it were crackling into flames,
His body half flung forward in pursuit,
And his long arms stretch'd as to grasp a flyer:
Nor knew he wherefore he had made the cry;
And being much befool'd and idioted
By the rough amity of the other, sank
As into sleep again. The second day,
My lady's Indian kinsman rushing in,
A breaker of the bitter news from home,
Found a dead man, a letter edged with death
Beside him, and the dagger which himself
Gave Edith, redden'd with no bandit's blood:
"From Edith" was engraven on the blade.

Then Averill went and gazed upon his death.
And when he came again, his flock believed —
Beholding how the years which are not Time's
Had blasted him — that many thousand days
Were clipt by horror from his term of life.
Yet the sad mother, for the second death
Scarce touch'd her thro' that nearness of the first,
And being used to find her pastor texts,
Sent to the harrow'd brother, praying him
To speak before the people of her child,
And fixt the Sabbath. Darkly that day rose:
Autumn's mock sunshine of the faded woods
Was all the life of it; for hard on these,
A breathless burden of low-folded heavens
Stifled and chill'd at once: but every roof
Sent out a listener: many too had known
Edith among the hamlets round, and since
The parents' harshness and the hapless loves
And double death were widely murmur'd, left
Their own gray tower, or plain-faced tabernacle,

To hear him; all in mourning these, and those
With blots of it about them, ribbon, glove
Or kerchief; while the church, — one night, except
For greenish glimmerings thro' the lancets, — made
Still paler the pale head of him, who tower'd
Above them, with his hopes in either grave.

Long o'er his bent brows linger'd Averill,
His face magnetic to the hand from which
Livid he pluck'd it forth, and labor'd thro'
His brief prayer-prelude, gave the verse
"Behold,
Your house is left unto you desolate!"
But lapsed into so long a pause again
As half amazed half frighted all his flock:
Then from his height and loneliness of grief
Bore down in flood, and dash'd his angry heart
Against the desolations of the world.

Never since our bad earth became one sea,
Which rolling o'er the palaces of the proud,
And all but those who knew the living God —
Eight that were left to make a purer world —
When since had flood, fire, earthquake, thunder, wrought
Such waste and havoc as the idolatries,
Which from the low light of mortality
Shot up their shadows to the Heaven of Heavens,
And worshipt their own darkness as the Highest?
"Gash thyself, priest, and honor thy brute Baal,
And to thy worst self sacrifice thyself,
For with thy worst self hast thou clothed thy God.
Then came a Lord in no wise like to Baal.
The babe shall lead the lion. Surely now
The wilderness shall blossom as the rose.
Crown thyself, worm, and worship thine own lusts! —
No coarse and blockish God of acreage
Stands at thy gate for thee to grovel to —
Thy God is far diffused in noble groves
And princely halls, and farms, and flowing lawns,

And heaps of living gold that daily grow,
And title-scrolls and gorgeous heraldries.
In such a shape dost thou behold thy God.
Thou wilt not gash thy flesh for *him;* for thine
Fares richly, in fine linen, not a hair
Ruffled upon the scarfskin, even while
The deathless ruler of thy dying house
Is wounded to the death that cannot die;
And tho' thou numberest with the followers
Of One who cried 'leave all and follow me.'
Thee therefore with His light about thy feet,
Thee with His message ringing in thine ears,
Thee shall thy brother man, the Lord from Heaven,
Born of a village girl, carpenter's son,
Wonderful, Prince of peace, the Mighty God,
Count the more base idolater of the two ;
Crueller : as not passing thro' the fire
Bodies, but souls — thy children's — thro' the smoke,
The blight of low desires — darkening thine own
To thine own likeness ; or if one of these,
Thy better born unhappily from thee,
Should, as by miracle, grow straight and fair —
Friends, I was bid to speak of such a one
By those who most have cause to sorrow for her —
Fairer than Rachel by the palmy well,
Fairer than Ruth among the fields of corn,
Fair as the Angel that said 'hail' she seem'd,
Who entering fill'd the house with sudden light.
For so mine own was brighten'd : where indeed
The roof so lowly but that beam of Heaven
Dawn'd sometime thro' the doorway?
whose the babe
Too ragged to be fondled on her lap,
Warm'd at her bosom ? The poor child of shame,
The common care whom no one cared for, leapt
To greet her, wasting his forgotten heart,
As with the mother he had never known,
In gambols ; for her fresh and innocent eyes
Had such a star of morning in their blue,
That all neglected places of the field
Broke into nature's music when they saw her.
Low was her voice, but won mysterious way
Thro' the seal'd ear to which a louder one
Was all but silence — free of alms her hand —
The hand that robed your cottage-walls with flowers
Has often toil'd to clothe your little ones;
How often placed upon the sick man's brow
Cool'd it, or laid his feverish pillow smooth!
Had you one sorrow and she shared it not ?
One burden and she would not lighten it ?
One spiritual doubt she did not soothe ?
Or when some heat of difference sparkled out,
How sweetly would she glide between your wraths,
And steal you from each other ! for she walk'd
Wearing the light yoke of that Lord of love,
Who still'd the rolling wave of Galilee !
And one — of him I was not bid to speak —
Was always with her, whom you also knew.
Him too you loved, for he was worthy love.
And these had been together from the first ;
They might have been together till the last.
Friends, this frail bark of ours, when sorely tried,
May wreck itself without the pilot's guilt,
Without the captain's knowledge : hope with me.
Whose shame is that, if he went hence with shame ?
Nor mine the fault, if losing both of these
I cry to vacant chairs and widow'd walls,
'My house is left unto me desolate.'"

While thus he spoke, his hearers wept ; but some,
Sons of the glebe, with other frowns than those
That knit themselves for summer shadow, scowl'd
At their great lord. He, when it seem'd he saw
No pale sheet-lightnings from afar, but fork'd
Of the near storm, and aiming at his head,
Sat anger-charm'd from sorrow, soldier-like,
Erect : but when the preacher's cadence flow'd
Softening thro' all the gentle attributes

Of his lost child, the wife, who watch'd his face,
Paled at a sudden twitch of his iron mouth;
And "O pray God that he hold up" she thought
"Or surely I shall shame myself and him."

"Nor yours the blame — for who beside your hearths
Can take her place — if echoing me you cry
'Our house is left unto us desolate!'
But thou, O thou that killest, hadst thou known,
O thou that stonest, hadst thou understood
The things belonging to thy peace and ours!
Is there no prophet but the voice that calls
Doom upon kings, or in the waste 'Repent'?
Is not our own child on the narrow way,
Who down to those that saunter in the broad
Cries 'come up hither,' as a prophet to us?
Is there no stoning save with flint and rock?
Yes, as the dead we weep for testify —
No desolation but by sword and fire?
Yes, as your moanings witness, and myself
Am lonelier, darker, earthlier for my loss.
Give me your prayers, for he is past your prayers,
Not past the living fount of pity in Heaven.
But I that thought myself long-suffering, meek,
Exceeding 'poor in spirit' — how the words
Have twisted back upon themselves, and mean
Vileness, we are grown so proud — I wish'd my voice
A rushing tempest of the wrath of God
To blow these sacrifices thro' the world —
Sent like the twelve-divided concubine
To inflame the tribes: but there — out yonder — earth
Lightens from her own central Hell — O there
The red fruit of an old idolatry —
The heads of chiefs and princes fall so fast,
They cling together in the ghastly sack —
The land all shambles — naked marriages
Flash from the bridge, and ever-murder'd France,
By shores that darken with the gathering wolf,
Runs in a river of blood to the sick sea.
Is this a time to madden madness then?
Was this a time for these to flaunt their pride?
May Pharaoh's darkness, folds as dense as those
Which hid the Holiest from the people's eyes
Ere the great death, shroud this great sin from all!
Doubtless our narrow world must canvass it:
O rather pray for those and pity them,
Who thro' their own desire accomplish'd bring
Their own gray hairs with sorrow to the grave —
Who broke the bond which they desired to break,
Which else had link'd their race with times to come —
Who wove coarse webs to snare her purity,
Grossly contriving their dear daughter's good —
Poor souls, and knew not what they did, but sat
Ignorant, devising their own daughter's death!
May not that earthly chastisement suffice?
Have not our love and reverence left them bare?
Will not another take their heritage?
Will there be children's laughter in their hall
For ever and for ever, or one stone
Left on another, or is it a light thing
That I their guest, their host, their ancient friend,
I made by these the last of all my race
Must cry to these the last of theirs, as cried
Christ ere His agony to those that swore
Not by the temple but the gold, and made
Their own traditions God, and slew the Lord,
And left their memories a world's curse
— 'Behold,
Your house is left unto you desolate'?"

Ended he had not, but she brook'd no more:
Long since her heart had beat remorselessly,
Her crampt-up sorrow pain'd her, and a sense
Of meanness in her unresisting life.

Then their eyes vext her ; for on entering
He had cast the curtains of their seat
  aside—
Black velvet of the costliest— she herself
Had seen to that : fain had she closed
  them now,
Yet dared not stir to do it, only near'd
Her husband inch by inch, but when she
  laid,
Wifelike, her hand in one of his, he veil'd
His face with the other, and at once, as
  falls
A creeper when the prop is broken, fell
The woman shrieking at his feet, and
  swoon'd.
Then her own people bore along the nave
Her pendent hands, and narrow meagre
  face
Seam'd with the shallow cares of fifty
  years :
And her the Lord of all the landscape
  round
Ev'n to his last horizon, and of all
Who peer'd at him so keenly, follow'd out
Tall and erect, but in the middle aisle
Reel'd, as a footsore ox in crowded ways
Stumbling across the market to his death,
Unpitied ; for he groped as blind, and
  seem'd
Always about to fall, grasping the pews
And oaken finials till he touch'd the door ;
Yet to the lychgate, where his chariot
  stood,
Strode from the porch, tall and erect again.

But nevermore did either pass the gate
Save under pall with bearers. In one
  month,
Thro' weary and yet ever wearier hours,
The childless mother went to seek her
  child ;
And when he felt the silence of his house
About him, and the change and not the
  change,
And those fixt eyes of painted ancestors
Staring for ever from their gilded walls
On him their last descendant, his own
  head
Began to droop, to fall ; the man became
Imbecile ; his one word was "desolate";
Dead for two years before his death was
  he ;
But when the second Christmas came,
  escaped
His keepers, and the silence which he felt,
To find a deeper in the narrow gloom
By wife and child ; nor wanted at his end

The dark retinue reverencing death
At golden thresholds ; nor from tender
  hearts,
And those who sorrow'd o'er a vanish'd
  race,
Pity, the violet on the tyrant's grave.
Then the great Hall was wholly broken
  down,
And the broad woodland parcell'd into
  farms ;
And where the two contrived their daugh-
  ter's good,
Lies the hawk's cast, the mole has made
  his run,
The hedgehog underneath the plantain
  bores,
The rabbit fondles his own harmless face,
The slow-worm creeps, and the thin
  weasel there
Follows the mouse, and all is open field.

SEA DREAMS.

A CITY clerk, but gently born and bred ;
His wife, an unknown artist's orphan
  child —
One babe was theirs, a Margaret, three
  years old :
They, thinking that her clear germander
  eye
Droopt in the giant-factoried city-gloom,
Came, with a month's leave given them,
  to the sea :
For which his gains were dock'd, however
  small :
Small were his gains, and hard his work ;
  besides,
Their slender household fortunes (for the
  man
Had risk'd his little) like the little thrift,
Trembled in perilous places o'er a deep :
And oft, when sitting all alone, his face
Would darken, as he cursed his credu-
  lousness,
And that one unctuous mouth which lured
  him, rogue,
To buy strange shares in some Peruvian
  mine.
Now seaward-bound for health they
  gain'd a coast,
All sand and cliff and deep-inrunning
  cave,
At close of day ; slept, woke, and went
  the next,
The Sabbath, pious variers from the
  church,

SEA DREAMS.

To chapel; where a heated pulpiteer,
Not preaching simple Christ to simple men,
Announced the coming doom, and fulminated
Against the scarlet woman and her creed:
For sideways up he swung his arms, and shriek'd
"Thus, thus with violence," ev'n as if he held
The Apocalyptic millstone, and himself
Were that great Angel; "Thus with violence
Shall Babylon be cast into the sea;
Then comes the close." The gentle-hearted wife
Sat shuddering at the ruin of a world;
He at his own: but when the wordy storm
Had ended, forth they came and paced the shore,
Ran in and out the long sea-framing caves,
Drank the large air, and saw, but scarce believed
(The sootflake of so many a summer still
Clung to their fancies) that they saw, the sea.
So now on sand they walk'd, and now on cliff,
Lingering about the thymy promontories,
Till all the sails were darken'd in the west,
And rosed in the east: then homeward and to bed:
Where she, who kept a tender Christian hope
Haunting a holy text, and still to that
Returning, as the bird returns, at night,
"Let not the sun go down upon your wrath,"
Said, "Love, forgive him": but he did not speak;
And silenced by that silence lay the wife,
Remembering her dear Lord who died for all,
And musing on the little lives of men,
And how they mar this little by their feuds.

But while the two were sleeping, a full tide
Rose with ground-swell, which, on the foremost rocks
Touching, upjetted in spirits of wild sea-smoke,
And scaled in sheets of wasteful foam, and fell
In vast sea-cataracts — ever and anon
Dead claps of thunder from within the cliffs
Heard thro' the living roar. At this the babe,
Their Margaret cradled near them, wail'd and woke
The mother, and the father suddenly cried,
"A wreck, a wreck!" then turn'd, and groaning said,

'"Forgive! How many will say, 'forgive,' and find
A sort of absolution in the sound
To hate a little longer! No; the sin
That neither God nor man can well forgive,
Hypocrisy, I saw it in him at once.
Is it so true that second thoughts are best?
Not first, and third, which are a riper first?
Too ripe, too late! they come too late for use.
Ah love, there surely lives in man and beast
Something divine to warn them of their foes: ·
And such a sense, when first I fronted him,
Said, 'trust him not'; but after, when I came
To know him more, I lost it, knew him less;
Fought with what seem'd my own uncharity;
Sat at his table; drank his costly wines;
Made more and more allowance for his talk;
Went further, fool! and trusted him with all,
All my poor scrapings from a dozen years
Of dust and deskwork: there is no such mine,
None; but a gulf of ruin, swallowing gold,
Not making. Ruin'd! ruin'd! the sea roars
Ruin: a fearful night!"

"Not fearful; fair,"
Said the good wife, "if every star in heaven
Can make it fair: you do but hear the tide.
Had you ill dreams?"

"O yes," he said, "I dream'd
Of such a tide swelling toward the land,
And I from out the boundless outer deep

Swept with it to the shore, and enter'd one
Of those dark caves that run beneath the cliffs.
I thought the motion of the boundless deep
Bore through the cave, and I was heaved upon it
In darkness: then I saw one lovely star
Larger and larger. 'What a world,' I thought,
'To live in!' but in moving on I found
Only the landward exit of the cave,
Bright with the sun upon the stream beyond:
And near the light a giant woman sat,
All over earthy, like a piece of earth,
A pickaxe in her hand: then out I slipt
Into a land all sun and blossom, trees
As high as heaven, and every bird that sings:
And here the night-light flickering in my eyes
Awoke me."

"That was then your dream," she said,
"Not sad, but sweet."

   "So sweet, I lay," said he,
"And mused upon it, drifting up the stream
In fancy, till I slept again, and pieced
The broken vision; for I dream'd that still
The motion of the great deep bore me on,
And that the woman walk'd upon the brink:
I wonder'd at her strength, and ask'd her of it:
'It came,' she said, 'by working in the mines':
O then to ask her of my shares, I thought;
And ask'd; but not a word; she shook her head.
And then the motion of the current ceased,
And there was rolling thunder; and we reach'd
A mountain, like a wall of burrs and thorns;
But she with her strong feet up the steep hill
Trod out a path: I follow'd; and at top
She pointed seaward: there a fleet of glass,
That seem'd a fleet of jewels under me,
Sailing along before a gloomy cloud
That not one moment ceased to thunder, past

In sunshine: right across its track there lay,
Down in the water, a long reef of gold,
Or what seem'd gold: and I was glad at first
To think that in our often-ransack'd world
Still so much gold was left; and then I fear'd
Lest the gay navy there should splinter on it,
And fearing waved my arm to warn them off;
An idle signal, for the brittle fleet
(I thought I could have died to save it) near'd,
Touch'd, clink'd, and clash'd, and vanish'd, and I woke,
I heard the clash so clearly. Now I see
My dream was Life; the woman honest Work;
And my poor venture but a fleet of glass
Wreck'd on a reef of visionary gold."

"Nay," said the kindly wife to comfort him,
"You raised your arm, you tumbled down and broke
The glass with little Margaret's medicine in it;
And, breaking that, you made and broke your dream:
A trifle makes a dream, a trifle breaks."

"No trifle," groan'd the husband;
"yesterday
I met him suddenly in the street, and ask'd
That which I ask'd the woman in my dream.
Like her, he shook his head. 'Show me the books!'
He dodged me with a long and loose account.
'The books, the books!' but he, he could not wait,
Bound on a matter he of life and death:
When the great Books (see Daniel seven and ten)
Were open'd, I should find he meant me well;
And then began to bloat himself, and ooze
All over with the fat affectionate smile
That makes the widow lean. 'My dearest friend,
Have faith, have faith! We live by faith,' said he;
'And all things work together for the good

SEA DREAMS.

Of those'—it makes me sick to quote
   him—last
Gript my hand hard, and with God-bless-
   you went.
I stood like one that had received a blow:
I found a hard friend in his loose accounts,
A loose one in the hard grip of his hand,
A curse in his God-bless-you: then my
   eyes
Pursued him down the street, and far
   away,
Among the honest shoulders of the crowd,
Read rascal in the motions of his back,
And scoundrel in the supple-sliding
   knee."

"Was he so bound, poor soul?" said
   the good wife;
"So are we all: but do not call him,
   love,
Before you prove him, rogue, and proved,
   forgive.
His gain is loss; for he that wrongs his
   friend
Wrongs himself more, and ever bears about
A silent court of justice in his breast,
Himself the judge and jury, and himself
The prisoner at the bar, ever condemn'd:
And that drags down his life: then comes
   what comes
Hereafter: and he meant, he said he meant,
Perhaps he meant, or partly meant, you
   well."

"'With all his conscience and one
   eye askew'—
Love, let me quote these lines, that you
   may learn
A man is likewise counsel for himself,
Too often, in that silent court of yours—
'With all his conscience and one eye
   askew,
So false, he partly took himself for true;
Whose pious talk, when most his heart
   was dry,
Made wet the crafty crowsfoot round his
   eye;
Who, never naming God except for gain,
So never took that useful name in vain;
Made Him his catspaw and the Cross
   his tool,
And Christ the bait to trap his dupe and
   fool;
Nor deeds of gift, but gifts of grace he
   forged,
And snakelike slimed his victim ere he
   gorged;

And oft at Bible meetings, o'er the rest
Arising, did his holy oily best,
Dropping the too rough H in Hell and
   Heaven,
To spread the Word by which himself
   had thriven.'
How like you this old satire?"

             "Nay," she said,
"I loathe it: he had never kindly heart,
Nor ever cared to better his own kind,
Who first wrote satire, with no pity in it.
But will you hear *my* dream, for I had one
That altogether went to music? Still
It awed me."

        Then she told it, having dream'd
Of that same coast.

      "—But round the North, a light,
A belt, it seem'd, of luminous vapor, lay,
And ever in it a low musical note
Swell'd up and died; and, as it swell'd,
   a ridge
Of breaker issued from the belt, and still
Grew with the growing note, and when
   the note
Had reach'd a thunderous fulness, on
   those cliffs
Broke, mixt with awful light (the same
   as that
Living within the belt) whereby she saw
That all those lines of cliffs were cliffs
   no more,
But huge cathedral fronts of every age,
Grave, florid, stern, as far as eye could see,
One after one: and then the great ridge
   drew,
Lessening to the lessening music, back,
And past into the belt and swell'd again
Slowly to music: ever when it broke
The statues, king or saint, or founder fell;
Then from the gaps and chasms of ruin
   left
Came men and women in dark clusters
   round,
Some crying, 'Set them up! they shall
   not fall!'
And others 'Let them lie, for they have
   fall'n.'
And still they strove and wrangled: and
   she grieved
In her strange dream, she knew not
   why, to find
Their wildest wailings never out of tune
With that sweet note; and ever as their
   shrieks

Ran highest up the gamut, that great wave
Returning, while none mark'd it, on the
    crowd.
Broke, mixt with awful light, and
    show'd their eyes
Glaring, and passionate looks, and swept
    away
The men of flesh and blood, and men of
    stone,
To the waste deeps together.

                    "Then I fixt
My wistful eyes on two fair images,
Both crown'd with stars and high among
    the stars, —
The Virgin Mother standing with her
    child
High up on one of those dark minster-
    fronts —
Till she began to totter, and the child
Clung to the mother, and sent out a cry
Which mixt with little Margaret's, and
    I woke,
And my dream awed me . — well — but
    what are dreams ?
Yours came but from the breaking of a
    glass,
And mine but from the crying of a child."

  "Child ! No !" said he, "but this
    tide's roar, and his,
Our Boanerges with his threats of doom,
And loud-lung'd Antibabylonianisms
    (Altho' I grant but little music there)
Went both to make your dream : but if
    there were
A music harmonizing our wild cries,
Sphere-music such as that you dream'd
    about,
Why, that would make our passions far
    too like
The discords dear to the musician. No —
One shriek of hate would jar all the
    hymns of heaven :
True Devils with no ear, they howl in tune
With nothing but the Devil !"

                    "'True' indeed !
One of our town, but later by an hour
Here than ourselves, spoke with me on
    the shore ;
While you were running down the sands,
    and made
The dimpled flounce of the sea-furbelow
    flap,
Good man, to please the child.. She
    brought strange news.

Why were you silent when I spoke to-
    night ?
I had set my heart on your forgiving him
Before you knew. We *must* forgive the
    dead."

    "Dead ! who is dead ?"

              "The man your eye pursued.
A little after you had parted with him,
He suddenly dropt dead of heart-disease."

    "Dead ? he ? of heart-disease ? what
        heart had he
To die of ? dead !"

              "Ah, dearest, if there be
A devil in man, there is an angel too,
And if he did that wrong you charge
    him with,
His angel broke his heart. But your
    rough voice
(You spoke so loud) has roused the child
    again.
Sleep, little birdie, sleep ! will she not sleep
Without her 'little birdie' ? well then,
    sleep,
And I will sing you 'birdie.'"

                    Saying this,
The woman half turn'd round from him
    she loved,
Left him one hand, and reaching thro'
    the night
Her other, found (for it was close beside)
And half embraced the basket cradle-head
With one soft arm, which, like the pliant
    bough
That moving moves the nest and nest-
    ling, sway'd
The cradle, while she sang this baby song.

    What does little birdie say
    In her nest at peep of day ?
    Let me fly, says little birdie,
    Mother, let me fly away.
    Birdie, rest a little longer,
    Till the little wings are stronger.
    So she rests a little longer,
    Then she flies away.

    What does little baby say,
    In her bed at peep of day ?
    Baby says, like little birdie,
    Let me rise and fly away.
    Baby, sleep a little longer,
    Till the little limbs are stronger.

If she sleeps a little longer,
Baby too shall fly away.

"She sleeps: let us too, let all evil, sleep.
He also sleeps — another sleep than ours.
He can do no more wrong: forgive him,
  dear,
And I shall sleep the sounder!"

Then the man,
"His deeds yet live, the worst is yet to
  come.
Yet let your sleep for this one night be
  sound:
I do forgive him!"

"Thanks, my love," she said,
"Your own will be the sweeter," and
  they slept.

THE GRANDMOTHER.

I.

And Willy, my eldest-born, is gone, you
  say, little Anne?
Ruddy, and white, and strong on his legs,
  he looks like a man.
And Willy's wife has written: she never
  was over-wise,
Never the wife for Willy: he would n't
  take my advice.

II.

For, Annie, you see, her father was not
  the man to save,
Had n't a head to manage, and drank
  himself into his grave.
Pretty enough, very pretty! but I was
  against it for one.
Eh! — but he would n't hear me — and
  Willy, you say, is gone.

III.

Willy, my beauty, my eldest-born, the
  flower of the flock;
Never a man could fling him: for Willy
  stood like a rock.
"Here 's a leg for a babe of a week!" says
  doctor; and he would be bound,
There was not his like that year in twenty
  parishes round.

IV.

Strong of his hands, and strong on his
  legs, but still of his tongue!
I ought to have gone before him: I
  wonder he went so young.
I cannot cry for him, Annie: I have not
  long to stay;
Perhaps I shall see him the sooner, for
  he lived far away.

V.

Why do you look at me, Annie? you
  think I am hard and cold;
But all my children have gone before me,
  I am so old:
I cannot weep for Willy, nor can I weep
  for the rest;
Only at your age, Annie, I could have
  wept with the best.

VI.

For I remember a quarrel I had with
  your father, my dear,
All for a slanderous story, that cost me
  many a tear.
I mean your grandfather, Annie: it cost
  me a world of woe,
Seventy years ago, my darling, seventy
  years ago.

VII.

For Jenny, my cousin, had come to the
  place, and I knew right well
That Jenny had tript in her time: I
  knew, but I would not tell.
And she to be coming and slandering me,
  the base little liar!
But the tongue is a fire as you know, my
  dear, the tongue is a fire.

VIII.

And the parson made it his text that
  week, and he said likewise,
That a lie which is half a truth is ever
  the blackest of lies,
That a lie which is all a lie may be met
  and fought with outright,
But a lie which is part a truth is a harder
  matter to fight.

IX.

And Willy had not been down to the farm
  for a week and a day;
And all things look'd half-dead, tho' it
  was the middle of May.
Jenny, to slander me, who knew what
  Jenny had been!
But soiling another, Annie, will never
  make one's self clean.

The Grandmother.

X.

And I cried myself wellnigh blind, and all of an evening late
I climb'd to the top of the garth, and stood by the road at the gate.
The moon like a rick on fire was rising over the dale,
And whit, whit, whit, in the bush beside me chirrupt the nightingale.

XI.

All of a sudden he stopt: there past by the gate of the farm,
Willy,—he did n't see me,—and Jenny hung on his arm.
Out into the road I started, and spoke I scarce knew how;
Ah, there's no fool like the old one—it makes me angry now.

XII.

Willy stood up like a man, and look'd the thing that he meant;
Jenny, the viper, made me a mocking courtesy and went.
And I said, "Let us part: in a hundred years it 'll all be the same, - You cannot love me at all, if you love not my good name."

XIII.

And he turn'd, and I saw his eyes all wet, in the sweet moonshine:
"Sweetheart, I love you so well that your good name is mine.
And what do I care for Jane, let her speak of you well or ill;
But marry me out of hand: we too shall be happy still."

XIV.

"Marry you, Willy!" said I, "but I needs must speak my mind,
And I fear you'll listen to tales, be jealous and hard and unkind."
But he turn'd and claspt me in his arms, and answer'd, "No, love, no";
Seventy years ago, my darling, seventy years ago.

XV.

So Willy and I were wedded: I wore a lilac gown;

And the ringers rang with a will, and he
   gave the ringers a crown.
But the first that ever I bare was dead
   before he was born,
Shadow and shine is life, little Annie,
   flower and thorn.

XVI.

That was the first time, too, that ever I
   thought of death.
There lay the sweet little body that never
   had drawn a breath.
I had not wept, little Anne, not since I
   had been a wife;
But I wept like a child that day, for the
   babe had fought for his life.

XVII.

His dear little face was troubled, as if
   with anger or pain:
I look'd at the still little body — his
   trouble had all been in vain.
For Willy I cannot weep, I shall see him
   another morn:
But I wept like a child for the child that
   was dead before he was born.

XVIII.

But he cheer'd me, my good man, for he
   seldom said me nay:
Kind, like a man, was he; like a man,
   too, would have his way:
Never jealous — not he: we had many a
   happy year;
And he died, and I could not weep —
   my own time seem'd so near.

XIX.

But I wish'd it had been God's will that
   I, too, then could have died:
I began to be tired a little, and fain had
   slept at his side.
And that was ten years back, or more,
   if I don't forget:
But as to the children, Annie, they're all
   about me yet.

XX.

Pattering over the boards, my Annie who
   left me at two,
Patter she goes, my own little Annie, an
   Annie like you:
Pattering over the boards, she comes and
   goes at her will,
While Harry is in the five-acre and Char-
   lie ploughing the hill.

XXI.

And Harry and Charlie, I hear them too
   — they sing to their team:
Often they come to the door in a pleasant
   kind of a dream.
They come and sit by my chair, they
   hover about my bed —
I am not always certain if they be alive
   or dead.

XXII.

And yet I know for a truth, there's none
   of them left alive;
For Harry went at sixty, your father at
   sixty-five:
And Willy, my eldest-born, at nigh three-
   score and ten;
I knew them all as babies, and now they
   're elderly men.

XXIII.

For mine is a time of peace, it is not often
   I grieve;
I am oftener sitting at home in my fa-
   ther's farm at eve:
And the neighbors come and laugh and
   gossip, and so do I;
I find myself often laughing at things
   that have long gone by.

XXIV.

To be sure the preacher says, our sins
   should make us sad:
But mine is a time of peace, and there
   is Grace to be had;
And God, not man, is the Judge of us all
   when life shall cease;
And in this Book, little Annie, the mes-
   sage is one of Peace.

XXV.

And age is a time of peace, so it be free
   from pain,
And happy has been my life; but I would
   not live it again.
I seem to be tired a little, that's all, and
   long for rest;
Only at your age, Annie, I could have
   wept with the best.

XXVI.

So Willy has gone, my beauty, my eldest-
   born, my flower;
But how can I weep for Willy, he has
   but gone for an hour, —

Gone for a minute, my son, from this
   room into the next;
I, too, shall go in a minute. What time
   have I to be vext?

XXVII.

And Willy's wife has written, she never
   was over-wise.
Get me my glasses, Annie : thank God
   that I keep my eyes.
There is but a trifle left you, when I shall
   have past away.
But stay with the old woman now : you
   cannot have long to stay.

NORTHERN FARMER.

OLD STYLE.

I.

WHEER 'asta beän saw long and meä lig-
   gin' 'ere aloän?
Noorse? thoort nowt o' a noorse : whoy,
   Doctor's abeän an' agoän :
Says that I moänt 'a naw moor aäle : but
   I beänt a fool :
Git ma my aäle, for I beänt a-gooin' to
   breäk my rule.

II.

Doctors, they knaws nowt, for a says
   what 's nawways true :
Naw soort o' koind o' use to saäy the
   things that a do.
I 've 'ed my point o' aäle ivry noight
   sin' I beän 'ere,
An' I 've 'ed my quart ivry market-noight
   for foorty year.

III.

Parson's a beän loikewoise, an' a sittin
   'ere o' my bed.
"The amoighty 's a taäkin o' you to 'issén,
   my friend," a said,
An' a towd ma my sins, an 's toithe were
   due, an' I gied it in hond ;
I done my duty by 'm, as I 'a done by
   the lond.

IV.

Larn'd a ma' beä. I reckons I 'annot sa
   mooch to larn.
But a cast oop, thot a did, 'boot Bessy
   Marris's bairn.
Thaw a knaws I hallus voäted wi' Squoire
   an' choorch an staäte,
An' i' the woost o' toimes I wur niver
   agin the raäte.

V.

An' I hallus coomed to 's choorch afoor moy
   Sally wur deäd,
An' 'eerd un a bummin' awaäy loike a
   buzzard-clock * ower my 'eäd,
An' I niver knaw'd whot a meän'd but I
   thowt a 'ad summut to saäy,
An' I thowt a said whot a owt to 'a said
   an' I coom'd awaäy.

VI.

Bessy Marris's bairn ! tha knaws she laäid
   it to meä.
Mowt 'a beän, mayhap, for she wur a bad
   un, sheä.
'Siver, I kep 'm, I kep 'm, my lass, tha
   mun understond ;
I done my duty by 'm as I 'a done by
   the lond.

VII.

But Parson a comes an' a goos, an' a says
   it eäsy an' freeä
"The amoighty's a taäkin o' you to 'issén,
   my friend," says 'eä.
I weänt saäy men be loiars, thaw summun
   said it in 'näste :
But a reäds wonn sarmin a weeäk, an' I 'a
   stubb'd Thurnaby waäste.

VIII.

D'ya moind the waäste, my lass? naw,
   naw, tha was not born then ;
Theer wur a boggle in it, I often 'eerd 'm
   mysen ;
Moäst loike a butter-bump, † for I 'eerd
   'm aboot an' aboot,
But I stubb'd 'm oop wi' the lot, an'
   raäved an' rembled 'm oot.

IX.

Keäper's it wur ; fo' they fun 'm theer
   a-laäid on 'is faäce
Doon i' the woild 'enemies ‡ afoor I
   coomed to the plaäce.
Noäks or Thimbleby — toaner 'ed shot
   'm as deäd as a naäil.
Noäks wur 'ang'd for it oop at 'soize — but
   git ma my aäle.

X.

Dubbut loook at the waäste : theer warn't
   not feeäd for a cow ;
Nowt at all but bracken an' fuzz, an'
   loook at it now —

* Cockchafer.   † Bittern.   ‡ Anemones.

Warn't worth nowt a haäcre, an' now
theer's lots o' feeäd,
Fourscoor yows upon it an' some on it
doon in seeäd.

XI.

Nobbut a bit on it 's left, an' I meän'd
to 'a stubb'd it at fall,
Done it ta-year I meän'd, an' runn'd
plough thruff it an' all,
If godamoighty an' parson 'ud nobbut let
ma aloän,
Meä, wi' haäte oonderd haäcre o' Squoire's,
an' lond o' my oän.

XII.

Do godamoighty knaw what a 's doing
a-taäkin' o' meä ?
I beänt wonn as saws 'ere a beän an'
yonder a peä ;
An' Squoire 'ull be sa mad an' all — a'
dear a' dear !
And I 'a managed for Squoire come Mich-
aelmas thutty year.

XIII.

A mowt 'a taäen owd Joänes, as 'ant nor a
'aäpoth o' sense,
Or a mowt 'a taäen young Robins — a
niver mended a fence :
But godamoighty a moost taäke meä an'
taäke ma now
Wi' 'aäf the cows to cauve an' Thurnaby
hoalms to plough !

XIV.

Loook 'ow quoloty smoiles when they
seeäs ma a passin' by,
Says to thessén naw doubt " what a man
a beä sewer-ly ! "
For they knaws what I beän to Squoire
sin fust a comed to the 'All ;
I done my duty by Squoire an' I done
my duty by hall.

XV.

Squoire's in Lunnon, an' summun I reck-
ons 'ull 'a to wroite,
For whoä 's to howd the lond ater meä
thot muddles ma quoit ;
Sartin-sewer I beä, thot a weänt niver
give it to Joänes,
Naw nor a moänt to Robins — a niver
rembles the stoäns.

XVI.

But summun 'ull come ater meä mayhap
wi' 'is kittle o' steäm
Huzzin' an' maäzin' the blessed feälds
wi' the Divil's oän teäm.
If I mun doy I mun doy, an' loife they
says is sweet,
But if I mun doy I mun doy, for I
couldn abeär to see it.

XVII.

What atta stannin' theer for, an' doesn
bring ma the 'aäle ?
Doctor's a toättler, lass, an a 's hallus i'
the owd taäle ;
I weänt breäk rules for Doctor, a knaws
naw moor nor a floy ;
Git ma my 'aäle I tell tha, an' if I
mun doy I mun doy.

TITHONUS.

THE woods decay, the woods decay and
fall,
The vapors weep their burden to the
ground,
Man comes and tills the field and lies
beneath,
And after many a summer dies the swan.
Me only cruel immortality
Consumes : I wither slowly in thine arms,
Here at the quiet limit of the world,
A white-hair'd shadow roaming like a
dream
The ever silent spaces of the East,
Far-fo ded mists, and gleaming halls of
morn.

Alas ! for this gray shadow, once a
man —
So glorious in his beauty and thy choice,
Who madest him thy chosen, that he
seem'd
To his great heart none other than a God !
I ask'd thee, " Give me immortality."
Then didst thou grant mine asking with
a smile,
Like wealthy men who care not how they
give.
But thy strong Hours indignant work'd
their wills,
And beat me down and marr'd and wasted
me,
And tho' they could not end me, left me
maim'd
To dwell in presence of immortal youth,

Immortal age beside immortal youth,
And all I was, in ashes. Can thy love,
Thy beauty, make amends, tho' even now,
Close over us, the silver star, thy guide,
Shines in those tremulous eyes that fill
    with tears
To hear me ? Let me go : take back thy
    gift :
Why should a man desire in any way
To vary from the kindly race of men,
Or pass beyond the goal of ordinance
Where all should pause, as is most meet
    for all ?

A soft air fans the cloud apart ; there
    comes
A glimpse of that dark world where I was
    born.
Once more the old mysterious glimmer
    steals
From thy pure brows, and from thy
    shoulders pure,
And bosom beating with a heart renew'd.
Thy cheek begins to redden thro' the
    gloom,
Thy sweet eyes brighten slowly close to
    mine,
Ere yet they blind the stars, and the wild
    team
Which love thee, yearning for thy yoke,
    arise,
And shake the darkness from their loosen'd
    manes,
And beat the twilight into flakes of fire.

Lo ! ever thus thou growest beautiful
In silence, then before thine answer given
Departest, and thy tears are on my cheek.

Why wilt thou ever scare me with thy
    tears,
And make me tremble lest a saying learnt,
In days far-off, on that dark earth, be
    true ?
"The Gods themselves cannot recall their
    gifts."

Ay me ! ay me ! with what another heart
In days far-off, and with what other
    eyes
I used to watch — if I be he that
    watch'd —
The lucid outline forming round thee ;
    saw
The dim curls kindle into sunny rings ;
Changed with thy mystic change, and felt
    my blood

Glow with the glow that slowly crimson'd
    all
Thy presence and thy portals, while I lay,
Mouth, forehead, eyelids, growing dewy-
    warm
With kisses balmier than half-opening
    buds
Of April, and could hear the lips that
    kiss'd
Whispering I knew not what of wild and
    sweet,
Like that strange song I heard Apollo sing,
While Ilion like a mist rose into towers.

Yet hold me not for ever in thine East :
How can my nature longer mix with thine?
Coldly thy rosy shadows bathe me, cold
Are all thy lights, and cold my wrinkled
    feet
Upon thy glimmering thresholds, when
    the steam
Floats up from those dim fields about the
    homes
Of happy men that have the power to die,
And grassy barrows of the happier dead.
Release me, and restore me to the ground ;
Thou seëst all things, thou wilt see my
    grave :
Thou wilt renew thy beauty morn by
    morn ;
I earth in earth forget these empty courts,
And thee returning on thy silver wheels.

THE VOYAGE.

I.

WE left behind the painted buoy
    That tosses at the harbor-mouth ;
And madly danced our hearts with joy,
    As fast we fleeted to the South :
How fresh was every sight and sound
    On open main or winding shore !
We knew the merry world was round,
    And we might sail for evermore.

II.

Warm broke the breeze against the brow,
    Dry sang the tackle, sang the sail :
The Lady's-head upon the prow
    Caught the shrill salt, and sheer'd the
        gale.
The broad seas swell'd to meet the keel,
    And swept behind : so quick the run,
We felt the good ship shake and reel,
    We seem'd to sail into the Sun !

III.

How oft we saw the Sun retire,
  And burn the threshold of the night,
Fall from his Ocean-lane of fire,
  And sleep beneath his pillar'd light !
How oft the purple-skirted robe
  Of twilight slowly downward drawn,
As thro' the slumber of the globe
  Again we dash'd into the dawn !

IV.

New stars all night above the brim
  Of waters lighten'd into view ;
They climb'd as quickly, for the rim
  Changed every moment as we flew.
Far ran the naked moon across
  The houseless ocean's heaving field,
Or flying shone, the silver boss
  Of her own halo's dusky shield ;

V.

The peaky islet shifted shapes,
  High towns on hills were dimly seen,
We past long lines of Northern capes
  And dewy Northern meadows green.
We came to warmer waves, and deep
  Across the boundless east we drove,
Where those long swells of breaker sweep
  The nutmeg rocks and isles of clove.

VI.

By peaks that flamed, or, all in shade,
  Gloom'd the low coast and quivering brine
With ashy rains, that spreading made
  Fantastic plume or sable pine ;
By sands and steaming flats, and floods
  Of mighty mouth, we scudded fast,
And hills and scarlet-mingled woods
  Glow'd for a moment as we past.

VII.

O hundred shores of happy climes,
  How swiftly stream'd ye by the bark !
At times the whole sea burn'd, at times
  With wakes of fire we tore the dark ;
At times a carven craft would shoot
  From havens hid in fairy bowers,
With naked limbs and flowers and fruit,
  But we nor paused for fruit nor flowers.

VIII.

For one fair Vision ever fled
  Down the waste waters day and night,
And still we follow'd where she led,
  In hope to gain upon her flight.
Her face was evermore unseen,
  And fixt upon the far sea-line ;
But each man murmur'd, "O my Queen,
  I follow till I make thee mine."

IX.

And now we lost her, now she gleam'd
  Like Fancy made of golden air,
Now nearer to the prow she seem'd
  Like Virtue firm, like Knowledge fair,
Now high on waves that idly burst
  Like Heavenly Hope she crown'd the sea,
And now, the bloodless point reversed,
  She bore the blade of Liberty.

X.

And only one among us — him
  We pleased not — he was seldom pleased :
He saw not far : his eyes were dim :
  But ours he swore were all diseased.
"A ship of fools," he shriek'd in spite,
  "A ship of fools," he sneer'd and wept.
And overboard one stormy night
  He cast his body, and on we swept.

XI.

And never sail of ours was furl'd,
  Nor anchor dropt at eve or morn ;
We loved the glories of the world,
  But laws of nature were our scorn ;
For blasts would rise and rave and cease,
  But whence were those that drove the sail
Across the whirlwind's heart of peace,
  And to and thro' the counter-gale ?

XII.

Again to colder climes we came,
  For still we follow'd where she led :
Now mate is blind and captain lame,
  And half the crew are sick or dead.
But blind or lame or sick or sound
  We follow that which flies before :
We know the merry world is round,
  And we may sail for evermore.

IN THE VALLEY OF CAUTERETZ.

All along the valley, stream that flashest white,
Deepening thy voice with the deepening of the night,
All along the valley, where thy waters flow,

I walk'd with one I loved two and thir-
   ty years ago.
All along the valley while I walk'd to-day,
The two and thirty years were a mist
   that rolls away;
For all along the valley, down thy rocky
   bed
Thy living voice to me was as the voice
   of the dead,
And all along the valley, by rock and
   cave and tree,
The voice of the dead was a living voice
   to me.

THE FLOWER.

Once in a golden hour
   I cast to earth a seed.
Up there came a flower,
   The people said, a weed.

To and fro they went
   Thro' my garden-bower,
And muttering discontent
   Cursed me and my flower.

Then it grew so tall
   It wore a crown of light,
But thieves from o'er the wall,
   Stole the seed by night.

Sow'd it far and wide
   By every town and tower,
Till all the people cried
   "Splendid is the flower."

Read my little fable:
   He that runs may read.
Most can raise the flowers now,
   For all have got the seed.

And some are pretty enough,
   And some are poor indeed;
And now again the people
   Call it but a weed.

REQUIESCAT.

Fair is her cottage in its place,
   Where yon broad water sweetly slow-
     ly glides.
It sees itself from thatch to base
   Dream in the sliding tides.

And fairer she, but ah how soon to die!
   Her quiet dream of life this hour may
     cease.
Her peaceful being slowly passes by
   To some more perfect peace.

THE SAILOR-BOY.

He rose at dawn and, fired with hope,
   Shot o'er the seething harbor-bar,
And reach'd the ship and caught the
     rope,
   And whistled to the morning star.

And while he whistled long and loud
   He heard a fierce mermaiden cry,
"O boy, tho' thou art young and proud,
   I see the place where thou wilt lie.

"The sands and yeasty surges mix
   In caves about the dreary bay,
And on thy ribs the limpet sticks,
   And in thy heart the scrawl shall play."

"Fool," he answer'd, "death is sure
   To those that stay and those that roam,
But I will nevermore endure
   To sit with empty hands at home.

"My mother clings about my neck,
   My sisters crying 'Stay for shame';
My father raves of death and wreck,
   They are all to blame, they are all to
     blame.

"God help me! save I take my part
   Of danger on the roaring sea,
A devil rises in my heart,
   Far worse than any death to me."

THE ISLET.

"Whither, O whither, love, shall we go,
   For a score of sweet little summers or so?"
The sweet little wife of the singer said,
   On the day that follow'd the day she
     was wed,
"Whither, O whither, love, shall we go?"
And the singer shaking his curly head
Turn'd as he sat, and struck the keys
There at his right with a sudden crash,
Singing, "And shall it be over the seas
With a crew that is neither rude nor rash,
But a bevy of Eroses apple-cheek'd,
In a shallop of crystal ivory-beak'd,
With a satin sail of a ruby glow,

To a sweet little Eden on earth that I know,
A mountain islet pointed and peak'd ;·
Waves on a diamond shingle dash,
Cataract brooks to the ocean run,
Fairily-delicate palaces shine
Mixt with myrtle and clad with vine,
And overstream'd and silvery-streak'd
With many a rivulet high against the Sun
The facets of the glorious mountain flash
Above the valleys of palm and pine."

"Thither, O thither, love, let us go."

"No, no, no !
For in all that exquisite isle, my dear,
There is but one bird with a musical throat,
And his compass is but of a single note,
That it makes one weary to hear."

"Mock me not ! mock me not ! love, let us go."

"No, love, no.
For the bud ever breaks into bloom on the tree,
And a storm never wakes in the lonely sea,
And a worm is there in the lonely wood,
That pierces the liver and blackens the blood,
And makes it a sorrow to be."

LITERARY SQUABBLES.

Ah God ! the petty fools of rhyme
That shriek and sweat in pygmy wars
Before the stony face of Time,
And look'd at by the silent stars :

Who hate each other for a song,
And do their little best to bite
And pinch their brethren in the throng,
And scratch the very dead for spite :

And strain to make an inch of room
For their sweet selves, and cannot hear
The sullen Lethe rolling doom
On them and theirs and all things here :

When one small touch of Charity
Could lift them nearer God-like state
Than if the crowded Orb should cry
Like those who cried Diana great :

And I too, talk, and lose the touch
I talk of. Surely, after all,
The noblest answer unto such
Is perfect stillness when they brawl.

THE RINGLET.

"Your ringlets, your ringlets,
  That look so golden-gay,
If you will give me one, but one,
  To kiss it night and day,
Then never chilling touch of Time
  Will turn it silver-gray ;
And then shall I know it is all true gold
To flame and sparkle and stream as of old,
Till all the comets in heaven are cold,
  And all her stars decay."
"Then take it, love, and put it by ;
This cannot change, nor yet can I."

2.

"My ringlet, my ringlet,
  That art so golden-gay,
Now never chilling touch of Time
  Can turn thee silver-gray ;
And a lad may wink, and a girl may hint,
  And a fool may say his say ;
For my doubts and fears were all amiss,
And I swear henceforth by this and this,
That a doubt will only come for a kiss,
  And a fear to be kiss'd away."
"Then kiss it, love, and put it by :
If this can change, why so can I."

II.

O Ringlet, O Ringlet,
  I kiss'd you night and day,
And Ringlet, O Ringlet,
  You still are golden-gay,
But Ringlet, O Ringlet,
  You should be silver-gray :
For what is this which now I'm told,
I that took you for true gold,
She that gave you 's bought and sold,
    Sold, sold.

2.

O Ringlet, O Ringlet,
  She blush'd a rosy red,
When Ringlet, O Ringlet,
  She clipt you from her head,
And Ringlet, O Ringlet,
  She gave you me, and said,
"Come, kiss it, love, and put it by :
If this can change, why so can I."
O fie, you golden nothing, fie
    You golden lie.

3.

O Ringlet, O Ringlet,
  I count you much to blame,

For Ringlet, O Ringlet,
 You put me much to shame,
So Ringlet, O Ringlet,
 I doom you to the flame.
For what is this which now I learn,
Has given all my faith a turn?
Burn, you glossy heretic, burn,
 Burn, burn.

A WELCOME TO ALEXANDRA.
MARCH 7, 1863.

SEA-KINGS' daughter from over the sea,
 Alexandra!
Saxon and Norman and Dane are we,
But all of us Danes in our welcome of thee,
 Alexandra!
Welcome her, thunders of fort and of fleet!
Welcome her, thundering cheer of the street!
Welcome her, all things youthful and sweet,
Scatter the blossom under her feet!
Break, happy land, into earlier flowers!
Make music, O bird, in the new-budded bowers!
Blazon your mottoes of blessing and prayer!
Welcome her, welcome her, all that is ours!
Warble, O bugle, and trumpet, blare!
Flags, flutter out upon turrets and towers!
Flames, on the windy headland flare!
Utter your jubilee, steeple and spire!
Clash, ye bells, in the merry March air!
Flash, ye cities, in rivers of fire!
Rush to the roof, sudden rocket, and higher
Melt into stars for the land's desire!
Roll and rejoice, jubilant voice,
Roll as a ground-swell dash'd on the strand,
Roar as the sea when he welcomes the land,
And welcome her, welcome the land's desire,
The sea-kings' daughter as happy as fair,
Blissful bride of a blissful heir,
Bride of the heir of the kings of the sea—
O joy to the people, and joy to the throne,
Come to us, love us and make us your own:
For Saxon or Dane or Norman we,
Teuton or Celt, or whatever we be,
We are each all Dane in our welcome of thee,
 Alexandra!

ODE SUNG AT THE OPENING OF THE INTERNATIONAL EXHIBITION.

UPLIFT a thousand voices full and sweet,
 In this wide hall with earth's invention stored,
 And praise th' invisible universal Lord,
Who lets once more in peace the nations meet,
 Where Science, Art, and Labor have outpour'd
Their myriad horns of plenty at our feet.

O silent father of our Kings to be
Mourn'd in this golden hour of jubilee,
For this, for all, we weep our thanks to thee!

The world-compelling plan was thine,
 And, lo! the long laborious miles
Of Palace; lo! the giant aisles,
 Rich in model and design;
Harvest-tool and husbandry,
Loom and wheel and engin'ry,
Secrets of the sullen mine,
Steel and gold, and corn and wine,
Fabric rough, or Fairy fine,
 Sunny tokens of the Line,
Polar marvels, and a feast
Of wonder, out of West and East,
And shapes and hues of Art divine!
All of beauty, all of use,
That one fair planet can produce.
 Brought from under every star,
 Blown from over every main,
 And mixt, as life is mixt with pain,
The works of peace with works of war.

O ye, the wise who think, the wise who reign,
From growing commerce loose her latest chain,
And let the fair white-winged peacemaker fly
To happy havens under all the sky,
And mix the seasons and the golden hours,
Till each man finds his own in all men's good,
And all men work in noble brotherhood,
Breaking their mailed fleets and armed towers,
And ruling by obeying Nature's powers,
And gathering all the fruits of peace and crown'd with all her flowers.

DEDICATION.

Dear, near and true — no truer Time himself
Can prove you, tho' he make you evermore
Dearer and nearer, as the rapid of life
Shoots to the fall — take this, and pray that he,
Who wrote it, honoring your sweet faith in him,
May trust himself; and spite of praise and scorn,
As one who feels the immeasurable world,
Attain the wise indifference of the wise;
And after Autumn past — if left to pass
His autumn into seeming-leafless days —
Draw toward the long frost and longest night,
Wearing his wisdom lightly, like the fruit
Which in our winter woodland looks a flower.*

* The fruit of the Spindle-tree (*Euonymus Europæus*.)

EXPERIMENTS.

BOÄDICEA.

While about the shore of Mona those Neronian legionaries
Burnt and broke the grove and altar of the Druid and Druidess,
Far in the East Boädicéa, standing loftily charioted,
Mad and maddening all that heard her in her fierce volubility,
Girt by half the tribes of Britain, near the colony Cámulodúne,
Yell'd and shriek'd between her daughters o'er a wild confederacy.

"They that scorn the tribes and call us Britain's barbarous populaces,
Did they hear me, would they listen, did they pity me supplicating?
Shall I heed them in their anguish? shall I brook to be supplicated?
Hear Icenian, Catieuchlanian, hear Coritanian, Trinobant!
Must their ever-ravening eagle's beak and talon annihilate us?
Tear the noble heart of Britain, leave it gorily quivering?
Bark an answer, Britain's raven! bark and blacken innumerable,
Blacken round the Roman carrion, make the carcass a skeleton,
Kite and kestrel, wolf and wolfkin, from the wilderness, wallow in it,
Till the face of Bel be brighten'd, Taranis be propitiated.
Lo their colony half-defended! lo their colony, Cámulodúne!

There the horde of Roman robbers mock at a barbarous adversary.
There the hive of Roman liars worship a gluttonous emperor-idiot.
Such is Rome, and this her deity: hear it, Spirit of Cássivëlaún!

"Hear it, Gods! the Gods have heard it, O Icenian, O Coritanian!
Doubt not ye the Gods have answer'd, Catieuchlanian, Trinobant.
These have told us all their anger in miraculous utterances,
Thunder, a flying fire in heaven, a murmur heard aërially,
Phantom sound of blows descending, moan of an enemy massacred,
Phantom wail of women and children, multitudinous agonies.
Bloodily flow'd the Tamesa rolling phantom bodies of horses and men;
Then a phantom colony smoulder'd on the refluent estuary;
Lastly yonder yester-even, suddenly giddily tottering —
There was one who watch'd and told me — down their statue of Victory fell.
Lo their precious Roman bantling, lo the colony Cámulodúne,
Shall we teach it a Roman lesson? shall we care to be pitiful?
Shall we deal with it as an infant? shall we dandle it amorously?

"Hear Icenian, Catieuchlanian, hear Coritanian, Trinobant!

While I roved about the forest, long and bitterly meditating,
There I heard them in the darkness, at the mystical ceremony,
Loosely robed in flying raiment, sang the terrible prophetesses.
'Fear not, isle of blowing woodland, isle of silvery parapets!
Tho' the Roman eagle shadow thee, tho' the gathering enemy narrow thee,
Thou shalt wax and he shall dwindle, thou shalt be the mighty one yet!
Thine the liberty, thine the glory, thine the deeds to be celebrated,
Thine the myriad-rolling ocean, light and shadow illimitable,
Thine the lands of lasting summer, many-blossoming Paradises,
Thine the North and thine the South and thine the battle-thunder of God.'
So they chanted: how shall Britain light upon auguries happier?
So they chanted in the darkness, and there cometh a victory now.

"Hear Icenian, Catieuchlanian, hear Coritanian, Trinobant!
Me the wife of rich Prasutagus, me the lover of liberty,
Me they seized and me they tortured, me they lash'd and humiliated,
Me the sport of ribald Veterans, mine of ruffian violators!
See they sit, they hide their faces, miserable in ignominy!
Wherefore in me burns an anger, not by blood to be satiated.
Lo the palaces and the temple, lo the colony Cámulodúne!
There they ruled, and thence they wasted all the flourishing territory,
Thither at their will they haled the yellow-ringleted Britoness—
Bloodily, bloodily fall the battle-axe, unexhausted, inexorable.
Shout Icenian, Catieuchlanian, shout Coritanian, Trinobant,
Till the victim hear within and yearn to hurry precipitously
Like the leaf in a roaring whirlwind, like the smoke in a hurricane whirl'd.
Lo the colony, there they rioted in the city of Cúnobelíne!
There they drank in cups of emerald, there at tables of ebony lay,
Rolling on their purple couches in their tender effeminacy.
There they dwelt and there they rioted; there—there—they dwell no more.
Burst the gates, and burn the palaces, break the works of the statuary.
Take the hoary Roman head and shatter it, hold it abominable,
Cut the Roman boy to pieces in his lust and voluptuousness,
Lash the maiden into swooning, me they lash'd and humiliated,
Chop the breasts from off the mother, dash the brains of the little one out,
Up my Britons, on my chariot, on my chargers, trample them under us."

So the Queen Boädicéa, standing loftily charioted,
Brandishing in her hand a dart and rolling glances lioness-like,
Yell'd and shriek'd between her daughters in her fierce volubility.
Till her people all around the royal chariot agitated,
Madly dash'd the darts together, writhing barbarous lineäments,
Made the noise of frosty woodlands, when they shiver in January,
Roar'd as when the rolling breakers boom and blanch on the precipices,
Yell'd as when the winds of winter tear an oak on a promontory.
So the silent colony hearing her tumultuous adversaries
Clash the darts and on the buckler beat with rapid unanimous hand,
Thought on all her evil tyrannies, all her pitiless avarice,
Till she felt the heart within her fall and flutter tremulously,
Then her pulses at the clamoring of her enemy fainted away.
Out of evil evil flourishes, out of tyranny tyranny buds.
Ran the land with Roman slaughter, multitudinous agonies.
Perish'd many a maid and matron, many a valorous legionary.
Fell the colony, city, and citadel, London, Verulam, Cámulodúne.

IN QUANTITY.

MILTON.

Alcaics.

O MIGHTY-MOUTH'D inventor of harmonies,
O skill'd to sing of Time or Eternity,

God-gifted organ-voice of England,
  Milton, a name to resound for ages;
Whose Titan angels, Gabriel, Abdiel,
Starr'd from Jehovah's gorgeous armories,
  Tower, as the deep-domed empyrëan
  Rings to the roar of an angel onset —
Me rather all that bowery loneliness,
  The brooks of Eden mazily murmuring,
  And bloom profuse and cedar arches
Charm, as a wanderer out in ocean,
Where some refulgent sunset of India
Streams o'er a rich ambrosial ocean isle,
  And crimson-hued the stately palm-woods
  Whisper in odorous heights of even.

Hendecasyllabics.

O you chorus of indolent reviewers,
Irresponsible, indolent reviewers,
Look, I come to the test, a tiny poem
All composed in a metre of Catullus,
All in quantity, careful of my motion,
Like the skater on ice that hardly bears him,
Lest I fall unawares before the people,
Waking laughter in indolent reviewers.
Should I flounder awhile without a tumble
Thro' this metrification of Catullus,
They should speak to me not without a welcome,
All that chorus of indolent reviewers.
Hard, hard, hard is it, only not to tumble,
So fantastical is the dainty metre.
Wherefore slight me not wholly, nor believe me
Too presumptuous, indolent reviewers.
O blatant Magazines, regard me rather —
Since I blush to belaud myself a moment —
As some rare little rose, a piece of inmost
Horticultural art, or half coquette-like
Maiden not to be greeted unbenignly.

SPECIMEN OF A TRANSLATION OF THE ILIAD IN BLANK VERSE.

So Hector said, and sea-like roar'd his host;
Then loosed their sweating horses from the yoke,
And each beside his chariot bound his own;
And oxen from the city, and goodly sheep
In haste they drove, and honey-hearted wine
And bread from out the houses brought, and heap'd
Their firewood, and the winds from off the plain
Roll'd the rich vapor far into the heaven.
And these all night upon the bridge* of war
Sat glorying; many a fire before them blazed:
As when in heaven the stars about tho moon
Look beautiful, when all the winds are laid,
And every height comes out, and jutting peak
And valley, and the immeasurable heavens
Break open to their highest, and all the stars
Shine, and the Shepherd gladdens in his heart:
So many a fire between the ships and stream
Of Xanthus blazed before the towers of Troy,
A thousand on the plain; and close by each
Sat fifty in the blaze of burning fire;
And champing golden grain, the horses stood
Hard by their chariots, waiting for the dawn.†

              Iliad VIII. 542-561.

* Or, ridge.
† Or more literally, —
  And eating hoary grain and pulse the steeds
  Stood by their cars, waiting the thronéd morn.

ADDITIONAL POEMS.

NOTE. — The Poems which follow include all those which have been omitted by the author from his latest revised editions, or never acknowledged by him. They are here printed, because, although unsanctioned by Mr. Tennyson, they have recently been collected from various sources, and printed *in America*.

TIMBUCTOO.*

"Deep in that lion-haunted inland lies
A mystic city, goal of high emprise."
CHAPMAN.

I STOOD upon the Mountain which o'er-
    looks
The narrow seas, whose rapid interval
Parts Afric from green Europe, when
    the Sun
Had fall'n below th' Atlantic, and above
The silent heavens were blench'd with
    faery light,
Uncertain whether faery light or cloud,
Flowing Southward, and the chasms of
    deep, deep blue
Slumber'd unfathomable, and the stars
Were flooded over with clear glory and pale.
I gazed upon the sheeny coast beyond,
There where the Giant of old Time infix'd
The limits of his prowess, pillars high
Long time erased from earth : even as
    the Sea
When weary of wild inroad buildeth up
Huge mounds whereby to stay his yeasty
    waves.
And much I mused on legends quaint
    and old
Which whilome won the hearts of all on
    earth
Toward their brightness, ev'n as flame
    draws air ;
But had their being in the heart of man
As air is th' life of flame : and thou wert
    then
A centred glory-circled memory,
Divinest Atalantis, whom the waves
Have buried deep, and thou of later name,
Imperial Eldorado, roof'd with gold :
Shadows to which, despite all shocks of
    change,
All on-set of capricious accident,
Men clung with yearning hope which
    would not die.

* A Poem which obtained the Chancellor's Medal at the Cambridge Commencement, MDCCCXXIX. By A. TENNYSON, of Trinity College.

As when in some great city where the walls
Shake, and the streets with ghastly faces
    thronged,
Do utter forth a subterranean voice,
Among the inner columns far retired
At midnight, in the lone Acropolis,
Before the awful genius of the place
Kneels the pale Priestess in deep faith,
    the while
Above her head the weak lamp dips and
    winks
Unto the fearful summoning without :
Nathless she ever clasps the marble knees,
Bathes the cold hand with tears, and
    gazeth on
Those eyes which wear no light but that
    wherewith
Her fantasy informs them.
                Where are ye,
Thrones of the Western wave, fair Isl-
    ands green ?
Where are your moonlight halls, your
    cedarn glooms,
The blossoming abysses of your hills ?
Your flowering capes, and your gold-
    sanded bays
Blown round with happy airs of odorous
    winds ?
Where are the infinite ways, which,
    seraph-trod,
Wound through your great Elysian soli-
    tudes,
Whose lowest deeps were, as with visible
    love,
Filled with Divine effulgence, circum-
    fused,
Flowing between the clear and polished
    stems,
And ever circling round their emerald
    cones
In coronals and glories, such as gird
The unfading foreheads of the Saints in
    Heaven ?
For nothing visible, they say, had birth
In that blest ground, but it was played
    about

With its peculiar glory. Then I raised
My voice and cried, "Wide Afric, doth thy Sun
Lighten, thy hills enfold a city as fair
As those which starred the night o' the elder world?
Or is the rumor of thy Timbuctoo
A dream as frail as those of ancient time?"
  A curve of whitening, flashing, ebbing light!
A rustling of white wings! the bright descent
Of a young Seraph! and he stood beside me
There on the ridge, and looked into my face
With his unutterable, shining orbs,
So that with hasty motion I did veil
My vision with both hands, and saw before me
Such colored spots as dance athwart the eyes
Of those that gaze upon the noonday Sun.
Girt with a zone of flashing gold beneath
His breast, and compassed round about his brow
With triple arch of everchanging bows,
And circled with the glory of living light
And alternation of all hues, he stood.
  "O child of man, why muse you here alone
Upon the Mountain, on the dreams of old
Which filled the earth with passing loveliness,
Which flung strange music on the howling winds,
And odors rapt from remote Paradise?
Thy sense is clogged with dull mortality:
Open thine eyes and see."
                I looked, but not
Upon his face, for it was wonderful
With its exceeding brightness, and the light
Of the great Angel Mind which looked from out
The starry glowing of his restless eyes.
I felt my soul grow mighty, and my spirit
With supernatural excitation bound
Within me, and my mental eye grew large
With such a vast circumference of thought,
That in my vanity I seemed to stand
Upon the outward verge and bound alone
Of full beatitude. Each failing sense,
As with a momentary flash of light,
Grew thrillingly distinct and keen. I saw
The smallest grain that dappled the dark earth,
The indistinctest atom in deep air,
The Moon's white cities, and the opal width
Of her small glowing lakes, her silver heights
Unvisited with dew of vagrant cloud,
And the unsounded, undescended depth
Of her black hollows. The clear galaxy
Shorn of its hoary lustre, wonderful,
Distinct and vivid with sharp points of light,
Blaze within blaze, an unimagined depth
And harmony of planet-girded suns
And moon-encircled planets, wheel in wheel,
Arched the wan sapphire. Nay— the hum of men,
Or other things talking in unknown tongues,
And notes of busy life in distant worlds
Beat like a far wave on my anxious ear.
  A maze of piercing, trackless, thrilling thoughts,
Involving and embracing each with each,
Rapid as fire, inextricably linked,
Expanding momently with every sight
And sound which struck the palpitating sense,
The issue of strong impulse, hurried through
The riven rapt brain; as when in some large lake
From pressure of descendent crags, which lapse
Disjointed, crumbling from their parent slope
At slender interval, the level calm
Is ridged with restless and increasing spheres
Which break upon each other, each th' effect
Of separate impulse, but more fleet and strong
Than its precursor, till the eye in vain
Amid the wild unrest of swimming shade
Dappled with hollow and alternate rise
Of interpenetrated arc, would scan
Definite round.
                I know not if I shape
These things with accurate similitude
From visible objects, for but dimly now,
Less vivid than a half-forgotten dream,
The memory of that mental excellence
Comes o'er me, and it may be I entwine
The indecision of my present mind
With its past clearness, yet it seems to me
As even then the torrent of quick thought

Absorbed me from the nature of itself
With its own fleetness. Where is he,
  that borne
Adown the sloping of an arrowy stream,
Could link hisshallop to the fleetingedge,
And muse midway with philosophic calm
Upon the wondrous laws which regulate
The fierceness of the bounding element?
  My thoughts which long had grovelled
    in the slime
Of this dull world, like dusky worms
  which house
Beneath unshaken waters, but at once
Upon some earth-awakeningday of Spring
Do pass from gloom to glory, and aloft
Winnow the purple, bearing on both
  sides
Double display of star-lit wings, which
  burn
Fan-like and fibred with intensest bloom;
Even so my thoughts erewhile so low,
  now felt
Unutterable buoyancy and strength
To bear them upward through the track-
  less fields
Of undefined existence far and free.
  Then first within the South methought
    I saw
A wilderness of spires, and crystal pile
Of rampart upon rampart, dome on dome,
Illimitable range of battlement
On battlement, and the Imperial height
Of canopy o'ercanopied.
           Behind
In diamond light up spring the dazzling
  peaks
Of Pyramids, as far surpassing earth's
As heaven than earth is fairer. Each
  aloft
Upon his narrowed eminence bore globes
Of wheeling suns, or stars, or semblances
Of either, showering circular abyss
Of radiance. But the glory of the place
Stood out a pillared front of burnished
  gold,
Interminably high, if gold it were
Or metal more ethereal, and beneath
Two doors of blinding brilliance, where
  no gaze
Might rest, stood open, and the eye could
  scan,
Through length of porch and valve and
  boundless hall,
Part of a throne of fiery flame, wherefrom
The snowy skirting of a garment hung,
And glimpse of multitude of multitudes
That ministered around it — if I saw

These things distinctly, for my human
  brain
Staggered beneath the vision, and thick
  night
Came down upon my eyelids, and I fell.
  With ministering hand he raised me up:
Then with a mournful and ineffable smile,
Which but to look on for a moment filled
My eyes with irresistible sweet tears,
In accents of majestic melody,
Like a swoln river's gushings in still night
Mingled with floating music, thus he
  spake:
"There is no mightier Spirit than I to
  sway
The heart of man; and teach him to attain
By shadowing forth the Unattainable;
And step by step to scale that mighty stair
Whose landing-place is wrapt about with
  clouds
Of glory of heaven.* With earliest light
  of Spring,
And in the glow of sallow Summertide,
And in red Autumn when the winds are
  wild
With gambols, and when full-voiced
  Winter roofs
The headland with inviolate white snow,
I play about his heart a thousand ways,
Visit his eyes with visions, and his ears
With harmonies of wind and wave and
  wood,
— Of winds which tell of waters, and of
  waters
Betraying the close kisses of the wind —
And win him unto me: and few there be
So gross of heart who have not felt and
  known
A higher than they see: they with dim eyes
Behold me darkling. Lo! I have given
  thee
To understand my presence, and to feel
My fulness: I have filled thy lips with
  power.
I have raised thee nigher to the spheres
  of heaven,
Man's first, last home: and thou with
  ravished sense
Listenest the lordly music flowing from
The illimitable years. I am the Spirit,
The permeating life which courseth
  through
All th' intricate and labyrinthine veins
Of the great vine of Fable, which, out-
  spread

* "Be ye perfect, even as your Father in heaven is perfect."

With growth of shadowing leaf and clusters rare,
Reacheth to every corner under heaven,
Deep-rooted in the living soil of truth;
So that men's hopes and fears take refuge in
The fragrance of its complicated glooms,
And cool impeachèd twilights. Child of man,
Seest thou yon river, whose translucent wave,
Forth issuing from the darkness, windeth through
The argent streets o' the city, imaging
The soft inversion of her tremulous domes,
Her gardens frequent with the stately palm,
Her pagods hung with music of sweet bells,
Her obelisks of rangèd chrysolite,
Minarets and towers? Lo! how he passeth by,
And gulfs himself in sands, as not enduring
To carry through the world those waves, which bore
The reflex of my city in their depth.
O city! O latest throne! where I was raised
To be a mystery of loveliness
Unto all eyes, the time is wellnigh come
When I must render up this glorious home
To keen Discovery; soon yon brilliant towers
Shall darken with the waving of her wand;
Darken and shrink and shiver into huts,
Black specks amid a waste of dreary sand,
Low-built, mud-walled, barbarian settlements.
How changed from this fair city!"
Thus far the Spirit:
Then parted heavenward on the wing: and I
Was left alone on Calpe, and the moon
Had fallen from the night, and all was dark!

POEMS PUBLISHED IN THE EDITION OF 1830, AND OMITTED IN LATER EDITIONS.

ELEGIACS.

Low-flowing breezes are roaming the broad valley dimmed in the gloaming:
Thro' the black-stemmed pines only the far river shines.
Creeping through blossomy rushes and bowers of rose-blowing bushes,
Down by the poplar tall rivulets babble and fall.
Barketh the shepherd-dog cheerly; the grasshopper carolleth clearly;
Deeply the turtle cooes; shrilly the owlet halloos;
Winds creep: dews fall chilly: in her first sleep earth breathes stilly:
Over the pools in the burn watergnats murmur and mourn.
Sadly the far kine loweth: the glimmering water outfloweth:
Twin peaks shadowed with pine slope to the dark hyaline.
Low-throned Hesper is stayed between the two peaks; but the Naiad
Throbbing in wild unrest holds him beneath in her breast.

The ancient poetess singeth that Hesperus all things bringeth,
Smoothing the wearied mind: bring me my love, Rosalind.
Thou comest morning and even; she cometh not morning or even.
False-eyed Hesper, unkind, where is my sweet Rosalind?

THE "HOW" AND THE "WHY."

?

I AM any man's suitor,
If any will be my tutor:
Some say this life is pleasant,
Some think it speedeth fast,
In time there is no present,
In eternity no future,
In eternity no past.
We laugh, we cry, we are born, we die,
Who will riddle me the *how* and the *why?*

The bulrush nods unto its brother.
The wheatears whisper to each other:

What is it they say? what do they there?
Why two and two make four? why round
　is not square?
Why the rock stands still, and the light
　clouds fly?
Why the heavy oak groans, and the white
　willows sigh?
Why deep is not high, and high is not deep?
Whether we wake, or whether we sleep?
Whether we sleep, or whether we die?
How you are you? why I am I?
Who will riddle me the *how* and the *why?*

The world is somewhat; it goes on some-
　how :
But what is the meaning of *then* and *now?*
　I feel there is something; but how
　and what?
I know there is somewhat : but what and
　why?
I cannot tell if that somewhat be I.
The little bird pipeth — "why? why?"
In the summer woods when the sun falls
　low,
And the great bird sits on the opposite
　bough,
And stares in his face, and shouts "how?
　how?"
And the black owl scuds down the mel-
　low twilight,
And chants "how? how?" the whole
　of the night.

Why the life goes when the blood is spilt?
　What the life is? where the soul may lie?
Why a church is with a steeple built :
And a house with a chimney-pot?
Who will riddle me the how and the what?
Who will riddle me the what and the
　why?

SUPPOSED CONFESSIONS

OF A SECOND-RATE SENSITIVE MIND NOT
IN UNITY WITH ITSELF.

O God! my God! have mercy now.
I faint, I fall. Men say that thou
Didst die for me, for such as *me,*
Patient of ill, and death, and scorn,
And that my sin was as a thorn
Among the thorns that girt thy brow,
Wounding thy soul. — That even now,
In this extremest misery
Of ignorance, I should require
A sign! and if a bolt of fire
Would rive the slumberous summer noon
While I do pray to thee alone,
Think my belief would stronger grow!
Is not my human pride brought low?
The boastings of my spirit still?
The joy I had in my free will
All cold, and dead, and corpse-like grown?
And what is left to me, but thou,
And faith in thee? Men pass me by;
Christians with happy countenances —
And children all seem full of thee!
And women smile with saintlike glances
Like thine own mother's when she bowed
Above thee, on that happy morn
When angels spake to men aloud,
And thou and peace to earth were born.
Goodwill to me as well as all —
— I one of them : my brothers they :
Brothers in Christ — a world of peace
And confidence, day after day;
And trust and hope till things should
　cease,
And then one Heaven receive us all.

How sweet to have a common faith!
To hold a common scorn of death!
And at a burial to hear
The creaking cords which wound and eat
Into my human heart, whene'er
Earth goes to earth, with grief, not fear,
With hopeful grief, were passing sweet!
A grief not uninformed, and dull,
Hearted with hope, of hope as full
As is the blood with life, or night
And a dark cloud with rich moonlight.
To stand beside a grave, and see
The red small atoms wherewith we
Are built, and smile in calm, and say —
"These little motes and grains shall be
Clothed on with immortality
More glorious than the noon of day.
All that is pass'd into the flowers,
And into beasts and other men,
And all the Norland whirlwind showers
From open vaults, and all the sea
O'erwashes with sharp salts, again
Shall fleet together all, and be
Indued with immortality."

Thrice happy state again to be
The trustful infant on the knee!
Who lets his waxen fingers play
About his mother's neck, and knows
Nothing beyond his mother's eyes.
They comfort him by night and day,
They light his little life alway;
He hath no thought of coming woes;
He hath no care of life or death,

Scarce outward signs of joy arise,
Because the Spirit of happiness
And perfect rest so inward is ;
And loveth so his innocent heart,
Her temple and her place of birth,
Where she would ever wish to dwell,
Life of the fountain there, beneath
Its salient springs, and far apart,
Hating to wander out on earth,
Or breathe into the hollow air,
Whose chillness would make visible
Her subtile, warm, and golden breath,
Which mixing with the infant's blood,
Full fills him with beatitude.
Oh ! sure it is a special care
Of God, to fortify from doubt,
To arm in proof, and guard about
With triple mailéd trust, and clear
Delight, the infant's dawning year.
Would that my gloomed fancy were
As thine, my mother, when with brows
Propped on thy knees, my hands upheld
In thine, I listened to thy vows,
For me outpoured in holiest prayer —
For me unworthy ! — and beheld
The mild deep eyes upraised, that knew
The beauty and repose of faith,
And the clear spirit shining through.
Oh ! wherefore do we grow awry
From roots which strike so deep? why dare
Paths in the desert ?   Could not I
Bow myself down, where thou hast knelt,
To th' earth — until the ice would melt
Here, and I feel as thou hast felt ?
What Devil had the heart to scathe
Flowers thou hadst reared — to brush the dew
From thine own lily, when thy grave
Was deep, my mother, in the clay ?
Myself ?   Is it thus ?   Myself ?   Had I
So little love for thee ?   But why
Prevailed not thy pure prayers ? Why pray
To one who heeds not, who can save
But will not ? Great in faith, and strong
Against the grief of circumstance
Wert thou, and yet unheard ?   What if
Thou pleadest still, and seest me drive
Through utter dark a full-sailed skiff,
Unpiloted i' the echoing dance
Of reboant whirlwinds, stooping low
Unto the death, not sunk ! I know
At matins and at evensong,
That thou, if thou wert yet alive,
In deep and daily prayers wouldst strive
To reconcile me with thy God.
Albeit, my hope is gray, and cold
At heart, thou wouldest murmur still —

" Bring this lamb back into thy fold,
My Lord, if so it be thy will."
Wouldst tell me I must brook the rod,
And chastisement of human pride ;
That pride, the sin of devils, stood
Betwixt me and the light of God !
That hitherto I had defied,
And had rejected God — that Grace
Would drop from his o'erbrimming love,
As manna on my wilderness,
If I would pray — that God would move
And strike the hard, hard rock, and thence,
Sweet in their utmost bitterness,
Would issue tears of penitence
Which would keep green hope's life.
Alas !
I think that pride hath now no place
Or sojourn in me.   I am void,
Dark, formless, utterly destroyed.

Why not believe then ?   Why not yet
Anchor thy frailty there, where man
Hath moored and rested ? Ask the sea
At midnight, when the crisp slope waves
After a tempest, rib and fret
The broad-imbaséd beach, why he
Slumbers not like a mountain tarn ?
Wherefore his ridges are not curls
And ripples of an inland meer ?
Wherefore he moaneth thus, nor can
Draw down into his vexéd pools
All that blue heaven which hues and paves
The other ?   I am too forlorn,
Too shaken : my own weakness fools
My judgment, and my spirit whirls,
Moved from beneath with doubt and fear.

" Yet," said I, in my morn of youth,
The unsunned freshness of my strength,
When I went forth in quest of truth,
" It is man's privilege to doubt,
If so be that from doubt at length,
Truth may stand forth unmoved of change,
An image with profulgent brows,
And perfect limbs, as from the storm
Of running fires and fluid range
Of lawless airs at last stood out
This excellence and solid form
Of constant beauty.   For the Ox
Feeds in the herb, and sleeps, or fills
The hornéd valleys all about,
And hollows of the fringed hills
In summerheats, with placid lows
Unfearing, till his own blood flows
About his hoof.   And in the flocks
The lamb rejoiceth in the year,

And raceth freely with his fere,
And answers to his mother's calls
From the flowered furrow. In a time,
Of which he wots not, run short pains
Through his warm heart : and then, from whence
He knows not, on his light there falls
A shadow ; and his native slope
Where he was wont to leap and climb,
Floats from his sick and filmed eyes,
And something in the darkness draws
His forehead earthward, and he dies.
Shall men live thus, in joy and hope
As a young lamb, who cannot dream,
Living, but that he shall live on?
Shall we not look into the laws
Of life and death, and things that seem,
And things that be, and analyze
Our double nature, and compare
All creeds till we have found the one,
If one there be?" Ay me ! I fear
All may not doubt, but everywhere
Some must clasp Idols. Yet, my God,
Whom call I Idol? Let thy dove
Shadow me over, and my sins
Be unremembered, and thy love
Enlighten me. O teach me yet
Somewhat before the heavy clod
Weighs on me, and the busy fret
Of that sharp-headed worm begins
In the gross blackness underneath.

O weary life ! O weary death !
O spirit and heart made desolate !
O damnéd vacillating state !

THE BURIAL OF LOVE.

  His eyes in eclipse,
  Pale-cold his lips,
The light of his hopes unfed,
  Mute his tongue,
  His bow unstrung
With the tears he hath shed,
Backward drooping his graceful head,
  Love is dead :
  His last arrow is sped ;
  He hath not another dart ;
Go — carry him to his dark deathbed ;
  Bury him in the cold, cold heart —
   Love is dead.

O truest love ! art thou forlorn,
 And unrevenged ? thy pleasant wiles
  Forgotten, and thine innocent joy ?
  Shall hollow-hearted apathy,
The cruellest form of perfect scorn,
 With languor of most hateful smiles,
  For ever write,
  In the withered light
  Of the tearless eye,
An epitaph that all may spy ?
No ! sooner she herself shall die.

For her the showers shall not fall,
Nor the round sun shine that shineth to all ;
Her light shall into darkness change ;
For her the green grass shall not spring,
Nor the rivers flow, nor the sweet birds sing,
Till Love have his full revenge.

TO ———.

 Sainted Juliet ! dearest name !
  If to love be life alone,
   Divinest Juliet,
 I love thee, and live ; and yet
Love unreturned is like the fragrant flame
Folding the slaughter of the sacrifice
 Offered to gods upon an altar-throne ;
My heart is lighted at thine eyes,
Changed into fire, and blown about with sighs.

SONG.

I.

 I' the glooming light
  Of middle night
  So cold and white,
Worn Sorrow sits by the moaning wave,
  Beside her are laid
  Her mattock and spade,
For she hath half delved her own deep grave.
 Alone she is there :
The white clouds drizzle : her hair falls loose :
 Her shoulders are bare ;
Her tears are mixed with the beaded dews.

II.

  Death standeth by ;
  She will not die ;
  With glazéd eye
She looks at her grave : she cannot sleep ;
  Ever alone
  She maketh her moan :
She cannot speak : she can only weep,

For she will not hope.
The thick snow falls on her flake by
　　flake,
　　The dull wave mourns down
　　　　the slope,
The world will not change, and her heart
　　will not break.

SONG.

I.

The lintwhite and the throstlecock
　Have voices sweet and clear ;
　　All in the bloomèd May.
They from the blosmy brere
Call to the fleeting year,
If that he would them hear
　　And stay.
Alas ! that one so beautiful
Should have so dull an ear !

II.

Fair year, fair year, thy children call,
But thou art deaf as death ;
　　All in the bloomèd May.
When thy light perisheth
That from thee issueth,
Our life evanisheth :
　　O, stay !
Alas ! that lips so cruel-dumb
Should have so sweet a breath !

III.

Fair year, with brows of royal love
Thou comest, as a king,
　　All in the bloomèd May.
Thy golden largess fling,
And longer hear us sing ;
Though thou art fleet of wing,
　　Yet stay.
Alas ! that eyes so full of light
Should be so wandering !

IV.

Thy locks are all of sunny sheen
In rings of gold yronne,*
　　All in the bloomèd May.
We pri'thee pass not on ;
If thou dost leave the sun,
Delight is with thee gone.
　　O, stay !
Thou art the fairest of thy feres,
We pri'thee pass not on.

* "His crispè hair in ringis was yronne."
　　　CHAUCER, *Knightes Tale.*

SONG.

I.

Every day hath its night :
　Every night its morn :
　Thorough dark and bright
　　Wingèd hours are borne ;
　　　Ah ! welaway !
Seasons flower and fade ;
　Golden calm and storm
　　Mingle day by day.
　There is no bright form
Doth not cast a shade —
　　　Ah ! welaway !

II.

When we laugh, and our mirth
　Apes the happy vein,
　We 're so kin to earth,
　　Pleasaunce fathers pain —
　　　Ah ! welaway !
Madness laugheth loud :
　Laughter bringeth tears :
　　Eyes are worn away
　Till the end of fears
Cometh in the shroud,
　　　Ah ! welaway !

III.

All is change, woe or weal ;
　Joy is Sorrow's brother ;
　Grief and gladness steal
　　Symbols of each other :
　　　Ah ! welaway !
Larks in heaven's cope
　Sing : the culvers mourn
　　All the livelong day.
　Be not all forlorn :
Let us weep in hope —
　　　Ah ! welaway !

NOTHING WILL DIE.

When will the stream be aweary of flowing
　　Under my eye ?
When will the wind be aweary of blowing
　　Over the sky ?
When will the clouds be aweary of fleeting ?
When will the heart be aweary of beating ?
　　And nature die ?
Never, O never ! nothing will die ;
　　The stream flows,
　　The wind blows,
　　The cloud fleets,
　　The heart beats,
　　　Nothing will die.

Nothing will die ;
All things will change
Through eternity.
  'T is the world's winter ;
    Autumn and summer
    Are gone long ago.
  Earth is dry to the centre,
    But spring a new comer —
  A spring rich and strange,
    Shall make the winds blow
    Round and round,
      Through and through,
      Here and there,
      Till the air
    And the ground
    Shall be filled with life anew.
The world was never made ;
It will change, but it will not fade.
So let the wind range ;
  For even and morn
    Ever will be
  Through eternity.
Nothing was born ;
Nothing will die ;
All things will change.

ALL THINGS WILL DIE.

CLEARLY the blue river chimes in its flow-
      ing
    Under my eye ;
Warmly and broadly the south winds are
      blowing
    Over the sky.
One after another the white clouds are
      fleeting ;
Every heart this May morning in joyance
      is beating
    Full merrily ;
Yet all things must die.
The stream will cease to flow ;
The wind will cease to blow ;
The clouds will cease to fleet ;
The heart will cease to beat ;
  For all things must die.

    All things must die.
Spring will come nevermore.
    O, vanity !
Death waits at the door.
See ! our friends are all forsaking
The wine and merrymaking.
We are called — we must go.
Laid low, very low,
In the dark we must lie.
The merry glees are still :

The voice of the bird
Shall no more be heard,
Nor the wind on the hill.
  O, misery !
Hark ! death is calling
While I speak to ye,
The jaw is falling,
The red cheek paling,
The strong limbs failing ;
Ice with the warm blood mixing ;
The eyeballs fixing.
Nine times goes the passing bell :
Ye merry souls, farewell.

  The old earth
  Had a birth,
  As all men know
  Long ago.
And the old earth must die.
So let the warm winds range,
And the blue wave beat the shore ;
For even and morn
Ye will never see
Through eternity.
All things were born.
Ye will come nevermore,
For all things must die.

HERO TO LEANDER.

O go not yet, my love !
  The night is dark and vast ;
The white moon is hid in her heaven
    above,
  And the waves climb high and fast.
O, kiss me, kiss me, once again,
  Lest thy kiss should be the last !
O kiss me ere we part ;
  Grow closer to my heart !
My heart is warmer surely than the bosom
    of the main.
O joy ! O bliss of blisses !
  My heart of hearts art thou.
Come bathe me with thy kisses,
  My eyelids and my brow.
Hark how the wild rain hisses,
  And the loud sea roars below.

Thy heart beats through thy rosy limbs,
  So gladly doth it stir ;
Thine eye in drops of gladness swims.
  I have bathed thee with the pleasant
    myrrh ;
Thy locks are dripping balm ;
Thou shalt not wander hence to-night,
  I 'll stay thee with my kisses.
To-night the roaring brine

Will rend thy golden tresses;
The ocean with the morrow light
Will be both blue and calm;
And the billow will embrace thee with a
    kiss as soft as mine.
No Western odors wander
  On the black and moaning sea,
And when thou art dead, Leander,
  My soul must follow thee!
O go not yet, my love!
Thy voice is sweet and low;
The deep salt wave breaks in above
  Those marble steps below.
The turret-stairs are wet
  That lead into the sea.
Leander! go not yet.
The pleasant stars have set:
O, go not, go not yet,
  Or I will follow thee!

THE MYSTIC.

ANGELS have talked with him, and showed
    him thrones:
Ye knew him not; he was not one of ye,
Ye scorned him with an undiscerning
    scorn:
Ye could not read the marvel in his eye,
The still serene abstraction: he hath felt
The vanities of after and before;
Albeit, his spirit and his secret heart
The stern experiences of converse lives,
The linkéd woes of many a fiery change
Had purified, and chastened, and made
    free.
Always there stood before him, night and
    day,
Of wayward vary-colored circumstance
The imperishable presences serene,
Colossal, without form, or sense, or sound,
Dim shadows but unwaning presences
Fourfaced to four corners of the sky:
And yet again, three shadows, fronting
    one,
One forward, one respectant, three but
    one;
And yet again, again and evermore,
For the two first were not, but only seemed,
One shadow in the midst of a great light,
One reflex from eternity on time,
One mighty countenance of perfect calm,
Awful with most invariable eyes.
For him the silent congregated hours,
Daughters of time, divinely tall, beneath
Severe and youthful brows, with shining
    eyes

Smiling a godlike smile (the innocent light
Of earliest youth pierced through and
    through with all
Keen knowledges of low-embowéd eld)
Upheld, and ever hold aloft the cloud
Which droops low-hung on either gate of
    life,
Both birth and death: he in the centre
    fixt,
Saw far on each side through the grated
    gates
Most pale and clear and lovely distances.
He often lying broad awake, and yet
Remaining from the body, and apart
In intellect and power and will, hath heard
Time flowing in the middle of the night,
And all things creeping to a day of doom.
How could ye know him? Ye were yet
    within
The narrower circle: he had wellnigh
    reached
The last, which with a region of white
    flame,
Pure without heat, into a larger air
Upburning. and an ether of black blue,
Investeth and ingirds all other lives.

THE GRASSHOPPER.

I.

VOICE of the summer wind,
Joy of the summer plain,
Life of the summer hours,
Carol clearly, bound along.
No Tithon thou as poets feign
(Shame fall 'em they are deaf and blind),
But an insect lithe and strong,
Bowing the seeded summer flowers.
Prove their falsehood and thy quarrel,
  Vaulting on thine airy feet.
Clap thy shielded sides and carol,
  Carol clearly, chirrup sweet.
Thou art a mailéd warrior in youth and
    strength complete;
  Armed cap-a-pie
  Full fair to see;
  Unknowing fear,
  Undreading loss,
A gallant cavalier,
Sans peur et sans reproche,
In sunlight and in shadow,
The Bayard of the meadow.

II.

I would dwell with thee,
  Merry grasshopper,
Thou art so glad and free,

And as light as air;
Thou hast no sorrow or tears,
Thou hast no compt of years,
No withered immortality,
But a short youth sunny and free.
Carol clearly, bound along,
  Soon thy joy is over,
A summer of loud song,
And slumbers in the clover.
What hast thou to do with evil
In thine hour of love and revel,
In thy heat of summer pride,
Pushing the thick roots aside
Of the singing flowered grasses,
That brush thee with their silken tresses?
What hast thou to do with evil,
Shooting, singing, ever springing
In and out the emerald glooms,
Ever leaping, ever singing,
  Lighting on the golden blooms?

LOVE, PRIDE, AND FORGETFULNESS.

Ere yet my heart was sweet Love's tomb,
  Love labored honey busily.
I was the hive, and Love the bee,
  My heart the honeycomb.
One very dark and chilly night
Pride came beneath and held a light.

The cruel vapors went through all,
Sweet Love was withered in his cell:
Pride took Love's sweets, and by a spell
Did change them into gall;
And Memory, though fed by Pride,
Did wax so thin on gall,
Awhile she scarcely lived at all.
What marvel that she died?

CHORUS

IN AN UNPUBLISHED DRAMA, WRITTEN VERY EARLY.

The varied earth, the moving heaven,
  The rapid waste of roving sea,
The fountain-pregnant mountains riven
  To shapes of wildest anarchy,
By secret fire and midnight storms
  That wander round their windy cones,
The subtle life, the countless forms
  Of living things, the wondrous tones
    Of man and beast are full of strange
    Astonishment and boundless change.

The day, the diamonded night,
  The echo, feeble child of sound,
The heavy thunder's griding might,
  The herald lightning's starry bound,
The vocal spring of bursting bloom,
  The naked summer's glowing birth,
The troublous autumn's sallow gloom,
  The hoarhead winter paving earth
    With sheeny white, are full of strange
    Astonishment and boundless change.

Each sun which from the centre flings
  Grand music and redundant fire,
The burning belts, the mighty rings,
  The murm'rous planets' rolling choir,
The globe-filled arch that, cleaving air,
  Lost in its own effulgence sleeps,
The lawless comets as they glare,
  And thunder through the sapphire deeps
    In wayward strength, and full of strange
    Astonishment and boundless change.

LOST HOPE.

You cast to ground the hope which once was mine:
  But did the while your harsh decree deplore,
Embalming with sweet tears the vacant shrine,
  My heart, where Hope had been and was no more.

So on an oaken sprout
  A goodly acorn grew;
But winds from heaven shook the acorn out,
  And filled the cup with dew.

THE TEARS OF HEAVEN.

Heaven weeps above the earth all night till morn,
In darkness weeps as all ashamed to weep,
Because the earth hath made her state forlorn
With self-wrought evil of unnumbered years,
And doth the fruit of her dishonor reap.
And all the day heaven gathers back her tears
Into her own blue eyes so clear and deep,
And showering down the glory of lightsome day,
Smiles on the earth's worn brow to win her if she may.

LOVE AND SORROW.

O MAIDEN, fresher than the first green leaf
With which the fearful springtide flecks
 the lea,
Weep not, Almeida, that I said to thee
That thou hast half my heart, for bitter
 grief
Doth hold the other half in sovranty.
Thou art my heart's sun in love's crystalline:
Yet on both sides at once thou canst not
 shine:
Thine is the bright side of my heart,
 and thine
My heart's day, but the shadow of my
 heart,
Issue of its own substance, my heart's night
Thou canst not lighten even with *thy* light,
All-powerful in beauty as thou art.
Almeida, if my heart were substanceless,
Then might thy rays pass through to
 the other side,
So swiftly, that they nowhere would abide,
But lose themselves in utter emptiness.
Half-light, half-shadow, let my spirit
 sleep;
They never learned to love who never
 knew to weep.

TO A LADY SLEEPING.

O THOU whose fringéd lids I gaze upon,
Through whose dim brain the wingéd
 dreams are borne,
Unroof the shrines of clearest vision,
In honor of the silver-fleckéd morn;
Long hath the white wave of the virgin
 light
Driven back the billow of the dreamful
 dark.
Thou all unwittingly prolongest night,
Though long ago listening the poiséd lark,
With eyes dropt downward through the
 blue serene,
Over heaven's parapet the angels lean.

SONNET.

COULD I outwear my present state of woe
With one brief winter, and indue i' the
 spring
Hues of fresh youth, and mightily outgrow
The wan dark coil of faded suffering —
Forth in the pride of beauty issuing
A sheeny snake, the light of vernal bowers,
Moving his crest to all sweet plots of
 flowers
And watered valleys where the young
 birds sing;
Could I thus hope my lost delight's renewing,
I straightly would command the tears to
 creep
From my charged lids; but inwardly I
 weep,
Some vital heat as yet my heart is wooing:
That to itself hath drawn the frozen rain
From my cold eyes, and melted it again.

SONNET.

THOUGH Night hath climbed her peak
 of highest noon,
And bitter blasts the screaming autumn
 whirl,
All night through archways of the bridgéd
 pearl,
And portals of pure silver, walks the moon.
Walk on, my soul, nor crouch to agony,
Turn cloud to light, and bitterness to joy,
And dross to gold with glorious alchemy,
Basing thy throne above the world's annoy.
Reign thou above the storms of sorrow
 and ruth
That roar beneath; unshaken peace hath
 won thee;
So shalt thou pierce the woven glooms
 of truth;
So shall the blessing of the meek be on
 thee;
So in thine hour of dawn, the body's youth,
An honorable eld shall come upon thee.

SONNET.

SHALL the hag Evil die with child of Good,
Or propagate again her loathéd kind,
Thronging the cells of the diseaséd mind,
Hateful with hanging cheeks, a withered
 brood,
Though hourly pastured on the salient
 blood?
O that the wind which bloweth cold or
 heat
Would shatter and o'erbear the brazen beat
Of their broad vans, and in the solitude
Of middle space confound them, and
 blow back
Their wild cries down their cavern
 throats, and slake

With points of blast-borne hail their heated eyne!
So their wan limbs no more might come between
The moon and the moon's reflex in the night,
Nor blot with floating shades the solar light.

SONNET.

The pallid thunder-stricken sigh for gain,
Down an ideal stream they ever float,
And sailing on Pactolus in a boat,
Drown soul and sense, while wistfully they strain
Weak eyes upon the glistening sands that robe
The understream. The wise, could he behold
Cathedraled caverns of thick-ribbéd gold
And branching silvers of the central globe,
Would marvel from so beautiful a sight
How scorn and ruin, pain and hate could flow:
But Hatred in a gold cave sits below;
Pleached with her hair, in mail of argent light
Shot into gold, a snake her forehead clips,
And skins the color from her trembling lips.

LOVE.

I.

Thou, from the first, unborn, undying love,
Albeit we gaze not on thy glories near,
Before the face of God didst breathe and move,
Though night and pain and ruin and death reign here.
Thou foldest, like a golden atmosphere,
The very throne of the eternal God:
Passing through thee the edicts of his fear
Are mellowed into music, borne abroad
By the loud winds, though they uprend the sea,
Even from its central deeps: thine empery
Is over all; thou wilt not brook eclipse;
Thou goest and returnest to His lips
Like lightning: thou dost ever brood above
The silence of all hearts, unutterable Love.

II.

To know thee is all wisdom, and old age
Is but to know thee: dimly we behold thee
Athwart the veils of evils which infold thee.
We beat upon our aching hearts in rage;
We cry for thee; we deem the world thy tomb.
As dwellers in lone planets look upon
The mighty disk of their majestic sun,
Hollowed in awful chasms of wheeling gloom,
Making their day dim, so we gaze on thee.
Come, thou of many crowns, white-robéd love,
Oh! rend the veil in twain: all men adore thee;
Heaven crieth after thee; earth waiteth for thee;
Breathe on thy wingéd throne, and it shall move
In music and in light o'er land and sea.

III.

And now — methinks I gaze upon thee now,
As on a serpent in his agonies
Awe-stricken Indians; what time laid low
And crushing the thick fragrant reeds he lies,
When the new year warm-breathéd on the Earth,
Waiting to light him with her purple skies,
Calls to him by the fountain to uprise.
Already with the pangs of a new birth
Strain the hot spheres of his convulséd eyes,
And in his writhings awful hues begin
To wander down his sable-sheeny sides,
Like light on troubled waters: from within
Anon he rusheth forth with merry din,
And in him light and joy and strength abides;
And from his brows a crown of living light
Looks through the thick-stemmed woods by day and night.

THE KRAKEN.

Below the thunders of the upper deep;
Far, far beneath in the abysmal sea,
His ancient, dreamless, uninvaded sleep,
The Kraken sleepeth: faintest sunlights flee
About his shadowy sides: above him swell
Huge sponges of millennial growth and height;

And far away into the sickly light,
From many a wondrous grot and secret cell
Unnumbered and enormous polypi
Winnow with giant fins the slumbering green.
There hath he lain for ages and will lie
Battening upon huge seaworms in his sleep,
Until the latter fire shall heat the deep;
Then once by man and angels to be seen,
In roaring he shall rise and on the surface die.

ENGLISH WAR-SONG.

Who fears to die ? Who fears to die ?
Is there any here who fears to die ?
He shall find what he fears ; and none shall grieve
For the man who fears to die ;
But the withering scorn of the many shall cleave
To the man who fears to die.

CHORUS.

Shout for England !
Ho ! for England !
George for England !
Merry England !
England for aye !

The hollow at heart shall crouch forlorn,
He shall eat the bread of common scorn ;
It shall be steeped in the salt, salt tear,
Shall be steeped in his own salt tear :
Far better, far better he never were born
Than to shame merry England here.

Cho. — Shout for England ! etc.

There standeth our ancient enemy ;
Hark ! he shouteth — the ancient enemy !
On the ridge of the hill his banners rise ;
They stream like fire in the skies ;
Hold up the Lion of England on high
Till it dazzle and blind his eyes.

Cho. — Shout for England ! etc.

Come along ! we alone of the earth are free ;
The child in our cradles is bolder than he ;
For where is the heart and strength of slaves ?

Oh ! where is the strength of slaves ?
He is weak ! we are strong : he a slave, we are free ;
Come along ! we will dig their graves.

Cho. — Shout for England ! etc.

There standeth our ancient enemy ;
Will he dare to battle with the free ?
Spur along ! spur amain ! charge to the fight :
Charge ! charge to the fight !
Hold up the Lion of England on high !
Shout for God and our right !

Cho. — Shout for England ! etc.

NATIONAL SONG.

There is no land like England
Where'er the light of day be ;
There are no hearts like English hearts,
Such hearts of oak as they be.
There is no land like England
Where'er the light of day be ;
There are no men like Englishmen,
So tall and bold as they be.

CHORUS.

For the French the Pope may shrive 'em,
For the devil a whit we heed 'em :
As for the French, God speed 'em
Unto their heart's desire,
And the merry devil drive 'em
Through the water and the fire.

FULL CHORUS.

Our glory is our freedom,
We lord it o'er the sea ;
We are the sons of freedom,
We are free.

There is no land like England,
Where'er the light of day be ;
There are no wives like English wives,
So fair and chaste as they be.
There is no land like England,
Where'er the light of day be ;
There are no maids like English maids,
So beautiful as they be.

Cho. — For the French, etc.

DUALISMS.

Two bees within a crystal flowerbell rocked,
Hum a lovelay to the west-wind at noontide.

Both alike, they buzz together,
Both alike, they hum together,
Through and through the flowered
    heather.
Where in a creeping cove the wave un-
    shockéd
    Lays itself calm and wide.
Over a stream two birds of glancing
    feather
Do woo each other, carolling together.
Both alike, they glide together,
    Side by side;
Both alike, they sing together,
Arching blue-glosséd necks beneath the
    purple weather.

Two children lovelier than Love adown
    the lea are singing,
As they gambol, lily-garlands ever string-
    ing:
    Both in blosmwhite silk are
        frockéd:
Like, unlike, they roam together
Under a summer vault of golden
    weather:
Like, unlike, they sing together
    Side by side,
    MidMay's darling golden lock-
        éd,
    Summer's tanling diamond eyed.

WE ARE FREE.

The winds, as at their hour of birth,
    Leaning upon the wingéd sea,
Breathed low around the rolling earth
    With mellow preludes, "We are free."
The streams through many a lilied row
    Down-carolling to the crispéd sea,
Low-tinkled with a bell-like flow
    Atween the blossoms, "We are free."

THE SEA FAIRIES.*

Slow sailed the weary mariners, and
    saw
Between the green brink and the run-
    ning foam
White limbs unrobéd in a crystal air,
Sweet faces, rounded arms, and bosoms
    prest
To little harps of gold: and while they
    mused,
Whispering to each other half in fear,
Shrill music reached them on the mid-
    dle sea.

* Original form.

SONG.

Whither away, whither away, whither
    away? Fly no more:
Whither away wi' the singing sail?
    whither away wi' the oar?
Whither away from the high green field
    and the happy blossoming shore?
Weary mariners, hither away,
    One and all, one and all,
Weary mariners, come and play;
We will sing to you all the day;
    Furl the sail and the foam will fall
From the prow! One and all
    Furl the sail! Drop the oar!
    Leap ashore,
Know danger and trouble and toil no
    more,
Whither away wi' the sail and the oar?
    Drop the oar,
    Leap ashore,
    Fly no more!
Whither away wi' the sail? whither away
    wi' the oar?
Day and night to the billow the foun-
    tain calls:
Down shower the gambolling water-
    falls
    From wandering over the lea;
They freshen the silvery-crimson shells,
And thick with white bells the clover-
    hill swells
High over the full-toned sea.
Merrily carol the revelling gales
    Over the islands free:
From the green seabanks the rose
    down trails
    To the happy brimméd sea.
Come hither, come hither and be our
    lords,
    For merry brides are we:
We will kiss sweet kisses, and speak
    sweet words.
O listen, listen, your eyes shall glis-
    ten
    With pleasure and love and revelry;
O listen, listen, your eyes shall glis-
    ten,
When the sharp clear twang of the gold-
    en chords
    Runs up the ridgéd sea.
Ye will not find so happy a shore,
    Weary mariners! all the world o'er;
        O, fly no more!
Hearken ye, hearken ye, sorrow shall
    darken ye,
Danger and trouble and toil no more;

TO ———.

Whither away?
Drop the oar;
Hither away
Leap ashore;
O fly no more — no more:
Whither away, whither away, whither away with the sail and the oar?

Οἱ ῥέοντες.

I.

ALL thoughts, all creeds, all dreams are true,
All visions wild and strange;
Man is the measure of all truth
Unto himself. All truth is change,
All men do walk in sleep, and all
Have faith in that they dream:
For all things are as they seem to all,
And all things flow like a stream.

II.

There is no rest, no calm, no pause,
Nor good nor ill, nor light nor shade,
Nor essence nor eternal laws:
For nothing is, but all is made.
But if I dream that all these are,
They are to me for that I dream;
For all things are as they seem to all,
And all things flow like a stream.

Argal — this very opinion is **only true** relatively to the flowing philosophers.

POEMS PUBLISHED IN THE EDITION OF 1833, AND OMITTED IN LATER EDITIONS.

SONNET.

MINE be the strength of spirit fierce and free,
Like some broad river rushing down alone,
With the selfsame impulse wherewith he was thrown
From his loud fount upon the echoing lea: —
Which with increasing might doth forward flee
By town, and tower, and hill, and cape, and isle,
And in the middle of the green salt sea
Keeps his blue waters fresh for many a mile.
Mine be the Power which ever to its sway
Will win the wise at once, and by degrees
May into uncongenial spirits flow;
Even as the great gulfstream of Florida
Floats far away into the Northern seas
The lavish growths of southern Mexico.

TO ———.

I.

ALL good things have not kept aloof,
Nor wandered into other ways;
I have not lacked thy mild reproof,
Nor golden largess of thy praise,
But life is full of weary days.

II.

Shake hands, my friend, across the brink
Of that deep grave to which I go.
Shake hands once more: I cannot sink
So far — far down, but I shall know
Thy voice, and answer from below.

III.

When, in the darkness over me,
The four-handed mole shall scrape,
Plant thou no dusky cypress-tree,
Nor wreathe thy cap with doleful crape,
But pledge me in the flowing grape.

IV.

And when the sappy field and wood
Grow green beneath the showery gray,
And rugged barks begin to bud,
And through damp holts, new flushed with May,
Ring sudden laughters of the Jay;

V.

Then let wise Nature work her will,
And on my clay the darnels grow.
Come only when the days are still,
And at my headstone whisper low,
And tell me if the woodbines blow,

VI.

If thou art blest, my mother's **smile**
Undimmed, if bees are on the wing:

Then cease, my friend, a little while,
That I may hear the throstle sing
His bridal song, the boast of spring.

VII.

Sweet as the noise in parchéd plains
  Of bubbling wells that fret the stones
(If any sense in me remains),
  Thy words will be ; thy cheerful tones
As welcome to my crumbling bones.

BONAPARTE.

He thought to quell the stubborn hearts
  of oak,
Madman! — to chain with chains, and
  bind with bands
That island queen that sways the floods
  and lands
From Ind to Ind, but in fair daylight
  woke,
When from her wooden walls, lit by sure
  hands,
With thunders, and with lightnings, and
  with smoke,
Peal after peal, the British battle broke,
Lulling the brine against the Coptic sands.
We taught him lowlier moods, when
  Elsinore
Heard the war moan along the distant sea,
Rocking with shattered spars, with sudden fires
Flamed over : at Trafalgar yet once more
We taught him : late he learned humility
Perforce, like those whom Gideon schooled
  with briers.

SONNETS.

I.

O beauty, passing beauty! sweetest
  Sweet!
How canst thou let me waste my youth
  in sighs?
I only ask to sit beside thy feet.
  Thou knowest I dare not look into
  thine eyes.
Might I but kiss thy hand! I dare not
  fold
  My arms about thee — scarcely dare to
  speak.
And nothing seems to me so wild and bold,
  As with one kiss to touch thy blesséd
  cheek.

Methinks if I should kiss thee, no control
  Within the thrilling brain could keep
  afloat
The subtle spirit. Even while I spoke,
The bare word KISS hath made my inner
  soul
To tremble like a lutestring, ere the
  note
Hath melted in the silence that it broke.

II.

But were I loved, as I desire to be,
What is there in the great sphere of the
  earth,
And range of evil between death and birth,
That I should fear, — if I were loved by
  thee?
All the inner, all the outer world of pain
Clear Love would pierce and cleave, if
  thou wert mine,
As I have heard that, somewhere in the
  main,
Fresh-water springs come up through
  bitter brine.
'T were joy, not fear, clasped hand-in-hand with thee,
To wait for death — mute — careless of
  all ills,
Apart upon a mountain, though the surge
Of some new deluge from a thousand
  hills
Flung leagues of roaring foam into the
  gorge
Below us, as far on as eye could see.

THE HESPERIDES.

"Hesperus and his daughters three,
That sing about the golden tree."
                Comus.

The North-wind fall'n, in the new-starréd
  night
Zidonian Hanno, voyaging beyond
The hoary promontory of Soloë
Past Thymiaterion, in calméd bays,
Between the southern and the western
  Horn,
Heard neither warbling of the nightingale,
Nor melody of the Libyan lotus flute
Blown seaward from the shore ; but from
  a slope
That ran bloom-bright into the Atlantic
  blue,
Beneath a highland leaning down a weight
Of cliffs, and zoned below with cedar shade,
Came voices, like the voices in a dream,
Continuous, till he reached the outer sea.

SONG.

I.

The golden apple, the golden apple, the hallowed fruit,
Guard it well, guard it warily,
Singing airily,
Standing about the charmèd root.
Round about all is mute,
As the snow-field on the mountain-peaks,
As the sand-field at the mountain-foot.
Crocodiles in briny creeks
Sleep and stir not : all is mute.
If ye sing not, if ye make false measure,
We shall lose eternal pleasure,
Worth eternal want of rest.
Laugh not loudly : watch the treasure
Of the wisdom of the West.
In a corner wisdom whispers. Five and three
(Let it not be preached abroad) make an awful mystery.
For the blossom unto threefold music bloweth ;
Evermore it is born anew ;
And the sap to threefold music floweth,
From the root
Drawn in the dark,
Up to the fruit,
Creeping under the fragrant bark,
Liquid gold, honeysweet, thro' and thro'.
Keen-eyed Sisters, singing airily,
Looking warily
Every way,
Guard the apple night and day,
Lest one from the East come and take it away.

II.

Father Hesper, Father Hesper, watch, watch, ever and aye,
Looking under silver hair with a silver eye.
Father, twinkle not thy steadfast sight ;
Kingdoms lapse, and climates change, and races die ;
Honor comes with mystery ;
Hoarded wisdom brings delight.
Number, tell them over and number
How many the mystic fruit-tree holds
Lest the red-combed dragon slumber
Rolled together in purple folds.
Look to him, father, lest he wink, and the golden apple be stol'n away,
For his ancient heart is drunk with over-watchings night and day,
Round about the hallowed fruit-tree curled —
Sing away, sing aloud evermore in the wind, without stop,
Lest his sealèd eyelid drop,
For he is older than the world.
If he waken, we waken,
Rapidly levelling eager eyes.
If he sleep, we sleep,
Dropping the eyelid over the eyes.
If the golden apple be taken,
The world will be overwise.
Five links, a golden chain, are we,
Hesper, the dragon, and sisters three,
Bound about the golden tree.

III.

Father Hesper, Father Hesper, watch, watch, night and day,
Lest the old wound of the world be healèd,
The glory unsealèd,
The golden apple stolèn away,
And the ancient secret revealèd.
Look from west to east along :
Father, old Himala weakens, Caucasus is bold and strong.
Wandering waters unto wandering waters call ;
Let them clash together, foam and fall.
Out of watchings, out of wiles,
Comes the bliss of secret smiles.
All things are not told to all.
Half-round the mantling night is drawn,
Purple fringed with even and dawn,
Hesper hateth Phosphor, evening hateth morn.

IV.

Every flower and every fruit the redolent breath
Of this warm sea-wind ripeneth,
Arching the billow in his sleep ;
But the land-wind wandereth,
Broken by the highland-steep,
Two streams upon the violet deep ;
For the western sun and the western star,
And the low west-wind, breathing afar,
The end of day and beginning of night
Make the apple holy and bright ;
Holy and bright, round and full, bright and blest,
Mellowed in a land of rest ;
Watch it warily day and night ;
All good things are in the west.
Till mid noon the cool east light
Is shut out by the tall hillbrow ;

But when the full-faced sunset yellowly
Stays on the flowering arch of the bough,
The luscious fruitage clustereth mellowly,
Golden-kernelled, golden-cored,
Sunset-ripened above on the tree.
The world is wasted with fire and sword,
But the apple of gold hangs over the sea.
Five links, a golden chain are we,
Hesper, the dragon, and sisters three,
Daughters three,
Bound about
The gnarlèd bole of the charmèd tree.
The golden apple, the golden apple, the hallowed fruit,
Guard it well, guard it warily,
Watch it warily,
Singing airily,
Standing about the charmèd root.

ROSALIND.

I.

My Rosalind, my Rosalind,
My frolic falcon, with bright eyes,
Whose free delight, from any height of rapid flight,
Stoops at all game that wing the skies,
My Rosalind, my Rosalind,
My bright-eyed, wild-eyed falcon, whither,
Careless both of wind and weather,
Whither fly ye, what game spy ye,
Up or down the streaming wind?

II.

The quick lark's closest-carolled strains,
The shadow rushing up the sea,
The lightning flash atween the rains,
The sunlight driving down the lea,
The leaping stream, the very wind,
That will not stay, upon his way,
To stoop the cowslip to the plains,
Is not so clear and bold and free
As you, my falcon Rosalind.
You care not for another's pains,
Because you are the soul of joy,
Bright metal all without alloy.
Life shoots and glances thro' your veins,
And flashes off a thousand ways
Through lips and eyes in subtle rays.
Your hawkeyes are keen and bright,
Keen with triumph, watching still
To pierce me through with pointed light;
But oftentimes they flash and glitter
Like sunshine on a dancing rill,
And your words are seeming-bitter,
Sharp and few, but seeming-bitter
From excess of swift delight.

III.

Come down, come home, my Rosalind,
My gay young hawk, my Rosalind:
Too long you keep the upper skies;
Too long you roam and wheel at will;
But we must hood your random eyes,
That care not whom they kill,
And your cheek, whose brilliant hue
Is so sparkling-fresh to view,
Some red heath-flower in the dew,
Touched with sunrise. We must bind
And keep you fast, my Rosalind,
Fast, fast, my wild-eyed Rosalind,
And clip your wings, and make you love:
When we have lured you from above,
And that delight of frolic flight, by day or night,
From north to south;
Will bind you fast in silken cords,
And kiss away the bitter words
From off your rosy mouth.*

SONG.

Who can say
Why To-day
To-morrow will be yesterday?
Who can tell

* AUTHOR'S NOTE.—Perhaps the following lines may be allowed to stand as a separate poem; originally they made part of the text, where they were manifestly superfluous.

>My Rosalind, my Rosalind,
>Bold, subtle, careless Rosalind,
>Is one of those who know no strife
>Of inward woe or outward fear;
>To whom the slope and stream of Life,
>The life before, the life behind,
>In the ear, from far and near,
>Chimeth musically clear.
>My falcon-hearted Rosalind,
>Full-sailed before a vigorous wind,
>Is one of those who cannot weep
>For others' woes, but overleap
>All the petty shocks and fears
>That trouble life in early years,
>With a flash of frolic scorn
>And keen delight, that never falls
>Away from freshness, self-upborne
>With such gladness as, whenever
>The fresh-flushing springtime calls
>To the flooding waters cool,
>Young fishes, on an April morn,
>Up and down a rapid river,
>Leap the little waterfalls
>That sing into the pebbled pool,
>My happy falcon, Rosalind,
>Hath daring fancies of her own,
>Fresh as the dawn before the day,
>Fresh as the early sea-smell blown
>Through vineyards from an inland bay.
>My Rosalind, my Rosalind,
>Because no shadow on you falls,
>Think you hearts are tennisballs
>To play with, wanton Rosalind?

Why to smell
The violet recalls the dewy prime
Of youth and buried time?
The cause is nowhere found in rhyme.

KATE.

I know her by her angry air,
Her bright black eyes, her bright black
    hair,
Her rapid laughters wild and shrill,
As laughters of the woodpecker
    From the bosom of a hill.
'T is Kate — she sayeth what she will:
For Kate hath an unbridled tongue,
    Clear as the twanging of a harp.
    Her heart is like a throbbing star.
Kate hath a spirit ever strung
    Like a new bow, and bright and sharp,
    As edges of the scymitar.
Whence shall she take a fitting mate?
    For Kate no common love will feel;
My woman-soldier, gallant Kate,
    As pure and true as blades of steel.

Kate saith "the world is void of might."
    Kate saith "the men are gilded flies."
    Kate snaps her fingers at my vows;
    Kate will not hear of lovers' sighs.
I would I were an armed knight,
    Far famed for well-won enterprise,
    And wearing on my swarthy brows
    The garland of new-wreathed emprise:
For in a moment I would pierce
The blackest files of clanging fight,
And strongly strike to left and right,
    In dreaming of my lady's eyes.
    Oh! Kate loves well the bold and
        fierce;
But none are bold enough for Kate,
She cannot find a fitting mate.

SONNET

WRITTEN ON HEARING OF THE OUT-
BREAK OF THE POLISH INSURREC-
TION.

Blow ye the trumpet, gather from afar
The hosts to battle: be not bought and
    sold.
Arise, brave Poles, the boldest of the bold;
Break through your iron shackles — fling
    them far.
O for those days of Piast, ere the Czar
Grew to his strength among his deserts
    cold;
When even to Moscow's cupolas were
    rolled
The growing murmurs of the Polish war!
Now must your noble anger blaze out
    more
Than when from Sobieski, clan by clan,
The Moslem myriads fell, and fled before—
Than when Zamoysky smote the Tartar
    Khan;
Than earlier, when on the Baltic shore
Boleslas drove the Pomeranian.

SONNET

ON THE RESULT OF THE LATE RUSSIAN
INVASION OF POLAND.

How long, O God, shall men be ridden
    down,
And trampled under by the last and least
Of men? The heart of Poland hath not
    ceased
To quiver, though her sacred blood doth
    drown
The fields; and out of every mouldering
    town
Cries to Thee, lest brute Power be in-
    creased,
Till that o'ergrown Barbarian in the East
Transgress his ample bound to some
    new crown: —
Cries to Thee, "Lord, how long shall
    these things be?
How long shall the icy-hearted Muscovite
Oppress the region?" Us, O Just and
    Good,
Forgive, who smiled when she was torn
    in three;
Us, who stand *now*, when we should aid
    the right —
A matter to be wept with tears of blood!

SONNET.

As when with downcast eyes we muse and
    brood,
And ebb into a former life, or seem
To lapse far back in a confusèd dream
To states of mystical similitude;
If one but speaks or hems or stirs his
    chair,
Ever the wonder waxeth more and more,
So that we say, "All this hath been before,

All this *hath* been, I know not when or where."
So, friend, when first I looked upon your face,
Our thought gave answer, each to each, so true,
Opposéd mirrors each reflecting each —
Altho' I knew not in what time or place,
Methought that I had often met with you,
And each had lived in the other's mind and speech.

O DARLING ROOM.

I.

O DARLING room, my heart's delight
Dear room, the apple of my sight,
With thy two couches soft and white,
There is no room so exquisite,
No little room so warm and bright,
Wherein to read, wherein to write.

II.

For I the Nonnenwerth have seen,
And Oberwinter's vineyards green,
Musical Lurlei; and between
The hills to Bingen have I been,
Bingen in Darmstadt, where the Rhene
Curves toward Meutz, a woody scene.

III.

Yet never did there meet my sight,
In any town to left or right,
A little room so exquisite,
With two such couches soft and white;
Not any room so warm and bright,
Wherein to read, wherein to write.

TO CHRISTOPHER NORTH.

You did late review my lays,
  Crusty Christopher;
You did mingle blame and praise,
  Rusty Christopher.
When I learnt from whom it came,
I forgave you all the blame,
  Musty Christopher;
I could *not* forgive the praise,
  Fusty Christopher.

FUGITIVE POEMS.

NO MORE.*

O SAD *No More!* O sweet *No More!*
O strange *No More!*
By a mossed brookbank on a stone
I smelt a wildweed flower alone;
There was a ringing in my ears,
And both my eyes gushed out with tears.
Surely all pleasant things had gone before,
Low-buried fathom deep beneath with thee, No MORE!

ANACREONTICS.*

WITH roses musky-breathed,
And drooping daffodilly,
And silver-leaved lily,
And ivy darkly-wreathed,
I wove a crown before her,
For her I love so dearly,

A garland for Lenora.
With a silken cord I bound it.
Lenora, laughing clearly
A light and thrilling laughter,
About her forehead wound it,
And loved me ever after.

A FRAGMENT.*

WHERE is the Giant of the Sun, which stood
In the midnoon the glory of old Rhodes,
A perfect Idol with profulgent brows
Far-sheening down the purple seas to those
Who sailed from Mizraim underneath the star
Named of the Dragon — and between whose limbs
Of brassy vastness broad-blown Argosies
Drave into haven? Yet endure unscathed
Of changeful cycles the great Pyramids

* From the Gem, a literary annual, for 1831.

* From the Gem, a literary annual, for 1861.

Broad-based amid the fleeting sands, and
sloped
Into the slumberous summer noon ; but
where,
Mysterious Egypt, are thine obelisks
Graven with gorgeous emblems undiscerned ?
Thy placid Sphinxes brooding o'er the
Nile ?
Thy shadowing Idols in the solitudes,
Awful Memnonian countenances calm
Looking athwart the burning flats, far off
Seen by the high-necked camel on the verge
Journeying southward ? Where are thy
monuments
Piled by the strong and sunborn Anakim
Over their crowned brethren On and Oph ?
Thy Memnon when his peaceful lips are
kist
With earliest rays, that from his mother's
eyes
Flow over the Arabian bay, no more
Breathes low into the charmed ears of
morn
Clear melody flattering the crisped Nile
By columned Thebes. Old Memphis hath
gone down :
The Pharaohs are no more : somewhere
in death
They sleep with staring eyes and gilded
lips,
Wrapped round with spiced cerements
in old grots
Rock-hewn and sealed for ever.

SONNET.*

ME my own fate to lasting sorrow
doometh :
Thy woes are birds of passage, transitory :
Thy spirit, circled with a living glory,
In summer still a summer joy resumeth.
Alone my hopeless melancholy gloometh,
Like a lone cypress, through the twilight hoary,
From an old garden where no flower
bloometh,
One cypress on an island promontory.
But yet my lonely spirit follows thine,
As round the rolling earth night follows
day :
But yet thy lights on my horizon shine
Into my night, when thou art far away.

* Friendship's Offering, 1833.

I am so dark, alas ! and thou so bright,
When we two meet there 's never perfect
light.

SONNET.*

CHECK every outflash, every ruder sally
Of thought and speech ; speak low
and give up wholly
Thy spirit to mild-minded melancholy ;
This is the place. Through yonder poplar valley
Below the blue-green river windeth
slowly ;
But in the middle of the sombre valley
The crispéd waters whisper musically,
And all the haunted place is dark and
holy.
The nightingale, with long and low preamble,
Warbled from yonder knoll of solemn
larches,
And in and out the woodbine's flowery
arches
The summer midges wove their wanton
gambol,
And all the white-stemmed pinewood
slept above —
When in this valley first I told my love.

THE SKIPPING-ROPE.†

SURE never yet was Antelope
Could skip so lightly by.
Stand off, or else my skipping-rope
Will hit you in the eye.
How lightly whirls the skipping-rope !
How fairy-like you fly !
Go, get you gone, you muse and mope —
I hate that silly sigh.
Nay, dearest, teach me how to hope,
Or tell me how to die.
There, take it, take my skipping-rope,
And hang yourself thereby.

THE NEW TIMON AND THE POETS.‡

WE know him, out of Shakespeare's art,
And those fine curses which he spoke ;
The old Timon, with his noble heart,
That, strongly loathing, greatly broke.

* Friendship's Offering, 1833.
† Omitted from the edition of 1842.
‡ Published in Punch, Feb. 1846, signed " Alcibiades."

So died the Old: here comes the New.
  Regard him: a familiar face:
I thought we knew him: What, it's you,
  The padded man — that wears the
    stays —

Who killed the girls and thrilled the boys
  With dandy pathos when you wrote!
A Lion, you, that made a noise,
  And shook a mane *en papillotes*.

And once you tried the Muses too;
  You failed, Sir: therefore now you turn,
To fall on those who are to you
  As Captain is to Subaltern.

But men of long-enduring hopes,
  And careless what this hour may bring,
Can pardon little would-be POPES
  And BRUMMELS, when they try to sting.

An Artist, Sir, should rest in Art,
  And waive a little of his claim;
To have the deep Poetic heart
  Is more than all poetic fame.

But you, Sir, you are hard to please;
  You never look but half content;
Nor like a gentleman at ease,
  With moral breadth of temperament.

And what with spites and what with fears,
  You cannot let a body be:
It's always ringing in your ears,
  "They call this man as good as *me*."

What profits now to understand
  The merits of a spotless shirt —
A dapper boot — a little hand —
  If half the little soul is dirt?

You talk of tinsel! why, we see
  The old mark of rouge upon your cheeks.
You prate of Nature! you are he
  That spilt his life about the cliques.

A TIMON you! Nay, nay, for shame:
  It looks too arrogant a jest —
The fierce old man — to take his name,
  You bandbox. Off, and let him rest.

STANZAS.*

WHAT time I wasted youthful hours,
  One of the shining wingèd powers,
Show'd me vast cliffs with crown of towers.

As towards the gracious light I bow'd,
They seem'd high palaces and proud,
Hid now and then with sliding cloud.

He said, "The labor is not small;
Yet winds the pathway free to all: —
Take care thou dost not fear to fall!"

SONNET

TO WILLIAM CHARLES MACREADY.*

FAREWELL, Macready, since to-night we
  part.
  Full-handed thunders often have confest
Thy power, well-used to move the public breast.
  We thank thee with one voice, and from
    the heart.
Farewell, Macready; since this night
  we part.
  Go, take thine honors home: rank
    with the best,
  Garrick, and statelier Kemble, and the
    rest
Who made a nation purer thro' their art.
  Thine is it, that our Drama did not die,
    Nor flicker down to brainless pantomime,
    And those gilt gauds men-children
      swarm to see.
Farewell, Macready; moral, grave, sublime.
  Our Shakespeare's bland and universal eye
    Dwells pleased, thro' twice a hundred
      years, on thee.

BRITONS, GUARD YOUR OWN.†

RISE, Britons, rise, if manhood be not
  dead;
The world's last tempest darkens overhead;
  The Pope has bless'd him;
  The Church caress'd him;
He triumphs; maybe we shall stand alone.
  Britons, guard your own.

His ruthless host is bought with plunder'd
  gold,
By lying priests the peasants' votes controll'd.

---

* The Keepsake. 1851.

* Read by Mr. John Forster at a dinner given to Mr. Macready, March 1, 1851, on his retirement from the stage.
† The Examiner, 1852.

All freedom vanish'd,
The true men banish'd,
He triumphs; maybe we shall stand alone.
Britons, guard your own.

Peace-lovers we — sweet Peace we all desire —
Peace-lovers we — but who can trust a liar? —
Peace-lovers, haters
Of shameless traitors,
We hate not France, but this man's heart of stone,
Britons, guard your own.

We hate not France, but France has lost her voice.
This man is France, the man they call her choice.
By tricks and spying,
By craft and lying,
And murder was her freedom overthrown.
Britons, guard your own.

"Vive l'Empereur" may follow by and by;
"God save the Queen" is here a truer cry.
God save the Nation,
The toleration,
And the free speech that makes a Briton known.
Britons, guard your own.

Rome's dearest daughter now is captive France,
The Jesuit laughs, and reckoning on his chance,
Would unrelenting,
Kill all dissenting,
Till we were left to fight for truth alone.
Britons, guard your own.

Call home your ships across Biscayan tides,
To blow the battle from their oaken sides.
Why waste they yonder
Their idle thunder?
Why stay they there to guard a foreign throne?
Seamen, guard your own.

We were the best of marksmen long ago,
We won old battles with our strength, the bow.
Now practice, yeomen,
Like those bowmen,
Till your balls fly as their shafts have flown.
Yeomen, guard your own.

His soldier-ridden Highness might incline
To take Sardinia, Belgium, or the Rhine:
Shall we stand idle,
Nor seek to bridle
His rude aggressions, till we stand alone?
Make their cause your own.

Should he land here, and for one hour prevail,
There must no man go back to bear the tale:
No man to bear it —
Swear it! we swear it!
Although we fight the banded world alone,
We swear to guard our own.

THE THIRD OF FEBRUARY, 1852.*

My lords, we heard you speak; you told us all
That England's honest censure went too far;
That our free press should cease to brawl,
Not sting the fiery Frenchman into war.
It was an ancient privilege, my lords,
To fling whate'er we felt, not fearing, into words.

We love not this French God, this child of Hell,
Wild War, who breaks the converse of the wise;
But though we love kind Peace so well,
We dare not, e'en by silence, sanction lies.
It might safe be our censures to withdraw;
And yet, my lords, not well; there is a higher law.

As long as we remain, we must speak free,
Though all the storm of Europe on us break;
No little German state are we,
But the one voice in Europe; we *must* speak;
That if to-night our greatness were struck dead,
There might remain some record of the things we said.

If you be fearful, then must we be bold.
Our Britain cannot salve a tyrant o'er.

* The Examiner, 1852, and signed "Merlin."

Better the waste Atlantic roll'd
  On her and us and ours for evermore.
What! have we fought for freedom from
    our prime,
At last to dodge and palter with a pub-
    lic crime?

Shall we fear him? our own we never
    feared.
  From our first Charles by force we
    wrung our claims,
Prick'd by the Papal spur, we rear'd,
  And flung the burden of the second
    James.
I say we never fear'd! and as for these,
We broke them on the land, we drove
    them on the seas.

And you, my lords, you make the people
    muse,
  In doubt if you be of our Barons' breed—
Were those your sires who fought at
    Lewes?
Is this the manly strain of Runnymede?
O fall'n nobility, that, overawed,
Would lisp in honey'd whispers of this
    monstrous fraud.

We feel, at least, that silence here were
    sin.
  Not ours the fault if we have feeble
    hosts—
  If easy patrons of their kin
  Have left the last free race with naked
    coasts!
They knew the precious things they had
    to guard:
For us, we will not spare the tyrant one
    hard word.

Though niggard throats of Manchester
    may bawl,
  What England was, shall her true sons
    forget?
We are not cotton-spinners all,
  But some love England, and her honor
    yet.
And these in our Thermopylæ shall stand,
And hold against the world the honor of
    the land.

HANDS ALL ROUND. *

First drink a health, this solemn night,
  A health to England, every guest;

* The Examiner, 1852, and signed "Merlin."

That man's the best cosmopolite
  Who loves his native country best.
May freedom's oak for ever live
  With stronger life from day to day;
That man's the best Conservative
  Who lops the mouldered branch away.
    Hands all round!
  God the tyrant's hope confound!
To this great cause of Freedom drink, my
    friends,
  And the great name of England, round
    and round.

A health to Europe's honest men!
  Heaven guard them from her tyrants'
    jails!
From wronged Poerio's noisome den,
  From iron limbs and tortured nails!
We curse the crimes of southern kings,
  The Russian whips and Austrian rods—
We likewise have our evil things;
  Too much we make our Ledgers, Gods.
    Yet hands all round!
  God the tyrant's cause confound!
To Europe's better health we drink, my
    friends,
  And the great name of England, round
    and round!

What health to France, if France be she,
  Whom martial progress only charms?
Yet tell her — better to be free
  Than vanquish all the world in arms.
Her frantic city's flashing beats
  But fire, to blast, the hopes of men.
Why change the titles of your streets?
  You fools, you'll want them all again.
    Hands all round!
  God the tyrant's cause confound!
To France, the wiser France, we drink,
    my friends,
  And the great name of England, round
    and round.

Gigantic daughter of the West,
  We drink to thee across the flood,
We know thee and we love thee best,
  For art thou not of British blood?
Should war's mad blast again be blown,
  Permit not thou the tyrant powers
To fight thy mother here alone,
  But let thy broadsides roar with ours.
    Hands all round!
  God the tyrant's cause confound!
To our dear kinsmen of the West, my
    friends,
  And the great name of England, round
    and round.

O rise, our strong Atlantic sons,
  When war against our freedom springs!
O speak to Europe through your guns!
  They *can* be understood by kings.
You must not mix our Queen with those
  That wish to keep their people fools;
Our freedom's foemen are her foes,
  She comprehends the race she rules.
    Hands all round!
  God the tyrant's cause confound!
To our dear kinsman in the West, my friends,
  And the great name of England, round and round.

THE WAR.*

There is a sound of thunder afar,
  Storm in the South that darkens the day,
Storm of battle and thunder of war,
  Well, if it do not roll our way.
    Form! form! Riflemen form!
    Ready, be ready to meet the storm!
    Riflemen, riflemen, riflemen form!

Be not deaf to the sound that warns!
Be not gull'd by a despot's plea!
Are figs of thistles, or grapes of thorns?
How should a despot set men free?
    Form! form! Riflemen form!
    Ready, be ready to meet the storm!
    Riflemen, riflemen, riflemen form!

Let your Reforms for a moment go,
Look to your butts and take good aims.
Better a rotten borough or so,
  Than a rotten fleet or a city in flames!
    Form! form! Riflemen form!
    Ready, be ready to meet the storm!
    Riflemen, riflemen, riflemen form!

Form, be ready to do or die!
  Form in Freedom's name and the Queen's!
True, that we have a faithful ally,
  But only the Devil knows what he means.
    Form! form! Riflemen form!
    Ready, be ready to meet the storm!
    Riflemen, riflemen, riflemen form!
                                    T.

* London Times, May 9, 1859.

ON A SPITEFUL LETTER.*

Here, it is here—the close of the year,
  And with it a spiteful letter.
My fame in song has done him much wrong,
  For himself has done much better.

O foolish bard, is your lot so hard,
  If men neglect your pages?
I think not much of yours or of mine:
  I hear the roll of the ages.

This fallen leaf, is n't fame as brief?
  My rhymes may have been the stronger.
Yet hate me not, but abide your lot;
  I last but a moment longer.

O faded leaf, is n't fame as brief?
  What room is here for a hater?
Yet the yellow leaf hates the greener leaf,
  For it hangs one moment later.

Greater than I—is n't that your cry?
  And I shall live to see it.
Well, if it be so, so it is, you know;
  And if it be so—so be it!

O summer leaf, is n't life as brief?
  But this is the time of hollies.
And my heart, my heart is an evergreen:
  I hate the spites and the follies.

1865 - 1866.†

I stood on a tower in the wet,
And New Year and Old Year met,
And winds were roaring and blowing;
And I said, "O years that meet in tears,
Have ye aught that is worth the knowing?
Science enough and exploring,
Wanderers coming and going,
Matter enough for deploring,
But aught that is worth the knowing?"
Seas at my feet were flowing,
Waves on the shingle pouring,
Old Year roaring and blowing,
And New Year blowing and roaring.

* Once a Week, January 4, 1868.
† Good Words, March, 1868.

THE WINDOW

OR, THE SONGS OF THE WRENS.

WORDS WRITTEN FOR MUSIC.

THE MUSIC BY ARTHUR SULLIVAN.

FOUR years ago Mr. Sullivan requested me to write a little song-cycle, German fashion, for him to exercise his art upon. He had been very successful in setting such old songs as "Orpheus with his lute," and I drest up for him, partly in the old style, a puppet whose almost only merit is, perhaps, that it can dance to Mr. Sullivan's instrument. I am sorry that my four-year-old puppet should have to dance at all in the dark shadow of these days; but the music is now completed, and I am bound by my promise.
A. TENNYSON.

December, 1870.

I.
ON THE HILL.

THE lights and shadows fly!
Yonder it brightens and darkens down
    on the plain.
A jewel, a jewel dear to a lover's eye!
O is it the brook, or a pool, or her win-
    dow-pane,
    When the winds are up in the morn-
      ing?

Clouds that are racing above,
And winds and lights and shadows that
    cannot be still,
All running on one way to the home
    of my love,
You are all running on, and I stand on
    the slope of the hill,
    And the winds are up in the morning!

Follow, follow the chase!
And my thoughts are as quick and as
    quick, ever on, on, on.
O lights, are you flying over her sweet
    little face?
And my heart is there before you are
    come and gone,
    When the winds are up in the morn-
      ing!

Follow them down the slope!
And I follow them down to the window-
    pane of my dear,
And it brightens and darkens and
    brightens like my hope,
And it darkens and brightens and dark-
    ens like my fear,
    And the winds are up in the morn-
      ing.

II.
AT THE WINDOW.

VINE, vine and eglantine,
Clasp her window, trail and twine!
Rose, rose and clematis,
Trail and twine and clasp and kiss,
Kiss, kiss; and make her a bower
All of flowers, and drop me a flower,
    Drop me a flower.

Vine, vine and eglantine,
Cannot a flower, a flower, be mine?
Rose, rose and clematis,
Drop me a flower, a flower, to kiss,
Kiss, kiss — And out of her bower
All of flowers, a flower, a flower,
    Dropt, a flower.

III.
GONE!

GONE!
Gone till the end of the year,
Gone, and the light gone with her and
    left me in shadow here!

Gone — flitted away,
Taken the stars from the night and the
    sun from the day!
Gone, and a cloud in my heart, and a
    storm in the air!
Flown to the east or the west, flitted I
    know not where!
Down in the south is a flash and a groan:
    she is there! she is there!

IV.
WINTER.

THE frost is here,
And fuel is dear,
And woods are sear,
And fires burn clear,
And frost is here
And has bitten the heel of the going year.

Bite, frost, bite!
You roll up away from the light
The blue woodlouse, and the plump dor-
    mouse,
And the bees are still'd, and the flies are
    kill'd,
And you bite far into the heart of the
    house,
But not into mine.

Bite, frost, bite!
The woods are all the searer,
The fuel is all the dearer,
The fires are all the clearer,
My spring is all the nearer,
You have bitten into the heart of the
    earth,
But not into mine.

V.
SPRING.

BIRDS' love and birds' song
    Flying here and there,
Birds' song and birds' love,
    And you with gold for hair!
Birds' song and birds' love,
    Passing with the weather,
Men's song and men's love,
    To love once and forever.

Men's love and birds' love,
    And women's love and men's!
And you my wren with a crown of gold,
    You my Queen of the wrens!

You the Queen of the wrens —
    We'll be birds of a feather,
I'll be King of the Queen of the wrens,
    And all in a nest together.

VI.
THE LETTER.

WHERE is another sweet as my sweet,
    Fine of the fine, and shy of the shy?
Fine little hands, fine little feet —
    Dewy blue eye.
Shall I write to her? shall I go?
    Ask her to marry me by and by?
Somebody said that she'd say no;
    Somebody knows that she'll say ay!

Ay or no, if ask'd to her face?
    Ay or no, from shy of the shy?
Go, little letter, apace, apace,
    Fly!
Fly to the light in the valley below —
    Tell my wish to her dewy blue eye:
Somebody said that she'd say no;
    Somebody knows that she'll say ay!

VII.
NO ANSWER.

THE mist and the rain, the mist and the
    rain!
Is it ay or no? is it ay or no?
And never a glimpse of her window-pane!
    And I may die but the grass will grow,
And the grass will grow when I am gone,
And the wet west wind and the world
    will go on.

Ay is the song of the wedded spheres,
    No is trouble and cloud and storm,
Ay is life for a hundred years,
    No will push me down to the worm,
And when I am there and dead and gone,
The wet west wind and the world will
    go on.

The wind and the wet, the wind and the
    wet!
Wet west wind, how you blow, you
    blow!
And never a line from my lady yet!
    Is it ay or no? is it ay or no?
Blow then, blow, and when I am gone,
The wet west wind and the world may
    go on.

VIII.
NO ANSWER.

Winds are loud and you are dumb :
Take my love, for love will come,.
  Love will come but once a life.
Winds are loud and winds will pass !
Spring is here with leaf and grass :
  Take my love and be my wife.
After-loves of maids and men
Are but dainties drest again :
Love me now, you 'll love me then :
  Love can love but once a life.

IX.
THE ANSWER.

Two little hands that meet,
Claspt on her seal, my sweet !
Must I take you and break you,
Two little hands that meet ?
I must take you, and break you,
And loving hands must part —
Take, take — break, break —
Break — you may break my heart.
  Faint heart never won —
  Break, break, and all 's done.

IX[b].
AY !

Be merry, all birds, to-day,
  Be merry on earth as you never were
    merry before,
Be merry in heaven, O larks, and far
    away,
  And merry forever and ever, and one
    day more.
      Why ?
  For it 's easy to find a rhyme.

Look, look, how he flits,
  The fire-crown'd king of the wrens,
    from out of the pine !
Look how they tumble the blossom, the
    mad little tits !
"Cuck-oo ! Cuck-oo ! " was ever a
    May so fine ?
      Why ?
  For it 's easy to find a rhyme.

O merry the linnet and dove,
  And swallow and sparrow and throstle,
    and have your desire !
O merry my heart, you have gotten the
    wings of love,
  And flit like the king of the wrens
    with a crown of fire.
      Why ?
  For it 's ay ay ay, ay ay.

X.
WHEN ?

Sun comes, moon comes,
  Time slips away.
Sun sets, moon sets,
  Love, fix a day.

"A year hence, a year hence."
"We shall both be gray."
"A month hence, a month hence."
"Far, far away."

"A week hence, a week hence."
"Ah, the long delay."
"Wait a little, wait a little,
  You shall fix a day."

"To-morrow, love, to-morrow,
  And that 's an age away."
Blaze upon her window, sun,
  And honor all the day.

XI.
MARRIAGE MORNING.

Light, so low upon earth,
  You send a flash to the sun.
Here is the golden close of love,
  All my wooing is done.
O the woods and the meadows,
  Woods where we hid from the wet,
Stiles where we stay'd to be kind,
  Meadows in which we met !
Light, so low in the vale,
  You flash and lighten afar :
For this is the golden morning of love,
  And you are his morning star.
Flash, I am coming, I come,
  By meadow and stile and wood :
O lighten into my eyes and my heart,
  Into my heart and my blood !
Heart, are you great enough
  For a love that never tires ?
O heart, are you great enough for love ?
  I have heard of thorns and briers.
Over the thorns and briers,
  Over the meadows and stiles,
Over the world to the end of it
  Flash for a million miles.

THE LAST TOURNAMENT.

Dagonet, the fool, whom Gawain in his moods
Had made mock-knight of Arthur's Table Round,
At Camelot, high above the yellowing woods,
Danced like a wither'd leaf before the Hall.
And toward him from the Hall, with harp in hand,
And from the crown thereof a carcanet
Of ruby swaying to and fro, the prize
Of Tristram in the jousts of yesterday,
Came Tristram, saying, "Why skip ye so, Sir Fool?"

For Arthur and Sir Lancelot riding once
Far down beneath a winding wall of rock
Heard a child wail. A stump of oak half-dead,
From roots like some black coil of carven snakes
Clutch'd at the crag, and started thro' mid-air
Bearing an eagle's nest: and thro' the tree
Rush'd ever a rainy wind, and thro' the wind
Pierced ever a child's cry: and crag and tree
Scaling, Sir Lancelot from the perilous nest,
This ruby necklace thrice around her neck,
And all unscarr'd from beak or talon, brought
A maiden babe; which Arthur pitying took,
Then gave it to his Queen to rear: the Queen
But coldly acquiescing, in her white arms
Received, and after loved it tenderly,
And named it Nestling; so forgot herself
A moment, and her cares; till that young life
Being smitten in mid-heaven with mortal cold
Past from her; and in time the carcanet
Vext her with plaintive memories of the child:
So she, delivering it to Arthur, said,
"Take thou the jewels of this dead innocence,
And make them, an thou wilt, a tourney-prize."

To whom the King, "Peace to thine eagle-borne
Dead nestling, and this honor after death,
Following thy will! but, O my Queen, I muse
Why ye not wear on arm, or neck, or zone,
Those diamonds that I rescued from the tarn,
And Lancelot won, methought, for thee to wear."

"Would rather ye had let them fall," she cried,
"Plunge and be lost — ill-fated as they were,
A bitterness to me! — ye look amazed,
Not knowing they were lost as soon as given —
Slid from my hands, when I was leaning out
Above the river — that unhappy child
Past in her barge: but rosier luck will go
With these rich jewels, seeing that they came
Not from the skeleton of a brother-slayer,
But the sweet body of a maiden babe.
Perchance — who knows? — the purest of thy knights
May win them for the purest of my maids."

She ended, and the cry of a great jousts
With trumpet-blowings ran on all the ways
From Camelot in among the faded fields
To furthest towers; and everywhere the knights
Arm'd for a day of glory before the King.

But on the hither side of that loud morn
Into the hall stagger'd, his visage ribb'd
From ear to ear with dogwhip-weals, his nose
Bridge-broken, one eye out, and one hand off,
And one with shatter'd fingers dangling lame,
A churl, to whom indignantly the King,
"My churl, for whom Christ died, what evil beast

Hath drawn his claws athwart thy face?
 or fiend?
Man was it who marr'd Heaven's image
 in thee thus?"

Then, sputtering thro' the hedge of
 splinter'd teeth,
Yet strangers to the tongue, and with
 blunt stump
Pitch-blacken'd sawing the air, said the
 maim'd churl,
 "He took them and he drave them to
 his tower —
Some hold he was a table-knight of
 thine —
A hundred goodly ones — the Red Knight
 he —
Lord, I was tending swine, and the Red
 Knight
Brake in upon me and drave them to his
 tower;
And when I call'd upon thy name as one
That doest right by gentle and by churl,
Maim'd me and maul'd, and would out-
 right have slain,
Save that he sware me to a message,
 saying —
'Tell thou the King and all his liars,
 that I
Have founded my Round Table in the
 North,
And whatsoever his own knights have
 sworn
My knights have sworn the counter to
 it — and say
My tower is full of harlots, like his court,
But mine are worthier, seeing they profess
To be none other than themselves — and
 say
My knights are all adulterers like his own,
But mine are truer, seeing they profess
To be none other; and say his hour is
 come,
The heathen are upon him, his long lance
Broken, and his Excalibur a straw.'"

Then Arthur turn'd to Kay the senes-
 chal,
"Take thou my churl, and tend him
 curiously
Like a king's heir, till all his hurts be
 whole.
The heathen — but that ever-climbing
 wave,
Hurl'd back again so often in empty foam,
Hath lain for years at rest — and rene-
 gades,

Thieves, bandits, leavings of confusion,
 whom
The wholesome realm is purged of other-
 where, —
Friends, thro' your manhood and your
 fealty, — now
Make their last head like Satan in the
 North.
My younger knights, new-made, in whom
 your flower
Waits to be solid fruit of golden deeds,
Move with me toward their quelling,
 which achieved,
The loneliest ways are safe from shore to
 shore.
But thou, Sir Lancelot, sitting in my place
Enchair'd to-morrow, arbitrate the field;
For wherefore shouldst thou care to
 mingle with it,
Only to yield my Queen her own again?
Speak, Lancelot, thou art silent: is it
 well?"

Thereto Sir Lancelot answer'd, "It is
 well:
Yet better if the King abide, and leave
The leading of his younger knights to me.
Else, for the King has will'd it, it is well."

Then Arthur rose and Lancelot follow'd
 him,
And while they stood without the doors,
 the King
Turn'd to him saying, "Is it then so
 well?
Or mine the blame that oft I seem as he
Of whom was written, 'a sound is in his
 ears' —
The foot that loiters, bidden go, — the
 glance
That only seems half-loyal to command, —
A manner somewhat fall'n from rever-
 ence —
Or have I dream'd the bearing of our
 knights
Tells of a manhood ever less and lower?
Or whence the fear lest this my realm,
 uprear'd,
By noble deeds at one with noble vows,
From flat confusion and brute violences,
Reel back into the beast, and be no
 more?"

He spoke, and taking all his younger
 knights,
Down the slope city rode, and sharply
 turn'd

North by the gate. In her high bower the Queen,
Working a tapestry, lifted up her head,
Watch'd her lord pass, and knew not that she sigh'd.
Then ran across her memory the strange rhyme
Of bygone Merlin, "Where is he who knows?
From the great deep to the great deep he goes."

But when the morning of a tournament,
By these in earnest, those in mockery, call'd
The Tournament of the Dead Innocence,
Brake with a wet wind blowing, Lancelot,
Round whose sick head all night, like birds of prey,
The words of Arthur flying shriek'd, arose,
And down a streetway hung with folds of pure
White samite, and by fountains running wine,
Where children sat in white with cups of gold,
Moved to the lists, and there, with slow sad steps
Ascending, fill'd his double-dragon'd chair.

He glanced and saw the stately galleries,
Dame, damsel, each thro' worship of their Queen
White-robed in honor of the stainless child,
And some with scatter'd jewels, like a bank
Of maiden snow mingled with sparks of fire.
He lookt but once, and veil'd his eyes again.

The sudden trumpet sounded as in a dream
To ears but half-awaked, then one low roll
Of Autumn thunder, and the jousts began:
And ever the wind blew, and yellowing leaf
And gloom and gleam, and shower and shorn plume
Went down it. Sighing wearledly, as one
Who sits and gazes on a faded fire,
When all the goodlier guests are past away,

Sat their great umpire, looking o'er the lists.
He saw the laws that ruled the tournament
Broken, but spake not; once, a knight cast down
Before his throne of arbitration cursed
The dead babe and the follies of the King;
And once the laces of a helmet crack'd,
And show'd him, like a vermin in its hole,
Modred, a narrow face: anon he heard
The voice that billow'd round the barriers roar
An ocean-sounding welcome to one knight,
But newly-enter'd, taller than the rest,
And armor'd all in forest green, whereon
There tript a hundred tiny silver deer,
And wearing but a holly-spray for crest,
With ever-scattering berries, and on shield
A spear, a harp, a bugle — Tristram —
late
From overseas in Brittany return'd,
And marriage with a princess of that realm,
Isolt the White — Sir Tristram of the Woods —
Whom Lancelot knew, had held sometime with pain
His own against him, and now yearn'd to shake
The burthen off his heart in one full shock
With Tristram ev'n to death: his strong hands gript
And dinted the gilt dragons right and left,
Until he groan'd for wrath — so many of those,
That ware their ladies' colors on the casque,
Drew from before Sir Tristram to the bounds,
And there with gibes and flickering mockeries
Stood, while he mutter'd, "Craven crests! O shame!
What faith have these in whom they sware to love?
The glory of our Round Table is no more."

So Tristram won, and Lancelot gave, the gems,
Not speaking other word than "Hast thou won?
Art thou the purest, brother? See, the hand
Wherewith thou takest this is red!" to whom

Tristram, half plagued by Lancelot's
    languorous mood,
Made answer, "Ay, but wherefore toss
    me this
Like a dry bone cast to some hungry
    hound ?
Let be thy fair Queen's fantasy. Strength
    of heart
And might of limb, but mainly use and
    skill,
Are winners in this pastime of our King.
My hand — belike the lance hath dript
    upon it —
No blood of mine, I trow; but O chief
    knight,
Right arm of Arthur in the battlefield,
Great brother, thou nor I have made the
    world ;
Be happy in thy fair Queen as I in mine."

And Tristram round the gallery made
    his horse
Caracole ; then bow'd his homage, bluntly
    saying,
"Fair damsels, each to him who worships
    each
Sole Queen of Beauty and of love, behold
This day my Queen of Beauty is not
    here."
Then most of these were mute, some
    anger'd, one
Murmuring "All courtesy is dead," and
    one,
"The glory of our Round Table is no
    more."

Then fell thick rain, plume droopt
    and mantle clung,
And pettish cries awoke, and the wan day
Went glooming down in wet and weari-
    ness :
But under her black brows a swarthy
    dame
Laught shrilly, crying "Praise the patient
    saints,
Our one white day of Innocence hath
    past,
Tho' somewhat draggled at the skirt.
    So be it.
The snowdrop only, flow'ring thro' the
    year,
Would make the world as blank as
    wintertide.
Come — let us comfort their sad eyes,
    our Queen's
And Lancelot's, at this night's solemnity
With all the kindlier colors of the field."

So dame and damsel glitter'd at the
    feast
Variously gay : for he that tells the tale
Liken'd them, saying "as when an hour
    of cold
Falls on the mountain in midsummer
    snows,
And all the purple slopes of mountain
    flowers
Pass under white, till the warm hour
    returns
With veer of wind, and all are flowers
    again " ;
So dame and damsel cast the simple white,
And glowing in all colors, the live grass,
Rose-campion, bluebell, kingcup, poppy,
    glanced
About the revels, and with mirth so loud
Beyond all use, that, half-amazed, the
    Queen,
And wroth at Tristram and the lawless
    jousts,
Brake up their sports, then slowly to her
    bower
Parted, and in her bosom pain was lord.

And little Dagonet on the morrow
    morn,
High over all the yellowing Autumn-tide,
Danced like a wither'd leaf before the
    hall.
Then Tristram saying, "Why skip ye
    so, Sir Fool ?"
Wheel'd round on either heel, Dagonet
    replied,
"Belike for lack of wiser company ;
Or being fool, and seeing too much wit
Makes the world rotten, why, belike I
    skip
To know myself the wisest knight of all."
"Ay, fool," said Tristram, "but 't is
    eating dry
To dance without a catch, a roundelay
To dance to." Then he twangled on
    his harp,
And while he twangled little Dagonet
    stood,
Quiet as any water-sodden log
Stay'd in the wandering warble of a
    brook ;
But when the twangling ended, skipt
    again ;
Then being ask'd, "Why skipt ye not,
    Sir Fool ?"
Made answer, "I had liefer twenty years
Skip to the broken music of my brains
Than any broken music ye can make."

Then Tristram, waiting for the quip to come,
"Good now, what music have I broken, fool?"
And little Dagonet, skipping, "Arthur, the king's;
For when thou playest that air with Queen Isolt,
Thou makest broken music with thy bride,
Her daintier namesake down in Brittany —
And so thou breakest Arthur's music too."
"Save for that broken music in thy brains,
Sir Fool," said Tristram, "I would break thy head.
Fool, I came late, the heathen wars were o'er,
The life had flown, we sware but by the shell —
I am but a fool to reason with a fool.
Come, thou art crabb'd and sour: but lean me down,
Sir Dagonet, one of thy long asses' ears,
And hearken if my music be not true.

"'Free love — free field — we love but while we may:
The woods are hush'd, their music is no more:
The leaf is dead, the yearning past away:
New leaf, new life — the days of frost are o'er:
New life new love to suit the newer day:
New loves are sweet as those that went before:
Free love — free field — we love but while we may.'

"Ye might have moved slow-measure to my tune,
Not stood stockstill. I made it in the woods,
And found it ring as true as tested gold."

But Dagonet with one foot poised in his hand,
"Friend, did ye mark that fountain yesterday
Made to run wine? — but this had run itself
All out like a long life to a sour end —
And them that round it sat with golden cups
To hand the wine to whomsoever came —
The twelve small damsels white as Innocence,
In honor of poor Innocence the babe,
Who left the gems which Innocence the Queen
Lent to the King, and Innocence the King
Gave for a prize — and one of those white slips
Handed her cup and piped, the pretty one,
'Drink, drink, Sir Fool,' and thereupon I drank,
Spat — pish — the cup was gold, the draught was mud."

And Tristram, "Was it muddier than thy gibes?
Is all the laughter gone dead out of thee? —
Not marking how the knighthood mock thee, fool —
'Fear God: honor the king — his one true knight —
Sole follower of the vows'— for here be they
Who knew thee swine enow before I came,
Smuttier than blasted grain: but when the King
Had made thee fool, thy vanity so shot up
It frighted all free fool from out thy heart;
Which left thee less than fool, and less than swine,
A naked aught — yet swine I hold thee still,
For I have flung thee pearls, and find thee swine."

And little Dagonet mincing with his feet,
"Knight, an ye fling those rubies round my neck
In lieu of hers, I'll hold thou hast some touch
Of music, since I care not for thy pearls.
Swine? I have wallow'd, I have wash'd — the world
Is flesh and shadow — I have had my day.
The dirty nurse, Experience, in her kind
Hath foul'd me — an I wallow'd, then I wash'd —
I have had my day and my philosophies —
And thank the Lord I am King Arthur's fool.
Swine, say ye? swine, goats, asses, rams, and geese
Troop'd round a Paynim harper once, who thrumm'd
On such a wire as musically as thou
Some such fine song — but never a king's fool."

And Tristram, "Then were swine,
  goats, asses, geese
The wiser fools, seeing thy Paynim bard
Had such a mastery of his mystery
That he could harp his wife up out of Hell."

Then Dagonet, turning on the ball of
  his foot,
"And whither harp'st thou thine? down!
  and thyself
Down! and two more: a helpful harper
  thou,
That harpest downward! Dost thou
  know the star
We call the harp of Arthur up in heav-
  en?"

And Tristram, "Ay, Sir Fool, for
  when our King
Was victor wellnigh day by day, the
  knights,
Glorying in each new glory, set his name
High on all hills, and in the signs of
  heaven."

And Dagonet answer'd, "Ay, and
  when the land
Was freed, and the Queen false, ye set
  yourself
To babble about him, all to show your
  wit—
And whether he were king by courtesy,
Or king by right—and so went harping
  down
The black king's highway, got so far,
  and grew
So witty, that ye play'd at ducks and
  drakes
With Arthur's vows on the great lake of
  fire.
Tuwhoo! do ye see it? do ye see the
  star?"
"Nay, fool," said Tristram, "not in
  open day."
And Dagonet, "Nay, nor will: I see it
  and hear.
It makes a silent music up in heaven,
And I, and Arthur and the angels hear,
And then we skip." "Lo, fool," he
  said, "ye talk
Fool's treason: is the king thy brother
  fool?"
Then little Dagonet clapt his hands and
  shrill'd,
"Ay, ay, my brother fool, the king
  of fools!
Conceits himself as God that he can make
Figs out of thistles, silk from bristles,
  milk
From burning spurge, honey from hornet-
  combs,
And men from beasts. Long live the
  king of fools!"

And down the city Dagonet danced
  away.
But thro' the slowly-mellowing avenues
And solitary passes of the wood
Rode Tristram toward Lyonesse and the
  west.
Before him fled the face of Queen Isolt
With ruby-circled neck, but evermore
Past, as a rustle or twitter in the wood
Made dull his inner, keen his outer eye
For all that walk'd, or crept, or perched,
  or flew.
Anon the face, as, when a gust hath blown,
Unruffling waters re-collect the shape
Of one that in them sees himself, return'd;
But at the slot or fewmets of a deer,
Or ov'n a fall'n feather, vanish'd again.

So on for all that day from lawn to lawn
Thro' many a league-long bower he rode.
  At length
A lodge of intertwisted beechen-boughs
Furze-cramm'd, and bracken-rooft, the
  which himself
Built for a summer day with Queen Isolt
Against a shower, dark in the golden
  grove
Appearing, sent his fancy back to where
She lived a moon in that low lodge with
  him:
Till Mark her lord had past, the Cornish
  king,
With six or seven, when Tristram was
  away,
And snatch'd her thence; yet dreading
  worse than shame
Her warrior Tristram, spake not any
  word,
But bode his hour, devising wretched-
  ness.

And now that desert lodge to Tristram
  lookt
So sweet, that, halting, in he past, and
  sank
Down on a drift of foliage random-blown;
But could not rest for musing how to
  smooth
And sleek his marriage over to the Queen.
Perchance in lone Tintagil far from all

The tonguesters of the court she had not heard.
But then what folly had sent him overseas
After she left him lonely here? a name?
Was it the name of one in Brittany,
Isolt, the daughter of the King? "Isolt
Of the white hands" they call'd her: the sweet name
Allured him first, and then the maid herself,
Who served him well with those white hands of hers,
And loved him well, until himself had thought
He loved her also, wedded easily,
But left her all as easily, and return'd.
The black-blue Irish hair and Irish eyes
Had drawn him home — what marvel? then he laid
His brows upon the drifted leaf and dream'd.

He seem'd to pace the strand of Brittany
Between Isolt of Britain and his bride,
And show'd them both the ruby-chain, and both
Began to struggle for it, till his Queen
Graspt it so hard, that all her hand was red.
Then cried the Breton, "Look, her hand is red!
These be no rubies, this is frozen blood,
And melts within her hand — her hand is hot
With ill desires, but this I gave thee, look,
Is all as cool and white as any flower."
Follow'd a rush of eagle's wings and then
A whimpering of the spirit of the child,
Because the twain had spoil'd her carcanet.

He dream'd; but Arthur with a hundred spears
Rode far, till o'er the illimitable reed,
And many a glancing plash and sallowy isle,
The wide-wing'd sunset of the misty marsh
Glared on a huge machicolated tower
That stood with open doors, whereout was roll'd
A roar of riot, as from men secure
Amid their marshes, ruffians at their ease
Among their harlot-brides, an evil song.
"Lo there," said one of Arthur's youth, for there,
High on a grim dead tree before the tower,
A goodly brother of The Table Round

Swung by the neck: and on the boughs a shield
Showing a shower of blood in a field noir,
And therebeside a horn, inflamed the knights
At that dishonor done the gilded spur,
Till each would clash the shield, and blow the horn.
But Arthur waved them back: alone he rode.
Then at the dry harsh roar of the great horn,
That sent the face of all the marsh aloft
An ever upward-rushing storm and cloud
Of shriek and plume, the Red Knight heard, and all,
Even to tipmost lance and topmost helm,
In blood-red armor sallying, howl'd to the King,
"The teeth of Hell flay bare and gnash thee flat! —
Lo! art thou not that eunuch-hearted King
Who fain had clipt free manhood from the world —
The woman-worshipper? Yea, God's curse, and I!
Slain was the brother of my paramour
By a knight of thine, and I that heard her whine
And snivel, being eunuch-hearted too,
Sware by the scorpion-worm that twists in hell,
And stings itself to everlasting death,
To hang whatever knight of thine I fought
And tumbled. Art thou King? — Look to thy life!"

He ended: Arthur knew the voice; the face
Wellnigh was helmet-hidden, and the name
Went wandering somewhere darkling in his mind.
And Arthur deign'd not use of word or sword,
But let the drunkard, as he stretch'd from horse
To strike him, overbalancing his bulk,
Down from the causeway heavily to the swamp
Fall, as the crest of some slow-arching wave
Heard in dead night along that table-shore
Drops flat, and after the great waters break

Whitening for half a league, and thin
  themselves
Far over sands marbled with moon and
  cloud,
From less and less to nothing; thus he fell
Head-heavy, while the knights, who
  watch'd him, roar'd
And shouted and leapt down upon the
  fall'n ;
There trampled out his face from being
  known,
And sank his head in mire, and slimed
  themselves :
Nor heard the King for their own cries,
  but sprang
Thro' open doors, and swording right
  and left
Men, women, on their sodden faces, hurl'd
The tables over and the wines, and slew
Till all the rafters rang with woman-yells,
And all the pavement stream'd with
  massacre :
Then, yell with yell echoing, they fired
  the tower,
Which half that autumn night, like the
  live North,
Red-pulsing up thro' Alioth and Alcor,
Made all above it, and a hundred meres
About it, as the water Moab saw
Come round by the East, and out beyond
  them flush'd
The long low dune, and lazy-plunging sea.

  So all the ways were safe from shore
    to shore,
But in the heart of Arthur pain was lord.
  Then out of Tristram waking the red
    dream
Fled with a shout, and that low lodge
  return'd,
Mid-forest, and the wind among the
  boughs.
He whistled his good warhorse left to graze
Among the forest greens, vaulted upon
  him,
And rode beneath an ever-showering leaf,
Till one lone woman, weeping near a cross,
Stay'd him, " Why weep ye ? " " Lord,"
  she said, " my man
Hath left me or is dead " ; whereon he
  thought —
" What an she hate me now ? I would
  not this.
What an she love me still ? I would not
  that.
I know not what I would " — but said
  to her, —

" Yet weep not thou, lest, if thy mate
  return,
He find thy favor changed and love thee
  not " —
Then pressing day by day thro' Lyonesse
Last in a roky hollow, belling, heard
The hounds of Mark, and felt the goodly
  hounds
Yelp at his heart, but, turning, past and
  gain'd
Tintagil, half in sea, and high on land,
A crown of towers.

      Down in a casement sat,
A low sea-sunset glorying round her hair
And glossy-throated grace, Isolt the
  Queen.
And when she heard the feet of Tristram
  grind
The spiring stone that scaled about her
  tower,
Flush'd, started, met him at the doors,
  and there
Belted his body with her white embrace,
Crying aloud, " Not Mark — not Mark,
  my soul !
The footstep flutter'd me at first : not he :
Catlike thro' his own castle steals my
  Mark,
But warrior-wise thou stridest through his
  halls
Who hates thee, as I him — ev'n to the
  death.
My soul, I felt my hatred for my Mark
Quicken within me, and knew that thou
  wert nigh."
To whom Sir Tristram smiling, " I am
  here.
Let be thy Mark, seeing he is not thine."

  And drawing somewhat backward she
    replied,
" Can he be wrong'd who is not ev'n his
  own,
But save for dread of thee had beaten
  me,
Scratch'd, bitten, blinded, marr'd me
  somehow — Mark ?
What rights are his that dare not strike
  for them ?
Not lift a hand — not, tho' he found me
  thus !
But hearken, have ye met him ? hence he
  went
To-day for three days' hunting — as he
  said —
And so returns belike within an hour.

THE LAST TOURNAMENT.   437

Mark's way, my soul! — but eat not thou
    with him,
Because he hates thee even more than fears;
Nor drink: and when thou passest any
    wood
Close visor, lest an arrow from the bush
Should leave me all alone with Mark and
    hell.
My God, the measure of my hate for Mark
Is as the measure of my love for thee."

    So, pluck'd one way by hate and one
      by love,
Drain'd of her force, again she sat, and
    spake
To Tristram, as he knelt before her, saying,
"O hunter, and O blower of the horn,
Harper, and thou hast been a rover too,
For, ere I mated with my shambling king,
Ye twain had fallen out about the bride
Of one — his name is out of me — the prize,
If prize she were — (what marvel — she
    could see) —
Thine, friend; and ever since my craven
    seeks
To wreck thee villanously: but, O Sir
    Knight,
What dame or damsel have ye kneeled
    to last?"

    And Tristram, "Last to my Queen
      Paramount,
Here now to my Queen Paramount of love,
And loveliness, ay, lovelier than when
    first
Her light feet fell on our rough Lyonesse,
Sailing from Ireland."

        Softly laugh'd Isolt,
"Flatter me not, for hath not our great
    Queen
My dole of beauty trebled?" and he said,
"Her beauty is her beauty, and thine
    thine,
And thine is more to me — soft, gracious,
    kind —
Save when thy Mark is kindled on thy lips
Most gracious; but she, haughty, ev'n to
    him,
Lancelot; for I have seen him wan enow
To make one doubt if ever the great
    Queen
Have yielded him her love."

        To whom Isolt,
"Ah then, false hunter and false harper,
    thou

Who brakest thro' the scruple of my
    bond,
Calling me thy white hind, and saying to
    me
That Guinevere had sinned against the
    highest,
And I — misyoked with such a want of
    man —
That I could hardly sin against the low-
    est."

He answered, "O my soul, be com-
    forted!
If this be sweet, to sin in leading-strings,
If here be comfort, and if ours be sin,
Crown'd warrant had we for the crowning
    sin
That made us happy: but how ye greet
    me — fear
And fault and doubt — no word of that
    fond tale —
Thy deep heart-yearnings, thy sweet
    memories
Of Tristram in that year he was away."

    And, saddening on the sudden, spake
    Isolt,
"I had forgotten all in my strong joy
To see thee — yearnings? — ay! for, hour
    by hour,
Here in the never-ended afternoon,
O sweeter than all memories of thee,
Deeper than any yearnings after thee
Seem'd those far-rolling, westward-smil-
    ing seas,
Watch'd from this tower. Isolt of Britain
    dash'd
Before Isolt of Brittany on the strand,
Would that have chill'd her bride-kiss?
Wedded her?
Fought in her father's battles? wounded
    there?
The King was all fulfill'd with grateful-
    ness,
And she, my namesake of the hands,
    that heal'd
Thy hurt and heart with unguent and
    caress —
Well — can I wish her any huger wrong
Than having known thee? her too hast
    thou left
To pine and waste in those sweet memo-
    ries?
O were I not my Mark's, by whom all
    men
Are noble, I should hate thee more than
    love."

And Tristram, fondling her light hands, replied,
"Grace, Queen, for being loved: she loved me well.
Did I love her? the name at least I loved.
Isolt?—I fought his battles, for Isolt!
The night was dark; the true star set.
Isolt!
The name was ruler of the dark——Isolt?
Care not for her! patient, and prayerful, meek,
Pale-blooded, she will yield herself to God."

And Isolt answer'd, "Yea, and why not I?
Mine is the larger need, who am not meek,
Pale-blooded, prayerful. Let me tell thee now.
Here one black, mute midsummer night I sat
Lonely, but musing on thee, wondering where,
Murmuring a light song I had heard thee sing,
And once or twice I spake thy name aloud.
Then flash'd a levin-brand; and near me stood,
In fuming sulphur blue and green, a fiend—
Mark's way to steal behind one in the dark—
For there was Mark: 'He has wedded her,' he said,
Not said, but hissed it: then this crown of towers
So shook to such a roar of all the sky,
That here in utter dark I swoon'd away,
And woke again in utter dark, and cried,
'I will flee hence and give myself to God'—
And thou wert lying in thy new leman's arms."

Then Tristram, ever dallying with her hand,
"May God be with thee, sweet, when old and gray,
And past desire!" a saying that anger'd her.
"'May God be with thee, sweet, when thou art old,
And sweet no more to me!' I need Him now.
For when had Lancelot utter'd aught so gross
Ev'n to the swineherd's malkin in the mast?
The greater man, the greater courtesy.
But thou, thro' ever harrying thy wild beasts—
Save that to touch a harp, tilt with a lance
Becomes thee well—art grown wild beast thyself.
How darest thou, if lover, push me even
In fancy from thy side, and set me far
In the gray distance, half a life away,
Her to be loved no more? Unsay it, unswear!
Flatter me rather, seeing me so weak,
Broken with Mark and hate and solitude,
Thy marriage and mine own, that I should suck
Lies like sweet wines: lie to me: I believe.
Will ye not lie? not swear, as there ye kneel,
And solemnly as when ye sware to him,
The man of men, our King—My God, the power
Was once in vows when men believed the King!
They lied not then, who sware, and thro' their vows
The King prevailing made his realm:—
I say,
Swear to me thou wilt love me ev'n when old,
Gray-haired, and past desire, and in despair."

Then Tristram, pacing moodily up and down,
"Vows! did ye keep the vow ye made to Mark
More than I mine? Lied, say ye? Nay, but learnt,
The vow that binds too strictly snaps itself—
My knighthood taught me this—ay, being snapt—
We run more counter to the soul thereof
Than had we never sworn. I swear no more.
I swore to the great King, and am forsworn.
For once—ev'n to the height—I honor'd him.
'Man, is he man at all?' methought, when first
I rode from our rough Lyonesse, and beheld

That victor of the Pagan throned in
    hall —
His hair, a sun that ray'd from off a brow
Like hillsnow high in heaven, the steel-
    blue eyes,
The golden beard that clothed his lips
    with light —
Moreover, that weird legend of his birth,
With Merlin's mystic babble about his
    end,
Amazed me; then, his foot was on a stool
Shaped as a dragon; he seem'd to me no
    man,
But Michaël trampling Satan; so I sware,
Being amazed: but this went by — the
    vows !
O ay — the wholesome madness of an
    hour —
They served their use, their time; for
    every knight
Believed himself a greater than himself,
And every follower eyed him as a God;
Till he, being lifted up beyond himself,
Did mightier deeds than elsewise he had
    done,
And so the realm was made; but then
    their vows —
First mainly thro' that sullying of our
    Queen —
Began to gall the knighthood, asking
    whence
Had Arthur right to bind them to him-
    self?
Dropt down from heaven? wash'd up
    from out the deep?
They fail'd to trace him thro' the flesh
    and blood
Of our old Kings: whence then? a
    doubtful lord
To bind them by inviolable vows,
Which flesh and blood perforce would
    violate:
For feel this arm of mine — the tide
    within
Red with free chase and heather-scented
    air,
Pulsing full man; can Arthur make me
    pure
As any maiden child? lock up my tongue
From uttering freely what I freely hear?
Bind me to one? The great world laughs
    at it.
And worldling of the world am I, and
    know
The ptarmigan that whitens ere his hour
Wooes his own end; we are not angels
    here

Nor shall be: vows — I am woodman of
    the woods,
And hear the garnet-headed yaffingale
Mock them: my soul, we love but while
    we may;
And therefore is my love so large for thee,
Seeing it is not bounded save by love."

Here ending, he moved toward her,
    and she said,
"Good: an I turn'd away my love for thee
To some one thrice as courteous as thy-
    self —
For courtesy wins woman all as well
As valor may — but he that closes both
Is perfect, he is Lancelot — taller indeed,
Rosier, and comelier, thou — but say I
    loved
This knightliest of all knights, and cast
    thee back
Thine own small saw 'We love but while
    we may,'
Well then, what answer?"

                He that while she spake,
Mindful of what he brought to adorn her
    with,
The jewels, had let one finger lightly touch
The warm white apple of her throat, re-
    plied,
"Press this a little closer, sweet, until —
Come, I am hunger'd and half-anger'd —
    meat,
Wine, wine — and I will love thee to the
    death,
And out beyond into the dream to come."

So then, when both were brought to
    full accord,
She rose, and set before him all he will'd;
And after these had comforted the blood
With meats and wines, and satiated their
    hearts —
Now talking of their woodland paradise,
The deer, the dews, the fern, the founts,
    the lawns;
Now mocking at the much ungainliness,
And craven shifts, and long crane legs
    of Mark —
Then Tristram laughing caught the harp,
    and sang:

"Ay, ay, O ay — the winds that bend the
    brier !
A star in heaven, a star within the mere !
Ay, ay, O ay — a star was my desire,
And one was far apart, and one was near:

Ay, ay, O ay — the winds that bow the grass!
And one was water and one star was fire,
And one will ever shine and one will pass.
Ay, ay, O ay — the winds that move the mere."

Then in the light's last glimmer Tristram show'd
And swung the ruby carcanet. She cried,
"The collar of some order, which our King
Hath newly founded, all for thee, my soul,
For thee, to yield thee grace beyond thy peers."

"Not so, my Queen," he said, "but the red fruit
Grown on a magic oak-tree in mid-heaven,
And won by Tristram as a tourney-prize,
And hither brought by Tristram for his last
Love-offering and peace-offering unto thee."

He rose, he turn'd, and flinging round her neck,
Claspt it; but while he bow'd himself to lay
Warm kisses in the hollow of her throat,
Out of the dark, just as the lips had touch'd,
Behind him rose a shadow and a shriek —
"Mark's way," said Mark, and clove him thro' the brain.

That night came Arthur home, and while he climb'd,
All in a death-dumb autumn-dripping gloom,
The stairway to the hall, and look'd and saw
The great Queen's bower was dark, — about his feet
A voice clung sobbing till he question'd it,
"What art thou?" and the voice about his feet
Sent up an answer, sobbing, "I am thy fool,
And I shall never make thee smile again."

THE END.

FSC
www.fsc.org
MIX
Papier aus ver-
antwortungsvollen
Quellen
Paper from
responsible sources
FSC® C141904

Druck:
Canon Deutschland Business Services GmbH
im Auftrag der KNV-Gruppe
Ferdinand-Jühlke-Str. 7
99095 Erfurt